THE DRUID

DRAGONSLAYER
BOOK THREE

JULES CORY

Troubador Publishing Ltd
Unit E2 Airfield Business Park,
Harrison Road, Market Harborough,
Leicestershire LE16 7UL
Tel: 0116 279 2299
Email: books@troubador.co.uk
Web: www.troubador.co.uk

ISBN 978 1 80514 464 9

British Library Cataloguing in Publication Data.
A catalogue record for this book is available from the British Library.

Printed by Printed and bound in Great Britain by 4edge Limited
Typeset in 11pt Minion Pro by Troubador Publishing Ltd, Leicester, UK

Matador is an imprint of Troubador Publishing Ltd

THE DRUID

For those who will always believe.

CHAPTER ONE

The swords screamed as they clashed together. Steel sliding against steel, trying to find purchase before being halted by the crossbars of their hilts. I dug my toes into the pale sand of the arena to gain extra grip before shoving my opponent backwards and gaining a respite to catch my breath. My opponent was taller than me by a head, his reach was longer and he was stronger, but I was quicker, lighter on my feet and agile. We were evenly matched and neither had yet to gain the advantage.

I twisted away from the slice he aimed towards my shoulder, bringing my blade down across his exposed back. He spun to block my move, forcing my blade harmlessly away before cutting back across my belly. I swiftly shuffled backwards but the edge of his sword still cut through the loose fabric of my shirt.

I wiped the sweat from my top lip while he flicked the end of his blond warrior's tail back over his shoulder. He taunted me with a smile while we circled each other, just out of reach of the blades. I rolled my wrists to loosen cramping muscles, twisting the sword in a figure-of-eight and *Saorsa* whispered a soft sigh as her blade cut through the air. I watched the muscles of his shoulders, looking for the tension which would predict his next lunge, as he watched me. He raised a mocking eyebrow over apple-green eyes that dared me to break.

We leapt at the same time. The blades scraped together and screeched discordant tones. I kicked at his knee, making little impact with my bare feet but causing him to stumble and break the hold on my sword. In the moment before he found his balance, I chopped at his neck. First left, then right, then left again. His reflexes reacted to my slashes and I forced him

1

backwards. He took four steps before ducking under my thrust and starting his counterattack. He swung his sword back and forth with enough force to make the air whine with each pass. I retraced the steps I had just taken, ineffectively swiping at his blade in an attempt to turn his strokes.

My heel caught in the sand and I fell heavily, but I continued the movement to roll back onto my feet. I spun in a circle to avoid the swing aimed at my hamstrings, catching his blade and turning it away from my body. I followed with reckless slashes to his head, his belly and his neck, straining to control the wild arc of my sword. *Saorsa* flashed in the weak sunlight as I forced him back across the arena. The muscles of my arms blazed in protest while the concussive forces slammed into them again and again. Sweat ran into my eye and I blinked to clear the sting, moving to create a safe space and rub the irritation clear.

He gave me no quarter. He closed the gap in a deep lunge, following through to chase me with a flurry of sweeps. Still blinded in one eye, he exploited the weakness and repeatedly attacked from the vulnerable side. I was forced to concentrate on my defensive moves, positioning my blade to protect my body. I tightened my grip and *Saorsa*'s embossed hilt bit into my palm.

I overbalanced and needed a heartbeat to regain my stance. It was enough for him to move within reach. With a predatory grin, he hooked a leg around my knee, taking my leg from under me. I landed heavily on my back and my sword fell from numbed fingers. His blade rested against my throat and with a slight flick of the wrist as the sword was withdrawn, he sliced a small cut on my chin.

'Ouch,' I protested, rubbing a bead of blood from my chin.

'First blood,' he declared, offering me a hand and hauling me back onto my feet. 'You're still holding back. You will never win if you refuse to attack me with your full strength.'

'I will never beat you, even then.'

Vallori was my *pháirtí*. It was an ancient title, given to those who would bind themselves to another. The sacred ritual allowed a deeper healing than that gained from simple solitude, and I had been in great need of that when I had arrived at the Sanctuary of The Moon Goddess and fallen at his feet five summers ago.

We rested on one of the stone benches that ran along the edge of the arena and watched the other pair training. Z'hara was a tall, lean woman

2

with dark skin that told of her history in lands far south of the Northlands. She had mahogany eyes and long eyelashes, with straight, black hair plaited into neat rows, each starting at her temples and extending through her tail to rest along her back. She was an excellent swordswoman, using two short swords with lethal elegance.

Z'hara sparred with her *pháirtí*. Bonash was a small, wiry man who was often teased for having more hair in his short, scraggly beard than on his almost-bald head. He was competent with his sword, but his calling was in learning and Z'hara was not testing him as hard as Vallori had pushed me. The session ended with Z'hara easily disarming him and his sword landed in the sand with a soft thud. They bowed deeply to one another before turning to join us on the bench.

Vallori smiled at Z'hara, clearly showing his pride and affection, and handed her a towel while Bonash slumped next to me. We frequently practiced together and regularly spent time in each other's company. Five years at the tranquil sanctuary had done much to erode my suspicious nature and the patient guidance given by my *pháirtí* had slowly removed the barriers I had erected to protect those around me from my destructive nature. Slowly, Vallori had rebuilt my trust and I now considered these people my friends.

I had shared almost everything with Vallori and I did not doubt that he would have discussed much of that with Z'hara, who in turn would have spoken to Bonash. I had learnt to accept this. The sanctuary was not a place of judgement or expectation. Information was shared simply to understand and allow appropriate guidance. I felt accepted and safe here, but there still some things that I kept hidden. I had buried them deep within me and would not discuss them. Not even with my *pháirtí*.

Z'hara looked at me with a mischievous smile. 'How did she do?'

Vallori huffed. 'She still insists on holding back.'

Her grin widened. 'Let's see what we can do about that.'

The tall woman grabbed my arm and ignored my dramatic groan of protest as she dragged me into the arena. Her technique was very different to Vallori's, not least in her use of two swords rather than the one. While his strength could be managed by my agility, Z'hara balanced her strength with being quick and agile. Strategies I commonly relied on with Vallori would not protect me from her. True to her word, she worked me harder than Vallori and within heartbeats I was struggling to keep up with her twin attacks. I was repeatedly forced to block her left strike and then her right. *Saorsa* flashed in a wild dance while Z'hara chased me across the arena. I had no time to think for tactical moves, needing to concentrate solely on avoiding first blood. My tired muscles protested anew and my lungs pleaded for air.

A familiar calm surrounded me when I saw the pattern to Z'hara's attacks. I could predict her moves. I knew of multiple ways to block and deflect her strikes. My technique became less reactive and more fluid. I adjusted my position before she started her attack, turning on my heel to slice at her back. She twisted out of reach but my blade sliced a small tear her shirt.

I grinned, feeling the rush of knowing I could beat her. I now dictated the rhythm of the dance. I slashed backwards and forwards, maintaining the momentum to power my swing. Z'hara was forced to retreat and it was my turn to chase her, rapidly changing between high and low slashes, left and right thrusts. Never repeating the same move. Forcing her to guess my plays. I no longer held my swing and aiming for the flesh that would give me the victory, I started my end game. Three moves that would twist me behind her and expose the back of her neck. Push one blade out wide. Force the other towards the floor. Spin around the unprotected side and slice for the base of the neck.

I stopped short as Z'hara's blade touched my neck, my sword quivering in empty air. She had turned around quicker than I had anticipated and in the opposite direction to the way I had predicted. She flicked her blade and nicked across the one made earlier by Vallori. She smiled and lifted her sword to show me the bead of red. The trophy of her victory.

'Made you work for that one,' I commented, encouraged to see sweat on her forehead.

'And you finally stopped holding back and showed what you are capable of.' She shoved me playfully. 'Or perhaps you were just happier to slice my head off?'

'Perhaps,' I agreed in false sincerity. 'Or maybe you are just a better fighter than Vallori.'

We had returned to the bench and continued to mock Vallori about his fighting prowess long after he found it amusing.

The sanctuary was separated roughly into four sections. The largest was dedicated to the training of warriors and those who taught there were among the best in the Northlands. Bordering this was the area where skilled elemental manipulators worked alongside gifted seers and visionaries. A large structure dominated this section and its tall, pointed roof could be seen from any point in the sanctuary. The building was covered in runes and sigils to contain the energies gathered, and they glowed a faint blue whenever incantations and elemental manipulations occurred within its walls. The sector dedicated to healing contained two long infirmary buildings and several gardens, growing medicinal plants such as feverfew, meadowsweet and sage. Common herbal therapies were used alongside more arcane methods and the magickal healing of illness and injury.

The final section was the oldest and most sacred area within the sanctuary. A natural spring had been dedicated to the Moon Goddess since before records had begun and this was lovingly sheltered within this space. Most gardens within the compound held some type of water, either as small circular ponds or enclosed within large ceramic bowls, and these were used to aid meditation and communion with the Goddess, particularly at night when the moon was reflected in their surface. This sector promoted spiritual awareness and offered an immense oval pool that fed from the sacred spring. Water plants floated on the surface while brightly coloured fish swam its gentle currents.

I walked through a quiet courtyard, having been summoned to attend the High Priestess, and reflected on how little time I had spent in this final quarter. It encouraged a more theoretical learning, housing many ancient and obscure texts, and I rarely had the patience for that. I was also reluctant to consider anything directly concerned with the Moon Goddess, content to spend my days fighting Vallori and Z'hara, teaching the basics of elemental control to those who had not benefitted from Drey's training, and to assist the healers whenever they had need. I had no desire to return to the expectations of my Goddess.

'You've been avoiding me,' Luella commented, opening the door to my hesitant knock.

The sanctuary's High Priestess was a small, unimposing woman with grey-streaked, dark hair and eyes that were full of compassion and experience. She invited me into her receiving chamber, a room comfortably decorated with a set of four well-padded chairs around a large fire. A sturdy oak desk was situated beneath the single window and candles of differing lengths told of many nights spent working beyond dusk. A silver quill rested on a wooden cradle and the beautifully carved bookcase contained a jumble of scrolls.

'Your academic studies have been neglected.' Luella guided me to one of the chairs and gestured for me to sit. 'We barely see you in the libraries and I don't believe you have ever attended a discussion on the merits of Moon Goddess's teachings on the preservation of a woodland.'

Distracted by anxious thoughts of why she had summoned me, I took a breath to apologise. I turned to face her and finally saw her mocking smile. I bowed my head in false shame.

'I have been a terrible student.'

She sat in the chair beside me. It was an informal gesture and I took comfort that this was probably intentional. She folded her slender hands in her lap, tilting her head to look at me with a slightly amused expression.

'You can relax, Tallen. You are not in trouble and I won't keep you long.'

'I'm very grateful for your time and for all that you have taught me,' I said in sincere gratitude for the shelter and acceptance I had found here.

'In turn, you have assisted our healers in developing new techniques and different ways to create potions and ointments.'

'I'm happy to help where I can. I had a good teacher.'

'Drey?'

The question was a gentle push for information. I had spoken little of my time at Liegeport and even less of the people I had grown up with there. I had not spoken of my relationship with the Faulknar heir, dismissing it as ancient history which was no longer relevant to my life and the choices I would need to make. I fooled no one but stubbornly held to my view. Drey had been discussed as my mentor in the knowledge of healing and herbal remedies. I had avoided mention of his other influences that involved stealing and spying. Luella waited a couple of heartbeats before a small smile rippled over her lips.

'Very well. That is not what I wanted to talk to you about.' She leaned forward in her seat and I nervously bit my lower lip. 'On Vallori's guidance, we have kept you ignorant of the concerns of the world outside of these walls. You came to us needing to recover physically and mentally. I understand why you still keep some secrets but I hope you have come to trust us here.'

My stomach clenched and old fears rushed to claim me. I had trusted them. I had wanted to find an escape from my problems so badly, I had easily accepted their assurances that this was a place of peaceful retreat. Perhaps I had been naive. I had been in this situation before, surrounded by people who I had thought cared for me. Had I been foolish enough to make the same mistake twice?

Luella continued with more noticeable caution. 'I would happily consent to you staying with us for the rest of your days, but I cannot deny that the Goddess has always had other plans for you. I fear we can delay that fate no longer.'

The older woman waited patiently while I reluctantly accepted that I could not be allowed to hide in seclusion, here or elsewhere. The priestess was aware of my triple heritage as an Empath, Moon Warrior and Dragonslayer. Empaths were rare. Moon Warriors even rarer. And as far as it was known, I was the only Dragonslayer. The Gods would not allow me the luxury of a quiet and uneventful life, no matter how much I craved it. I had not even begun to meet the challenges they had planned for me.

'There have been some developments that affect you, and I feel it is time you were made aware of what has been occurring within the Three Kingdoms. The war between Faulknar and Lindvane has continued with increasing aggression on both sides. I know you have friends in Liegeport.'

I felt myself curl my shoulders and my tone was equally defensive. 'Had.'

'Have,' she persisted. 'All entrance to the port by sea has been blocked by Gallowgla for some time. I'm sure you will appreciate the implications for food supplies, as well as other requirements. Some cargo has been able to reach Kingsport and this has been sent overland. Faulknar has lost around a third of its territory from when you were last there and many seek the capital for protection.'

Again, she waited while I considered the information. How did I feel about the war and the fact that Faulknar clearly seemed to be losing? I had made friends at Liegeport, with most being unaware of how the king, and Drey, had exploited my abilities for their own gain. People I knew would be suffering and dying. I took a deep breath and I shut those thoughts behind a door in my memory.

'Lindvane has been taking full advantage of some unprecedented natural events. Earth tremors have crumbled town walls allowing Hayton's troops access without the need for siege. Rivers have changed course to deny water to villages and their crops. Windstorms batter against forests felling ancient trees. Winters have been long and cold, while summers have seen drought and wildfires. Diseases are spreading readily and are claiming the lives of the vulnerable. It seems nature herself is fighting against Faulknar.'

I would not tell of the Empathy Crystal and Villermir's desire to use it to control the elements. How I had retrieved the stone from its mountain crypt and allowed Villermir to defect with it to Hayton. I would not tell of my fear that the priest of Baila would corrupt every magick he could tear from the crystal.

'And then there is Hilman. The kingdom's current ruler has declared complete allegiance with Hayton. We can pray that there will be another rebellion and someone with the interests of their people will replace Averill, but that is looking very unlikely.' The priestess sighed and closely examined her nails for several heartbeats. 'It started as rumours. Easily dismissed as the exaggeration of people's fears during troubled times. The stories became more frequent, with consistent details, so we sent scouts to determine the truth of the situation. The truth was worse than we feared. Dark magick has travelled from Gallowgla. We have found evidence of at least twenty shamans practising again in the kingdom, with probably many more who we are unaware of.' She paused again. 'Tallen, we need your dragon.'

I froze, hardly daring to breath. I had told no one about Megin.

'How do you know?'

She smiled sadly. 'You are not the only one that the Goddess talks to. This is what your dragon was created for. This is why you were sent to release her from the mountain on Wyrm Island. The Gods have need of you both and the time has come for you to answer their call.'

CHAPTER TWO

The waning moon shone brightly onto the forest clearing. The breeze barely disturbed the leaves in the canopy and shadows moved slowly. Two adult deer and their three juveniles nibbled at the short grass, stamping their legs at flies buzzing in the still night and flicking their tails in irritation. Their ears twitched, constantly searching for the slightest sound of danger. At least two heads were always raised while they slowly moved back towards the safety of the trees. The juveniles drifted a few paces away from the adults.

Seven wolves waited the undergrowth. The gentle wind blew towards them, hiding their scent from their grazing prey. Their bodies were held low to the ground with their muscles tense. They separated the scents of the deer from those of the forest. They listened for the sound of their breathing and the soft tread of their steps. All senses were focused on the deer as they crept closer. The three leggy adolescent wolves were enclosed by the four muscular adults, containing the risk that their enthusiasm would spook the deer, but all were quiet and no hint of threat reached the herd. The shading within the wolves' coats provided excellent camouflage, allowing their small movements to be easily dismissed as shadows in the dappled moonlight.

The wolves began to slink forward. They remained close to the ground and they flowed as one sinuous being towards the clearing. They slowly spread out, weaving between the tree trunks and the scrubby bushes. Their ears rotated towards their prey and their eyes fixed onto the target. Each foot was carefully placed to avoid making any sound and the deer remained unaware. They moved ever closer, their mouths open in anticipation. Step by tentative step, they crept to the edge of the forest. Two adult wolves were joined by the darker adolescent and they adjusted their position to flank the adult deer. The remaining four wolves stalked their young.

The largest deer lifted its nose to sniff the air. Danger. The alarm was barked and animals exploded into movement. The deer fled towards the far end of the clearing and the wolves burst out of the shadows to follow them. The pack split, forcing the younger deer away from the protecting adults. The zig-zag pattern of the deer's flight was mirrored by the wolves and the juveniles were divided again. The three groups crashed into the forest; two adult deer were pursued by three wolves, two juvenile deer were chased by the remaining two adults, and a single juvenile fled from a pair of young, inexperienced wolves.

The two juvenile deer lost sight of the other groups as they crashed through the bushes and bracken, each desperate to avoid the wolf that harried them. Slowly getting closer. Waiting for the fatal stumble or misstep. The silver male leapt and snapped at a hind leg, catching it below the large thigh muscle and flipping the animal over. He rushed in and seized the neck, holding tight while the deer thrashed in panic. The strength of the wolf's bite crushed the throat and the rhythmic clenching of his jaws took the power from hind limbs that scraped at his ribs. The deer's twitching became less frequent and then finally stopped. All was still except the heaving of the wolf's chest.

It was some time before the wolf lifted its head and panted, with his muzzle coated in blood. His mate stood over the other juvenile deer and the young wolves squabbled over their kill a short distance away. He lifted his nose and howled in triumph. Answering calls sounded from deeper into the forest. It had been a successful hunt.

I recognised Vallori's scent a heartbeat before feeling the firmness of his chest pressed against my back. The early morning sun streamed through the window, creating a square of light on the thin rug of my room, and I could faintly hear waves crashing against the rocks far below the sanctuary. I took a deep breath and, realising I was awake, Vallori tightened his grip around my waist.

Vallori had spent many nights in my bed. At first, it was the only way to manage the night-terrors that had plagued my sleep. He would be there when I woke, screaming and thrashing, and would endlessly repeat a calming mantra until I settled. His presence had softened the nightmares and they became blessedly infrequent until I no longer needed his comfort.

Following my meeting with Luella, the nightmares had resurfaced in vivid, violent detail and Vallori had returned.

'You were twitching in your sleep,' he mumbled. 'Bad dreams?'

'No, good dreams. The wolves took down a small group of deer.'

'Your wolf?'

'He's not my wolf,' I denied without much conviction. 'The cubs weren't with him this time and one of the youngsters was missing. But the other adolescents took down their own prey. They're getting much better.'

Vallori huffed at my obvious pride. 'The dreams are always about him, aren't they? The one that brought you here.'

'I can't believe you've never dreamt about your badger?'

I had frequent dreams involving the wolf that had guided me to the Moon Goddess's sanctuary. I had never quite believed he had been real but the way I had watched him grow in my dreams, bond with a female and start a pack, suggested that I had not imagined him. The wolf had been claimed as my sprit guide, while Vallori's was a badger. As far as I was aware, he had never had contact with the animals in life or in his dreams.

'I did once,' he started slowly.

I rolled onto my back so I could see his face. 'You've never told me this.'

He shrugged one shoulder. 'It was only the once and a long time ago. I had been at the sanctuary for a while but was still a little lost. I didn't know which direction to turn. I did not want to return to being a hired sword but without the structure of a defined role, I felt adrift. I was questioning whether my future belonged to the Goddess. I believe she sent the dream to encourage me to stay.'

'What did the dream show you?' I prompted gently when he fell silent.

'It was a winter's night. Snow had covered the valley in white and it had settled on the branches of a small copse nestled at the base of a hill. The badger was very thin and I could tell that he was weak. The season had not been kind to him. In my dream I could smell what he was attracted to. The woods smelt warm. There was food there and the musk of a female. His need for companionship was almost as great as his need for food.'

'And you could relate to that?'

His smile was small and brief. 'I could. The dream seemed to connect with something that I had denied for a very long time. I needed to be part of something. To belong and have a purpose. I could be more here than just a short-term fix to a problem.'

'And so you stayed, to bond as *pháirtí* to the most hopeless of helpless cases,' I teased gently. 'This is your calling. I give you purpose. But I am grateful to that badger for keeping you here. Tell me again about the spirit guides.'

He had explained the system to me many times, but the comfort of the wolf-dream was fading and the sound of his voice never failed to calm me. The myths told of three animals bound to the Goddess. I carried the spirit of the wolf, Vallori had the badger, and Z'hara and Bonash both claimed the owl.

'There are three spirit guides to reflect the three aspects of the Moon Goddess.' Vallori patiently retold the information. 'The wolf is associated with the protective nature of The Lady. Those that have the wolf as their guide show qualities of loyalty and will fiercely defend their territory and those they care about.'

'I've been called a protector before,' I stated quietly.

Villermir had cultivated my fear of him when I was a child so he could use it to gain access to my guarded mind. He had taken my connection to the Empathy Crystal and used me to control the powers locked within. He had burrowed into my mind and violated every memory, including those I had not been aware of. The mere thought of him still had the ability to hurl me into a whirlpool of panic.

Vallori knew who had named me a protector. His voice was barely above a whisper when he continued. 'You will need to talk about what happened at some point. It will continue to haunt you until you share it.'

I took a steadying breath. 'Later.'

'It's been five years, Tallen. And don't think to claim it's because you're trying to protect me.'

I smiled at his mild rebuke. 'Tell me about the badger.'

'Ah, the badger. The noblest of creatures. Badgers represent the nurturing aspect of the Goddess. Those of us blessed with them as spirit guides are said to provide food and shelter. We provide for the physical while the owls take care of the spiritual, offering knowledge and counsel. The official facet is prophecy but I think that it was just a convenient "P" to fit with protection and provision. You will have found Z'hara and Bonash extremely knowledgeable on wide range of subjects.'

I suddenly remembered that I had arranged a training session that morning, and I was now late. 'Mainly, I find Z'hara very knowledgeable on the reasons why I should be punctual for her lessons.'

I wanted nothing more than to remain in the warm bed with Vallori but I knew I would regret staying any longer. I hastily dressed and ran, leaving him grinning smugly.

After a punishing session with Z'hara, I decided to continue my torture with a visit to the stables. Animals had always disliked me and I struggled to find a horse that did not bite or kick at me whenever I was near. There were numerous horses at the sanctuary. A few were exclusively ridden by a priest or priestess or a specialist equine fighter, but most were shared by any who had need of them. There were large and small horses, placid and temperamental ones, stallions, geldings and mares. All of them hated me.

After repeatedly complaining to Vallori about the horses' behaviour, he suggested I spent a season working with a few to build their trust. I was over half-way through the available horses and none had warmed to my approach, much less my handling. I was still no closer to finding one that I could ride without it trying to throw me at the first opportunity. Despite considering myself to have fast reflexes, I had gained several scars from equine teeth and hooves.

I started at the far end of the barn and decided that dealing with the most aggressive one first would be the best course of action. Hex was a large, black stallion with feet the size of plates, accentuated by long, black hair covering each hoof. He towered over me and, assuming he ever submitted to me riding him, I had little hope of controlling him. For completeness I had included him in my selection but I did not try very hard to become his friend. He snorted as soon as he recognised my scent and by the time I was outside his stall he was circling the confined space in agitation. I barely managed to avoid his snapping teeth when I quickly removed a discrete pile of dung and, when his flying hind feet narrowly missed my head, I decided that his stall was clean enough.

My next challenge occupied the stall opposite and had been watching Hex's behaviour. He was already wary, drawing his ears back and showing the whites of his eyes. Swale was slightly smaller than Hex but shared his colouring and hairy hooves. Being a gelding, his temperament was less volatile but he had still given me a couple of sharp bites. I entered his stall calmly and quietly, avoiding any sudden movements. I kept my gaze lowered while I watched him from the corner of my eye but Swale stayed in the furthest corner of his stall while I cleaned his straw bedding and I respected his choice by keeping as far away from him as I could.

Our fragile truce was broken when I came to groom him. Unlike Hex, Swale had patches of dried mud in his coat and several tangles in his mane and tail. I could not avoid getting closer to him and resigned myself to gaining a few more bruises. I collected a brush and comb from the grooming box and slowly invaded his space. His ears were pinned flat to his neck and he snorted his displeasure but remained still when I reached to touch his shoulder, the muscles quivering under my hand. He stomped a hind foot in warning when I started brushing his coat and a stubborn patch of mud on his rump required more vigorous scraping, earning me more than one slap from a swishing tail. Pleased with my progress, I started on untangling his mane. Making sure not to startle him, I carefully walked my hand up from his neck and took a handful of hair close to his ears. He whipped his head around so fast that I was unable to dodge out of the way and the bony ridge of his eye socket connected with my forehead. I staggered backwards, with Swale following me across the stall. His head was lowered in an unmistakably threatening posture and I was more than happy to take the hint.

I felt a small sense of satisfaction to discover my next horse was not in his stall. The straw was clean and fresh so I quickly moved to the next. Kelpie was a rich red, chestnut mare who was as changeable as the weather. One day she would tolerate my presence, while the next day she would try to kick my head to splinters. I soon realised that this was one of her more difficult days when I looked into her stall to find her already baring her yellowed teeth. Rubbing my tender head, I took a deep breath to firm my courage and entered her stall. Having ignored her initial threat, she contented herself with watching me suspiciously while I cleaned and freshened her bedding. When I started to groom her, however, she decided I was a plaything to be repeatedly snapped at or pushed into the walls. She managed to step on my feet twice and cause significant bruising to my shoulder when she grabbed at my tunic, crushing a finger-length of skin. I was physically battered and mentally drained by the time I had finished with her.

My final horse was a fine-boned, blue roan mare named Trefin. She was smaller than the others so that my head was almost as tall as her withers. She was even-tempered and worked hard for those she accepted, but she could be nervous and reactive around those she had little experience of and those who were too abrasive around her. She had once broken a young student's leg, kicking out as she reared because he had shouted across to his friend while holding her head-collar. She was the calmest of the five but I still respected the damage she could do if spooked.

Trefin stared at me with wide eyes. One ear remained flat while the other followed my movements as I removed her waste and added fresh straw. I spoke in soft tones and watched her closely when I moved in to groom her, working steadily at the small clumps of dried mud while her tense muscles twitched and she anxiously flicked her tail. She raised her hind leg a couple of times when I brushed her sensitive belly and flung her head up to narrowly miss my chin when I moved to her opposite side, but otherwise she held firm. Sweat had darkened her neck and shoulders by the time I was finished and she snorted noisily, shaking out her tension when I left her stall.

Bonash leaned against the wall opposite having watched my efforts with some amusement. I replaced the grooming box to its shelf by the barn door before returning to lean beside him.

'How long have you been there?'

'A while.' He nodded his head towards Trefin. 'She's a good horse.'

'Yes, she is. She let me do a lot more than I thought she would. All the others have tried to kick me senseless. Kelpie succeeded in battering me against the wall.'

'And you've gained yet another bruise.' He pointed to my forehead. 'It's because they see you as a predator.'

I carefully prodded the swelling. 'I try to act calm and avoid sudden movements.'

'It's not that.' He waited for me to stop playing with my throbbing injury. 'I've read a few old texts that describe how animals behave around some people. Specifically, those associated with wolf guides. It seems the horses are sensing your connection to a threat and are reacting accordingly.'

'I doubt that's the reason. They just don't like me. It's always been this way. Horses, dogs, goats. None of them tolerate my presence.'

'Spirit guides are with you since you are born so it would explain why animals have always feared you. It's unclear why, but some have suggested it may be because you have a wolf-like scent. Or maybe they sense something in your aura.'

We stood in silence while I considered his words. I had always assumed that my lack of skill with animals had been down to a flaw in my personality. Drey had once described me as someone waiting to erupt and I could easily believe beasts would respond poorly to that. I very much doubted that my scent or aura would reflect a wolf's and that they saw me as any more of a predator than any other human, but stranger things had proven true.

Bonash nudged me with his elbow. 'And then there's you being a Dragonslayer. Imagine if horses perceived you as a dragon. That would certainly explain why they fear you so much.'

I turned to look at him in false horror. 'I've got no hope of finding a horse that will accept me!'

'You need to treat Trefin like the precious creature she is.' He laughed and pushed himself away from the wall. 'Anyway, the reason I came to find you is that there has been a tree-felling accident in Lithie. There will be at least ten injured and Calor called for you to help. They are likely to need as many hands as they can get.'

I arrived at the infirmary just as the sun was touching the tops of the trees, having cleaned myself of horsehair and random pieces of straw. I went to the larger of the two infirmaries, a long, timber building which had been divided into several separate rooms. Some areas were large enough to allow for several individuals to receive prolonged care, while smaller rooms were available for minor treatments such as the application of bandages or the cleaning of wounds. The first two rooms were empty so I tried one of the long-stay areas to see if I was needed there. The dimming light from the tall window at the far end of the chamber cast the room into a shadowy gloom and three apprentices were lighting lamps at the side of the occupied beds. I walked over to the bed of Howe, a soldier who had been injured in a practice fight and had a large gash on his leg. The leg was heavily bandaged and rested on top of the sheet. He grinned at me and I nodded in greeting.

'You must be bored if you have come to visit me,' he laughed.

I shook my head in false sympathy. 'Sorry. I'm not here to see you. My pride could not handle the shame of being associated with someone so clumsy he nearly chopped his own leg off.'

'That's not true! Rommie sliced at me after I had taken first blood. Cursed fool forgot to hold his blade. He's the clumsy ox you should be avoiding.'

I patted him on the shoulder. 'Good advice. I'll avoid both of you.' I caught the eye of the disapproving apprentice who was lighting the lamp next to Howe's bed. 'I was told that there were people coming in from Lithie. Calor wanted some extra help?'

The apprentice sniffed. 'They are setting up in other infirmary.'

I politely thanked her, rolling my eyes at a smirking Howe before quickly leaving. I was not sure whether the apprentice was irritated by me personally, that I was disturbing her patient, or that she had been tasked with caring for the minor injuries rather than being asked to help with the more critical new arrivals. Whatever the reason, she wanted me gone and I was happy to obey.

The second infirmary was of a similar size to the previous building, but the internal layout was different with no rows of beds for those needing long-term care. There were a few smaller chambers that could be used for private healing or used as teaching and practice areas, but the main role of this building was to allow more intensive healing where teams of healers could work on as many as six individuals. There were three rooms available for such sessions, although it was unusual for all three to be used at the same time.

One of the larger chambers hummed with quiet efficiency as they prepared for the injured. All six beds were already draped with clean sheets. Two apprentices had been assigned to each bed and would be responsible for the basic but important tasks of ensuring all was ready for those about to arrive. Jars of ointment and strips of bandage were placed on the small tables positioned within the working area, alongside bowls of water and cloths for cleaning. Small, sharp blades used for cutting open flesh were arranged beside the tongs and pinchers used to remove debris from wounds. A tray of needles sat next to skeins of sinew so fine you could almost see through them.

Lulled by their calm and methodical preparations, I startled like a flushed bird when Calor bustled into the room followed by a flock of students, several experienced apprentices and two masters of healing. Calor was a small man but he made up for his lack of height with his bustling personality and wild gestures when speaking. He strode into the chamber directing apprentices and students to different work areas, flapping his arms in the directions he wanted them to go. I smiled at the whirlwind of chaos he had brought into a space that a moment before had been so tranquil.

'Tallen,' he boomed, although he was less than two paces away from me. 'Thank you for coming. We have need of many hands and most of my teachers have gone to Glensend for the horse fair. You know how these youngsters get around untrained horses. I've set so many broken limbs from kicks and falls, not to mention the fights and brawls, to spend any more of my time there. But it's good training for the students and I'm sure they will all be kept very busy.'

The masters took the opportunity of Calor's distraction to melt away and join their colleagues. It seemed that each master would oversee one of the beds, with one or two of the experienced apprentices to help them. The students had aligned themselves around the remaining four beds while Kallie and Tobee, who were almost at the point of moving from student to teacher, each took a bed for themselves. The younger apprentices waited around the perimeter of the room, ready to fetch further supplies as required.

'So, with that many gone, I need you to take the lead on one of the tables.' Calor had continued to talk, guiding me to one of the two remaining beds. 'Stile will be your anchor and you will have experienced students as your feelers. I have every confidence that they will be adequate for your needs.'

He patted me on the shoulder and left for his own work area before I could stutter my objections. I had never led a major healing before and, despite having performed a healing at the Isle of Serpents on my own, I was not confident in my skills to perform one which involved leading other healers. I had assisted on several magickal healings since I had come to the sanctuary but I had always been the anchor or a feeler. I had been guided and protected by those leading the healing, a task Calor had just given to me. Feelers acted as extended fingers, probing into the damaged body to identify sections that needed replacing or repairing. Skilled healers, such as Calor, could use up to twenty feelers to monitor a patient and guide the magick. I felt overwhelmed at the five he had given me. The anchor was required to control the flow of magick into the healers and the patient; too little would be inadequate for the healing, too much could burn the flesh from the patient and the thoughts from the healers' minds. Stile was a quiet, competent and compassionate healer and I had no doubt that she would keep us safe. My fear was in my ability to keep her safe. Although she would be responsible for monitoring the flow of energy during the healing, it was the leader who summoned the power and contained the forces within the protective circle. It would be my ability to balance the magick and ensure no one individual received more than they could handle, while ensuring that the healing promoted health and repair rather than destruction and death. I wished I had even a small portion of the confidence that Calor seemed to have in my ability.

Stile smiled at my obvious apprehension. 'You'll be fine,' she reassured. 'Just start with your circle and we'll take it from there.'

I smiled my sincere gratitude for giving me something to focus on. Circles I could do. I took the block of chalk from the table the apprentices had prepared and drew a large circle around the bed. The head of the bed was facing north and I drew the symbol for water – three wavy lines, one on top of the other separated by a finger-width. Moving to the east, I drew an inverted arrowhead to represent earth before coming to the south and drawing the triangle in a square for fire. Finally, for the west I drew the pentagram sigil for air. I walked around the outside of the circle to ensure my lines were clear and distinct, that my circle was joined perfectly and would provide the containment I would require when handling the magick. I checked and checked again that all was prepared correctly and that my team of feelers were ready. Stile gave a quick nod of approval and I had time to look over and compare my circle with Calor's. He caught me studying his work and waved away my attention.

I heard the commotion rushing towards us. Instructions were shouted and a bustle of people burst through the doors. The injured were being carried on blankets, they were held under the shoulders and knees by pairs, and they were carried in the arms of a single carer. One of the senior students quickly prioritised their needs and directed them to an appropriate bed. All looked severely injured and in urgent need of help. Some were groaning in pain and these were taken to the beds of the senior apprentices and the masters. Others were more worryingly silent. I had just enough time to see one with blood-stained hair being taken to Calor's space before another was placed on the bed in front of me. I took a deep breath and concentrated on the task in front of me.

With a nod from my team to confirm they were ready, I started to engage the circle of protection while the patient's clothing was removed and his superficial wounds were cleaned. I breathed the words of power to activate the sigils I had drawn in chalk and connected with the energy contained within the elements of fire, air, water and earth. The words had no magick in themselves. They were an old language that was rarely spoken beyond the far fringes of the Northlands. The terms simple and descriptive, guiding the user in shaping the magick they invoked, while allowing a purity of thought without the memories and emotions which could be triggered by more commonly used words and phrases.

I suppressed the information coming from my physical senses and the sounds and smells from the infirmary drifted away. With each repeat of a word, I felt a wave of exhilaration sweep through my body. Picturing the wavy line symbol, I breathed *deuraich* and felt the thrill of clear water rushing through my veins. Moving onto the inverted arrowhead, I whispered *tathasg* and was rewarded with crisp mountain air tickling my nose and filling my lungs. The image of the pentagram and the word *gealbhan* caused a flash of fire to rage through my muscles, melting them with the warmth of the sun. The circle was completed with *talamh* and the symbol of the triangle within a square, making my bones feel as solid as mountains. Having gathered the elements, I bound their energies with the intention of the circle, *blàthaich* – protection. The circle blazed with a silver fire so bright I had to rapidly close my eyes but still an after-image floated behind my closed lids. The energy lifted the hairs on my arms, settling into a ghostly glow which outlined the chalk images as they gently hummed.

With the protection circle in place, I turned my attention to the patient. The auras of the feelers glowed with the emerald shade of their healing energy, tendrils of this green extended from their hands into the patient on the table. Stile was a pale gold that expanded and darkened as she connected with energy radiating around her. The patient's aura was a dark, sickly blend of colours. Dark indigo swirled around the head and throat before blending into a forest green surrounding the chest. Deep crimson rippled over the abdomen, threaded with veins of black in the areas of greatest damage. I lowered my palms to either side of his head, a finger-length away from each ear, and connected with his pulsing energies. The man was instantly known to me. No barriers to his *self* prevented me from exploring his memories, his aspirations, his regrets and fears. I saw the person he was and the one he hoped to be. The struggles he had overcome and the times when he had failed. I observed the accident that had brought him to the sanctuary with the clarity of his frustration and despair. A young man had enthusiastically chopped at a large horse-chestnut that had contained a rotten core, despite repeated advice to leave the tree alone. The lad had been pushing to show his worth to his older brother and had ignored the warnings of hollow bark. Seeing the danger, several had run in to stop him but the tree had fallen the wrong way and crushed those who had tried to help. The man whose head I cradled had tried to free those trapped under the heavy trunk, only for him to lose his footing and roll the weight onto himself and three others who had been assisting him. His guilt at causing more harm weaved more dark veins through his aura.

Moving my thoughts away from his mind, I turned my attention to the damage to his body. With a final word of permission – *cead* – I drew on the energy supplied by the elemental forces radiating from the protective circle. I drew strength, warmth, clarity and flow, easing my way into the turbulent aura of my patient. His essence sucked greedily at me, snatching strands of my aura which were instantly consumed. The desire to plunge into the maelstrom chipped away at my resolve. A wave of nausea washed over me as my vision splintered into a swirling mass of vibrant colours. I felt myself fraying at the edges by his need to devour my energy. The tendrils of my feelers became wrapped around each other and they circled a whirlpool created by my disorientation. I knew a moment's panic before I felt the steady presence of my anchor and the chaotic storm eased. Guided by Stile, I carefully gathered the emerald strands of my team and addressed the needs of my patient.

I worked methodically, moving from one area of concern to another. Stile remained a calm focus in the manner of an experienced sailor on the tiller, appearing to do very little but skilfully navigating around the turbulent currents. I drew on the offerings of the elements to settle the fractious energies twisting around broken bones, torn tissues and severed vessels. I encouraged the fibres of the man's body to untangle and pull in the appropriate directions. I reduced swollen organs so that blood could flow and coaxed the ragged edges to weave together to make firm bonds, ensuring they would not break when the man started moving again. I released the trapped toxins, guiding their natural release through kidneys and guts. I continued until there were no more green threads to guide me.

I withdrew my awareness to encompass the body in its entirety. Checking the strength of each area and inspecting the energy flow to ensure all was as it should be. I touched his mind to ensure he felt peace and was focused on repair rather than survival. Content that my patient was as ready as we could make him, for the final repairs would be done by him, I checked on those who had aided me. Two of the feelers had dimmed auras, testifying to the depletion of emotion and reserve taken during the healing. The other three hummed gently but still glowed brightly. Stile's golden aura pulsed with glistening threads of sunlight.

I allowed myself a small smile of pride and withdrew contact, releasing the auras of my team. I cautiously re-established my connection to my physical senses and gradually became aware of the smells and noises of the room. The gentle throb of aching muscles brought my awareness back to the needs of my own body. I swayed slightly, grabbing the edge of the bed to support myself before a couple of deep breaths steadied my vision. I was glad to see my patient was staring at those around him as if he had been suddenly awakened from a deep sleep. I released the power of the circle with a word of gratitude – *taing* – and the energies faded to a gently pulsing glow, allowing the man to be safely removed from the circle by the attending apprentices. He required their support and was still very weak, but the broken bones of his hips held firm and he limped to a nearby chair to be bandaged.

We snatched time for a shared sense of achievement and a quick mouthful of water before the next patient arrived.

CHAPTER THREE

A chill breeze blew off the sea, bringing a light rain with it and the low clouds drifted across the darkening sky to briefly expose the first stars. I wrapped my arms around my chest a little tighter and huddled into the long, warm cloak while the wind played with my raven black hair. The weather had discouraged anyone else from venturing onto the exposed walkway and I was grateful for the solitude. I remembered the many times I had climbed onto the roof of the royal house at Liegeport seeking to be alone. Perching up high could always settle my turbulent thoughts, calming the noise in my head which constantly buzzed when I was around others.

A few strands of my long hair had escaped the cloak to gently lash at my face. I tucked them back inside the collar, studying my arms as they returned to rest on the stone in front of me. My nails had been bitten down as far they would go and scabs flecked my hands where they had been abused by fighting partners or disgruntled horses. A network of white scars, extending over my wrists and up my arms, told of my habit of clawing at those scabs when anxious. They added to the shiny skin of older damage that served as a reminder of my foolish visit to Mobis's Hell, where I had retrieved Kade's soul and the darkness that remained deep within his spirit. At Liegeport, I had covered the unsightly scars with leather vambraces, but many at the sanctuary had seen the destroyed flesh and it now seemed a vanity to hide them.

I looked out over the endless sea, listening to the rhythmic sound of water crashing onto the rocky shoreline, and returned my thoughts to the conversation with Luella. Despite having spent days considering what had been said, I had reached no conclusion on how to respond. I was not concerned for Megin. I had broken our link and I had not felt her presence since then. The debilitating headaches I had suffered before releasing her from Wyrm Island had gone and I was no longer troubled by the nightmares of being trapped within its mountain. Megin was safe. My instruction for her to leave me had been for this reason and I could not call her back, no matter who demanded it from me.

My restless thoughts circled around what choices I had regarding Faulknar's war and Villermir's abuse of the Empathy Crystal. Luella had reminded me that my refuge at her sanctuary was temporary and it seemed the time had come for me to leave, but I had no idea where I could go. There were few who would welcome my return and I dreaded the thought of Villermir turning his attention to me once again.

I turned at the soft sound of footsteps. 'I thought you were with Z'hara.'

'I was,' Vallori confirmed as he came to stand beside me. 'But I was missing this beautiful evening.'

I grinned at his obvious discomfort. 'You didn't have to come.'

The rain had already darkened spots on the shoulders of his tunic and I was sorry that he had felt the need to follow me to my uncomfortable perch, particularly as I had specifically chosen the position to be uninviting. Vallori understood my need to be alone, however, and he would not have come without thought.

'Have you made your decision?' he asked quietly.

I shook my head. 'No. Not yet.'

He hesitated before asking the question I suspected he had come to ask. 'Will you tell me what you are so afraid of out there?'

I remained silent. It was an old conversation, held many times since I had arrived broken and battered. As my body healed, Vallori had carefully gathered the shattered pieces of my mind and offered a way to move forward. I was reluctant to betray his trust in me by telling him about the darker side to my powers.

'You have to face this,' he continued quietly. 'If Luella is right, we need to be ready for what is coming. What is coming for you.'

'I know,' I said in a tone barely above a whisper.

'Tell it to me as if you are making a report.'

I played with the loose stone chips that littered the surface of the wall under my fingernails while I tried to convince myself that talking about it would not make it any more real. I had nothing to fear from words. My *pháirtí* stood as still as a statue and made no comment, allowing me the illusion that I was talking to myself.

'So,' I began. 'Where to start? Chronologically, proximity, or degree of threat. Well, if this is a tactical report, perhaps we should start with proximity. Luella mentioned that Gallowgla shamans had come to Hilman, bringing their blood rites with them. At the very least, they will be corrupting the flow of energy through Hilman. At worst, they will have discovered a way of raising daemons to terrorise the population into doing whatever the shamans want of them. I doubt that will be pleasant for us.'

I saw that my hands were trembling and laid them flat on the wall, concentrating on the rough texture of the stone beneath my palm. I used the rate of Vallori's breathing to tell of how he was responding to the information. It remained deep and regular.

'My fear… My fear is that these shamans have been taught by the old woman I met when we were taken to Gallowgla.'

Vallori turned to look at me with small frown creasing his head. 'Where were you taken?'

I shrugged. 'A place called Freisholm. Sheltered bay, three mountains.'

'I know it. They call her Sálaforn. It means ancient soul.'

'Well, that definitely suits her.' I turned to look at him. 'But how do you know Freisholm? What do you know of her?'

He smiled. 'This is not my story and you will not distract me that easily. It is enough for now that I know of Freisholm, and I know of Sálaforn.' The smile faded as his frown returned. 'The question is, what did she want with you?'

I picked at the loose skin on my thumb. 'At first, I thought she wanted to ransom me to Villermir but I don't think she had known who I was. What I was. I was stupid to play my hand so early. I showed her what I was capable of but I just needed her out of my head.'

I wilfully tried not to recall the terrors she had placed in my mind. Visions that would enable her to access my memories and gain knowledge of my power. Villermir had tried that before, with greater success, but the torments she used were bad enough. I had forcefully ejected her from my mind and revealed a strength she had not known was there. And she had wanted it.

'Once she knew what power I had, she wanted to know more. She wanted to use it for her own ambitions. She used me to summon the Fates. Mobis, Taranis and Sluagh. Standing right in front of me.'

25

Vallori had been still before but I felt him become rigidly motionless. I felt the pressure contained within him and worried that his careful control would shatter. This was the reason I had kept my secrets. This was why I had never told him. I had no right to burden him with this. I had seen the hate and disgust in Kade's eyes when he saw who I was. What I was capable of. I could not bear to see it again. Not in Vallori.

But I could no longer protect him from this, so I continued.

'She needed my blood to summon the Fates and I know she saved some of it. Maybe she called them again, compelling them to release their daemons or perhaps she had enough of my blood to summon the monsters for herself. No matter how she is doing it, I gave her that power. And there will be daemons in Hilman or Luella would not need Megin.' Vallori's breathing was still deep and regular despite his rigid composure. 'I assume that she told you about my dragon?'

'We knew the dragon had returned. We assumed it was yours. Luella has told us nothing else.'

'Dragons were created to deal with the threat of daemons. If we have daemons, we will need a dragon to destroy them. And with Megin being the only dragon… But I sent her away. I cannot call her back even if I wanted to. Which I don't.' I took a breath to calm my racing heart. 'Luella expects me to be the Dragonslayer of legend, calling my dragon to slay the monsters of Mobis's Terrors. I can't do it. I just can't.'

'Then we will find another way.'

'Do you have much experience fighting daemons?' I instantly regretted my tone and gave him a sad smile to soften the impact. 'Me neither.'

I remained silent, hoping that Vallori would be content with the horrors I had already shared. That he would accept the need to confront the daemons and leave my other secrets safely hidden. I continued to look over the dark sea while I remained acutely aware of his posture, willing for him to leave. He made no move to go.

'You are not going to let me avoid this anymore, are you?' A smile briefly lifted the corner of his lips. 'Don't say I didn't try to warn you. If Sálaforn and her daemons aren't enough for you, there is also the threat of Villermir. That vile priest has unfinished business ripping my mind into shreds, snatching whatever he can to bend and twist and—'

I stopped. My heart was racing too fast and it stabbed into a chest that felt crushed by thick iron bands. I fought for air but my throat remained closed. My mind screamed to hide, to bolt from the danger rushing in to claim me. *Villermir had found me. He was coming for me.* My legs trembled, desperate with the need to run. My vision dimmed as I frantically searched for signs he had broken through my mental barriers.

'You are safe. I am right here. No one is hurting you. You are safe.'

The sound of Vallori's voice provided a focus at the centre of the storm raging within my mind. It was a familiar mantra. The frequently spoken words he used to calm my panicked episodes after tormented dreams or when unpleasant memories surfaced. They occurred less often than when I had first stumbled into the sanctuary, but they had lost none of their impact.

His quiet persistence had broken through my defences. My lungs were released and I took several cautious breaths. The noise in my head faded and my muscles relaxed. The remembered horrors of my time as Villermir's captive were safely returned to the bolted depths of my mind. I took a last deep, cleansing breath and fully returned to Vallori, who stood patiently beside me. I gave him a small, apologetic smile which he quickly dismissed.

'I'm sorry. I did not mean to push so hard.'

I dismissed his apology as quickly as he had dismissed mine. 'It's fine, but I would appreciate not having to think about what waits outside these walls for a while longer.'

'For a while,' he agreed.

'And, although I appreciate the gesture, you don't need to stay.'

'You don't have to face this alone.'

'I know. I'll find you if I need you.' I smiled at his scowl. 'Go back to Z'hara.'

'Don't stay up here too long,' he started before seeing my expression and shaking his head. 'Why I would I think that you would listen to me?'

Despite Vallori's pessimism, it was not long before I decided to descend from the wall. Memories of Villermir were still too close and I doubted that spending more time with my thoughts would be a sensible idea. My body was as restless as my mind so I made my way to the practice arena. The central portion of the training ground had an open roof and the sand had been darkened by the insistent rain, but an overhang circled the perimeter and these areas had remained dry. I was in the mood to hit something so, after removing my baldric and placing *Saorsa* gently on the ground, I went to train with a padded post. The target for my frustrations was a wide tree trunk that had been rammed into the earth. Thick rope had been tightly coiled around the pole before being covered by a heavy sacking, containing the straw which would protect knuckles and shins as they pummelled against it. Over the years the straw had fallen out in many places and had not been replaced.

I selected a rod from the stack, grasped it firmly in both hands and smacked the timber target as hard as I could. The concussion vibrated up my arms but the trunk barely moved. Arcing the pole around my head, I slammed it against the opposite side and more stuffing was forced out of the threadbare sacking. I attacked the post again and again. Faster and faster. I twirled and danced. I struck with both forehand and backhand. I aimed high and then low. I never attacked the same spot twice. My awareness narrowed to the pattern of the swing and the accuracy of the contact.

The force behind my beating became channelled by images of those who still held the power to haunt me. Despite Vallori's counselling, the hours I had spent training, and my ability to shape magick, I still could not control the fear that surfaced whenever I thought of them. The shaman – *thwack*. The one Vallori had named Sálaforn – *thwack*. What was his connection to her – *thwack*. Villermir – *thwack*. The thought of him smothered my mind in choking ash – *thwack*. Why was I still so terrified of him – *thwack*. Rolyan – *thwack*. Despicable, festering little rat – *thwack*. How could that insignificant bully still turned my belly to water – *thwack*. Kade – *thwack*. Kade, Kade, Kade – *thwack*. Why was I still thinking about Kade – *THWACK*!

The pole snapped. I blinked at the short end, momentarily confused as to why it had broken. Thoughts of my tormenters drifted away and the reality of the training session slowly reasserted itself. My hands were pierced with needle-stabs and my arms trembled from the force with which I had pummelled the padded target. The sacking looked like it had been mauled by an angry forest cat and there was a good amount of straw on the floor.

'You rely too heavily on a two-handed grip.'

I turned at the sound of an unfamiliar male voice and instinctively raised the broken stick in defence. It was a ridiculously ineffective weapon; the man was a giant. Even casually leaning against a column with his muscular arms folded across his broad chest, I could tell he was more than a head taller than Vallori. His eyes were so dark that they appeared completely black. His scarred face was framed by short, black hair and he had a thick, black beard.

He was well-armed with a broadsword, long knife and short axe, and the thin handle of another blade was sticking out from the top of his boot. The rim of a round shield showed above his head. I glanced towards *Saorsa*, wondering if I could reach her before the warrior threw the axe. He noticed and slowly raised empty hands.

'I respect the laws of sanctuary.' His deep voice rumbled softly around the arena. 'You have nothing to fear from me.'

'Why are you here?'

He grinned. 'At the Sanctuary of the Moon Goddess or spying on you?'

'Both,' I snapped, failing to see his humour.

He inclined his head at my tone but remained mockingly challenging. 'I'm here as a guest of the High Priestess. And I'm spying on you because of your reputation. A Dragonslayer has not been known for many generations.'

'Sorry to disappoint.'

I moved slowly towards *Saorsa*, watching closely as he pushed himself away from the column and walked towards me, matching my speed. He stopped a safe distance away with his palms still facing me when I released my sword. The blade's runes caught the dim light and flared for a heartbeat before fading back into the dusky-grey of the blade. I held the weapon in a relaxed grip, pointing the tip towards the floor. The threat was clear but he remained unintimidated and unimpressed.

'That remains to be seen. You have the anger and the suspicion, but–'

'But I favour a two-handed grip.'

He inclined his head again, his taunting smile refusing to leave. 'It will be a weakness against Gallowgla.'

'And what do you know of Gallowgla?'

'I know they are settling in Hilman. I know they use shields. They will block your sword and leave you vulnerable to their blades.'

'I can fight against two swords.'

'It won't be enough. The techniques are different.' He shrugged the shield off his shoulders. 'I could show you.'

I glared at him. 'You want to fight the Dragonslayer?'

'By the Gods!' He threw his head back and laughed. 'Of course, I do.'

He moved into the centre of the sanded arena, drew his sword and threw his arms wide in a clear invitation. Wide straps held the shield tight to his forearm and palm and he held his broadsword loosely in the other hand. I held no illusions that I would be able to beat him but the static post had offered no challenge and I still retained my restlessness. This warrior was unknown and dangerous. Giving a quick laugh at my own foolishness, I dipped my head in acceptance and joined him in the arena.

We started to circle each other, assessing stance and gait for signs of weakness, but he did not delay. He punched his shield forward and I quickly raised *Saorsa* in response. My blade skidded over the stained hide and was forced to the side, allowing him to swipe his sword at my waist. I twisted out of range, driving back at his unprotected side, but again he caught my swing on his shield. I was forced back several paces with the strength of his push.

I started the next attack. Always aiming for his unprotected side, I swung at his legs, his head, his back. Each time he easily batted my sword away. His sword's swing was hindered by the shield so I changed technique to exploit this. He easily deflected my strokes with the wooden barricade. No matter what I tried, I could not break through his defences and I was using much more energy than he was. It was not a sustainable strategy.

His mocking smile returned, knowing I had reached the conclusion he wanted. He moved his shield half a hand-width further from away his body and I snatched at the invitation. I sliced *Saorsa* into the gap between shield and shoulder, aiming for the middle of his upper arm. A heartbeat before I connected, he stepped in and closed the space, trapping my arms between the shield and keeping *Saorsa* safely away from his shoulder. I was effectively restrained. Enjoying my frustration, he slowly raised his sword to tap the flat of its blade against my head.

'You're dead,' he grinned.

I huffed in defeat and he released his grip, taking a step away from me. Switching his sword to his shield hand, he removed the axe from his belt and I lifted *Saorsa* in a two-handed stance in preparation. I briefly wondered how I was supposed to defend against the combined threat of axe, sword and shield, but he tossed the axe in the air to reverse the hold and presented the handle to me.

'Use this to catch the rim of the shield.'

'Just like that?'

'It won't be that easy.'

We circled each other again while I got accustomed to the weight of the axe. I opened with a feint with *Saorsa*. The one-handed hold felt unnatural and my attacks were sluggish and inelegant, but the power of my strikes grew as I gained confidence. I found the rhythm of slashing with the axe and slicing with the sword and the speed of my dance increased. Left hand, right hand. Alternating back and forth to force my opponent back. I twisted and turned and chased him across the sand until I saw my chance. I hooked the axe head over the upper rim of the shield and pulled it down. I pushed his sword wide, quickly flicking my wrist to angle *Saorsa*'s blade against his neck.

And still he grinned.

'You let me win.'

'Aye,' he admitted when I pushed him away. 'But I made my point.'

'And did the Dragonslayer meet with your expectations?'

'You held back–' I groaned in frustration, replacing *Saorsa* in her sheath and handing back the axe. 'And I see I'm not the first to say that. But it remains true.'

'You held back too,' I snapped.

'Many would think that a weakness,' he continued, ignoring my comment. 'That you lack the ability to commit to a kill.'

His mockery had gone and his tone carried a hint of sadness. His head was tilted slightly, watching with dark, unreadable eyes.

'I can kill,' I said quietly.

'Aye,' he replied, equally softly. 'I daresay you can. You have no reason to prove yourself. For you, the act of killing is too easy. You fear to lose control. That your anger could kill all those around you. Friend and foe alike. As easy as crushing a beetle. For you, it takes more strength to step back from that precipice. To resist the temptation.'

I shivered with a sudden chill. 'Who are you?'

He gave a wide genuine smile and extended his arm. 'Friends call me Bear.'

It was not the question I was asking but I clasped his wrist anyway. 'Well met, Bear. I think.'

I slept late the next morning and was awoken by loud banging on my chamber door. At my grunted instruction, a girl's head poked around the barely opened door.

'Master Thringal requests your presence as soon as possible,' she informed me.

'Now?' I queried petulantly, still struggling to free myself of the tangled blankets. 'What does he need me for?'

'He has a project he needs your help with. I think he's been up all night.'

I dressed quickly and made my way to the area where Thringal preferred to work. I enjoyed the craftsman's company and had spent several hours with him developing the basic magicks I had learnt from Drey. Under his guidance, my ability to manipulate the elements had been tempered and channelled until I could easily control several at once. I could create both offensive weapons and defensive barriers; heating metals to make thin, sharp blades which would not buckle or snap, or compressing air to make shields which no arrows could penetrate. I could nurture the ideal climate for plants to grow or to send them into hibernation, ensuring there was an abundance of food at the sanctuary. I could keep people safe and I could feed them, but I found most pleasure in shaping fire into spirals and whirlwinds while animated animals danced within the flames.

I found Thringal curled over his desk cradling his head in his hands, his curly brown hair in more disarray than usual. He looked up at my entrance and I agreed with the runner's assumption that he had been up all night. He smiled in embarrassment and gestured towards the lump of rock in front of him. It was a large as his head and speckled with shades of grey, ranging from almost white to almost black. Four spiked lumps jutted out from the stone, making it look like a misshapen, overturned beetle with legs pointing towards the ceiling. I inclined my head at him with an enquiring smirk.

'I know,' he pleaded, shaking his head. 'I know. I've been at this all night and all I've done is turn a square lump of rock into a round lump of rock.'

'What were you trying to do?'

He sighed and sat back in his chair, his round face sagging in defeat. 'It is my granddaughter's naming day and I wanted to make something special for her.'

'So, you made her a lump of rock?'

He waved a hand at me. 'I know. I should not have been so ambitious. I should have gone for a wooden one.'

'A wooden what?'

'Effie loves the stories of faraway lands and princesses in castles. I was trying to mould a building of stone. To make it more like the tales with their citadels of rock than the plain structures she's used to.'

I picked up the boulder, surprised at its weight. 'You chose one with this much granite?'

He gave me a small smile. 'I know how stubborn that rock can be...'

'But you wanted it to be special.'

32

I required no more explanation. His intentions were good, granite would make a beautiful castle, and he was one of the most skilled in reshaping rock. I frowned in concentration and wove tendrils of thought within the stone, searching for reasons why it would resist Thringal. Strands of energy threaded throughout the layers of quartz and feldspar to create a jewelled matrix. The channels were clear and bright, showing no hint of distortion which would inhibit its restructuring. I probed deeper. Rock held the memory of every event since its formation and would often fester on any perceived slight or resentment. I gently teased apart the information stored over the lifetime of the boulder, from its creation in a deep magma cauldron until it was hammered from the fire-mountain. I saw the miner hack into the seam with ancient tools and place the rocks into a wooden cart. I smiled, recognising a hint of ancestry in the shape of the nose and the set of the mouth. I felt the stone's indignation; Thringal's ancestor had not asked permission before removing the rock from its brethren. He had not known of magick and had not been told of the sentience of stone. It had been an unintentional insult.

The granite still held a grudge against Thringal and his family, but was happy to accede to my requests and I began to mould it. I extended the four lumps into graceful towers with pointed roofs similar to those at Liegeport, and heated small grains of stone to produce glass in the windows. I selected some of the palest mineral and made tiny doves that perched on the turrets. I moulded the main bulk of the stone into a hilled enclosure. A walkway ran the length of the outer stone wall, patrolled by little soldiers with minute swords and spears. Within the walled fortress, buildings of different shapes and sizes were created to represent homes, shops and storehouses. I crafted a small forge, heating darker minerals to create the effect of glowing coals before sealing it behind glass to preserve the colour. A market was placed in the centre with the covered stalls of Liegeport, adding livestock pens with small groups of sheep, cattle and pigs. I teased each shade from the stone to provide individual colouration for each of the animals and people. To finish the gift, I took some water from the cup on Thringal's desk and added it to make a moat. I covered this with glass so the water could flow when the castle was tilted, adding a sense of movement to the frozen scene.

I withdrew my connection from the rock and appraised my work. The small characteristics given to the animals and people made the gift resemble the tales Thringal's granddaughter loved. The stone had held a wide variety of colours and had given texture to the buildings, resulting in a realism I had not expected. I smiled, pleased with what I had achieved. I looked up to see Thringal watching me with a strange expression on his face.

'What?'

'After all this time, you still have the power to surprise me,' he told me quietly. 'That is truly beautiful.'

I shrugged dismissively. 'You know I like making things. The rock had some beautiful colours to work with. You chose well.'

'But I couldn't mould it.'

I grinned. 'That was because your ancestor mined it without seeking permission, and it still hasn't forgiven your family. I hope Effie likes it.'

'She will love it. The moat is perfect.'

I shrugged. 'I was showing off.'

Chapter Four

I arrived at the training session the following day to find Vallori, Z'hara and Bonash already there, along with Bear. All four were sharing a joke, laughing and relaxed, and I was irrationally irritated that he had already won the respect of my friends. He looked up to see my bad-tempered scowl and widened his grin, delighted to resume his taunting.

'Tallen,' Vallori began. 'This is Bear. He has come from—'

'We've met,' I interrupted rudely.

Bear rumbled a laugh. 'I told her that she favoured a two-handed grip.'

'Ha!' crowed Z'hara. 'I told you.'

I rolled my shoulders and released *Saorsa* from her scabbard. 'Are we here to highlight my many faults, or shall we work on correcting them?'

Vallori frowned. 'I'm not sure I want to be at the sharp end of your blade this morning.'

Bear raised a challenging eyebrow. 'Then let's make this fun. Vallori and Tallen against me, Z'hara and Bonash?'

I did not relish the thought of facing the combination of Bear and Z'hara, and the damage they could inflict. Not to mention Bonash's tendency to sting like a wasp when your attention was engaged elsewhere. Bear gave me no time to dwell, however, immediately swinging for my head with his broadsword. I cursed, reacting instinctively in defence before concentrating on three, constantly moving targets whilst avoiding Vallori.

Bear quickly gauged our strengths and weaknesses, moving fluidly to complement Z'hara's natural style while compensating for Bonash's shortcomings. Vallori and I easily read each other's moves following years of fighting, but Bear pushed both of us hard by repeatedly exploiting our weaker areas and interrupting our set pieces. Bonash soon reached the limit of his endurance and was granted respite to critically evaluate us as we reverted to two-on-two.

Over the next few days, Bear trained us hard. We were required to fight singularly, in pairs and in threes, learning the different skills required with and against multiple partners. We learnt to fight using one-handed and two-handed grips, and practised with daggers, short axes and shields. Bear quietly transformed us from a group of individuals into a team, able to predict each other's moves and act to support or compensate as required. I had learnt so much from Vallori and Z'hara, adding to that Langdon had taught me in Liegeport, but that had always focused on individual fighting skills. Bear showed us tactics and strategy until we reacted without thought as a complete unit. I burned to know who he was and what he was doing at the sanctuary.

Despite all the different combinations, it was unusual for Bear to fight me one-on-one. It seemed he had learnt all he needed to on the night of our first meeting and had no desire to repeat the match, so I was surprised when, after a particularly bad-tempered fight with Z'hara, he suggested I take my frustrations out on him instead. I suspected a trap to punish my lack of control but I was unable to resist the temptation. I now knew of his weaknesses and was keen to test myself against them. I inclined my head in acceptance and gestured for him to join me.

Z'hara hesitated, understanding that something was about to happen. The cohesion of the team, which Bear had carefully cultivated, caused her need to protect me to conflict with her desire to avoid the score that was about to be settled. After several heartbeats of indecision, she moved to stand with Vallori and Bonash.

I started to circle Bear. Just as we had done before, we assessed each other. I was tired after my punishing bout with Z'hara while Bear had fought little that morning and was still fresh. I had a dagger sheathed at my hip but chose to use *Saorsa* in a two-handed grip while Bear had his broadsword and shield. I would have to work twice as hard to protect all areas and I knew I would lose stamina quickly. I would need an aggressive strategy to ensure a quick victory.

'You have been itching to face me since I let you win,' taunted Bear. 'Now is your chance to show your friends that you can beat me.'

'With pleasure.'

I leapt forward, swinging *Saorsa* in a feint to his knees which caused him to lower the shield as I had predicted. I reversed the angle of my blade and slashed at his neck. Bear caught my blade with his, but his mocking smile had gone and he was forced to concentrate on my offensive play. I kept him on the defensive, repeatedly forcing him to use his shield to block me and denying him the chance to use his sword. I pushed him back several paces but could not find the opening I needed. My opening gambit had failed and I accepted that this was going to take longer than I had hoped.

My thrust faltered and Bear seized his opportunity, bringing his sword up to slice at my ribs. I twisted to place *Saorsa* between me and his blade, forcing me off balance and allowing him to push me back with the shield. I stumbled but flowed into a roll and returned to my feet before his blade could bite my neck. I pushed his weapon away, clattering *Saorsa* against his shield then slicing back at his sword in one smooth serpentine movement. I caught his blade against his shield and my two-handed grip was a match for his back-handed hold. The test of strength, however, was not one I could sustain and I relinquished the hold, stepping nimbly out of range of the sword that flew towards my head.

We circled again and I took the time to recover my breath, smiling to see he was breathing hard as well. I considered my options. I was unlikely to outlast him, so using agility to tire him would probably fail. He was stronger and had a greater reach, so brute force would also be a losing strategy. I decided that I would need to rely on my wits and hope to catch him off-guard.

I used every technique I had learnt from Laken and Langdon, Vallori and Z'hara, as well as a few I had previously kept to myself. Blades clashed together. *Saorsa* bit deep into the wooden shield and I drew blood from his forearm, but we were a long way past first-blood rules. The mocking smiles and taunting glances had been replaced by fixed snarls and poisoned glares. We both sought to end the contest. Again and again, we battered each other without finding the weakness that would lead to the final stroke. The opening that would force the other to surrender.

I broke contact and stepped back, needing a moment to recover my breath. I was coming to the end of my endurance and I was barely able to match him. I could not hold Bear for much longer. I fought with my desire to win at all costs, knowing I was approaching the point where I had always shied away.

Bear exploited my hesitation and attacked with a parry of slashes to my head. I reacted without thought, batting away his strikes as I moulded my aura into a scaled tail. I forced the arrow-tip through the sand of the arena, into the soil below and continuing through into the bedrock until I pierced the magma chamber at the core of the earth. I took a deep breath in and raw power travelled up the tail, wrapping around my spine and settling into a ball of energy at the base of my ribs. My limbs felt rejuvenated and I slashed at Bear with the gained strength. I saw his smile of triumph and realised I had fallen into the trap he had set for me.

He threw away his shield and used his free hand to create a boulder of compressed air, hurtling it towards my chest and sending me flying across the arena. I threw a fireball and forced him to drop to the ground, giving me time to race back to him. I swung *Saorsa* while he was still climbing to his feet, with all pretence at fair play having vanished. I could fight Bear with a blade and effortlessly control the elements, but I could not control my anger while attacking with both. My blood surged, seeking to annihilate the threat in front of me. My rage suppressed all thoughts of Bear as a tutor and ally. Blades whistled through the air and connected in a spray of sparks as we hammered at each other. We twisted and turned in a lethal dance while his whirlwinds sucked my fireballs into a ranging inferno. I buckled the sand beneath his feet causing him to stumble and I smiled in triumph. He may exceed my skill with the blade but he came nowhere close to my ability with magick. He could only manipulate one element while I played with all four.

I toyed with him but still he battled on. We sliced with blades while we battered with magicks. It was inevitable that I would beat him and yet he continued to resist me. It was time to finish this.

'Enough!' I screamed.

With a flick of my hand, the sand of the arena rose to encase Bear leaving only his head free. I compressed the individual grains until they set like stone, making him a statue with his sword arm frozen in extension. My heart pounded in triumph at the sudden fear in his eyes. I raised *Saorsa* above my head, swinging her down to take off his head.

'Tallen! NO!'

I pulled the swing, tilting the blade to whistle harmlessly over Bear's head and continuing the turn to see Vallori being restrained by Z'hara and Bonash. I lowered my sword in confusion and struggled to grasp the reason for his cry, but his expression wiped all other thoughts from my mind. His look of horror mirrored Kade's after I had brought him back from Mobis's Hells, and seeing it in Vallori felt like being punched in the stomach. All air was knocked from my lungs and I could not claw it back. The sand statue dissolved and Bear stumbled away from me. My mind raced to recover the context. I was at the sanctuary not in Villermir's base at Burford Hythe. The anger that had driven me to viciously attack Bear had no place here. I had violated a sacred trust, almost killing a guest of the High Priestess.

I looked at faces that showed fear and distress. Overwhelmed with shame, I ran.

I had retreated to the cliff point overlooking the rocky shore, where the rhythmic crashing of the waves gently eroded my guilt into a heavy numbness. I had picked my seclusion well and it was late afternoon before someone found me. I reluctantly returned to the compound but was grateful that I had been summoned by an anonymous runner to a scholar who I had not encountered before. I was still not ready to face Vallori.

I knocked at the sturdy oak door of Master Kien's study and received a gruff command to enter. I cautiously stepped into a cluttered room that smelt faintly of leather and parchment. Tall bookcases covered two of the walls, filled with leather-bound books and rolled scrolls, and dotted within by lumps of crystal and carved wooden structures. A long table was placed in the centre of the room and was covered with open texts, scattered parchment, stained quills and dried inkwells. A raised platform, angled for writing, was set in the light from the window. Several crates stood open, showing the straw packing used to protect their contents, and amongst these stood an average-sized man. His shoulders were slightly curved from spending too much time hunched over desks and his slate grey hair touched the collar of his tunic. His clothing was covered in a fine layer of dust to suggest he had just returned from travelling.

He turned to face me with a scowl that deepened the creases around his eyes and mouth, making his weathered face look like crumpled leather. The intensity of his gaze made it feel as if he was judging the very core of me. I defensively took a step backwards but he waved me in with a flap of his hand.

'Well, don't just standing there,' he blustered. 'Come and help unpack these things.'

'I can get someone to help you,' I stammered, slightly annoyed that I had been summoned for such a routine task.

'You're here now, aren't you?' he replied sharply. 'And close the door behind you. Some of these items are not for public viewing.'

Having given his orders, he proceeded to ignore me and returned to rummage through a crate in search of some treasure. He moved a section of straw and the sunlight caused a large ruby to glint invitingly, causing my magpie heart to flutter and my fingers to twitch with the desire to hold it. I decided that this would not be such a tedious task after all and closed the door as instructed.

I moved to investigate the nearest box, disappointed to find only ledgers and bound journals. I placed these neatly in spaces within the bookcases before moving onto the next container. A delicate creation of fine wood lay under the surface packing, containing layers of interconnecting discs with notches carved around the edges so that I only needed to turn one disc to make all the others move. It was a pretty toy, but I dismissed this along with the texts and gently placed it on a shelf. The crate contained various carved items, including jointed models of animals which could be used for educational purposes. Other strange curiosities involved acrobats who flipped and tumbled when the supporting posts were squeezed, and an impossibly fragile sphere carved into fine strips which could turn independently to create a confusing number of different pattern combinations. While I dismissed these along with the rotating discs, I could not help but admire the craftsmanship that had gone into their creation.

I was almost at the base of the crate before I made the discovery I was looking for. A rough chunk of rock, the size of my hand, lay nestled in the straw. It was so black it seemed to absorb all the light from the room. The stone was uniformly jet and it was hard to discern the sharp edges despite being a roughly chiselled stone. It seemed to flow like ink, but contained none of the variances in colour. Just a deep black that sucked at my awareness. I was drawn towards the slightly malevolent presence of the crystal, rocking forward to peer into the endless darkness.

'The Infinity Stone.' Kien's voice startled me, tearing my gaze from the stone. 'It will suck the soul right out of you. You've seen one of these before?'

'Not as big.' I made a circle with my thumb and first finger to describe the size. 'It was egg-shaped.'

He frowned. 'Infinity Stones are very rare. Especially shaped ones. Where did you encounter this egg?'

'Drey had one.'

Kien considered for a moment. 'Faulknar?' I confirmed with a nod. 'Yes. I've heard of him. He has made a bit of a name for himself acquiring powerful artefacts. Albeit a very small collection.'

I scowled at his dismissal of my friend, but the frown quickly faded when I wondered if Drey had ever been my friend. I had accused him of merely wanting to exploit my talents and claim my dragon. I was certain he was not my friend now.

'Try not to touch the crystal when you move it,' Kien continued patronisingly. 'You will be unable to break the connection from a touch.'

I maintained eye contact with him, raising a challenging eyebrow while I created a cushion of air to lift the artefact and glide it to the top of the bookcase, setting it down without as much as a wobble. Kien sniffed before turning back to his crate without another word. I allowed myself a small, triumphant smile before returning to empty my own container of the remaining small stones. I used a more mundane method to place the smaller rocks on the bookshelves and passed by the table containing the scroll and open texts. I gave them little attention but an illustration caught my wandering gaze. The image was over half the size of the page and the colours were still vivid despite its obvious age. The scene showed a small village nestled within a wide valley, with craggy cliffs stretching towards the sky on either side of a wide river. The detail was such that small figures could be seen in the boats fishing on the water, but the artist's skill was not what had attracted me. Flying over the valley was an orange dragon with blood-red wings. It was banking on a thermal, mouth open to roar a challenge as it extended its talons towards the fishermen.

'Where's Baniskarou?' I asked, reading the inscription under the picture.

'Don't touch that!'

I looked up to see Kien marching towards me at a surprisingly fast pace. His face was contorted in such anger that I took a couple of guilty steps away from the text. The small man waved me back further as he approached the table, carefully examining the pages to ensure they were undamaged. Having confirmed all was in order, he turned his attention back to me.

'You have no idea how old this is,' he began. 'If you had damaged—'

41

'I wasn't touching it,' I snapped back. 'By the Gods, is it any wonder I avoid libraries? Your precious book is fine. I'm not going to harm it just by looking at it.'

'That remains to be seen,' he persisted before narrowing his eyes at me in suspicion. 'What do you know of Baniskarou?'

'Nothing. It says in the text—'

'Impossible,' the old man dismissed. 'Who told you about Baniskarou?'

'No one,' I repeated, raising my voice in frustration. 'The picture shows a dragon that is marked differently from those that flew over the Three Kingdoms. The inscription states that the village of Baniskarou is being attacked, and I wondered if there were dragons there, then maybe there were Dragonslayers too. Maybe there still are?'

'Nobody has been able read that language for generations. Scholars have devoted their whole lives and not one has been able to translate more than a handful of words.'

I sighed at the expression on Kien's face, having seen it too often. The crease of a frown, the wide-open eyes, the half-formed question on the lips. I resisted the urge to apologise and instead focused on the writing in the book. To me, the writing looked like the common language used throughout the Three Kingdoms and the Northlands. I rubbed the back of my head, my scalp prickling at the memory of Villermir teaching me to read and the smacks he had given when I failed to meet his demanding standards. I remembered how I struggled to see the common language symbols within the mess of lines and boxes inscribed on the paper.

I tilted my head and relaxed my gaze until the letters shimmered and their edges blurred. A small smile crept onto my lips. I was seeing what everyone else saw, the characters of an ancient language my brain automatically converted into common speech. A language I had known but had been suppressed by Villermir's teachings. My smile widened. I could now switch between the two languages as easily as shifting my focus.

I looked up to see Kien still staring at me. 'You can read this?'

'The translation is not literal but the meaning is clear.' I returned to the table, taking care to hold my finger above the text to avoid touching the parchment. '… and so the dragon came to the village of Baniskarou. Its destruction was swift and devastating. The village that had stood for countless generations was reduced to ash. Not a soul survived—'

Kien held up his hand. 'Merciful Mother,' he breathed. 'How can you know this language? Our best guesses date the linguistic style back to the time of the Ancients. Perhaps your Dragonslayer blood remembers it?'

He shook his head in disbelief. I considered it was more likely that Megin remembered the language and the link with my dragon enabled me to translate. I felt no need to share my opinion so kept quiet and scanned the remaining text for anything of interest. Much of the account recalled the destruction of the village, providing clear detail of the violence caused by the dragon, but three lines up from the bottom of the first page was a mention of daemons. The writing described how it was thought that a swarm of daemons had infested the village prior to the dragon attack, subjecting the villagers to torments of the mind and corrupting their normally placid natures. The character used to portray the word *daemon* reminded me of one of the runes cast into *Saorsa*. I drew my sword from her scabbard, looking up as Kien took a step back into a clear defensive position and raised his hands in a pose more of a warrior than that of a scholar.

'Peace,' I reassured, laying the sword on the table next to the book. 'I'm just testing a theory.'

I rocked the blade until the light picked up the faint carvings. The shapes were not those of the ancient text in the ledger, but there was enough similarity for me to guess at the meaning of *Saorsa*'s sigils.

'This one must mean daemon,' I suggested pointing to a character towards the end of the inscription. 'And this looks like the one for blood.'

The remaining symbols were less clear, and I felt that I was guessing more than translating when Kien pointed to other runes.

'Swim or wash?' I suggested hesitantly. 'That could be me or self?'

Kien raised an eyebrow. 'Self-swimming daemon blood.'

I smiled at him. 'Doesn't sound that fearsome.'

I returned to the script to try to decipher the remaining characters. The one before daemon could be *within*, while the one between self and swim could be *should* or *inevitable*. I felt a cold finger stroke the length of my spine at the truth of my interpretation. I looked up to meet Kien's eyes.

'I shall bathe in daemon blood.'

I watched the colour drain from his face as he, too, felt the certainty of my translation. 'Is that a promise or a curse?'

'I guess that depends on whether you are a daemon.'

I got the second summons at dusk. I knew Luella would expect me to account for my behaviour that morning but I still had no idea how I would justify my actions. I could not forgive myself for the lack of control that nearly killed Bear. The sanctuary was not harsh on its students, and misdemeanours were to be expected in a learning population, but there was no chance of Luella dismissing my behaviour easily. I had been very close to beheading a sanctioned guest of the High Priestess. My mind offered a range of options that could be taken against me, so that by the time I knocked on her door I was convinced I would be burned as a warning to other students.

I entered to find Luella sitting at her desk leafing through a mound of papers. She looked up when I walked in and I tried to gauge her mood, but I could tell nothing from her composed expression. She carefully replaced her pen in the wooden holder and indicated the comfortable chairs by the hearth. I took it as a good sign that she was not expecting me to stand while she passed her judgement, although my heart still raced as if I had just run up five flights of stairs.

'Thank you for joining me,' she began, selecting the chair that was positioned opposite me.

'Of course, High Priestess.' I thought it appropriate to maintain formality. 'I apologise for my behaviour this morning. I can assure you that it will not happen again.'

She lifted an eyebrow. 'Can you? It was quite an impassioned display from what I have heard.'

I avoided her challenging gaze. 'I had not used magick in that way before. I was unprepared for my loss of control. I will not allow it to go that far again.'

Luella folded her arms. 'Is that so? You would deny the use your magick to defend yourself? To defend others? No matter what the provocation?'

I frowned. 'I don't understand. I attacked a guest. I should not have put Bear in danger. I cannot put anyone in that position again.'

'I'm not sure that will be your choice.' She relaxed her arms, letting them fall into her lap as she softened her tone. 'You are here to learn the limits of your abilities. To learn to control them. Vallori has pushed you as far as he can but he is reluctant to press you beyond what you are willing to give. Bear could see you were holding back and he does not share Vallori's concerns. I daresay, he enjoys pushing people beyond their comfortable limits.'

'I nearly killed him,' I persisted.

'And he is not happy about that.' She chuckled. 'It has been a long time since anyone has bested that mountain of a man. A lot of people will be pleased to remind him that he was beaten by such a small, young woman.'

I was beginning to think that I had missed something. 'I don't understand,' I repeated. 'I lost control.'

'That is all part of learning. Finding your limits. Managing *all* elements of your abilities. How to exploit *everything* you have.' She looked down at her hands and examined her fingers. 'It is a lesson you will need to learn quickly, I'm afraid. I left it too late to summon Bear.'

I rubbed at the ache in my temples that was deepening with each comment Luella made. It seemed that not only was she not angry at me, but that she was actually pleased that I had finally confirmed something she had expected all along.

Luella sighed. 'Let me try this a different way. I told you that you would soon have to leave here. You will be tested against foes that are not restricted by the rules taught here. You must know what you are capable of. How to use it. And how to come back from it.'

The priestess knew me well enough to know that my silence was more than an acceptance of her words, and that my stillness was more than a lack of movement.

'Why are you so afraid of letting go?' she pushed gently.

I gave a sharp, bitter laugh. 'Apart from killing everyone within a day's ride of me?'

She leaned forward and waited until I lifted my eyes to look at her. 'When everyone thinks of the moon, they see her bright face and the silvery glow she casts over the earth. They forget that for most of the cycle over half her surface is shrouded in shadow. The greater part of her is dark and unknowable. You are a Moon Warrior, Tallen, and that means embracing the dark side of your nature. The Goddess requires you to do those tasks that others shy away from. To go places where others choose not to travel. You are the dark aspect of her moon.'

'And if I kill everyone in the process?'

'Do you really think that is a possibility?'

'I nearly killed Bear!'

'But you did not.'

I did not have her faith that I would be able to stop myself again. That it was only Vallori reminding me of Kade, and how Faulknar's heir would be so disappointed in me. She did not know of his disgust at what I had done to him. Or the fact that he wanted to hang me as a traitor.

'It's not just the potential for killing.' I took a shaky breath, trying to make her understand the danger. 'I feel it drawing me in. The freedom of just letting go. Of giving in to all that rage. No consequences. Just destruction. It felt… right.'

The priestess studied me while she considered her words. 'The path of the Moon Warrior is dark and dangerous. I cannot imagine what is required of a Dragonslayer but I suspect that, in some way, your rage may be required. We have not faced daemons since a time before the Rebellion and people started turning their backs on the Gods. The knowledge of that time was lost in the destruction that followed and we have no way of knowing what the cost will be. I can see how it would sit uncomfortably alongside your Empathic understanding, but perhaps your anger will be needed to protect you from what you will have to do.'

I shook my head. 'You're just guessing. Are you willing to bet the lives of Bear, and Vallori, and the others on a suspicion that my rage will be sated once I have an appropriate target? You have no idea what's lying inside me waiting to burst out.'

'I understand that you are scared—'

'You have no idea!'

She sat back in her chair as I struggled to control my breathing and slow my pounding heart. I clenched my fists in an attempt to stop them visibly shaking. I avoided looking at Luella although I knew she was staring at me, waiting until I knew my voice was steady enough to continue without shouting.

'Let's pretend that you are right. That I will be able to direct the power towards daemons and not any innocents who may be near me. What happens when it no longer becomes my choice?'

'How do you mean?'

'There have been… some people that have… explored my mind.' I was finding it hard to find the appropriate words when all my senses were screaming at me to avoid this conversation. 'What if someone could make me do things against my will?'

I was still looking at the floor but heard the soft rustle of fabric as Luella leaned forward. 'They would need your permission to—'

I looked up and echoed her words. 'Not everyone is restricted by our rules.'

I saw the thoughts ripple within the priestess's eyes: disbelief, doubt, questioning, acceptance. My heart started to race again when I saw her make the connection.

'Tell me about Villermir.'

My head throbbed with sudden heat. The room tilted and my vision constricted to a small area of clear detail. My stomach twisted and I swallowed against the nausea rising up my throat. I wiped my wet palms on my trousers and concentrated on the breathing exercises Vallori had taught me.

'He's the High Priest of Baila–'

'I know who he is,' snapped Luella, before taking a breath and continuing more calmly. 'Stop dissembling. What is he to you?'

My leg would not stop trembling and I dug my nails into my palm, but I forced myself to continue. 'He introduced me to magick. He showed me what was possible. Both within myself and by others.'

'But you are the most powerful person I know and you have not even begun to use your full capabilities yet. Surely after all you have learnt here, he could no longer harm you.'

I heard the note of hysteria in my bitter laugh. 'I could be as powerful as a God and he would still be able to do whatever he liked. He has cultivated my fear since I was a child. It is as natural for me to fear him as it is for me to breathe. I have no choice in it. Just like a fear of heights or a fear of drowning. You can tell yourself that you will not fall and you can be the best swimmer there is, but you still fear the possibility that you could be wrong. That this will be the time when you die. I cannot do anything other than fear him. And that gives him total control over me.'

My mind replayed images from my time in Burford Hythe at the hands of Villermir; winged daemons that tore at my skin, flames that scorched my lungs, insects that crawled over my body. All manipulated from my mind to ensure my primal fears were exposed and used to torment me. All designed to give the access that my natural defences had denied him. To enable him to access my power and use it as he wished. To make me the puppet that Kade had accused me of being.

My eyes stung with unshed tears at the frustration and helplessness he still had the power to instil in me. I focused again on my breathing, willing myself to hear Vallori's steadying mantra as I battled the emotions which threatened to overwhelm me. Gradually, my heart slowed and my breathing steadied but I could not stop the tremors that ripped through my body.

'Villermir will use everything I have to destroy me. To destroy Faulknar and finish what the Rebellion started. He aims to annihilate the old Gods and have total dominion for Baila. He has corrupted the natural flow of energy in the Three Kingdoms and is causing monumental changes in weather and landscape. He will stop at nothing, *nothing* to get his way.'

I looked up to see Luella had paled. 'He's controlling all that?' she asked quietly.

'Who else could it be? Unless the Gods are set on their own collapse, he seems to be the only one to benefit.'

She shook her head slowly. 'How?'

I hesitated before realising that I had told her about Villermir's effect on me, there was no reason for her not to know it all. 'He has the Empathy Crystal. He has the conduit to make those changes.'

'How is he accessing it? He can't be an Empath, surely?' She was clever, she quickly made the connection. 'You?'

'He used me to unlock it. It seems he no longer needs me to employ it.'

The priestess was quiet for a long time. She maintained her gaze and I searched for her intentions. The muscles around her eyes remained relaxed and I saw no accusation. A slight frown creased the skin across her forehead and her lips were pinched into a thin line as she debated with herself on how to proceed. I hoped I had convinced her that it was safer for me to stay hidden within her sanctuary, but accepted it was beyond the control of either of us. I knew that I could not ignore the changes that Villermir had wrought, any more than I could leave the shamans unopposed in Hilman. If I was honest, I was surprised that the Goddess had left me here so long.

Luella took a deep breath then gave a small nod to confirm her decision. 'It is no coincidence that the Goddess brought you here. We have trained all the Moon Warriors and I believe you are destined to complete the tests before you leave us. But it seems we have run out of time and you will be judged before I would have chosen to do so.'

'What tests?'

'What I tell you next must not be told to anyone else. Not even your *pháirtí*. Do you understand?' I nodded, and she continued. 'To qualify as a Moon Warrior, you will need to complete three tasks. I cannot tell you what they will be other than to say that they will challenge your strength and battle skills, your magickal abilities, and your knowledge and loyalty. You will either succeed or you will be killed.'

She waited for me to appreciate the consequences of attempting the ritual. 'Why do I need to be tested? Surely the knowledge I have gained here should be enough. Why take the risk that I will be killed?'

'Completion of the rites has always been used to determine the character of those given the title of Moon Warrior. I agree that you possess many of skills already and are clearly chosen by the Goddess, but I believe she would not have sent you here if she did not wish you to be tried in this manner.'

I tried to find the reasons to avoid these trials but I rarely made the best choices and perhaps I should trust the Goddess's plan. I did not believe that she would have brought me all this way just so I could die in some pointless assessment.

'When?'

The older woman sighed and uncharacteristically ran her fingers through her hair in a nervous gesture. 'As I mentioned before, events are moving fast and I fear we no longer have the time to delay. The tests are held on the first day of the full moon when the Goddess is at her strongest.'

'That's tomorrow night.'

'And we cannot put this off for another cycle. I suggest you spend the day with your friends.'

Chapter Five

I had retreated to my usual refuge on top of the sanctuary walls, looking out over the ocean and watching the dark night give way to a grey dawn and then to a rose-pink sunrise. The seabirds' caws drifted on the swirling breeze, first blowing towards me then back over the water, and the wind's fickle nature seemed to match my turbulent mood. I could leave the sanctuary, perhaps find another community further north where I could pretend that the fate of the Three Kingdoms was not my concern. I could decline the Moon Warrior tests, denying my heritage as a Moon Warrior and try to avoid being a Dragonslayer. I could stay on the walkway forever and refuse to acknowledge anything other than the birds and the wind.

The last option was as plausible as the rest and I knew the decision had been made the previous evening, even if I did not want to accept it. Luella had been right. The Goddess had brought me here for a reason and I was not arrogant enough to think that any decision I made would be better than hers. I would face the challenge of the tests and, if I survived, I would address the threat to the Three Kingdoms. I could not deny the call of my blood; as Empath, as Dragonslayer, and as Moon Warrior.

'You've been avoiding me.' Vallori had come to find me as he always did.

'Will you not let me brood in peace?' I smiled to soften the accusation, grateful for his company despite my mocking words.

'Do you want to talk to you about what happened yesterday morning?'

'When I nearly killed a guest of the Sanctuary of The Moon Goddess?'

'Yes, that. Bear admitted he provoked you. He takes full responsibility.'

'That's unnecessarily generous of him, but Bear is not the problem.'

'Then tell me.'

I took a deep breath. It was easy to bite at Vallori and use a sharp tongue to avoid his difficult questions. Under the shadow of the Moon Warrior tests, I did not want to do that. He was just trying to understand and as my *pháirtí,* he had a right to know.

'It's not just that I nearly killed him,' I started carefully. 'It's not even because it would have been *so easy* to kill him. The problem is, I wanted to do it. There was no question in my mind that Bear would die and it felt like the most natural thing I had ever done.'

'But you didn't kill him.'

I sighed in frustration. I could not make him understand. He rested a hand on my arm, waiting until I turned to look at him before continuing.

'I do understand, Tallen. Everyone understands. You are a capable fighter and I know you have killed before. And I know this is different. Your magick is greater than anyone's and that makes you so much more dangerous.'

'Then you understand why I cannot use it. It's not just the potential. I'm so angry. All the time. And if I let that bleed into the magick... I'm scared, Vallori.'

'Everyone is scared. Even Bear, and he's the most powerful warrior I have ever seen. We should be scared. But *you* should not. I can't begin to understand what lies in store for you, but the way Luella has been pushing me for information—'

'Have you been telling tales on me?'

Vallori smiled. 'She has received no secrets from me. But she has been asking more frequently lately.' He studied me for a few heartbeats before continuing softly. 'She has something planned for you and I suspect it will test every skill you have. We have always told you that you're holding back. Bear was willing to take you to the point of losing control.'

'And look how that turned out.'

'I know you're afraid of what could happen when you release your power, but you need to know what you are capable of. What you will need to do to crush the daemons and stop the foul magick that's destroying the Three Kingdoms.'

'And if I can't?'

He hesitated again. 'I suspect you will not be able to avoid using your full power for much longer. I know you are scared of what you might find, of what's hidden deep within yourself. But we're just frightened you won't come back from it.'

'You should be more afraid that I will burst your head like a ripe tomato.'

'There have been days,' he admitted with a brief smile. 'But don't pretend to yourself that people don't care about you. That it would be of no consequence if you walked away from us.'

'Didn't work out too well last time.'

'Things are rarely that simple, Tallen.'

Luella may not have mentioned the Moon Warrior trials but Vallori, Z'hara and Bonash were certainly aware that something was about to occur. After much encouragement and promises that Bear would not be at the session, I was convinced to train with them and Vallori led us to a smaller room off the main corridor. The space was generally used for more intimate practice and was quieter than the main training arena. The four of us were the only people there.

The private training room was not the only acknowledgement of their suspicion that fate was starting to reclaim me. I was barely challenged, with neither strength nor skill being put to the test. The exercises were aimed at loosening up joints and reviewing muscle memory rather than teaching new skills or correcting bad habits. The session finished without releasing any of my nervous tension.

The second half of the day continued in much the same manner. Aware of my restlessness, Bonash suggested meditation to help calm me. I had always struggled to sit still and was rarely able to sufficiently quieten my mind so, predictably, I continued to fidget throughout Bonash's tranquil guidance. Thoughts of what was waiting for me that evening stung my body with anxiety, while my mind freely roamed to conjure the various horrors I might face. Eventually, Z'hara grew tired of my constant twitching and frustrated sighs, and dragged me out of the secluded garden.

Z'hara proposed a more domestic distraction and, despite being the last one I would have chosen, her attentions made me feel more relaxed than either the meditation or the fighting. She took me to her chamber and instructed me to sit while she brushed my hair. The repetitive rhythm of the brush eased the tension in my muscles and watching her nimble fingers braid small silver rings into the plaits created a sense of contentment I had not expected. We chatted while she worked, mainly commenting on Vallori's many annoying habits while being fully aware that we both deeply cared for him. I no longer constantly checked the passage of the sun and was surprised when Vallori and

Bonash arrived to escort us to the evening meal. My anxiety hit with a greater intensity after the short period of absence, resulting in awkward conversation and uncomfortable silences, with little appetite in any of us.

The apprentices had started lighting the candles and lamps when Luella came in person to escort me. My sense of dread was not helped by the hush that settled over the hall upon her arrival, with whispered conversations regarding why she was here rippling around the room. What little food I had eaten turned sour in my stomach and my legs were trembling by the time I stood to greet her. She gave a small incline of her head then walked away without having spoken a word. I looked at my friends, briefly wondering if I would see them again, then obediently followed the High Priestess.

Luella walked briskly towards the large central building with the pointed roof. The sigils around the main door glowed dimly in the fading light while the full moon hovered above the walls of the sanctuary, seeming to watch my approach to a familiar structure which suddenly felt threatening. Luella did not hesitate, continuing through the wooden doors and into the darkened corridor. Small, flickering flames from flat oil-jars caused shadows to creep along the dark wooden panels.

We entered a side room and I released the breath I had not realised I was holding. The chamber was comfortably furnished with padded chairs and was brightly lit with tall candles. The priestess closed the door behind me, allowing her shoulders to drop for the first time since entering the dining hall. She gestured for me to sit in one of the chairs.

'I have told you the reasons why I believe you should progress with the Moon Warrior tests,' Luella began as she sat in a chair next to me. 'And I have explained that these will result in success or failure. No second attempts. Either you will pass through to the next trial or you will be killed. Do you understand?'

'I understand.'

'The decision has to be yours, are you sure you want to proceed?'

I gave a weak grin. 'No. I want to run away and never have any responsibilities. Ever.'

Luella remained serious despite my feeble attempt at humour. 'You could have left today but you are still here.'

'You spoke the truth earlier. There must be a reason I was sent here. And I suspect that if I avoid these tests, there will be others later. I agree to proceed.'

'There will be three challenges. You must complete each before moving to the next. Once you start the first, there will be no going back. You will succeed or you will be killed. There will be no breaks between them and you will continue until you have completed all three, for as long as that takes. You will receive no help or aid, and you must complete them yourself. Do you understand?'

I felt that she was reciting a well-rehearsed speech, giving the rules of the game without actually telling me how to play it. I nodded my reply but realised she needed verbal confirmation when she remained silent and still. I repeated my agreement to proceed. Her face softened with concern for an instant before quickly returning to the controlled composure of a High Priestess, giving a firm nod.

'Follow me.'

She led out of the chamber and along the rest of the main corridor, stopping in front of a heavy door surrounded by protective symbols. With one last look at me, she opened it wide and indicated that I should enter. The light from the corridor continued for no more than a pace before darkness claimed the room. The hall should have been familiar, having spent many hours studying there, but I could not determine the dimensions of the space, much less any items contained within it. I briefly wondered whether it had become a portal to another time and place, where hidden dangers lurked to trap me, but I had agreed to continue and there was no conflict in my mind when I stepped through the doorway.

The door closed quietly behind me and I felt instantly smothered by the total darkness. I extended an arm in front of me to assess whether any barriers lay directly ahead. I could not see anything, not even the movement as I moved the limb up and down. I extended my awareness and searched for the elements I could manipulate into lighting the room. Something was blocking my magick and I was unable to gather the energy or shape it to my will. I waited for several racing heartbeats in the completely silent darkness, then took a tentative step forward.

I reacted by instinct when the blade whispered through the air. I twisted to one side and the lethally sharp edge sliced through the fleshiest part of my cheek rather than anything more vital. I spun in a quick circle, drawing *Saorsa* and slashing at the air around me. The room returned to being as empty as it had a heartbeat before. I could not see or hear anything to indicate where the attacker was or when they might strike again. I rubbed at the wound in irritation. I lacked a target and stood helpless until the next assault. I strained my eyes looking for any hint of light that would betray my challenger but I remained blind.

The softest of breaths provided warning when the weapon spun towards me once more. I took a step backwards and arched my back to avoid the steel tip that aimed for my neck. I lifted *Saorsa* to intersect with my opponent's weapon, releasing a scream of protest when it caught the edge. I judged the slant of the blade and the angle at which the pressure was exerted, and predicted where the slice would come next. The next few parries were purely based on reaction. I was knocked one way and then the other while I tried to keep my blade in front of me. The concussive forces sent stinging waves up my arms as the weapons collided, but I managed to avoid any further injury.

My sword swung against nothing but air and I had the chance to recover my breath. My eyes refused to adjust to the dark and I could detect no sign of my opponent. I scowled at the futility of this exercise; how was I supposed to demonstrate my skill when I could not see my target, much less anticipate their moves? I wished for the senses of an owl and the ability to locate my prey in complete darkness. Perhaps I had bonded with the wrong spirit.

The thought born of frustration made everything clear. I had spent many nights with the wolf pack tracking deer and rabbits. Vision was of primary use once the animals had been flushed, but it had limited benefit in dappled glades when dawn and dusk muted all to variations of grey. With a small smile, I closed my eyes to remove the temptation and let the other senses colour my world. I smelt the sweet scent of beeswax that had been used to polish the wooden panels of the floor and walls. I inhaled the mustiness of a room that was rarely exposed to fresh air. I caught the faint sour taste of the powdered minerals used for incantations, along with the bitterness of the herbs smoked to expand the human perception. And I detected the musk of male sweat.

Having found the general location of my opponent, I tilted my head and focused my hearing on that area. The chamber was protected to prevent the energy created through summoning or elemental manipulation from leaking into the compound. It also prevented any noise from entering. The room was as silent as a tomb. I stilled my mind and slowed my breathing to allow the slightest wisp of air to guide me. I extended my sense of touch, enlarging my aura but nothing interrupted the flow of energy enveloping my body. I pushed further and further until I felt the smallest hint of increased pressure. Not wanting to alert my prey, I kept close control on my probing and gave as little impression of my presence as he did. I kept my breathing shallow and silent. I heard the whisper of a breath and finally knew where to find him.

I made my first offensive move. I darted forward as quietly as I could, leaving the swing of my sword until the last moment to prevent any avoidable noise. *Saorsa* flew in a move that would slice him from hip to opposite shoulder, but his blade blocked mine while still low to the ground. His sword cut through the air and created turbulence within my auric fields. The soft whine of displaced air allowed me to predict his attack. Up or down, left or right. We were evenly matched and neither gained an advantage. I placed my feet carefully to avoid unseen obstacles as we danced around the room.

Saorsa whistled through empty air but I kept track of his location. I was fully tuned to his breathing, his smell and the disruption of my auric currents. Like bats hunting insects in the night, I no longer needed vision to see where he had retreated to. I pressed with a vicious slice that would disable his sword arm and I did not need *Saorsa*'s contact to know the move had hit true. My senses exploded with the release of blood. He switched his blade to the other hand and I pushed again, knowing my quarry would not be disadvantaged for long. I exploited the time it took to find his new rhythm, attacking fast and erratic, and preventing him from choosing his own strategy. His parries were reactive and lacked force but he was not lacking in skill. He soon repaid the injury I had given with a deep gash over my ribs.

I skipped back out of his reach. We were both too spent to control our breathing, clearly identifying our positions and he did not refuse the invitation. I was forced to defend while protecting against the sharp sting of the wound. He followed my retreat and I was pushed backwards several paces before I could twist away from his sword. I quickly switched from the chased to the chaser, slashing *Saorsa* across his back then reversing the blade to hamstring him when I met no resistance. I dropped into a low crouch and his blade skimmed over my head. I kicked out to strike at the side of his knee and he gave a satisfying grunt of pain when he hit the ground. I stamped hard on his wrist, releasing his sword and kicked it away before he had a chance to reclaim it.

The loss of his sword seemed to signal the end of this trial, with light returning to illuminate the room. The dimly glowing lamps caused my eyes to protest after so long in the total darkness and I blinked rapidly as I held the tip of *Saorsa* against the hollow of my opponent's throat.

'Bear?'

I glared at the large man as he lay on the floor. He raised himself onto his elbows and I immediately responded, lifting the point of my blade into the fleshy tissue between his lower jawbones. He opened his hands, palms towards me in submission. Dark blood ran freely down his sword arm.

'You must complete the test,' he said quietly.

'I beat you fairly,' I countered. 'Without the use of magick.'

'Not exactly without magick.' He shrugged a shoulder. 'But yes, you did beat me fairly. Now you must complete the challenge.'

I frowned in confusion. 'What else is required?'

Bear shifted his weight towards his uninjured arm. 'I'm sure you were told the instructions for these trials. You have won, so you must now kill me.'

I took a step back in horrified shock. 'What? I was told that *I* would die if I failed. There was no mention of having to kill anyone.'

'Do you lack the strength of character to complete the task?'

I gave a short, bitter laugh. 'You, of all people, should not need to ask that. Have you forgotten our sparring session so quickly?'

'You failed to kill me then. It remains to be seen if you can kill me now.'

I moved to kick his sword to within his reach, then stood several paces away to allow him to stand without threat.

'I have the required *strength of character*,' I snapped. 'I have nothing to prove there. And we gain nothing by your death.'

'I am a Moon Warrior, Tallen nic Duane. I have stood where you are now. Your abilities exceed mine. It is appropriate that I relinquish my place to you.'

'That's the stupidest thing I've ever heard. What possible benefit could there be in reducing the number of trained warriors? Especially one of the few chosen by the Goddess. It makes no sense.'

Bear raised his blade and moved into an offensive position, one which I immediately mirrored. He made no move towards me and we stared at each other for several heartbeats, each waiting for the other to make the first move.

'Only one of us gets to leave this room,' growled Bear. 'If you want to proceed with the Moon Warrior trials, you must do this.'

'Not if it means killing a skilled warrior who is of value to the Goddess.'

'You are a Dragonslayer!' he roared. 'Are you prepared to die and throw away your potential, on a principle?'

'That is your choice, not mine.'

I turned at the sound of a sharp click. A door was standing slightly ajar in a wall that I knew was solid only a moment early. Bear lowered his sword and relaxed his shoulders.

'Congratulations. You have shown that you do not crave the title of Moon Warrior above all else and have completed your first test.' He gave an elaborate bow, extending his arm towards the exit. 'You may proceed.'

I stared at him with a blank expression, struck mute by indignant disbelief. One moment he was demanding that I kill him, the next he was congratulating me for not killing him.

'This is ridiculous! You seem to be making the rules up as you go along. If this is some foolish game you are all playing, I fail to see the humour.'

'This is no game, Tallen. But I'm sure you can appreciate that to tell you the answer before asking the question would defeat the point of the test. You have to be free to make your own choice, without being influenced by what you think is required of you.'

He inclined his head towards the plain door. A soft, yellow light outlined the threshold to the next room, and the next test. After the darkness of the first trial, the light appeared welcoming but I did not trust its blatant invitation. I hesitated for several heartbeats while Bear waited patiently and my mind frantically searched for alternative options. There were none, of course. I had agreed to complete the three assessments at the forfeit of my life so, after exhaling a noisy, exasperated breath, I walked over to the door and opened it wide.

The light burned as an impenetrable barrier preventing any view of what lay ahead until I entered into the room. I turned back at the quiet click to find that the wall was once again solid, confirming that there would be no way back.

I swiftly surveyed the room and the flicker of recognition choked my breath. My heart stuttered and my guts clenched in response to a fear so much greater than that of the first test. I took an involuntary step back and my mind whimpered that there was danger here. Deep, irrational fears awoke, born in a time before I knew about magick and dragons and the power within me. Before I knew of the evil within the one who haunted that room. I saw the library at Liegeport and it still held the power to paralyse me.

I drew a shaky breath and the stabbing pain over my ribs reminded me that a current threat lurked here. Gathering my panicked thoughts, I focused on the detail and searched for the challenge within this trial. Tall bookcases lined all four walls and seemed to crowd the large space, although it was the long, dark wood table which dominated my attention. Silently judging and finding me lacking. The smell of parchment and ink sent a wave of nausea and I swallowed against the burn in my throat. I scanned the shadows looking for the one who had orchestrated the nightmare. No movement alerted me to his presence, but I found him all the same.

Somehow knowing he had been discovered, he stepped into the light. He was hooded in a dark grey cloak that shrouded his face. Strands of dirty-blond hair poked out at the collar and was the only feature identifiable in the voluminous robe. I could not tear my eyes from him. All my nerves were aflame with the rapidly alternating need to run or curl into a protective ball. He did not move, standing as still as a statue as my mind fought my body and tried to convince me that this could not be him. I would not have been sheltered so long at the sanctuary if they meant to betray me to Villermir. Holding my breath to brace my ribs and with every muscle tensed for the inevitable attack, I took a tentative step forward and lifted *Saorsa*.

The response was immediate and I screamed. Fire engulfed my wrists and burned the scarred tissue of my hands. I dropped my sword with the agony of blistering skin twisting my hands into claws. I stared in horror but the fire extinguished as quickly as it had started. Villermir had changed his tactics. This was no mind-game. The flames had caused real damage and the pain throbbed up my arms in time to my racing heart.

'Your weapons will not help you here,' he purred.

He had not moved a single step. His hands still hung loosely at his side and his face remained hidden by the hood. His stance was relaxed and arrogant, silently watching while I struggled to get my breathing under control. The fears of my childhood flooded my brain and combined with the crippling pain of my arms to tear my concentration into a whirlwind of tattered shreds. I reached for my anger to smother the pain and allow my mind focus, building layer upon layer of barriers to keep him out of my mind.

My reinforced defences provided no protection against elemental forces and his fire had just been the beginning. With a small flick of a finger, Villermir created buffeting winds which slammed me into the wall and knocked the air from my lungs. I cowered as ledgers and ink pots pummelled me, bruising wherever they smashed into flesh. I regressed to the quivering child who was helpless against his onslaught. My thoughts skittered away from ways of protecting myself and returned to the despair that had been nurtured in this room. The inevitability of my torment. That I deserved this.

I recalled the crippling attacks that had plagued me when I first came to the sanctuary. The physical debility that drained all defence against the crushing weight of my failure and the total conviction that the world would be better off without me. The constant dialogue that claimed I destroyed everything and I should remain far from those I would end up hurting. That I would always be alone.

But I was not alone. Vallori's deep voice had talked me through the endless nights when my body shook from the overwhelming despair, and had shone like a light on a stormy night. He offered a promise of safety and his gentle persistence had broken through the noise. He had stayed, immovable, while I thrashed and raged.

Using the memories of Vallori as a shield, I took control of the elements. I compressed the air that was pommelling me, agitating a tiny spark until it ignited within the plentiful fuel available. A blanket of flame raged above my head. My anger at Villermir whipped the fire into a blazing inferno – *how dare he invade the place where I had felt safe.* I sent the raging wildfire hurtling towards my tormentor. All my hate blazed in release and I sent the destruction that would incinerate the despised priest.

He transformed his gale into a solid wall of protection, deflecting my flames into the bookcase behind him. It exploded into a rain of burning leather, parchment and waxed wood. Stray sparks caught in the hem of his robe and the cuffs of his sleeves, smouldering as he urgently patted them out. I gave him no respite. I created a volley of fireballs and sent them racing towards him. He swatted them away but the bookcases were starting to produce significant amounts of smoke.

My chest constricted in pain and I choked in an effort to force air into my lungs. My body spasmed and I coughed up water. My thoughts spiralled out of control again as I struggled to understand how I could be drowning. My vision blurred and I fell to my knees, coughing more water from my mouth. I fought to breathe. My flailing mind remembered a raging wall of sea, sent by Villermir in anger at my escape from Freisholm. Kade and I had survived the tempest and I had funnelled the air into the sail to blow us back to safety. *Air. Precious air.* I connected with the element and flowed a cloud of the life-giving gas around the water filling my throat. It seeped into my lungs, expanding to expel the water.

As fast as a striking snake, Villermir changed tactic again. I staggered to my feet while the floor tilted and swayed. The polished wood planks buckled and split in a straight line from Villermir to me. I stumbled to one side, instinctively reaching out to save my fall and hissing a curse when several small blisters on my hand burst. The flare of pain summoned the cold fury that had consumed me when facing Bear in the training arena, and I welcomed it as a familiar friend.

Villermir's arrogance swirled around him like an aura. He had not moved from his place on the boundary of shadow. He had not even raised his arms. I lifted boulders from the exposed earth and threw rock after rock, shattering them into razor sharp fragments before he was given the chance to deflect them back at me. I stalked towards him, a smile of triumph twisting my lips as he finally lifted his arms, showing numerous cuts on his callused hands. I ignored the flutter of a discordant memory and whipped the shards of stone into a whirlwind that slashed at him. I tore apart the ground beneath him and he sank waist-deep into the hole. The hood dropped over his face but I paid little attention when he pulled the material away to reveal a yellow lining. I stood over him and drew the edges of the crack together. He braced his arms against the sides of the crater and looked up with pleading hazel eyes.

'Tallen nic Duane.' A voice unlike Villermir's coughed against the smoke and the debris. 'Remember where you are.'

I blinked at him. The illusion shattered and my mind scrambled to make sense of what I was seeing. The clues that had triggered my fear of Villermir were laid bare; the hint of a lining that suggested blond hair, the large robe that hid a shorter, stockier body, the set-up of the room used to prejudice my mind towards deception, the commanding tone of voice that I was too ready to believe belonged to the priest. I had been a fool, succumbing so easily to a trick of light and shadow.

'Kien?' I stuttered, still feeling sluggish and confused.

'Yes, yes,' he blustered. 'Your aid would be appreciated.'

The hem of his robe had caught under his foot and he struggled to disentangle himself in the constricting space. I clasped his offered hand and pulled him free of the pit.

'I agree that the tests can seem unnecessarily cruel,' he began quietly. 'But they have been used for generations to determine the resilience within the most gifted of students. They are designed to expose your weaknesses. Do not believe yourself needlessly misled.'

My anger still simmered just within my control. I did not want to argue the merits of facing my fears while I continued to feel vulnerable and exposed. I desperately wanted the Moon Warrior tests to be done so I could go back to avoiding the terror they were so mercilessly provoking.

'Is this where you tell me I have to kill you before I can proceed to the next stage?' I asked despondently.

A hint of a grin was quickly suppressed. 'No. You have already come too close to killing me already, I have no desire to press you further. Congratulations, you have shown you can master your fear and have completed the second test. You may proceed.'

At a gesture from his hand, I turned to see a bookcase had silently moved away from the wall by a hand-width and I needed no further encouragement to escape the library and face the final trial.

I stepped through the bookcase into a room that seduced with its warmth and comfort, amplifying the weariness I felt after the two brutal tests. A thick patterned rug covered the floorboards while a fire crackled quietly in a corner. Two deeply upholstered chairs in fabrics to match the rug faced the glowing embers. In one, Luella turned to smile at me.

'Welcome, Tallen.' She gestured the empty seat. 'Please join me.'

I felt exhausted. My body ached deep within the muscles of my back and shoulders. The pain in my hands had returned and the damaged tissues throbbed with an insistent torment. The wound over my ribs was still oozing. The blood had stiffened the material surrounding it to cause further discomfort whenever it rubbed against the injury. My mind remained foggy and clouded, and I was suspicious that the image in front on me was simply another illusion. As tired as I was, I would not take the docile scene at first impression and I looked for the trap hidden within the apparently harmless invitation. Luella inclined her head in appeasement.

'Please,' she persisted, encouraging me to take the empty chair. 'There is no deceit here. You have completed the physical aspects of the trials and you are bleeding.'

I remained cautious but crossed the room and collapsed into the chair. My body craved the support of soft cushions and I involuntarily released a sigh as I relaxed into the padded fabric. I closed my eyes, suddenly overwhelmed by the promise of sleep. It would be so very nice to rest my body and mind and forget the hurtful manipulations of the Moon Warrior tests.

I snapped open my eyes and jerked forward away from the seductive embrace of the cushions. The flash of pain over my ribs effectively chased away any drowsiness. I stretched my back and made myself focus on the final test. A small table was placed next to the priestess's chair, with the contents covered by a dark cloth.

'What's the third task?' I asked bluntly.

'You have shown skill with sword and elemental control.' She smiled when my eyes widened in horrified realisation. 'Peace. *Saorsa* will be returned to you when your trial has finished. As well as demonstrating your abilities—'

'Which you already knew from my work here over the past few years.'

She inclined her head in acknowledgement but still did not react to my accusatory tone. 'You have shown your strength of character. There are boundaries to how you use your abilities. You will not kill needlessly although you are more than capable of defending yourself and destroying your enemies if required. You have faced your darkest fears—'

'You used me. You turned the content of our discussions against me.'

'And those with Vallori and Z'hara and Bonash, and everyone else at the sanctuary.' Her tone hardened in response to my accusations, reminding me of the High Priestess's strength of character. 'The methods used to train Moon Warriors are arcane and absolute. I warned you that very few complete the tests, not because their abilities were lacking but because they could not overcome the personal torments they were presented with. You have denied your bond with the wolves and you refused to acknowledge your fear of Villermir. Not to mention your reluctance to use your talents because you risk losing control. You have addressed all those aspects of your character here. And you have conquered them!'

I sat in stunned silence and she paused to allow me to consider how thorough the trials had been. She waited until my body relaxed into a less defensive posture before continuing in a quiet manner.

'The final test will not test your physical strength or magickal ability. But it will confront another of your key fears. And, for you, I fear this may be your hardest.'

She turned slightly in her chair and removed the cloth from the table, folding it neatly and placing it on the floor beside her. She leaned forward to place the small silver pot on a stand over the embers before lifting the table to place it between us. Three bundles of green leaves, two with berries, were laid in neat piles. The first contained flat, veined leaves that were the shape of a teardrop and a number of shiny black berries. In the second pile were thin stemmed plants, with small three-spiked leaves and purple flowers. The final selection was again a long-stemmed plant, this time with slender, ribbed leaves and white berries. All three were poisonous; nightshade, wolfsbane and mistletoe.

'Your final task,' confirmed Luella. 'You are required to ingest the tincture of at least one of these plants.' I watched a trail of steam drift from the spout of the pot and avoided the priestess's direct stare. 'This is a trial of trust. I betrayed your confidence to arrange the previous two tests. Will you trust me enough to brew a tea from your chosen plant?'

The steam curled into delicate spirals, dancing gracefully in the warm currents produced by the embers. The final assessment was a test of knowledge, involving an understanding of the properties of the plants and their effects on the body. The difference between a plant's therapeutic dose and its lethal effects was a fine line. All three had the ability to stop the heart, but at the correct concentration they could also be used to strengthen the heart muscle and correct abnormal rhythms. I would have to trust Luella to infuse the leaves for the appropriate length of time to avoid a killing dose.

I did not doubt her technical ability but I was not sure I could rely on her motivations, particularly after the previous tests had been specifically designed to force feelings that I would prefer to stay hidden. I did not know her intent with the use of these plants. I could be required to summon the will to heal myself from a lethal dose. I could be taken to the very edges of death and back to Mobis's Hells. This could be the final judgement as to whether I was worthy, and the cause of her warning that those who were deemed lacking would not emerge alive.

'I select all three.' I turned to face her. 'You stated that I had to choose at least one. I choose all three.'

A ghost of a smile was hastily controlled and she inclined her head at my decision. If she was going to poison me, then I would make it as difficult as possible. Nightshade would cause my heart to race, wolfsbane would slow it down, and mistletoe would strengthen the beats to keep the blood pumping around my body. Of course, there were other side effects and it would depend on the dose that was delivered, but I had no control over that. It was the best I could do.

I watched closely while Luella carefully selected the required number of leaves from each group, trimming them of their fibrous stems and discarding the berries which had helped to identify the plants. She sliced her gathered collection into thin strips before using the cloth to remove the lid from the pot, careful to avoid the billowing steam that was released. Once the leaves were sprinkled into the warmed water, she used the blade of the knife to agitate the mixture to the desired colour. Content that she had the correct strength, she poured the infusion into the cup and handed it to me. I could not fault her preparation but still I hesitated to drink from the offered vessel. I waited almost a dozen heartbeats before I was able to conquer my distrust and take the poison, sipping until all the liquid had been consumed.

The dark, brown brew tasted sharply on my tongue and the bitter aroma irritated my nose. The dose was strong and it was not long before my stomach cramped in protest. My heart pounded painfully in my chest and my head flushed with blood, with the pulses throbbing at my temples. Sweat beaded on my upper lip and I clumsily swiped at it in irritation as a headache started to form behind my eyes. The room became clearly defined within my vision, with the edges becoming sharper and the colours more vibrant. I frowned in confusion while Luella's face seemed to lengthen and her eyes grew larger. I flopped back into the chair and the cup fell to the floor, forgotten. My arms stretched away from my body, the limbs narrowing into twig-like structures which no longer belonged to me. I watched them drift away from my body. I looked up to a ceiling that had been transformed into a perfect night sky, sprinkled with gently rotating diamond-bright stars. I was enthralled by the slow movement of the flickering lights, content to watch them for the rest of my life.

A polite cough interrupted my whimsical musings on the starry kingdom of the Gods. I dreamily lowered my gaze and found that the dark panelled, comfortable room had been replaced with a forest glade, dappled with moonlight. I inhaled the scent of crushed grass and night-blooming flowers; evening primrose, night-blooming jasmine and moonflower. It was a beautiful and peaceful place, and as comforting as warm embrace.

The gentle cough was repeated with a more insistent tone. I reluctantly concentrated on focusing my wandering vision to the person in front of me. Recognition brought a sudden clarity. A midnight blue cloak with a purple silk lining covered the graceful frame of the Goddess of the Moon, and she was staring impatiently at me with her ice-blue eyes while a gentle breeze played with the ends of her silver hair.

'Oh,' I gasped irrelevantly.

'Indeed,' she responded, her voice sounding like water flowing over ice. 'It would appear you have met the criteria required to become one of my warriors. A Dragonslayer and a Moon Warrior. Doubly bound to my service. The usual reward for completing the trials is a vision from me but we are long passed that. So what else can I give you?'

She tilted her head in a manner strangely similar to Luella while she considered me. I did not need to be told that her question was rhetorical. This was not a granting of wishes, but an honour to be bestowed. Time seemed to move differently in this space and I could not tell whether I waited a moment or a lifetime. Either way, I was content to watch as her eyes probed into my core.

'I give you the one thing you lack. Faith. If you cannot believe in those around you, and cannot believe in yourself? Then you will believe in me.'

CHAPTER SIX

I awoke in the warm grip of soft sheets and a padded mattress. I took a deep breath, releasing a soft moan when all my stiffened muscles flared in complaint. Reluctantly, I opened my eyes to see a sunlit chamber and Bear leant against the wall. His expression was mildly challenging and his arms were folded across his chest, cradling the injury I had given during the Moon Warrior test.

'At last, she is finally waking up!' he grumbled.

'Hush,' Luella replied softly. 'You are as much to blame as anyone else.'

The High Priestess placed a cool towel on my forehead, easing the ache that throbbed behind my eyes. Kien stood behind her. The cuts and bruises I had inflicted were clearly visible but, in contrast to Bear, he offered me a small, apologetic smile.

'Neither Bear nor Kien would leave your side until they knew you were awake,' Luella continued. 'We have all been through the trials. We know the cost.'

I returned Kien's smile. They were not my enemies despite having manipulated my emotions to make it seem that way. In truth, I was equally to blame. I had been quick to react instinctively and with anger, and the familiar fault had blinded me to the truth.

I had aimed to sit up, but that required releasing my arms from the sheets and I stopped abruptly when I saw my bared flesh. The traumatised tissue I had hated for so long had been replaced with clean, healthy skin. The scars had smoothed and faded into a delicate pattern that gave the impression of soft flames. I stared in disbelief. The red, angry welts had gone, as had the shiny craters which had formed between them. Subtle tones of rose and apricot coloured the space within the raised, rounded white lines to turn the ugly blemishes into beautiful art. I rotated my hands and examined the inside of my forearms, marvelling at the transformation from disliked imperfections into graceful design.

Luella waited patiently while I inspected my new arms and I looked up to see her watching me with an indulgent smile.

'We healed your more serious wounds and purged your system of the poisons you ingested. We all get a token from the Lady of the Moon on becoming her warrior, but it seems she gave you the additional gift of healing your arms.'

I was not really listening to her. My gaze had returned to my healthy limbs and I turned them this way and that, catching the sunlight on the skin and stretching the joints to enjoy the increased flexibility of supple tissue. I felt a smile creep onto my face and was suddenly self-conscious, unwilling to admit that my injuries had affected me so much. They were a visual reminder of how I had failed to protect the Empathy Crystal from Villermir. How retrieving Kade from Mobis's Hells had triggered the visions he despised. I should not feel such pleasure at the vitality of my limbs when Kade was still having to deal with the cost of my actions.

I abruptly realised that Luella had stopped talking and my mind raced to capture the last fragments of the conversation.

'What tokens?'

The priestess laughed softly. 'She will have known you wanted them gone but you should be proud of your scars and the journey you took when obtaining them. As for the token, you have been marked as one of her warriors. The glowing should disappear by the next full moon.'

She inclined her head towards my abdomen, currently hidden by the thick sheet, and I lifted the covers to belatedly realise I was naked. I had been bathed and my wounds had been dressed, but I stared at the turquoise glow which radiated across my belly and, for the second time, I felt my mouth drop open in wonder. A shaded outline of the crescent moon curled around the left side of my navel. The brightness of the mark blurred the edges a little but I could make out subtle shading which perfectly matched that of the moon. I released the sheet and returned to look at the High Priestess, shaking my head at the impossibility of the gifts I had been given.

'Your medal of merit,' she explained. 'We all receive them after completing the tests. As she did with us, I assume she visited you to confirm her acceptance of your sacrifice?' She smiled at my nod of agreement. 'You will find that being a Moon Warrior for The Lady is not an insignificant oath. You will be compelled to follow her command.'

'Does the mark burn if I resist?'

'No. Nothing like that. You feel her will, sometimes in visions but more often as a feeling. A calling or compulsion. A sense that something is wrong and you have an urgent desire to fix it.' She flicked a look at Bear. 'For the most part, you are unaware of what the Goddess requires until the task is complete. Then you realise that, what you thought were random choices, all turned out to be connected and have brought you, irrefutably, to that point.'

'So, it's just decoration?' I smiled. 'I've been claimed by the Goddess. It is very pretty.'

Her face smoothed into a more sombre expression. 'The marks are a little more than that. They work as a connection between us, as her Moon Warriors. They serve to let us know if one of us falls.'

The priestess fell silent and Kien moved to stand beside her. 'We are each given the mark in a different place, and we feel an incapacitating wound at that site when a Warrior dies. The last one to leave us was Mattian.' His eyes were fixed on Luella. 'His mark was on the inside of his wrist. When he was burned by those false priests of Baila, our arms felt encased in molten metal.'

'My mark is on my abdomen.' His words weighed heavily and the sound of my voice felt like an intrusion. 'If I was to die, you would feel a pain in your belly?'

Unexpectedly, my comments raised an indulgent smile from the graceful lady sitting beside me. 'It is appropriate that your mark is located there. Your talents are instinctual. You react in response to the feelings in your guts.' She inclined her head towards the large man standing quietly in front of her. 'Bear is marked over his heart. His skills come from the big, old heart of his namesake.'

He huffed in dismissal. 'The Lady has such a sense of humour.'

Luella's smile widened before she nodded towards the Moon Warrior standing protectively at her shoulder. 'Kien favours the academic. He is more at home in the library and hunting for lost manuscripts to widen his, already vast, knowledge. His mark is nestled at the base of his skull.'

'And yours?' I prompted.

She gave a short laugh. 'Mine reminds me that I have a habit of stepping into trouble.'

Kien sniffed. 'That's not the reason your mark is on your ankle and you know it,' he chastised affectionately. 'Luella's is there to remind her that she is always ready to step up to the challenge of making difficult decisions, and to do that needing to be done.'

'Which brings us nicely to the difficult decision of what is required next,' continued Luella. 'Your body will need several days of rest to recover from the healing, but you will soon need to honour your commitment to the Goddess. There is a lot of work that needs to be done and, as I stated before, we can no longer afford to wait.'

Luella and Kien, with occasional input from Bear, went on to explain the situation outside of the sanctuary. I had been told about the daemons and the invasion of Gallowgla into the most northern territories of the Three Kingdoms. It was a natural progression for the Gallowglass. Their homelands were almost directly east of Hilman and I appreciated that the rich, fertile soil would be appealing to those who farmed a rocky, mountainous terrain. The resident population were understandably unsettled by the invasion, but tensions had already been running high with a volatile mixture of prejudice, poverty, fear and anger. Averill's rise to power had helped to ignite the simmering resentments. Reports told of swift justice, with the brutal annihilation of his rivals and the indiscriminate destruction of property and livestock for those who angered him. Harsh penalties were dispensed upon those who transgressed the increasing number of laws and restrictions. Public executions had returned, with deaths by hanging, stoning or burning becoming common in market squares across the kingdom. Failure to attend one of these events could itself lead to severe punishments. I thought of the welcoming bustle of the port I had seen when crossing Hilman with Drey and Kade, and grieved on many different levels.

I was informed that, while the kingdom would be hostile, Moon Warriors were rarely required to counter the politics of a region, despite the blatant need in Hilman for a more tolerant system of governance. I was being sent solely to defend these people against the daemons raised by the Gallowgla shamans and their blood rituals. Bear had watched Hilman change from a land of production, prosperity and peace into a cauldron of hate, slavery and murder. He would lead me, along with Vallori, Z'hara and Bonash, into this dangerous place and try to prevent us all getting killed.

'Of course,' Bear concluded cheerfully. 'We have to get across the border first.'

It was a warm, sunny autumnal day when we finally left for the border with Hilman. I had received two gifts from Luella in acknowledgement of completing the Moon Warrior tests; an obsidian-black velvet cloak with a purple lining which was stored safely in my saddlebags, and a padded leather jerkin with a high collar to protect the neck which I wore with pride. A crescent moon was stamped into the leather on the collar and delicate stitching bought the garment in to sit snugly against my ribs and waist. I appreciated the practical nature of the gift and that it would provide good armour for the coming fight, but I treasured the craftsmanship and the beautiful design.

The little blue roan waited in the small courtyard in front of the double wooden gates, along with the other horses who stood patiently awaiting their riders. Trefin would be for me as the quietest of the group. I had worked hard to gain her trust and she now tolerated me in most situations. I had grown quite fond of the little mare.

Vallori and Z'hara had already claimed their mounts and chatted amiably as their horses affectionately nibbled at each other. Z'hara's chestnut gelding stood a hand-width taller than Vallori's mare, but it was the smaller horse that seemed more striking with her coal-black colouring and the dramatic white star on her chest. Bonash was tightening the girth strap of a stocky bay mare that noisily chewed at her bit, and had created a thick foam of saliva to coat her lips. To compliment his imposing frame Bear had chosen a large, black battle-horse, complete with a long, jet fetlock which covered the eyes and long, ebony hair which encircled each hoof. I had a moment's fear that he was taking Hex, but the gelding was placid and he calmly watched the activities of the courtyard. The bulky man grinned at me. He swung effortlessly into the saddle and was fully aware of how he towered over everybody else. He wore a jerkin that resembled mine and I suspected it would also carry the embossed moon on the collar.

There was no denying that our small group would be leaving on a military campaign. While our horses were lightly burdened with shelters, sleeping mats and provisions, we carried an array of lethal weapons strapped to backs, hips and saddles. I was armed with *Saorsa* and a thick bladed dagger at my waist. Several throwing knives were concealed beneath the hem of my new jerkin and a small blade was tucked into my boot. I had also stashed a few small bottles of poison within Trefin's saddlebags, along with a range of healing herbs and ointments. Z'hara conspicuously carried her twin swords strapped to her back and I knew her to have several daggers tucked into her boots, waistband and sleeves. Vallori and Bonash carried heavy swords, with Bonash also taking a small axe. Bear bristled with weapons. In addition to his broadsword, he carried an axe at his waist. A bow, a quiver full of arrows and his shield were lashed to his horse. He also concealed several knives within his clothing. I was left with no doubts concerning the reality of the danger we were about to face.

I felt a rising dread as we completed the last of our preparations and nudged our horses towards the large, wooden gates. I had developed an irrational fear over the previous few days that I would be struck down by a bolt of lightning the moment I left the sanctuary and returned to the world beyond its protective walls. That somehow, I had been shielded from a divine backlash that was due to me for ignoring my obligations for so long. I knew it was my own guilt that tormented me, but I could not shake the heavy feeling in my stomach which grimly predicted some impeding catastrophe. I mocked myself for being a fool and left the compound with no disaster befalling me. I had left the enclosure on several occasions to visit the cliffs and the rocky shore when I needed solitude, and I had suffered no mishap. I shook off my worries and appreciated the warm morning sun on my back.

We had gone no further than halfway across the grassland when the feared thunderbolt struck. My head burst with the buzz of a swarm of angry bees and needle-stab pains exploded in every area of my skull. My eyesight darkened so the image I saw seemed cloaked in dense smoke while I inhaled the smell of rancid decay. I choked, gagging against the cloying taste of foulness that coated my mouth. My skin felt ice-cold. My vision tilted and I rolled off Trefin. The contact with the ground caused a new eruption of hostile sensations to batter against my body. Cramping spasms ripped through my guts and my heart fluttered erratically within my chest. My fingers and toes curled tight against the pain while a roaring wind raged within my ears.

At some point I became aware of Vallori's voice. His gentle tone created a rhythm that insistently wove through the chaos, slowly working his way through the noise. He repeated the familiar mantra and I focused on the words, listening carefully as he confirmed that I was safe and that he was with me. My muscles started to relax and the pounding of my blood eased to a murmur. The blanketing grey mist receded and I could, once again, make out the grassy meadow that bordered the forest. Vallori was sitting next to me. One hand protectively cradled my head while I grasped his free arm with enough force to leave bruises. I forced myself to release my grip, clenching my fists to prevent myself from scraping at the buzzing which still stung deep within the skull.

'That was a bit dramatic, don't you think?'

I looked up to see Vallori offering a weak grin, unable to reassure him with one of my own. The fury of the storm had receded but I still felt flailed and raw. I felt crushed by the emotions of despair and malevolence, of suffering and injustice.

'Everything is in pain. Everything is dying.'

'What do you mean—' began Vallori before Bear interrupted him with a growled curse.

'Of course,' he grumbled. 'I've been such a fool.'

The movement of Bear dismounting caused another wave of dizziness, dimming my vision once more. I breathed deeply through my mouth and the sensation passed quickly. The big man's face loomed into view when he squatted down in front of me.

'My apologies, Tallen.' His face was creased with remorse. 'Luella warned me that you felt it, even protected by the sanctuary's wardings. I forgot you were an Empath and that you would pick up the land's distress.'

'The soil. The stones. The rocks. They are all screaming. I feel their fibres being torn apart. Every tree, bush and plant. Every blade of grass. All of it is dying. I can taste their decay.' I built layer upon layer of mental barriers to reduce the sensations that were assaulting at me. 'I feel him everywhere. Villermir is using the Empathy Crystal to corrupt the energy lines and I can feel his presence clawing at me.'

'The changes are occurring across the Three Kingdoms. Their effects are muted but they still resonate this far north.' Bear watched me closely as my reinforced defences softened the distress. 'Landscapes that have taken an unfathomable length of time to mould are being ripped up and reshaped in a matter of hours. I haven't seen the effects in Faulknar or Lindvane, but Hilman has suffered terrible changes over the past few years.'

Bear explained how Hilman had been subjected to tremors that had shaken the sides of great hills. Craters had opened up large swaths of earth, destroying farmland and killing livestock so that many communities would face starvation during the winter months. Weather changes had amplified the effects. Rainstorms lasted for days and caused flood water that ruined homes and spread disease. The people of Hilman were already suffering from Averill's brutal regime, and the looting and violent reprisals that had followed. They were poorly equipped to deal with the ground under their feet taking their property and livelihoods as well.

Bear talked long enough for me to gather my scattered wits and adapt to the waves of torment battering against my mental walls. A pulsing tension remained but, with Vallori's support, I was able to regain my feet. Trefin needed considerable coaxing to allow me near her, having bolted when I fell and Bonash had struggled to herd her back to the group and catch her flapping reins. Vallori held her bridle to prevent her from dancing away from me and her whole body quivered when I mounted.

The day passed slowly. We travelled away from the sanctuary and through the ancient forest surrounding it. My companions tried to make conversation, but I found it difficult to concentrate on their words and failed to respond to their questions. It did not take long for them to cease their attempts. Despite my strengthened defences, the information continued to overwhelm me. The trees stabbed my skull with blades of fire. The bracken whipped with barbs that flayed my skin. The soil erupted in flashes of blinding light every time the horses placed their feet. Stilted conversations floated around me with the sharp irritation of a swarm of insects, before faltering to a stop. We camped by a gentle-flowing stream that sounded like the screeching of nails on slate to my sensitised ears. Bear, Bonash and Z'hara soon retreated to their beds, while Vallori loyally stayed until I could no longer tolerate his presence and told him to join Z'hara.

The next day I found it easier to block the messages coming from the land, sealing it into a small section of my mind so I no longer felt constantly attacked and overwhelmed by its suffering. I became able to follow the gentle banter of my companions and, while it took an exhausting amount of will, I was able to feel part of the group again. Their conversation became a welcome distraction, with Z'hara informing Bear of her reason for being at the sanctuary.

'The island had few resources,' she explained, 'so most families were either ocean-faring merchants or fishermen. As soon as I was old enough, I left my nagging mother to join my father and trade across all the sea-bordered territories. Apparently, she was furious but I never went home again to find out.'

'Which port was your favourite?' Bonash prompted, knowing she loved to tell stories of her travels.

'Well,' she purred. 'That's like asking who your favourite lover is.' She laughed freely as Vallori raised an eyebrow. 'The ports on the mainland closest to home were equal parts chaotic and exotic. The fragrant scents of spices drifted on the sea breezes to mingle with the smell of fresh fish and baked bread. The clothing of the people matched the different colours of the spices and fruits available in the markets. Bright oranges, radiant reds, vibrant greens and intense yellows all merged as the jumble of the crowds jostled to grab a bargain. Hawkers would have to shout over the buzz of conversation and the sharp bursts of laughter. The heat of the midday sun blurred everything to a shimmering haze.'

'So, which is your favourite?' Bonash grinned, playing the game of Z'hara's storytelling.

'Ferica is generally considered the finest for food. But for craftsmanship you would need to go to the western edges of the Namori lands. A trading culture of their own, the Travellers know quality when they see it and their ability to decorate pottery and design jewellery is unmatched by that of any other region. And the tales they tell over a campfire always make for a welcome visit.'

She continued for some time, praising the virtues of the different ports she had visited along the southern coasts bordering the kingdoms south of the Namori, and those along the western shores of Lindvane and Hilman. Z'hara's father had rarely travelled inland and, in order to reach the waters between Faulknar and Gallowgla, he would travel around the northern tip of the Northlands. As well as being a journey that would last the best part of a year, the seas around the Northlands were often too dangerous to sail. Violent, unpredictable storms would strike without warning during all seasons.

'Why did you stop trading?' inquired Bear.

Z'hara's face clouded and her voice softened with the story told less often. 'Father was open-minded with what I did when I was a girl but as soon as I reached marriageable age, he could only think of profit.' She shook her head, her braids rippling in defiance. 'Well, I wasn't going to stick around for him to sell me off to the highest bidder. I left him.'

The next part of her tale involved a nightmarish journey across Hilman and the Northland territories as she avoided numerous attempts to coerce her into prostitution or sell her into undesirable marriages. Z'hara had an exotic beauty that was rarely seen in the busy ports of Hilman, much less the poorer communities inland. She attracted the attention of many who sought to profit from her youth and looks. The confident, competent warrior I knew was battered and scarred, both physically and emotionally, by the time she was found by a healer journeying to the Sanctuary of The Moon Goddess.

Bonash gallantly interrupted before she was required to describe this part of her history to Bear. 'Unfortunately, the reason I came to be at the sanctuary is less exciting than Z'hara's. My village ran me out for asking too many questions.'

As intended, Bonash's flippant comments lightened the mood and Z'hara smiled at his false modesty. 'You are such a liar, small man. Your family adored you and you know it.'

'Perhaps.' Her *pháirtí* grinned at her before turning back to Bear. 'The village is close to the border with the Northlands so we all knew about the Moon Goddess's sanctuary and its reputation as a place of learning. Despite Hilman's long history of restrictions on any religious faction, my parents were still open to the old ways and suggested I studied there when they could no longer provide me with the answers I was seeking.'

'And have you been home since?'

'I've returned a few times but it is safer not to draw the attention of the priests' to the village.' Bonash shrugged. 'Strangers are no longer welcome in Hilman. Especially those coming from the north.'

'True,' Bear agreed sadly. 'The border has been effectively closed for several seasons now. Some traders can still cross but it is getting increasingly difficult to arrange the appropriate paperwork and bribes. Unfamiliar faces have almost no chance of gaining access to the Three Kingdoms via the land border.'

'So how are we going to get there?' I asked. 'We're heading away from the coast.'

Bear's beard split in a grin. 'Eager to see your Gallowglass friends again? The pirates hold most of the ports along the east coast. Nothing gets in or out that they don't know about. No, I'll take the fanatical amateurs on the land over the professional thugs on the water.'

It became clear what Bear meant by *fanatical amateurs* when we reached the border five days later. A small hill descended into a wide, flat plain dotted with areas of scrubby gorse and heather. An abandoned farmhouse had been ravaged by the weather so that part of the roof had collapsed and the wooden fencing had decayed from persistently damp rot. The dominating feature in this large, open space, however, was the clear border between Hilman and the Northlands, marked by rows upon rows of sharpened wooden stakes. Even from a distance and squinting against the setting sun, I could tell that the defences stood taller than a horse and were angled towards those coming from Hilman. At least five layers ensured that very few massed assaults would penetrate, while darkened depressions behind the spears suggested pits lined with similar spikes to trap any foot-soldiers who made it through. A thick strip of churned earth told of the archer's range, their arrows capable of cutting down the enemy if they dared to approach. The presence of a number of dark scavenging birds testified to recent casualties and my sensitised nerves drummed with the ground's torment and the tortured energies of death.

Behind the spiky barrier were two walled fortifications, barely in sight of each other. The nearer one appeared to be a more recent structure, with wooden walls and small squat towers. A flag showing the joined clans of the Northlands could be seen flapping in the gusting breeze but the blue cross was the only clear feature, with the totem animals reduced to blotches of colour by distance. The distant fort seemed a more permanent structure, larger and primarily made of stone. A tall platform rose from the centre of the compound. It was open to all sides but had a tiled canopy, covering what looked like a large cone of stacked wood to suggest a signal tower. The fort's surrounding walls were crenelated at regular intervals to allow archers to pick off invaders both in front of and caught within the spiked barriers. I saw no sign of occupation within either fortress as everyone remained safely hidden inside.

It was neither the spiked border nor the menacing fortifications that captured my attention and foretold of the violent conflict we were about to engage. Countless numbers of men and numerous rows of canvas tents waited beyond the barren strip of disputed land. Five wooden trebuchets were aimed at the Northlands' stone fortress, along with a number of smaller catapults. A similar army was stationed in front of the wooden fort, although the numbers of soldiers and the weapons of war were significantly less. Large, black banners fluttered in the wind, displaying the red oval and radiating silver shards of their God. Baila had sent his warriors to destroy the kingdom that had thought to deny him.

CHAPTER SEVEN

We made a cold camp on the small rise, none of us wanted to cross the scrubby grassland in the dark and risk the hidden traps waiting there. Conversation became stilted with everyone's thoughts drifting to the hostile army camped less than a day's ride away. Eventually Bear abandoned all attempts at distracting us with wild tales of catching fish in frozen rivers or chasing foxes through shrieking farmyards and addressed the cause of our discomfort.

'Well,' he said, finally admitting defeat. 'As you're all set on filling your minds with increasingly horrific ways in which the Army of Truth will slaughter you, I may as well give you a history lesson.'

I smiled, that was exactly what I was doing.

'Army of Truth?' questioned Z'hara, with an amused expression.

Bear huffed a bitter laugh. 'You would have thought all those educated priests could have come up with a better name, but they seem to like that one.'

The big man stared towards the army concealed by the darkness and told of how the peaceful religion had transformed into a focal point for people's frustrations and prejudices. He remembered a time when the Baila faith was a small religion, living harmoniously with those who believed in the old Gods. They preached love and compassion, honouring your neighbour and performing acts of charity. As the religion grew, some saw the priesthood not as a vocation involving a sacred duty, but as a pathway to money and power. Subtle undertones of greed and corruption floated underneath the surface, but the majority maintained their belief in peace and charity.

'That all changed about ten, fifteen years ago.'

'Villermir.' I spat the word. I could still feel his presence invading the damaged land, festering like an open sore.

'Indeed,' Bear confirmed. 'That stinking pile of rotting guts changed everything. Looking back, it seems so obvious but at the time it all made perfect sense. How could we have been such fools?'

'Not all were fooled,' offered Vallori quietly.

'True. Some continued in their belief of compassion and peace. But this was often at odds with the teachings of their priests. Under the guidance of Villermir and his growing band of sycophants, sermons started to emphasise the differences between those following Baila and those of other faiths. The religion came to be seen as the one, true faith. Those who did not see this were deemed inferior. Deserving of pity or, more dangerously, contempt. Neighbours and friends, who had always lived happily together now became targets of suspicion and distrust. Those not of the faith were denied goods or services. Many abandoned their previous beliefs just so they could remain in their own communities.'

The big man fell silent and I suspected there was a story behind his silence. Perhaps he had been driven from his home by Baila fanatics, although I doubted that he would have gone easily. Perhaps his family took up the faith and he was no longer welcomed. I felt certain that this would be a frequent occurrence throughout Hilman and Lindvane, and I hoped it had not progressed into Faulknar. We waited patiently while he stared at nothing, confronting what seemed to be uncomfortable memories.

He took a breath and continued. 'That was all some time ago. This army is a relatively new addition to the faith. With power and money comes the need to protect it. Several of the larger priesthoods have long had their own guards. Hired thugs really, to protect them and theirs. Over the last few years this has grown into something else. Something darker. More organised. Priests started calling for the faithful to demonstrate their faith by challenging everyone who was not openly devoted to Baila. Started saying it was their sacred duty to defend their principles.'

Bonash sighed. 'Nothing more motivating than piously dying for your God.'

'Or killing for him,' added Z'hara.

We fell into a sullen silence before quietly retiring to our beds. I tossed and turned long after everyone else was still, restless after the talk of Villermir and his holy army. My thoughts circled around the image emblazoned on their banners: the black background with the fiery oval at its centre. A memory tugged at me but I could not capture it. I chased it round and around, placing it in different settings to force the connection. I was almost asleep when the link finally surfaced and I was jolted fully awake again.

In his vision, Kade had seen men dressed in black attack Liegeport and kill his brother. And I had seen uniformed soldiers, all in black, attack Kingsport. Both had worn the Army of Truth crest. All hope of sleep was lost and I became increasingly angry at how deep Villermir's hooks had dug into my past. The arrogance of his manipulation of anyone who did not agree with him. How sour his ambition, that it could include the assassination of the Faulknar heir.

I rolled onto my back, staring miserably at the stars so very far above me. They remained unaware of the turmoil we inflicted on ourselves. The eternal drive to be bigger and better, eagerly embracing the need to balance on the broken backs of others so we could snatch at the reward. The Gods could be cruel and capricious, but humans alone had the capacity to dehumanise others just for the promise of power.

The dark waters of despair beckoned once more and it would have been easy to let myself drift into their dark embrace but, as much as I wanted to run away from the thought, Villermir was my problem. Somehow, I had to stop the evil he was spreading through the land and its people. Their fear and anger and hate needed healing as surely as any diseased body. The poisoned heart of the Three Kingdoms had to be removed. My Goddess expected me to do this and I had to try.

Keeping my blanket wrapped around my shoulders, I sat up and considered whether it would be safe to create a small fireball to brew a tea. Bear was a mound of dark shadow with only the whites of his eyes showing bright in the moonlight to reveal he was watching me.

'You've made your decision then?'

I gave a small smile. 'Is it that obvious?'

He lifted a shoulder in a small shrug. 'The Lady can be very persuasive. You have been fighting with yourself since we left the sanctuary. I had begun to think that your frown would become a permanent feature.' His teeth flashed in the dim light when he grinned, knowing I would have scowled at his comment. 'The Lady does not ask for simple favours. She expects us to pay dearly for her blessings, but we pay willing nonetheless.'

I examined the backs of my hands and wrists where the Goddess had turned my scars into an image of faded flames. I considered all the gifts she had given to me, not least being a belief in the path she had chosen for me. All I had to do was follow her guidance.

'I still have no idea how to make it through our friends across the border,' I confessed, 'much less get past countless shamans and daemons and all the other horrors I don't want to consider. I then need to find and kill possibly the most powerful sorcerer there is.' I sighed at the enormity of the challenge, producing a small, bejewelled fireball and making it slowly rotate above the palm of my hand. 'But I have been given these skills for a reason. I have as good a chance as any, and maybe better than most.' I closed my fingers and extinguished the fireball. 'Let's see how far I make it before he squishes me like a bug.'

Bear sniffed at my bleak humour. 'Don't discount your dragon.'

My tone became sharper. 'There is no decision to be made there. Megin is free. She has no part in this.'

'That might not be your decision to make.' His shadow shifted as he rolled his shoulders and stretched his back. 'But for now, I believe it is your turn to take watch.'

He settled down to sleep and I thought of Megin. I hoped she was safe, soaring over the northern mountain ranges and flying high in the endless skies. I did not regret my decision to send her away but the constant ache of her absence throbbed a little more deeply in the core of my soul.

The next morning, we descended the rise and crossed the heathland that stretched towards the wooden fort. We all kept a wary eye on the Army of Truth but at a distance, all appeared quiet. The horses picked up on the anxious mood and I had to concentrate on keeping my flighty mare calm. I watched her ears, trying to predict what she would startle at, and became fascinated by the way they constantly flicked, catching the slightest sound and taking only a heartbeat to determine its source before turning towards a new one. I softened my vision and let my ears tune into the small details, using Trefin to guide my focus towards the information she was reacting to. The soft creak of leather tack and armour, the quiet clink of metal bits and weapons, the soft thud of the horses' hooves, and all the other noises associated with our group. I dismissed these and became aware of the less intrusive sounds. The buzz of an insect flying too close, the alarm call of a bird hidden within the bushes further to the north, the muffled shouts of those patrolling the fort. I smiled as Trefin's world was revealed to me, showing me a new perspective on her cautious nature. She gave attention to so many tiny activities that I had been completely unaware of.

The afternoon sun was in our faces as we approached the fort. The structure stood defiantly against the enemy camped at their feet, with large timber poles placed upright to create the defending walls. Each was sharpened to a point that reached into the sky and each stood uniformly at four times the height of a man. The heads of the soldiers could be seen patrolling the walkways that ran below the spiked tops. Infrequent glints told of arrows, notched and ready within the slots of the two towers placed overlooking the border. I saw no Northlands' soldier outside the fort and our approach was the only thing this side of the spiked barrier to disturb the carrion birds searching for an easy meal.

A dirt track guided us to the gates, curving around towards the rear of the fort with no other entrance visible. Any attack would have to travel along the fort's wall before being able to gain entry, having to dodge spears, arrows, rocks and burning pitch. Bonash's mare jogged in response to his increased tension when we rode up to the double wooden doors, each studded with large, triangular metal rivets to destabilise a battering ram. Bear rode a horse-length in front of the rest of us, clearly showing that he was the one with authority. He hailed the sentries in the watch towers either side of the gates.

'Tell your general that Lord Westmoorland has arrived.'

All four of us turned our heads toward Bear in a synchronised show of amazement; none of us had known that he was nobility. I released, belatedly, that Bear would not have been his real name and only now did it occur to me to wonder what it was.

The sentry in the right tower raised his crossbow. 'You appear to come from the north but Westmoorland is a Hilman name.'

Bear – *Lord Westmoorland* – sat straighter in the saddle, using his full height to ensure the man understood he had been given a command and not a request. 'Inform General Wick that I am here.'

The suspicious guard opened his mouth to reply but was halted by an older soldier clapping him on the shoulder. An incline of the head by this taller man succeeding in getting the first to lower his weapon and send him to report. The remaining soldier leaned casually over the wall.

'I'm sure you understand our caution,' he said, waving an arm behind him to indicate the army camped at his back.

'True.' Bear relaxed into his saddle, content to wait for the general. 'But it also helps to welcome friends when you find them.'

'Aye,' the guard nodded amiably. 'The trick is knowing friend from foe.'

The large gates soon creaked open to reveal a stocky man in leather armour that clearly showed the damage and cuts inflicted from hard use. His long hair was tied at the base of his neck, bordering a weathered face which wore a deep scowl. His arms were crossed over his chest and displayed the bunched biceps of a powerful fighter. He did not wait for the gate to fully open before he strode purposefully towards us, his confrontational manner directed at Bear.

'It's about time you got your lumbering bulk here,' he grumbled in ill-temper. 'Was beginning to think you'd forgotten your manners and decided to take up sheep farming.'

In stark contrast to the bristling nature of the fort's general, Bear grinned with uncharacteristic joy. He jumped off his horse and embraced the smaller man in a bone-crunching hug, which his victim fiercely returned. The two men separated reluctantly, firmly clasping the other's forearm to maintain the contact for a while longer.

'By the Gods, Wick,' sighed Bear. 'It's so good to see you.'

'Aye,' replied the general. 'I daresay my heart is lighter for seeing your ugly face, too.'

Bear threw his head back and laughed, slapping the shorter man on the back with such force that Wick had to take a step to rebalance himself. I found myself smiling at the obvious friendship between the two, grateful we had found a welcome here. And one that was much more exuberant than I had expected.

In contrast to its sombre external appearance, the inside of the fort was a buzz of activity. Soldiers purposefully strode across the main courtyard while servants scuttled around them, performing all the domestic duties required by the fort. Bed linen passed by firewood and water was carried in buckets, while sacks of grain and potatoes wove between them all. Dogs barked, chickens clucked and horses whinnied. After the calm order of the sanctuary and the measured silences during the ride across the Northlands, this chaotic scene assaulted my senses and I felt tossed around like a leaf in a gale. Trefin jigged in response to my tightened grip on her reins while I reacted to every shouted command, every banging door and every crack of the fluttering flags. I found myself constantly looking for the dangers that could be hidden within all this frantic activity and wished I could escape back to the safe tranquillity of the sanctuary.

I took a deep breath and rolled my shoulders to relax the muscles. We dismounted and the horses were efficiently taken by the fort's grooms. Bear and Wick continued to talk companionably and led us into the main building, where the central hall continued the fort's general attitude of hastily built functionality. A large fireplace dominated the far wall. The blazing fire was the width of a cartwheel and yet barely covering half of the hearth. Several benches were scattered around the room, varying in size and involving all different types of timber. They appeared to have been made with whatever materials were available. An assortment of chairs, stools and upturned barrels had provided additional seating as the need arose. The hall was dark and smoky. Only a few narrow windows provided light so that, despite being early in the afternoon, candles were required to illuminate the darker corners.

We followed Wick through a door that hung unevenly and refused to close, up the stairs and along the hallway to a small private room. More mismatched chairs were scattered in front of a long desk, which the general ignored in favour of perching on the windowsill. He appraised us with his arms folded and a slight frown creasing his forehead.

'So,' he said eventually, addressing Bear. 'Have you brought me a gift of five trained soldiers or are you just passing through?'

'We're just passing through.' The dark man stretched out his long legs. 'But we could bide a while if needed. You have a fortress full of soldiers and another in view. Would our small party make that much of a difference?'

Wick grumbled deep in his chest. 'Apart from being outnumbered and Baila's forces seeming to grow bigger every day, nearly all these fighters are new recruits. We send inexperienced children against disciplined soldiers and the slaughter rate is correspondingly high.' He looked up at the ceiling, hoping to find the inspiration to solve his problems. 'The Northlands is not a heavily populated territory and those we have are remotely scattered. The Army of Truth pulls from Hilman, Lindvane, and who knows where. We have farmers and fishermen wanting to do their bit.' He grinned in dark humour at his friend. 'Aye, five trained soldiers would make that much of a difference.'

Bear dipped his head. 'Then tell us how we can be of aid.'

The conversation weaved into a tapestry of strategies, suffering and slaughter. With each skirmish, Baila's army would advance into the Northlands where significant losses would be taken by both sides, only for the advancing host to seamlessly replace their numbers within days. The fort was solely focused on maintaining the stalemate and denying a full-scale breech into the free lands of the north, but the incessant nature of the struggle was seeping away morale. Wick feared it was only a matter of time before he would have to deal with desertions.

Bear and Z'hara gently steered the conversation towards the logistics for the next inevitable attack. It was decided that the garrison would divide into five companies, each having one of us embedded to provide support to the captains. We would enforce their commands. We would encourage their fighters. We would be used to plug the gaps where inexperience left them vulnerable. We would be needed everywhere.

The shout came a little before dusk and the fort buzzed like a kicked wasps' nest. Men and women burst into activity, grabbing weapons before heading to the rear gates. Horses and people gathered in five loose groups and the sinking sun flashed on breastplates and blades. Some held short axes while a few carried a mace. Most were barely able to cover the fear within their fixed masks of determination.

I made my way to my allotted company, where we would file around the left side of the fort to face Baila's attacking force. The first cries of the injured floated towards us when the archers rained their arrows into the advancing ranks. I looked to see Bear pound his captain on the back then scanned the group for Vallori, finding him within a few heartbeats as he clasped his captain by the forearm. I took a deep breath and turned my attention to my own company. Men and women, both young and old, stood side-by-side, nervously waiting for the order to advance. My captain was one of the three within my group that were mounted, making him easily visible above the crowd of soldiers. His dark mare, flecked with silver, stood patiently while he stroked his beard, a thick scar pulling down his right eye. His hawk's gaze hovered over those in his command until he found me. He frowned, holding eye contact as he considered the addition of this unknown factor. I was small and unimpressive, and I did not blame him for questioning my place there. I withdrew *Saorsa* and watched him straighten in his saddle, appraising my right to hold such an impressive sword. He gave me a brief nod of acknowledgement, having made his decision, and I returned the gesture.

Wick cantered out of the fort on an excitable bay battle-horse, raising his broadsword high above him to attract the attention of all within sight. The general's wide smile sought to fill his soldiers with confidence and promised the glory found in battle. His horse had circled twice before he yelled for his soldiers to engage. I ran in the centre of the group with my captain at the front, holding his horse to the pace of the runners. We flanked the wall as Bonash's company veered out to the right of us, aiming to attack the outer edge of the advancing army. The fifth unit was mounted and half this number thundered past us to encircle Baila's troops, engaging them from behind to divert attention and divide the thrust of their attack.

I slammed into Baila's front line. Arrows flew over my head and I slashed *Saorsa* at the shoulder of the soldier in front of me. Warm blood splashed over my face, and I welcomed the heat of my rage which sharpened my vision and flooded my limbs with energy. My slashes, parries and stabs became a macabre dance and the dehumanised bodies fell in front of me. I briefly noted the change of direction when the arrows were moved away from the clashing ranks and aimed further into the Army of Truth, causing many to fall and become obstacles to those who would reinforce the attacking line. I saw my captain's horse rear up, striking out with its hooves to smash at a man's face. Baila's soldier was lost to my view as he fell on his back, to be crushed by those fighting around him. I rotated in a circle of calm while I cut and sliced at those who would dare to oppose me. The ruby eyes within my blade's hilt flashed in appreciation of the blood sacrifice I was giving her.

A young soldier to my right stumbled and fell beneath the onslaught of an older man. My face pulled back into a rictus snarl and I marked him for mine. I pushed, punched and elbowed my way through the wall of bodies that stood between us. Friend and foe were cast aside as irrelevant, and I kept my gaze locked on the one raising his blade, two-handed, to drive its steel through the fallen soldier's chest. The point was less than two hand-spans from the boy when I forced his blade sideways. Baila's soldier looked at me with a fleeting expression of surprise before his upper lip lifted into a disgusted sneer. I mockingly inclined my head, inviting him to try his luck against me, while the young recruit scrambled to his feet and moved to guard my back.

'Woman.'

His voice dripped with distaste and my smile widened. This was going to be fun.

I made the first move, slicing at his shoulder in a move he easily blocked. My second and third parries tested the range of his swing and the speed of his recovery. By the fourth I knew where he was vulnerable and pushed my attack to his weaker side. Two quick slashes to his left, before a decoy to his right opened the space for a deep bite into the side of his neck. *Saorsa* cut into the major blood vessels and dissected his windpipe. His eyes widened in shock and he fell to his knees, his sword falling from nerveless fingers. I grabbed his collar, shaking him until he looked at me with rapidly glazing eyes.

'Give my regards to Baila,' I whispered into his face. 'Tell him I'm coming for him.'

I pushed the dead man away, discarded like a broken toy. I snatched a moment to survey the battle, we had barely advanced more than halfway along the wall of the fort. We attacked the Army of Truth on three sides but they managed to stand firm. More soldiers pushed through the spiked defences to join the mass seething around the fort. The Northlands' soldiers were disorganised and chaotic. They had regressed to fight as individuals, no longer presenting as a united force, but they fought with a passion I had not expected. Neither side seemed in control. Both sides fought against the surging tide.

A glancing blow to the side of my head caused my vision to spin for a heartbeat, but *Saorsa* had bitten into the man's ribs before my view stabilised. A twist of my wrist caused him to cough blood and I moved on to the next. I pushed through the press of bodies. The black uniforms made each enemy target easy to identify and I carved from one fighting pocket to another. I used my sword to defend and attack, covering the weaknesses as my company tired, became injured or left gaps which could be exploited. The scents of sweat, leather and oiled metal weaved through the more pungent smells from the dead and dying. The ground grew slippery. Horses and soldiers screamed in agony, spilling the vital contents of their bodies.

I ignored the tendrils of chaos and confusion that wove throughout the battlefield. I refused to acknowledge the dark energies released by the suffering and slaughter. I suppressed the emotions that tugged at me. The fear and pain and despair. The wrenching disorientation of a soul being torn from its body. Years of training allowed me to close off my mind, with my body flowing through the movements without conscious thought. It allowed a needle-sharp focus on the subtle tells of another's weakness, blocking out all other distractions. It allowed me to avoid the horror I created as I hacked and punched and gouged and ripped.

My rhythm was interrupted by a cheer rolling from my left, racing towards me, around me, and then off through those on my right. My opponent pulled back along with all the rest of Baila's army, melting into the gloom of fading twilight. We had beaten them back to the spiked defences marking the border, and the enemy retreated beyond the treacherous barrier. It appeared that the rules of the game stated this signalled the end of the encounter and commands were relayed instructing us to return to the fort. Most gratefully obeyed the orders, although a few remained to relieve the suffering of those yet to succumb to their injuries. I saw one optimistically searching those of Baila, perhaps hoping for loot or information about their future intentions, but I doubted much of benefit would be found there.

I stood, twitching in frustration while indecision prevented me from retreating. I still raged for blood, needing to press the advantage and chase the enemy back to their base where I would burn everything the cowards had, but I would not last long on my own and any support I had was already halfway back to the safety of the fort. The tide of combat had already flowed away from me, yet I could not deny the burning ember of my anger which refused to be extinguished. I absently pushed past a fighter, my mind occupied by strategy and stealth, of infiltrating into the heart of the camp where I could cause the most confusion and panic.

The fighter persisted and I was halted by a surprisingly firm palm pressing against my chest. I gripped the wrist to twist it out of my way, frowning in annoyance when the offending limb did not move. I finally turned my full attention to the increasingly irritating distraction, and found Bonash meekly smiling at me. His steady gaze drilled into me until he had calmed the noise and I could hear reason once more.

'Bonash. What are you doing here?'

His smile melted into his usual half-frown of exasperation, deliberately misunderstanding the questioning of his presence in my section of the battlefield when he should have been further to the right.

'Are you concussed? You do remember we rode here together? With Bear, and Z'hara, and Vallori?'

'Funny man,' I grinned, breathing out the last of my anger. 'I'm not concussed and you know very well what I meant.'

Bonash moved his hand from my chest onto my shoulder and gently guided me back to the fort. I reluctantly appreciated the small man's tactic, using his quiet presence to stop me blindly charging into a situation I had no hope of surviving. It was very subtle, much like his owl spirit-guide. I thought of how Bear would have handled the situation differently, probably choosing to sit on me until I had calmed down. The image made me chuckle and caused Bonash to once again question whether I had received a significant blow to the head.

'I was just thinking how frustrating it is to be surrounded by people who can so easily read emotions in the colours of your aura.'

'Well, you do burn particularly bright when you're angry.' He gave me a sly grin. 'Especially when you are about to do something incredibly stupid.'

My mouth dropped open in mock-offense. 'Is that so? And what is my aura telling you right now about my stupid intentions? Comments like that have consequences, little man.'

Bonash's laugh seemed more poignant in such an incongruous setting. He skipped out of reach of *Saorsa*'s blade, angled to slap his retreating rear, and I chased him back to the fort.

He was not laughing, some considerable time later, when I was still obsessing about why we had not pushed the advantage and ran the host back to their camp. I could not understand why they insisted on stopping at the border. They were the enemy. They should be crushed and sent back to their ugly little temples of pompous piety. Ignoring the visible effort it was taking him to remain calm, I restarted the cycle of conversation for the countless time and triggered a chorus of frustrated groans from all within hearing.

'I still don't understand why the border is so important,' I began, waving the remains of a chicken thigh at him to emphasise my point. 'It's not even a physical barrier. Not like a river or a forest. It's just a line, on a map, that somebody decided was the limit of the Northlands.'

Bear slammed his head onto his arms that were folded on the table in front of him. 'By the Gods. Somebody keep her away from the wine and ale. Preferably forever.'

I immediately turned on him in a desperate attempt to gain an ally, causing my vision to blur for a heartbeat. I may have drunk too much, too quickly but I was not ready to concede my point.

'You, of all people, have to understand. The stalemate will never be broken if we let them just stroll back to their side of the border. Congratulating them on a game well played. Why can't anyone see this?'

Bonash took a steadying breath before starting his explanation. Again. 'The Northlands encompass a territory of wide-open spaces and poorly tamed landscape. The land has remained unchanged since memory began. Maintaining its connection with the Gods so that every mountain, every moorland, every vale, stream and thicket remains sacred. The people that live here have no desire for ownership. They consider themselves guardians. And while the clans may fight amongst themselves, and have done for countless generations, each and every one of them would die to preserve the sanctity of a single tree.'

I interrupted impatiently. 'And the sacred land stops at the border. I understand that, despite the arbitrary allocation of this hallowed boundary. My point stands. Baila's chosen are not going to stop because the land is seen as the provenance of Gods they don't believe in. They will happily chop down all the sacred trees, seeing them as nothing more than available firewood. They will never uphold the beliefs of the Northlands. Baila's faithful will take the soul from every man, woman and child until the last tribe has converted, while the priests take every last rock that can be turned into gold for their temples.'

'And that is why the clans will defend the border. What happens in Hilman is not their concern but Baila will not be permitted to enter the Northlands unless they respect the Gods and the land they inhabit.'

'And that's never going to happen!' I clenched my fists at Bonash's infuriating acceptance of this insane situation. 'This pointless slaughter will never end. Baila will always push to convert those that don't follow their ways. Are the clans prepared to fight this futile war forever?'

The small man shrugged sadly. 'If that's what it takes.'

I rolled my head, groaning in unrelenting frustration. Vallori slapped his palms on the table and made everyone startle.

'Enough of this. Tallen, we all know you disagree but nothing will be changing tonight. I suggest we all get some rest. Let us discuss our options again tomorrow and decide on an appropriate course of action when we have clear heads.'

I opened my mouth to protest but the glare Vallori directed at me was enough to stop me from being that particular kind of stupid. He rose and walked over to stand behind me, grabbing a fistful of my jerkin when I made no effort to rise in a clear statement that we were leaving. Bonash gallantly raised his tankard to salute our debate, causing Z'hara to smirk. Vallori applied a little more pressure to get me moving and I mumbled my farewells, swaying slightly as he guided me out of the dining hall. He wrapped his arm around my shoulders in a more companionable gesture and he led me to the long room where I would sleep.

'I like you drunk,' he said, smiling at my indignant frown. 'You're funny.'

'Yeah? Well, I hate you.'

I was going to tell him exactly why I was not funny and how it would have been nice if he had defended me rather than treating me like a child and escorting me from the room as if I was having a tantrum and…

I stopped. His smile had faded and his eyes had softened with obvious concern. The intensity of the look made me feel exposed and a little uncomfortable, but the moment quickly passed. I sat on the edge of the bed and he knelt before me to remove my boots, remaining on his knees when he had finished so that his face was level with mine. The look had returned but it did not feel uncomfortable this time. It felt safe.

'I know you, Tallen. I'm your *pháirtí*.' He spoke quietly with the cadence of the calming mantra, and the ghosts crowding around me drifted away. 'I know the drink merely numbs the pain. I know you feel the suffering of the land. That this fed into the storm that raged when you fought. I know you've never faced death on this scale before. And you fear losing yourself to the anger and hate that you use to protect yourself from it.' He hesitated and I reached out a hand to cradle his face. He looked so sad. 'I also know that when the storm passes, you feel the presence of every soul that was taken. Tallen, I *know* you.'

He let his words soak into a hidden place deep within my chest. He removed my hand and gently encouraged me to lie down, with a touch as light as that used to sooth a nervous horse. He pulled the blanket to cover me, before sitting beside me and resting his hand on my cheek. I closed my eyes against the painful throb coming from my chest, its beat strengthened by the warm connection of his cupped palm. I craved the acceptance in its intent but feared my need for it.

'I know everyone talks about your destiny. That you need to save everyone. That you need to solve all their problems.' He bent down to place a feather-light kiss on my forehead. 'You don't have to win every battle, Tallen. And you don't have to do it alone.'

I must have been more drunk than I thought because, between one heartbeat and the next, I forgot to ask how he could read all that from my aura and fell asleep instead.

CHAPTER EIGHT

It took three days of pointless skirmishes before we finally accepted that we were making no difference to the fates of those at the fort. The choreographed dance of advance and retreat was repeated under a suffocating weight of doomed inevitability, so we moved our thoughts away that of the Northlands' defence and towards how we could enter Hilman.

We considered fighting past the border during the daily confrontation with the Army of Truth but rejected it as the five of us would not get far without the support of the fort's soldiers, and they had made it very clear that they would not cross into Hilman.

We attempted to creep past the camp on the night of a new moon, choosing stealth rather than strength and hoping that the darkness would hide us within the barren scrubland of the border. This was also rejected when we felt the warning of a powerful warding, the hairs on my arms standing erect whenever I ventured within three horse-lengths of the invisible barrier. I suspected Baila's army had brought their priests, although I had not seen any since arriving, and they would alert the soldiers as soon as we attempted to cross. We travelled half the night to test the limits of the protection and found no weakness that could be exploited. In frustration, I suggested we incapacitate the enemy by loosening their bowels and forcibly ejecting their stomach contents. This resulted in such a scathing glare from Bear that I instantly felt like a child again, having been caught stealing warm biscuits from Mistress Narran's kitchen at Liegeport.

We finally concluded that the use of magick could not be avoided, although we would need to ensure we did not attract the attention of the priests; I had no doubt they would readily inform Villermir that five had crossed into Hilman, even if they did not know our intentions. We returned to the plan of crossing during an assault when the priests' barrier would be disabled for their soldiers to engage. We hoped the chaos of the battle would mask our unnatural use of energy.

As the alarm sounded for another early evening attack, we held back from the main fighting and waited for both sides to be fully engaged. At a brief nod from Bear, we divided into two groups; Bonash moved to the left to join the big man while Vallori and Z'hara moved to join me. We gently guided our horses so each group advanced on one side of the fighting, advancing slowly but steadily. I focused my mind on the rhythms of Trefin's movements and timed my breathing with the bunching and releasing of her muscles. I extended a calming warmth throughout her skin and watched the involuntary ripple when her nerves shuddered in response to the gossamer contact. I swiftly thanked the Gods, grateful she had not resented the subtle control of my will over hers, then carefully extended a bubble of calm around my mare. The chaotic river of energies created by the battle divided to flow around us.

Bonash's mare violently tossed her head on the far side of the battlefield and the small man struggled to control her sudden panic. Bear was mirroring my protective sphere and the unseen touch of his contact had triggered her distress. I quickly dismissed them. It was what we had anticipated. Bonash's bay was the most reactive and presented the greatest risk of being noticed despite the enchantments Bear and I wove to glide any attention away from our group. The glamour would work, allowing us to pass as if invisible, only if there were no sudden movements to invite a closer look. We needed the horses to remain quiet despite the stench of death and the screaming of dying horses all around them. Bear had total control over his powers and could easily manage Bonash's mount, but he would need to use his energy to calm rather than conceal and would be unable to hide more than the two horses. While my powers were unpredictable and would not sustain the illusion against Trefin's nervousness and the bay's changeable temperament, they were easily capable of concealing myself, Vallori and Z'hara. Vallori and Z'hara's horses were battle-trained and remained steady despite the chaos surrounding them and the extra pressure of my contact. We would remain safe, provided I could maintain my concentration.

A teardrop of sweat rolled slowly between my shoulder blades and down my spine. I maintained the perfect circle around my group, keeping it stable as we passed the final cluster of fighting. I ignored the throbbing ache behind my eyes and tested carefully for any presence of the warding barrier. My energies remained undisturbed and we crossed the border, entering Hilman without incident. While the battle continued behind us, unaware of our escape, we maintained a steady pace through the barricades, around the enemy camp, across the open heath and towards the cover of a small woodland. My shoulder muscles were twitching from the sustained tension by the time we joined Bear and Bonash in the shadow of the trees, and I tentatively lowered our illusion. I heard Bear's sigh of relief echo mine when we finally relaxed our control.

My relief did not last long. Within a heartbeat, I was assaulted by a cramping bout of nausea. Acid burned at the back of my throat and I swallowed several times before the feeling would subside. My body's reaction was to be expected from the prolonged use of power, but the painful twist in my belly persisted. The constant pressure I felt from the land had developed a sharper edge on crossing into Hilman, and Villermir's presence prodded as a malicious thread throughout. I inspected my mental defences. The barriers were intact but they were covered with a black mesh that crept over sections like strands of burnt ivy. Cords of dark vine invaded through several areas of the outer walls, burrowing into any gaps found. I feared this infestation was connected to the nausea and built more layers of walls.

Bear stretched his back, reminding me of a hound shaking to release the tension after a stressful event. Without anyone speaking, we turned our horses to face into the woodland and continued our journey. Bear was the last to move but halted when I turned Trefin back to face the fort. It was not finished here and I was still angry that lives would continue to be lost in this futile game of to-and-fro. I understood our duty, and my promise to the Goddess required fighting a different enemy, but it pained me to leave with so little achieved.

Taking considerably less effort than it had taken to create the illusion of invisibility, I floated several small fireballs above my palm. I rotated them slowly and they burned like a cluster of small suns. The frustrations of the past few days fed into their heat until they crackled and snapped with angry fire sprites. Trefin snorted and shook her head, stamping her front hoof in alarm at being so close to my flaming orbs.

'Fly my little firebirds.'

I released them and they flew towards the oiled canvas of the camp's tents.

Bear had placed his horse alongside Trefin's shoulder and I saw a look on his face that hovered somewhere between annoyance and disappointment. He did not dissolve the fireballs, however, and we watched together as the flames caught and were fanned by the breeze into blazing towers. The ravenous sprites gorged on the rich offerings supplied by an army encampment, with tents, bedding, clothing and personal items greedily consumed. The smoke blew gently towards the fort, interrupting the flow of battle when it became clear the camp was alight. The Northlands jeered at their enemy fleeing to save whatever they could. The fires had already spread to engulf half the camp.

I knew that this was only a temporary reprieve and the Army of Truth would replenish their losses within a few days, but it gave a small sense of having achieved something.

Bear leaned over to pull at Trefin's reins. 'Time to go.'

We travelled deep into the night, choosing the smaller tracks through the forest rather than risk the larger roads, and under the thick canopy, the half-hidden images ghosting at the edges of my mind were easily dismissed as shadows. They were harder to ignore when we left the shelter of the trees and they added to the persistent feeling of despair that had clung to the back of my throat since crossing into Hilman. It made me miserable company but the others were equally sombre.

In a landscape where farmers had ploughed the earth into regular sized squares and sheep grazed on the lower slopes of the hills, wide stretches of earth had been ripped into long crevices. Deep craters sunk into fields that had previously grown grains or vegetables, and had now been left abandoned. Many of the farmhouses and barns had been destroyed by fire, with possessions scattered in the long grass as if abandoned by owners hastily fleeing their homes. The sheep warily kept their distance from us and we could see they were unhealthily thin despite the abundance of grazing. Wild animals were conspicuously scarce, with only small field birds left to chase insects and forage in the hedgerows. Hungry families would have hunted the larger game and I feared the numbers taken would irreparably damage some populations.

We rode through a damaged, abandoned landscape that felt unnaturally quiet. We saw nobody on the track. No soldiers marched towards the border. No farmers carried their goods to market. No merchants offered their wares in the hope of trade. The few farms still inhabited showed little sign of occupation other than the thin drifts of smoke from cook-fire chimneys. The farmers stayed well hidden from the strangers passing by. Only once did we encounter anyone during that first day. A thin man in oversized clothes stood in his doorway, tightly holding a scythe in both hands while his wife remained mostly concealed within. His stance radiated angry defiance, while hers was one of defeat with her head lowered and her shoulders curled. But it was their flat eyes which named the emotion that had stalked at me since leaving the Northlands. Grief. The farmers grieved. The landscape laid heavy with grief. The air was so saturated with grief that it made it hard to breathe. Everything was pulled out of shape. Fractured. Dissonant. The land was grieving.

We remained subdued when we finally made camp later that evening. Bonash made a small fire, more for its brightness than for its warmth. None of us wanted to hunt in this persecuted countryside so we chewed mechanically on the dried meat and cheese taken from the fort. The dull ache in my stomach leeched any pleasure from the food and I gave up after a few bites, taking some comfort from a warm tea instead. Conversation was forced and we soon retired to our beds to avoid the pretence of normality when we all felt overwhelmed and pessimistic.

The dream that night came with such a force that I felt I was drowning in its vibrant imagery. I readily joined my wolves, stretching and yawning in preparation for the hunt. The family loped, loose-limbed, through the sun-dappled forest, following well-used tracks to cover the ground quickly and increase their chances of finding deer. My male's nose rose, twitching, and caught the first scent of musk. A female. Not far. The posture of the group changed. The wolves' muscles tensed and they increased their speed. They effortlessly covered the distance to their prey who remained unaware of the danger. The scent grew stronger when they reached the thicket where the hind was browsing. She sensed the wolves' approach and became a flash of movement.

The wolves raced after her a heartbeat later, spreading out to funnel her in the direction they wanted her to go. The colours of the forest blended into a harsher palate. The softness of early morning was replaced by more garish tones. The yellow of the gorse was a little too bright. The green of the pines was a little too vivid. The sky became darker and the wolves crashed through the bracken. Their lungs strained to fill with the air needed to fuel their pumping muscles. Their tongues flapped as gaudy splashes of red, moving up and down in rhythm with their racing limbs. Brambles raked at their flanks and they strained to run faster, swiftly changing direction between one step and the next.

Chased by a darkness that seemed to rush towards us, we pushed faster. The cohesion of the pack faltered around me and we each ran to save ourselves. My heart raced with horror as beasts hidden in the shadows waited to snatch at any stumble or misstep. Their taunting shrieks echoed around the trees, from behind me, and now on both sides. Malice pulsed as a heartbeat. It goaded me into a dwindling tunnel of sharp light, surrounded by the cloying darkness trying to swallow me. I ran through vines that waited to trip me. I pushed past branches that scratched at my face. My head pounded with each beat of my heart and my lungs screamed for more air. I had reached the limit of my endurance.

My foot caught on a root and I fell, twisting to land on my back and face the evil that stalked me. My wolf leapt out of the dark and I raised my hands to protect my face when he stood over me. Globules of saliva dripped from yellowed teeth, exposed when the lips curled back into a terrifying snarl. Large ears were held flat to a head with an overly long muzzle. Black, leathery wings were tucked tight to his back and amber eyes seethed with the molten lava of hatred. He lunged for my throat.

I choked on my sharply inhaled breath, coughing as I sat up and my brain frantically tried to make sense of the images which were still clinging to my mind. My breathing slowed and reality replaced the fear. Z'hara was on the opposite side of the fire with Vallori asleep beside her. Bear and Bonash were sleeping a little further away. I watched Z'hara pour hot water into a cup, making a tea which released a sweet aroma. Her calm, methodical movements soothed the remaining turmoil although my hand still trembled when I took the offered brew.

'Bad dreams?' she asked softly.

'I didn't mean to disturb you.'

She dismissed my apology, shaking her head so the small charms braided into her hair flared briefly in the firelight. 'That's not what I meant.' She looked towards Vallori. 'Do you need him?'

Vallori was turned away from me, curled on his side. He appeared peaceful and untroubled by the darkness of bad dreams. It was a generous offer and I was sorely tempted to accept. I did need him. But Z'hara continued to watch him with a sadness in her expression that was clear, even in the dim light. She needed him too.

'No. Not yet.'

She turned back to study me, taking a sip of her own drink before continuing. 'We all feel it. This land. It feels wrong. Like it's twisted and deformed. When you left the sanctuary… Well, I'm guessing it's worse here.' She offered me a small smile. 'I'm sure the Goddess's gift of empathy is not always a blessing.'

I shrugged. 'Are they ever?'

'True.'

Several moments passed in an uncomfortable silence while I watched the other woman bite on her cup, struggling with some inner conflict. Her dark eyes seeing things from a different time.

'I've seen it before,' she began hesitantly. 'The farmer's wife. From earlier. I've seen that before. The last time I was in Hilman, the women had that look. I'd forgotten. I've spent so much time in the sanctuary where we are treated as equals. Even in the Northlands. But here. Hilman has always been different. That woman was scared and not just because of the war. Or whatever is causing the destruction of the land. Or whoever is burning their properties. She was scared of him.'

'People get nasty when they get scared.' I said carefully. 'When they get hungry. When they don't feel safe.'

'True.' She moved her sight from unseen memories to look at me. 'But I guarantee that we will see more of this before long. It's in their history. Their culture. Hilman has always seen women as less than men. Men rule here. In everything from the court and counsel, in trade and business, in the home. Women cannot own property, do not own possessions. Everything is given to them by their fathers, their husbands, their brothers. Women are expected to defer to the man's wishes in everything. Every aspect of their lives. What they do, what they wear, who they marry.'

I remembered what little Z'hara had told us about her time in Hilman, and of the attempts to marry her to a stranger. I thought I understood the hurt but I struggled to understand how the women would meekly accept this. Her words explained the attitude of the soldier I killed at the fort and his clear contempt at confronting a woman in battle. I had shown him a fair amount of contempt of my own, but I could not dismiss the helplessness I felt around men such as Villermir and Rolyan. I should not be so quick to judge.

'We are not going to be welcome here,' she continued, holding herself very still. 'Many will try to control us. I tried to fight them. Succeeded on a few occasions. But there are always too many. You strike at one and the whole town will rise up against you. Just as you would beat a disobedient horse or hound, it is expected that you would beat a disobedient woman. Girls are taught from the moment they can crawl that they have no purpose other than to serve the needs of the male. Brothers take their toys, their friends, even their food. Girls are not educated. They rarely attend social events, and then they are closely managed. They have no say in the shape of their lives. Everything is controlled, permitted only by the male, with girls given in marriage as soon as they reach puberty.'

Z'hara ran out of words, or perhaps the will to remember any more. She was quiet for a long time before softly speaking to the fire.

'Be very careful, Tallen.'

We travelled for two more days before the farms showed signs of more effective management, although the livestock remained unhealthily thin. Farm workers now toiled in the fields and watched us with suspicion when we rode past. Following Z'hara's words, I became acutely aware of the absence of women, seeing none in the fields or farmyards where I expected them to be working alongside the men.

The track had widened into a well-used road and we approached the first market town. Farmers and merchants had joined us but the lack of women in these groups was still uncomfortably conspicuous. Danger simmered close to the surface and I became more conscious of myself and Z'hara, with each movement causing me to anxiously check the reactions of those around us. Without having discussed it, both Z'hara and I pulled up our hoods to become less obviously female and avoid drawing attention to ourselves.

In surprising contrast, the few soldiers we saw were completely uninterested in five armed travellers. We had been careful to avoid the Army of Truth near the border but when open countryside had forced us to pass a group heading north, it was a complete non-event. They barely noticed us when we moved aside to let them through, finding us as interesting as the wind lifting their horses' manes. Their attitude became apparent when we neared the town and saw that almost every merchant had a least one guard with a sword or axe for protection, with many farmers also carrying long hunting knives. In a kingdom where much of the food, livestock, horses and anything else that could be used was taken to feed, clothe and transport the army, desperate people would readily relieve traders of their goods. But despite the hardships caused, any soldiers encountered were treated with respect and men scrambled out of the way with a reverential bow. I was surprised to see expressions of gratitude rather than those of fear.

We entered the market town without challenge. Unlike the heavily populated areas I was familiar with in Faulknar, the trading centre was not fortified or protected by defendable walls and gates. The town seemed to have grown organically from the land around it. Buildings gradually got closer together, pathways randomly diverged from the main track, and frequent small areas had been created for meeting and trading. We followed the flow of people towards the more organised centre of town, heading for the slightly raised hill where several stalls could be seen. The sounds of complaining cattle and squealing pigs drifted towards us along with the smells of food and commerce.

I looked at Z'hara, to find her watching me. The women within the crowds were enclosed in a long, plain dress of a dark brown or black material, with a matching headdress which covered their head and neck. The dress fell straight from their shoulders in a shapeless tube that gathered in at the ankles. The restrictive garment meant that the woman could only extend her legs for a short pace with each step and the shuffling gait was a disturbing addition to the submissive posture shown by the all the women. The outward appearance of the town reflected every busy, noisy, chaotic trading place I had seen, but there was also a barely contained undercurrent of violence which tightened the muscles of my shoulders and made my fingers grip *Saorsa's* hilt a little tighter.

It became harder for Z'hara and me to blend in as the streets got busier, and we received more disapproving looks at being mounted and wearing clothes which allowed free movement. Glares and tuts of disapproval became scathing comments, aimed at Bear, Bonash and Vallori regarding their acceptance of our non-conformity; they should show more control over us, it was a disgrace to allow us to look or act like that in public, we should be taught the appropriate way for a woman to behave. Trefin nervously fought the bit and I struggled to prevent her from pushing into the men who came too close, provoking a tirade of complaints involving how, if they insisted on giving me a horse, they should give me one of a suitably placid temperament that I could manage to control. Their conviction that the male was the superior sex and that women needed to be governed like wilful children should have been laughable, but being surrounded by the consequences of their oppressive attitude, where women were afraid to raise their heads or look anyone in the eye, was sufficiently sobering. The men's rigid belief in their absolute authority kept their women walking a step behind, docilely carrying his purchases in oversized baskets while uttering no word of conversation, much less in protest. I felt sick and it had nothing to do with my empathic link to this damaged land.

The sound of a whip cracking a short distance to our right startled Z'hara and her horse shook her head in protest. A ripple of agitated jostling flowed through our horses and a chorus of curses followed as those around us were forced to move swiftly to avoid being stepped on. Z'hara pinched her lips into a thin line and she gripped the leather of her reins tight enough to turn her knuckles white.

She turned to me with a dangerous expression. 'Are you ready to see the meaner side of Hilman?'

I felt that Hilman was already showing itself to be sufficiently ugly but we obediently followed when she turned her horse down a claustrophobically narrow side street. Z'hara had taken us to a large, grassed area that was divided roughly into two sections, with a platform on either side. The crowds in front of these platforms were exclusively male, reflecting much of the town, and we were the only ones mounted.

The huddle of desperate people behind the platforms made me catch my breath and I could feel the heat radiating from Z'hara's stiffly controlled anger. She jerked her chin towards the larger of the two groups, quietly confirming what I suspected and filling in the details so I could fully appreciate the horror.

'That's the wife market. Men sell their sisters, daughters and nieces. Farmed off to the highest bidder for a short life of servitude before they die in childbirth.'

The cluster of quiet women, all contained within the restrictive dresses, were mainly older girls and young adults but I saw some that were as young as eight or nine summers. A woman roughly my age was helped onto the platform, showing a calm acceptance with no look of distress, no tears or wailing. I saw no resistance of any kind in the woman on the stage or in those who waited behind her. She passively accepted the touch of the man who was cajoling the crowd to part with their coin, turning her in circles or lifting her chin so those bidding could get a better look at her face. She maintained a posture of deflated inevitability. A dejected understanding that this was how it was meant to be.

Z'hara indicated the other group. 'Over there is the labour market. Brothers, sons and nephews sold for a fixed term to provide the muscle for farming or livery. If unlucky, they get bought for the quarries or mines. There they have only the false hope of freedom at the end of their tenure. Most will die of exhaustion, or malnutrition, or disease, or will be crushed by rocks long before then.'

The young men and boys in this group held their heads high, seemingly proud of the services they could offer. They paraded themselves in the hope of getting a higher bid based on how hard they would work or how strong they were. Their pride contrasted sharply with my memory of the sailors and fishermen forced into slavery by the Gallowglass pirates. These had not been forcibly taken to serve in distant lands, but were local men being sold by their families and traded for their health and strength.

I turned to look at Bonash, finding it hard to understand how this quiet, thoughtful man came from a culture that bought and sold people in the same way I would buy or sell a horse. The pretty woman invited bids that suggested significant value, but the lanky boy was offered less than the cost of a yearling pig. As hard as I looked, I saw no reflection of this flippant attitude to human life in the scholarly man currently rubbing circles with his thumb into the shoulder muscle of his horse. Bear saw me watching.

'Hilman has always accepted trade in others as a practical solution in a kingdom where resources can be scarce,' he offered quietly. 'Bartered labour can sometimes be the only way to feed a family or ensure a child gets cared for when there is no money for food, or clothing, or heat. A dowry gets paid to the wife's family rather than needing to be provided by them. Workers are paid for the years of their lives rather than their days. Traditionally, the practice was less formal with everyone coming to a mutual arrangement. But this...' He hesitated and I anxiously looked to see if anyone was paying too much attention or taking offence at implied criticism. 'These markets started a couple of winters ago. Someone saw an opportunity to make some money, creaming the coin before passing it to the families. A change of attitude that spread like a plague across the whole kingdom. All it took was a suggestion here, an offer there. Soon, people could no longer see it as being any other way.'

Vallori was the first to break, turning his horse more sharply than was necessary. Men grumbled as they moved out of our way and we headed back to the main route through the town. We joined the flow with no more thought than to get away from the slave markets and the unbearable sadness they caused. I focused on Z'hara's rigid back and readily fell into old habits of making myself small and inconspicuous, letting the hood fall low over my face and keeping my head down. I let Trefin find her own path and we pushed through areas that seethed with contempt and hate.

Trefin stopped abruptly and I looked up to see what new horror was being offered by this hateful place. We had been herded into a wide street that was lined by tall buildings, funnelling a large, closely packed crowd towards a high wall. Men were sitting on the roofs of the overlooking houses with their legs hanging over the edge, giving the impression that something important was about to happen and they wanted to have a good view of it. The crush in the street was halted by a row of guards using the shafts of their ceremonial spears as a barrier to ensure a clear space remained in front of the wall. The noise in the confined area became painfully loud with men pushing and shoving in an unproductive attempt to get closer to the front. They were forced together so tightly that turning to leave would be impossible, and yet more pushed past our horses to join the crush.

A hush from the front rippled towards us when a door to the side of the wall opened and a tall man walked into the cleared space. He was tonsured and wearing the robes of a Baila priest, and was followed, three paces behind, by a pair of black uniformed guards who were followed, three paces behind them, by another pair of soldiers. Held between them was a small, slight woman in a loose-fitting gown of undyed linen that brushed against her bare feet as she walked. Her light brown hair was uncovered and fell around her shoulders in an unkempt tangle. In contrast to the other women seen in the town, she carried her head high and looked defiantly at the hostile crowd. Her face clearly showed the marks of rough handling.

The hush turned to murmuring before growing louder, and the threat of violence increased with each step. The woman was led to the centre of the priest's stage before being turned to face the jeers and taunts of the baying crowd. She stood bravely with her back pressed against the wall and her hands tightly clasped at her waist, enduring the abuse for some time before the priest raised a hand and the mob fell silent.

'My children,' he began in a condescending tone that reached the back of the crowd. 'My children. It is with a heavy heart that we must attend to this matter today. Despite the care of Baila's chosen, and the best efforts of the good men of Hilman...' He paused as his congregation dutifully nodded in agreement that they were giving their best efforts. 'It is regrettable that a few refuse to embrace the benevolence of Baila and take comfort from his teachings.'

Trefin shifted under me and I tensed, tightening my grip on her reins. I consciously relaxed my body but could not remove the loathing twist to my mouth. Time spent absorbed in the serene tolerance of Luella's sanctuary had done nothing to remove the hate I had for these vicious priests and their vile, corrupted religion.

'This woman...' I heard an echo of the scorn directed at me by the soldier at the fort and Trefin danced sideways. '...has been accused of practising the fallacious herb-lore of the forbidden ways. She has been seen, unaccompanied, in the fields and hedgerows after dark. Collecting dangerous plants and moulds for malignant potions. Her man cowers in the shadows of their dwelling, where graven statues of false idols watch with malevolent intent. Seeding death and disease into the very heart of this community.'

Vallori moved his mare closer to Trefin. The nervous roan was reacting to my increasing fury and Vallori continued to push until his thigh pressed against mine. I turned to him in irritation. He gave a slight shake of his head, maintaining a hard glare which reminded me that my aura was boiling with the vibrant hues of my anger. Although they could not see it, those closest were already glancing at me in suspicion, feeling the radiant discomfort of power despite being beyond their five senses. The priest would almost certainly be able to detect the raging storm-cloud surrounding me if he chose to look in my direction. Grinding my teeth in frustration, I gathered the simmering energies and forced them deep within my core. The need for an avenging fireball dissipated and the tingle in my palms faded.

The priest finally came to his conclusion.

'The church of the most gracious Baila condemns this woman as a witch.'

A murderous cheer thundered through the crowd, causing Bonash's horse to swiftly reverse out of the street and the small man was happy to let her go. The woman had bravely faced her accusers throughout the priest's speech but crumbled when the first stone hit her. Rocks ranging from the size of a quail's egg to that of my fist were thrown at her in zealous spite. They smacked into her belly and smashed her chest. They pounded against her arms and ribs when she curled to protect herself. They cracked against her head to leave bright red outlines on her too-pale skin. Tears streamed down her bruised face and she cried out in pain with each stone that struck her. The rain of rocks continued, with fear and hatred strengthening the arms that threw them. The woman collapsed under the assault. She rolled onto her side and hugged her knees in the pitiful posture of a frightened child. And still they threw. Their faces were pulled back into cruel masks, while blood stained her dress. It seeped from her mouth and nose. It leaked from countless cuts on her arms and face.

Vallori grabbed Trefin's reins and we followed as Z'hara turned her horse away from the fanatically violent crowd. Those nearest quickly turned their frustrations towards us when we pushed our way through. Being too far away to effectively strike at the victim, they readily focused on us. Specifically, on Z'hara and me. A large stone hit the rump of Z'hara's mare and I felt one bash painfully into my lower back. Vallori released his hold on Trefin and I set my heels to her flanks, uncaring of who she crashed into or stood on while we bullied our way out of the street and back the main road. People leapt out of the way as Bear ploughed after Bonash, already halfway to the outskirts of the town. Z'hara, Vallori and I gave our horses' their heads and thundered out of the putrid market town, ignoring the shouts of protest from those who scrambled out of our way.

Chapter Nine

We did not travel far and made camp in a sparse woodland by the side of the main road. We had encountered no vigilante gangs prior to the town and had no reason to suspect that any would come after us, and yet I found it hard to concentrate on the small tasks of collecting firewood or clearing a smooth area for our bedding. I was tight with nervous energy and my attempts at grooming the horses resulted in Bonash's mount baring her teeth, Trefin kicking out with her hind leg, and Vallori's steady black mare flattening her ears and showing the whites of her eyes. Eventually, Bonash tactfully suggested he take over the horses' care.

I sat. I stood. I paced. I sharpened and oiled my weapons with an intensity that was unnecessary. None of it erased the festering discomfort I felt after witnessing such primal savagery. Z'hara had a need to expel some frustrations of her own and proposed that we spar with each other. We sought release through the physical exertion, clubbing at each other with no finesse and minimal technique. My mind was quieter following the exercise but my soul remained heavy.

Darkness crept in while I ate a tasteless meal and I was still restless when I retired to my bed. I laid on my back, listening to the rhythmic breathing of those around me and willing myself to relax. I fought the insistent urge to do *something* but it was not long before I gave up any pretence of sleep. I could not deny the need to avenge the woman who had been so viciously stoned. I had no clue as to how I was to do that, but felt returning to the town would be the best place to start.

Vallori's face was illuminated by the soft glow from the fire's embers. He watched me gather my knives. 'If I asked you not to do anything stupid, would you listen?'

I smiled at him. 'Now, what you call stupid, I call fun. You are going to have to be more specific.'

'Your hands are twitching. That normally means you are about to set fire to something.'

'Or steal something.' I ignored his look of disapproval. 'I haven't decided yet.'

'This is not a good idea.'

'I know. But I rarely have good ideas so the bad ones will have to do.' I stretched my hands towards the warmth of the small flames and gave him an apologetic look. 'I have to do something. This feeling won't stop biting at me.'

'I could come with you?'

I had considered this, and should have welcomed the company, but I considered Vallori more strength rather than stealth. I could not deny my old habits and I still considered remaining unseen as my best protection. I gently refused his offer.

'I work better alone.'

I waited several heartbeats for Vallori to offer more reasons for me not to go but he remained silent, only quietly asking me to be careful when I left to saddle Trefin.

The soft beat of the mare's hooves on the dry ground gave rhythm to the need pulsing inside me. By the time I left the little roan tethered to a small hedgerow, my palms itched in anticipation and I absently scratched at them while I walked the short distance to the market town. It was quieter than I had been expecting, with only a few walking the streets. The undercurrents of violence that were so visible during the day were hidden behind closed doors and shuttered windows.

It had been some time since I had explored a town at night but the familiar network of streets and alleys allowed me to quickly orientate myself. I easily found the heart of the town, keeping to the shadows and carefully avoiding the sites of the slave markets and the stoning. I slipped down a narrow passageway and emerged in a large open street dominated by Baila's temple. Surrounded by predominantly timber buildings, the faint moonlight reflected off the pale sandstone to arrogantly radiate its importance. It stood over twice the height of the neighbouring structures and was lavishly adorned with large carved figures standing amongst smaller mythical beasts. I was still several paces away, but I could already feel the temple's protective wardings, stabbing with needle-sharp points all along my arms and clashing with the stinging of my palms.

The feeling became overwhelming when I approached the building and I quickly retreated to the far side of the square, climbing onto the roof of the largest house where I could study the temple. I searched for a way in, knowing the hateful priest would be hiding there. I crouched on the edge, mirroring the pose of the half-human creatures which had been carved at the corners of the building to scare away evil forces. I appreciated the irony of the biggest evil residing within the temple.

Two guards stood either side of the main doors. Their posture was relaxed and bored, but they were wearing the uniform of Baila's army and I would not discount them as being purely ceremonial. *Hired thugs*, Bear had called them. With Vallori's caution to be careful echoing Z'hara's earlier warning, I rejected the front door and looked for a more subtle way in. The far side of the temple was pressed against the adjoining building but a narrow alley ran along the opposite wall. Two doors offered a way in, one placed towards the rear of the temple and another leading to an enclosed courtyard. I stayed in the shadows but the guards continued their conversation and seemed completely unaware that I approached.

The temple's wardings were powerful and stronger than I had expected. I was still some way from the building when the unpleasant energies hammered into the base of my skull. I checked my mental barriers, confirming they were intact despite new vines covering the outer layers. I wove more protective sigils into the defences but the pounding pressure persisted. I cautiously advanced towards the building, fighting for each step against the forces pushing to keep me away. My skin crawled and my chest ached by the time I reached the temple's door and grasped the handle.

Pain raced up my arm as if it had been thrust into a blazing fire. I leapt back and bit the inside of my cheek hard enough to avoid crying out in agony. The throbbing discomfort in my mouth dispelled the false pain of my arm, and I looked at a limb untouched by fire and with no evidence of burns. I stared at my shaking hand, repeatedly flexing and extending my fingers, still unable to believe it was whole and healthy. I cursed quietly. Taking vengeance on the priest was no longer an option and I left, choosing no particular direction other than one which would take me away from those malignant energies.

The town reminded me sufficiently of Liegeport that I was soon recognising familiar characteristics. The poorer areas were furthest from the main road and the trading spaces, while more prosperous homes bordered the larger squares and meeting places. A narrow river flowed sluggishly through one side of the town and several houses backed onto this, appropriately distanced from the less favourable districts. Small patches of well-tended grass allowed their owners to sit on a summer's evening and watch the swans float majestically on the water. It stank of mockery, that they could find pleasure in this natural beauty when the ugliness of an exploited landscape was less than a morning's walk away.

I made my decision. As satisfying as setting fire to the rancid place would be, with the closely packed wooden buildings igniting in a maelstrom of flame and burning ashes, it would not benefit those who were already suffering. The anger at lost property and destroyed possessions would be swiftly aimed at those most vulnerable, and that was not what I wanted. I selected a path that involved intense annoyance rather than dramatic chaos, and Vallori and Z'hara's cautioning voices became silent.

I chose a house that shamelessly proclaimed its wealth with a pair of stone lions standing either side of the main door, each with a gilded collar and coloured glass eyes. Using the small knife tucked in my boot, I prised open the window and crawled into the wide area where guests would be received. Expensive rugs covered the floor and my feet made no sound when I landed softly. A pair of thick tapestries matched the quality of the rugs, but I was attracted to the array of decorative items displayed on shelves and small tables around the edges of the room. Carved wooden figures stood beside similarly crafted stags and a large, tusked boar. A matched pair of rearing horses, sculpted into a pale stone, sat within crevices at each end of the far wall. Small mounds of salt crystal had been moulded into intricate spiralling shapes and dyed with a rainbow of colours that were beautiful even in the muted tones of the dim lighting. The amount of decoration in the room should have been crassly overwhelming but it somehow managed to retain a sense of elegance.

I moved into a side room where the furnishings and solid oak desk suggested the room was used as a study. A few scrolls lay loosely rolled on the table along with an open ledger, and stained quills poked out of a plain leather tumbler which sat beside a half-filled glass inkwell. I found nothing of interest there so turned my attention to the modest fireplace and the shelf above it. A few smooth, round pebbles were scattered within the functional items required for lighting and maintaining a fire. Intrigued as to why they would be there, I picked them up and rolled them between my fingers to catch the subdued light. The stones were highly polished and the thin bands, the colour of walnut, russet and sand, shone like glass. I placed a couple of the more attractive ones in my pocket.

My foot pressed a loose floor plank when I crossed the room, releasing a short squeak. I froze for several heartbeats, but the house remained quiet and there was nothing to suggest I had been heard. I gave a small smile in anticipation before curling back the rug and levering up the wood slat, revealing the hidden cache beneath. I removed a dark leather pouch that fit easily into the palm of my hand but felt heavy enough to contain a reasonable number of coins. I added it to the stones in my pocket. A plain wooden box held a few glass beads and small gems, along with a dark blood-red stone. It had been shaped into a teardrop, with flattened sections chipped throughout like worked flint. I stroked the polished jewel with my fingertips.

'Now you're pretty,' I breathed, and placed it safely within a small pocket.

Nothing else in the room deserved a closer look so I returned to the reception area. A high-pitched whine was becoming increasingly insistent and I sought to locate its source, despite the nagging suspicion that a seemingly mundane house would house a magick artefact. The hum started undulating and it was almost a softly lilting tune by the time I entered the room at the back of the house, not at all like the unpleasant sensations I normally felt around magickal items.

While the first room had presented as functional, this one embraced me as I walked in. Several comfortable chairs were placed strategically: beside the window, either side of the fire, cradled within a curve of the wall. All had been arranged so they faced into the room. All set to create the feeling of inclusion and belonging. A shared space. Soft pelts from thickly furred seals draped over some of the chairs, quietly displaying the wealth of the household where trade with the cold, harsh lands beyond the Northlands provided comfort for a family in Hilman. They triggered an unwelcome memory of Gallowgla.

This room was clearly for the woman or women of the house and I reviewed my judgement of the town. Significant coin had been spent to provide these luxuries, suggesting a fondness which had not been apparent with the controlling behaviour and restrictive dress forced on the women when in public. Small portraits of children, both girls and boys, were placed on tables around the room along with sculptured figures of family: embracing couples, cradling babies, a mother being hugged by a child. Perhaps what I had seen was, in part, an attempt to placate Baila's priests and their suffocating doctrines, and not a true reflection of how these people felt. Maybe it was not what they hoped and dreamed for their families.

The humming became noticeably louder and, irritated by the blatant nagging from the magick, I relented and let myself be guided to a low door which could easily be overlooked. It fit snugly below the window and had been carved with symmetrical patterns so it looked more like a decorative panel than a functioning door. An indentation to one side allowed a fingertip to flick open the flap, opening smoothly to reveal a shallow cave with two narrow shelves. The top shelf held trinkets that looked like they had been made by children as playthings and I suspected these were personal treasures that held fond memories of a growing family. A small wicker sewing basket rested on the floor amongst scraps of embroidered linen.

An unremarkable, roughly made wooden box was partially covered by the scraps of cloth and spools of thread that were scattered over the middle shelf. The humming had faded to the sigh of a pleasant melody, and I smiled at the impression of self-importance radiating from this inconspicuous item. I reached towards it carefully, testing for protective wardings, but this box wanted to be found and allowed me to retrieve it without reprimand. The music fell silent when I opened the box, or maybe I no longer noticed it. I was captivated by the exquisite beauty of the pendant. A delicate dragonfly stretched its wings, nestled on a cushion of snow-white silk. Threads of gold encased the thin shards of emerald within its wings and along the top of its back. The underbelly rippled with the low light reflecting off pearl. Its eyes were tiny drops of jet. Time stopped for a heartbeat and I basked in the splendour contained within this miniature masterpiece. I reluctantly closed the lid and placed the treasure in my pocket, knowing I had achieved what I had needed to that night. I was uninterested in anything else the house may have had to offer and left without further investigation.

I had planned on quickly leaving the town but the closer I got to the market areas, the busier it became. Shadows moved in the alleys and side streets, and by the time I bordered the poor district I could no longer ignore the clusters of children huddled into sheltered corners. They warily watched me, deciding whether I was a threat or a target. Dirty, skeletal limbs protruded from fraying clothes that would not keep them warm in winter. They were surrounded by filth and rotting debris, with the resultant disease and sore-pocked skin clearly evident. Hair was shorn short to ensure an anonymity that would protect the girls from unwanted attention. Their ages ranged from perhaps six or seven years up to young adults, and I suspected there were many who had run to avoid arranged marriages, preferring the threat of starvation or freezing in cold, stinking passageways. I closed my eyes, crushed by the desperation of it all and the fear that it would be reflected across Hilman.

I reached for the coin purse I had taken from the rich, warm, well-fed family, removing a coin to toss at the nearest child. The dead look in his eyes upon seeing the disc confirmed what I already knew. Coin would not help them. It would be taken from them and they would be beaten as thieves. I replaced the coin and cursed the wasted time, but spent the rest of the night raiding for blankets, food and clothing. Items that could be used immediately or easily defended. The first tones of dawn forced me to leave but I returned to Trefin feeling a warm satisfaction from the night's work.

The camp was busy with the familiar routines when I returned. Bear was boiling water for the tea that would take away the morning's chill. Bonash was beside him, rummaging through our stores for nuts and seeds. Vallori rolled his bedding and gathered his pack before joining Z'hara, who was scooping grain into buckets for the horses' morning rations. Trefin eagerly joined the group and nibbled Z'hara's sleeve to ensure she received her share. I barely had time to remove her bridle before she started munching happily, shaking when I slid the saddle from her back. Vallori offered me a brush but maintained his grip to ensure I had noticed his questioning raised eyebrow.

'The town is not burning so I judge that as *not-stupid*.' I snatched the brush from him. 'And I left when only the bakers were awake so no one noticed me and there are no guards chasing me. So, again, I'm going with *not-stupid*.'

Z'hara smirked as she took the brush, offering to groom Trefin and sending me to get some food. I gratefully thanked her and joined Bear and Bonash by the fire, declining the handful of seeds offered by the smaller but accepting the tea offered by the larger. I closed my eyes in appreciation when the warm liquid settled in my stomach.

'Did you kill him?'

I looked up to see the dark Moon Warrior watching me intently, patiently waiting for me to answer and noting my frown.

'I wanted to,' I admitted, perhaps for the first time to myself as well as to Bear. 'But I couldn't even get close. There was a very nasty sting hiding in the temple's wardings. Stronger than I was expecting.'

Bonash grinned while he passed a handful of hazelnuts to Vallori who had come to sit by me. 'I suspect it may be a result of how shockingly overdue your devotions to Baila are. He takes these kinds of things personally.'

I shook my head in mock contrition. 'It is true that I have been very remiss in my platitudes. It has been some time since I last visited a temple. Not since I left Faulknar.'

Bear grunted. 'His ambitions have risen since then. Faulknar still falls far behind in their worship of the false God but, even there, Baila's influence is growing. Particularly in these last few years. In Lindvane and Hilman, it is effectively without competition. And Baila's priests are clever. They siphon the energies that their followers pour into their worship and use it to fuel their magick. The more the faithful pray to their God, the more powerful the priests get. The energy you felt surrounding the temple was just a small slice of the power they have trapped within the countless artefacts they've obtained.'

I shifted uncomfortably at the thought of all that power being leeched into the grasp of the corrupt priests. The energies were supposed to flow freely through people, into the Gods, and through the land before returning to the people. An unbroken chain that replenished and repaired what it took and consumed. The coin pouch pressed uncomfortably against my hip and I retrieved a disc, watching as I rolled it over and through my fingers.

'Can I look at that?'

Bonash reached for the coin I was playing with, turning it over to examine both sides. Eventually, he nodded to himself with a small smile and flicked the coin to Bear.

'It's more than that. See what they've done? One side is stamped with Averill's image and the stag of Hilman. Standard for coins within a kingdom and used for generations to remind its subjects of who rules over them. But look on the reverse. There's an image of the oval of Baila. A clear statement concerning the influence of that religion. Faith and Crown. Equal. Governed by one as much as the other. At the forefront of everything you do.' He grinned at Bear, leaning forward to emphasise his point as Z'hara came to stand behind Vallori's shoulder. 'Do you understand the scale of this? Every time one of these coins is handled, touched, traded, even looked at, a small fragment of that person's soul is sent to Baila. With the priests collecting the toll.'

We travelled in a roughly south-easterly direction. We remained on small roads and diverted around towns and larger villages while not actively avoiding anyone. Those we met were suspicious and wary but they were too concerned with their own affairs to waste time on us. Provided we did not threaten them or attempt to steal their possessions, they were happy to ignore us.

Our days quickly fell into a routine. We would wake early and Bear would leave camp before us to scout the surrounding area for possible threats or alternative ways through the craggy hills. He generally returned by late morning to confirm we were still taking the best route. He stopped this ritual after a few days, with the open countryside within the valley and the lack of hostile intent from those we encountered negating the need for his vigilance. We would travel beyond dusk each night and took infrequent breaks to rest the horses, each of us feeling a nagging urgency despite not having a clear destination.

I found the days dull and monotonous but still welcomed them over the nights. The dreams persisted so I would often stay awake deep into the night trying to avoid them. Unseen terrors stalked dark forests and enclosed spaces provoked echoes of the nightmares Villermir had manipulated. Occasionally the wolves would chase me, turning into orange-eyed, winged daemons that snapped at my face and throat. Less frequently, the horses hunted. Turning into grotesque parodies of our mounts. Muscular bodies would bulge so that sinuous necks attached to bull-like bodies, and thickened limbs ended in cloven hooves. Tusks as long and thick as my arm extended from lower jaws, advancing with lowered heads to rip open my belly. These dreams made me more reactive around Trefin, who would become more nervous around me, and this resulted a lot of frustration and cursing. Vallori gave me an evening drink containing valerian and camomile to encourage a deeper, more restful sleep, but it proved difficult to get the infusion right. If it was concentrated enough to suppress the dreams, I would remain slow-witted until late in the day. A more dilute mix would allow me to function adequately, but the dreams would break through to haunt me. I eventually accepted that the night-terrors would remain until I dealt with their cause and I refused the offered brew.

My distressing dreams were not the only thing to disquiet the group. Almost half the nights were disturbed by an event that was difficult to explain as a natural occurrence. Flashes of green light would dance amongst the clouds, becoming more vivid as the sky darkened. The sheets of emerald split the sky like lightning, each flare stretching as wide as a banner. The display would continue deep into the night and I feared that this was in some way connected to my dreams. We all felt unnerved that the lights were always in the south-eastern sky. And that we seemed to be drawn towards them.

The mood within the group deteriorated from sombre silence to sulky brooding and then to petulant squabbling once the rain started. It persisted for days without respite so that everything became saturated and covered in mud. Damp clothing chaffed. Dried rations softened and developed mould. Oils were rubbed into leather and grease was applied to the horses' pasterns. We spent more time on caring for the permanently moist skin on our horses' legs than we did for ourselves, and we were all stinking and miserable. When we came to a tavern, situated at an isolated trade route crossroads, we agreed in less than a heartbeat that we would be staying there for the night.

The tavern was of a moderate size and had a similarly sized barn to one side for horses. Many of the stalls were empty and we housed our mounts in peat-lined beds covered with clean straw while a wide-eyed boy anxiously stared at Bear. Sweet smelling hay was provided and we removed the saddles, inspecting their backs for reddened skin and prodding for any sore areas. The lad smiled shyly when the big man winked at him, tossing him a coin in exchange for grooming the horses while we went in search of hot food. I did not doubt the boy would do a good job. Z'hara's chestnut was already nibbling at his sleeve in relaxed companionship, something the mare had never done to me.

Entering the tavern released a warmth that made me sigh in contentment and I was not the only one to do that. The dark timbers of the ceiling shimmered slightly with the smoke from two fires, one set at each end of the main room, and from the pipes of many who crowded within the inn to avoid the rain. The soft murmur of noise did not do justice to the number of farmers, labourers and merchants seated around tables and in alcoves throughout the space. We barely aroused more than a quick glance before they returned to their quiet, intimate conversations.

It took some time to locate a free table, set into an alcove, which could accommodate all five of us. Wooden barriers had been placed to create a degree of privacy around the table so, as I took the small space that backed onto the outer wall, Z'hara sat at an angle on my left while Bonash repeated this on my right. Bear and Vallori took the outside spaces to complete the horseshoe.

Bonash surveyed the tavern, shaking his head slightly. 'There's not more than a farm or two within a day's walk of here. Most of these men will be staying the night. There might not be any rooms left.'

'I need a bath!' Z'hara groaned dramatically. 'I'll happily sleep on the floor, but I really want a bath.'

Vallori leaned down to sniff at her shoulder. 'Yes, you really do need a bath.'

He received an outraged slap on the arm. 'You don't smell so great yourself.'

I smiled at their banter, appreciating how quickly our tempers had improved simply by being warm and out of the rain. Z'hara extended her hand to me.

'Hand it over, Tallen.'

'Hand over what?' I asked innocently.

She wiggled her fingers. 'Hand over that nice, fat pouch of coins that you... *found*. I think you should be paying.'

'Oh, you think that do you? I thought we had an equal arrangement where everyone contributes. If I pay for the food, drinks, stables, rooms, baths, what will you be contributing?'

Z'hara smiled sweetly. 'My contribution is not stabbing you in the leg for being selfish.'

Vallori nodded sagely. 'That sounds fair.'

I scowled at him. 'Thanks for your support.'

In truth, I was not reluctant to let the purse go. Since Bonash had shown me the image of Baila and told of its potential to drain a fragment of your soul when touching one coin, much less a whole pouch of them, I was eager to find a way of getting rid of them. I went to pass it to Z'hara's outstretched hand but Bear intercepted to enclose it within his palm. It felt strangely appropriate that he should be the one to take care of the coins. I noticed a quick look pass between Bonash and the Moon Warrior before being distracted by the tavern owner approaching our table. He was a slightly rounded man with a large nose and flushed red cheeks, framed by a mass of dark hair. He frowned at Z'hara and me but made no comment.

'What can I get you?'

Bear, naturally, spoke for the group. 'Ale and a hot meal for all of us would be gratefully received.'

'Meat's scarce but we have a hot broth that's filling.'

The big man politely smiled. 'Sounds ideal. And we will require rooms for the night.'

The owner tilted his head to indicate the crowded room. 'You and everyone else here. Rain's brought everyone off the road. We've no room spare but there's space in the barn to keep you dry and the horses' heat will make sure you stay warm.'

'Then we will take that gladly.'

Bear agreed the fee and poured the required amount directly into the man's hand, being careful not to touch the coins himself. The man nodded in acceptance and left to fetch the ale.

Vallori turned to look forlornly at Z'hara. 'Looks like you are going to have to stay smelly.'

She shrugged a shoulder in response. 'At this point, I'm prepared to jump into a horse trough.'

The ale was well watered but the broth contained a respectable amount of vegetables, along with some grain to provide more substance. I agreed that it was hot and filling. I sat back, content to watch the different groups gathered in the tavern. There was little interaction between the tables beyond the occasional polite acknowledgement. The owner served everyone himself but people remained patiently seated until he could attend to them. It was not like the inns I had visited in Faulknar. There was no minstrel or storyteller. There were no games of chance provoking animated exchanges between the contestants. It was polite and orderly and respectful, and showed none of the rough chaos I was familiar with. I felt saddened by its loss, and maybe more than that. I missed Tawpin. This place would certainly benefit from the presence of my wild-haired, roguish friend and the mischief he would cause.

Bonash nudged my arm. 'What were you thinking? You were smiling. A fond memory?'

I looked to find all my companions watching me and felt suddenly self-conscious, unwilling to compare the possible friendships here with those I had lost in Faulknar. I looked into the serious, deep apple-green eyes of Vallori that were so different from the open, laughing sea-green of Tawpin's.

'This tavern is way too respectful for my taste. I prefer something a little more rowdy.'

Z'hara chuckled. 'Why doesn't that surprise me?'

'I was remembering a friend. Tawpin. We used to drink at the Blue Boar. And, oh, could we drink! He taught me many things. Hangovers. Vomiting on an empty stomach is worse than having something to bring up. He showed me how to set the tanners against the sailors so that, when they inevitably started throwing punches, we could get free drinks while the barkeep was busy elsewhere. A good night was measured in black eyes and split knuckles.'

Bonash looked horrified. 'He sounds awful.'

I laughed. 'He was thoroughly dreadful. He taught me how to steal. How to read people and exploit their weaknesses. To cause chaos and mayhem wherever we went. But he always did it with a smile. A wide-mouthed, too many teeth smile that made you forgive him everything. He loved people and everyone knew it. He never took it too far. He never caused more than a temporary inconvenience. He was safety at the centre of a storm.'

I stopped talking. My thoughts had taken me down a path I was unwilling to go and was less willing to share. Thinking of all that Tawpin had taught me and of how safe I had felt with him reminded me of the one lesson he had not taught me. He left the lesson of betrayal to Kade.

I returned to watching the tavern's crowd to break the river of thought that threatened to drown me, careful to avoid eye-contact with Vallori. I quickly scanned the quiet tables and the quiet conversations that were taking place there, finding nothing of interest, but my fitful attention was captured by a figure half-hidden in the gloom of a booth. He sat alone, his hood still covering his head so his features were shadowed, with both hands cradling his tankard. He sat very still and he was unmistakably watching us.

We watched him back. It had not taken long for the others to follow my sustained gaze, also becoming intrigued by the stranger's guarded nature which contrasted sharply with the others in the tavern. He controlled his movements carefully. He deliberately maintained a relaxed attitude that would prevent any misunderstanding, ensuring he would not provoke more than our mutual assessment of how much of a threat the other posed. He drank enough to keep the tavern owner content with him taking up space, but not so much that the weakened ale would cloud his thoughts or slow his reactions. Searching deeper, I noticed a slight catch to his right shoulder when moving that could suggest a recent wound or a more chronic injury. His posture was angled in a way that would allow an immediate answer to any threat or danger. He reminded me of my wolf, with an attitude that spoke of confidence in his physical ability. I suspected a body of fighting muscle was carefully hidden under the loose-fitting cloak.

It was late in the evening before the stranger hid some coins under the base of his tankard and rose to leave. He gave us a slight nod of acknowledgment that bordered on arrogance, then made his way to the exit without looking back. We made sure there was sufficient time for no suggestion that we were following him before leaving to spend the night in the barn, finding him waiting for us.

He was casually leaned against the half-door of the stable, scratching the base of a thin-boned skewbald's ear while it pressed its head against his chest. He paid no attention to us and continued to fuss the horse, unconcerned when we fanned out in a blatantly offensive pattern. The wide-eyed lad nervously flicked his attention between us and the stranger, his eyes even bigger than before. The big warrior noticed and quietly addressed the boy's anxiety, flicking his head towards the open double-doors and allowing the lad to skitter past us while sticking as close to the far wall as possible.

The man turned towards us after the boy fled, easing off his hood to reveal a long face and a small, amused smile. He had straight, dark hair that brushed his shoulders, separated in the middle so that a curtain fell to either side of his face. A single braid sat in front of each ear, containing a small blue bead at its tip to weight it in place. The blue of the beads was the same colour as the eyes that silently challenged us.

He suddenly threw off his cloak in a flourish of fabric, causing a reflex of drawn steel. Five swords aimed at his chest before the garment touched the ground.

'Easy there,' he laughed.

He remained undisturbed by our response but showed the palms of his hands in a token gesture, claiming he was not a threat despite clearly being one. Despite intentionally provoking us to test our reactions. His smile widened when we maintained our raised blades.

Bear was the first to lower his weapon, although he did not sheath it. The others followed his example a heartbeat later but I waited until I had the man's full attention before lowering *Saorsa,* making sure he understood the damage she could inflict. I took some satisfaction to see his arrogant smile falter just a little.

'What do you want?' Bear demanded.

'Well, you look like fighting people so I thought I'd offer you a fight. Not me, although...' he lifted an eyebrow at Vallori, '...maybe later.' He shrugged the idea away, ignoring Vallori's scowl, and became serious for the first time. 'Hilman's at war. I was hoping you would want a piece of it.'

'You don't look like one of Baila's devoted,' Vallori scoffed, with an expression that suggested he would be happy to fight later.

The man spat in the dirt beside him. 'Those puffed-up dandelions. That is truly insulting if you think I would join them.'

'So, you want our help to fight these *puffed-up dandelions*?' I asked. 'You could certainly do with the help. You've barely made a mark. The soldiers we've met have given us no more than a disapproving look, despite being obviously armed. And with two of us being women. Your little insurrection does not seem to be causing them much concern.'

He reluctantly moved his attention away from Vallori, where the two had maintained their staring contest, to fully look at me. He blinked several times before answering.

'Insurrection is a big word, and those are truly...' He struggled to find the word he was searching for. '... strange eyes. We are dealing with more than whatever flea is currently biting at the priests' tender areas. We don't have enough resources to deal with Baila's Army of Truth.'

'You don't feel the need to protect your people from the beatings, starvation, oppression, slavery?' Z'hara challenged quietly.

He turned to her, softening a little. 'Honestly? No. We don't have the time to fight Baila, or Averill, or all the weak-minded who would use them as an excuse to bully others. There are bigger, more devastating dangers to worry about. Ones I can't begin to explain or know how to fight. So, yes. The petty nastiness that's spreading through Hilman is not my concern. It won't matter when there's no one left to bully.'

Bear sheathed his sword. The man's bleak passion in answering Z'hara had deflated our offensive posturing and we started to see him as less of a threat. He walked up to the stranger, standing uncomfortably close to the significantly smaller man. Only Bonash and I stood shorter, with Z'hara being roughly a similar size and Vallori being at least a head taller. Bear intentionally towered over the man, who frowned slightly at having to twist his neck to look the Moon Warrior in the eye but showed no sign of being intimidated.

'Did they cradle you in manure to get you to grow so big?'

Bear grinned at the poor attempt at humour. 'Perhaps you should tell us who, or what, you would like us to fight.'

While we checked our horses and gathered our supplies for the night, we heard about the horrors that were being inflicted on the eastern regions of Hilman. The area we had been drawn towards since leaving the Northlands.

'There are not enough of us,' he began. 'There will never be enough of us. Most come from the west where the threat is lessened and the grip of Baila is looser. Too many in the east cannot understand how nightmares can be made real, cannot explain what they've seen. They cling to religion in the hope of salvation.' He looked at Z'hara. 'That's why the people accept the beatings. And the starvation. The oppression and the slavery. It's better than an alternative that is so overwhelming, so beyond their comprehension. They choose to put their faith in an unjust God in order to maintain some hope of control. He has to save them because they have no chance of saving themselves. And the priests feed on their fears at every opportunity, just to satisfy their hunger for power and control.'

'So, what is this danger? What has the people so scared?' Bear prompted gently.

The smaller man shifted his gaze to look at me. 'Daemons. Orange-eyed daemons. They are summoned by the shamans who came across the Northern Sea with the Gallowglass pirates.'

I reflexively flicked a look at Vallori to see him already watching me. The stranger noticed our exchange.

'The raids started on the coast,' he continued, 'but soon moved inland, taking those Gods-cursed shamans with them. They dance half-naked, covered in ash and lime, gathering power like the summoning of storm clouds. Calling their creatures from Mobis's Hells to come and play.'

I shivered, suddenly ice-cold.

'You will have seen the green lights at night. The monsters glow when we cut them. Bleeding green light that dances in the sky.' He grinned with grim humour. 'It's very pretty and it costs them nothing. We hack off a limb and it grows back. We cut off a head and it turns into a new beast, so we have twice as many to deal with. We have a few old blades that seem to carry a little magick and can deliver a sting. And we have a growing number of spell-weavers who help distract the monsters from their slaughter. But they are no match for the shamans. It's carnage. Time after time. We get ripped to shreds while they get stronger.'

He fell silent and the soft noises of the sleeping horses sounded uncomfortably loud in the empty space left by his words. The air seemed to press in around us.

'So?' The challenging grin returned as the fighter stood. 'Do you want to come and join the fun?'

Bear gave a wry smile and Vallori slowly shook his head. Z'hara and Bonash shared the same look of quiet determination. It was what we were here for. It was what we had been sent to do. I was a Dragonslayer, created to fight daemons. Again, it was Bear who spoke for the rest of us by saying it out loud.

'We will fight with you.'

'Splendid!' He paused halfway up the ladder taking him up to the hay loft. 'My name's Elyos. We leave at dawn.'

Chapter Ten

Any relief from the heavy rain of the previous days quickly evaporated as the low mist penetrated collars and wicked up sleeves. By mid-morning I was already damp and miserable, and so I welcomed the distraction when Elyos slowed his horse to walk alongside me. The mist had curled the ends of his hair and his nose was a little red, but otherwise seemed unaffected by the unpleasant weather.

'Tallen,' he said with a grin.

'Elyos,' I replied suspiciously.

I waited for him to continue while he studied the backs of the others. Bear and Bonash rode together at the front, with Vallori and Z'hara riding side-by-side behind them.

'Tell me. Do you ever feel left-out? Ignored?'

Vallori turned to scowl at him, being close enough to hear our conversation and not liking the obvious provocation. Elyos's grin widened but I gave a small shake of my head and Vallori returned to looking forward.

'What do you mean?'

Elyos flapped his hand to indicate those in the lead. 'Well, the giant and the weasel are together.'

I turned to face him, irritated by the implication in his use of the term *together* and the mildly insulting description of Bonash despite having just advised Vallori to ignore his baiting.

'Are you always this rude?'

'Generally.' He shrugged a shoulder but carried on regardless. 'And blondie and beautiful have each other. So where does that leave you?' He looked at me with a mockingly pitying expression. 'Do you not have anyone to warm your bed?'

Before I had the chance to respond to his goading, Vallori whipped round so suddenly that his mare shied sideways. Elyos crowed in victory.

'Ha! I knew it. You have slept with him. What a truly genial arrangement.'

Vallori's glare turned murderous, and I was sure it was only Z'hara's softly spoken words that kept him from riding over to punch Elyos's insolent mouth closed. I decided to adopt a more subtle rebuke and sent a blast of compressed air towards the skewbald's face. The gelding violently raised his head and unbalanced his rider before pirouetting on his hind legs. I grinned at the overly self-confident man fighting to keep his seat, flustered into gathering his reins and cursing with an impressive vocabulary. It was testament to his skill as a rider that he remained in the saddle and returned to walk his calmed horse beside me within a few heartbeats.

'What was that?'

I kept my smug smile in place, asking innocently, 'What was what?'

'Moss spooks at a gust of wind while your blue, who has been twitching at grasshoppers all morning, doesn't flick an ear?'

I watched his face while I lifted some dirt from the road, opening my hand and making it dance in my palm as little whirlwinds. I separated the colours so that lighter shades weaved around darker tones and rotated the grains, faster and faster, into dizzying patterns. My smile became more genuine when Elyos's jaw dropped in wonder. I released the dirt to drop back on to the trail, but he continued to stare at my empty palm for some time before raising his eyes to mine.

'You've just become a lot more interesting.'

I raised a challenging eyebrow. 'And you should be more respectful. Will you stop playing games now?'

He gave a small nod of acceptance and we rode in a more comfortable silence, before I relented to the urge and asked.

'Do you always look to cause trouble? And by that, I mean offend. For what? Fun? Relieve the boredom? Or do you just want people to hate you?'

I had expected a return of his mocking arrogance but he replied with a hint of sadness in his tone. 'Have you ever seen a flintknapper work? Seen how they take a block of flint that looks so perfectly complete. A creamy shell surrounding dark rock that's as smooth as water. Solid. But then, just a tap at the right spot. At the right angle. And it splinters.'

'Is that what you are doing? Testing to find our fracture lines. To see if we'll splinter.' I scowled at his presumption, remembering Tawpin's return to Kingsport. 'I've seen those games played before and I don't care for them.'

He just smiled in response.

The weather cleared soon after midday, bringing an afternoon of watery light which provided a little warmth and slowly dried us. Elyos guided us further away from the main road and onto tracks that flowed up and down small, lush hills dotted with sheep, aiming towards the large ridge which dominated the horizon to the east. It took us the rest of the day to reach it, and the sun was low in the sky before Elyos led us off the trail and across the grassland.

We had not travelled far across the flat plain when people started to line up along the summit of the ridge, to stand directly in front of us. I counted thirty warriors and, while I could see no drawn swords, there were several spears held pointing to the sky. The central two figures were cloaked, making them seem more ceremonial, but all looked capable of fighting if they deemed us a threat. They silently appraised us and we spread out to ride alongside each other in a defensive line, with Bear and Vallori at the edges and Elyos riding a horse-length in front having taken the centre.

He halted his gelding when we were a spear-throw away from the base of the ridge and time seemed to slow with both sides remaining still. We waited for something that would suggest a hostile intent, where the raising of a spear or the releasing of a sword could signal either the salute of welcome or the start of a battle. We waited. Then waited longer.

Eventually, the taller of the two cloaked figures started walking down the slope towards us, taking a mostly diagonal route on an unseen path. Half of the group followed him in a procession while the other half, which included the spear-bearers, remained on the ridge to guard their descent. Elyos hissed the release of a breath I had not realised he had been holding when the cloaked leader reached the flat land. His shoulders relaxed and when the elder stopped, with his people fanning out behind him, he slipped his leg over the front of the saddle and dismounted with his usual arrogance.

The two men stopped a sword-length from each other. Elyos stared with his habitual mockery while the other's glare was more hostile. The older man was at least a head taller than Elyos but, even with the bulk of his thick cloak, he seemed somewhat fragile next to the solid presence of the younger. Dark eyes drilled into blue with a challenge Elyos did not back away from.

I had ample time to notice that the long slate-grey hair held no braids or beads. The shrewd face suggested that he held his position through cunning more than strength, although an embossed hilt above his shoulder spoke of practical use as well as skilled craftsmanship. A thick rope of gold hung around his neck and caught the evening sunlight.

'What manner of danger have you brought us this time?'

Elyos did not flinch at the spite in the words and continued to use his flippant manner as an effective diversion.

'I've brought five strangers who could betray us to the Army of Truth, who would be happy to hang us all, and five extra mouths to feed.' He paused for a heartbeat, before adding as if it was an afterthought. 'Oh, and they are five experienced, trained fighters and at least one of them has magick.'

The anger was unmistakable despite being nothing more than a subtle tightening of the muscles around the eyes. I gripped *Saorsa*'s hilt a little tighter while Elyos blatantly provoked this dangerous opponent. A man who obviously hated him.

Their antagonistic posturing lasted several heartbeats before it was interrupted by the second cloaked figure, who had been standing quietly beside the elder throughout the exchange. With an exasperated roll of her eyes, she strode confidently between the two, breaking their eye contact and shaming them both into more civilised behaviour.

'Enough of this pissing contest, you two. You are being rude to our guests.' She turned to us with a pleasant smile. 'Be welcome and accept our gift of hospitality.'

She ignored the elder when he turned on his heel and strode back to the ridge, the others following like ducklings. She looked at Elyos and her smile softened. She stepped forward to wrap him in a fierce hug.

'It's good to see you, brother.'

Carys, Elyos's sister, led us up the deer track that cut faintly into the ridge's slope. On reaching the summit, I looked down on a temporary settlement of crude structures which could be quickly dismantled and moved. The ridge had effectively hidden a camp that buzzed with people busily performing their late evening duties. With the sun hidden behind the rise, numerous small fires burned to brighten the descending twilight and provide warmth against the rapidly chilling air. Several horses were corralled to one side of the camp and a large communal area spread along the other side, where two long fires were being used for cooking and the food was freely shared with any who asked. The adults watched over the children and dogs who ran in play. The atmosphere reminded me more of a spring fair than a war barracks.

We were taken to the corralled horses and a freckled youth offered to attend to our mounts. I had noticed the affection Elyos gave his gelding so I readily followed his lead, handing over Trefin's reins with only a flicker of concern that she would be adequately cared for. Having settled the horses, Carys suggested food and hot drinks, and led us towards the communal fires, explaining, with some pride, about how people had come together to form the camp and how everyone shared a responsibility to support each other. Many had arrived with little but a desire to be useful and help protect their kingdom in any way they could, soon finding a role within the community and a renewed sense of purpose.

Carys was a similar size to her brother, with the same dark hair and blue eyes. She also wore the blue beads in her hair, although her braids were weaved together into a single rope at the back of her head and neck. She appeared to be a few years older than Elyos and he frequently deferred to her in a number of small, subtle ways. We were met with looks of polite curiosity with only a few more suspicious glances and I did not feel unsafe despite having been greeted with assertive posturing on the ridge. We seemed to have been readily accepted, but stares that were openly unpleasant were regularly aimed at Elyos. Several of the men knocked into him in an intentional slight, while many more moved to give him an exaggeratedly wide berth. I was not the only one to notice this and I also saw questioning expressions on Bonash and Z'hara, but Carys and Elyos ignored the behaviour as if it was of no importance. Elyos's familiar arrogance, however, was conspicuously absent.

The broth was warm and the bread was fresh, and both were greatly appreciated. Elyos and his sister left to perform whatever duties were required of them and we sat as a group on the edge of the communal area, watching to determine strengths and weakness, rivalries and alliances. Most of the interactions within the community seemed to be amicable and, apart from the elder who had challenged us earlier, there was no evidence of formal hierarchy present. Everyone helped with the tasks of running the camp. People moved freely between groups, chatting companionably with each other. All except for Elyos. He moved alone through the bustle of people as though he was the outsider, talking to few and having short, functional conversations when necessary. My brain was itching to know the story behind his extreme change of character, but I was distracted by a conversation within a group a short distance from us.

'You heard about the stoning of that healer over in Herringsford?' A bushy-haired man leaned into the group, eager to share his gossip.

The woman to his left huffed her disapproval. 'Happy to call her a witch when it suits them, but how many of them had she helped with her knowledge and her ointments?'

The other four nodded in sad agreement before the first took control of the conversation again.

'I heard, a couple of days after the stoning, that priest was called to attend some meeting or sermon or something. Anyway, he left town with only a few guards. Thinking that his God would protect him.' He paused to ensure he had the full attention of his companions. 'Didn't get more than a day out before he was killed.'

'How?' asked the youngest. 'By one of his guards? I mean, who else would dare?'

'All the guards were killed too. No one knows what happened. But it was a frenzied attack, that much is sure. Ripped apart. Some are saying it was a bear but nobody's seen one of those this far south for generations.'

I looked at Bear, to find him carefully watching me. He maintained my gaze and I knew with absolute certainty how those men had died.

It was not long after full dark that the flashes began, changing the mood from one of a trading fair to something more subdued. The separate groups moved closer together. Conversations became less animated. Children huddled closer to their parents. The cook fires were piled with more wood to become higher and brighter, blazing their defiance at the unnatural light show. Even we were affected, now that we knew what the emerald lightning meant. Z'hara leaned into Vallori and he draped his arm over her shoulder, resting his cheek on her head to watch the eastern sky. Bear and Bonash sat close together, not quite touching but comfortably sharing the space while they talked quietly about the threat we faced. Recalling Elyos's comments, I smiled at the unlikely match of the big, blustering Moon Warrior and the quiet, thoughtful scholar. I startled as someone grasped my shoulder, turning to see Elyos grinning at me and offering a bottle containing a dark liquid.

'For your dreams,' he explained before walking away.

I scrambled after him. 'Wait. What is this? What do you mean, for my dreams? Elyos!'

I followed him to a log placed lengthways on the ground to offer a long seating space. It was partially hidden in the gloom and sufficiently far enough away from the main area that we could be easily ignored. He sat, quietly challenging me to join him with raised eyebrows and I managed to resist for several heartbeats before, inevitably, dropping down next him.

He indicated the bottle. 'Try some.'

Maintaining eye contact, I took a large mouthful. Then coughed. I spluttered as tears suddenly stung my eyes and my throat flamed. This was not the herbal tonic I had been expecting and the harsh drink burned the back of my mouth. Liquid fire flowed down my throat to settle as warm embers in my chest. I looked at Elyos's widening grin, suddenly fearful that he may have just poisoned me.

'It's fermented longer than ale,' he explained before taking the bottle and having a long swallow of his own. 'Kicks like a mule, doesn't it?'

Once the fire had dimmed, the drink had sweet undertones and a mellowness that was not unpleasant. I snatched it back and took another, smaller, mouthful.

'And this will help my dreams?'

His smile slowly faded. 'I saw you last night. Your body was twitching like it was trying to fight the Hordes of Hell. I had those terrors hunting me when I was a child. I know how they feel.'

I lifted his gift. 'And this was your answer?'

'No,' he smiled briefly. 'I still get haunted occasionally. Images of things I've seen. Things I've done.'

He took back the bottle and had another swallow before returning it to me. We were quiet for some time, each thinking about the visions that tormented us, but the bite of my curiosity could not be ignored.

'So, why does everybody hate you?'

Elyos threw back his head and laughed loud enough to cause those who were nearest to turn and scowl at him, making him laugh again.

'And you call me rude! They don't hate me. They would just prefer me to be elsewhere.' He shrugged. 'They think I'm unlucky.'

'Unlucky? I would have gone with rude, arrogant, obnoxious.' I grinned to soften my words. 'Why do they think you're unlucky?'

He paused and took another drink before deciding what to say. Once decided, he chose to talk to the ground rather than look at me.

'It would seem that the Gods have chosen to curse me. It started when I was just a baby. I'd crawled off somewhere and my father died saving me from an angry boar. Then my mother and younger brother died in a fire after I had failed to bank it properly. I had lit the fire, got bored, and just left it. They thought a log fell out of the grate, setting the house on fire. Trapping everyone inside.' He took a deep breath, continuing in a more flippant tone. 'And, ignoring all the many mistakes and bad decisions I've made that have caused damage, injury and various other harms. Other highlights include breaking a friend's arm so that it didn't heal properly and he never regained full use of it. Or the time when I got one person killed and another severely maimed during a hunt.' He gave a sharp, bitter laugh. 'So many to choose from.'

'I'm sorry. You've had so much tragedy in your life and it's awful. But it doesn't mean you're cursed. You shouldn't be judged on your past. Surely these people can see—'

'Carys and I arrived with enough from Scarpvale to warn everyone of the curse, but you are right. People don't tend to worry about accidents that occurred somewhere else and a long time ago. Particularly when there are more immediate dangers. So, they didn't heed the warnings and found out for themselves. I get people killed on the battlefield. I make bad decisions and I don't follow orders. I once brought back a group of travellers, like you, thinking they would be useful fighters. Only, we never found out. They never got the chance to fight. They had gut-rot and they all died. But not before spreading the disease to half the camp, and a third of those dying as well.'

He had watched Carys make her way towards us, stopping to talk or touch a shoulder of those she passed, and affected a lighter, but still bitter, tone once she was close enough to hear us.

'And the only one who still refuses to listen to the warnings is my beloved sister. She could have the pick of anyone she wanted but no one wants to be associated, however loosely, with the cursed one. So, my *luck* to her is to live forever alone.'

Carys had joined us in time for the last comment and rewarded it with a decidedly unimpressed look.

'I see he is telling you about his supposed curse.' She took the bottle, taking a long swallow without flinching before passing it back to me. 'Don't listen to him. He always gets morose when he drinks this venom.'

She sat beside him and linked her arm through his to take the bite from her words, smiling indulgently when he pressed against her.

'You should have someone to care for you.'

She gently pushed him back. 'I have lots of people that care for me. This is the life I choose so stop thinking that it's all about you.' She leaned forward to look past him at me. 'And as for this stupid curse. People die from boar attacks and house fires all the time. Well, not all the time, but enough that he cannot be the cause of these accidents. The *boar* was a pregnant sow and she would have gored anyone who went near her. It was just unlucky that he was involved with both tragic situations.'

'Unlucky and cursed are kind of the same thing,' he countered quietly.

She ignored him and continued talking to me as if he was not there. 'And as for Jym's arm. Honestly, that boy was a walking hazard. It was going to happen sooner or later. And maybe it was you who challenged him to jump off the cliff ledge. But he chose to do it. Everyone knew that ledge was too high, but Jym merrily threw himself off it anyway.' I had the feeling I was an incidental listener to an argument that they had been having for years. 'It's not like you had any control over his mind and made him do it.'

Elyos leaned forward to break my view of his sister. 'Can you control people's minds?'

'No,' I denied emphatically, suddenly wondering if I did have the ability to influence someone else's behaviour. This seemed no more unlikely than creating fire or being a Dragonslayer. I tried to make Elyos lift his right arm and was disappointed when it remained stubbornly motionless.

Carys had continued talking. 'Anyway, both of you hush. Gallian is about to begin with his story.'

I smiled at Elyos, liking his spirited sister, then turned to look at the storyteller who had gathered a clutch of small children at his feet. He was a tall, thin man with long legs that stretched out before him and a sharp face that reminded me of a heron. His grey hair covered his ears and a silver pendant at his throat glinted when it caught the fire's light. He wore an old storyteller's cloak that was embroidered with a variety of animals, both real and imagined. He waited, gathering the expectant silence as a fisherman gathers his nets.

'In a time before memory, the Gods walked amongst us. Brennus explained the workings of the natural world, a raven perched on his shoulder and nibbling at his ear. Goraith recited poetry and sang beautiful melodies as she walked the marbled streets. Achaius would bring the finches and the squirrels to play with the children while his unicorn stood majestically by his side. Beathan conveyed the warmth of belonging and purpose with a touch of her hand. It was a time of peace, and plenty, and joy.

'But while the Gods are unknowingly different from us. Powerful beyond our imagination. Intricate tapestries woven of knowledge and understanding. In some ways, they are very much like us. With darker threads of greed and jealousy and pride. In time, some of the Gods got bored. Drunst would release wind and fire sprites to poke and prod at people as they worked or slept, just for his own amusement. Arduinna would set her hawks and hounds to chase people through the forests just for the pleasure of watching her creatures hunt. Camlun fanned the flames of small inconveniences until they became violent confrontations and planted the seeds for family feuds that would last generations.

'The Sun God and the Moon Goddess indulged their antics as if they were the actions of high-spirited children. Unconcerned with the harms done. The Gods were powerful and they were worshipped. They had no care for the woes of a few humans. But those we now call the Fates saw an opportunity. Taranis saw the chaos produced by Drunst, and twisted and distorted it to cause torment. Sluagh took Arduinna's hunt, and corrupted and polluted it into abuse. And Mobis sat watching over it all. Deciding who would join him in his hellish realms. Tainting the meaning of death from that of a blessed departure from one reality and a welcome into a golden land of enchantment. Warping it to create a fear of having your soul violently ripped from your flesh to suffer for all eternity.

'The Sun and the Moon felt a ripple in the fabric of existence. The people started praying to the Fates, begging for protection from these horrors. The energy that fed the Gods' power faded as the Fates absorbed the people's pleas and devotions. They became weaker while the Fates grew stronger. And that could not be allowed. The Gods decided to give a small number of favoured humans limited powers. Gifts that could be used to defend the people from the spiteful games of the Fates. The twisting of the mind into hate. The grim satisfaction to be gained from needlessly hurting or killing. The contempt for others not like you.

'Few were selected to become the Favoured, but those few shone like a beacon in those dark times. As bright as the Sun God on a cloudless summer's day. Hope was born as Empaths revealed the path back to peace and harmony and joy. Firewalkers ignited strength and courage within the soul to provide light and warmth in the darkest of days. The Aqualine calmed the turbulent waves of fear and dread until the tranquillity of a midnight lake washed the life's blood clean of hate.

'And then there were the Dragonslayers. Only five were chosen to control the magnificent creatures that gleamed like jewels in firelight. That flew with the grace of an eagle and the precision of a hawk. That stood as tall as a mountain and as long as a valley. That breathed the flames of the tallest fire, glowing in all the colours of a rainbow. The Dragonslayers did not inspire or comfort the people. Their role was to protect them from the creatures the Fates released. The daemons. Monsters created from rage and despair that played with humans as a cat plays with a mouse. The Dragonslayers and their beasts preyed on the daemons until they were chased back to Mobis's Halls. And the Gods were pleased.

'But the Favoured were humans. And they answered the needs of humans above all others. They stopped seeing the difference between the Gods and the Fates. Seeing all as unnecessary interference in the lives of the people. The hope of freedom from the Fates became the hope for independence and choice. Courage in the face of daemons turned into leadership and governance. The calm of confidence developed into determination and strength of will. And the Dragonslayers oversaw it all by adding ambition. The ambition to rule your own destiny. The ambition to manage the landscape to meet human needs. The ambition to honour your clan or tribe above your duty to the Gods. And the Gods were not pleased.

'They grew angry at this rebellion. Their toys no longer wanted to be played with and had developed teeth and claws with blades and spells. In temper, the Gods spewed fire from the mountains. Covered vast swathes of land in ice and snow. Burnt forests into deserts. Caused the land to shake, cracking the ground to leave behind deep crevasses which dropped down into the darkness of the abyss. Having shown their wrath, the Gods withdrew. Leaving the broken land to the weak humans. Expecting them to fail and beg the Gods to help them. To plead for a return to the old ways. The days of peace and plenty and joy.

'But the people thrived. The Gods had made the Favoured too powerful and they inspired the people to create towns and ships. They encouraged the people to spread around the world, mastering the extremes of desert and frozen wastes. The people grew rich, trading in all the wealth the land had to offer. The Gods were no longer needed and their influence faded to that of myth and legend. A story to be believed as true rather than a known truth that had been experienced. As the Gods' authority melted away, so did their power. Only a few could still feel their touch. The druids and the priestesses alone held the knowledge to access the sacred energies. Only the Favoured shared the promise of what was, until they, too, became seen as too powerful. Too influential in the politics of the kingdoms. Shunned and dismissed, most gracefully receded to sanctuaries and places of healing. The Dragonslayers remained, refusing to leave the people unprotected. But the festering resentment of those with power led to the destruction of the magnificent dragons and the Dragonslayers became a myth alongside that of their Gods.'

The storyteller stopped, leaving the crackling of the fires to be the only sound. The children in front of him stared with large, round eyes and mouths open in anticipation. Even the adults had paused with tankards half-raised and food half-chewed. They were captivated by the images conjured by his words and bound by the tone and rhythm of his voice. They were transported to times long past.

I also found myself ensnared by his spell. I knew the story of the Gods but still felt the wonder of them walking alongside humans, and the despair of the Fates releasing their daemons. Monsters that had come to play with us once again. I had heard of the Rebellion but had not listened to its tale and was unsettled by the Dragonslayers' part in it. Faulknar had considered the fall of the Gods as almost inevitable. As if they had just got tired of us and walked away. I belatedly realised that *rebellion* inferred a more violent separation. Hearing that my Empath and Dragonslayer lineage may have been the reason for the Gods' departure sat sourly in my belly. Particularly when considering my current, intimate association with the Goddess. I suspected she would not have forgotten my ancestors' part in her decline.

In Hilman, the subject of the Rebellion was clearly a tale well told and the audience waited for the conclusion to the storyteller's fable. Nobody had moved while the man deliberately took a slow drink of ale to refresh his throat. A conspiratorial smile crept over his face and he replaced the tankard by his feet.

'There are some that say not all dragons are dead.'

There was a collective sigh of relief when the storyteller finished his tale.

He turned to look over his shoulder at the eastern sky where the green flares could still be seen. He waited for the cluster of flashes to fade before turning back to his listeners.

'Legend has it that in our time of greatest need. When the Fates return to claim the souls denied them. When their daemons devour mankind to feed the fires of Mobis's Hells. The Dragonslayers will return. They will remember their oath to protect us from these evils. To fight by our side and rid us of these nightmares that walk during the day. To send the monsters back to the Seven Hells for good!'

The children clapped excitedly while the adults stamped their feet and cheered their approval. I scanned the crowd. All faces beamed at the storyteller in appreciation of a tale well told by a skilled orator. All faces except one. Vallori was looking straight at me.

CHAPTER ELEVEN

I awoke before dawn, walking through a quiet camp with only those responsible for the morning meal's preparation awake with me. I grudgingly admitted that Elyos's fire-in-a-bottle had helped and, although I was a little thick-headed, I felt more rested than I had since entering Hilman. The dreams had still visited but I had felt as an observer, rather than victim to the visceral terror which normally accompanied the images. The residual headache was soon cleared with a few beakers of cold water and I was able to face the day with some optimism.

I took a bitter tasting hot drink, declining the offer of warm bread, and went to watch the horses as the first lines of grey stretched across the eastern horizon. I kept a sufficient distance so as not to disturb them and absorbed their calm while they dozed on a flexed foot or nibbled at grass still covered in dew. Their soft snorts released puffs of steam into the low-lying mist. A few birds heralded the dawn, hidden within a scrubby heath which extended beyond the horse field to a small, triangular woodland. The rolling hills in the distance looked to be carpeted in brown and green velvet below the jagged peak that rose in the centre.

I turned my attention to a camp slowly coming to life. The banked fires at the centre of each small cluster of shelters were coaxed into producing the heat needed to warm water. Some went to collect hot food from the communal kitchen while others sharpened weapons and waxed leather armour. A few children carried buckets to hidden streams within the heather and bracken. Animated conversation scattered throughout, perhaps discussing of the previous night's battle and the possibility of another that night. I watched Bear approach several of these groups, clasping a shoulder or the forearm in a warrior's greeting, and adding his opinion on the debate. Vallori and Z'hara would occasionally join him but also spent time on their own to talk with groups, perhaps offering advice or promising support.

The calm, efficient organisation shown the previous evening was still evident but it was frequently interrupted by pockets of unrest, with Elyos invariably at the centre. The minor altercations I had seen the previous day had descended into posturing and petulant shoving, with some resulting in punches being thrown. I looked for a pattern that would explain why Elyos radiated such disharmony. His challengers were mostly around the same age as him and, surprisingly, it was they who would instigate the argument, not Elyos. They taunted him with a childish provocation, pushing into him or taking an item he was reaching for. Less surprisingly, Elyos never backed away from an insult, whether that involved simply maintaining a glare or a more physical confrontation. He always ended the encounter as the victor, and I was sure this seeded more resentment that would flare up at another time. A few of the more confident ones tried the same tactics on Vallori, who simply stood his ground with a slightly bored stare until they slunk off in defeat.

Having grown cold watching the small displays of dominance, I returned to the communal area for another hot drink and reassessed the attention aimed towards me. The looks remained curious but there was no open challenge in the way it was being directed at Elyos and Vallori. I had always encouraged people to dismiss me as small and unimportant, and I was not surprised to see this reflected in their attitude towards me. Z'hara had an exotic presence that made people respect her, even before they knew what she was capable of, and no sane person would challenge Bear. I suspected that Bonash would be another that many would underestimate, and realised I had not seen the small, wiry man all morning. I began actively searching for him but had failed to locate him when Z'hara joined me.

'They've invited us to join them in their morning drills.' She smiled wickedly. 'Care to show them what we can do?'

I grinned back, welcoming the opportunity to surprise a few who were quick to judge us. 'I would be honoured.' I extended my arm with a dramatic flourish. 'Lead the way.'

Z'hara started to turn but stopped with a slight frown, tilting her head to look over my shoulder. 'Is he fighting again?'

I laughed, not needing to ask who she was referring to, and followed her to a cleared area on the far side of the camp. The fighters had been divided into groups of four where they were using both swords and axes to attack their opponents. One woman was using two long-bladed knives that she dangerously twirled around her. Bear and Vallori stood to one side talking to a thick set man and a slightly smaller woman. Bear introduced us.

'Tallen, Z'hara. This is Laggan and Annan. They are in charge so do as they say.' Bear stared at me with raised eyebrows to emphasise his point.

'What?' I smiled back. 'I always do as I'm told.'

Z'hara snorted at my comment, which I ignored. I released *Saorsa* from her sheath and, enjoying the gasp of wonder that my sword always elicited, rolled my wrist so the runes caught the morning sunlight. I gave a wicked grin when a young man cursed, having been distracted by the sight and consequently nicked by his opponent. Vallori loudly cleared his throat, drawing attention away from my blade and back to the practice session.

'How shall we begin?' he asked. 'All four of us together?'

Laggan shook his head. 'You know how to fight each other. Let's mix things up.'

He passed control to Annan, whose clear and confident manner invited no challenge to her authority. She placed us in pairs within different groups, matched two-on-two, so that we faced a variety of opponents and a range of fighting styles. She changed our pairing frequently so I rotated through fighting alongside Bear, Vallori and Z'hara as Annan watched us with a critical eye. Once satisfied we could work together, she divided us again so that we fought alone against three opponents. The resistance fighters lacked the technical skill I had learnt at Liegeport and could not match the precision I had been taught at the sanctuary, but they showed a passion and tenacity that made them unpredictable and dangerous. They may have lacked Elyos's dramatic flair, but each was just as efficient at finding cracks within our defences and exploiting any weakness they found.

I took the opportunity to watch the training session during a rest break, assessing those we were to fight beside in the way Annan and Laggan were evaluating us. They were listened to with respect, providing clear instructions with swift correction when needed, and created cohesion within the groups by including all in the praise or criticism given. Overly confident individuals were quietly paired against more experienced fighters. The more hesitant ones were encouraged to take supporting roles that allowed others to be the first to attack. The resistance fighters were rough and lacked the instinctual reflexes that came from years of practice, but I had no concerns about fighting alongside them.

My attention lingered on Vallori, surrounded by two with swords and one with both sword and axe. He moved with an easy grace, effortlessly parrying their strikes and deflecting attacks from all sides. He placed his feet as delicately as a dancer and maintained his space despite all that they threw at him, which, for the one with the axe, involved some considerable skill.

I watched Bear, roaring with delight while his challengers attacked him with as much success as if they were attacking a mountain. He merrily played with those surrounding him, making them run in circles until they were exhausted and panting. Z'hara was the total opposite. Quietly skilful, she patiently waited for the lunge before neatly deflecting the blade and striking at her opponent as quick as a snake. She controlled her group by making them cautious and forcing them to overthink their actions. I wondered which came first; the fighting style that mimicked their spirit animal or the spirit animal that influenced their fighting style. Vallori, the badger, was solid and immovable. Bear, as powerful and passionate as his namesake. Z'hara, the owl, silent and elusive but striking with deadly precision.

I looked back towards the camp and found the elder watching my companions like a hawk studying its prey. He did not seem to be pleased despite our obvious skill, and I wondered if we were not playing into the story he was trying to sell his people. He saw me watching him and turned away, returning to the camp with quick strides.

The first wave arrived before the sun had yet to reach its peak. The practice session was interrupted by the news that fighters from the night's battle had returned and we quickly made our way back to the camp, finding the population had almost doubled. Many had visible wounds. Several were lame. All wore the expressions of those who had seen unspeakable horrors. Most went quietly to their shelters to get whatever rest sleep would offer them. A few stayed to describe what happened in dull, disconnected voices. Their eyes constantly moved but focused on nothing. They spoke of monsters, over twice the height of a man that ripped people in half. Of daemons bigger than the largest bulls that tore chunks of flesh from their victims. Flying beasts that stabbed with beaks longer than the length of a sword, filled with teeth as sharp as daggers. They described a scene sent straight from the depths of Mobis's seventh hell.

The second wave came a little after midday. Those who had been more seriously injured were accompanied by those carrying wooden staffs or wearing chains of small bird skulls around their necks. I saw a few with the crude tattoos of a raven dotted on a forearm or a face, advertising their trade as spell-weavers. Those struggling to walk were supported with shoulders to lean on or steadying arms around the waist. Behind these, crude sleds were being pulled, carrying those unable to walk and who groaned in pain when jostled by the bumpy ground. Blood seeped through the dressings hastily placed over gaping wounds. Bone poked through the skin in limbs snapped like twigs. The more concerning ones were quiet, already too close to the borders of death.

Old habits from years of working alongside Drey had me several paces towards the injured before I hesitated, remembering who I was with. Bear waved his hand in dismissal.

'Go. You are the best healer. You should be with those worst affected. I'll help deal with those still able to stand.'

He was already walking before he had finished talking and I saw Vallori and Z'hara move to join him. I made my way to the slow procession and followed them to a structure that would provide some privacy and protection. I hesitated on the threshold, suddenly overwhelmed by the sight of so many injured and so few to care for them. I watched patients being carefully transferred to pallets. Bowls of water were quickly gathered along with clean linen and bandages. The too few spell-weavers tried to be everywhere as they determined those most in need. Bonash, who had been absent all morning, appeared at my side. I turned to him in growing despair.

'They're just children. Pretending that whatever talent they have makes them healers. Playing at having the knowledge required by staining their skin and wearing a few bird skulls. They know nothing.'

He cradled my elbow and gently pushed me towards the nearest bed. 'Then we should teach them.'

Runners were sent for charcoal while Bonash and I took a side each, moving from patient to patient and determining the ability of the spell-weavers who attended to the swellings and bleeding. I found two who had some experience of using magick for healing and possessed suitable crystals with which to empower their words and sigils. I showed how to draw the rune that would allow the patient to sleep while bones were set and wounds were cauterised. I watched them tentatively draw the three rings within a

141

spiral on the forearm. I guided the use of their crystal to activate the sign and smiled at their look of wonder when the soft, blue light pulsed in response to their words of permission – *cead*. I sent them to work throughout the infirmary alongside the three who Bonash had similarly tutored.

Satisfied that the injured could be worked upon while suspended in a pain-free slumber, I turned to the remaining spell-weavers and those who would help them, showing how to carefully realign bones so they would heal straight. I taught how to search for the injuries hidden deep within the chest or abdominal cavities. How to identify those needing immediate attention to stop the bleeding and those who could be managed by the application of tight bandages. They were already proficient at suturing and could effectively close deep wounds as well as they could superficial lacerations, needing only brief guidance on the key places to ensure blood would flow to the vital areas. They knew to frequently check those with head wounds, using conversation to determine whether the patient was deteriorating and relying on physical clues on those unable to talk.

They were soon confidently performing the tasks I had set them. Spell-weavers sent the patient into a slumber with charcoal and crystal. Helpers set broken limbs, bound displaced joints and sutured wounds. Others cleaned and cauterised, dressed and splinted. Runners removed blood-soaked clothing and soiled linen, returning with clean supplies and fresh water. The spell-weavers returned when the treatment was complete, using spring water to wash away the charcoal and air as they breathed the word of release – *fuasgail* – to disperse the energies safely back into the earth.

The last patients were being cared for when the shouting began. I turned to Bonash, finding him looking as confused as I was at the sudden commotion, and joined a few of the helpers to see what was occurring. A thin man had his back to me, angry at the man in front of him.

'You should not have brought her here.'

'You have to help her. Please.'

'She is beyond help. She's already dead, you fool. Take her back before it's too late.'

'She's not dead. She's not. Please, somebody help her.'

'You idiot. You've endangered us all. Leave! Now!'

The thin man emphasised his point with a shove, causing the other to stumble. The fallen man protectively cradled a woman in his arms. She had darkened lips and her shadowed eyes had sunk deep into their sockets, giving her face the disturbing appearance of a skull. A large volume of blood had soaked into her clothing and covered the arms of the man who carried her. Tears washed tracks through the dirt and dried blood on his face, and his eyes were full of heartbreak as he implored those around him for aid. A small crowd had gathered but no one moved to help him.

'I said leave! Before you kill us all.'

The angry man repeated his command and went to encourage the other to leave with a kick but, without truly considering it, I had already placed myself between them.

'These people need help,' I began, belatedly realising how outnumbered I was. 'If you are not prepared to offer it then stand aside so others can.'

He snarled at my interference. 'She's already dead. And this fool has brought her here so we can all be damned to Mobis's Hells along with her.'

The crowd shouted their agreement, calling for the pair to be driven from the camp, and Bonash came to stand beside me. I cautiously knelt to feel for the pulse that would determine if she was still alive, or if Bonash and I would be lynched alongside her companion. I waited for several of my rapid heartbeats but felt no flicker of life under my fingertips. I removed my hand, took a breath, and tried again with a lighter pressure. My fingers barely pressed the skin as I waited. There. It was so weak. And again. Faint, but life was definitely still present. I looked up into a face that showed more fear than hatred.

'She's still alive. But barely. If she is to be helped, I need to do it now.'

I stood up but the thin man failed to move. I tensed my muscles and waited for the tell that would predict his intent to strike. I intended to land the first punch before being smothered by the surrounding mob.

Bonash leaned in to whisper in my ear. 'Are you sure about this?'

I shrugged a shoulder. 'No. But I feel we should do something.'

The man heard the exchange and his anger flared once more. I reacted before he had barely moved his arm, grabbing his wrist and twisting it with enough pressure to force him to his knees. Bear was ploughing his way through the mob, followed by Vallori and Z'hara, and I released my hold, content to leave them to manage the situation while I turned back to the sobbing man who gently rocked the dying woman.

'Can you stand?' He did not seem to hear me so I repeated the question with greater insistence. 'Can you stand?'

He looked at me with dazed eyes, taking a while to focus, then nodded. With the assistance of Bonash, I managed to get him and the woman into the infirmary and place her on a pallet. Released of his burden, the man backed himself against a pole and slid down it to sit on the floor, his arms wrapped around his knees while he stared blankly at the woman's ashen face. I sought the aid of a helper to take care of him or a spell-weaver to assist me, but everyone had moved away. Those who had readily followed my instructions now looked at me with fear. I sighed in disappointment before returning to the problem I had given myself, suddenly unsure of how I was going to save this woman who was one breath away from death. Bonash, once again, came to stand at my shoulder.

'I will be your anchor,' he said quietly.

I closed my eyes in relief before turning to face him. 'Are you sure?'

'No.' He smiled. 'But I feel we should do something.'

'Then let us do this.'

I drew a circle around the bed while Bonash cut away her blood-soaked clothing, revealing long, deep gashes across her abdomen and ragged sections of raw flesh. I left Bonash to deal with her body and completed the protective barrier. Three parallel waves at north – *deuraich*. The inverted arrowhead at west – *tathasg*. The pentagram at south – *gealbhan*. The triangle within a square at east – *talamh*. I breathed my request to access the powers – *cead* – and was answered by a blinding flare from the charcoal circle that swiftly faded to a faint blue glow. I knelt at the head of the woman and laid my hands on the flat surface of her skull, my fingertips resting just above her ears. I looked over at Bonash, who nodded to confirm he was ready, and took a last steadying breath before whispering the last word of power. May the Gods protect us – *blàthaich*.

I closed my eyes and opened my sight to see the woman's aura slowly pulsing in time with her weakened heart. Dark crimson and indigo surrounded her while her body fought to heal with a heart unable to respond to its needs. I slowly extended my aura to meld with hers but as soon as I made contact, her energies greedily sucked at mine. I was caught unprepared and struggled against her pull. I sought to maintain control over what was me and what was her. I sank deeper into the tangle of energy lines at the base of her skull, becoming stretched almost to the point of snapping. I was caught in a web of writhing black that pulsed with flashes of green. I was tossed and twisted, shaken and stretched, until all sense of *self* was shredded away.

A fading star was glimpsed for a moment then lost, leaving only a faint glow far in the distance. A gentle pressure pressed against my thoughts and they snatched at the return of *self*. I became more substantial and more defined. I embraced the light and became *me* again. I became aware of where I ended and where others began.

Bonash.

I'm here.

His calm presence allowed me to focus and, once again, I could see the ribbons of energy pulsing slowly at the base of the woman's head. Her natural energies were choked by the black-green tendrils. I cautiously reached to touch one, recoiling quickly at the malevolence radiating from it. Her heart was constricted by these vines and its vital beat was slowing. I infused some of my energy into the tired muscle, giving it strength while I worked to remove the vile mesh surrounding it. It consumed any energy I targeted at it, neither growing nor diminishing. I could not physically remove it and it clenched tighter whenever I tried to pry it away.

With the lack of any other options, I considered that if it looked like a vine and acted like a vine, perhaps it could be destroyed like a vine. I had once seen the groundsman at Liegeport torch a particularly virulent strain of ivy that had smothered the royal house so, focusing on a small section, I offered the word for fire – *gealbhan*. Orange flares sparked within the parasitic cords, causing the tendrils to shrivel and dissolve. The woman's heart fluttered at the sudden release of pressure and I hastily coaxed it back into a regular rhythm. The energies woven around and within it slowly melted into a vibrant yellow glow.

I reluctantly moved my attention away from the foul corruption, knowing her haemorrhaging body would kill her faster than the malign vines. I moved to her chest where fluid had leaked into her lungs and gently pushed it back into the surrounding blood vessels, allowing her to breathe more easily and provide the air for her strengthening heart. The colours of her abdomen throbbed with sickly tones where flesh had been torn by monstrous claws and I sent my healing energy into the tissues. I took the time needed to repair damaged organs and reconnect torn muscle.

Once content that her body would not deteriorate further, I returned to the invading corruption. I sent pulses of energy into every vine, chasing the green-black pollution with my cleansing fire. I followed it as it wrapped around the major blood vessels. I hunted it up her spine and into her skull, scouring it from the peaks and valleys of her brain. I blazed through her muscles and into her limbs. I felt an irritating pull, but I ignored it and searched for foulness in the lungs and between the ribs. Finding nothing, I tracked back to the heart. The pull became an insistent tugging but still I resisted. A surge of energy hit me like a slap.

Time to come back now.

Bonash's voice in my head brought sufficient awareness to realise I was exhausted. I whispered my gratitude – *taing* – and felt the words on my lips. I returned to my body, swaying slightly as I withdrew my aura. I spoke the word of release and the protective circle flared for a heartbeat before it was extinguished. I looked at my trembling hands, noting that the skin had become almost translucent and I could see the energy flowing around my veins as a softly glowing, butter-coloured thread. I saw Bonash reach for me when I tried to stand, but his face distorted and the world slipped sideways. I fell into a soft blanket of darkness.

The sun was hidden behind the ridge when I emerged from the infirmary. The healers and helpers had quietly tended those who needed to remain in their care while I recovered my strength. They had respectfully left me to sleep and I had awoken to find them regarding me with subservient glances, replacing the fear which had been present earlier. I did not see the woman anywhere but feared to ask how she fared.

Camp life had continued without me and people gathered supplies for the evening meal. The smell of roasting hog caused my stomach to grumble, adding to the residual light-headed feeling and reminding me that I needed more than sleep to replenish spent reserves. I deemed food to be less important than the incessant thirst, so I went in search of water, aiming in the general direction of Bear who I could see standing head and shoulders above the people around him. Beyond him, the training arena had been marked by a ring of small fires to leave a large, cleared area within it. Bear saw me approach and invited me into the conversation with a wave of his hand but each member of the group quietly made their excuses and departed. The dark warrior grinned at their sudden embarrassment.

'You've given them something to talk about,' he began, appraising my slightly unsteady condition. 'They've never seen anything like it before.'

'Is the woman well?'

'Oh, she's more than well. I would say she's the healthiest one here.'

He took my wrist and turned it over to show a faint, creamy glow where the skin was thinnest. I pulled back my hand, folding my arms over my chest to hide the evidence that I had expended too much energy during the healing.

'You exceeded sensible limits,' he chided gently. 'You went too far.'

I dismissed his concern with a shrug. 'There was more than tissue damage. Daemon wounds seem to cause some form of infection. Its fingers were wrapped around all the vital centres of the body. Polluting the energies into something else.'

Bear nodded. 'There was certainly a fear she had brought some disease into the camp. Nash felt traces of it—'

I blinked at him. 'Nash?'

The big man's face curled into an embarrassed smile. 'Some of the children have started following him around like orphaned puppies and they've taken to calling him Nash. I like it and I've kind of adopted it.'

I laughed at the absurdity of this mountain of a man giving Bonash a pet-name. 'Where is *Nash* anyway? He keeps disappearing and I wanted to thank him for being my anchor.'

'He's with the dream-walkers. They've been teaching him how to scout for shamans. Seems they create quite a disturbance in the ley lines when they call their daemons. He's been learning how the dream-walkers can walk the ethereal plane and spy on them. Gives an early warning system of when they'll strike, allowing the fighters to confront them away from the camp.'

I scanned the settlement that seemed full of people. 'No daemons tonight?'

He shook his head. 'All quiet apparently. Seems even evil shamans respect the feast days.' He rolled his eyes at my confused scowl. 'It's the equinox. I swear, you show no respect to the Gods.'

He clasped my shoulders and turned me towards the communal kitchen with the suggestion that I get some food, before leaving to join another small gathering that wanted his advice. I reluctantly admitted that my body needed sustenance and collected some slices of roasted hog and a heel of bread. The food sat heavily in my belly so after eating only half of that taken, I threw the rest to the dogs and decided that ale would be a more satisfactory option. I found a quiet place a short distance from the training ground's ring of fire and watched an atmosphere of expectation start to build in anticipation of the night's ceremony.

The autumn equinox was one of three ceremonies to honour the Gods for a bountiful harvest, traditionally involving offerings of apples or wheat at waterfalls or woodland shrines. The equality of day and night specific to this festival was reflected in the blessings of the ancestors, balancing the past and the present. Decorative straw cones would be made from stems of wheat or barley and given as tokens for a plentiful supply of food that would last throughout the winter months. The stalks could also be woven into small figures in a representation of the ancestors and to encourage their protection from evil spirits during the long, dark nights.

I was reminded of the latter when a pretty girl with long blonde hair and sharp blue eyes, of perhaps five summers, ran up to me. She hesitated for a moment, suddenly shy, then passed me a straw doll of a man. In the absence of farmed grain, she had taken long stems of dry grass, weaving them into a rope before twisting it into a figure roughly the size of my hand. Having given me her gift, she ran back to the arms of her mother; the woman I had helped earlier and who was, indeed, looking well. She gathered her daughter close to her body, closing her eyes and kissing the top of the child's head. The man, who had been so overcome with grief, stood protectively next to them. He maintained my gaze, placing a hand over his heart and offering a deep bow. I raised the grass token and nodded in appreciation, mouthing my thanks for the heartfelt gesture. He bowed again before placing an arm around the woman's shoulders and guiding his family to a nearby group who had already noisily started their celebrations. A hand rested on my shoulder and I turned to see Carys smiling at me, carrying a bottle.

'It's nice to see you finally making friends with someone other than my idiot brother.' She sat next to me, watching the couple and their daughter. 'That was an amazing thing you did. People will remember this day for a long time.'

I toyed with the little grass-stem man. 'It was one person. I wish I could do more.'

She dismissed my comment and continued as if I had not spoken. 'Power like that does not belong in the secluded valleys of Hilman.' She turned to study me. 'Why are you here?'

For the first time, I became wary of this unassuming woman. Her blue eyes radiated an intelligence I did not want to challenge. The strength of her gaze confirmed her position of authority in this community, which included many strong-willed fighters. I answered carefully.

'We were invited.'

'Perhaps. But the question remains. A backwater tavern seems an unlikely place for one capable of doing what you did today. So, I ask again. Why are you here?'

I hesitated while I considered how much I should tell her, deciding on that which would soon become obvious to all. 'We're here to fight daemons.'

She paused for a while before raising her head with a sniff, breaking eye contact and dissolving the tension between us.

'That I believe,' she declared, offering me the bottle. 'A gift from my idiot brother.'

I gratefully accepted the potent drink, asking, 'It all seems unnaturally harmonious. Where is Elyos?'

Carys laughed. 'He does like to poke the wasps' nest. But you are right. He's not here. He left earlier while you were sleeping.' Her face grew serious, and a little sad. 'Tonight is a time for calling the ancestors. Elyos always keeps his ghosts close. He has no desire to see them manifest. He will have found a place to get drunk where he cannot hear the drums.'

She left me to my fiery drink and soon after, the autumn equinox ceremony began. A slow drumbeat started behind me with the rhythm timed to every fourth heartbeat. I turned to see a dark-haired man, bare-chested to reveal a pattern of clay symbols, using a small stick with padding on each end to keep the beat. His drum was the length of his arm. A circle of thin pale calfskin pulled tight as he rocked the stick so alternating ends measured the timing. He was followed by six male drummers, walking in pairs and holding their double-ended batons in silent suspension above their smaller circular drums. They marched in time with the beat as the marked man led them towards the arena. The elder walked behind the drummers and was again cloaked to create an imposing ceremonial presence. His face was hidden by a large deer skull that swayed when he paced to the hypnotic beat. Its antlers reached up into the night sky.

At the rear of the procession came three men and three women, again walking in pairs. They followed the drummer inside the circle of fires and their white robes seemed to writhe with the flickering shadows. They marched to the centre before separating, becoming another ring within the fires' boundary. They had arranged themselves so that the elder stood at the east facing west, while the painted drummer stood at the west facing east. Between the two, the drummers and singers alternated until the circle was complete.

The six drummers joined in and the rhythm was increased to every other heartbeat. I felt my heart throb in reply. Two streams of women dancers skipped through the crowd and into the ring, turning one way and then the other in time with the drums. They wove between each other in a serpentine dance, making half bows to those they passed. Two revolutions of the ring had been completed before the beat doubled its pace again. The dancers stamped bare feet as they bowed, adding a soft rhythm to the heavy beat of instruments which caused reverberations deep in my chest. The people watching started to sway, called by the power of the drums and their rate doubled again. The dancers swirled in front of the fires in a dizzying spiral of light and shadow. Heads raised and lowered. Arms flowed and twisted. Feet stamped and spun. Energies gathered as a storm, inviting the Gods to attend. The drummers increased their beat to an intoxicating rhythm and a few in the crowd became spellbound, dancing into the arena to participate in the ceremony.

At the height of the frenzy, the elder started to chant. A low moaning that wrapped around the beat of the drums and wove into the patterns of the dancers. The chant rose and fell so that it felt like the pull of a tide. Up and down. In and out. Quietly, the singers joined him. Adding harmonies that ached the heart. They increased their volume and the power built within the crucible. Complex melodies threaded through the elder's stabilising tones. Calling the spirits to walk again. Cajoling them to leave the Halls of Eternity and be with their descendants on the night when the Sun God and the Moon Goddess existed in balance. To spread love and belonging to all those present. To bless those held dearest to them.

The shadows deepened between the dancers and these ghostly figures moved alongside them, drawn by the rhythm of the dance, before silently leaving the fire-circle to join those gathered to watch. Those touched by their ancestors closed their eyes in rapture, unable to see their shades but feeling their presence. More and more spirits appeared until the camp was full of ghosts sharing space with their loved ones. Forming a connection between what is and what was. People swayed in the ecstasy of the unseen but deeply felt affection.

And the drums continued to beat. The singers continued to chant. The dancers continued to sway. And the ghosts continued to arrive.

I saw Vallori sitting alone at the edge of the crowd. He was hunched forward with his elbows resting on his knees and his hands covering his mouth. I looked for Z'hara and, not finding her, went over to him. He wore a pained expression that confirmed my concerns.

'Hey,' I began, sitting next to him. 'You seeing ghosts as well?'

He immediately changed his posture, straightening his back and dropping his hands to smile warmly at me. I raised an eyebrow at his sudden care-free attitude and he soon realised he was not going to fool me, curling again to rest his chin into cupped hands.

'Anyone you know?' I prodded gently.

He gave me a sad smile, shaking his head slightly. 'No. Fortunately, my ancestors remain far from these shores. My family are still very much alive and unlikely to trouble me tonight.'

I leaned against his shoulder. 'Then why so melancholy?'

He remained quiet for a while before answering. 'I was remembering different equinox ceremonies. Those of home are in many ways similar to this.'

'Freisholm?' I guessed. 'You still consider that your home?'

He turned to smile at my less than subtle probing for information. He rarely talked about his life before the sanctuary and I suspected he had some painful memories that he was reluctant to share.

'Yes Tallen. I still consider Freisholm my home. I was born there. It moulded me into who I am. For better or worse.' The smile slowly faded. 'We observe many of the same rituals as you. The equinox, the solstice, a few in between. But ours were often more primal. More...' He struggled to find the appropriate word. 'More visceral.'

I thought about my own time in Freisholm and the disturbing memories created there. 'Blood sacrifice.'

Vallori continued to look away, watching the ceremony within the fire-ring. His face was partially hidden by shadow and his eyes saw distant images.

'Blood sacrifice. And Bane at the heart of it.'

I was surprised by the uncharacteristic bitterness in his tone. 'Bane?'

I felt a shudder ripple through him. He took a breath, forcefully retrieving his thoughts to continue in a detached tone. 'My brother was chosen as a favourite, a plaything, by the grandmother. You remember Sálaforn?'

I involuntarily clenched my hands into fists at the reminder of the old shamanic crone who had tormented me during my detention in the Gallowgla settlement. Vallori reached over, gently forcing his hand into mine and intertwining our fingers to relax my grip.

'She had her claws into him from the moment she saw him. Filling his head with stories and promises.'

'He performed the blood sacrifice?'

'He was the reason I left. It became clear that neither of us would back down. I wouldn't join him in serving Sálaforn. And I couldn't get him to see what he was becoming. There would only ever be one way out. And while Bane would have happily spilt my blood, I was not ready to take his.' He shrugged as if it was of no importance. 'So, I left.'

'And you've never been back?'

He shook his head. 'I can't go back.'

I squeezed his hand. 'I'm sorry. It seems family is haunting you tonight after all.'

He smiled sadly, raising our hands to kiss my knuckles. 'Indeed. But enough of that. Who is this?'

He was looking over my shoulder so that I turned to see who he was referring to. Finding nobody there, I turned back to him with a confused frown.

'Who's who?'

He tilted his head and mirrored my confused expression. 'Can you not see?'

I waved my free hand at the spirits who were mingling throughout the gathering. 'I see these. I don't know who they are though.'

Vallori laughed quietly. 'You see everyone else's ghosts but not the one who stands by your side.' He looked over my shoulder again. 'Perhaps you should invite them in. I don't think you need to be afraid of this one.'

He rose, leaning in to kiss my forehead and bowing to the shade behind me before he left. I refused to acknowledge its presence, not yet ready to face anyone who had died because of me. The sailors at Gallowgla. The healers on the Isle of Serpents. Tawpin's family. I closed my eyes, unwilling to face the harm I had brought so many people.

I took a breath. Tonight was not Samhain. Tonight was about family. I hardly dared to hope that the Goddess would grant a visit from my father, someone she had kept hidden for so long. I felt the presence at my shoulder take form and become solid. My body was rigidly fixed against the disappointment that it would not be my father who waited for me, but a vengeful spirit come to claim penance. The ghost stepped in front of me, hesitating for a heartbeat before sinking to kneel before me.

I opened my eyes and time stopped. The breath caught in my throat and my heart contracted painfully. Tears stung my eyes before escaping to roll down my face. I stared in wonder at his strong face. His clear, blue eyes. His short, blond hair. His perfect face. I could not believe what I saw in front of me. He was as solid as Vallori had been moments, or a lifetime, before.

'Laken?'

He smiled, crinkling the skin at the edges of his eyes. 'Hello, little one.'

CHAPTER TWELVE

I awoke late the next morning and the camp was already busy with activity. Bonash was surrounded by a cluster of children who were trying to show him how to play a game that involved pebbles and string, while he was trying not to listen to the argument between Elyos and the elder.

'Good morning, *Nash*,' I teased.

'Good morning, *Tal*,' he returned, giving a shy smile.

'I see Elyos is back.'

'The shamans are gathering the power they need to summon their daemons. There will be a battle later.' He dipped his head towards the arguing pair. 'Our friend is not happy that his elder does not consider us ready to fight in his army.'

'What? That makes no sense. Surely they need all the help they can get.'

'That's what Elyos is so eloquently trying to explain.'

To prove Bonash's point, Elyos threw his hands up in frustration. 'Has old age finally taken your wits? You'd throw away the best fighters here because you're too proud to admit you were wrong. Do you not care about the consequences of your decision? What this will cost in lives?'

'You accuse me of costing lives? *You*?' The elder lowered his voice and his mocking tone turned harsher. 'Do I have to remind you of all those who have died because of your decisions? Because of the curse you carry? How many lives have you taken, boy?'

I thought for a moment that Elyos was going to punch the older man but someone had already run to fetch Carys. She hurried over to stand between them as she had at our first meeting, and probably on many other occasions. She placed a restraining hand on her brother's chest and gave a slight shake of her head, maintaining eye contact with him while she addressed the elder.

'That was not called for, Sheehan. We are all trying our best.'

The elder huffed and crossed his arms over his chest. 'Some to better effect than others. Chaos is not a recognised strategy for keeping people safe. Your brother is a liability. And we cannot trust that the new arrivals will not disrupt the chain of command, causing confusion at a time when clarity is required.'

'Sheehan!' Carys turned to glare at him. 'You have made your point. They will not take part today. But we will use them. And soon.'

She continued to stare at the older man, challenging him to debate further. After a few heartbeats, Sheehan relented and strode away. She looked back at her brother, offering a softer challenge until he also submitted to her will and walked off in the opposite direction. Carys saw Bonash and me watching the exchange and came over to join us.

'I'm sorry that you heard that,' she apologised. 'It has nothing to do with you. We are grateful you are here.'

'So why are we not being used?' I pushed.

Carys sighed, suggesting it was an old argument. 'Simply? Because you're Elyos's. The more detailed explanation involves a rivalry that has festered for some time.'

She looked at our expressions and quickly realised we were expecting the more detailed version. Not wanting the children to overhear our conversation, she suggested that we walked with her to a more private location.

'We have a lot of good people here,' she began. 'Some who take care of people's physical needs. Some who can fight unimaginable horrors over and over again, with some of those able to inspire others to face those same horrors. Some speak to the Gods, protecting the souls of those who are taken and giving courage to those left behind. There are very few who can combine all those things.'

'Sheehan?' Bonash suggested.

The dark-haired woman nodded. 'Sheehan excels at inspiring faith and using it to bring people together as a community. He pays attention to the details so that people stay fed and warm, which is no easy feat in an abandoned valley. His fighting days may be behind him but he still has a quick mind and a way of seeing the entirety of a battle, with all the possible outcomes.'

Bonash interrupted. 'He is clearly a natural leader, but that does not explain why he refuses to use us.'

'There are two, maybe three, here who could challenge Sheehan for his role. He possesses all the traits I've just listed, but he is also insecure and feels vulnerable when he is not in total control. Above all else, he needs order and structure.'

I smiled. 'Not words associated with Elyos.'

'My brother's special kind of chaos causes Sheehan extreme anxiety, but it's more than that. Despite all his bluster, Elyos pays attention and he knows how people work. Given the chance, he could lead people into the very halls of Mobis's Hells and they would willingly die for him. And that scares Sheehan more than anything.' Her face became harder. 'So he denies him that chance. He discredits Elyos with every opportunity he gets. You are just the latest in a long line of hints and rumours. You were brought here by Elyos so who knows where your loyalties lie? You are renegades and will not listen to those directing the battle's strategy. You will choose to follow your own rules and challenge the chain of command. And so it goes on. Sheehan stokes the fires of people's fears, feeding on Elyos's *curse* so that they turn away from him. Shun him. Ostracise him.'

'And turn to Sheehan instead.' Bonash nodded in appreciation. 'It's a clever strategy. It unites them against a common threat.'

'The threat should be those bastard shamans and their monsters,' she snapped. 'Instead, we turn on ourselves. Isolating one of our most effective fighters while he doubts every decision he makes. Convinced that the stupid curse is real.'

Having uncharacteristically shown some of Elyos's temper, she forcefully calmed herself and returned to the agreeable manner she more commonly assumed. She made her excuses about helping to organise those about to leave and purposefully walked away.

'She's the one truly keeping this place together,' Bonash commented. 'People are often blind to what's right in front of them.'

'Then why doesn't she just take charge? She is more than capable of handling both their egos.'

The small man looked at me sadly. 'This is Hilman.'

He also made his excuses and returned to the dream-walkers, with the hope that observing the gathering energies could offer more of an advantage. Left on my own, I decided that helping in the infirmary would be the best way to spend my time. My path took me past a shelter where I could hear Elyos grumbling and cursing. I looked inside and grinned at his ill-tempered searching, throwing clothes and blankets into a heap on the floor.

'You'd better hurry,' I suggested. 'They're leaving without you.'

He spun around sharply with a face that was full of anger, but his expression softened when he saw it was me and he returned to his search.

'I'm not going with them. They don't want me fighting with them.'

'Because of your curse?'

He found his dagger, placing it with some force into its sheath, and turned to me with a resigned sigh. 'Something like that.'

'This is ridiculous. We can't fight. You can't fight. What are we expected to do, look after the children and the dogs?'

He shrugged. 'You could heal those who are more than half dead.'

'You heard about that then?'

'Yes. I heard.'

'And yet they still don't trust us.'

'Of course they don't trust you. They've only seen that kind of power from the shamans, who are raising an army of monsters from their worst nightmares. They have no idea what you are capable of. And that scares them.'

'Scares them or scares Sheehan?'

His face darkened as his sister's had done earlier. 'I have to go.'

'Go where? Nobody will let you do anything and your army is leaving without you.'

He moved to leave but I remained standing in the entry and blocked his exit. He glared at me in frustration.

'They may not want me with them but that doesn't mean I'm not going to fight. Now move or I will shove you out of the way.'

I stayed where I was, and his expression changed when he started to critically appraise me. As always, I had dressed so I was ready for any event. *Saorsa* was sheathed on one hip and my dagger was on the other. Two small throwing knives were positioned at the base of my spine and the small knife was hidden inside my boot.

'You want to come?' I grinned my response, to which he jabbed a finger into my chest to emphasise his point. 'You swear you will do everything I ask. No debate. You do as I tell you.'

I placed a hand over my heart. 'Of course.'

He frowned, not trusting my sincerity, but nodded anyway. 'Come on then.'

I turned towards the horse fields but Elyos had already left in the opposite direction. He called after me when I hesitated in confusion.

'We can't risk the horses near the daemons. They are too valuable to be killed, not to mention the risk that they would trample us in their panic.'

I belatedly realised that the paddocks were still full. 'But...'

He grinned wickedly at my disappointment. 'We run.'

We ran out of the camp, through the scrubland and into a woodland carpeted in squirrel-chewed pinecones. We continued running along a drover's trail that led through the lower slopes of two overlapping hills. I had never had the need to run for extended periods and could not match Elyos's easy lope. He took great pleasure in mocking my ragged panting while I repeatedly pointed out that this was why we have horses.

We crawled on our stomachs to the summit of a small, heather-covered rise and kept our profile low while we looked down on the scene below. The site of the battlefield had been well chosen. A narrow river bordered one side and a rocky wall framed the other, while the armies gathered in a large, flat grassland between the two. The resistance fighters faced their enemy in long rows, with the spear-carriers scattered throughout the front ranks and the archers protected at the rear. Many were nervously checking and rechecking the slide of blades within their scabbards or tossing their axes from hand to hand as they looked for the strengths and weaknesses in their opponents.

The invading army numbered less than half of that offered by the resistance. The way the enemy wore their hair, their style of dress, and the mean double-headed war axes confirmed who they were. And that the reduced number would be small comfort once they started fighting.

'Pirates,' I snarled.

'These pirates have raided far from the coast,' Elyos confirmed quietly. 'Most have taken land and settled to create new Gallowglass communities, driving out those who can trace their claim to Hilman through countless generations. Enough have followed their mystics inland to offer subjugation or annihilation.'

I looked beyond the raiders, who were assembled in a more casual fashion with no spears or archers, and saw something much more frightening. Two male shamans were dressed in loincloths and wolf-skin capes, with the wolf's head flapping macabrely as they danced their ritual. Their hair was spiked into peaks at the crown of their head but fell in thick cords down their backs. Pale grey symbols decorated their twisting bodies. They strutted and paraded and gestured, with their bare feet stomping the ground. Each performed a dance independently of the other, giving courage to the raiders and sowing fear into their enemies.

'Why is everyone just standing there?' I asked after some considerable time. 'We have greater numbers. We should attack now. Before the monsters turn up.'

'Nobody is any rush to die.'

And so, we waited. And waited. Then waited some more.

My body reacted to a sudden change in the energies rippling around the clearing and I felt Elyos tense beside me. The shamans continued to prance and gesticulate, but the ground between them started to shimmer and a dark grey fog began to rise from the turf. It spread out behind the raiders until it filled the space between the fighters and their sorcerers. The fog thickened and I watched in fascination as flashes of green lightning briefly illuminated the dirty cloud. It shifted and swirled, becoming rounded shapes which writhed and twisted. Crude limbs and torsos became identifiable.

A screeching war-cry from the invaders signalled the start of the battle and both sides ran, shouting incoherent challenges and insults. The first row threw their spears when the raiders came within range, immediately followed by the second and third waves. The raiders raised their heavy shields, capturing the weapons as the spear-heads drove deep into the hide-covered wood. Both shield and spear were discarded and the raiders continued their charge. The first screams of the dying sounded when the archers fired into an enemy no longer protected by their shields. Moments later the two armies clashed in a deafening crash of noise. Shouts of rage blended with screams of pain while the steel of sword and axe tore through armour and flesh.

The shamans continued to dance, calling a pale green mist to drift between the fighters. The mist separated into countless shapes that each turned into a horrific phantom of a person. Clear, individual features could be seen within the ribbons of skin that hung from their skeletal faces. The blades of the resistance fighters passed harmlessly through these tattered wraiths, as if passing through smoke, while the ghost swords hacked into human flesh with devastating effect.

'For the love of Mobis, what are those?' I asked, barely able to breathe as the full extent of the hellscape unfolded.

'Those are what we don't talk about.'

Elyos was pale and trembling, watching his army courageously fight against the raiders while having to avoid the wraiths. An enemy which now outnumbered them.

A terrible roar echoed around the clearing. The first daemon bellowed its challenge and I saw the visions of my night-terrors become terrifyingly real. Giant, human-shaped creatures thundered over the battlefield, carelessly crushing both raider and resistance. Muscular horse-like monsters tore at those around them with vicious tusks that protruded from thick, square jaws. Leathery-winged birds, the size of a large hound, flew overhead to stab randomly with sword-like beaks. The lethally sharp teeth ripped away chunks of flesh when the beak was withdrawn. The daemons created mayhem and slaughtered both armies.

A pair of piercing whistles caused the monsters to pause, then a series of short blasts restarted the carnage. The creatures' callous destruction was now consistently directed at the resistance. I dug my fingers into the soft ground in frustration and watched the fighters battle desperately against the triple threat of raider, wraith and daemon.

Elyos jerked violently and I turned to see him visibly twitching.

'Elyos?'

He turned to look at me with a face distorted with panic, his hands clenched into fists.

'You have to stay here.'

'Elyos, what's wrong?'

'I have to go,' he stammered. 'Swear you'll stay here.'

I was starting to understand Sheehan's fears regarding the safety of Elyos within the horror of this nightmarish battle, but then I noticed his eyes. The light should have reduced his pupils to small circles in the centre of his eyes, but they had expanded so that only a thin ribbon of blue encircled the black. His gaze moved constantly, unable to focus on a single point, while his head jerked with involuntary movement. Beads of sweat dotted his forehead and temples. And suddenly it all made sense.

'You're a *miann cath*. That's why everyone is afraid of you. Oh Elyos, you have the battle-lust. The battle-fury.'

He rose to a crouch, snarling in what seemed more pain than anger.

'You have to stay here,' he instructed for the third time, jabbing a finger at my face. 'Swear it.'

'All right. I swear. I'll stay here.'

Elyos lowered his hand and gave a quick nod, accepting my promise but still unable to control the tremors. He looked down at the battle for several heartbeats with an agonised expression that rippled between longing and despair. Eventually he could resist no longer and, apologising, he slipped over the rise and down the slope. He drew his sword and ran towards the fighting, submitting to the madness. He crashed into the conflict, no longer able to tell friend from foe. He slashed at those around him, both raider and resistance, as he barrelled into the heart of the chaos. He became a bubble of destruction and people separated to let him through, twisting out of the way of his deadly blade.

He carved a path towards the nearest daemon. The monster was the size of a large horse but carried the muscle of a bull. It raced towards him, lowering its head to tear open the man's belly. Elyos became still, staring at the beast until it was almost within touching distance. He lifted his blade and sliced across the daemon's throat, twisting away from the tusks which would have disembowelled him. Green fluid flooded out of the gash, bursting into iridescent sparks which rose into the sky and became small ribbons of emerald light. The creature roared as it turned, the wound on its neck already healing. Elyos slashed again, then again. He kept its attention on him and away from those close by, but he was only one small distraction in a field of monsters and wraiths. *Saorsa* was humming at my hip, reminding me that this was why we were here. That this was what she was made for. And what I was born to do.

I cursed, then rolled over the rise to follow Elyos down the slope and into the battle. *Saorsa* sighed at being released and the runes on her blade glowed. My world shrunk to those before me and heartbeat decisions were made; raider or resistance, enemy or ally. I welcomed the chance to release my frustrations and made for the nearest monster with the hum of my sword vibrating through my body. *I shall bathe in daemon blood.* Her song reached its crescendo as she bit into the thigh of a man-daemon and it echoed around my head as emerald sparks flew around me.

Saorsa's song soared with a clear expression of joy and I heard a screeching cry echo her call. The sound flooded through every cell of my body, filling me with warmth and acceptance and belonging. I reached to remember where I had heard that cry before but my mind slammed the door closed on the memory, denying its existence.

I had no chance to chase the source of the familiar sound. A pirate had exploited my momentary lapse in concentration and slashed her knife along my side. I swung my sword, deflecting her blade when she brought it up to slice open my chest, then swiftly reversed *Saorsa's* angle to push up through her belly and into her chest.

The man-daemon had not forgotten me and followed up its attack. The pirate had barely hit the ground when it reached down to crush my skull. Raising *Saorsa* with all the strength my rage was pumping through my muscles, I cut through its arm. It curled over the haemorrhaging stump and I rammed my sword into its chest, ripping the blade free to create a large gash and clouds of emerald mist. The monster crashed to its knees, bringing its throat within my range and I roared in triumph, slashing open its neck. *Saorsa* bit deep and the beast dissolved into sparks.

Movement to my left caused me to spin around. A wraith raised his sword, ignoring my attack when *Saorsa* passed through his skeletal body with as little resistance as passing through a waterfall. I twisted away from his lunge but the ghostly blade scraped against my shoulder. The wound burned ice-cold in an unsettling, unnatural contrast to the warm blood seeping down my arm. I created a fireball sent it towards the wraith, hoping the distraction would buy time for my numbed arm to regain feeling. The fire stuck to the ghost like burning pitch. It writhed and squealed in what seemed to be agony before it dissolved into green smoke.

I hacked at raiders and daemons while I ignited any wraiths I could see. I became hopeful that we could win, now we had ways of defeating all three threats; the raiders could be killed by the resistance, fire could kill the wraiths, and *Saorsa* could kill the daemons. I had total control of the space around me, ignorantly unaware of the slaughter which continued elsewhere.

The battle ended at dusk without warning or explanation. The daemons dissolved and the wraiths faded. The raiders withdrew, protecting those who were injured or unconscious. No one went to chase them. The clearing was littered with bodies and the fighters around me were exhausted. A few moaned in pain but most were silent. I scanned for Elyos but could not locate him in those close enough to be recognised. As the feverish sensations of battle faded and I was able to assess more than the immediate threat surrounding me, I felt the nudge of Drey's training and turned to those who were wounded and needed my help. I moved from fighter to fighter, resistance and raider, determining whether they could be attended to or whether a more permanent solution was required.

I knelt beside a man, holding his hand as he slipped into the Halls of Eternity, when a hand settled lightly on my shoulder. I turned to look up at Elyos. The battle-lust had left his eyes and he appeared to have only superficial injuries. He gave me a small smile and helped me to rise, clasping my arm in a warrior's greeting.

'You promised to stay on the hill.'

I shrugged. 'I lied.'

He shook his head, releasing his grip to cradle the back of head. 'I'm going to be in so much trouble.'

I covered his hand with mine and grinned. 'Nothing new there.'

He released a bitter laugh and we went to join the spell-weavers. We quickly bandaged those who could walk and sent them back to the camp, then turned to those who needed more involved care. Three from the previous day were present and were able to work alongside me, placing those more seriously injured into a suspended slumber which allowed bones to be set and wounds to be cauterised. Those who required extensive healing would remain asleep until we reached the infirmary and more invasive methods could be safely performed within a protected area. It was deep in the night and I was bone-achingly weary by the time we returned to the settlement and passed our patients to those waiting for them.

Elyos nudged my arm. 'Looks like I'm not the only one in trouble.'

I looked to where he indicated and saw Vallori striding towards us, clearly displeased. Z'hara, Bear and Bonash trailed a few paces behind him. Elyos tried to leave but I grabbed his arm.

"Oh no. You got me into this. The least you can do is provide me with some support.'

'If I remember correctly, I told you to stay out of the fight. In fact, you swore that you would stay on the rise. So, this is all for you.'

He bowed with unnecessary flourish and left me to face Vallori alone.

'For the love of Mobis, Tallen. What, in all his Torments, were you thinking?'

I blinked at his rare display of anger and responded with some of my own.

'What was I thinking? Well, maybe I was thinking that I would go and kill some daemons. That is, overall, what we are here for. What *I* am here for.'

'Without us to protect you?'

'There was a whole army! And since when do I need protecting?'

'You were specifically told not to go. If the shamans had taken you... By the Gods, you know what would happen then!'

I took a breath to argue that nobody had specifically told me not to go and the shamans were too busy summoning their daemons to notice I was even there, when Z'hara came to stand by Vallori.

'They said you were dead.' Her eyes flicked to Elyos who was a few paces away, talking to his sister. 'When the fighters returned without you, we thought you were dead.'

'This is because I went with Elyos. Let me take a guess at who was spreading those rumours.' I glared at Bonash who was intently studying his feet. 'You know the game Sheehan is playing, Bonash, and you walked straight into his trap.'

The small man looked up at me apologetically before scurrying off to the infirmary. I immediately turned on Bear.

'And you? Wasn't it you who told me to embrace my inner darkness and do whatever it takes? Do *you* think I was being reckless or is this what we've all been training for?'

He was saved the need of replying by Carys, who coughed politely to interrupt. She held a firm grip on her brother and had been more successful in preventing him from escaping. I saw the stain of distrust in the eyes of my companions when they looked at him and hatefully admitted how quickly Sheehan had opened the cracks between us.

'There's a council to discuss the battle,' she explained. 'I think you should all be there.'

We followed Carys to a shelter only slightly larger than those around it and it did not take many to make the space seem crowded. Sheehan sat on a large, embroidered cushion beneath the sloping roof at the far side of the room and Carys went to sit on another beside him. Several fighters from that day's battle were already sitting around the edges of the room, along with a few who had stayed behind; the system being that two cohorts would alternate to allow some rest before being required to face the daemons again. We awkwardly shuffled in, trying to avoid stepping on those already seated as we created a space for the four of us.

Elyos had dropped back and entered last. He tried to remain unnoticed but a woman lunged over several people in an attempt to get at him. She managed to land a punch before she was adequately restrained.

'He is not welcome here,' she snarled.

'Breana, peace.' Carys tried to placate the woman while sending an apologetic look at her brother. 'Elyos has as much right as anyone else here. Please be seated.'

'He has a *right*? What about Gil? Did he have a right before you killed him?' She lunged at Elyos again, requiring another to assist in preventing her from attacking him a second time. 'What about Fionn, you monster? What about all those you hacked at as if they were the enemy? You should be hanged for what you did!'

Elyos remained motionless but had paled, taking the woman's anger without comment. Carys repeated her call for peace and requested that everyone be seated so they could commence the council. After much persuasion, the woman allowed herself to be guided back to her place while Elyos slunk into the darkest part of the shelter. Sheehan watched it all impassively while Carys waited for everyone to settle before calling for the most senior fighter to report.

'Despite the battle being shorter than most, we still lost fifty-eight and have another twenty-seven in the infirmary who will not be able to fight again for some time. The raiders seemed to have taken a similar toll but, as we have seen before, I'm sure they will be replaced before long. It's like trying to fight the tide. Sooner or later, we will not be able to hold them. We should leave for the higher ground where we can have the advantage.'

Carys sighed, replying softly. 'If we leave now, we will only have to fight them at another site later. This is an old discussion, Teiryn. They have no need to follow us into the hills and will look to the towns of Cambrien and Moorsend instead. The aim of the council tonight is to see what we have learnt and how we can increase our successes while minimising our losses.'

The discussion circled for some time. People offered strategies and tactics, many of which had been tried before with minimal impact. Battle plans that had been effective for generations could be used against the raiders, but they were woefully inadequate against the unnatural horrors raised by the shamans. The resistance could only hope to distract the daemons and avoid the wraiths while targeting the raiders, attempting to reach the shamans who remained protected and free to summon and control their monsters. The arguments flowed in one direction, then the other, before returning to the first. Eventually, frustration loosened my tongue.

'We can kill the wraiths with fire.' The atmosphere became instantly colder but, assuming it was in response to me mentioning the threat that nobody talked about, I continued. 'We could use the archers with fire-arrows, even if only in the initial stages before it gets too chaotic to risk. I tried fire on the daemons but it had no effect at all. The wraiths, however, shrivel to nothing once you torch them.'

There was a collective intake of breath and murderous looks were directed at me. Some had paled but many showed the hatred normally aimed at Elyos. I looked at Carys to see what social taboo I had broken.

'The wraiths are the ghosts of our fallen.'

I blinked. 'What?'

'When someone is killed by a wraith, some of their corruption gets transferred. The person's spirit becomes trapped and is unable to leave. Their shade is taken and transformed into one of these apparitions.'

'The torments of Sluagh,' breathed Bear with uncharacteristic despair.

Sheehan spoke for the first time. 'Those you *torched* were our friends. Our family.'

The true depths of the horror explained why the skeletal army was not talked about. It explained why there had been such evident fear at the possibility of the dying woman being brought into the camp. And the reluctance to start a battle where you faced the torture of fighting a familiar face who was dispassionately intent on killing you, helpless to defend against the ghost of someone you cared about.

'I didn't know.' My apology sounded hollow and it was only accepted by a few.

Carys allowed a moment for people to grieve before carefully returning the council to the discussion of ways that would allow us to attack the shamans. They were the key to everything, with the monsters dispersing once their masters had depleted their energies. The more the resistance could engage or injure the daemons, the sooner the sorcerers would lose their ability to maintain the creatures. This would provide the best opportunity to strike at the shamans directly. Bonash joined us when the conversation turned to potential strategies to weaken the daemons.

'Arrows, blades, spears, all do little,' stated a fighter with a bandaged arm and a recent wound showing on his face. 'There's maybe a dozen swords that can cause noticeable harm.'

Bear leaned forward. 'Why these swords? What do they have to make them special?'

The fighter shrugged. 'Nothing that stands out. They all seem to be old, family-owned blades, but other than that they are like any other.'

Bear frowned, stroking his beard while he thought. 'I would like to take a look at these blades.'

I searched for Elyos, catching his attention while he remained partially concealed and forgotten in the gloom.

'Someone should give Elyos one of those blades.'

I spoke quietly, talking to myself and not meaning to be heard, but my words carried further than I had intended. Once again, all attention was on me and I became the target for their distrust and resentment.

Sheehan scoffed. 'The sword would be wasted on the cursed one. He seeds destruction not salvation.'

'Oh, for the love of Mobis,' I blurted. The old man's blatant prejudice overrode my caution despite the hostile atmosphere, and my previous disrespectful comments. 'Stop hiding behind this stupid curse and call it for what it is. He's a *miann cath*. What you insist on calling a curse, others would claim to be the touch of the Gods. He's your best weapon and you are too scared to use him.'

I felt the shocked stares of all and immediately regretted my outburst. It was not my place to name Elyos for what he was and I doubted the additional judgement I had created would be kind. I was the only one who saw him leave. Everyone was looking to me, considering what I had said. The resistance may not have known the title but they had seen him in the throes of the battle-lust and had cause to fear him. Those of the sanctuary knew the full implications of the name and were now aware of the danger he posed to those around him. I felt Vallori's glare drill into me and I chose to ignore it. Instead, I looked to Carys and held her gaze. I was unsure if she knew the old term and feared for what it meant for her brother, or whether she just feared her people's reaction to it and how it would drive him further away. I saw her take a shaky breath, visibly fighting to calm herself.

'What Elyos is or is not, is not for discussion here,' she said eventually. 'If we are incapable of finding new ways of defeating these creatures, I suggest we retire and get some rest for whatever the dawn may bring.'

She looked at the exit, clearly wanting to follow her brother, but Bonash had come to the meeting for a reason.

'The dream-walkers may be able to help.' He started quietly but fell silent when he was met with scorn, being judged alongside me.

'The spell-weavers are useless against the daemons,' countered a woman who folded her arms across her chest in dismissal. 'The best they can offer are curses and insults.'

There were no spell-weavers present to defend themselves. All were in the infirmary caring for the wounded and performing a vital task that had been conveniently overlooked in the aggressive mood of the council.

'They provide more than that,' Bonash defended. 'But the dream-walkers offer a different form of magick. We know the shamans call energies and gather the power to summon the daemons. It is how we can predict when to fight and when to rest. There may be an opportunity there. If we looked at more than observing the pull of energies, we might be able to disrupt them. It would make it harder for the shamans to access this energy or, maybe even interfere with their connection to the daemons. Perhaps we could make them a little less of a threat.'

'There are a lot of maybes in that,' grumbled the woman.

'But any advantage should be exploited,' commented Sheehan, keen to take control of the council. He nodded towards Bonash. 'I would be grateful if you and your companions could look towards using your magick to aid us in this matter.'

I bristled at the clear instruction for us to stay away from the battlefield and stay hidden from view with the dream-walkers. I was also aware, finally, that I had caused enough problems and no one would listen to my protests. There was a hush while people considered whether the unfamiliar world of magick that we had brought to their world could be the hope that they needed. Allowing them to face the torments that awaited them.

'How does that even work,' asked someone quietly. 'How do you summon a monster from the Seven Hells?'

Bonash sighed, wondering how to explain the principles of magick and the realms of the Gods, but it was Vallori who spoke.

'There is a tale told by the Gallowglass,' he began, making my heart beat a little faster. 'An old grandmother was obsessed with blood magick and the raising of daemons. She sacrificed countless people. Those of her community as well as slaves. She used their blood to please the Fates and have them grant her wish. Sending their souls as payment for the daemons she would use to crush her enemies. She would perform ancient ceremonies where the sacrificial blood would run until it soaked into the ground. Shamanic chanting was used to summon the dark spirits and malevolent souls. Ancient words bound those tortured wraiths to her. But she failed to raise the daemon army she craved.

'An older tale is told in Gallowgla. Darker than the one shared a few nights back. It tells of the Gods and the Fates, the Favoured and the Rebellion. But it also talks of how the Fates used the blood of the Dragonslayers to create their daemons. How they used the Gods' chosen to bring about their destruction. Used their most powerful weapon to bring about their demise.' He looked up and scanned the faces of those watching him in fascinated horror. 'The grandmother knew of this story and it fuelled her ambitions. I know that she obtained a vial of Dragonslayer blood.'

I fled the shelter, suddenly unable to breath in the claustrophobic space and needing to escape Vallori's words. I slammed into Elyos, who had remained outside the exit and had heard all that Vallori had said.

'Dragonslayer?' he whispered.

'And you think you're cursed,' I hissed. 'My ancestors have lived for generations without causing any harm to anyone. So far, I have given Villermir the Empathy Crystal and he is using it to destroy the Three Kingdoms. And I've given Sálaforn enough blood to summon the entire daemon horde from Hell.' Elyos blinked at my dire confession. 'Drey should have left me to die at Methhold.'

I stormed off. Away from the judgement of Vallori and the council. Away from the shock in Elyos's eyes. I kept walking until I could no longer see the light from the camp's fires. Until I could pretend I was the only person in existence.

CHAPTER THIRTEEN

The next morning, the wound inflicted by the wraith throbbed incessantly.
I had left it open, with even the light touch of a bandage or sleeve rubbing
painfully, but it still stung and festered under the surface. I could feel its
foulness burrowing into my arm. I was tired and miserable.

'You look like week-old horse dung,' greeted Bear cheerfully. 'You
manage to get any sleep?'

'Some,' I shrugged. 'You?'

He shrugged back, grinning. 'Some.'

He studied the wound for a moment, then took hold of my arm to
examine it more closely. The movement was slight and he was gentle but I
still hissed at the pull of sore tissues. He frowned at my reaction, raising his
other hand to hover above the wound. I felt the warmth of his aura while he
assessed the unseen effects of the unnatural injury. It was not long before he
withdrew, tilting his head slightly in question.

'It looks like a normal scrape on the surface but below… There are
energies there that feel very wrong. And its spread into the muscle is not
like normal inflammation.'

'Wraith-wound,' I confirmed. 'It feels like some kind of moss or algae
has been stuck on my arm. I can feel the roots of it pushing into me. And
there is a strange pulling sensation. It's faint but it seems like something is
tugging at it. At me.'

'We should get Nash to look at it.'

I agreed but became distracted by Sheehan and Elyos talking by one
of the shelters. Bear soon followed my gaze, shaking his head sadly at the
familiar scene.

'There's a whole heap of trouble between those two.'

'I should apologise for what I said last night.' I started walking towards the pair. 'I should try to make right the trouble I caused.'

Bear groaned. 'Aye. Splendid idea. What harm could possibly come of that?'

Elyos and Sheehan were standing close together and keeping their voices low, but it was the usual topic of discussion.

'If it wasn't for your sister,' the elder hissed, leaning threateningly into the smaller man. 'I would have chased you out of here long ago.'

'You've been trying to do that for years, old man. Even in your prime you could never make me do anything I didn't want to.' His voice became dangerously soft. 'And you should treat my sister with more respect. She's the only one keeping these people together and you know that.'

Sheehan hesitated at the blatant threat, looking up to see us approaching. Now knowing that we were watching, he instantly replaced his mask and greeted us with a warm smile.

'A good morning to you,' he said cheerfully.

'It is indeed morning,' replied Bear before I had a chance to speak. 'Although, I'm not sure it will turn out to be a good one. The dream-walkers have sensed the gathering energies. There will be daemons today.'

The elder dipped his head in acknowledgement and remained overly pleasant. 'This presents an opportunity for you and your companions to study these energies. Perhaps you will be able to find a way of hobbling these shamans like some unruly yearling.'

He looked at me but Bear continued to address him. 'Bonash will stay behind but the rest of us will be going.'

Sheehan opened and closed his mouth in a good imitation of a stranded fish. I knew the elder would have argued if it had been me or Elyos who had spoken. I suspected he would have taken both of us together. But nobody argued with Bear.

'Well,' he stuttered. 'I don't think that's wise.'

'So you have said.'

Bear could be as unmovable as a mountain when he wanted and the older man soon realised he would not be able to change our minds. He huffed in frustration and turned to leave.

'And Elyos fights with us,' I stated.

Sheehan snapped back to face me, both he and Elyos protesting in unison.

'Are you crazy?'

'That's absurd.'

'He fights with us,' I calmly repeated.

Sheehan looked back and forth between Bear and me while we patiently waited for him to reach the inevitable conclusion. His face clouded when he realised he could not bend us to his will, and he conceded with a poisonous glare directed towards Elyos.

'The deaths will be on your hands,' he snarled before marching off.

Elyos ran his fingers through his hair in a nervous gesture. 'Tallen,' he sighed. 'This is not a good idea. You've seen what I am. Gods, you've told the whole camp what I am.'

I cringed at the gentle rebuke. 'When the tribes were building this land and creating the Three Kingdoms, *miann cath* were celebrated as being favoured by the Gods. For being incredible warriors who were unbeatable in battle. For protecting their tribes against overwhelming odds.'

He hopelessly shook his head. 'Those times have long since passed. There's no room for me in these more civilised times.'

'Civilised is not going to kill daemons.'

He turned to look at Bear. 'You can't believe this is a good idea?'

The big warrior grinned wickedly. 'I *believe* that you are going to need this.'

He reached behind his back and retrieved a blade. The sword was small and had a plain wooden handle, stained from the oil of countless hands. Bear offered him the weapon.

'I already have a blade.'

'Not like this one.'

I smiled. 'A daemon blade.'

Bear shrugged. 'Maybe. I think we're about to find out.'

Elyos stared at us with mild disbelief. 'You're both crazy.'

We left before mid-morning and marched through the pass to the clearing, as Elyos and I had done the previous day. We returned to a site that showed little sign of the battle other than the churned earth and the deep divots left by the daemons. The spell-weavers had explained that the wraiths appeared to remain tethered to their former bodies, denying their families the small comfort of performing the funeral rites. I looked over the battlefield and the scale of the wraiths' torment reached a new level. I shied away from what the shamans had done with all the bodies. A sense of evil permeated the area that went beyond the rows of raiders lined up to kill us. It went beyond the knowledge that we were about to be torn apart by daemons or taken to serve in the ghostly army. A malevolent presence seemed to be waiting, just out of view, so that even the carrion birds avoided the place. My wraith-wound's persistent tugging increased its intensity.

I searched for Vallori and Z'hara, positioned within the opposite flank at Vallori's request. He had been predictably displeased to learn of Elyos's inclusion in the army and then became angry on discovering that I had agreed to fight alongside him. We had parted in ill-temper, with my childish promise to get crushed by a daemon before I would let a shaman bleed me dry. I regretted my words now that the threat of death was all around, but there was little I could do now to fix our quarrel. I sent a prayer to Camlun to keep everyone safe and I rubbed *Saorsa*'s ruby-red eyes for warriors' luck.

Elyos and I had been placed at the far edge of the right flank, aiming to balance the risk of having him close enough to assist the main driving force while avoiding being so close that he would attack our own fighters. He had started to twitch as soon as the shamans began chanting and I was beginning to doubt the wisdom of my decision. Bear quietly positioned himself between Elyos and the fighters nearby.

'Do you think you can focus on the raiders?' I asked nervously. 'And the daemons when they come?'

'Do you think you can avoid incinerating our ghosts?'

Guilt stabbed painfully into my chest but I turned to see him wearing a mocking smile, taking the sting out of his words.

'I guess I deserved that.'

'You weren't to know,' he shrugged. 'Maybe we should burn them. Maybe that would release them into the Halls of the Gods, saving them from an eternity of slavery. Nobody knows. And I think that hurts the most.'

We remained silent for some time and I tried hard not to think about whether the wraiths were aware of their situation. Whether they watched helplessly while they killed their friends, unable to do anything to stop it. I looked past the pirates to the two shamans who were dancing and prancing behind their human army, calling their ghost soldiers. I repetitively rubbed circles over one of *Saorsa*'s smooth eyes with my thumb in an attempt to calm my racing heart. They were too far away. It was not possible for me to see a small bronze bowl on the ground between them, into which they could dip their fingers when they periodically reached for the ground. I shook my head, irritated that I was letting my imagination paint images to feed my fears, but could not remove the echo of Vallori's words and the memory of the old crone taking my blood at Freisholm.

'A *miann cath* and a Dragonslayer,' commented Elyos quietly. 'What are the chances of that? I feel the Gods are playing a merry game with us.'

The energies reached their peak and Elyos twitched violently. His eyes had darkened to black circles and they could no longer focus on one point. Bear glanced at me with a look of concern while Elyos fought to control the battle-fury, and I tightened my grip on *Saorsa*'s hilt.

The enemy charged and I ran towards them. All coherent thought vanished and I screamed insults, slashing at the raiders and twisting away from wraiths. I kept Elyos in view, satisfied that he was being kept busy with the invaders while Bear shouldered away any resistance fighters who got too close. With me on one side and Bear on the other, we created a protective barrier around the *miann cath* so he was free to cleave at those in front of him.

I heard the call again. It was louder this time, more insistent. The screeching cry beckoned and I searched the sky, yearning to join with it. The hint of leathery wings brushed against my mind with tantalising familiarity, but the knowledge of its name remained stubbornly hidden from me.

The ground shook with the stampede of man-daemons and horse-daemons. A bird-daemon swooped down to pierce my chest and I swung *Saorsa* up to slice open its neck. Her runes blazed, bathed in the daemon's blood, and the creature dissolved into mist before it hit the ground. I dealt with two more raiders on my way to join Elyos and his battle with a man-daemon. The monster swiped at me, and I sliced a deep bite into its chest when it hunched over. Elyos stabbed into its neck, angling his sword as he withdrew to gouge a large hole in its throat. His borrowed weapon flared and the runes on its blade accepted the daemon blood. I grinned at him, delighted that we may have found the secret to the ancient swords.

Then froze. He looked at me with wide, staring eyes and a terrifying, rictus snarl, and I did not doubt that he no longer recognised me. I feared that his battle-lust would gladly accept me as its next target. The moment only lasted for a heartbeat, and I breathed again when he turned to engage a group of raiders who had thought to surround him.

I turned to slice open the belly of a flying daemon that was swooping

174

down to stab at a resistance fighter before twisting away to avoid having my own belly opened by a wraith, cursing at being unable to defend against the ever-present ghosts. A horse-daemon galloped past, crushing all in its way. Bear paid no attention to the monster and it crashed into a wall of earth that had suddenly appeared in front of it. I laughed at my own stupidity, having been presented with what should have been obvious. Magick may not harm the beasts, but it could hold them long enough for the runed blades to destroy them.

I left the resistance to deal with the raiders while I danced to avoid the wraiths and concentrated on creating a range of obstacles to frustrate the ground-based daemons. I opened pits for them to stumble into and built barriers to corral them. I funnelled them towards the charmed blades of a Dragonslayer and a *miann cath*. I sliced at the wings of the bird-daemons that dove to attack, cutting off their heads when they crashed to the ground. I buried man-daemons in mounds of earth, stabbing through their eyes into their massive skulls. I gloried in the song of my sword, and we slashed and tore and ripped and shredded. We danced in emerald clouds of daemon blood.

Once again, the monsters faded and the raiders withdrew, carrying their collapsed shamans. Once again, I looked around a battlefield covered with the dead and dying. I felt dizzy with relief to see Vallori and Z'hara covered in blood but seemingly free from serious injury. Bear roared in triumph at the retreating raiders while Elyos was hunched over a few paces away from him. Both men were bruised and bloodied but still standing. I assessed my own injuries; the sting of a cut on my cheek, the tenderness of my ribs, the throbbing of a wound on my upper thigh, and the relentless pulsing of the wraith-wound on my shoulder. Thanking Camlun for allowing all of us to survive with only minor injuries, the healer in me turned my attention to those who had not been so favoured and joined the spell-weavers in caring for those most seriously wounded.

I was joined by Bear and Elyos for the walk back to camp, the two men having stayed to help the healers while Vallori and Z'hara had returned with the main group. I saw a reflection of my own exhaustion in their faces, with Bear also showing a hint of grim satisfaction on routing the raiders and their abhorrent creatures. Elyos looked down at the ground, but the set of his shoulders suggested some relief at having avoided harming any resistance fighters. The memory of him fighting tirelessly against the massive daemons reminded me of a more important point.

'Oh!' I shouted excitedly, backhanding Elyos in the ribs and making him grunt in discomfort as I hit a sore spot. 'I know what it is. It has to be that.'

'It has to be what?'

All exhaustion vanished and I had to resist the urge to bounce up and down, knowing I had found the answer to the daemon swords. I slapped him again, this time avoiding his tender ribs by aiming for his shoulder.

'Your sword. Why it can kill daemons when the other swords can't. It's so obvious, why didn't we think of it before?'

'What are you talking about? You're making no sense. What is so obvious?'

I turned to Bear. 'You saw them too, right? Just like *Saorsa's* but not as many.'

The big man nodded. 'I was a little busy to notice the details but aye, I saw them. It does ring of the truth and would definitely mark them as different to the other swords.'

Elyos was still confused and not in the mood to be ignored. 'Are you going to tell me what you two are talking about or should I leave you alone so you can discuss your secrets?'

'Elyos. Your blade glowed every time you struck a daemon and activated its runes. Did you not see that?'

'I think I would have noticed.'

'And that would explain why no one has made the connection before,' suggested Bear. 'Perhaps it is only those with sufficient magick who can see the runes activate, so that not even the spell-weavers would be able to see them. With no runes visible on the blade, they would just look like normal weapons.'

'They must be really old,' I commented. 'Why would you need a daemon-killing sword unless there were daemons to kill? And there haven't been daemons since–'

'The Ancients,' finished Bear. 'Those swords are more special than I thought. Just think how many could be still around. It would take hundreds being forged to result in the few we have here, but there's no reason to believe they are the only ones. There could be countless more, lying forgotten in the barns and storerooms across the Three Kingdoms.'

'And you think they would make that much of a difference?' asked Elyos.

'We are barely touching the surface with the daemons we're facing. And we are not the only ones getting slaughtered by these monsters.'

My excitement faltered and I considered the scale of the problem. The night sky was frequently painted green, suggesting daemon battles throughout the eastern territories of Hilman. Who knew how many were taking place beyond that. Even believing there were more daemon-swords waiting to be found, would it be enough to prevent the creatures advancing across all of the Three Kingdoms.

'It would be better than what we have at the moment,' offered Bear quietly and without any real conviction. 'Would your scouts be able to spread the word? Get people searching for their family blades? Ones that have been passed through many generations?'

Elyos shrugged. 'Perhaps. We could suggest that merchants were sourcing old weapons to supply a noble collector. Give the interfering priests no reason to be suspicious.'

'The last thing we need is for them to get hold of that much power,' I agreed grimly. 'I doubt they would use it to help defeat the daemons when they have shown no interest so far.' I growled in frustration. 'With all their resources, they could annihilate the shamans and send the raiders fleeing from our shores. But instead, they're too busy protecting their own interests and stoning herb-witches.'

Bear sighed. 'One impossible battle at a time please, Tallen.'

Elyos shook his head and voiced the defeat we were all thinking. 'It would take too much time. Assuming that we could find any, most of what we would get would be brittle with rust or broken and useless.'

We walked in silence for some time, each of us trying to make the knowledge of the runed swords increase our chances of destroying enough daemons. Even if we just looked at causing sufficient distraction so the shamans would become vulnerable, there was no way of determining which weapons would be effective at harming the daemons until the runes activated. That would require the presence of daemons and would make the information that identified the charmed blades redundant. I could only think of one option where the knowledge of the runes could be used in a more proactive way.

'We could make our own?'

'You could do that?' asking Elyos hopefully.

'Aye,' mocked Bear. 'We just need to have the skills of those who originally created the swords. Skills that have not been known since the time of the Ancients.'

I refused to be so easily dissuaded. 'We know how to make runed blades, Bear.'

'But not all runed blades can kill daemons,' he countered. 'My sword contains a number of runes. It can't kill daemons.'

'Maybe they are just the wrong runes?'

'And do you know the correct ones? Did you clearly see the precise sigils that would need to be accurately inscribed so that they kill the daemon and not the bearer?'

'No,' I reluctantly admitted. 'But I know *Saorsa*'s runes. We could start with those.'

'*Saorsa* is a dragon-blade. She was forged in the fires of Mount Kahlua with the breath of the Gods.'

'And Dragonslayers and *miann cath* are just myths,' I snapped back, frustrated by his pessimism. 'Your element is air. Perhaps you could sing to the metal and get it to reveal what runes are needed.'

I knew I was desperately searching for ideas and I failed to even convince myself. Bear did not bother to point out the many faults in my suggestion, choosing to let his scowl confirm that we did not have the skills to make our own charmed blades. Elyos waited for us to continue proposing ideas and, when we remained sullenly silent, offered a suggestion of his own.

'As someone who has no idea what you are discussing or understands the consequences if this goes wrong, I think it's worth trying. Anything to help reduce the slaughter we're suffering at the moment.'

We made a start as soon as we returned to camp, with Bear reluctantly agreeing to determine how we could engrave the plain swords. There was no forge within the settlement and the nearest was over a day's ride away. The occasional trip to replace lost arrows or repair broken spearheads was deemed an acceptable risk, but nobody wanted to increase the chances of discovery by making more frequent visits. Not to mention the fact that inscribing runes onto weapons would definitely been seen as heretical practice by the Baila fanaticists, with the resultant violent repercussions. Instead, Bear arranged for rocks and boulders to be collected from the surrounding area and he built a small, circular oven that could create enough heat to soften the blades for engraving.

While Bear worked on the problem of carving the runes into the swords, I addressed the issue of what sigils to engrave. *Saorsa* had six runes embedded within her blade while Elyos's seemed to only have three. My first challenge was to determine which of the six, if any, were present on the smaller sword. I was fairly confident that the daemon rune had been there, but I was sure the other two were not on *Saorsa*. I closed my eyes and slowed my breathing, concentrating on the image of Elyos using his blade to cut into the flesh of a man-daemon. At the flare of the runes, I again heard the faint sound of large, leathery wings flapping above my head despite being sat within the temporary forge. The feeling of warmth and belonging flushed my skin once more, but still my mind refused to acknowledge the invisible presence and the memories it threatened to provoke. I forcefully returned my focus to the frozen image of Elyos's sword and the glowing runes. The first was the inverted trident; *kalc* – underworld. The second was the familiar three-sided box sigil that was indented top and bottom; *peorth* – daemon. The last was the paired chevrons, the top one rotated to open to the left and the lower one open to the right; *jera* – harvest.

We faced the daemons twice more before Bear was ready to engrave the sigils and we used this time to confirm that I had correctly identified the runes contained within the ancient swords. I noticed a change seep through the camp as we worked. Rumours spread about what we were hoping to achieve and people came to watch us attempt to mark the plain blades. I also noticed a change in Elyos, who was more relaxed when working alongside Bear to maintain the oven and evenly heat the metal. I watched his attitude soften when the petty challenges towards him ceased and the hostile glares became less frequent. They had seen how effective he could be when they worked with him. When they gave him the space he needed on the battlefield. When they no longer expected him to follow their rules. I looked up one morning to find Vallori watching from the entrance as Bear, Elyos and I adjusted the alignment of the runes along a blade. He gave a small smile of approval when Elyos suggested a template that could be used to ensure consistency across all weapons, reducing the risk of reproduction errors confusing what would activate and what would remain ineffective.

Vallori gave me a quick nod. 'You've done good work here.'

I dismissed his comment. 'Bear and Elyos have done most of the hard work. Getting the oven built. Finding the engraving tools.'

He laughed and turned to leave, calling over his shoulder. 'Take the apology, Tallen.'

By the third encounter we were willing to try the first engraved sword. Bear had been able to soften the metal enough for the sigils to be scratched into the blade, but it was crude and we had no way of knowing if they would work until it was used against a daemon. Vallori volunteered to try the weapon but Bear would not allow anyone else to carry the risk of an untested blade. We could have caused the blade to weaken and shatter on contact, making it more of a liability than the original sword. He was right to have been concerned. The runes did not activate and Bear received a crushing blow that would numb his arm for almost two days. He threw the sword across the make-do forge in frustration.

'I knew it wouldn't work,' he growled. 'I can't get the blade hot enough. The sigils are sitting *on* the blade. They're not part of it. There's no magick there.'

I placed *Saorsa* on the slab of rock that was serving as an anvil, hoping for inspiration on how to seal in the magick. Bear was right. The runes in both Bear's sword and *Saorsa,* although visible, were melded into the steel. I could feel no trace of them when I ran my fingers over the inscription. There was nothing visible or tactile in the other charmed swords to reveal their engraving until the moment of contact with daemon flesh. It seemed the magick needed to be a part of the blade, embedded within it, and that would mean forging new blades which we could not do within the camp.

Elyos had placed his sword alongside *Saorsa* to provide a comparison between the two weapons. I was intent on trying to determine the similarities that may hold the key to unlocking the runes, and I missed the look in Elyos's eyes when his hand brushed across the dragon-sword. I did not notice the desire to hold her that was shown by all who saw her. I did not recognise the peril within the soft chime when he lifted her from the surface.

'Be careful with that,' warned Bear.

But Elyos was no longer listening to anything other than the enticing call of the blade. He rotated his wrist to frame her in a golden light and I took a breath to warn him, but it was already too late. Elyos's grip slipped and *Saorsa* fell to the floor, drawing blood from his thigh.

'It appears you are cursed after all, my friend. Terminally cursed to be clumsy.' The injured man started to protest but Bear continued. 'Peace. She does that to everyone. Lures you in with those seductive hues rippling over her blade. Winks at you with a flash of those ruby eyes. Then bites you for your presumption! It seems only Dragonslayers can hold dragon-blades without fear of reprisals.'

I retrieved *Saorsa* and replaced her alongside the plain sword, only half-listening to Bear's commentary. I was distracted by the sharp, almost gloating, note made by my weapon when she took her blood-fee.

'You should get some ointment for that,' I said absently. 'It's likely to fester.'

My thoughts had already moved on, comparing her discordant tone to the harmonies she sang when tasting daemon blood. I closed my eyes and searched for the song in the memory of Elyos's blade flaring at the contact with a daemon. There it was. The glow of the runes had been so obvious that it had hidden the song woven within. I opened my eyes to look at the blades lying side-by-side. So different, with one being exquisitely beautiful while the other was common and plain. And yet, they were also so similar. I smiled at the two men who were watching me expectantly.

'Well?' prompted Bear.

'Music,' I replied.

'What?' questioned Elyos.

'Music,' I repeated, laughing at his exasperated expression. 'The blades sing when the runes are activated. Both of them. The same song.' I grinned at Bear. 'And I hear it now. It's quiet. Very quiet. But it's there. Just waiting for another taste of daemon blood.'

Without releasing my gaze, Bear reached out a hand. 'Elyos. Fetch the blade.'

The engraved sword was retrieved and placed into the big man's hand. He twisted the hilt so that the carved sigils caught in the light of the oven's fire.

'How do we make this sing?'

'Air is your element, fire is mine,' I offered tentatively. 'You breathe your magick into the runes and I'll fuse it into the blade.'

Bear hesitated for a heartbeat before nodding in agreement and setting to work, pumping the bellows to increase the temperature within the oven. Once the blade was sufficiently heated, Bear deepened the inscription. He breathed the words of power over the sigils when the marks were cut deeper into the metal. I felt the vibrations of the runes fade as the blade cooled and gained confidence that this was why the magick had failed.

'Let's see how much heat you can take,' I challenged the sword.

The forge and the men working in it blurred, my vision narrowing to the glowing characters etched into the blade. I added to the energy within the residual heat to make the sword burn brighter and hotter. I slowly increased the power within the runes, careful not to go too fast and cause the blade to become brittle and crack. The metal rippled around the engravings and the colour changed from orange to yellow to white. I whispered words of power and the molten steel flooded the runes, making them an integral part of the blade. Ignoring the pain in my head, I searched for the song within the weapon and compared it to that of *Saorsa*. The pitch was too low. The harmonies were not blending as they should. I increased the flow of power, making the blade boil as I dragged the vibrations into the correct tone. The song reverberated through my chest and confirmed that the magick was right.

I looked up from the warmly glowing blade, the movement causing the room to tilt and forcing me to grab at the make-do anvil to avoid failing while my vision steadied. Bear dowsed the sword in water and steam rose with an angry hiss. I wiped the sweat from my face while we all stared at the cooling weapon. The blade was smooth, showing no sign of the runes hidden within. Bear and I grinned, both convinced that this time it would activate when carving at daemons. Elyos remained wide-eyed in awe of the magick he had just witnessed.

'And the song?' Bear asked cautiously.

I nodded. 'It's there. It should work.'

'Can we make more?' asked Elyos in a reverentially hushed whisper.

'No,' declared Bear before I had the chance to respond. 'You almost collapsed creating this one. Let's see if it works before we ask for more.'

The blade proved successful and the mood within the camp changed once again. People snatched at the hope the new sword had given, desperate to believe it could be the answer to defeating the daemons. Their expectations added weight to the next problem of how to create enough enchanted weapons for all who wanted them. Vallori, Z'hara and Bonash had joined us in the forge and we sat surrounded by donated swords, arrows and spears, trying to find a way of embedding the required sigils into all those blades.

'We don't need all of them runed,' suggested Vallori. 'Most of the battle involves human raiders and avoiding the wraiths. We don't need special weapons for that.'

'Having a daemon-sword increases everyone's confidence, whether fighting monsters or raiders,' countered Z'hara. 'And we can't leave our fighters defenceless when we know of a way to avoid that.'

Vallori persisted. 'We cannot charm all these weapons. We can't protect the whole army this way.'

'I could–' I started.

'No,' came the unified response of those from the sanctuary.

Vallori continued, ignoring my interruption. 'We only need enough to allow the most capable fighters a fair chance with the daemons.'

Bear shook his head. 'With the blades we already have, we would need at least fifty to make even a slightly noticeable difference.'

Z'hara rubbed at her eye in frustration. 'Even rotating the swords between the two cohorts, that would still leave more than eight out of every ten unprotected.'

'Not to mention the time it would take to make those fifty,' added Bonash quietly.

The conversation faltered so I tried again. 'I would just need–'

'No!'

Elyos looked at each of us in turn. 'What are you not saying? Is the problem with the swords? Would arrowheads be quicker to mark?'

Bonash sighed tiredly before patiently explaining. 'It's not the size of the weapon but the power needed to embed the magick. Each rune contains a reservoir of energy that needs to be supplied by Bear and Tallen. To activate the runes and make them sing requires more than Tallen can give.'

'One sword took more than was safe,' confirmed Bear, carefully avoiding looking at me. 'Two swords could leave her unconscious for days. More than that could be fatal.'

I watched everyone contemplate how much power would be required to activate all the weapons needed, and how I was woefully lacking that much power. I saw the small creases in their foreheads deepen when they tried to find an effective way of overcoming the problem while avoiding the one I already knew would work.

'Have you all finished thinking of what will *not* work?' I asked sharply. 'Can we do it my way now?'

'The rules are there for a reason, Tallen,' Bonash protested. 'The backlash of taking too much power–'

'The rules are there to protect people who are already safe.' I turned to

Bear as a potential ally. 'Sometimes the rules need to be broken when safe is no longer an option.'

Bear dipped his head in acknowledgement and I knew that, although he hated it, he agreed with me. The only possible way we could enchant enough weapons was for me to access a source of energy outside of myself. I had accessed that power before but never on this scale. If I lost control while in contact with the core's massive energy reserves, I risked not only my destruction but also that of everything within a day's ride.

Z'hara broke first. 'I don't have much magick but you can have whatever I possess.'

I smiled my appreciation. 'Thank you. I don't need your power but I would welcome you as an anchor.'

She nodded in agreement and Vallori sighed in defeat. 'I won't let you two handle this alone.'

His face remained passive and I suspected that only Z'hara and I noticed the slight tensing of his eye muscles that told of his concern. Bonash conceded shortly after.

'You'll need a fourth,' he offered quietly, flicking a look towards Bear.

Elyos, knowing nothing of what we were agreeing to, bravely offered himself to the cause but Bear clapped him on the shoulder.

'You'll be kept busy enough helping me,' he rumbled. 'This is going to be a long night.'

While the two men went to stoke the oven and collect the blades for engraving, the four of us arranged ourselves into a protective circle hoping to mitigate any disaster I may inadvertently unleash. I sat at the south, representing fire. Vallori sat opposite, at north and representing water. Z'hara took the east, representing earth. Leaving Bonash the west, representing air. I whispered the word for permission and extended my aura to encompass those of the circle, weaving our golden strands together to make a tethering rope. I concentrated on my breath, inhaling deeply and holding it for three heartbeats before releasing. I felt the others match my rhythm and their heartbeats adjusted to synchronise with mine. By the fourth breath we were as one and the energies flowed freely between us.

I felt myself smile when my auric tail extended from the base of my spine and its arrowed tip dug into the ground beneath where I was sitting. With each exhale I pushed it further into the earth, caressing the shimmering scales against the pebbles and the moist soil as it burrowed towards the warmth hidden in the depths. I felt my wings unfurl when I stretched my back in anticipation of the power I was about to absorb. The energy vibrated through the ground and into my tail, and it caused my body to hum in delight. I broke through the outer crust and into the magma chamber, exploding into blinding shards of light. I basked in the sulphurous gases that filled the cavern and the towers of flame that erupted from the churning river of fire. I plunged my tail into the molten rock and power raced up my spine, crashing into my brain. I breathed in the intoxicating energies. Opal droplets dripped from wings that shimmered and sparkled. I luxuriated in the sensation and greedily embraced the power of the stars.

The distant ring of a hammer on metal snapped my attention back to the reason why I needed to access this magnificent wonder. I used my inhaled breath to siphon the power, using my companions as vessels to contain the energies, and funnelling the overflow into the runes Bear was carving into the first blade. It took no time at all to meld his sigils into the metal and bind the energies within to make the runes sing. I smiled when I heard him curse at the speed at which I completed the work, sliding the blade across the bench for Elyos to dowse in the bucket while he pulled a second blade from the fire and shouted at Elyos to heat a third. The men moved quickly but I was frustrated at the time it was taking Bear to carve the runes. He had barely finished engraving the last sigil when I melted his work into the steel, binding the runes with words of power. The big man swore at me when I burnt his fingers in my haste but my attention had already moved to the arrows stacked in a corner. The small arrowheads were easily heated and I rapidly softened the metal, carved the characters and absorbed them into the point. It was now Elyos's turn to curse. The heat I had created ignited the wicker basket storing the arrows, making him rush over to smother the flames while Bear yelled for another sword.

Eventually there were no more weapons to inscribe. A large heap of swords, arrows and spears lay cooling on the ground. Bear was hunched over the work-surface and Elyos sat slumped against a pole. I whispered the word of gratitude and reluctantly withdrew my tail from the boiling river of magma. My wings withdrew back into my corporeal body and, taking a deep cleansing breath, I unravelled the bound auras and released my companions. It took another breath to quieten the pounding in my head and dim the flashes of light that danced across my vision. I grinned drunkenly at the look on Z'hara's face as she slowly flexed and extended her illuminated fingers. A blue mist of residual energy bathed all four of us in a shimming light.

'You're all glowing,' I giggled, still euphoric from the connection with the cavern's immense energy source.

She smiled back, sharing the exhilaration of having so much power course through her. Our mutual ecstasy was interrupted by a polite cough. Carys stood on the threshold of the forge, with her arms crossed and wearing a mildly amused expression. She was surrounded by as many as could press in to watch the creation of magick that burned brighter than the dawning sun.

CHAPTER FOURTEEN

I should have known. I should have been prepared. But I had become very good at denying the reality of the situation we were facing. The success of the enchanted weapons gave everyone hope that we could win against the shamans and their daemons. We were able to employ more strategy now the battles had become less of a struggle for a survival. On one occasion a fighter had managed to get close enough to a shaman to inflict a wound, albeit a superficial one, and we began to feel that it was only a matter of time before we would be able to kill one of them. A grudging cooperation had even developed between Sheehan and Elyos now that the elder could no longer sustain the division between the fighters and the *miann cath*. The mood in the camp was optimistic, and there was talk of sending fighters with runed swords to other resistance groups to train them in the methods we had found to be effective. We allowed our successes to blind us.

Z'hara and I were practising in the early dawn mist when Bonash came running up to us, flushed and visibly anxious. 'This is big,' he announced. 'They've called a council. This is going to be bad.'

'What are you talking about?' asked Z'hara, sheathing her swords. 'Why have they called a council this early?'

Bonash had already turned to leave and his agitation increased when we failed to follow him. 'Come on,' he pleaded. 'We can't waste any time.'

We shared a look of confusion but, trusting the small scholar, we followed him to the main shelter. We fed off his distress and had developed significant concern of our own by the time we entered the crowded space. Sheehan and Carys were already seated on their honorary cushions when Z'hara and I joined Vallori and Bear. Bonash left us to join two of the most experienced dream-walkers within the camp. A gentle buzz of conversation rippled around the room but quickly faded when Sheehan raised a hand.

'Thank you all for your prompt attendance,' he started formally, surveying the crowd before gesturing the dream-walkers. 'Wallace, perhaps you can explain why we are all here.'

A tall man with short, dark hair rose to stand beside Bonash and address the council. He nervously played with the hem of his tunic while his eyes flickered around those gathered.

'A few of us dream-walkers prepared to search for the energies of the shamans as they summoned their daemons. Just like we do every morning. It generally takes a while to separate the natural flow that weaves through everything. The grasses, the trees, the animals, and such like.'

'Wallace,' Carys interrupted gently and the man swallowed to moisten his dried mouth. 'Why don't you tell us about how today was different?'

'Yes. Yes, of course,' he stammered. 'Well, as I said. It normally takes a while to identify the corrupted energies but this morning we were overwhelmed as soon as we made contact.' His voice became stronger when he described what had occurred. 'The shamans were already leeching power from around their camp and had extended their range to include most of the distance between them and us. But it's not just the extent of their gathering, they are probing deep into those resources. Draining the life source of everything they touch. The damage will take generations to recover.'

'Are you trying to tell us there will be more daemons?' asked a red-haired woman.

The tall dream-walker looked at her apologetically and nodded. 'I would say considerably more. The energy being gathered is so much greater than anything we've seen before. They could summon hundreds.'

The council erupted as the fighters voiced their anger and fear. More than a few called for the abandonment of the camp and a retreat into the mountains. Many others, falsely confident following the success gained from the runed weapons, denied that this posed a new problem.

'Seems to me they are just levelling things out,' said one. 'We kill some of their daemons, they create more. Just like they keep replacing the cursed raiders.'

'We've got them running scared,' claimed another. 'They know we are winning and they are over-playing their hand.'

'Listen to yourselves. We can barely deal with the daemons we already face,' countered a third. 'More daemons will mean more death. Are you willing to throw our lives away so cheaply?'

Sheehan raised his hand and again the room fell respectfully silent. 'And when the shamans have drained the land dry, will we be free of the daemon problem?'

Bonash hesitantly rose to stand alongside the taller dream-walker. 'There is an unlimited amount of power that the shamans can draw on if they are willing to take the risk. Today's careless depletion of energy suggests that they are prepared to continue, whatever the cost. The only way to stop the daemons will be to stop the shamans.'

Previous arguments regarding the risks of continuing to fight and the uncertain safety of retreat flared again. Old opinions were traded until a young fighter stood up to address the council, voicing what I was feeling and what I suspected many others were as well.

'I cannot leave others to face what I am unwilling to face myself. I will stay and fight. To make whatever difference I can. Alone if I have to.'

Bear remained seated but his deep voice carried easily. 'You will not be alone.'

The fighter gave him an appreciative smile before sitting again, blending back into the silent crowd. I looked at the faces that quietly considered the stark choice and whether they would choose survival over sacrifice. I was surprised to see that most chose to fight, with expressions of grim determination outnumbering those of sad regret. I saw Sheehan and Carys had noticed as well, giving each other a nod before the elder confirmed the decision.

'We make a stand,' he declared to his subdued audience. 'Both cohorts will cause as much damage as they can while we move the camp to safer ground. This may be our last act of defiance. Let us give them something to remember.'

No rallying cry followed his words. No cheer of victory or glory. Just a sombre quiet brought by the grim realisation that it was always going to end this way. We battled overwhelming odds against an enemy we were poorly equipped to face. I shared a concerned look with Z'hara, but the warrior had trained at the Sanctuary of The Moon Goddess. She hesitated for only a moment before lifting her head in determination.

'We have a better chance than most.' She winked at me. 'We have two of the Goddess's Moon Warriors.'

I smiled back at her unfaltering optimism. 'Then let us go and kill some daemons.'

The battle started like any other and it initially appeared that we had overestimated the threat. The pirates had increased their number, but this was still less than what we presented. Vallori and Z'hara had again positioned themselves within the ranks of the far left while Elyos and I remained on the far right, leaving Bear and Bonash to support the centre. Carys and Sheehan had stayed to organise the relocation of the camp further into the hills, along with the elderly, the injured and the very young. Almost a quarter of the spell-weavers and dream-walkers stayed with them but the rest had gathered at the rear of the army to wreak whatever mayhem they could with spells and curses and disrupted energies. Anyone capable of holding a weapon stood and faced the raiders, including any child taller than the length of Bear's sword. Hunting knives were given to the youngest, although many were already proficient archers and it was hoped they could remain on the fringes of the battle. The men, women and children of the resistance waited anxiously for the fighting to begin, with many poorly hiding their fear.

The air almost shimmered with the energies being compressed within the cauldron of the clearing. Despite days of rain, the grasses were as brown and dry as if it was the height of a summer's drought. The only animals seen on the march to the battlefield were dead, dried husks on skeletal frames. No birds flew in the sky. No insects skimmed over the wilted stems of wildflowers. The ground was dusty and had cracked in many places where the shamans' desecration had deeply penetrated. I watched the two sorcerers dance behind the enemy and lowered my protective barriers slightly, channelling the land's pain into my rage and welcoming the warmth that seeped into my muscles. I tightened my grip on *Saorsa*'s hilt while she hummed quietly in anticipation.

The smaller shaman shrieked an undulating cry that carried shrilly over the battlefield and caused more than a few of our fighters to take a reflexive step back. A wave of noise flowed through the raiders as they drummed swords and axes against their shields or stamped their feet in provocation.

'Look,' Elyos said quietly.

He dipped his head towards the rocky wall bordering the clearing and the reason for the pirates' arrogance became clear, with more and more raiders lined up along its edge. The prancing shamans crowed with delight when another group appeared around the far end of the wall's base. The raiders now outnumbered us three or four to one but, more worryingly, each company had their own pair of shamans, including one old woman who reminded me of the Freisholm crone. All six twisted and gestured and chanted and shrieked, calling their monsters to come and destroy us.

'Merciful Mother,' I breathed, losing the last frayed threads of hope.

The raiders charged and those on the cliff descended on ropes. I ran to engage the nearest pirates while spears whistled over my head, and the chaos quickly engulfed me. The numbers contained within the clearing compressed everyone into a heaving mass and I was crushed by both raider and resistance fighters. It was unable to swing *Saorsa* effectively, restricted to slashing at legs while I stabbed with my dagger. The fighting was primitive and brutal. The dance of swordplay was replaced with clubbing and shoving and gouging and jabbing. An endless stream of violence with a new enemy immediately replacing the one just fallen.

The closeness of the fighting meant the wraiths were impossible to avoid. I resorted to shoving raiders towards them as a shield, but still received many glancing blows from the ghosts' swords and a deep wraith-wound over my hip. I finally conceded that I could not fight the double threat of wraiths and raiders, and I ignored the implications of calling my fire. I ignited all the skeletal shades within several arm-lengths and created a small respite, with any fighter nearby being singed. I buried the twist of guilt and proceeded to torch any wraith I could see, caring less about the souls of the ghosts than those of the resistance currently being slaughtered by them.

The daemons created carnage wherever they rampaged, crushing all as the mass of people denied any escape. The shrill whistles of the shamans failed to achieve any control over the beasts and they trampled raider and resistance alike. Bones shattered when man-daemons charged over those who had fallen. Flesh was ripped and gouged by the horse-daemons' stampede. People were impaled by the circling bird-daemons swooping down to stab with their blade-sharp beaks. The monstrous bellows and shrieks added a paralysing fear to that already smothering the clearing.

I used magick to contain the nearest daemons, fighting through the raiders until I was close enough for *Saorsa* to finish the monsters, but I was burning my power at an alarming rate. I was struggling to focus on the many threats that were pushing in on me; fighting with sword and dagger, creating fire to incinerate the wraiths, moulding air and earth to trap the daemons. Black spots danced across my vision and a pounding headache made it difficult to concentrate, but the creatures kept coming and pirates gave no respite. I gathered my energies and fought on.

At some point the crush of bodies lessened and *Saorsa* created a small space around me. I took a moment to look beyond my immediate circle and across the battlefield. I saw the hellish scene from a nightmare. Countless bodies were crushed and torn, lying in a swamp of blood and waste. The daemons tossed their victims like toys while the silent wraiths claimed more souls. The noise was deafening, with the screaming and shouting and crash of weapons merging into one dreadful wall of sound.

In the midst of all this horror my attention was caught by a child, frozen in terror as a horse-daemon thundered towards him. His pitifully inadequate knife was gripped before him in shaking hands while fighters battled around him. He was abandoned in a strange circle of calm while disaster charged towards him. I started running, knowing I was too far away and too many fighters blocked my path. I would never reach him in time. I shouted at him to run but my voice was lost within the roar of the battle. I screamed my throat raw when the daemon lowered its head, its tusks positioned to tear the boy in half. It galloped ever closer. Four horse-lengths away. Three. Two.

Elyos barrelled out of the crowd, slashing at the beast's throat with enough force to lift him off his feet. Emerald sparks flew when his runed blade bit into the monster and the momentum was sufficient to twist the creature off its path by just enough. Elyos slammed into the child to spin him out of harm's way, but the man was dragged along with his sword still embedded in the daemon's neck. Jewelled daemon-blood continued to spray for several paces until the creature stumbled and collapsed, gouging a deep trench in the ground. Elyos tugged his blade free and limped clear of the thrashing hooves. He snarled at the terrified boy to run.

I reached the pair, sliding to a halt as Elyos turned towards me. He had raised his sword and taken two paces towards me before he hesitated, blinking with wide black eyes and a small frown as he seemed to find some recognition. Without a word he turned back to the fighting and I repeated his instruction to the cowering boy, needing a third command before the lad recovered enough wits to scurry away. I followed Elyos to fight alongside the whirlwind of a *miann cath*.

The call for retreat eventually came. The battle had been short and bloody and we were all exhausted. The daemons continued to crush and gouge and stab. The wraiths continued to harvest their victims. The runed blades had bought us some time and we had fought heroically, but we had achieved nothing. We were still devastatingly outnumbered by the raiders and had failed to get anywhere close to the shamans. We were no longer able to stand our ground, much less gain any form of advantage. We fell back to the rear of the clearing and I was shocked to see how few of our fighters were able to respond to the call. The spell-weavers and dream-walkers had also suffered major losses when raiders had broken through to them.

'Why do they not follow us?' asked a young fighter as the enemy jeered at our ragged retreat.

'They don't need to,' came the tired reply. 'They know we're already finished.'

I looked around and saw the same emotions repeated throughout. At best, there was quiet resignation. At worst, there was fear and despair. It would take a long time for this community to recover and it would never be the same. I turned to Elyos, who wiped blood and sweat from his face but only succeeded in smearing it into streaks. The blood from a deep head wound added to the smudging, in a face drawn tight with anger and frustration while he fought the fading battle-lust. We watched in impotent silence while the shamans dissolved their daemons and the gloating raiders withdrew. They callously left the atrocity of the wraiths floating among the bodies that covered the clearing.

The taunting of the wraiths' presence, freely roaming around our dead, cut deeply. It was a blatant reminder that our companions were now bound to the shamans. The pain twisted sharply when ghosts started to rise from the newly slain, joining the spectral army and creating a hellish barrier between us and the six sorcerers who had remained to glory in our agony. Their casual cruelty kindled a fire within my core and a writhing ball of flame appeared in each of my palms in response. I rotated them slowly while I fought the desire to ignite the abhorrent shades, knowing the decision did not belong to me. I was surrounded by people who had cared for the souls now suspended in a reality where they were neither alive nor dead. I felt sick with the torment of either option.

'Burn them,' growled Elyos. 'Burn them all.'

I turned to see him looking at the wraiths with such hatred that I did not doubt the conviction in his decision. I felt guiltily relieved that the choice had been made and gratefully released the flaming spheres, increasing their size and the intensity of their heat so that the skeletal army exploded into a wall of fire. The ghosts quickly evaporated, leaving the flames to feed on the bodies in a communal funeral pyre. The stench of burning flesh and bone was terrible and many fell to their knees in grief. Black, acrid smoke darkened the sky while the fire consumed the bodies and released their souls to rest.

We stood watching for some time before Elyos guided me over the rise where the spell-weavers had created a base to care for the more seriously injured, away from the visual reminder of our defeat. Unlike the orderly dispersal after previous battles, those able to stand had not left to report to those who had stayed behind. A detached state of shock seeped throughout, with some standing, others sitting, all staring vacantly at nothing. All were lost in bleak memories and were unwilling, or unable, to move on to an unknown future. The spell-weavers quietly moved among them to assist where needed but left most to their grief. I felt numb, looking at the blank faces of people who had been so optimistic just the day before. I felt unable to connect with any of them, walking as a stranger in an unfamiliar land. I aimlessly followed Elyos's back through the unbearable pain and suffering.

Bear bellowed in incoherent rage. I searched the crowd and found him towering over a spell-weaver, leaning threateningly over the smaller man who sadly shook his head. I went cold at the thought of what would make the big warrior so angry with a spell-weaver, finding the distressing conclusion that Bonash must be seriously wounded. I hurried towards him, catching snatches of their conversation.

'You need to do something,' Bear roared. 'And do it now!'

The spell-weaver's reply was lost but I could see his expression as he courageously met the intimidating glare. His look of regret suddenly made it difficult to breathe. There were still too many people crowded around the pair for me to see clearly but I was now certain that Bonash was grievously hurt. I started running, uncaring of who I pushed out of the way in my haste. I gathered my remaining power into a ball at the base of my ribcage, praying to Nathair for guidance so I could heal whatever damage had been inflicted.

'The only thing I can offer now,' continued the spell-weaver, 'is providing whatever comfort I can before the passing of–'

I did not hear his last words. I had crashed through the ring of people and was finally able to see who was on the ground. Vallori sat with his back to me, his legs curled to the side to carefully avoid touching the person lying in front of him. Bonash rested on bent knees cradling Z'hara's head.

My mind shouted in denial for several heartbeats before it finally accepted the details of her face and the fact that my friend was still alive. One side of her head was a matt of bloodied hair to suggest a cracked skull. Her face was pulled into a grimace and her eyes were clamped closed against the pain. I took this as a positive sign that she had not drifted beyond the point of feeling. I had dealt with head injuries before and, while they could be fatal, I was confident I could repair the damage. Vallori was blocking my view of Z'hara's body so, following the principles of obtaining a full assessment before commencing a healing, I moved around Bonash to stand beside Bear.

I should have been warned by their expressions. Bonash was skilled in healing and could have assisted a spell-weaver with repairing the injuries. Bonash and I had healed potentially fatal wounds on many occasions. He should have called for me. They should have been relieved that I had arrived. But I saw the extent of the damage and everything became clear.

The mess of flesh had once been a lean, graceful body. Her chest had been crushed, causing her infrequent breaths to be shallow and erratic. A large gash, clearly made by a daemon, ripped across her abdomen to expose a mash of tissue no longer identifiable as skin or muscle or organ. I could not believe she was still alive after sustaining that much damage. I looked at Bonash and saw the sheen of sweat on his forehead, telling of the desperate effort needed to keep her this side of death.

Shamed into action, I ignored my exhausted body and reached out to connect with Z'hara. My senses screamed at the touch of her tormented energies and I was pulled into the turmoil of her pain. Stabbing flashes of light blinded me as a kaleidoscope of angry colours swirled in nauseating spirals. I focused on a thread of black-green that snaked around her spine. I had seen that particular shade before and it had no right to be there. I followed the strand to a major blood vessel at the base of the ribs, finding the essence of Bonash woven within the tissues to prevent a catastrophic loss of blood. The wraith-wound would be the injury that killed her and I did not need reminding of the consequences of that.

I released a flare of golden light to burn the corruption. Darkness crowded in from the edges of my vision and my view became a small circle of energies, but my cleansing fire shrivelled the black-green veins infiltrating my friend's body. It was not enough. The pollution receded for barely a heartbeat before flooding back. I drew more power and forced the tendrils away from the damage being held together by Bonash. It was a temporary reprieve. I needed to remove all the corruption before I could even begin to think about repairing the daemon injuries, and I was so tired. I felt my sense of *self* dissolving into Z'hara's energies as they greedily sucked at my vitality. I was finding it harder to resist the pull but knew I had to remove the stain if I was to prevent her transition into a wraith. I gathered the final strands of my energy.

I screamed. The sudden wrenching of my aura from Z'hara's flayed my senses into a tidal wave of torment. Every cell in my body felt scalded. My panicked mind tried to separate from the fading presence of Z'hara's energies while I tried to return to her, needing to complete the healing. Elyos's blurred face was too close to mine. The roar of noise raged in my head and deafened me to his words. He shook my head, rattling my traumatised mind and causing the world to tilt sharply. I closed my eyes and swallowed against the threat of vomiting. My senses slowly settled and, by the time I opened my eyes, my vision had steadied.

'Mobis's Torments, Tallen.' His hands cradled my face so that I looked directly into his concerned eyes. 'Killing yourself is not going to save her.'

I knocked his hands away and, irritated by an itching nose, rubbed at my face. I spent too long looking at the blood on my fingers, trying to understand why I was bleeding when it was Z'hara who was hurt. Elyos shook me again to return my attention to him.

'Her injuries are too severe,' he continued. 'Not even you can repair that much damage.'

Despite my obvious condition, I refused to believe him and pushed him away. I drunkenly rose from the kneeling position, having no recollection of collapsing several paces from Z'hara, but quickly realised I had made no difference to her terrible injuries. I swayed slightly, vaguely aware of Elyos's support, and watched the tears stream down Bonash's face. It seemed my strength had been enough to ease her suffering a little, and it had allowed her to open her eyes and see Vallori looking back at her. So much was spoken in that shared gaze. I stood paralysed by the emotions distorting Vallori's face. I felt more helpless than when facing the daemons of my night-terrors. The burning in my chest was worse than any wound I had ever received. The agony was all-consuming, knowing there was nothing I could do to ease his pain.

Z'hara took a rattling breath and Vallori squeezed her hand tightly in response. 'I need you to do it,' she whispered.

Vallori shook his head, a single tear rolling down his cheek when he blinked. 'I can't.'

'Please. I can feel it. It's taking me.' She paused while a tremor rippled through her body. 'I don't want to be one of those.'

I miserably relaxed my focus to reveal her tortured aura. Wisps of green were already weaving around her, drawing her soul into the realm of the wraiths. I had achieved nothing.

'You can't ask me to do that.' Vallori's voice cracked as he pleaded. 'I can't.'

Z'hara struggled to talk but persisted, causing more of her aura to fade while the wraith-mist grew thicker. Bonash would not be able to hold her for much longer.

'A mortal wound. It means a clean death. I need to die by human hands.'

Her body arched in a spasm of pain, causing Vallori to grip her hand so hard his knuckles showed white through the skin. His face was contorted by intolerable grief. Her aura was almost gone.

'I need you to do this,' she whispered so very quietly. 'I want to go. While I still know you. While I still love you.'

My body refused to breathe. Vallori's face shifted, having made his decision. A fixed mask covered his agony when he raised her hand and gently kissed her knuckles. Maintaining eye contact with her, he slid his hunting knife from its sheath and placed the point over her heart. She gave him a small smile and he plunged the blade into her heart. My own heart shattered in response. Sharp shards of glass embedded into my chest so they ripped afresh on every tortured breath. Vallori seemed so very far away. I watched his rigid expression fight with the uncontrollable trembling that wracked his body. He carefully removed his knife for Z'hara to exhale her last breath and her eyes glazed into sightlessness.

My mind became disconnected. I was no longer able to acknowledge or process the destruction of Vallori's spirit when he lifted the bloodied blade and hacked at his hair in the traditional Gallowgla display of extreme grief. A high-pitched ringing hurt my ears and my body started to shake in a poor reflection of Vallori's despair. I roughly shoved away from Elyos's support in a sudden need to get away from the unbearable misery. My breathing was too quick and too shallow. My heart was racing uncontrollably. I was sweating and I was light-headed. My eyes restlessly searched for the unseen threat while my mind screamed that there was danger everywhere. I had to escape. I had to run. I stumbled backwards. Hostility surrounded me. Someone grabbed my arm. I tried to pull away but the grip was too strong. My body shook violently and my mind screamed with the warning of imminent disaster.

I looked at Bear. Solid, familiar Bear.

He maintained his hold, preventing me from bolting while I fought to control my panic. I repeatedly told myself that there was no danger here. I was amongst friends. Over and over. But my heart continued to race and the broken pieces of my heart continued to rip into my chest.

'Tallen?' he asked gently.

My panic flared in response to his voice and I struggled again to remove his grip. 'I can't...' I stammered. 'I can't.'

'Don't do this,' he pleaded. His expression stabbed new holes in my heart, adding more sorrow to this hateful day.

'I can't stay here. I just can't.'

'You have the soul of a wolf, Tallen. Wolves need a pack. They do not do well on their own.' He sighed sadly. 'Remember that we are here, waiting, when your revenge is sated. Or you find it is not enough.'

CHAPTER FIFTEEN

My feet followed the trail without thought while my body fought against the surging tide of fatigue. I was cold and shivering and I stumbled several times when I failed to notice where I placed my feet. I was tired. So very tired.

The small shepherd's hut was not far from the trail. No light was visible from the windows and there was no smell of smoke. I needed no further convincing to investigate more closely. The single-storey structure was constructed from tightly packed stone and a turf roof that made it look crude and basic, but it had withstood generations of harsh weather and would offer a welcomed shelter. The plain wooden door fit snugly and opened with ease into a single room. A central fireplace sat within the far wall, with a table and chairs arranged to the right and a narrow bed to the left.

The place had been effectively cleared when the occupant left with even the mattress missing. A cloak had been carelessly thrown over a rough-cut chest and the reason it had been discarded became clear when I lifted it up. The bottom half was almost completely separated from the main part of the garment, with only two areas holding the material attached so that one firm tug would have reduced its length by half. The coarse wool was scratchy and some creature had chewed several small holes, but it was more than I had and I gratefully wrapped it around my chilled body. I curled into a ball, succumbing to the physical exhaustion of expending too much magick.

I awoke cold and cramped but feeling much restored. My next priority became one of food and I searched the hut for what it had to offer. The shelf above the table and chairs contained a number of small containers but these only held a few stale crumbs and a single, dry, shrivelled mint-leaf. I sharply regretted all the small possessions I had abandoned. The basic supplies of cups and clothing, the herbs and ointments used for healing, and my store of poisons. I was surprised by how much I regretted losing Trefin.

I followed a drover's trail around the base of the mountains and hills that formed the spine of Hilman, separating the more fertile farming lands of the west from the desolate moors of the east. The corruption of the land was grimly evident. I walked in a dead landscape of decaying hedgerows and diseased woodlands. Less frequently, but more disturbingly, I saw changes on a massive scale. The sides of hills had been sheared by massive rock-falls to expose stark, lifeless cliffs. Vast areas of mountain had been blackened as if burnt by intense wildfires, leaving cemetery forests of dead, skeletal trees. The sense of *wrongness* clung like a lingering bad taste.

The exhaustion had returned by late afternoon and I could no longer ignore the lack of food. The devastated land could offer nothing, with even berries and seeds being beyond its ability. I surrendered to my body's needs and reached out for the energies within the soil and stones, finding it disturbingly easy to justify my violation as insignificant when compared to that of the shamans. Villermir's vile presence battered against my defences when I made the connection but still I soaked in the invigorating energy, savouring the power which warmed my muscles and revitalised my stamina. It was with some reluctance that I withdrew contact.

My dreams swiftly returned me to a landscape where malice hid within the encroaching darkness and I was chased through twisted woodlands. Wolf howls became distorted into chilling screams that promised torment and pain. Branches snatched at me, slicing my skin with sharp twig-fingers. Shadows flickered at the edges of my vision, disappearing if I turned to look. Malevolent orange eyes glowed from the dark fog that was racing to engulf me. Monstrous bat-winged wolves leapt to snap at my legs. Over and over, I would stumble or trip. The ground falling away and my vision turning so I would see the wolves pounce, ripping and tearing a body that had once been mine.

On many occasions, the terrifying dreams were replaced with ones where the colours were more vibrant, more defined. In these I soared over battlefields, able to identify the small differences that separated raider from resistance despite the great height. Sluagh's wraith army floated throughout but I had no interest in them. I shrieked my challenge to the foul daemons that rampaged in their panic. The stupid creatures were aware enough to fear my presence. I opened my mouth and released rivers of fire. I ripped and bit and hunted and crushed. My blood sang with the joy of doing what I was created to do. What I had been denied for so long. I roared, rejoicing with the glorious pleasure of annihilating daemons.

Rarely, the dragon's dream took a darker turn and these I hated the most. A firestorm would be released that would cover half the battlefield. Wraiths evaporated instantly and daemons burned. Humans, both raider and resistance, were reduced to charcoal silhouettes or melted away to nothing.

My path headed roughly south-east, towards the green lights and their promise of daemons. I walked, day after day, with the trail becoming progressively more damp and more muddy. The carpeting moss had retained much of the moisture from recent rains to create a saturated turf that sucked at my boots. The land became flatter and drainage became stagnated, turning large areas into bog where I skipped from grassy tussock to wiry heather to avoid the more water-logged sections.

The open moorlands clearly displayed the damage Villermir's abuse of the Empathy Crystal had caused. Long ridges dominated the blighted landscape where the earth had shifted and the ground had buckled. The scars stood as tall as a man in many places, revealing the dark, peaty soil and looking as if massive claws had scratched into the land. I crossed the desolate moor, feeling exposed and vulnerable. I increasingly used magick to raise my temperature against the biting, icy winds and to replenish my energy in the absence of adequate food and rest. I ignored the implications of my sustained exploitation of the land's power and focused on the ways in which I could kill as many daemons as possible. I analysed strategies to find the most effective methods at my disposal; what traps would work best for containing man-daemons, which sword strokes would cause the greatest damage to stampeding horse-daemons, what magicks would be most useful for destroying bird-daemons.

The presence of a treeline on the horizon was a welcome distraction from the monotony of bleak moorland, promising a return to more populated areas where I may be able to steal food. At the very least, it promised shelter from the relentless wind. I had not travelled far into the forest before I detected the subtle signs of human activity, flattened bracken where someone had walked off the trail, broken twigs when held for support, and a footprint left in the mud. I found it easy to follow the two men and one woman as they scouted the eastern edges of the forest. They were inexperienced and rarely looked up, allowing me to remain safely hidden within the branches above them when they stopped for a hasty meal. They discussed the danger of a raider's camp nearby but, having assured themselves that no attack was imminent, the conversation quickly turned to the domestic concerns of people I did not know. I soon became bored and moved to wedge myself deeper between the trunk and its surrounding branches, dozing into an uncomfortable sleep.

The scouts had gone by the time I awoke but I had a reasonable idea of where their camp was situated and found it easily enough. The camp was small and hidden within a dell that created a natural bowl around a gently flowing stream. Their shelters were crude, with some having simply thrown blankets over the branches to form a basic tent. I saw only two women in the group of around twenty, and all lacked the carriage and awareness of trained fighters. I felt no desire to join them, having total conviction that it was better for everybody that I remained on my own, but the smell of their cooking had my stomach cramping. The sweet aroma of warm oats was mouth-wateringly seductive and I siphoned some energy from a nearby tree in order to silence my hunger. I had almost decided to abandon caution and join the group when a scout ran into the dell.

'They've found us,' he declared, sliding to a halt while the others gathered around him. 'The raiders are in the forest. They're heading this way. We need to leave. Now!'

The camp fractured into a chaotic frenzy, with each fighter wavering between grabbing weapons and collecting personal possessions, and they had still not prepared themselves by the time the enemy was heard crashing through the trees. The raiders were not quiet. Their howling and taunting fanned the panic that had already been simmering close to the surface. The fighters finally realised that their possessions would be of no use to them if they were dead, but it was already too late. The raiders had divided into two groups and moved to surround the camp. Cursing, I randomly chose the group to my right and slipped through the woods to engage them. I struck quickly and lethally, stabbing at a pirate then blending back into shadows, but the raiders had people to spare and I made little difference. They efficiently herded us towards the edges of the woodland.

The desperate group fought for their lives, and managed to kill a few, but the raiders could have easily overwhelmed us had that been their intention. Instead, they played with their victims. They inflicted superficial wounds and minor injuries while they laughed and jeered, gleefully pushing us out of the trees and into the open heathland. The fighters were focused on the raiders and they failed to see the single shaman who danced at their backs. They did not see the wraith-army materialise. Only when a man-daemon roared its challenge did they turn, standing frozen in terror. My lips curled into a snarl when two of the monsters charged towards the hapless fighters.

'My turn,' I growled.

I ran out of the treeline, releasing a fireball to incinerate the wraiths while I raced towards the daemons. The shaman shrieked in anger, or pain. I did not care which. I embraced the opportunity to confront the monsters whose attention was now firmly placed on me, leaving the group to face the fully engaged raiders. *Saorsa*'s exquisite song filled my mind and I sliced her blade into the giant thigh of the first daemon. Pearls of green floated into the sky as I ducked under the descending fist of the second daemon. I twisted and spun around the two beasts, darting around them like an annoying insect. I played with them as the raiders had toyed with the fighters, finally able to release my frustration and pain at a deserving target. I bathed in emerald rain as *Saorsa* took bite after bite of daemon flesh. I finally severed the neck of one, allowing me to give my full attention to the other. I danced around his crushing fists, jumping away from his stamping feet, and laughing at its impotent rage. I roared in triumph as my sword opened its belly, using the backswing to remove its head when it curled forward.

I released a fireball into the remaining wraiths and searched for my next daemon victim, but the raiders had recognised the risk I presented and a number were surrounding their vulnerable sorcerer while they guided him away. I ignored the flicker of disappointment at being denied more daemons and turned to assist the fighters in encouraging the final raiders to retreat.

I withdrew my blade from the belly of the last pirate and turned to find myself surrounded by eight of the fighters. All had their swords pointed at my chest. Appreciating the irony of having just saved their miserable lives, I slowly lowered *Saorsa* and carefully raised my free hand in a gesture of peace.

'I'm not a raider. I mean you no harm.'

An older man pushed through the ring of blades to confront me. He held a wound below his ribs that seeped blood through his fingers and I saw that almost half the fighters had fallen, along with the five dead raiders.

'What are you?' he accused.

'I'm just here to help.'

'We want none of your magicks,' snapped a bloodied fighter. 'Your kind are the reason these monsters are here.'

His words carried the echoes of Baila's rhetoric, and others nodded and mumbled their agreement. Fear had been swiftly replaced by hate now they held the perceived advantage of numbers.

'My *kind* are the only ones that stand a chance of saving your sorry souls.' I raised my voice, persisting when they started to protest. 'You want to fight? Find a resistance group that knows how to deal with this enemy and do everything they tell you. Find one with dream-walkers who can warn you of attacks. One with spell-weavers who can heal your wounds. One with enchanted blades that can kill the daemons before they crush you like bugs.'

A young fighter, brave with righteous anger, stepped forward to rest his weapon on my shoulder. The blade trembled where he held it close to my neck. 'Or maybe we should kill you now and have one less heretic to worry about.'

My mocking glance was enough to provoke his growl of outrage. I easily stepped to the side when he drew back for a backhanded slice, bringing *Saorsa's* hilt smashing onto his shoulder and numbing his arm. The remaining fighters closed in when his sword dropped from nerveless fingers, but they never stood a chance. I was a trained soldier. A Moon Warrior. They were farmers and labourers, and I disarmed them with embarrassing speed. I scanned all their faces. All looked at me with fear and hatred used to cover shame and helplessness.

'Go home,' I told them. 'Your deaths will only serve to feed their wraith-army.'

I turned to leave, confident that not one would follow.

The camp contained, perhaps, fifty pirates and they were confident in their numbers. No scouts patrolled the surrounding area. No guards scanned the trees that bordered the small clearing where they had set up their base. It made it laughably easy for me to watch them cook their evening meals or repair torn clothing and damaged armour. I dismissed the fighters and studied the shaman who sat in an island of calm, surrounded by the flow of domestic activity. He was less intimidating, dressed in leather trousers and a plain woollen shirt which covered the clay symbols marking his body. His hair remained spiked with lime and ash but his small frame, in contrast to the heavy-set soldiers, made him look deceptively vulnerable. His shrewd eyes were hidden as he crouched over a set of engraved stone tiles and studied them for portents and auguries. I was not fooled by his meek demeanour, clearly seeing the swirl of energies which buzzed around him like flies on a dung heap.

I waited until the moon was high in the sky and bathing the camp in light and shadow. The raiders had noisily drunk themselves into a snoring slumber, wrapped in blankets around the embers of the small fires with only a few left on watch. I remained hidden within the shadows and slipped amongst the sleeping bodies to where the shaman had claimed the only shelter. No light escaped from the canvas tent and I heard no sounds to suggest he was awake, but still I listened for the slow, rhythmic breathing which would confirm he was asleep. I checked one last time to ensure none of the raiders were looking in my direction and, satisfied that my entrance would remain unnoticed, slipped inside. The moon escaped from the cover of a cloud when I carefully closed the flap, and its light briefly illuminated the rim of a bronze bowl. My heart thumped painfully in confirmation of my fear that a bowl of my blood was used to call the daemons, before cursing myself as a fool. The bowl could be used for any number of routine reasons that did not involve the ritualised summoning of ghosts and monsters. The items placed alongside the bowl, a hand-mirror, a fine-toothed comb and a small dagger, certainly suggested a more mundane use.

My eyes adjusted to the dim lighting and I turned my attention to the shaman. He was curled on his side facing away from me. Beneath him a sheepskin provided some protection from the damp ground while a woollen blanket covered him to provide warmth. I stood over him for some time, watching his chest rise and fall in a peaceful sleep. He did not appear to be troubled by the torments his creatures unleashed. No night-terrors played behind his closed eyelids. No ghosts haunted his dreams. It was so tempting to blame this individual for all the horrors created by the Fates. This slight old man became the focus for all my frustration and hatred and pain.

I calmly removed my dagger from its sheath. I wanted to see his face when he realised that all his power could not protect him from a blade in the dark. I grasped his shoulder and pulled him towards me, quickly clamping his mouth and nose closed when he rolled onto his back. I watched his eyes snap open then widen in fear and I rammed my knife into his throat. He thrashed in choking panic, but his limbs were restricted by the blanket and the thickness of the sheepskin muffled the sound of his drumming heels. No one came to his aid and suffocation quickly dimmed his sight. I withdrew the blade at an angle to sever the major artery, ensuring massive blood loss would finish the kill. One less shaman to terrorise the Three Kingdoms.

A peal of thunder rumbled around the forest in the absence of any lightning or rain. I remembered that daemons were Taranis's creatures and the shamans would work on his behalf. I half-expected to be struck down in divine retribution, but all remained calm and the single boom faded away.

I remained standing over the dead sorcerer for some time, waiting for an inner acknowledgement that I had achieved something significant. I eventually accepted that this was just one of many shamans and there was much work left to do. I turned to leave but my attention caught on a pendant that hung around the sorcerer's neck. I reached forward, using my bloodied dagger to cut the leather cord, and retrieved the small glass vial. It was a little over half-full of a thick, dark liquid and a plug of cork contained the fluid. It smeared the glass with a sticky coating when I rotated the item. As with the bronze bowl, I had no way of knowing the purpose of the item but I doubted it was for simple decoration. I searched its energies, swiftly withdrawing when the familiar aura of blood sucked at me with a foul, corrupted presence. I dropped the vial and crushed the glass under the heel of my boot, again waiting for some dire repercussion as the blood seeped into the dirt. No vengeful spirit claimed justice for my destruction and I grinned smugly in the darkness; killing shamans was a lot easier than trying to kill Baila's priests.

I became a ghost. Guided by the green lights, I located the pirate settlements and crept in to kill their shamans while they slept, destroying the vile cylinders of blood that each wore around their neck. It took a while but rumours spread of a wandering spirit who could enter armed camps undetected, killing shamans while leaving no other trace of having been there. The fighters became superstitious and more vigilant, and guards were set to watch, but I gained confidence with each attack and readily avoided their precautions. I started to feel invincible, siphoning power from the land to give me increased stamina and a heightened awareness. I used the stolen energies to maintain my body, no longer searching for the mundane needs of food and drink, and my mind completely focused on the goal of eliminating the sorcerers who danced to the call of the Fates. I moved readily from those with a single shaman to camps that boasted a pair, finally moving to ones that contained three or four. I took pride in my ability to dispatch one without waking the others. As the number of shamans increased, the camps grew to contain hundreds of fighters who were more disciplined and better organised. It became a welcome challenge to approach without being seen, to enter without alerting the scouts who patrolled the boundaries, and to evade the guards who had been set to protect the valuable enchanters. I could no longer move quickly between camps, forced to spend longer observing their routines, identifying their weaknesses, and finding opportunities to exploit. Their increasing measures of protection remained contemptuously within my capabilities.

It required no thought to move from killing shamans to ruthlessly dealing with any raider who stood between me and that goal. Scouts would be removed to allow access into the camp. Those on watch would be arranged in poses that, at a glance, would be seen as bored dozing. The guards defending the shamans were dealt with, and I did not hesitate to use magick when a single sentry became two, or three, or four. I casually used my elemental control of air to subdue any sorcerer that woke, taking cruel pleasure in their naked fear when they watched me kill their brethren. I justified my actions against the horror they had released with their foul monsters, and I wrapped myself in the blanket of my righteous crusade against their invading evil.

The village sat nestled between the base of a rolling hill and a wide, fast-flowing river. A pair of river barges were tied to a large jetty that extended far across the water. The settlement was large enough to hold a tavern by the waterside, a communal hall in the centre of the village, and a busy forge which filled the air with the smell of ash and hot metal. A small market square in front of the hall contained a few stalls selling food and drink, leather goods and farm tools, and a merchant offering jewellery and decorative items. I walked anonymously through the streets. My hood was pulled low along with everyone else's while the rain lashed down and forced people to hurry about their business. No one was concerned with a stranger brought in by the weekly market. I stood uncomfortably close to those with strong Gallowgla accents while they negotiated prices or terms of barter. The villagers seemed content to trade with the outsiders and showed no signs of fear or distrust, much less hatred or oppression. Their easy acceptance of the raiders was unsettling when shamans were raising daemons less than a week's walk away. People were very good at ignoring the horrors that stalked them, preferring to focus on the day-to-day tasks which gave an element of control over their lives. The calm domesticity of the market contrasted sharply with the factional hatred I had seen in the towns, where Baila's priests fed on fears and prejudices.

I did not linger long and retreated to a shepherd's hut further up the hill that had been abandoned for the winter months. I had obtained a small amount of food from the market, and a large bottle of a spirited drink that was close enough to Elyos's fiery brew. I was in a constant state of twitching agitation from being alone in a tormented land and surrounded by enemies. I slept fitfully, with recurring dreams of daemons and unseen terrors hunting me. The fire-in-a-bottle drink was the only thing that quietened the noise for a while, allowing me to get some of rest. The chronic fatigue and persistent tremors caused by my reckless use of power, combined with my frequent need to leech energy from the abused land, made me increasingly reliant on the fermented liquid. I greedily welcomed the warm comfort it gave whenever I could obtain it, as well as its ability to silence the small, nagging voice of guilt that warned of my pending self-destruction.

I scratched at a scab and felt the sticky fluid ooze out of the wound. I wrinkled my nose in disgust as I lifted my sleeve to look at the inflamed mess of my lower arm. My nails had clawed away the covering tissue and a malodourous, yellow paste leaked from the infected gash. The numerous wraith-wounds itched incessantly and my scratching had caused them to fester. Large, red blotches radiated heat, encircling each of the smaller cuts that covered my arms and ribs. A particularly frustrating one throbbed in the centre of my back, so that I would rub against surfaces like a horse scratching against a fence to relieve its itch. Cauterising the wounds would silence their irritation, and I had initially dealt with the smaller wounds, but I always found an excuse to delay the painful procedure until I lacked the courage to address the festering mess.

I had never found the strength to burn the deep wound on my hip. It was swollen and discoloured, with the skin pulled painfully tight by the pressure of inflamed tissue and a significant amount of thick pus. I was finding it harder to mask the pain through the use of magick and my lameness was becoming a significant issue. I swallowed a large mouthful of the spirited drink, finally accepting that I needed to address these injuries.

Starting with the one I had just traumatised, I created a thin sheet of flame and smothered the wound. I gasped as the fire scorched the damaged tissue and sent tendrils of pain throughout my arm. I gagged on the stench of burnt discharge, the foul odour mixing nauseatingly with that of roasted skin. The room tilted and I cracked the back of my head against the rough wall behind me. The sudden flare of pain acted as a distraction from the agony throbbing in my arm and stabilised my vision. I took several rapid, shallow breaths. Sweat beaded on my forehead and between my shoulder blades.

It was some time before my heart rate slowed and my breathing returned to normal, and I dared to look at the damage done. The skin was blistered, with areas that were open and oozing, but the fluid was clear. All trace of the thick pus was gone and I no longer felt the invasive feelers infiltrating the surrounding tissue. I tentatively stretched and flexed my fingers. I felt the pull of traumatised skin but without the pulsing ache that had previously accompanied any movement.

Addressing the next wound took more courage now I knew of the pain involved. I debated whether to cauterise one at a time, leaving the next until the first had healed, but I knew well enough to recognise this as an avoidance tactic. I had created one reason after another to avoid the discomfort, and this had resulted in the damage I was currently facing. The hut was sheltered and the rain hammering against the roof would discourage any casual traveller. I was unlikely to find such protection again and I could not delay any longer.

It had been dark for some time before I had finished treating all the smaller wounds, each throbbing in time with my heartbeat to create a symphony of dull pain. I was exhausted, slumped against the cold stone wall while my legs twitched with frequent tremors. I held myself very still but took some comfort that the torment came from healthy, natural damage rather than the corrupted touch of the wraiths. I focused on the small details of each injury, carefully avoiding the fact that the worst one was yet to come. The flame required to cauterise that one would need to be so much bigger, so much hotter than the previous attempts. I had barely managed to stay conscious with the previous attempts and I had no doubt that I would get only one chance at cleansing that injury. The angry mess throbbed defiantly, as if mocking my cowardice. Taunting me with my fears that I was not strong enough to complete the final treatment.

I bashed my head against the wall once more in frustration, briefly distracted by the thought that there was going to be a sizeable lump there. The sharp pain gave me a focus and I gathered my depleted resources, committing to the final burning. I drained the bottle of fiery courage and anxiously created a fireball. I rotated and compressed it until it filled my cupped hand and blazed white-hot. My face felt tight with the sphere's radiating heat as I watched the colours ripple beneath the surface. I spun it slowly, admiring the beauty of its power. I delayed until I could delay no longer.

Channelling all the rage and frustration I felt, I slammed the blazing fireball into the wraith-wound. I momentarily smelt the stench of scorched tissue and heard the sizzle of burning flesh, before my scream sounded very distant and I gratefully plunged into the waiting oblivion.

CHAPTER SIXTEEN

With the raiders' camps becoming increasing more secure, my path gradually drifted westward. The scenery changed when I crossed the base of Hilman's spine and normal life persisted with the return of more managed farmland. I regularly shared roads with merchants and farmers who were travelling to the towns and villages to trade. In contrast to those I'd seen further north, the lowland towns readily welcomed strangers and buzzed with colourful, noisy markets and stores. I was able to walk the streets, raising nothing more than mild distaste at my dishevelled appearance.

My priorities also changed with the return of civilisation. I still destroyed any raider camp I encountered but I no longer actively sought them. I became increasingly exposed to the presence of Baila and, with my crumbling mental defences leaving me vulnerable to the land's suffering at the hands of Villermir, I readily transferred my hatred to his priests. The religion's influence wove through the towns like dark threads in a vibrant tapestry, agitating my already sensitised state. The restrictive dress and cowered demeanour of the women may have been absent, with female stallholders hawking their wares as brashly as any in Liegeport, but the markets selling young men and girls remained and I saw the women repeatedly defer to men in numerous different ways. Baila's temples dominated the towns as a constant reminder to the people that their actions were being judged. The subtle message was reinforced by the number of priests who walked among the crowds. Their austere robes and tonsured scalps added to their paternal benevolence to create the impression that they were something more than those around them. I watched with contempt while the townspeople bowed and flattered, belittling themselves to gain favour while the priests remained condescendingly aloof.

The confidence I had gained from raiding the shamans' camps had slipped easily into arrogance, and I followed a particularly querulous priest along a row of stalls. I smiled at his frequent searches for something he could not find, unable to determine its source as the ripples of energy I constantly radiated. I stood within five paces of the old fool and he still could not locate the cause of his irritation, quickly dismissing me as a noisome beggar who was so far beneath him that I warranted no more than a cursory glance. He took his frustration out on the stallholders, increasing his offensive behaviour to women in particular. He talked over them, rejected their opinions and disregarded their advice. He refused to accept the true value of any item, claiming extortion, and would only agree to less than half of its true worth. He carried a tall staff and used it to painful effect on anyone who was slow to move out of his way, freely chastising any who failed to give due reverence.

He remained a bleakly amusing distraction, confirming many of my prejudices concerning Baila's priesthood, until he stumbled into a young boy who was sitting beside his family's stall playing with a small wooden hare. The priest had not paid attention to where he was placing his feet and had tripped over the boy's legs, tumbling into the stall. I suspected that embarrassment was a potent motivator when his conceited blustering took a nastier turn.

'You vile whelp,' he spluttered, using his staff to deliver a stinging blow to the lad's arm. 'You tripped me on purpose.'

The child sat frozen while the old man towered over him. The disturbance had attracted everyone's attention and the boy's gaze fearfully darted from the priest to the crowd, to his parents, and back to the priest. The boy's father tried to calm the situation while his mother rushed to remove her son, but the spiteful old man had jabbed his staff into the child's belly and had effectively pinned him to the ground.

'What manner of heresy is this?' he continued, kicking the toy hare. 'Do you pray to your false Gods and curse an old man to stumble? Does your hare idol govern you to cause harm to a priest of Baila?'

The accusation was absurd. It was a child's toy. His words, however, resonated with a crowd who were subtly, but constantly, influenced by Baila. The family became isolated with the crowd swiftly turning into a menacing mob. The prejudices and hatred so evident in the northern towns may have been masked earlier, but they sat close to the surface and were readily released on finding a suitable target. What better way to reinforce your allegiance than by rapidly distancing yourself from those who are different, claiming you never trusted them, and you always knew there was something strange about them. The child's parents shared an anxious look, aware of the danger they were in, while people they had known all their lives crowded in to hurl accusations.

'My apologies, your eminence,' offered the father, bowing in subservience. 'He's just a silly boy. He meant no harm. It was just an unfortunate accident.'

The priest snapped his glare from the young lad to the father. 'This was no accident. This is witchcraft. You allow your child to meddle with graven images of foul Gods. You have brought evil to this place.'

The mob muttered in agreement and pressed in, excited by the promise of violence. The mother cuddled her son, afraid to move and draw attention to herself and her child. The father stuttered and flustered while he tried to find a way to placate the priest. He had remained behind his stall and grasped desperately at its offered solution.

'You misunderstand, your eminence. We are simple wood carvers making decorative items to bring small pleasure in these dark times.' He spread his arms wide to encompass his goods. 'Please. Take whatever you wish as a meagre gesture. An apology for an inconvenience caused.'

It was the wrong decision. The old man's face clouded with the suggestion of a bribe, but turned thunderous when the gesture highlighted the contents of the stall. Several beautifully carved wooden ornaments were displayed; engraved bowls, polished wooden eggs and orbs, long thin containers ending in delicate spirals. Amongst these innocuous items, however, were several animal statues; hares, hounds, owls, stags, squirrels. Creatures of the countryside. Creatures that had been used since the beginning of memory to symbolise the Gods.

The priest screamed in rage. 'Idolatry!'

He slammed his staff down on the carvings, smashing several of the more delicate items. He swiped the rod across the surface, causing many more items to break when they fell to the floor, and clubbed at the statues left standing. The mother chose his petulant distraction to slip behind the stall, aiming for some protection from the priest's wrath and the crowd's hostility. Her movement returned the old man's attention to her son who was still grasping his toy in a vain attempt at comfort. The priest viciously cracked the staff over the boy's hands, making him drop the toy, then turned it to strike the child's head. The boy folded, crying, into his mother's lap while blood trickled down his temple. The priest smashed the base of his staff down onto the toy, breaking off the ears. He growled in frustration, raising the stick to deliver greater damage to the offensive carving and the sobbing child.

He stopped with his arm still in the air and gagged. Then choked. He gagged again, coughing up a mouthful of water which he spat onto the ground. His eyes grew wide when he choked again and his chest heaved with the effort of trying to get air into his lungs. More water was coughed out of his mouth and he grasped the stall for support. I calmly watched while he struggled to breathe, filling his lungs with the fluid I forced out of the surrounding tissues and drowning him in his own liquids.

I remained overlooked in the chaos that surrounded the dying priest, staying only long enough to see the family slip away to safety while they were forgotten in the confusion.

The wind howled through the rocky peaks of the mountain. I perched on the towering precipice and its lashing turbulence caressed my skin. I stretched in pleasure, flexing my toes so my talons chipped stones from the boulder. I breathed in the icy cold air and looked down on the forest so very far below. More pebbles tumbled down the rock-face when I pushed off, spreading my wings to glide before catching the warm thermals which lifted me high into the sky. I flew east over hills and heath. I drifted down to skim over a massive lake that extended far across the narrow waist of this northern landscape, almost separating the top section from the remaining land. I continued over a rolling mountain range where snow dusted the upper slopes. I flew as far as the sea before banking and following the coastline south. The strong winds created white peaks on the waves and the dark grey water crashed into the rocky shoreline. Further out, dolphins crested the stormy surface. I briefly harassed a pod before moving on. I had more important matters to address.

Further down the coast, a small fleet of five ships aimed for a sandy beach and the protection of a narrow cove. Their sails were snapped taut by the strong winds that propelled the vessels towards their landing. I lazily drifted out to intercept the ship in front, amused by the sailors who skittered about like insects when they saw me. Without interrupting the rhythm of my wingbeats, I released a river of my glorious fire and the ship became engulfed in flames. The waterproofing oils readily ignited and funnelled the flames into a tall inferno. A few sailors managed to jump overboard, but I disregarded them and the remaining ships as unimportant. The prickle of energies was becoming insistent so I increased my speed to race along the shoreline.

I screeched in delight when I saw them. The ships had landed on a long, shingle beach where gently rolling dunes created a border against the moor. The invaders had not been able to travel far from their vessels, an army had waited in ambush and the two now clashed close to the dunes. I screamed again on seeing the number of daemons present. All five shamans had raised their monsters to wreak destruction. There were so many for me to play with. So many for me to destroy. I turned and banked towards the moor, releasing a torrent of fire to incinerate the four bird-daemons that dared to confront me.

I ripped. I bit. I slashed. I tore. I flew through clouds of daemon blood. My fire smothered the abhorrent ghost-army. My talons sliced into daemon flesh. My teeth grasped and my jaws crushed. I chased after a pair of horse-daemons that stampeded through the humans. I swiped at the haunch of the nearest, flipping it so it crashed into the ground and twisted its neck into an unnatural position. I swept in before it had the chance to repair itself and emerald mist surrounded me. I turned towards the second daemon. It foolishly thought to challenge me, ungracefully kicking out with its thick forelimbs. I extended my rear talons and descended, striking into the beast like an eagle pinning a hare. Its horn grazed my belly when it thrashed its head. I slammed down to crush its chest.

The shamans continued to prance in the dunes. I rumbled in contempt at their juvenile antics. Insignificant humans pretending to be Gods. I spat a globule of fire at them, already rising into the air as they burned. Only one had been aware enough to run from me. He had avoided the worst of the flames but his back had still blustered from the heat and he had collapsed from the pain, scrabbling into the coarse grasses in his attempts to drag himself away from the carnage. It was pathetic. I swooped down and grasped his head, shaking him like a terrier with a rat. His neck was already broken before I dropped him. A discarded, broken toy.

I soared over the battlefield. The daemons and the wraiths had dissolved. A few humans wandered amongst the many dead. I dismissed them as unimportant, climbing high into the air to pirouette in smug satisfaction following the destruction of so many daemons.

You should be here. You should be with me.

I woke with my heart pounding, frantically grasping after the retreating warm emotions of safety and belonging, desperate to obey the voice that asked me to join her, while denying it was anything more than a dream. I refused to accept that the painful thumping of my head was in any way the same as that I had felt on my journey to release Megin. I clenched my eyes tightly closed to prevent the stabbing light from entering, but my vision still swam with sickening flashes of red and white. My entire body felt pierced by sharp needles, creating a constant disharmony of small agonies that discouraged even the slightest movement. I tried not to breathe, trying to limit the movement of my chest, but this only resulted in increasing the pressure in my head and caused the flashes to dance at dizzying speeds.

I slowly extended my arm to place the palm onto the cold ground. I gasped as the contact sent burning sparks racing along my limb and into my chest. My hand clenched into the dirt and my body arched in response to the land's torment. I clutched at the power vibrating beneath my hand, drawing it into my fingertips and letting it twist around my aura. I used the stolen energy to carefully rebuild my mental barriers, using the poisonous tendrils as part of the structure to hold the decaying walls together and plug the increasing number of holes.

The noise of the abused land subsided. I took a deep breath and my body returned to its normal, trembling state. I opened my eyes to see the sheltered rocky overhang I had crawled into and grounded myself in the reality of stone and moss. My face pulled into a feral snarl. I needed to hunt.

The raiders had pushed far into Hilman territory. The surrounding farms had been abandoned, with their victims herded towards the timber barricade protecting the village. The invaders had broken the double-doored gateway into the settlement by the time I arrived and I strode the main road towards the clash of conflict, no longer concerned with stealth and subterfuge. I knew what I was capable of and the raiders were not a threat to me. Their shaman danced on a small rise to the left of the village, but I was in no rush to deal with her. A welcome calm diffused through my body and I released *Saorsa*, having already selected the first to die.

I carved through the rear ranks, moving quickly to avoid being surrounded and trapped. The raiders' attention was on those in front of them and were too late to recognise the danger at their backs. My advance was stalled temporarily where a bottleneck had been created between the broken gates. I pushed through, relying on elbows and fists and the occasional forehead to force my way into the enclosure. Once past the obstruction, the fighting opened up and I joined villagers who were too busy to notice one more in the crowd, grateful I was killing their enemy and not them.

Fighting in the village was different to that on the exposed flatlands of the moors. The conflict was separated into multiple small groups within the structure imposed by buildings and streets. Enemies remained hidden behind walls and it was easy to get trapped with your back against an immovable barrier. Options became limited and strategies became blocked, and I abandoned any conscious plan or direction. I spent too much time reacting to threats that suddenly appeared, but the restricted environment worked for the disorganised rabble defending their homes. A few showed some training and ability, although most were farmers, merchants or labourers fighting with farm tools and kitchen cleavers. They would have been cut down in moments by an assembled force, but the confined spaces between shops and homes ensured they only ever faced one or two raiders at any time. Desperation gave them a ferocity that adequately compensated for their lack of skill.

Fighting within a settlement also affected the raiders. This was not the open expanse of a battlefield and they did not only encounter fighters. Mothers, children and the elderly had also taken shelter within the walled enclosure. Dogs ran wild, biting anything that moved and adding to the general chaos. Livestock squealed and bleated and lowed and squawked. They assaulted the senses with their frantic cries and the noxious stench of manure mixed with spilt blood. Smoke hung thick in the air from torched buildings and the flames drove their occupants into the slaughter. Surrounded by the madness, raiders were easily distracted and readily abandoned their companions for the treasures on offer. They raped as freely as they stole, consumed in a drunken hedonism fuelled by the intensity of the life-and-death battles all around them. The pitiful attempts to protect loved ones from such abuse sharpened my rage and I let *Saorsa* swing again and again.

In the overwhelming confusion, the wraiths were barely noticed. They eerily ghosted through the village, appearing from a building or wall to deliver a deep wound before vanishing again. I ignited any I saw but most remained elusive and I was unwilling to send fireballs blindly into structures that could contain terrified villagers. I moved from section to section, from one battling group to another, searching for the vile green spectres. Frustration added to the fury of my attacks on the pirates while the ghosts remained evasive. My efforts to destroy the shaman's foul creatures were as effectively thwarted as the raiders' attempts to crush the villagers. The sorceress seemed content to play with her victims, requiring only the skeletal army to haunt and maim and instil gut-chilling fear.

I had given up the hope of taking my anger out on any daemons when the ground trembled, heralding the arrival of the monsters. They thundered towards the enclosure and *Saorsa* sang in anticipation. Bird-daemons swept over the small market square, plucking screaming villagers and carrying them high into the air, before dropping them from a height to crush those frozen in horror below. I sliced *Saorsa* into any daemon neck that came too close.

The sound of shattering timber was soon followed by the stampeding land daemons, and the rhythmic crashing of destroyed buildings moved towards me in the centre of the settlement. I grinned in feral pleasure when the first horse-daemon appeared. The raiders and villagers ceased to exist, and all my attention turned to the monster charging towards me. Its head was lowered, moving from side-to-side to create a lethal dance with tusks slicing into any who were near it. Its giant feet crushed baskets and carts and people alike, never breaking the rhythm of its stride. I waited patiently, swiping in irritation at any raider who thought to attack while I focused on the beast. I waited until the last possible moment before twisting out of its way, casually dragging my blade across its neck and along its side. It bellowed and green daemon-blood haemorrhaged from the deep gash I had inflicted. It skidded to a halt, scattering people when it turned to face me, and pawed at the ground. It charged again and my grin widened as I played with the stupid creature, scoring a matching wound on its opposite flank. It tossed its head and snorted its annoyance, charging at me for the third time. I let *Saorsa* have her kill. She sliced so deep into the neck that her blade remained stuck within the tissues and I was dragged a few paces before the beast collapsed, dissolving into an emerald mist.

More daemons thundered into the square. Monstrous arms swung into walls, causing timber structures to snap like twigs and large boulders to fly from stone buildings. I no longer had time to play and destroyed the creatures quickly and efficiently. Weeks spent fighting the beasts had shown me their weaknesses; blind spots that could be exploited, thinner hide at the armpit and groin that could be easily opened, an inability to turn quickly that left them vulnerable to my agility. The settlement burned around me, with the timber quickly succumbing to the flames. The walled enclosure ceased to offer protection, now trapping the villagers inside a killing arena of sword and fire, wraith and daemon. Having no other option, they fled to the open land surrounding the village, carrying children and supporting the old and injured.

I ran through a destroyed section of wall to see a hellscape of bodies littering the ground. The majority of the raiders had withdrawn at the arrival of the daemons and they had waited for the fleeing villagers. They were experienced at fighting in the open and it had been a massacre. Almost all had been slain, including the parents who still cradled their children. My heart ached for the last few, battered fighters who were determined to inflict as much damage as they could, knowing their lives would not be spared.

I roared in frustration and anger and despair. I forced the air out of my lungs with such force that it caused a ripple to race away from me. The ring of compressed air sucked in all sound for a heartbeat before returning in a ground-shaking boom. The concussive wave knocked the air from the chests of all who surrounded me and I watched everyone collapse to the floor, gasping like stranded fish as they tried to force their lungs to inhale. They soon became still, with the daemons and wraiths evaporating when the shaman died.

I stood at the edge of a field covered with bodies and was sharply reminded of the carnage caused by the dream-dragon. I felt repulsed by the meaningless waste of life. I hated the pirates for having brought their sorcerers. I despised those who summoned their daemons to the Three Kingdoms. I clenched my fists in impotent rage.

The ground rippled. Then heaved. Then flowed to slowly smother the bodies and hide them from my sight. I turned in a half-circle and the earth moved to engulf the remains of the shattered village. It smoothed into a low, broad curve of turf that became a gently rolling hill. A barrow to cover the dead.

I wandered aimlessly after the burial of the village, gradually moving further into the heart of the kingdom and closer to the border with Lindvane. The rocky mountains of the north had smoothed into gentle hills and the fertile farmland had encouraged the population to grow. I blended easily with the merchants and their mercenaries who intermittently shared the roads. I encouraged their natural reticence around armed strangers and they did not look at me too closely.

The increasing presence of Baila's soldiers was harder to dismiss. The indifference seen in those further north was noticeably absent in these more populated areas. Travellers were frequently questioned and their wagons inspected, with the pious deference of those targeted now carrying a hint of fear. I avoided the soldiers wherever I could and when required, I slipped into the old habits of remaining invisible; avoiding eye contact, remaining small and unimportant, never being in a direct line of sight, making no sudden movements. I effectively concealed myself by being unremarkable and instantly forgettable.

The town was of a significant size, sitting proudly at the top of a hill that rose above a large area of flat farmland. It had attracted a number of travellers, with most being traders with pots or poultry, although some were family groups seeking the protection of the town. These carried their possessions on their backs or in single-wheeled handcarts, and they glanced anxiously at those around them. It had been many days since I had last seen any raiders and it seemed unlikely that these people were running from pirate attacks. I spent time watching them with mild curiosity and found them more concerned with their fellow travellers than with scanning the horizon for danger. I saw little suggestion of malicious intent within the group, although all were edgy and suspicious. They were wary of strangers, of any who were not personally known by them and were considered *other*. The hospitality of offering comfort to a stranger was noticeably lacking here, and it carried the stench of Baila's teaching to fear the unknown. This now seemed to include their own countrymen.

Long queues had formed at the gates to the town and people waited to be granted access. A pair of black-clad soldiers assessed all who requested admission and inspected all goods and possessions. I moved closer to a family group, quietly amusing the young children with slight-of-hand tricks while their parents explained their reasons for being there and pleaded for entrance. As hoped, the soldiers gave only a cursory glance in my direction before waving us through, assuming I was part of the family. Once through the gates, I was able to slip away into the crowds without the parents ever noticing me.

Despite the many soldiers patrolling through the streets, remaining anonymous in such a bustling, chaotic environment was easy. Their distinctive uniforms meant I had no problem detecting and avoiding them. Their presence was also clearly marked by the reverential bubble that surrounded them. People moved out of their way, dipping their heads and avoiding eye contact whenever the soldiers walked by. Stallholders presented items of food or clothing as if they were making offerings to a God, and the soldiers were happy to take anything that pleased them without even the pretence of making payment. Their casual disrespect for those trying to feed their families made the muscles of my shoulders rigid with barely suppressed resentment. I headed to the nearest tavern to wash the foul taste from my mouth.

The tavern was busy. A mix of merchants, labourers and others of the town mingled freely with the lack of inhibition commonly seen in those who had been steadily consuming fermented drinks. The atmosphere was loud and claustrophobic, and the heat of the fire after the chill outside caused my head to spin. It took more concentration than it should to make my way to the counter without stumbling into anyone and I was grateful to grasp its solid surface for support.

It took a while for the tavern-owner to attend to me and I spent the time watching her tease and mock her customers. Her face was flushed with the heat of the room and her hair was piled on top of her head in a mess of curls. She moved with the grace of a fighter, twisting away from reaching hands and stepping smoothly to avoid unsteady drinkers. I felt the flicker of a smile at the thought that kingdoms could descend into Mobis's realms but taverns would still be riotous islands of normality.

'Yes dear,' she said once she finally found the time to serve me. 'What can I get you?'

Before I had the chance to answer, she looked up from cleaning the spotless counter to see me clearly for the first time. And hesitated. My hood was still pulled low over my face to conceal my eyes and I maintained an unremarkable appearance, yet something had triggered suspicion in a woman who had happily socialised with everyone else in the tavern. The place was predominantly filled with male customers, although there were enough females present for me to reject my gender as the focus of her disquiet. *Saorsa* and my other weapons were carefully concealed under my cloak, and there were others who carried blades, so I dismissed this as well. With the obvious reasons excluded, I followed her gaze to find her staring at a small length of back hair that had escaped my hood. She tilted her head as if to consider its significance and if she should react to it. I remained still, unwilling to provoke a reaction with a sudden movement, but very slowly moved my hand closer to the hilt of my sword. The tension remained for a few heartbeats before she made her decision, raising her gaze away from my hair and towards my partially covered face.

'What will it be?' she asked quietly.

I requested a bottle of her strongest wine, sharing another awkward moment when I exchanged payment. My sleeves were pulled low over my hands so I could avoid touching the accursed Baila coins when I poured them from the pouch, but my fingers shone like lanterns with dull-amber threads of energy. The skin was almost translucent and it no longer concealed the veins of power that weaved through the tissues. I carefully watched the woman's face, relieved when she seemed not to see the unnatural appearance of raw energy. I took my drink and quickly retreated to a corner where I could watch the entire room yet still make a quick exit if the need arose. I spent several moments paying particular attention to the tavern-owner but she soon returned to her previous gregarious nature, seemingly no longer concerned with the strange woman she had just served.

The wine was bitter with a sharp aftertaste but it was sufficient to quieten the noise in my head and I listened to the gossip of those nearby, disregarding most of it when it concerned local problems and personal hardships. The same stories were told in every tavern I had been in. The pressures of working under the authority of Baila's priesthood and the infiltration of the religion into the lives of those in the centre and west of the kingdom. There was little talk of raiders, and none of daemons, but Baila's priests and their soldiers were woven through every aspect of town life. Taxes to be paid. Devotions to be made. Due reverence to those in the service of their God. Despite the apparent civility of the tavern, suspicions ran close to the surface with talk of neighbour turning on neighbour and the priests' encouragement of reporting any perceived wrong. It seemed that factual evidence or proof was no longer required. The simple people of the town just needed to inform those best suited to judge the actions of others against the demanding standards of the scriptures. The priests ordered swift and severe punishments for those deemed lacking, creating fear and suspicion which bubbled away like a poisonous stew.

I swallowed the last of my wine and left the tavern, no longer taking comfort from the agreeable atmosphere now it had proven to be so superficial.

The news was nothing I had not heard before, offering no solution to the problem and little hope of anyone rising to fight the blatant injustices. The insidious nature of Baila's teachings and the clear consequences of failing to comply resulted in a suitably compliant population. Life carried on and people did the best they could with the options given to them. It was all so depressingly inevitable.

I had every intention of leaving the town to its miserable fate, but the flow of people swept me away from the gates and towards an area where tall houses were closely pressed together. It was only when I emerged from a side alley and stepped into the main street that I realised I had been herded to the town's temple. Flanked by high buildings, it still radiated power with its elaborately pious stone carvings and promised salvation. A crowd was forming and there was an atmosphere of expectation that was becoming bleakly familiar. A timber platform, which appeared to have been hastily built, stood to one side of the building and was raised so it was level with the top step of Baila's temple. A solid, triangular-shaped wooden support extended from the ground, passing through the platform for its point to finish higher than the tallest man. Iron shackles hung from just below the join at its apex.

I started to pay attention to those around me, hoping for information on who the unfortunate victim was, and I became more uncomfortable with each snippet of conversation heard. It seemed news of my petty attacks against Baila's chosen had spread. Wicked magick was being used to harm Baila's heroic soldiers. Malicious forces guided the hands killing his devoted priests. Ancient evil walked the streets of Hilman's towns and villages. All of it was being firmly placed on the woman about to be executed. It was a clear statement that my actions against Baila's army and his priesthood would not go unpunished, despite being unable to locate me.

The noise of the crowd increased with jeers and insults, aimed at the accused who walked towards the platform. She remained mostly hidden by those in front of me, but a ripple of movement marked her passage as she was escorted towards her fate. Several stones were thrown by people releasing pent-up frustrations and fears. The braying of the mob reached its crescendo as the leading pair of guards stepped onto the raised stage to be followed, two paces behind, by the condemned and then, two paces behind her, the final pair of guards.

I stared, not quite believing what I was seeing. The woman was slightly built, wearing a simple white gown and soft shoes. She was a little older than me, with straight, black hair brushing her shoulders and a pale complexion. She was led to the wooden structure and her wrists were locked into the shackles. She raised her head to fearfully look out over the mass of people calling for her death and I saw that her eyes were brown but, otherwise, she bore a remarkable resemblance to me. I tasted bile when I realised it was not just my deeds that were being told to all who would listen, my appearance was also being widely circulated. I had been careful to remain hooded and anonymous, and yet Baila's chosen had known exactly who had been targeting them.

Movement at the temple's entrance heralded the arrival of a high-level priest and his two attending acolytes. Their banded robes and solemn movements reinforced their superiority over the hostile crowd they had gathered. The high priest played into the spectacle of the occasion with his posturing and the positioning of his two attendants, each a respectful two paces behind and standing one to each side of him. He basked in the potent energy of the mob before raising his hands for silence.

'My children. Evil walks amongst us.'

His words echoed those of the crowd and I had no doubt as to where the peoples' fears had originated. The faces of the men and women around me showed a desperate need for the parental protection offered by the priest.

'This woman has been judged and found guilty of using arcane magick to harm those devoted to the One True God.' A buzz of pious outrage flowed through the crowd. 'Magick used to summon evil spirits that poison your crops and sicken your livestock. Magick used to draw fire from the depths of the ground. Fire to burn the brave soldiers that oppose her. Fire to burn the priests in your streets as they try to protect your children from her evil. Delivering such agony against those with a selfless love of Baila's devoted children.'

While I reluctantly had to accept that I had set fire to several priests and their acolytes, none had died protecting any other than themselves. And, apart from the one time when I had toppled a wall onto a group of soldiers, I had rarely used more than plain steel to kill those of the Army of Truth. The irony of that title was sharp-edged when they repeatedly lied to provoke prejudice and hatred. I had assessed the woman's aura, she had no magickal ability and the priest would know that. Being unable to punish me, he had taken the first woman who bore a likeness and decided to execute her, just to reinforce his authority. I felt the heat of my anger flood through my veins while the priest continued his diatribe.

'This witch may be one of many,' he proclaimed. 'We have no clue what number plague our towns and villages. But I promise we will hunt down every last one of them. Baila's devoted will not die in vain. Their sacrifice will be remembered and avenged.' The mob roared their approval, caught up in the storm of righteous rhetoric. 'This evil woman will feel the heat of her fire. Will feel the agony of the flames she has inflicted on our brothers. Her soul will burn forever, denied the release of Baila's mercy.'

The crowd chanted for the woman's death and the priest was handed a long, thin rod of bloodstone. The green crystal was streaked with red so that the stone appeared to have trapped fire within it. He drew on his meagre magick to channel energy into the artefact, amplifying the power into a swirling mass of dark red threads. With a dramatic flourish, the priest jabbed the rod towards his victim and she screamed as the flames engulfed her, wrapping around her body to block her from view. The crowd cheered and I was sickened by more than just the stench of burning flesh. The devouring fire symbolised their defiance against terrors of their own imagination. The blaze of my rage cried out to add to the inferno and show these cowering cowards what true magick looked like. I wanted to cleanse the land of their self-righteous piety and their hypocritical bloodlust.

With images of dragon-fire filling my mind, I released a smothering blanket of rippling flame that consumed everyone in the street. The roar of the firestorm I created muted their tormented screams and the heat of the inferno quickly extinguished their cries. The platform swiftly disintegrated into ash and Baila's temple smoked over the charred bodies of its priest and acolytes. The neighbouring streets succumbed to the blaze and the fire quickly spread throughout the town.

CHAPTER SEVENTEEN

I was actively hunted and I maintained a constant state of tension. Baila's soldiers routinely patrolled the roads and even small villages now retained some as a permanent deterrent. People were quick to condemn strangers and it rarely took long before someone would alert the authorities to an unfamiliar face, particularly those who bore a resemblance to my description. I avoided the more populated areas but still found no respite, with soldiers patrolling almost all routes and closely inspecting anyone wanting to enter a settlement larger than a few houses. I inverted my daily routine. I would travel at night when the cold drove most people inside and the dark would hide me from the soldiers, using only farm tracks and deer trails across open farmland and scrubby hills. I slept fitfully during the day, hidden from casual observation within the rocky rubble of a landslide or the prickly shelter of a hedgerow. I dreamt of dragon-slain daemons releasing a green mist over bloody battlefields.

It became increasingly harder to find the motivation to continue. I was painfully cold and soul-achingly weary. It took so much effort just to keep walking and the constant threat of discovery weighed heavily. I deeply missed the guidance of my wolf, wanting him to lead me to safety as he had the last time I had felt this adrift and alone. I yearned for his company but feared the temptation offered by my dreams. It would be so easy to answer the dragon's call and abandon this failing body to be absorbed into her loving embrace. But a renewed connection to Megin would place her in danger and I would not risk that.

No danger. I will protect you.

I stumbled and fell heavily to my knees. The sharp stones dug painfully into my hands and knees, dissolving the fantasy of joining my dragon and returning me to the reality of the deer track. I was shivering despite the clammy perspiration that had become a constant feature. A cold wind forced its way through my clothing to bite at my skin and I clenched my jaw against the chattering of my teeth. I stubbornly continued towards the distant light from a farmhouse window and the promises it offered. It had been some time since I had been able to obtain more than scraps of barely edible food, and the energy I siphoned from the land had become steadily less effective at sustaining me as my physical body deteriorated. I needed warmth and a meal and this was the quietest farm I had seen in days.

The farm was the smallest in a cluster of three nestled within the valley, and it was the last before a large rocky landslide interrupted the flow of workable farmland. I burrowed into the hedge bordering its muddy paddock just before dawn and assessed the risk. An older man appeared to share the property with a younger woman. A stocky horse and a thin cow were led to the sparse pasture and a number of chickens were chased out of a barn that leant against the far wall of the farmhouse. The pair spent most of the day inside the sturdy building and I dozed during their long periods of inactivity.

The cow was returned to its night's shelter at dusk and I thanked Sucellos for his blessing when the man saddled the piebald horse. The woman stood in the doorway and wrapped her shawl a little tighter around her shoulders while he mounted. He gave her a swift nod of farewell then cantered into the deepening gloom in the direction of the nearest village. The woman watched him until he faded from sight, nervously surveying her farm and the bordering hill slopes before disappearing back into the house. A blast of cold wind triggered a bout of violent shivering and I did not delay in crossing the muddy field and shadowy yard into the barn. The small warmth generated by the cow within the confines of the crude, draught-ridden shelter was sufficient to provoke a deep sigh of relief.

The placid beast was contained within the main stall by an unstable barrier of broken gates and poorly fitting fencing, and a narrow passageway ran in front of this along the length of the barn. A jumble of farm tools and old leather tack was stored at one end. At the other, a small stall was piled with straw bales upon which the chickens quietly warbled in indignation at my intrusion. I moved to the cluttered end where a latched window overlooked the yard. Gaps between the shutters allowed a chilly draught to knife into the shelter, but also allowed me to see the glow from the farmhouse windows where they projected patches of light onto the dark ground. I would be able to tell when the lamps were extinguished and the woman had retired to her bed without having to leave the protection of the barn. Satisfied at this small token of luck, I stole some straw from the cow and made a comfortable nest before settling in to wait.

I woke to the sound of horses' hooves clattering on the stony track. The warmth had lulled me to sleep and now I had to deal with the increased risk of the returning farmer, and whoever he had brought with him. I eased open the shutters so I could see the yard more easily. The streaks of light from the farmhouse were still visible and the woman remained inside, apparently not yet having heard the riders' approach, so it seemed I had not slept for long. I anxiously waited for the new arrivals to come into view, concerned that the horses would need stabling alongside the cow. While the straw bales offered a potential hiding place, I suspected the chickens would readily betray me to anyone within hearing. It would also be difficult to hide my constant glow. The prolonged use of power had abraded away my corporeal body so that the coils of my energy were now visible to any with the smallest hint of ability.

The woman opened the door and riders' dark uniforms were highlighted by the light. The two men were young, perhaps a little older than me, each armed with a single sword. I prayed to all the Gods that they were merely conducting a routine patrol and would soon leave. I would have accepted the soldiers being invited in, allowing me to slip away despite having to abandon the hope of food, but the woman's rigid posture and folded arms suggested an irritation which was unlikely to offer hospitality. While the taller one questioned the farm-owner, the smaller of the two looked towards the barn. He dismounted smoothly, confident enough in his mount's training to leave the reins loose over its neck, and he walked towards me. I churlishly thanked the Gods for their complete lack of assistance and distractedly placed my palm to the ground to siphon the land's power, failing to set the appropriate defences which had become increasingly necessary.

The violent backlash raced through my body. Intense pain crushed my chest and flames exploded in my skull. I reflexively clenched my fist into the dirt and the ground screamed again at my trespass. Sorrow and hate tore through me. I was made to understand the offence caused by the unnatural landslide. I felt the agony of the distorted flow of energy, haemorrhaging from brutalised earth and splintered boulders. I snatched my hand away and severed the connection. My vision cleared as I gasped air into my traumatised lungs and the pain gradually receded. I had gained little power but I would not go back for more. It would have to be enough.

I swiftly crossed the short distance to the ill-fitting doors, pushing them open to find the soldier already standing on the other side. His eyes widened slightly in surprise but he immediately stepped back and drew his sword. *Saorsa* was already in my hand and I wasted no time in pressing my small advantage. He blocked my initial strike and parried my second, quickly adapting to take the offensive by the third. I welcomed the simplicity of a purely physical fight, without the interference of priests or shamans, and the challenge of a worthy opponent.

We separated. The second soldier had already dismounted and was coming towards us with his blade drawn, but I kept my attention on the man in front of me. His stance was relaxed and I saw his confidence in being able to deal with anything I could throw at him. I slowly rotated my wrist, happy to prove him wrong.

He darted in and I was forced back several paces before I twisted away from his attack and came back to lead the dance. He retreated but recovered quickly and we separated again as the other soldier joined us. The taller man also carried the frame of an experienced fighter but, while the first had shown a quiet determination, this one displayed a slightly amused insolence that still managed to radiate danger.

'Well, look at you,' he mocked while we circled each other, assessing the relative strengths and weaknesses in this new dynamic. 'So corrupted by power, you shine like a signal beacon.'

I glanced at my glowing hands and the smaller one pounced on the small distraction with a flurry of strokes to my head and chest. His taller companion followed a heartbeat later to attack with a ferocity of his own and I spent several moments scrambling backwards in response to the paired threat. The soldiers worked well together, matching their swings to keep me defensive and prevent me from selecting a strategy of my choosing, but I was a Moon Warrior and I had spent a long time fighting against multiple opponents. I pushed back. I found their rhythm and guided it towards mine. I turned and twisted and flowed around their blades, letting *Saorsa* sing when steel clashed against steel. I let my attack of one opponent meld seamlessly into my defence against the second and held my distance while I slowly moved them closer to each other. My sword flowed from shape to shape; circles, figures-of-eight, serpentines, arrowheads. My muscles confident in manoeuvres drilled during countless sessions with Bear and Bonash. Vallori and Z'hara.

I hesitated at the thought of those from the sanctuary and my denied grief returned to stab at my heart. The taller one pounced and sliced a deep wound along my ribs. Reflex saved me from the opposing thrust and it took some time to regain my rhythm. I slammed the door shut on the invasive memories, but not before I yielded to Bear's comment that I relied too heavily on my two-handed grip of *Saorsa*. I parried one-handed against a volley of strikes while I bought time to release my dagger. Two swords would have been better but it would suffice, and I could now address their simultaneous attacks.

The soldiers were good. They readily adapted to the new tactic and increased the aggression of their assault. The farmyard echoed with the concussive clash of steel and my synchronised dance of one-before-the-other collapsed under the combined force of their blades. Any attempt at strategy dissolved once more, with the fight descending into a brutal match of strength and agility. Habit and reflex dominated the choice of parry or block, strike or retreat. Gains were quickly won and lost, with any advantage passing equally between the three of us. We had barely moved from the front of the barn.

The taller soldier slipped, twisting his foot so he fell on one knee. I swiftly dismissed the fleeting weakness but the smaller one was momentarily distracted, and it was all I needed. I attacked with a renewed force that drove him away from his companion, giving me the space I needed to concentrate on just the one foe. It was his turn to defend against two blades and I mercilessly pushed him backwards. I sliced and slashed, one side and then the other. I encouraged his attention towards my sword and waited for the slight loss of balance as I lured him beyond his reach. He stretched too far and I twisted around, burying my knife up to its hilt into his back. He stood, frozen, for several heartbeats before crumpling to his knees.

I ignored the dying man and returned my attention to the remaining soldier. He stood, staring at his fallen colleague, and I watched while he considered whether he was willing to risk his life to take mine. Baila's faithful had always been eager to become martyrs and the decision was made with a raised head and a thin smile.

'I will take pleasure in being the one to claim your life, sorceress.'

I opened my arms wide in provocative invitation. 'Come and take it then.'

We both advanced for the final bout. I had left my dagger embedded in the soldier's back and gratefully returned to my favoured two-handed grip. I noted the first signs of desperation in my opponent's assault but accepted that I was equally tired and saw more than a hint of desperation in my own attack. We were evenly matched for a while. Thrust and slice effectively blocked and parried. Fatigue closed the gap between us and hilts became clubs while elbows threw punches. It was time to finish this.

I feigned a stumble, provoking him to over-reach at my exposed right side while I rotated inside his thrust. *Saorsa* glided smoothly up through his belly and into his chest. His face was so close to mine, contorted in pain before consciousness left him. His body slumped backwards, slipping from my sword and falling to the ground. I stared at him with a numbed detachment. Somewhere distant I knew I should have felt more. Some sorrow or remorse, but I lacked the ability to feel anything other than exhausted.

I eventually turned away from him, stumbling when the exhilaration of the fight left me as a cold tide flowing from my head to my feet. My vision swam and I staggered a few steps before falling to my knees. I cradled my head in my hands and a stabbing pain behind my eyes muted all other senses. The sensation passed and I opened my eyes to find the woman had approached, and was standing a few paces away with the blade of my dagger pointing towards me. I left *Saorsa* lying on the ground and slowly raised my hands in the universal gesture of peace.

'I'm not going to hurt you,' I promised, too tired to care if she was about to stab me with my own knife. 'I just wanted food but I will leave without further trouble.'

I waited on my knees while she considered my words. The blade was unexpectedly still in her hands, and I briefly wondered whether she was a credible threat, but she soon made her choice and lowered the knife.

'The soldiers come, wanting...' She paused to glance at the dead soldier behind me and her voice was harder when she continued. 'They often come wanting favours. Some food seems fair payment for what you may have prevented.'

She reversed the weapon and I rose to re-sheath it along with *Saorsa*. The woman turned and walked back towards the farmhouse, unconcerned with whether I was following. I hesitated, debating whether it was a good idea to enter the building when I had no way of knowing what awaited me there, but I had come here for food and she had just offered it to me freely. Besides, I had just killed two of Baila's soldiers, I doubted this night could get any worse.

The front of the farmhouse was one big room. There was a long table to the left of the door and a banked fire to the right, with two chairs placed beside it. A thin curtain partially separated the front of the house from a small passageway leading to the rear. The room spoke of function and of work, and there were few luxuries to provide comfort. The woman was collecting a bowl as I entered, indicating for me to take one of the chairs when I hesitated on the threshold. A cauldron of broth simmered gently over the embers and the savoury aroma caused my stomach to clench, swiftly followed by a wave of nausea and light-headedness. It had been too long since my last meal.

I carefully removed my cloak and dropped gratefully into the chair nearest the fire. I inspected the deep gash over my ribs. My jerkin and shirt were already stiff with blood, and it pulled painfully when I folded them back from the wound, but it had been a clean slice and it should heal well enough. There was still some oozing when I pressed the skin around it but I did not think I would lose much more blood from the injury. I tore a strip from the shirt and bound the edges of the wound together so the flesh could start to knit.

'We have bandages,' stated the woman, passing me a small beaker of watery ale. 'Farm work leads to frequent injuries. I could take proper care of that.'

I dismissed her offer. 'I've had worse. But the food and drink are appreciated. Thank you.'

She was equally dismissive of my gratitude, turning to ladle broth into the bowl while I took a welcome swallow of the ale. I was thirsty enough to have readily accepted stale pond water and greedily drained the cup. My host gave a flicker of a smile when she reclaimed the empty beaker and passed me the filled bowl. Taking cautious, small sips of the broth so as not to offend my complaining stomach, I watched her refill the cup and place it on the floor beside me. She claimed the spare chair and we sat in silence while I reappraised my initial impression of her, judging her to be older than I had initially thought. There were shallow creases at the corners of her eyes and mouth, and her hands were calloused from years of hard labour. She maintained a tightly controlled posture but I was unsure whether this was her normal carriage or a response to my presence in her home. Her light brown hair was pulled into a functional tail with a few loose curls framing her face. Shrewd nut-brown eyes evaluated me and I found it surprisingly hard to read her intentions. I did not feel safe here. She seemed a little too composed after what had just happened in her yard. Perhaps a hard life had taught her how to deal with unexpected violence. Perhaps I was too suspicious and too tired to accurately judge. My cramping belly was certainly no aid in clarifying my thoughts.

I failed to suppress a satisfied sigh when the warmth of the meal softened my muscles and I saw the woman twitch another small smile. The heat from the fire and the comfort of the food had suffused my body with a pleasant softness, and I felt a dangerous temptation to curl in front of the embers like a contented cat. I sat straighter in the chair, using the pull of the wound to chase away those seductive thoughts. Her expression did not change but I sensed there was some amusement at my obvious tactic. My irritation at her smugness washed away the remaining drowsiness.

'Two of Baila's soldiers are lying dead outside your door,' I declared sharply. 'What are your intentions?'

She paused, as if to consider when I was sure she had already evaluated all her options and decided on her course of action.

'I shall tell the truth to any who ask.' She confidently maintained my gaze. 'The soldiers came here to follow up reports of a stranger in the area. They found the intruder in the barn and were killed to trying to apprehend the trespasser.'

'And this trespasser? What will you say about that?'

Her eyes flicked briefly to look at my wrists, still glowing a dark amber but no longer pulsing. I had no doubt that she knew who I was.

'I didn't get a good look. They had some skill with the sword but beyond that I couldn't tell.'

'And in return?' She continued to look levelly at me, expecting me to ask the question. 'What do you want from me?'

The small smile lingered longer on her face and she relaxed back into the chair. 'I didn't lie when I said the soldiers come looking for favours. Despite preaching purity, the priests do nothing to discourage their soldiers from taking whatever they want. Two less rapists are no great loss.'

'My guess is that you could have taken care of yourself.'

She shrugged. 'Maybe. But there are plenty who cannot. I remember a time when women didn't live in fear. I would welcome a return to those days.'

I shook my head. 'You think I'm some kind of saviour?'

She gave a bitter laugh. 'Mobis's Torments, no. If only half the rumours about you are true, you could be the most dangerous person alive. Understand, that while I will not hand you over to those sanctimonious priests, we are not on the same side.'

The peril I had sensed was laid wide open. The only reason she had offered respite was because she hated Baila's oppression more than she hated me. I did not trust that her promise not to expose me would last long once her own interests were challenged.

'I should go. The soldiers will be missed and they will send others to look for them.' I rose and offered her back the bowl. 'Thank you for your hospitality.'

She hesitated, seeming to regret having spoken so freely. 'My apologies. I did not mean to be rude. You should have more broth before you go. There is time yet.'

The strength of longing for warm food and comfortable shelter unsettled me, confirming that there were many layers of threat here. I needed to leave.

'It's time I left,' I repeated, more firmly than I was feeling.

She nodded, accepting my decision and she took the empty bowl. 'At least take some food with you. There is cheese to spare and a little bread. It's not much but more than you have now.'

It seemed childish to refuse so I graciously accepted. She bundled the supplies in a square of cloth while I adjusted the strapping over my wound and replaced my cloak. She walked with me to where the soldiers' horses had remained in obedient alertness.

'You could take one of the mares,' she suggested. 'They are sufficiently ordinary that no one will think to trace them back here.'

I gave a small smile; the two bays had stood firm while their riders had been killed and had waited patiently while we were inside, but they both spooked when I approached.

'I have nowhere to go and I'm in no hurry to get there. Do what you will with the horses.'

She nodded in agreement, wrapping her arms around her against the cold. She called after me as I crossed the yard.

'Stay off the main roads. They are too well patrolled. There's a shepherd's trail on the other side of the landslide that will take you further into the hills.'

I turned to give a nod of acknowledgement but continued at a brisk pace away from the farm, ready to place this evening behind me. I followed the main track to the rocky scar, fighting the feelings of sorrow and despair when I clambered over the desecrated earth and scrambled over the violated boulders. The promised trail was barely visible in the shadowy, shrubby grassland of the lower slopes and I had to concentrate to avoid drifting off its path, but it offered a direction and I readily followed it as it wound gently up the hill and into the safety of the dark countryside.

I first suspected that something was seriously wrong just after dawn when my stomach forcefully ejected what was left of the broth. My belly had been cramping since leaving the farmhouse but I had dismissed it as the result of prolonged fasting. The healer in me, however, would not deny the fact that I should have vomited soon after eating if my body was merely rebelling against the sudden volume. Frequent episodes plagued the morning and I expelled foul liquids, the vomiting turning to dry heaves once all fluid had been removed from my stomach. My guts twisted into tight knots that forced me to wait, hunched over, until the pain subsided. I spent a miserable day violently shivering and I fought the urge to crawl under the nearest bush until the malady passed, fearing Baila's faithful would come searching once the dead soldiers were discovered.

My condition calmed during the night and I snatched a few hours' sleep, awaking cold and shaking to another day of strong winds. The gusts swirled around me and constantly tried to push me from the poorly defined track. I found it increasingly hard to concentrate and my feet were frequently left to take the easiest route, drifting away from the uneven shepherd's trail and back to the valley floor. My head throbbed to the beat of my racing heart and my belly felt like it had been repeatedly kicked by a horse, with any attempt made to replenish lost fluids provoking immediate expulsion and debilitating cramps. I knew I was trembling from more than the cold, with severe dehydration adding to my perpetual state of malnutrition, but any connection with the land flamed against my raw senses to cause an agony and despair I could no longer defend against. The numbing discomfort of exhaustion was preferable to the intense torment it cost to obtain a short reprieve.

My mind wandered. I was comforted with visions of snow-capped mountains where the air was so crisp and clear that it hurt to breathe it. Dark lakes were cradled within valleys and shimmered with gentle waves that sparkled like jewels. Groups of tawny deer browsed in meadows surrounded by tall pines that stood as straight as spears, pointing into the dark blue sky. Wide rivers carved through the glens, raging and frothing around the boulders that dared to interrupt their flow. Peaceful landscapes that were so very far from the deformed, ravaged earth where I walked, depleted and vulnerable. Where the land stabbed me with misery and haunted me with accusatory shadows each time I stumbled and my flesh touched the ground.

Another wave of cramps drove me to my knees and the world turned black while I waited for the episode to pass. Eventually the spasm eased and I opened my eyes to a muddy road that bore the deep depressions of numerous wagons' wheels. The path was not wide, seemingly more of a communal farm track than a well-used road, but it still risked greater exposure than I was comfortable with. I quickly stood up but this triggered another flood of nausea that left me gasping and unable to move for several anxious moments.

The ringing in my ears faded and I heard the sound of hoof-beats. I could not afford to be caught in the open. I was unable to defend myself against an elderly merchant, much less a soldier. I reached for my sword and swiftly turned to confront the threat, but I had moved too quickly and my world tilted. I stumbled backwards and tried to will my vision to settle. My mind screamed at the danger I was unable to avoid while I fought just to keep standing. A pair of hands firmly gripped my upper arms and gently forced me to sit, maintaining their support when I swayed unsteadily. The contact provided a focus for my scattered thoughts and silenced the storm of my panic.

My vision cleared and I saw an aging face close to mine, watching me with concerned nut-brown eyes. His head was slightly tilted and a small frown had formed a crease between his eyebrows. I studied the details of his face while I calmed my breathing and waited for my heartbeat to slow. I searched for a sign that he was a threat and for any feeling of danger, but found none. I relaxed my shoulders and removed my grip on his wrists, for which he rewarded me a satisfied smile. He released my arms and sat back on his heels.

'Better?' He had a soft, deep voice. 'You look awful.'

'I think—' My throat was raw and I coughed against its sting. 'I think I must have eaten some spoiled food.'

He looked at me for a while, his head tilted again while he considered my story. 'It can happen. And it is rarely pleasant.'

I felt such longing, sitting on a hard road with a concerned stranger, and I wanted nothing more than to curl up and rest, but I did not dare succumb to the temptation. Either this man was more than he appeared or I would be led by him into greater danger. I needed to stay alone and hidden. I would not be safe here no matter how much I desired it. I started to rise but he immediately reached over and easily pinned me to the spot.

'I don't think it's wise for you to be going anywhere just now. Let me get a fire started and warm you up at least before you decide to travel on.'

The sun had dropped behind the hills and the warmth it had offered was gone with it. Despite the warnings, I was easily convinced to accept his invitation. The man hummed quietly to himself, setting a small metal container over the flames to heat the water. He returned to the wagon where two horses stood patiently, a bay in harness at the front and a piebald tied to the wagon's end-rail, and collected a pair of mugs. He brought them back to the fire when the water started to boil.

'Mint tea,' he proclaimed, handing me one of the mugs. 'Good for the digestion.'

The aroma of the tea caused my stomach to clench, but it offered no further protest and I tentatively sipped the blissfully warm liquid. We both waited to see if the drink would be accepted. The traveller smiled when I took a second swallow.

'So, what brings you to the middle of nowhere? On your own?' he asked softly, warming his hands around his mug. 'Where are you headed?'

I had decided on my alibi while the stranger had prepared the tea, but still felt a swift twist of guilt at stealing some of Z'hara's story.

'My family wanted to marry me off to the highest bidder. I wasn't prepared to be bartered like a surplus sow. So, I ran.'

His eyes flicked to *Saorsa's* hilt and I doubted he accepted my tale, but his reply remained unchallenging. 'I imagine that you could be quite determined when you set your mind to something.'

We continued to watch each other while I slowly finished the drink, neither fully trusting the other, but I could find no fault with his hospitality. The tea had released the tightness in my belly and had provided some much-needed warmth, causing my fingers to tingle with a sensation that was not unpleasant. I dared to indulge in this respite a little longer, knowing I would benefit from the heat of the fire and the recuperative effects of the tea. I promised myself that I would risk more fires, finally accepting that the cold was as likely to kill me as any patrol.

Another wave raced through my guts and the tea was violently expelled from my stomach, continuing long after the drink had gone. The man sat patiently, a small frown of concern showing despite offering no assistance. I fought the nausea pulsing from the ground where I rested my head against the cool earth, and I breathed carefully until the dry heaves settled. I slowly uncurled to look at the traveller. He leaned forward to place his mug on the ground beside him and I finally understood.

'The farm,' I accused. 'You were at the farm.'

He nodded in agreement. 'And I'm sure you've realised by now that it was not spoiled food that you received there.'

My mind raged in vindication of its suspicions. I had been so desperate for food and warmth that I had been easily fooled. Twice. I was in more danger now than I had been fighting the two soldiers. I scrabbled backwards, thinking only of getting away but the stinging sensation in my hands had grown more intense and I was having difficulty in rising. My head pounded and dissolved any coherent thoughts. The man from the farm calmly walked over to press me down.

'Don't fight it,' he advised, deceptively soft. 'The first dose debilitated you more than expected. You will not get far after a second dose.'

My esteemed destiny had come crashing to a halt beside a muddy track in the deserted hills of Hilman. I fought for as long as I could, but had little strength to sustain my anger and I soon floated away on a midnight-blue river.

CHAPTER EIGHTEEN

The sound of voices disturbed my blissful nothingness and dragged me back to a reality I did not want to embrace. The ground below me was hard and I had been covered by a blanket. My head throbbed but my belly had settled and for that I was grateful.

'We should move.'

I recognised the voice but my thoughts were gossamer threads and they evaded my attempts to contain them. A male voice answered with a chuckle and I remembered the man. And the wagon. And the tea.

'Always in a hurry,' he replied lightly. 'And yet, you are content to warm your hands by my fire.'

'Your fire will attract patrols.'

'I have full confidence in your ability to deal with anyone we may encounter.' The voice carried more than a hint of mockery. 'Besides, I was up and down this road for nearly two days before she stumbled into my path. I saw no one. You chose the direction well.'

The pieces slid together; the woman from the farm, they had worked together. The fog receded from my mind and I became fully aware of my vulnerability. I opened my eyes to look directly into the face of the woman I no longer believed to be a farmer. Her practical leathers and the glint of her sword's hilt in the flickering of the fire confirmed her as a fighter, and I did not doubt that she was a good one. She narrowed her eyes on discovering I was awake.

'How much did you give her?'

'She could barely stand.' The traveller stripped a twig of its bark. 'A half-dose was sufficient.'

'Clearly not.'

The woman moved to the rear of the wagon where one of the soldiers' mares was tied alongside the piebald, collecting a short length of thin rope and a small wooden box. Guessing her intentions, I tried to stand but my sluggish limbs struggled to escape the blanket. The man remained where he was while I scrambled away from the fire, unconcerned with my attempt at freedom, and his confidence was depressingly justified with the pathetic resistance I offered the woman when she returned to subdue me. My body acted a heartbeat after the intent and it gave her amble time to slap away my feeble punches and kick my legs out from under me. She placed a knee into my tender guts, effectively pinning me while she tightly bound my wrists, and then dragged me back to the discarded blanket. The brief struggle had merely succeeded in making my head swim and intensifying the crushing headache.

'Is that necessary?' he asked softly. 'She's no threat like this.'

'Don't be so sure,' the fighter warned, accepting the mug he offered and adding a small amount of grey powder from the box to the swirled liquid. 'Even half-dead, she easily killed two of Baila's soldiers. I'm not prepared to take the risk.'

Satisfied the drink was as she wanted it, she returned to my side and restrained me with embarrassing ease. She poured the uncomfortably warm liquid to the back of my mouth before clamping it shut, raising my chin so my head was forced back and the liquid flowed down my throat. I choked and gagged and choked again, finally swallowing when my lungs demanded air. She held my head until she was sure I had consumed the full dose, then released me to return to the traveller's side. I miserably curled onto my side while my captors continued to talk as if I was no longer there.

'She scares you.'

'Of course she does' she snapped, before continuing in a softer tone. 'She should scare you too.'

'Maybe. But it's hard to see all the stories in one so frail.'

'She may look weak now. Drugged and starving. But she has access to power...'

'Her power's fading. And what little she has is barely maintaining her body. It seems improbable that she is still able to function at all.

The woman grumbled a response but my mind had been distracted by a night sky full of stars and the cold, crisp mountain air. Nearby, two mountain peaks could be seen as dark, grey shadows. It was so quiet that the rhythmic *hush* of the wind was the only sound. The details of the forest below were faded by distance, offering the freedom of wide, open spaces. I could smell the remains of a seal carcass nearby. The scent of salt and blood blended comfortably with my full dragon-belly.

Safe.

Safe, I agreed, feeling the warmth of that word deep in my soul.

A contented rumble reverberated around my chest. Megin's chest? The distinction was blurred. Irrelevant. We were one. I relaxed into the peaceful majesty of the mountain peak.

I thought dragons were supposed to like caves.

Stupid ape. I smiled at the different shades of mockery, exasperation and fondness she had put into the comment. *After generations of being within that mountain, I have need of the big sky above me.*

Of course, I replied sleepily. *Stupid me.*

I was so tired. It was too hard to follow my thoughts to their conclusions. Fragments came and went and I had no desire to understand their meaning or context. I floated, happy to drift wherever the currents took me. Lulled into a numbing doze by the feelings of acceptance and belonging. Megin's concern brushed against me like a caress.

Don't go back, she pleaded. *Stay with me.*

So much love. I was vaguely surprised that my heart could contain a dragon's worth without bursting. I felt blessed by the gift of this wonderfully pleasant dream, before letting it fade away.

The swaying refused to follow the rhythm of my spinning head. My back was pressed against the wooden board at the front of the wagon, the plank of the raised seating area sat close above me, and my legs were slightly bent with the width of the cart preventing me from fully straightening them. I was held in place by rolled blankets and filled sacks and much of the other baggage needed to support two travellers and their horses. The barrier would have been easily pushed aside but I doubted anyone would be tempted to assist my escape, so I remained being gently jostled in the slightly cramped space.

I counted the horses' footfalls and decided there were still three, suggesting that the woman still accompanied the older man. I heard no voices but felt it was likely that she rode while he drove the wagon. We were not moving in haste and it was day. Beyond that I was unable to tell.

I assessed my physical condition. I found the inner glow of my strength was depressingly faint and I had very little with which to restore it. My body was a symphony of discomfort, with the prolonged immobility offering cramping back and leg harmonies to the underlying throb of my bloated belly and the pounding of my head. My heart raced with an irregular beat that clashed against the stinging of my palms and the soles of my feet. I felt as weak as a new-born kitten.

But all this was just background noise to the tormented chaos in my mind. Insufficient power had drained my ability to maintain my mental barriers and the harder I tried to repair them, the faster they melted away. It was like trying to hold onto water. The empathic connection to the land attacked with a force that left me gasping in pain or sobbing with despair. Tortured harmonies knifed into my skull from the twisted and distorted energies. Burning heat enflamed me where power had been abruptly obstructed, to be swiftly followed by a freezing cold where currents no longer flowed. The stench of rot and decay caused me to gag, assaulted by fouled rivers and polluted streams, with the vile taste coating my mouth so I felt as despoiled as the land.

I became absorbed, smothered by the dense earth. I was crushed by rocks that aimed to break my bones and crack my skull like the shell of an egg. I was blinded by flares of light that stabbed into my mind with daggers of vibrant ruby, gold and jade. Toxic obsidian vines threaded through a landscape of corpse-grey where shadowy creatures hissed and snarled. Gelatinous, tubular bodies slithered around me, their rounded heads and unseeing eyes rising up to sway in front of me. Accusing. Judging. Condemning. Their high-pitched squeals tore through my thoughts and I was faced by one horror after another. I was trapped in the nightmare of the land's suffering and made witness to each sordid violation.

The screams of the creatures subtly changed. The sounds no longer seemed to smash against each other in jarring dissonance. The tone softened slightly and I became drawn towards it rather than being repulsed by it. I identified repeated rhythms and the howling noise grew less angry, more sorrowful. The different voices started to merge and blend, complimenting each other as they wove into a melody that ebbed and flowed in hypnotic swirls. The sirens' song coaxed and pleaded, and I was swept along by the promise within their music. I willingly followed when one voice rose above the rest, guiding the way. The soft tenor carried the tune and the harmonies quietened, then faded. Shapes formed within the sound, almost recognisable as words. Repeated phrasing tugged at a memory. I had heard this song before. An old song. Sung generations ago by farm workers toiling in the fields.

The grey mist evaporated into an image; the memory of where I had heard the song before. The outer room of Kade's chambers at Liegeport were bathed in gentle afternoon sunlight. His long fingers danced over the twelve-stringed lute to create harmonies that were painful in their beauty. His head was tilted and his eyes closed as he appreciated the exquisite tone of the instrument. A relaxed smile betrayed his joy in the music he made. He opened his eyes and he lifted his head, widening his smile when he looked at me. His warm, brown gaze melting the very core of me even before he added his velvety voice. The words added colour to the tapestry of his music, creating images of late summer harvests and the companionship of neighbours working towards a common goal.

I was distracted by a movement at the collar of his shirt. A slim finger of black stroked the base of his neck, extending to wrap around his throat before disappearing behind his back. Kade seemed unaware as I watched more dark extensions clutch at him. The light in the scene changed from a soft glow to a harsh glare. The instrument was gone and Kade was now standing in front of the window. His head was tilted again but the expression of contentment had been replaced by one of cruel mockery. His face was gaunt so that shadows ringed his eyes and an unhealthy paleness coloured his cheeks. He started to pace with jerky movements, surrounded by a malevolent darkness that swirled around him.

'Why do you haunt me?' he snapped. 'Why do you return to remind me of my failures?'

He turned to brace himself against the windowsill, letting his head fall forward to reveal a section of the tattoo he had received at the Isle of Serpents. The sharp, clear lines of the protection sigils had smeared and blended into a mass of tangled threads. Areas of thin, faint lines bled into fat, globular veins. The mark was shifting and sliding like a nest of vipers, reaching out to obscenely caress his neck and probe into the base of his skull.

'I close my eyes but I still feel you,' he continued. 'All of you. Crawling over my skin with your condemnation and disappointment.'

He snapped round to glare at me with enough hatred to freeze my breath. Such intense anger distorted his face into a twisted mask of loathing.

He stalked across the room, angrily throwing a chair out of his way, and raised a finger in accusation.

'You will be gone,' he roared. 'I will suffer your ghosts no more. I banish you, evil spirits!'

I awoke to see the jumbled chaos of the wagon bed. The sharp daylight hurt my eyes and stabbed into my head, and I raised my bound fists in an attempt to block out the light. I felt flushed with fever and was desperately thirsty. My thoughts sluggishly connected to remind me where I was, and I became aware that my head rested against a shoulder and a strong arm held me pressed against a chest. The man was humming quietly. The song. The one Kade had been singing. Before it all changed. I tried to push away but the traveller firmly held me and I lacked the will to protest.

'Steady now,' he crooned. 'I'm not sure you are fully back with us. You were thrashing around like you were possessed by crazed serpents and I thought you were going to smash my wagon into pieces.'

'You should have left her twitching like a stranded fish.' The woman spoke from somewhere outside the wagon but I was too comfortable to attempt to locate her. 'You are too soft, old man.'

'And you are too harsh,' he mocked gently. 'That is why we make such a good team.'

She huffed but made no further comment. The man seemed content to wait and resumed his humming, lulling me into a relaxed dose when I followed the path of the melody. Returning to my memory of Kade.

'That song.' My voice cracked and I swallowed against my sore throat. 'I've heard it before. You were singing it?'

He chuckled. 'The tune is stuck in my head and I've been singing it for days. The rhythm of a plodding horse is much the same as that of scything wheat. It helps to be reminded of warm summer days on chilly winter ones.'

The wagon rocked when the woman climbed up into the bed, rolling a sack out of her way. She crouched down in front of me, holding a beaker, and critically assessed my condition.

'I don't think that is wise,' her companion cautioned.

'She can't keep thrashing around. The roads are getting busier. Someone will notice. We cannot afford to have anyone looking too closely.'

'Her power is almost gone and her body is barely capable of sustaining her. It may be more of a risk than you think.'

The fighter left her appraisal of me to glare at the older man. 'I know my job.'

His tone remained calm. 'I have no doubt about that. I'm just offering information that you may not have.'

'The dose is sufficient.'

I obediently took the beaker and drank the toxin. My vision refused to stop spinning and I knew I would be unable to stand. The poison had robbed me of my ability to move effectively and had scrambled my thoughts. I was rapidly heading towards the point when my erratically beating heart would fail completely.

'There are easier ways to kill me,' I commented quietly.

She scoffed, taking back the empty cup. 'If I wanted you dead, you would never have left the farm.'

The fluid sat heavily in my stomach and I concentrated on my breathing to prevent vomiting away the precious liquid. I listened while the traveller detailed the trap that had been set for me, weaving a tale with a storyteller's magic.

'You're a bard,' I declared, the thought suddenly occupying my whole mind.

The woman hissed but the man merely sighed sadly. 'Accusations like that will get me burned. I'm a storyteller. A minstrel, on occasion. But when the need arises, yes. I can track someone with, shall we say, enhanced abilities. Your careless use of power meant you were not hard to find. The difficulty lay in getting you to trust. We considered poisoning you with food from a market stall, but you barely ate. We thought a dose slipped into a drink at a busy tavern would be more successful, but you stopped visiting towns and accepting their hospitality. You avoided merchants' camps that could offer a shared meal, choosing quieter paths that discouraged travellers. We were starting to consider poisoned darts as an option.' He chuckled to himself at such a preposterous thought. 'Your desire for warmth and your need for food was plain to see, however. We simply used the farmhouse as a trap, with the soldiers providing the bait. What better disguise than a grateful farmwife offering to repay the debt of saving her from those brutish soldiers?'

'You talk too much,' cautioned the woman gently.

'It's a habit I find hard to deny,' he admitted, continuing to talk as I drifted into a drugged sleep.

Tallen.

The darkness was peaceful and soothing. I felt wrapped in a soft blanket and lying on a comfortable bed. My mind floated freely in no particular direction. I luxuriated in the pleasure of nothingness.

Tallen!

The peace turned brittle. Cracks radiated away from me to shatter the uniformed darkness like breaking glass. Sensations and emotions leaked through to tug my thoughts in countless different directions. I did not want to listen to them. I tried to block them but my protests were insubstantial and the feelings dragged me from my sheltered oblivion. Back into the realm of memory. Of recognition. Of Megin.

Tallen?

I noted a hint of fear in her call. She was a dragon. Why would she be fearful?

I could not find you.

What a strange thing for a dream to say. Dreams do not exist unless you think of them. If it exists, I must be thinking of it. If I'm thinking it, I must be here. If I'm not here, I can't be thinking of it. If I'm not thinking it, it can't exist. If it doesn't exist, it can't be looking for me. If it's looking for me, I must be thinking it. If I'm thinking it, I must be here. If I'm here, how can I be missing?

Stupid ape. The fear had been replaced with annoyance. *I am not a dream, as you are fully aware. Denying it does not make it any less true.*

More thoughts. More sensations. More noise.

You should not be here. I sent you away. I forbade you. I forbidded you? No, forbade. I forbade you!

My dragon snorted. *You may have rejected me but I did not abandon you. You are my Slayer. Dragons do not relinquish that bond so easily.*

Guilt. So much guilt. Layers and layers of guilt.

I have watched while you destroy yourself with self-loathing. Reached out when you chose to ignore the wisdom of your teachers, drowning in what was not yours to take.

I continued to run from the truth that I had not protected her. That the connection had remained and had left her vulnerable to exploitation through me. I chose to focus on her last comment.

I took nothing I did not need. My protest sounded feeble.

Annoyance flared into anger. *Lies! You tell yourself so many lies. You denied the cautions told to you. You took too much power from the land. You claimed the land's suffering and despair as your own. You used it to fuel your hatred of the black priests. Using stolen power to fight stolen power.*

I felt myself shrinking. She challenged me with the truths that I could no longer cover with my thin web of deception. I was shamed by her reminder that I knew my actions were wrong. I had justified them over and over in order to violate the land again and again. I had held myself to a higher purpose that I had created solely to excuse my behaviour, when I was no better than those I claimed to despise. I had taken one step beyond acceptable limits. Then another. Then further still. Until I could no longer see a path back.

Megin's anger had gone. *Your body is dying. You no longer need it. Do not hold on to it anymore.*

The sudden thought of dying abruptly halted my continued monologue of self-disgust, igniting a fierce protective instinct I had not been aware of.

What do you mean?

The question sounded harsher than I had intended. It was not Megin who had caused my flesh to decay.

We were created by the Goddess for one purpose. We can be more effective without the weakness of your corporeal container.

My dragon stretched her wings, glorifying in her magnificence. She unashamedly declared her size and strength as a statement of undeniable fact rather than as a prideful boast. A body that could crush daemons. That could rip them in two. She promised a life devoted to slaying our daemonic enemies, unconcerned by human frailties. The longing I had previously felt for food and warmth was as nothing compared to the aching need deep in my soul that craved for a permanent joining with my beautiful dragon. To become absorbed into her protection. To be so utterly accepted. Strangely, it was the thought of *Saorsa* and her ruby eyes glinting in the sunlight that calmed the tide into a clear purpose.

No. I projected as much love as I could to soften the blow of another rejection. *I cannot. I have unfinished business that I need to address.*

With the acceptance that I needed to return to my body came the understanding that Megin was still dangerously exposed. The pulsing waves of misery and distress that I now accepted as belonging to the land and were not mine to claim, provided confirmation that my barriers were badly weakened and needed urgent repair if I was to hide Megin's presence. Feeling wretched with regret, I pushed my dragon's consciousness away from mine and turned my attention to the neglected boundary that surrounded my mind. I entered a landscape of pale grey that was as vast and featureless as the black oblivion I had earlier embraced. Anxiety crept into my soul like the cold of a frosty morning and I spun in a circle, frantically searching for any sign of my protective walls. There was nothing. Just endless grey. My defences were completely gone.

The pale mist swirled around my ankles, lustfully rising up to lick at my calves. Darker threads snaked through the ground-covering cloud like a swarm of eels, caressing my feet as they swam past me. Sections of the grey shifted and shaped to reveal foggy landscapes through frosted windows. They shimmered out of focus and I strained to make sense of the blurry images. Fragments became almost recognisable before evaporating back into the blank expanse. More and more windows floated around me; some hovering just above the swirling mist, others hanging far above me, more crowded the space between the two.

I stared at a vision that formed a little to my left, concentrating on the unstable images while I tried to make sense of what I was seeing. A tavern. Dark wooden tables were covered in empty tankards and dirty bowls. Someone was placing the items on a tray before cleaning away the scattered crumbs of a previous meal. The loaded tray was carried to a narrow passageway at the rear of the room, continuing into the kitchen where it was placed on a large table covered with shallow score marks. Several tankards were selected and taken to a smaller bench by a window where they were submerged in a wide bucket of soapy water. Another had entered the room while the items were being washed. Quietly standing behind the first. Standing uncomfortably close. The image spun and I looked into a face that sent my mind swirling into spirals of panic. Dag. His shaven head with its hard features leered at me. As I remembered him from the Mermaid Tavern in North End.

I was seeing a memory that I had bolted behind an iron-rimmed door, deep within the vaults of my mind. The realisation slammed into me and I frantically scanned the other floating visions, revealing so many memories which should have been safely locked away in my hall of doors. They were all open now. Visible to anyone entering my thoughts.

The terrifying thought brought a memory flying towards me at a dizzying speed. It became a doorway and I entered a library lined with bookcases that held the musty smell of old leather-bound tomes and vellum scrolls. I obediently sat at the dark wood table, taking my allotted place before a square of plain parchment, a damaged quill and a half-empty inkwell.

'So nice of you to join me,' purred the deep, nasal voice of Villermir. 'It has been too long since you last addressed your studies.'

I turned to see the priest towering over me as he had when I was a child, but the memory was subtly different. His hair was a lighter shade of blond and his prominent nose seemed more pronounced in a face that was thinner than before. His spitefully mocking eyes, however, were exactly as I remembered them and the cold chips of slate dared me to challenge him. I suppressed the fear that threatened to paralyse me. I was no longer that easily intimidated girl. I gave him the challenging glare he invited and he rewarded me with a smugly satisfied smile that was more disturbing than the scorn. The image of the library, and the illusion of memory, faded and we returned to the bland landscape of my open mind. He continued to tower over me so that I retained the impression that I was still a child in his stern paternal presence.

'You've grown,' he commented benignly.

'And you've grown old,' I replied churlishly.

His smile faltered and his tone became harder. 'Yet, still with the wicked tongue. Still so quick to judge.'

'You shouldn't be here.'

'Here? Where is here? Is this a private space to be jealously guarded? Or is this a shared consciousness where thoughts and ideas can be freely exchanged?'

His placid manner had my thoughts spinning. This was not a memory but was this real? Had Villermir entered my mind as easily as Megin or was this simply my imagination conjuring up the danger I feared? The vision of Villermir continued to smile indulgently while I wrestled with the confusion of reality and deception.

'Why are you here?' I asked, deciding it was a valid question in either situation.

'Tallen,' he mocked gently. 'Why waste time asking questions to which you already know the answers? A more pertinent question would be why do you resist that which is inevitable?'

'And what would that be?'

'We are so very alike, you and I.'

'I am nothing like you!'

'Are you so sure? Do we not both have divine power flowing through us? Do we not both follow the decree that is given to us? Will we not both do whatever it takes to realise that mandate?'

I shook my head in denial but without any real conviction. 'It's not the same thing.'

'Then tell me. How are we different?'

I struggled to unite my thoughts, each justification melting as I tried to reinforce it.

'You hurt people.'

'And you do not?'

The many faces of those that I had harmed ghosted around me in silent accusation. Those I had hurt. Those I had killed.

'You violated the land.'

'And you have not?'

My mind spun faster and faster, viciously judging me while Villermir waited patiently for me to explain how I was unlike him. How my selfish actions were more acceptable than his. How I was maintaining some moral code when I could find no evidence to support that. I chased after every example trying to find an adequate explanation but valid reasons continued to evade me. Eventually, Villermir took pity on me and offered his hand.

'Tallen. We are both aiming for the same goal. Imagine what we could achieve if we pulled in the same direction?'

His words made sense. Despite everything I knew – *thought I knew* – about him. Despite everything I believed, I still found myself doubting my convictions. Perhaps we were trying to achieve the same ending. My obsession with the need to punish Villermir's priests had distracted me from my true goal. My divine goal. The shamans were able to unleash their daemons freely while I had been forced to hide from the Army of Truth and their retribution. Maybe we could, *should*, work together. I needed to stop my campaign of victimising his priests. I needed to return to my primary purpose of ridding the world of daemons. His hand loomed invitingly in front of me, appearing large as my smaller hand reached for it. It seemed so powerful compared to mine. It offered me a confidence in the path I needed to travel.

A shriek of rage caused me to snatch my hand back, reaching up to cover my ears when the scream echoed painfully around my head. The flap of angry, plum-coloured dragon wings caused small tornadoes throughout the grey mist as her scarlet belly arrowed towards us. Megin released a torrent of fire at Villermir, causing his image to evaporate, and I fell backwards into the void.

CHAPTER NINETEEN

The gentle pressure was persistent and I had no effective way of refusing. I followed its guidance to a bright white space that vaguely resembled a room. There appeared to be wall-like structures but the edges were blurred so that there was no clearly visible joining to define the space. It could have been as small as a thimble or as large as a kingdom.

A slight woman faced me with an expectant expression on her face. She wore a long cloak that was the colour of summer oak leaves and it was beautifully embroidered with images of many of the forest's leaves, including those of the beech, hawthorn, sycamore and hazel, along with the oak. She wore practical hunting leathers of the same colour under the rich cloak. Her uncovered hair draped around her shoulders in loose, dark ginger curls and framed a teardrop shaped face that was the colour of hazelnuts. Freckles were freely scattered over her cheeks and around her spring-grass coloured eyes. She was mesmerising.

She gracefully raised her arm and a sparrowhawk glided in to rest on her gauntleted wrist. A rough-coated, blue hound curled around her feet while a white stag strode calmly to stand by her shoulder, his twelve-tined antlers towering above her. Hawk. Hound. Hart. Arduinna. The hound yawned loudly as if bored with my delay in recognising his goddess. I lowered my head in formal obeisance, provoking a sigh of frustration that echoed that of her hound.

'We do not have time for this,' she chastised, causing the hawk to ruffle its feathers. 'I do not understand why she has so much patience with you.'

I was still finding it hard to concentrate and struggled to make the required connections between thoughts. I did not understand why she was annoyed with me and my mind sought the distraction of the warm, brown eyes of the stag that stared fearlessly back at me.

'You are a hunter,' the goddess stated, sharp enough to force my attention back to her. 'It is time you started acting like one.'

'I don't underst–'

'Enough! You abandon your trail as soon as the terrain gets tough. You lose sight of your prey and believe it gone for good. You starve because you lack the strength to overcome the challenges.'

I felt ashamed of everything and nothing. I knew the goddess was disappointed in me, but I was unsure of what in particular I had done to offend her. What crime I needed to do penance for and what I should do to appease her.

'It is not me you need to appease.' Her tone had softened but her expression remained judgmental. 'You need to stop this apathy and start behaving like a hunter. Search the trail for tracks. Listen for the sound of your prey. Fight through the marsh and the brambles. Stalk your quarry.'

Her instructions were clear, I should be able to do as she asked, but the voices of doubt continued to circle my thoughts and drain my will. I had tried to remain strong and keep moving when each step had been exhausting. I had fought to hear the truth behind all the noise proclaiming my weaknesses. And I had failed again and again. I was not strong enough. I could never be what was needed of me. It was too much.

'You are a Dragonslayer, a Moon Warrior and an Empath.' Her voice was as taut as a drawn bowstring. 'These are not empty titles. They are your heritage. The spirits of your ancestors flow in your blood. Do you think they had it easier than you? Do you think they surrendered once the terrain became hard? You fight for every step because it is woven into each fibre within your muscles. You stand tall because your soul is threaded with those who came before you. Your path is long because you are the only one who can walk it.'

Her words ignited the tiniest spark deep inside me. The faintest hint of a defiance. I would not give up that easily. I would face my doubts and overcome my failings. I would accept the guilt for what I had done and strive to be better. The tiny spark inflamed another, spreading to kindle a third. An ember glowed within my chest with just enough warmth to slow the downward spiral into helplessness. Just enough light to see outside of myself and acknowledge my responsibility to others.

I took a deep, decisive breath. 'One step.'

'Every hunt starts with a first step.'

I was still unsure of what I needed to do, much less in my ability to do it, but I knew the first step involved waking up. I had been asleep for far too long and it was time to stop avoiding my reality, whatever shape that currently presented. I just needed to open my eyes.

The soft edges of the empty space sharpened to become clearly defined walls and the harsh, white light softened to a warm, creamy glow. I lay on a thinly padded mattress and looked at the mottled plaster of a wall. A small square table had been placed near my head, on which there was a plain pitcher and a matching shallow bowl. A girl dressed in a long-sleeved linen dress fussed with sections of cloth, folding and arranging them neatly on the table. Her hair had been cut short in a careless fashion, with some chunks hacked shorter than others, and I estimated her age to be around eleven or twelve summers. I watched her careful movements while she finished arranging the cloths to her liking and selected one to dip into the basin, submerging it a few times before wringing out the excess water. She turned towards me with big eyes that sat within a round face, eyes that became wider on finding me looking at her.

'Oh. You're awake.' She stuttered before smiling shyly. 'You're awake.'

I tried to respond but was unable to do more than croak, sending her into a flutter of nervous activity. She scrunched the wet cloth in her fist and raised it as if to drip water into my mouth, before reminding herself that I was awake. She returned to the table to retrieve a cup and poured a small volume of water into the vessel. She awkwardly supported me while trickling the liquid into my mouth, careful enough to prevent me from choking. Satisfied that I had taken enough, the girl replaced the cup and retrieved the cloth to wipe my face. She sat on the side of the bed once she had finished and appraised me with a healer's regard.

'You're a healer?'

'No.' She dipped her head, embarrassed by the claim. 'I could never. But I have seen some work. I watch and do what I can.'

I cleared my throat again and asked the question I had attempted earlier. 'Where am I?'

She stopped anxiously fidgeting with her dress and looked up to smile proudly at me. 'Peverill.'

'Peverill? Peverill Hall?' She nodded happily. 'In Roebaneswood?'

'That's right. King Averill's court is just up the hill. He rarely comes down here, of course, but the queen frequently visits.'

I slumped back into the pillows in muted frustration. I should have stayed in my blissful oblivion where I could ignore the caustic jests of the Gods. I had been captured by the King of Hilman. Ally of Lindvane, where Hayton ruled at Villermir's command. I cursed the goddess and the spider's web she had returned me to.

'Yes,' continued the child cheerfully, misunderstanding my invoking of the goddess's name. 'This used to be a shrine to Arduinna. That was before we found Baila's Truth, of course. There's a spring in the courtyard where people would place their tokens as an offering.'

She looked up and I followed her gaze to where a panel of carved images separated the wall from the ceiling. Hawks, hounds, hares and harts. The creatures of the hunt. Arduinna's symbols.

'What is your name?' I asked the girl, wryly amused at the game the Gods were playing.

'I can't remember my given name,' she replied without any trace of regret. 'Everyone calls me Owl.'

I smiled at another layer being added. I accepted that her name could relate to her wide, owl-like eyes but, with such overt references to the Gods and their schemes, I suspected more than a simple pet-name. I would happily wager than this girl watched everything and knew more than she chose to reveal.

'Thank you, Owl.' She frowned in confusion. 'Thank you for taking care of me.'

She seemed suddenly very young and her cheeks coloured with the embarrassment of someone who was not often shown gratitude.

Under the attentive care of Owl, the poison gradually left my body and I regained my strength. I sacrificed the nutrition in the food I was given to repair the barriers around my mind, placing layer upon layer while I laid helplessly in the bed. Mercifully, I had no more visions of Villermir but Megin was more persistent. Her presence pushed against the excluding walls, pressing into my skull to trigger the crushing migraines I had not felt since releasing her from Wyrm Island. We circled old arguments involving rejection, abandonment, vulnerability and control. Eventually she accepted that I had sufficient strength to block her and she reluctantly left, although I added several more layers despite Megin's confirmation that my protections were adequate. The black vines that told of the land's corruption were still threaded throughout but I was now able to separate their influence from my thoughts. They became a background note of sorrow that served to remind me that I still had work to do.

With my mental fortifications repaired and my memories safely contained behind sturdy doors that had once again been locked and bolted, my attention turned to rebuilding my body. I was shamefully weak, with just the movement needed to sit being enough to make the room spin. Little by little, my aura faded from the dull, sickly brown to a healthier, pale orange, before finally being covered once more by pale skin. Day by day, I spent less time asleep and more time concerned with where I was and the implications of that. I was being kept, comfortably enough, in a small room with a narrow, securely barred window placed high in the wall above the bed. The walls were painted white with no adornment other than the carved frieze that ran around the top of the room, where Arduinna's animals watched in stony silence. The room contained the bed and the small table beside it, as well as a thin straw mattress placed in the corner by the door where Owl slept. The room reminded me of the priests' cells within the temples of Baila, except for the locked door and the barred window.

Muted voices were heard though the thick door moments before it was unlocked and pushed open. Owl had returned with a bundle of clean laundry tucked under her arm and carrying a pail of fresh water. The female guard gave me a fleeting, condescending glance before closing and locking the door. The sound caused a momentary tightening within my chest but the girl seemed unconcerned by her confinement. She dropped the linen at the base of the bed and filled the basin with the fresh water, chatting encouragingly while she helped me to sit. I shivered when my feet touched the cold stone floor.

'I'll be quick,' Owl promised, collecting the soap and cloth and dipping both into the basin.

'I can wash myself,' I protested weakly, having started this conversation several times before.

'I'm sure you can,' she predictably replied. 'But I'm faster.'

She smiled at my discomfort knowing how much I hated being treated like an infant. She methodically scrubbed my face and neck before moving onto my hands and arms. As always, she took care of the scars on my wrists

256

with almost reverent cleaning of their faded ridges and troughs. She gently slid my shirt over my shoulders to expose my back and hesitated, just for a moment, on seeing the pale lines as she had on every occasion before. I sighed, unwilling to let it pass this time.

'They're old scars, Owl,' I chided gently. 'They don't hurt anymore. You do not have to be so careful.'

She smiled shyly, accepting her foolishness. 'I know. It's just…'

'You have scars like these?' I guessed tentatively. 'On your back?'

She nodded, pausing again before continuing. 'How did you get yours?'

I shrugged. 'I've made some bad decisions. One of my more notable mistakes led me to a place where the beating of children was an acceptable practice.'

I noted her slight nod of agreement, confirming her scars had been delivered in similar circumstances. She returned to washing my back but still treated the marks with exaggerated care.

'Owl. You know the scars have nothing to do with you. Or with me. They are not who we are. We just happened to be in range when an angry, frustrated, scared person needed to ease their pain by lashing out at a soft target.'

The girl nodded but remained quiet, her downcast eyes briefly flicking towards my arms and the story told within the faded scars there that made a lie of my words.

'As I said, many bad decisions. Some I would take back if I could. Some were necessary.' I turned my hands over to reveal the inner surfaces of my arms. 'Some I'm still not sure of.'

The Goddess may have softened the visual appearance of the damaged tissue but the meaning remained. I was still uncertain of whether retrieving Kade from Mobis's Hells had been a good or bad decision. From a selfish viewpoint there was no debate, I would readily sacrifice my skin to keep him safe. But I was not entirely convinced that he was safe. And whether he was still tormented by the visions that resulted from his time there. I had not hesitated to extract him from Mobis's realms but grieved for the horror he had brought back with him.

Owl had finished cleaning my back and had moved on to other areas. I continued the conversation as much to cover my awkwardness as to dispel uncomfortable thoughts about Kade.

'You're a good person Owl. You look after me a lot better than I deserve.'

I had hoped to distract her from her dark thoughts and was rewarded with a hint of her shy smile. 'And as a reward for your diligent hard work, you get to stay confined with me day and night.'

'I've had worse tasks,' she admitted quietly.

'I'm sure you have but I don't need continued watching anymore. Are you not needed elsewhere?'

The unassuming girl stopped her ministrations and looked me straight in the eye. 'I've had worse tasks.'

I tilted my head enquiringly and her smile turned from shy to sly. 'Are you misleading your elders, claiming I am more indisposed than I am? How very remiss of you.'

She shrugged and passed a clean shirt to me. 'You are much less demanding than Mistress Keesa. That woman is never satisfied. Even the soldiers hide from her. She has everybody running for fear of her walking cane. She'd have me scrubbing and polishing and carrying.' She smiled again at me. 'It's much quieter in here so I may have exaggerated how much you need my help.'

'Clever girl.' I leaned against the table while she changed the linens on the bed. 'How long have you been here? At Peverill?'

'Since I was five,' she said without concern. 'I was sold to the estate. Not really to the king but I guess I'm part of his possessions. Master Skellin runs everything in Peverill, and most of Roebaneswood, so he would have bought me, but it would have been on behalf of the king.'

I had naively assumed that Owl was a servant or an orphan who had been given shelter in return for her labours. The slave markets that I had seen should have warned me that many in the service of the great estates of Hilman would be slaves, but I had been conveniently ignoring them.

'I'm so sorry,' I started, but the child's confused frown halted me.

'What for? Working for the king's estate is a great honour.' She pushed up the sleeve of her dress to reveal the slave mark branded into her wrist, pointing to the dots below a stylised deer head. 'See? I was bought for ten years labour so I only have four more summers to go before I can start looking for a trade. I'm hoping to be a seamstress. The ladies have such pretty gowns. It would be such an honour to be apprenticed to Mistress Annele.'

She chatted happily about fine tailoring for some time while she helped me back into bed and fussed to ensure I was comfortable. She finally took a breath to stand back and judge her work.

'What about your family?' I asked gently.

She shrugged. 'I don't remember much, other than they were starving. I think I was meant to remember that. I wouldn't have fetched much, being so young, but I'm sure it helped. And I have so many opportunities here that I would never have had, had I stayed in those crowded, smelly streets.'

I smiled at her resilience. She bundled up the dirty laundry, banging on the door in order to be let out so she could take it to the washers. I did not doubt that she was an informant for those holding me captive, but I could not help but like the girl.

I paced the small room. What had started as luxury had now become confining and claustrophobic. I no longer needed its warmth and shelter and I had started to look for ways of escape. The options were depressingly slim. There were only two exits from the cell, the barred window and the locked door. The window may have been just big enough for me to squeeze through but, even if I had the tools needed to prise the deep-seated bars from the wall, it was too high for me to reach even when standing on the bed. The walls were solid stone and I could smash everything in the room against them without causing more damage than some chipped paint. The door was locked from the outside with no access to a handle from the inside, much less the locking mechanism. It fit snugly into the frame so I was unable to see the bolt that secured the door or gain access to the hinge fittings on the opposite side. The craftsman who had designed the door was frustratingly skilled in his work. Secretly leaving my confinement was not going to be an option.

I took a breath.

'No.' Owl spoke before I had the opportunity to ask the question, having asked it many times before. 'I don't know where they have taken your weapons. No one is talking and the boys that clean the armoury haven't noticed anything new.'

The girl sat cross-legged on her thin mattress, quietly sewing a hem into a shirt, and ignored my cursing as she had on all the previous occasions. My thoughts circled on a familiar path while I paced another circle around my side of the room, allowing Owl some degree of privacy around her sleeping area. Plans and strategies were reassessed and rejected in a futile attempt to discover a feasible method of escape. My attention caught on a feature that did not seem to fit my understanding of the Hilman court and had been nagging me for some time.

'Hilman doesn't allow women to be soldiers, does it?' She nodded without interrupting her focus on her needlework. 'But I've only seen female soldiers guarding my door?'

'I told you.' She waved her hand vaguely in the direction of the wall carvings. 'This was Arduinna's place. Men don't come here.' She looked up and smiled at my confusion, happily placing her work aside at the opportunity to share some gossip. 'The goddess is said to protect her site as a sanctuary for women. Any man or boy that comes here says they hear unsettling whispers and feel like they are being watched, even when they are alone. Any that step through the gates say they are cursed with sleepless nights and develop painful rashes and sores. It's said that their manhood shrivels to nothing more than a dried twig.'

'You don't believe that.'

'Of course not,' she grinned mischievously. 'There are hidden passageways in the houses and the barn has a hidden room. The herb garden has a number of plants that can cause rashes and these are easily slipped into the food of anyone foolish enough to eat here.' The smile faded. 'Generally, we give them no reason to come here. It is regarded as a place where women gather to talk about women's things, and these are of no concern to men. The queen has her chambers in the great house, of course, but there are very few places in Roebaneswood where women can be without the overlooking presence of men. This place is protected by any means we have available to us.'

'So, while the men think you are talking about needlework and child-rearing, you are what? Raising an army?'

My mocking tone was harsher than I intended and Owl responded by returning to the shirt, fussing at the straightness of a perfectly straight hem. I continued in a softer tone.

'I'm sorry. I didn't mean to be dismissive. I just don't understand why you would go to so much trouble. What are you hoping to achieve?'

She looked at me with her large, round eyes.

'Your home must be very different from mine,' she said quietly. 'This place is safe for us. This place is freedom. Even someone as unimportant as me can relax without worrying about how I look or how I act. I don't have to be constantly aware of whether I'm being submissive enough or standing too straight. I don't have to constantly judge how close I am to other people, having to make sure I maintain the appropriate distance and not enter a man's personal space. I don't have to scan a room while not lifting my eyes from the floor in order to avoid those that would give me too much attention. Or those who would pay too little and stumble into my path when I could be punished for entering his space. Trying to anticipate every possibility is tiring. Here I can stop to smell a flower or laugh at kittens playing. Here I can learn to protect myself, with a weapon if needed. But there is so much more to it than that.'

She stopped, suddenly aware that she was saying too much, tantalisingly close to revealing what this sanctuary was truly used for. While I still struggled with the reasons, I had seen enough of Hilman to understand how precious a refuge away from men would be for the women here. The woman who had captured me and the female guards outside the door confirmed that there was a faction that showed no subservience, but Owl was too clever to use force when surrounded by those who were stronger than her. This place was not held by strength. I knew that more subtle methods of manipulation would be favoured here, presenting more of a threat to me than those standing outside my door. I needed to know more about the skills offered here, other than the poisons grown in the herb garden, but was unwilling to push Owl further when I had already caused her to anxiously avoid looking at me. I chose a different path.

'You get to run all over Peverill?' She nodded but continued to avert her gaze. 'You must have seen some sights. All those rich people coming to court.'

She smiled at some remembered event and, as I had hoped, her shoulders relaxed. I waited impatiently while she carefully determined what information could be shared and where she should remain silent. Eventually, her love for gossip triumphed and she placed the shirt to one side again.

'The whole town buzzes like a hive when one of the lords arrives. And that's almost all the time. The market here is usually small with only the essentials on offer but when the lords visit, it grows to twice the size. All the craftsmen set up their stalls. Merchants travel for days to get here just for the opportunity to sell to someone important. There's decorated leatherwork, fine pottery and tableware, carved woodwork, everything you can think of. Oh, but the cloth. The softest fabric you will ever touch.' Her wide eyes sparkled. 'My hands turn bright red from all the slaps I get from touching the cloth, but I don't care. Some feel like water flowing through your fingers. Others are as soft as kitten fur. There is every colour you can imagine. Some even have patterns of different colour within the same length of cloth. Not woven but one cloth dyed different colours. Without smudging into each other. And, of course, there are the scarves and shawls and jewellery to match.'

She sighed in happy remembrance of all the treasures she had seen. I gently pushed her for more information.'

'And the lords come all the time?'

She nodded, reluctantly pulling her thoughts away from the stalls of beautiful cloth. 'They come to show their fealty to the king and to Baila. There are always rumours that some lord or other is planning to depose the king or is secretly worshipping the old Gods. Some are called to confirm their allegiances and publicly honour the One True God, but most come to avoid suspicion. Declaring their loyalty before anyone thinks to suspect them. The temple is overflowing with gold and jewels as each tries to outdo the others in showing their devotion to the True Faith.'

Having been impatiently dismissive of Owl's indulgence with soft cloth and dyed fabric, I found myself equally distracted by all those beautiful, precious gems which would be wasted on those pious priests. I wondered if I would have time during my escape to visit the temple and liberate those pretty jewels. It took some effort to refocus my thoughts on gaining information about Peverill and Averill's court.

'Do these lords and their retainers sweep into town like a grand festival parade? Or is that deemed unseemly?'

The girl giggled, sounding more like the child she was rather than the careful Owl she needed to be. 'Everyone loves the spectacle except the grumpy priests. The lords show their loyalty with lavish proclamations and dramatic gestures, each trying to be more extravagant than the last. Not that anyone would dare say so, but much of the fun is watching the priests squirm and scowl and sneer. Pretending it's all far beneath them while trying not to appear too greedy when they snatch the valuable offerings. I mean, it's all done on the steps of the temple where everyone can see, not as a modest private devotion.'

'And they renew their fealty to Averill? Does he fear for his throne?'

Owl fell silent again while she filtered what she believed from that she felt able to tell. When she continued, her words were slower and more considered.

'Our king took the throne. He did not inherit it so I would guess that he would fear someone doing the same to him. But I don't think anybody would want to take it.' She shifted a little on the mattress, clearly uncomfortable talking about this topic. 'Averill has Baila's favour. The priests regularly declare his support for our king. No one would dare to challenge that.'

'And yet they still come to declare fealty,' I wondered aloud. 'What has got the nobility so scared?'

Owl resumed her work on the shirt and I was content to leave her in peace. She had given me much to consider, not least regarding her avoidance of the key details about Averill and his supporters. She had been well trained, revealing enough to satisfy my curiosity but retaining any information which could destabilise the kingdom. I felt my suspicions had been confirmed, that my carer saw everything that happened in Peverill and reported this to someone more senior. I knew that she understood the implications of the things she saw and how they influenced both the town and the court. I had no reason to doubt that she was aware of the ripples this information caused throughout the kingdom. I also knew that Drey would have sold half of his soul to have someone like Owl. I was certain someone here would be equally aware of her talents and was training her as Drey had once trained me.

I awoke to a vision of a tall, graceful woman bathed in a golden light so that her face and hands glowed, softening the features and appearing as a goddess. On seeing me awake, she took a step back out of the sunlight coming through the window and broke the spell. The effect had been intentional and I was instantly aware that the main player in this game had finally arrived.

In a vain attempt to reduce my obvious disadvantage, I kicked off the blankets and rolled to sit on the edge of the bed, careful to hide the pull of protesting muscles, although I was sure Owl had told of my increasing exercise to strengthen my body and sharpen my reflexes. The woman remained impassive and we both assessed each other, circling like two rival hounds despite both of us remaining stationary. She had a long face with deep-set brown eyes and framed by wisps of light brown hair, the main weight of which was coiled elegantly around her head. Her gown was a dark, wine-red and richly tailored with embroidery and gems. This was covered with a thick cloak of a matching shade. Her direct gaze and contained posture radiated confident authority, while her hands remained loosely clasped at her waist. She seemed content to watch me while she waited for me to make the first move.

Reluctantly, I lowered my gaze first and I quickly scanned for Owl, who was absent so that we were the only two in the room. There would be guards waiting behind the door, of course, but it seemed our conversation was to be private. She shifted her position slightly, causing a flare of sunlight to highlight a silver circlet which was mostly covered by her hair. The central portion of the decoration had been left visible above her forehead to show the embossed image of a stag.

'Your highness.' I inclined my head with the acceptable level of respect. 'Am I to finally know why I'm here and why my head is not mounted on a spike?'

A small smile flickered at the corner of her mouth at my mild impertinence. 'So direct.' Her voice was slightly accented but hidden well beneath a lifetime's training in court etiquette. 'But to be expected in one rumoured to be a Dragonslayer.'

My skin flushed with the danger hidden within that statement but I had not been killed so far, it was unlikely that she would change her mind now. I continued with the mildly challenging tone.

'You shouldn't believe all that you hear.'

She inclined her head. 'The stories are quite persuasive. Daemons and ghost armies. A Dragonslayer to save us all. There are even tales of a dragon flying along the east coast. Stories like these have not been told for many generations.'

Her knowledge was extensive. Peverill was located in the mid-south region of Hilman, far from the north-eastern territories where the shamans hunted freely. I doubted that the raiders had been able to infiltrate this far into the kingdom during the time I had been held captive. It was more feasible that Averill had informers throughout his kingdom and Queen Delaina was privy to this information. I took a breath to disingenuously deny my involvement, but the queen continued in a harsher tone.

'You draw too much attention to yourself. Very few are capable of the destruction you have caused. And only one has the colour of your eyes.'

'Your people are being slaughtered by those daemons,' I accused.

'Heretics and outcasts. They are of no consequence. You could have stayed in the north and have been of no consequence as well. But your public humiliation of the priests gave them the excuse they needed to become militarised. And that could not be allowed to continue.'

The thought that I had made the Baila priesthood more powerful threw cold water over my righteous anger at her callous dismissal of those fighting the raiders. My confinement had given me plenty of time to consider my actions as I had travelled across Hilman, and I had plenty to atone for.

'So why am I still alive?' I continued in a quieter, more respectful tone. 'Why have you not handed me over to the priesthood for a public execution?'

She took a breath, shifting her position again to give me the impression that her regal dignity was fighting with her desire to pace the room in irritation.

'That is still an option,' she cautioned. 'There are many who would eagerly claim your death. And one who very much wants you alive.' Her eyes narrowed at my involuntary reaction. 'You present an opportunity to claim much wealth and influence depending on whom I deliver you to.' She shrugged, enjoying my discomfort. 'Or maybe I will keep you for myself. One with your talents could prove very useful.'

She paused, letting my mind explore the implications of being handed over to any one of my many enemies. She watched me carefully to ensure I had understood the fragility of my situation, where she held all the control. I briefly wondered what lengths I would be willing to go to, and how many I would be prepared to kill, in order to avoid being used as a game-piece in her political schemes.

'And then there is this.'

She rotated her hands, turning them to reveal the jewelled dragonfly pendant I had stolen many months ago. The slender gold chain wrapped around the delicate wings and across its body and the cut emeralds flashed as they caught the light. The queen absently stroked the pearl underbelly with the edge of her thumb. I looked up to see an expression that may have been gratitude or relief ripple over her face before it was swiftly masked by her royal impassivity.

'You should not have this,' she stated, closing her hands protectively over the treasured object. 'It was taken from me a long time ago. I had thought it destroyed.'

While I mourned the loss of the pretty piece, it clearly meant more to the queen than just an item of decoration. 'I found it in a town not far from the border with the Northlands. In a merchant's home. Stored with other small items of some sentiment.'

'You stole it,' she accused harshly before softening her tone once again.

'And yet, I find myself grateful for your transgression. I had not expected to see it again.'

'What is it?' I pushed gently. 'Why does it mean so much to you?'

She hesitated. 'I am sure that one of your reputation will be aware that this is more than a simple family heirloom.'

The pendant had called to me, wanting to be found, and I could still feel the energy that contentedly hummed within it. It was not unusual for families to retain powerful artefacts without being aware of their ancient function.

'How does a pious devotee of Baila know about that?'

'Step carefully,' she snapped in response to my dangerously provocative comment. I inclined my head and, satisfied with my apology, she continued. 'This has been passed from mother to daughter for longer than anyone can remember. The connection ties me to my maternal ancestors. It is of great importance.'

'Do you know what it does?' I asked, more carefully this time.

She hesitated again, considering how much to reveal to me. 'I was a child. I cannot be certain what I saw. My mother explained that the dragonfly was said to travel between worlds. Water and air. Present and past. I remember being surrounded by many women.' She shook her head to banish the heretical memories. 'When I become betrothed to Averill, his high priest confiscated it. Claiming that it was a symbol of the old Gods. I had presumed that he had destroyed it.'

'Sold it for a healthy profit instead.'

'Apparently so. And creates the question, what to do about you?'

'You could give me back my weapons. In exchange for the jewel.' She gave me such an icy glare that I could not contain the smirk. 'It was worth a try.'

'Hardly. I should use you to gain political favour, as was my initial intention. But I feel this presents new possibilities. A thief with the ability to detect magickal items could prove advantageous. Heretics would pay well for such trinkets. The priests, even more so. I can see long term profit from having the services of one as skilled as you. The question becomes one of trust. Will you run at the first opportunity? You would be foolish to reject my protection, surrounded as you are by enemies from Hilman and Lindvane. Not to mention some very angry priests.'

The proposal sounded depressingly familiar, with the skills required by the Faulknar crown being equally useful for other kingdoms.

'Consider this,' the queen concluded. 'Work for me and you get to live. Refuse and I will toss you into the feeding frenzy that craves your head.'

Chapter Twenty

I was awarded more freedom following Queen Delaina's visit and regularly left the small room to exercise around the courtyard that was central to the former sanctuary. High stone walls enclosed the compound and effectively shielded its daily routines from those outside, with a double-gate within the south wall guarded by two sentries. There were two main buildings and a small barn within the compound. The larger one backed against the west wall and seemed to provide a domestic arrangement with a bustling stream of cooks and cleaners continually entering and exiting. I was surprised to see a number of well-dressed ladies leaving the two-storey house and walking amongst the courtyard's raised gardens, although Owl had told me that the queen frequently visited the compound so it would make sense that other noblewomen would also make use of the private space.

The small stables were situated opposite the main house, alongside the smaller of the main buildings which seemed primarily used as some form of dormitory or barracks. Meeting rooms flanked the main entrance and there was a partially submerged level where a long corridor contained many doors; some opened into sleeping quarters for the soldiers, some remained closed and may have housed other captives. The courtyard nestled between these two main structures and reflected the strange merging of refined domesticity and underlying violence. Those wearing heavy gowns and soft slippers were content to walk the narrow paths between grassed squares where those in fighting leathers and sturdy boots wrestled or trained with padded staffs. Small gatherings frequently contained both groups, sitting near the raised flowerbeds or beneath one of the few trees to discuss topics common to both courtiers and soldiers. I could only judge the women by their clothing but wondered at how many freely moved between the two sets.

The remaining wall was interrupted by a rocky section of the hill jutting into the compound, and this was the reason for the sanctuary's creation. The spring emerged from the moss-covered stones to trickle into a deep basin, where the pool of water at its depths remained dark and mysterious. Occasionally, the sun would shine at the correct angle for the light to penetrate and highlight the ancient metal tokens, partially hidden by the encroaching algae, which had been offered over countless generations. Fragments of coloured cloth had been forced into the cracks surrounding the spring, in a display that suggested a respect for the old ways had not been as suppressed as much as the priests would like to believe. I could sense the power humming within the shrine, diffusing into those who gathered around it to give a sense of belonging and purpose. I wondered how much this unseen influence was having on the women that came here and their determination to resist Hilman's rigid patriarchy.

My walks around the courtyard, while providing a distraction from the bare walls of my cell, did little to ease my growing impatience. Owl no longer spent all her time with me and I had extended periods to strengthen and tone my body. As I regained my physical fitness, my thoughts turned to the feasibility of escape and I started looking for ways to prepare myself so I could take full advantage of any opportunity that presented itself. I was always accompanied by one or two guards whenever I left the locked room and, while I felt I could overpower these, I would still be surrounded by a number of skilled soldiers as well as those who had come here to learn. The gates were adequately protected and the walls were sufficiently high to prevent a quick exit. The buildings offered a way to scale the east and west barriers but I would be visible to all in the courtyard, always being safely contained within the room long before the protective cover of night. I was unwilling to disrespect the shrine by using that as a means of escape, especially as it presented the same drawback as climbing the buildings. The sanctuary and its surrounding walls may have been selected to avoid observation by those outside, but it was also very effective at keeping people in.

I reluctantly accepted that I would have to wait for whatever errand the queen chose to send me on. Multiple options could become available once I was released from the confines of the compound and I needed to be ready to react when the opportunity came. The basic training I had been able to do within the cell had given me some confidence in my strength, but I had no way of knowing whether my stamina and reflexes would be sufficient. I needed an opponent to test myself against.

I sat on the edge of the raised herb-garden, the pleasant aromas doing nothing to ease my irritation, and my leg rhythmically twitched in frustration at the two students training with padded weapons. Nyx, the woman who had been sent to capture me, glared as my erratic movements disrupted her sense of order and control. She had remained at the sanctuary, taking personal responsibility for my security and always accompanied me whenever I left my cell. She was a quiet and sullen companion but her sense of duty could not be faulted. I had tried to provoke her on many occasions, mainly just to relieve the boredom, but she was steadfast in her dedication and remained stoic and alert despite my antics. I had been appropriately obedient on the last few outings so that Nyx was my only guardian, although I counted five of the more experienced soldiers closely observing me.

'Nyx. Will you spar with me?'

She gave me a suitably withering look. 'I am not going to give you a weapon.'

'Padded sticks are hardly a weapon,' I protested.

'The padding is there to muffle the sound not to soften the blow. They can still do damage.'

I smiled sweetly. 'I promise not to use magick.'

'I'm not giving you a weapon.'

'Wrestling, then. Please? I'm going crazy here. I need to do something other than sit and smell the rosemary.'

The fighter had been cooped up in the compound for as long as I had with only a few who matched her ability. I had gambled on her desire to stretch her skills, knowing she had wanted to test herself against me since the night at the farm, and watched her face while her strict sense of duty battled with her need to best me.

'Where's the risk?' I asked, baiting the trap. 'I'm surrounded by stone walls, at least twelve capable fighters, and double that number of students.'

I saw her quickly survey the courtyard, checking to see who was close enough to hear our conversation and who would be able to react if I proved more than she expected. I suppressed a smug smile of satisfaction and closed the trap.

'Of course, if you think I would pose more of a challenge than you could handle. Despite being so recently half-starved and poisoned. It's probably best that you don't show your failings to your new recruits. I'm not sure that would be good for morale.'

I had to respect her self-control at not growling in response to my blatant insult but her thunderous expression told me I had snared her.

'No weapons. No magick.'

'Agreed.'

Nyx wore her usual fighting leathers and appraised my attire as she removed her cloak and bound her hair into a tail. I was wearing my leather trousers and boots that had been returned, but my Moon Warrior jerkin had remained confiscated along with my weapons so my shirt hung loosely and would be easily grabbed. I had little confidence that I would be able to win the contest so did not deem it a major concern, and was surprised when the older woman called for a close-fitting jacket to be found for me. It seemed her persistent sense of duty would not allow her to benefit from such an advantage. I dipped my head in acknowledgement and mirrored her actions in removing my cloak and tying back my hair. I noticed that everyone in the compound turned to watch when we entered the nearest square of neatly trimmed grass and I welcomed the familiar apprehension, fearing I would make a fool of myself, but knowing I had nothing to lose and much to gain.

We carefully circled each other, neither wanting to make the first move. Wrestling had never been an effective skill for me, I was too small and my reach was too short. We completed another circle. Nyx was relaxed and confident, her steps carefully placed and well balanced. I noted that we had gathered an audience and let my gaze linger a moment longer than was necessary, drawing my opponent in to making the first move. She smiled a predatory sneer, fully aware of my ploy but taking the bait anyway.

The taller woman lunged for the collar of the jacket she had arranged for me. I easily twisted away from the obvious play, trapping her outstretched arm while I moved behind her. She slithered free to move behind me, grabbing the back of my collar and dragging me backwards. I rolled with the momentum, feet over head, breaking her grip and springing back up to face her.

We returned to our circling having taken the initial assessments of each other's preferences and flaws. She had used her superior height and strength but I was not fooled into thinking this would be her only tactic.

I darted in, dipping under her reaching arm and using my speed to twist it behind her. I kicked at the back of her knee to force her to the ground but she grabbed my collar and took me with her, rolling so I was thrown over her head to land on my back. I quickly moved to the side when she leaned forward to pin me to the ground, swinging my arm around as I rose to a kneeling position to add strength into my forearm block against her chest. She raised her arms to trap mine and pulled me into her, twisting so I would fly over her shoulder. I had anticipated the move and braced against her throw, wrapping my free arm around her neck. She reached up to twist the wrist pressed against her neck and easily removed the choke-hold, before turning away, completing her roll, and dragging me with her. Her shoulder slammed painfully into my chest when we hit the ground. I quickly moved to straddle her, flipping her so her face was pressed into the grass. I caught a wrist and twisted the arm behind her back, but she placed a hand beneath her and pushed backwards. I landed heavily and the air was forced out of my lungs when she landed on top of me. I shoved her off me and gained my feet.

We stood facing each other, a few paces apart, and circled again while we recovered our breath. She smiled when I rubbed my sore chest and I returned the gesture when she rolled her shoulder to release the protesting muscles. I searched for a strategy that would give me an advantage, but she gave me no time to consider my options.

She reached for my collar as before and I raised my arms to cover the grab, but she immediately changed tactic and crouched low. She extended her leg while she rotated and her shin caught the side of my knee. I was forced to the ground once more. Nyx immediately pounced to pin me on my back, sitting on my chest and placing a knee on each of my upper arms. She closed her hands around my throat with more strength than was warranted for a training bout and I felt a moment of panic.

My anger flared and flooded my muscles with new energy. I grabbed her thumb, twisting it back to release her grip and sucked in a breath. I snaked my other hand inside her arm to push against her shoulder. She leaned forward to counter, giving me the space to squeeze my knee under her hip. I replaced my hand at her shoulder with my foot and extended my leg to force her backwards, quickly flipping her over and holding her there with a knee pressed into the base of her spine. I twisted one arm around her back and rotated the wrist painfully in retribution for my sore throat, but she exploited my key weakness, easily pushing against my lighter weight and disrupting my balance. I leant forward to counter and she snapped her head back to strike my face. I felt the sting of a torn lip.

'This is starting to feel personal,' I stated dryly, wiping the blood from the corner of my mouth when we circled each other once more.

Nyx glared at me, cold hatred hardening her eyes. 'How very observant of you. Of course this is personal. Are you aware of the harm you have caused?'

'I'm aware,' I answered cautiously.

'Really?' she snapped back. 'You're aware that you've given those priests the perfect excuse to slaughter anyone they choose? You are aware that you've given them a reason to hunt down rumours and false accusations? You are aware that you have condemned everyone who would dare to dream of being free?'

Months of frustration erupted within the fighter and she launched at me. I had no opportunity to attack as she threw a storm of punches and kicks, but I was more comfortable with the methods of a tavern brawl than I was with a wrestling bout. I blocked her punches, letting my forearms absorb the hit and deflect her fists away from my face. I batted straight kicks away from my stomach and twisted away from her rotating kicks, so they fell against the firm muscles of my belly instead of the softness of my side or the vulnerable area over my kidneys. I even managed to connect with a few punches and kicks of my own, but I was tiring fast. My anger had abandoned me and it became increasingly difficult to protect myself. I needed to end the contest before I sustained significant damage.

Nyx brought her elbow down on my shoulder, cracking against my collarbone and causing my arm to go numb. She swiftly moved to stand behind me, wrapping her arm around my neck in a choke-hold and locking it in place with a hand behind my head. I feebly clawed at her arm but my head was already throbbing from the lack of air. I tried pushing her backwards, hoping to topple her onto her back, but she was immobile and my legs could not sustain the effort. The edges of my vision darkened and the centre became blurred. The strength melted from my muscles.

'Stop!'

Nyx turned, dragging me off my feet so that her grip on my neck was the only thing keeping me from falling. She relaxed her hold just enough to allow the blood to return to my head in thunderous pulses. My vision sharpened to find Owl standing within the ring of onlookers, nervously gathering the fabric of her dress within her clenched fists.

'Nyx, stop,' she continued bravely, albeit in a quieter, more pleading tone. 'The queen needs her.'

I felt the woman shiver and she took a calming breath, releasing her hold so I fell to the ground. I braced my hands against the grass and used the gentle tickling sensation as a focus while I closed my eyes and tried to get my ragged breathing under control. The pounding in my head eased and I felt Owl dab at a cut on my swelling cheek. I opened my eyes to see her face close to mine. Red blotches marked her face and neck, displaying an anger she had never shown even the smallest hint of before.

'Was it worth it?' she demanded. 'Was death what you were hoping to achieve? Or did you just wish for the pain of the beating?'

I sighed and let the girl fuss over me. I had achieved my intention, determining that while my strength and reflexes were sufficient, my stamina was still discouragingly lacking. Owl's words, however, highlighted a deeper concern. I had felt a sharp flare of resentment towards the child for having stopped Nyx from killing me.

Owl bustled into the room carrying a small bag and armfuls of rich cloth. Her anger at me after the fight two days previously had disappeared as quickly as it had arrived, although she remained quiet and guarded. Something had triggered her excitement, however, and she chatted without pause while she placed the clothing carefully on the bed and removed items from the bag. A mortar the size of her hand and its matching pestle were placed on the table, swiftly joined by a wide glass jar containing white cream and a cork-stoppered ceramic vial. I watched, quietly amused, while she gossiped about a new lord's recent arrival to Peverill and used the pestle to remove a globule of the cream from the jar, tapping it on the mortar's rim until the paste slid gelatinously into the bowl. She un-stoppered the ceramic vial and sprinkled some of the pale brown powder over the paste. She repeatedly glanced at me while she stirred the mixture, adding more powder until she was satisfied with the colour she had created.

'Sit,' she said, flapping her hands in the direction of the bed.

'What is all this?'

She flashed me a rare, full-mouthed smile that wrinkled the skin around eyes sparkling with barely contained eagerness. She impatiently grabbed my arm and pushed me towards the edge of the bed, placing a finger into the paste before rubbing it into my face.

'The queen is coming to talk to you.' She frowned slightly, adding a little more powder to the mixture to produce an imperceptibly darker shade. 'She wants you to look presentable.'

'I am presentable.'

Owl merely raised her eyebrows at me, rubbing another portion of paste onto my cheek which gained her nod of approval. 'Presentable to the nobles not looking like you've just come from a soldier's barracks.'

'I am in a soldier's barracks.'

The girl tutted and smeared cream over the cuts on my cheeks and at the corner of my mouth, retrieving more from the bowl to cover the bruises that surrounded them.

'She's the queen,' she scolded sternly. 'You are required to look nice for her.'

Content that she had concealed the more visible injuries on my face, Owl turned to the clothing she had brought and bullied me into wearing the dark amber gown. The dress was expertly tailored with pleats and panelling to fit snug but comfortably, and had a high collar which effectively hid the discolouration across my throat. Short, black boots and gloves complimented the gown, with the gloves extending beyond my elbows to cover both the bruised knuckles and my distinctive scars. I tolerated Owl's fussing over my hair while she talked about the latest fashions worn by the ladies of the court, reassuring me that I would compare well with those who had accompanied Lord Kett, the minor noble who had just arrived and who was considered stylish despite being from one of the poorer estates.

She was placing the last restraining pin into my hair when the door swung open and the queen swept into the room. I had thought my dress was luxurious but the queen's outfit was truly magnificent. Tiny pearls were dotted throughout her cornflower-blue gown and these were connected with silver thread to create a diamond pattern within the front panel. Her cloak was a darker shade but the shimmering lining matched the dress perfectly. The queen also wore long gloves that were the colour of an untouched snowfall; no dirt would dare to blemish their perfection. The points of delicate shoes showed at the hem, matching the silver of her gown's needlework and the royal circlet in her hair. Combined with her regal grace, the effect was captivating.

'Walk with me,' she commanded, ignoring Owl's curtsey, and immediately turned to exit the room.

I gave a quick smile of gratitude to Owl and hurried after Queen Delaina. Nyx, as usual, was waiting for me and smoothly joined us to walk the expected two paces behind. The fighter had also changed from her usual leathers into a fine gown of emerald green. I grinned at her obvious discomfort, receiving a poisonous glare in return.

'To what do I owe the pleasure of your company, your highness?' I asked, following the required half-pace behind the queen.

Delaina flicked a look at me out of the corner of her eye. 'I find your directness refreshing, even if it does border on rudeness.'

I dipped my head, offering minimal humility. She maintained her brisk pace along the corridor and chose to ignore my *borderline rudeness*.

'I have been told that your health has improved sufficiently and that refreshes the question as to what to do with you. An opportunity has presented itself where you may demonstrate your talents.' She flicked another look. 'And your loyalty.'

'And what is it that you require of me?' I asked cautiously.

'We will come to that. But first, I feel you should understand the context in which I ask for this service. I sincerely doubt that you would have considered the politics of your actions against Baila's faithful or have taken the time to understand how delicate a balance is being maintained between the ruling families and the priesthood in order to prevent a civil war.'

We had climbed the steps to the main hallway and arrived at the main doors, where the queen continued into the courtyard without pause. I had expected her to take a circuitous route through the gardens, involving several circuits with the pace she was setting, but we headed directly to the gates. I flashed a look at Nyx, who remained impassive, but snapped my attention fully back to the queen when she mentioned Faulknar.

'Faulknar remains divided on the subject of religion, stubbornly holding onto the ways of the past. The Supreme High Priest has his puppet king fight a holy war against his neighbour to ensure Baila succeeds and the old Gods are forgotten.'

'Hayton is no puppet,' I protested. 'And when did Baila get a Supreme High Priest?'

The queen turned to glare at me in sudden annoyance. '*King* Hayton is not who he once was. Faulknar has proved remarkably resilient and Lindvane is increasingly requiring the wealth offered by the priesthood to fund his war. The king has lost power and influence, and he resents it deeply.'

We had reached the exit of the sanctuary and the guards opened one of the gates to allow us to pass. I hesitated despite her clear intention for me to follow. Even dressed in fine clothing, my appearance was far too distinctive to safely venture into a busy town, in clear daylight, which was crawling with priests. The queen turned at my uncertainty and gave me a predatory smile, enjoying my unease.

'Do not flatter yourself,' she mocked. 'People will pay little attention to you, readily assuming you are one of Kett's women.' The smile widened. 'Although it may be prudent to keep your eyes lowered.'

I set my jaw against the frustration of having to play her game and followed her into the street. After all the time I had spent travelling across sparsely populated areas of Hilman and within the peaceful seclusion of the compound, the town threatened to overwhelm me. My senses were bombarded with movement and colour and noise and smells. I feared I was gawking like a country simpleton having never seen a thriving settlement before, but the queen was content to remain quiet while I adjusted to my surroundings and absorbed the splendours of her town. People chatted merrily and greeted their queen with bows and curtsies that showed some level of affection for her. While there remained a visibly strict hierarchy, with women walking a pace behind their men and deferring to them on many occasions, I also saw a level of freedom I had not expected. I sensed no fear or hostility within the busy markets and streets. I suspected I was being shown the more palatable areas, but the town was clean and the people looked well-fed when compared to the other Hilman towns I had seen. It appeared to be a contented, bustling place that reminded me sharply of Liegeport.

Despite the ordinariness of the scene, something struck a dissonant note. I calculated a rough estimate of how long it had been since I had left Elyos's resistance camp. My cloak was thin and the sun was warm on my back. The leaves had been shed from the trees but a number of small green buds were appearing on their branches and the first bulbs were pushing through the ground.

'What season is this?'

Queen Delaina's shoulders stiffened for a heartbeat before she resumed her regal posture. 'We are approaching midwinter.'

I looked around me. 'But it feels like spring?'

She gripped her hands a little tighter. 'The seasons have run differently during these past few years. Each year has been getting noticeably warmer with mild winters and blazing summers. It gets more extreme the further south you travel and many areas of Lindvane have suffered from a prolonged drought. No snow has fallen there for the last two winters. Over half that kingdom has been sucked dry. The season here has been particularly mild this year so that we have barely seen frosts, much less the snow we would usually expect. There seems to be no explanation for it. But I am certain the Supreme High Priest has something to do with it.'

Her voice had turned hard on the last statement and she flicked another sideways glance at me. She resumed the conversation she had started in the sanctuary with a more calculating tone.

'The priesthood has become extremely large and the traditional framework of acolytes, priests and high priests no longer fulfils its requirements, despite the ever-increasing number of ranks within each of those levels. Each town has one or two high priests. We have five here in Peverill. The priesthood was a squabbling nest of egos and there was deemed a need for a higher power to ensure the high priests stayed dedicated to their calling. A Supreme High Priest was created as the ultimate power within Baila's religion.'

'Villermir.'

'Indeed. And he is very interested in you.'

We lapsed into an uncomfortable silence and the queen allowed me to ponder the implications of such a valuable prize being held within her grasp. My thoughts of Villermir, however, focused on the Empathy Crystal and how his use of it to drain the land of its power seemed to be greater than simply diverting rivers and creating large holes in the ground. It seemed he had managed to interrupt the normal cycle of the seasons to create warmer temperatures. I did not want to consider what effect this would have on the production of food within the Three Kingdoms.

'Regardless of whatever he is doing to the weather,' she continued, 'he has cultivated civil unrest throughout the Three Kingdoms. Faulknar and Lindvane are at each other's throats, with Lindvane being backed by the religion's finances to push Baila's doctrine further into Faulknar territory. Leaving Hilman to suffer the ambitions of Baila's priests.'

'What do you mean?'

She paused to consider how, or how much, to explain. 'There are many within Baila's devoted who desire more than they currently have.'

'That sounds close to heresy,' I commented cautiously.

'Many within the priesthood grab what they will and judge any who question them as heretical. The religion runs on power and there are plenty who have insatiable appetites for it. Baila's religion is getting dangerously influential in Hilman, challenging the accepted rule of the nobility.'

'How very annoying for you.'

She gave me a dangerous look to remind me of how precarious my situation was and I regretted my insolent tone, dipping my head in appeasement.

'The nobles are unsettled and that can lead to unfortunate events. The priests have suitably indoctrinated the people and they exert considerable influence of their own. I am sure you are aware of the more *devout* towns in the north. Public beatings and executions are routine punishments for any who step beyond the confines of the scriptures. Any noble who tries to curtail the expansion of the priesthood is faced with their people being incited to riot. Hilman is walking a fine line between acquiescing to the religion's demands and provoking a revolt.'

I had never taken an interest in court politics or the measures required to rule a kingdom, my talents being needed for different purposes. My head hurt as I tried to merge all the actions and consequences involved with this complicated puzzle box.

'You seemed to know a lot about this,' I wondered aloud.

'For a woman? In Hilman?' Her tone was blatantly mocking. 'Do you think we are so different from the women in your Faulknar? Do you think we are less able to see the truths in our situation? The histories may not tell our stories but it does not mean we lack them. Our influence may be expressed in more subtle ways but it can be equally powerful. Women are invisible in Hilman, this is true.' She smiled at me. 'But you cannot expect me to ignore the opportunity that presents.'

'And how do I fit into that?'

We had looped around the main trading area of Peverill and the queen started making her way back to the compound.

'High Priest Maylon has been causing some trouble recently.' The queen glanced at Nyx and I turned to see the older woman scowl. 'He has been accusing people of crimes they did not commit, with the pretence of searching out heretics. A particular interest of his. Good people are being burned and the court is unable to officially intervene. I am inclined to try other methods.'

She paused when a group of people passed close enough to hear our sensitive conversation, allowing them to show their appropriate deference before continuing after they had moved on.

'Maylon has a list of people he intends to target. Noble families he intends to exploit through fear of reprisals. He has become very skilled at manipulating alliances and encouraging ostracism to ensure he gets what he wants. One accusation can destroy a family that has governed for generations. This cannot be allowed to continue.'

'What do you require from me?'

'You are to retrieve that list.'

I blinked at her. 'You want me to steal from a high priest? A fanatically ambitious high priest?'

We had returned to the compound and Hilman's queen waited outside the gates, turning to look at me. The woman's cunning intelligence seemed to radiate from her as her eyes forced her will upon me.

'I see you appreciate the consequences should you fail to complete this task. I expect the document to be presented to me tomorrow morning.'

With Owl absent from the room, I took full advantage and paced the entire space while my mind churned. I tried to formulate plans and strategies for infiltrating one of the most heavily guarded buildings in Hilman, but was repeatedly presented with suggestions on how I would be discovered and my head mounted above the town gates.

Much of my anxiety centred on my concern about using magick once more. After repairing my protective walls, I had avoided touching my source of power and I was unsure of the reaction I would get. I worried that the pain of the land would debilitate me with its continued sorrow and accusation. I feared my walls would crumble, allowing the return of Villermir and his disturbing half-truths. I was scared my guilt would cause me to hesitate when I needed to access it, leaving me fatally vulnerable to the priests and their magickal artefacts, or causing me to fail the queen's task and suffer her swift retribution. I circled the room as the doubts circled my mind, my frustration twisting tighter and tighter inside my chest until I wanted to scream.

I took a deep breath and forced myself to sit in a corner and be still. I pressed my back into the wall and concentrated on my breathing, counting the rhythm of each inhale and exhale until the noise had faded enough for me to focus on the problems I could control rather than those I could not. I had broken into temples before, there was no reason to believe that this would be any different. I was an experienced thief and I was a good one. I had faced dangerous situations before and had somehow managed to escape them. I chose to believe that this would hold true. It would be fine. It would be fine. It would be fine.

I was still trying to convince myself when Nyx came to collect me. I was not surprised that she would accompany me but still felt a flare of irritation that I would be supervised. I worked better alone and did not appreciate the distraction of her evident disapproval. I allowed my hostility to colour my tone.

'It seems I am to have the pleasure of your company, once again.'

'I do not fear that you will run,' she responded, with some hostility of her own. 'You would never reach the town gates. I am here solely to ensure you do not fall into the clutches of Baila's priests. I will kill you before I let them take you.'

'I'm not sure how to take that,' I replied with heavy sarcasm. 'Thank you?'

'I do not do it for you. You have caused enough harm to my kingdom. I will not let you betray this compound or my queen.'

'The task will be easier if I had my weapons. At the least, I will need a knife to lever open locks.'

'I have faith you will be able to adequately improvise,' she replied, stepping aside to give access to the open doorway. 'You waste time. I advise you to go and prove how useful you can be.'

The compound was quiet and a single guard stood by the gate, opening it slightly so we could slip into the deserted street outside. Light shone from a few houses but it was late and many had already taken to their beds. Despite the presence of Nyx, who moved as silently as I, and the insistent doubts I had felt within the cell, I felt a calmness at the familiarity of stalking dark alleys in a town at night. Old habits soothed my anxieties to a small glow deep in my belly and I focused on the information coming from my senses, attending to immediate concerns rather than unknowable future ones. I stayed in the shadows. I scanned for patrols. I assessed each noise for the possibility of danger. All remained safe and we quickly travelled towards the temple that stood at the centre of Peverill.

The building was easily located, with an excessive number of torches burning to defy to the darkness and the evils it contained. We paused, crouching in a secluded doorway close to the illuminated stone steps while we waited for an opportunity to approach. Nyx had previously scouted the temple and advised me of the guards' routines and a possible route of entry. The soldiers changed twice during the night, with two sentries permanently placed either side of the main double-doors. The rest of the building was left unpatrolled, being sufficiently protected by a wide alleyway between it and the neighbouring buildings, and the curve of the front wall which allowed a good view of the temple's sides. We would be noticed by those standing beside the door without them having to move position. The rear of the building pressed against the rocky scarp that wound around the lower half of the hill, leaving a small blind-spot at the far end of each wall. Nyx believed we would have a short window of opportunity during the shift change when the soldiers' focus would be on the front of the building, giving us access to an unguarded side door. I was certain that this would not be without defences but ignored the implications while I determined the safest route to the narrow blind spot.

Without waiting to see if my persistent companion followed, I left the shelter of the doorway and, using doorframes and window-ledges, climbed vertically up the three-storey building and onto its tiled roof. I moved quickly across the adjoining houses before perching on the edge closest to the steep rock-face. I could still see the guards standing on the top steps in front of the temple. A row of iron brackets held the flaming torches that illuminated the passageway with semi-circles of flickering light, but the overlapping sections of light were placed conveniently too far apart to expose the access door. I frowned at the one area of vulnerability being hidden within shadow and did not trust my luck enough for this to have been a simple oversight.

I cautiously lowered my barriers and heard the dissonant throb of the twisted land beneath the louder discord of the temple. I was able to ignore the land's presence and concentrate on the energies being emitted from the building. The seemingly unremarkable wooden door, slightly recessed into the plain stone wall, was vividly covered by lines of power to create a pulsing web over its surface. I could feel its rhythmic malevolence stabbing into my reinforced protections, confirming that the entrance was effectively warded. I focused on the handle and the lock beneath it, defining its distinctive pattern and searching for the key to unravel its defences. The layer was complex but there seemed to be an underlying sigil that centred the matrix.

'What are you waiting for?'

Nyx's sharp whisper so close to my ear fractured my concentration and the interwoven energies disappeared from my vision.

'The guards are changing,' she goaded. 'We have to move. Now!'

I forcibly suppressed my irritation as she was frustratingly correct and our window of concealment was already shrinking. In the absence of any windows facing the temple, we swiftly moved across the roof to the hill and used the narrow cracks within the rock to slow our descent. We barely had time to press our backs against the wall before the dismissed soldiers descended the steps, giving one last glance down the passageway when they left. They crossed the square still unaware of our presence and I heard Nyx release a soft sigh of relief at no alarm having been raised. I smiled at the audible slip in her normal confidence but swiftly returned my focus to the sigil protecting the door, filtering the overlapping energies to reveal its specific characteristics. If I could identify its core signature, I could counter its effects and open the door without igniting my hands, or alert those inside who were sensitive to its power. I gently probed the final layer, careful not to reveal my own questing energy.

'Stop stalling.'

I flinched at Nyx's hissed whisper, clenching my fists in barely contained anger. I turned to face her, our noses almost touching.

'You are not helping! Either you leave me to do this or you may as well hand me over to those guards right now. Stay out of my way or you'll get us both killed.'

The older fighter glared at me but remained silent. I waited a heartbeat longer to emphasise my point before returning to the symbol. It was not one I had seen before although I knew of one that was similar and prayed to Sucellos for his good fortune. I tentatively wove a portion of my aura into what I hoped was the disabling pattern and waited for the violent backlash that would tell me I was wrong. Nothing happened for the space of three, very long, heartbeats, but then a sharp click released the wardings and the energy-web faded. I glanced towards Nyx but she showed no sign of having heard, continuing to glare with impatience at my unwarranted delay. I checked the open end of the alley to confirm that we were still undetected and tentatively reached for the handle. I grasped the metal, feeling no more discomfort than a mild tingling from the residual power, and I encountered no resistance when I turned the handle and opened the door.

Baila's temples were conveniently built to a consistent design and we stepped into the main space, close to the lectern which faced the many rows of seats where the faithful would listen to the prescribed sermons. The gold accentuating the pedestal's carving gleamed in the soft light radiating from the oil lamps placed in niches along the walls. The temple was deserted and I did not feel the need to hide in the shadows as I led Nyx to the far side where there would be a passageway leading to the administrative areas. I was certain that any incriminating lists would be kept within the high priest's study, and hoped that many of the treasures given in tribute would also be stored there. I ignored the side rooms that remained hidden behind sturdy doors and aimed for the one located towards the rear of the building. A hum of power predicted a defensive warding but the threat to this door was considered less than that of the external one, and a commonly used protection sigil had been deemed sufficient. I quickly formed the acorn-styled rune and dissembled the warding without having to break my stride, entering the room without incident.

The high priest's study was similar to those I had encountered before and I felt the usual contempt for the lavish ornamentation that clashed with the religion's message of pious austerity. A sharp intake of breath from my unwelcome companion reminded me that outsiders rarely entered this private space.

'Not what you were expecting?'

She refrained from replying and I left her to explore while I focused on my assigned task. A slightly unpleasant sensation irritated my nerves, suggesting there were numerous magickal artefacts contained within the cabinets and drawers that crowded the room. I avoided investigating those too closely, as much due to my reluctance to tamper with their power as my desire to avoid drawing Nyx's attention to them. She continued to roam the room, completely unaware of the potential wealth of these items to her queen, while I moved to the functional, carved oak desk which dominated the space. I felt certain that a list of heretical sympathisers would be political rather than magickal and would not warrant any special protection. A simple lock denied access to the long, narrow drawer that sat beneath the entire length of the table's top. I scowled at Nyx, resenting the denial of my small blade which would have easily prised open the compartment. I briefly wondered if she would loan me the dagger that rested on her hip, but her answer was too predictable to even bother asking the question and I searched for an alternative. A plain wooden stand sat between two inkwells and held a thin disc embossed with Baila's radiating image. I retrieved the item, testing to see if it was soft silver or a more durable metal, and was pleased to find it was made of highly polished steel. Nyx turned to me with a questioning frown when I flicked the disc.

'I'm improvising.'

My guardian remained suspicious and watched while I slid one end of the object into the thin gap above the lock and pushed it up against the desktop. The device resisted and I adjusted the angle slightly before trying again. I smiled smugly at the resultant snap and Nyx came over to join me as I slid open the drawer, hovering expectantly at my shoulder. Several sheets of parchment littered the space within the compartment, along with other items involved with writing and record keeping which I readily dismissed. I moved a few documents aside, only finding accounts of the mundane purchases needed for the upkeep of the temple and its staff. I stood back to allow Nyx the space to continue looking while I reviewed my assumption that the list would be within the desk. I frowned at the drawer's dimensions that suggested it should be deeper, and smiled when I suddenly realised my error. I pushed the fighter's hands away and trailed my fingernails along the join between the front of the drawer and its base. Just to the left of centre, I was rewarded with the small depression I had expected. I pressed harder and a soft click announced the lifting of the entire base by the width of my finger. I slipped my fingertips under the thin wooden layer and raised it to reveal the hidden compartment. I pulled out the folded sheet of parchment, not bothering to open it and inspect its contents before passing to Nyx.

'I believe this is what you were after.'

The woman snatched the document, unfolding it to read the information recorded. The muscles of her face relaxed and I knew I had found the required list.

'Congratulations,' she stated eventually. 'You get to live a little longer.'

I inclined my head in mock humility, feeling little satisfaction at having discovered the important item. The exercise had proved only mildly challenging and I was still unsure of my ability to fully access my power without unpleasant repercussions. I was uninterested in the politics involved with the names contained within the list, being unaware of the main players in Hilman and caring even less. I scanned the room while Nyx evaluated those mentioned and what it would mean to her kingdom, cursing quietly at some of the names she read. I was hoping for something more than a dull list but dismissed the items that buzzed with power, finding no use for them. I lingered in front of a large cabinet that almost touched the high ceiling. The double-doors were secured at waist height with a substantial lock, and this was reinforced by a small bolt just above my head.

'What are you doing?' asked Nyx when she noticed my hesitation in front of the cabinet. 'We have what we came for. We should leave.'

'I'm just being thorough,' I replied, distracted by the thoughts of what I hoped was inside. 'There might be other items that could prove valuable.'

I was still holding the Baila token and used it to lever open the doors, having drawn back the bolt. It gave easily with a little pressure and the doors swung open to reveal shelves overflowing with gold and silver and jewels and pearls. A nobleman's treasury was carelessly arranged with goblets resting against decorative ornaments, draped in thick chains and sparkling pendants, sitting amongst gaudy rings and studded bracelets. My magpie's heart fluttered with joy at having found the treasure trove I had been hoping to find. I was so absorbed in the beauty of the hoard that I startled guiltily when Nyx closed the doors.

'We have no need for trinkets. It's time we left.'

I did not agree with her dismissal of the sparkling tribute and was reluctant to leave all the precious items to lie unappreciated in a dusty cupboard. I eased open one of the doors for a final look at the pretty jewels, gaining another icy stare from Nyx. After a moment's hesitation, I secured the cabinet and followed her out of the chamber. We left the temple without incident and waited in the shadows for the final change of guard. The climb up the rock-face was more difficult than the descent, with the cracks barely wide enough to support my questing fingers and much less at providing effective leverage for my toes. I scrambled the short distance, anxiously listening for the shout that would announce our discovery, but we both reached the safety of the roof with nothing worse than broken nails and scraped fingers.

Nyx quickly herded me back to the compound and secured me into my cell without further comment, being eager to deliver the list to her queen. I welcomed the sound the door being locked behind me, no longer able to contain a small, satisfied smile. I removed the heavy gold chain from my pocket and stroked the rubies and diamonds that were embedded within its pendant.

CHAPTER TWENTY-ONE

It seemed that my visit to the temple was deemed a success and my next assignment was to be two days later. The midwinter ball was a spectacular event that attracted nobility from across Hilman, often hosting a few from the border towns of Lindvane as well. Queen Delaina had decided to increase the peril within her game by insisting I attend; an important guest would be bringing a magickal artefact and I was to acquire it. I hated the task from every angle that I looked at it.

Owl, on the other hand, was practically bursting with excitement and talked about little else, especially because she had been selected as one of the serving girls for the event. She coached me in the names of the key players who would be attending, providing extensive detail on their estates and marital alliances. She explained the courtly etiquette I would be expected to perform, seemingly unaware that I had grown up in Faulknar's court, but I noted a few differences which would help my guise as a minor noblewoman visiting from a remote estate on the northern moors. Mostly, Owl described the current fashions and trends, and how she would be able to view the fine tailoring when the lords and ladies displayed their importance in silks and velvets, gold and jewels.

I sat impatiently, paying little attention to her instructions and observations while she applied her pastes and powders to cover the discoloured bruises, adding brighter shades to my lips, cheeks and eyelids.

'Is this really your first time at the midwinter ball?' I asked, surprised that the capable girl had not been utilised before.

She nodded, wearing a slight frown of concentration as she dabbed at my face. 'Yes. I can't wait to be so close to those gowns. I've served at other occasions, of course, but never at the main events. Not at the midwinter, the midsummer, or the King's coronation anniversary balls. These are the important ones where people always dress in their finest clothes. The styles and patterns will be copied by the merchants. I'm hoping Mistress Annele will let me help with the designs, seeing as I will have first knowledge of the best gowns.'

'You have not been selected to gather information about ballgown fashion,' I stated a little harshly. 'The queen will be expecting you to spy on her rivals.'

She did not hesitate at my blunt accusation. 'Of course. Both the king and the queen will have informants working as servers, as well as key places elsewhere. People readily overlook those offering delicacies and drink. They are less cautious in their conversations and we can hear information they would normally keep guarded.'

She ignored my resigned sigh and assessed her work, fussing with my hair. She had avoided any ornamentation but had washed it with scented oils and brushed it until it shined. Content with what she saw, she bid me to rise and helped me into the gown that had been chosen for me. Despite my apprehension at going to the event, I had to admit that the dress was beautiful. The soft cloth flowed over my skin when I stepped into the skirt and Owl lifted the material to cover me. The pale lemon colouring was highlighted with tiny beads of clear glass that sparkled when they caught the light. Owl tightened the laces at the rear of the gown to achieve a snug fit around my waist and chest, with several thin straps radiating over my shoulders to leave my neck and collarbones exposed. The skirt hung straight from my hips to brush the floor with its hem, with pleats at the waistband to allow unrestricted movement while maintaining the modest slim outline. Long gloves of cream and matching slippers completed the outfit.

'Here,' the girl said after she had finished adjusting the straps over my shoulders to exactly where she wanted them. 'The gown has pockets.'

She lifted the edge of one of the pleats at the waist to reveal a small metal catch. She unhooked the top section and folded back the cloth, encouraging me to place my hand inside. My fingers slipped easily into the silk-lined space that separated the lining from the outer surface of the dress, extending to a point in the middle of my thigh.

'There is another deep pocket on the opposite side,' she informed me.

'And two smaller ones at the back. You probably didn't need all four but I kept them in case you needed them.'

I withdrew my hand and Owl re-clasped the pocket, smoothing the material although I could see no trace of the hidden compartment. I smiled at the latest skill within the range of her talents.

'This is not the first dress you have made with added layers.'

She looked at me as if I had asked the silliest question she had ever heard. 'Of course not. Not everyone is as stubborn as Nyx. Most enjoy the social occasions and attend as many balls or regal events as they can. Always wanting a new gown.'

'So, Nyx won't be going to the ball?' I asked hopefully.

The girl giggled. 'I don't think she's trusted not to cause a scene. Her scowl alone would be enough to turn the sweet pastries sour.'

I grinned back, thinking that would be a scene worth seeing, but quickly turned to consider the possibilities without my persistent guardian watching my every move. With so many people contained within a small space, it offered an ideal time to disappear into the crowd and slip away unnoticed. That was, of course, if I had not been discovered and claimed for a very public execution by the high priests who would be in attendance.

Owl had moved to the box she had placed carefully on the table, opening it to reveal the last element of my disguise. Having protested that the busy event would leave me exposed to recognition, with my description being frequently discussed throughout Peverill, I was calmly informed that the danger would be minimal as the midwinter ball was to be a masquerade. I remained unconvinced, fearing my distinctive amber eyes would be enough to condemn me, but found myself gasping at the beauty of the creation Owl removed from its case. The mask was big enough to cover most of my face. The vibrant reds and yellows of the phoenix's body would sit over my nose while the wings, which wrapped around my face, contained shades of orange and gold that perfectly matched my eyes. The creature's neck extended between my eyebrows in a graceful arch so that the head laid flat against my forehead. It was exquisitely crafted with each feather stitched carefully into the fabric to give the impression of a real bird that could take to flight if startled. I held the mask in place while Owl fastened the laces behind my head, the material flexible enough to fit smoothly against my skin and allow unhindered vision. Nobody would be looking at my eyes.

Owl appraised me with her head tilted and her eyes slightly narrowed as if something was not to her liking. I nervously smoothed the fabric over my belly, concerned that I was causing the blemish in her perfect creation. She nodded to herself after a few heartbeats and shooed me away from beside the bed. She went, without hesitation, to the third plank from the top, lifted the mattress and slid the wood within the joint which secured the base to the frame. I stared as she hooked her small fingers into the space I had created there and retrieved the stolen pendant.

'How did you know about that?'

She shrugged. 'I clean your room and there are only a few places where you can hide things.' She smiled shyly at me before placing the oval pendant around my neck. 'You are a thief.'

I shook my head, sadly impressed by the skills trained into this clever girl. 'Promise me that you'll be careful.'

'With what?'

I hesitated, unsure of how much of my concern was due to my own experiences. Uncertain of whether I would have benefited from someone warning me when I was her age.

'The people who are training you. When they ask you to do these things, they will not consider whether it's in your best interests. You are just another tool to them, to be used purely to meet their own needs.'

She frowned in confusion. 'I don't understand.'

I struggled to find the right words to clearly convey my unease. 'You should watch those who would befriend you as carefully as those you are sent to spy upon. You need to protect yourself from some of the things you will be asked to do.' Her frown deepened and I knew she did not understand what I was trying to warn her of. 'Just… don't trust anyone.'

'No one?'

'Preferably.'

'I trust you.'

I threw my hands up in exasperation. 'My point exactly! Owl, I'm the last person you should trust.'

She scowled at my pessimism but said no more and left soon after to prepare for her duties. I was unwilling to sit and crease the fine gown while I waited so I paced, reviewing once more the next impossible task the queen had given me. I had been told that an important guest would have a magickal artefact and that I was to steal it. I had not been told who the guest was, why they had brought the item to a ball, or what that object would be. I trusted that the artefact would emit an energy signature and hoped it would not be too well hidden, I would not have the time or the excuse to roam the royal building at leisure. My main concern, however, were the priests who may also be aware of the item and would be hoping to obtain it for themselves. I did not want to draw attention to myself by searching for something that they also sought. I hated the assignment, preferring to sneak into Peverill Hall unnoticed instead of parading in the snake pit of a royal court. My social skills were painfully inadequate for the posturing ambitions I would need to infiltrate. Something I had no doubt Delaina was maliciously aware of.

It was not long before I was collected and the charade commenced. A curvaceous blonde opened the door, attractively filling her gown in a way that made me feel like a bony, malnourished street rat in comparison. I snatched the cloak from the bed and wrapped it around my bare shoulders to protect them from the chilly air, hurrying after the woman who was already some way along the corridor.

'No Nyx tonight then?' I asked casually.

The woman did not break her stride and refrained from turning to face me as she replied. 'Nyx is busy elsewhere tonight. She has, however, informed me not to let you out of my sight and to let you know that I have a number of different ways with which to kill you without attracting undue attention.'

Following her last comment, she turned to flash me a challenging smile and my thoughts of an easy escape faded. She returned to ignoring me and I was left to study the back of her ice-white gown, convincing myself that I could see Owl's hidden pockets, with the possible outline of a dagger.

We left the sanctuary, gaining the protection of a single guard, and we made our way to the main house. I saw no suspicion in his expression as he adopted his position two paces behind us, but had no way of knowing whether this was because he had been informed of who he was escorting or if my mask sufficiently obscured my distinctive features. I dismissed my nagging concern and focused on my companion. She had secured her mask when we left the compound, with the creation being less flamboyant than mine but still beautifully made. The white feathers of the swan matched both the gown and the ermine trim that wrapped around her shoulders. There were few other people about in this part of the town and none who were dressed for the ball, so I was unable to judge whether our outfits reflected the fashion expected or whether, knowing the queen's passion for games, we were conspicuously dressed.

Dusk darkened into night and we left the town to walk the winding road that led up the hill. Tall iron braziers held blazing beacons of fire at regular intervals to light the way, flickering against the occasional sharp boulders which poked through the turf. The scar that cut across the mound provided a natural border between the town and the more affluent areas of Peverill. The closer we got to Averill's hall, the larger and more elaborate the houses became. Each was distinctly separated from its neighbour, initially by walls and fences to mark the boundaries but later by the significant distance between the properties.

Evidence of the evening's festivities only became noticeable when we neared the Hilman king's residence. The midwinter celebrations in Faulknar had been a riotous affair, with the whole of Liegeport gathering to bid farewell to the long nights and welcome the anticipation of spring. Food and drink were freely available, with the music and dancing starting early in the afternoon and lasting well into the following day. It seemed the occasion was more strictly controlled in Hilman so that even the grand houses we had passed on the climb had little decoration to herald the longest night of the year. Their austerity made a clear statement when compared to the extravagant display that awaited the favoured guests.

I saw expressions of admiration and delight on the faces of the expensively dressed noble men and women approaching the estate. Peverill Hall was encircled by high walls that funnelled attention through the open iron gates and along the well-maintained road to the house. We were guided towards the large manor by colourful banners that had been strung between the illuminating beacons. The sundry buildings required to maintain the royal estate were carefully hidden by the darkness so the hall stood proudly at the centre of everyone's view. Lights shone invitingly from all the front-facing windows of the tall house, and from the round towers which stood to each side of the building to add a sense of strength and command. The main entrance jutted forward from the main structure and greeted visitors with four imposing, decorated columns that supported a square roof, crenulations running along the top. The heraldic rearing stag and crown was carved into the stone block above the doorway. It seemed to dance in the flickering light of the two large braziers that burned with powders to create a rainbow of coloured flame.

My companion stayed close by my side and we moved with the flow of people into the entrance area. Our cloaks were taken by liveried staff before being ushered into a reception hall, ornamented with evergreens and winter berries to match the decorations adorning the dominating wide, stone staircase. An intricate tile mosaic covered the floor, with complicated geometric patterns bordering scenes of the hunting and slaying of exotic beasts. The guard, who had shadowed us from the compound, left to join the other attendants and they made for a nearby side door, while I obediently followed the stream of guests towards the main ballroom.

I paused under a decorated archway that led into the hall, dazed by a dizzying kaleidoscope of people in colourful masks weaving amongst each other and the torrent of noise that pulsated throughout the room. The heat generated by the press of so many people within the confined space added to the thick cloud of cloying perfume and I found it difficult to breathe. I was buffeted by the cacophony of too many conversations and harsh laughter clashing against the music of three musicians playing beside a stage, the elegant seating remaining abandoned. Panic bubbled within my chest from being surrounded by so many people and being unable to identify the potential threats within the roiling mass of distractions. I took a step backwards, my mind screaming that this was too great a risk. I should not be here. I should flee while I still had the opportunity.

My companion slipped her arm through mine, firmly guiding me to one side and away from the busiest area around the entrance. She led me to a space by a large glass window, smiling politely at those around us and greeting a few by name. The relatively secluded spot created a little distance from those nearby and I was able to take a calming breath, drawing on her relaxed confidence to slow my racing heart.

'A trained solider, said to have battled Mobis's daemons, and you look ready to bolt from a routine social gathering.'

I looked to see unexpected humour in her expression and felt embarrassed by my unnecessary reaction. 'I doubt the skills I have on the battlefield would be appropriate here.'

Her grin widened with wicked amusement. 'But it would be very entertaining.'

She kept her arm firmly linked through mine in a gesture that felt slightly more restraining than companionable, and quietly advised me on the key players in attendance. I studied the dynamics and the subtle signs of Hilman society that permeated the room, only half listening to her coaching. The hall was full of sophisticated men and women who were elegantly dressed in pale shades that contrasted sharply with the vibrant darker colours of the room's decorations, and I wondered whether this had been by design.

Despite the press of people within the restrictive space, three distinct groups seemed to have developed. An exclusively male group had gathered closest to the stage, seeming to talk about important matters with their serious expressions and grave nods of agreement. I quickly dismissed them and moved my attention to the central area where both men and women had gathered. I frowned in disappointment at the blatant patriarchy displayed, with the men doing most of the talking and the women remaining quietly submissive a half-pace behind. Most of the women remained permanently attached to their man, although there was a minority who confidently moved between the groups to chat amiably with all. The final group was exclusively female and I had been placed within this section. The postures and conversations that surrounded me were more relaxed and animated than within the other groups, remaining refined and polite but showing more freedom than I had anticipated.

'Lord Sandbroke is the one wearing the badger mask.'

My guardian's comments interrupted my casual observations and I looked to see a short, lean man accompanying an equally short woman with a raven disguise.

'He is being watched by the priesthood,' she continued. 'Seen as a potential threat, so has come to Peverill to reaffirm his loyalty. He is the third lord who has felt the need recently, following Kett, and Pollard before him. Those three will not be seen in each other's company but will favour those more overtly devout. Those such as Boxhill, there with the ram mask, or Gelven, the one with the horse.'

I found it hard to concentrate on her narrative about people I did not know or care about. My attention drifted to the more superficial aspects, noting that there seemed to be no distinction between different classes of guest. All were similarly dressed in expensive tailoring and demonstrating impeccable courtly etiquette. While my facial covering was elaborate, it was not so different that it would invite special attention. The masks were beautifully crafted and many included fur or feathers to complement the shading within the outfits. Creatures of the forest blended with those of the farm, land beasts were represented amongst those of the air. I welcomed the concealment offered by my mask while resenting it in others, finding it impossible to read the expressions which informed me of a person's intent. I idly wondered how many of the noblewomen present were working for the queen and I scanned the servers searching for Owl.

'You're not listening to anything I'm telling you, are you?'

I smiled apologetically. 'I have no idea who you are talking about, and I've seen three rams and at least five horses. I'm not here to learn of the politics involving minor nobles.'

She lifted her head at my mild insult but her tone remained polite. 'There are more here than minor nobles, but you are probably correct. You will not find what you need hiding in a corner. It is probably time you circulated among Hilman's finest families.'

Continuing to tightly clasp my arm, she led me away from my circle of relative safety and aimed for three women who were standing at the border between the female-only section and that containing the mixed groups. The women separated smoothly to include us when we approached, smiling politely at the interruption of their conversation.

'Nallin. How lovely to see you,' greeted a brunette to my left who was wearing a delicate fawn's mask. 'My dear, your swan is truly delightful.'

My chaperone dipped her head in acknowledgement. 'Thank you, Fliss. I'm hoping to channel some of its grace.'

Her comment received a polite murmur of laughter before a black-haired woman wearing a black-cat mask turned to me. 'I don't believe I have seen you at court before. Although it is hard to tell behind these masks, of course.'

'Ladies,' Nallin began before I had a chance to respond to the mildly accusatory tone. 'May I present Lady Keelan.'

I demurely inclined my head but the cat pursued her enquiry. 'And what brings you to our court, Lady Keelan?'

'I'm just here for the midwinter celebrations,' I replied cautiously.

The woman tilted her head. 'Have you come far? I can't quite place the accent?'

'My father owns a small moorland estate near the Northland's border.' I resisted the temptation to snarl at her condescending tone while increasing the lilt I had mimicked whilst at the Sanctuary of The Moon Goddess, hoping it would cover my native Faulknar drawl. 'He thought it was appropriate for me to become accustomed with more esteemed company.'

She inclined her head at my flattery and seemed to accept my story. The woman beside her, wearing an extravagant woodpecker mask, tapped her lightly on the wrist.

'Come now, Salome. You are far too suspicious of everybody. Give the girl mercy.'

'Melody's right,' agreed Fliss. 'We are all aware of the disquiet rippling through the kingdom and, Baila knows, you have more right than most to be cautious. But can we not enjoy the simple pleasure of each other's company for one night?'

Salome looked over my shoulder to the hall's entrance and her posture stiffened in response to what she saw there. 'Apparently not.'

We all turned to see the new arrivals and the room became quiet, leaving only the musicians to disturb the uncomfortable hush. My apprehension was echoed throughout the hall when three high priests walked confidently into the crowded space, creating a respectfully clear area around them as they made their way to the raised platform. They remained unmasked and their grey, banded robes seemed to silently imply that our costumes were frivolous and gaudy. Their manner was similarly condescending when, after taking their seats at the near side of the stage, they critically surveyed those gathered before them. Slowly people returned to their conversations, albeit maintaining more sombre tones under the priests' glared judgement of anyone deemed to be having anything more than minimal enjoyment.

The event remained subdued and the guests stayed within their allotted sections, suitably inhibited from any casual mingling for fear that it may draw the attention of the high priests, until the final and most important guests arrived. Their delayed appearance increased the level of anticipation and drew a whisper of approval when Hilman's king and queen emerged from the private entrance at the far end of the platform. The pair dazzled in lavishly tailored outfits of white, showing flashes of the crimson and jade inserts. They ascended the steps and walked to the front of the stage, with the queen's hand resting lightly on the king's arm. Both had selected masks that acknowledged their heraldic crest. The antlers of Averill's stag extended far above his brow, while those of Delaina's doe bordered the elaborate weaves which coiled through her hair. The king gallantly escorted his queen to the smaller of the two central, richly upholstered, high-backed chairs before turning to address his audience.

'Welcome,' he began, spreading his arms wide to heighten his already commanding presence, 'to the annual midwinter ball. Tonight, we celebrate all that we have achieved since last midwinter and, by the grace of Baila,' he turned to incline his head to the priests before returning to the attentive crowd, 'look to the spring and the promise of continued prosperity. Let us forget the troubles of yesterday and rejoice in this night's blessing of such distinguished guests.'

A polite murmuring acknowledged the king's speech, increasing in volume when he remained standing. With a small smile on his face that hinted of further dramatics, he turned back towards the door from which he had entered. The light flared on his gold coronet, retained beneath the stag's head mask, and people started to question the delay in commencing the festivities. When the door opened, Averill returned to address his expectant audience.

'Our midwinter ball has been especially favoured this year by the grace of two very honourable guests. May I present their highnesses, King Hayton Lindvane and his King-in-Waiting, Hulce Lindvane.'

A ripple of surprise spread throughout the hall, quickly followed by polite applause when the two men ascended onto the stage. My heart raced with the implications of Faulknar's enemies being so close and the increased jeopardy of my situation. I looked to the queen, finding her maliciously amused by my obvious discomfort at the very public reveal of yet more layers within her dangerous game. I turned to see Nallin share a glance with Fliss. It seemed that Hayton's presence was as much as surprise to them as it had been to me. Melody fluttered at Salome, enthusiastically expressing her hope that she would be introduced to the King-in-Waiting while seemingly oblivious to the older woman's deepening scowl. Their contrasting attitudes were repeated throughout the ballroom and I saw expressions of pleasant surprise alongside those of guarded mistrust. In light of my conversation with Delaina and the list of names I had acquired for her, I suspected that many were swiftly calculating how to use access to Lindvane's royalty to their advantage.

Averill bid the festivities to commence and this signalled the arrival of a new army of servers to join those offering drinks, each carrying a tray of bite-size delicacies still warm and soft. Small tables had been placed beside the royal guests' comfortable chairs so that a selection of delights could be placed within easy reach. The priests refrained from sampling either food or drink, and remained apart from the more celebratory atmosphere which had resumed in the presence of Hilman's regal couple. People had returned to chatting freely and the separate groups started to blend, with individuals drifting in and out of the central area to introduce or be introduced.

I ignored the politics on the floor and studied the dynamics on the platform. Averill and Delaina were faultless in their performance as benevolent rulers, watching parentally over their guests and giving dignified nods or generous smiles to those they favoured. The high priests remained impassive but had dampened their silent condemnation following the king's explicit instruction to celebrate. I had no interest in their displeasure and instead turned my focus to the Lindvane pair.

I had spent my childhood fearing Hayton and hating him for the war that had taken Laken from me. The person on the stage did not match the monster I had created in my mind. The years of war seemed to have taken a hard physical toll on the man and he looked older than I had expected. In contrast to Averill's imperious confidence, Hayton looked small and tired, with a slightly stooped posture and wandering gaze. Lindvane's king had personally led many military campaigns, and much of the stiffness he had shown when mounting the platform's steps and taking his seat was probably due to old injuries which now restricted his joints. Despite all this, he had a fearsome reputation in Faulknar and I did not believe that he was as defeated as Delaina had suggested. I remained reluctant to dismiss him and saw that behind the tusked boar mask his shrewd eyes judged anyone caught in his scathing glare.

Hayton's eldest son, however, was a completely different matter. His manner and bearing were arrogant and confrontational. He had chosen a dark cobalt tunic above black shirt and trousers, appearing gaudy and antagonistic among the subdued shades of the other guests. He had forgone the expected facial covering, with his head decorated by a heavily jewelled circlet upon his curling black hair and a number of diamond studs in his ears. There was more than a hint of casual cruelty in his dark stare, and this was reinforced by the slight sneer with which he appraised the nobility paraded in front of him. A thick gold rope hung from his neck and bejewelled rings adorned several fingers, decoration which would easily fund a garrison of soldiers to bolster his father's war. Delaina seemed to consider him an immature fool who was easily influenced by those around him, but I doubted that he was any less of a threat because of this. Villermir would certainly appreciate such an impressionable pupil.

The noise level within the hall rose. Conversations and discussions resumed and the numbers within each group swelled. Nallin continued to talk with Fliss, commenting on who was spending time with whom and who was being avoided. I was content to stand quietly nearby, essentially forgotten, and considered what it was that queen was wanting me to acquire and where it would be hidden. I doubted anyone would be foolish enough to bring it to the festivities where three high priests would be aware of its presence, but I felt obliged to lower my mental defences a little to determine whether there was anything interesting within in the room. Apart from Hulce, the jewellery worn by both lords and ladies was discreet, understated and unimportant. I doubted the queen would have engaged my services for those of routine status, no doubt having other thieves who she could call upon. I feared I would need to gain closer access to the Lindvane pair to rule out any charmed amulets or enchanted crystals, but I would only risk exposing myself that way once all other options had been exhausted.

My attention sharpened when two of the priests rose and descended the platform, mingling with the guests in the male contingent in front of the stage. Hulce, having ignored his father's attempts at conversation, swiftly moved to one of the vacated chairs and engaged the remaining priest in deep discussion, leaning forward to ensure he heard every word of the man's quiet speech. Averill shared a humorous comment with Hayton that I suspected was at Hulce's expense, while Delaina maintained her quiet majesty of regal ornamentation. I ignored the games being played on the stage. I was more concerned with the roaming priests, particularly as one seemed to be heading directly towards me. Nallin noticed when I tensed and looked to see what had prompted my reaction.

'It will be nothing to worry about,' she dismissed. 'He's probably just looking for information about those newly arrived in Peverill. You know how they are? They want to know everything about everyone.'

She returned to her conversation with Fliss, with Salome and Melody joining them. The woodpecker linked her arm through my guardian's, proceeding to guide her to the central area and a mixed group where both men and women chatted amiably. Nallin was dragged away, turning back to glare a silent command for to me to stay where I was, but I had decided it was time I left the festivities and explored the house where the magickal trinket was more likely to be found. I placed my untouched drink on the tray of a passing server and moved towards the archway.

I had barely made three paces before the priest stepped from behind a pair of tall guests and blocked my exit, knowing I could not avoid him without causing offence. I dipped my head in acknowledgement but refrained from feeding his ego by giving him his title. He waited throughout an awkward pause, eventually deciding not to highlight my implied insult by correcting the oversight.

'I don't believe you have attended the temple.' His voice was tight as he mildly chastised my disobedience. 'Although, it is difficult to recognise faces with all these masks.'

'My apologies. I've not been in Peverill very long and I confess that I have been distracted by the preparations needed for this evening's entertainment.'

He frowned slightly at my poor excuse and his gaze dropped to the pendant around my neck. I resisted the sudden urge to protectively curl my hand around it, knowing I would only draw more attention to it.

'Are you a member of Kett's delegation, perhaps?' he persisted. 'Correct me if I am wrong, but the styling of your decoration appears similar to that offered in tribute.'

I was not surprised that a Baila priest would remember the treasures given in tribute, despite their pious protests against material value.

'It's a popular style.' I mimicked Owl's interest in fashion and casually stroked the central ruby. 'Many noblewomen have similar designs, I believe. I prefer the red but I have seen the coloured glass in many different shades. The merchant of this piece had ones in green and blue and yellow.'

My mindless chatter sufficiently bored the priest and he took a step away to conclude our conversation. I felt more than a little satisfaction at the suspicion starting to tighten the corners of his eyes, having planted the seed of doubt that Kett's tribute was worth as much as it had seemed. I wondered how long it would take before he felt the need to check that the jewels were authentic and not cheap alternatives.

'Well,' he said, turning away having already dismissed me from his concerns. 'You should attend the temple while you are here, giving your devotions as appropriate.'

He did not wait for my answer and disappeared within the mass of people. I relaxed, smoothing the front of my gown in a release of nervous tension before moving once more towards the exit. My path was blocked yet again, this time by a grinning Owl.

'Pastry?' she asked innocently, lifting a tray of savoury delicacies.

'No thank you,' I replied sternly, although I could not contain a small smile. 'I assume your sudden presence is not purely to appease my hunger?'

She lowered the plate and stepped aside to return my access to the archway. She lowered her voice and leaned in with a more serious expression.

'The queen asks that you go to the ladies' receiving room.'

'Why?'

She dramatically rolled her eyes. 'How would I know?'

'Because you know everything.'

She smiled again before merging into the crowd, immediately assuming the demeanour of an unimportant servant. I shook my head at the ease at which people accepted her insignificance while she readily gained information from those who deemed her practically invisible. I made my way through the last few guests and finally escaped into the quieter reception area. A few people conversed in small groups, scattered around the walls to leave the central area free for the hurrying serving staff who carried full platters to the main hall and empty trays to the kitchens. There were three wooden doors along the wall opposite the ballroom, elegantly carved to compliment the scenes within the mosaic tiles. I heard quiet music coming from the middle door and moved towards its brightly illuminated room, less interested in the female conversations which confirmed the receiving room I had been called to attend, and drawn more to the melody which sang above the strings. It was a voice I recognised.

The room was tastefully decorated with soft furnishings and large tapestries. Several women remained standing, chatting freely, while others relaxed on the many comfortable chairs and couches which filled the space. Small braziers burned in the corners of the room to provide heat and added a softer light to the bright, pleasantly scented candles that were placed generously throughout the chamber. The atmosphere was refined and graceful and my arrival elicited little more than a cursory glance, albeit one sharpened with political ambition. The underlying current of constant judgement under the facade of polite sophistication made my head ache, and reminded me of why I had avoided social gatherings whenever possible during my time in Liegeport.

I scanned the different groups and, finding none that were keen to include me, I made my way to the elderly man who sat to one side where he was mostly ignored. His melody wove delicately around the mellow tones of his lap-harp and he smiled in acknowledgement of my approach. He continued to sing so I sat on a padded stool beside him and idly watched those in the room. I thought I recognised a couple from the compound but it was difficult to be certain under the masks and I soon grew bored, letting my attention drift to the jewelled ornaments displayed on tall, narrow tables. I contemplated stealing the little golden bird that stood no taller than my first finger. It had small sapphire studs for eyes. It would fit easily into one of my pockets.

'It's a pretty decoration,' the singer commented, having finished his song. 'But the queen is very fond of it and it would be missed.'

I ignored his accusation, unconcerned that my thieving nature was so obvious to him and offered an observation of my own.

'A minstrel on occasion, you said.' My comment provoked a depreciative smile in the man who had brought me to Peverill. 'This is certainly some occasion.'

'I feel the need to formally introduce myself. The appropriate opportunity not having previously presented itself.'

'With me being poisoned, bound and abducted.'

He dipped his head in acknowledgement. 'Indeed. My name is Laryn Agalan. I am the queen's official musician, although I am occasionally employed as a storyteller.' He leaned towards me, lowering his voice conspiratorially. 'These ladies rarely have the patience for a good tale.'

'Minstrel for formal receptions, stories for the tavern. Your skills prove beneficial for a variety of situations.'

'I can legitimately go to places where others would be conspicuous. Such as attending a female-only reception. My purpose generally involves relaying messages, but I also hear things that may prove useful for my queen.'

'Such as the location of the person causing so much trouble for Baila's priesthood?'

'Your activities were certainly well discussed and you have already guessed my additional, hidden advantage. My queen had need of my services and I complied.' His expression softened while he appraised me. 'It is good to see you have recovered since I last saw you. There is even some colour to your cheeks.'

'How can you tell under all this?' I waved a hand at the mask obscuring my face. 'It's so difficult to tell what people are thinking, but perhaps that's the point in this snake pit.'

He smiled at my petulant tone. 'It's easier when you know what to look for. People are predictable and they often chose characters that reflect their nature.' He indicated a group a few paces away. 'Have you noticed that those wearing mouse masks are generally the quieter ones within the group? Or that those who chose cats are the ones spreading gossip? Those wearing birds-of-prey like to control the conversation.'

As if to prove his point, a lady wearing a hawk disguise laughed loud enough to draw all attention in the room before snatching control of the discussion within her group. Laryn turned to me with a mischievous grin.

'Have you noticed that you are the only one who is wearing a creature from legend?' He chuckled at the expression I must have shown beneath the phoenix. 'My queen is endlessly amused by these games. A mythical Dragonslayer disguised as a mythical firebird.'

I failed to see the humour in my unique facial covering when three high priests and Lindvane's king resided in a room not fifty paces away. The minstrel sighed at my obvious displeasure, straightening his posture before continuing.

'Nevertheless, I am the queen's messenger and she has bid me to relay a message to you. Hayton will soon tire of the celebrations. You have until his boorish son drinks enough to forget that his lecherous nature runs counter to the political piety he coverts, and appropriates the nearest beauty he can snare. At which point, his father will excuse himself from the ball. You need to retrieve the crystal from his room and present it to the queen before this.'

I was not surprised by his message but still felt the weight of the task assigned to me. 'You want me to steal from the King of Lindvane.'

'The Queen of Hilman requires you to steal from the King of Lindvane,' he clarified. 'And I suggest you do it soon. His suite is located in the west wing.'

The minstrel started a lively tune and I took my cue to leave. The ladies remained indifferent to my presence and I made my way back to the reception hall without incident. I watched the staircase for a while, hoping it would not be unusual for a guest to ascend to the private chambers, but they remained deserted and there would be no way of remaining unnoticed as I made my way to Hayton's rooms. I normally distained the nobility's air of condescending authority but prayed it would work in my favour, having decided to brazen my way to the upper level and trusting that others would presume I had a reason for being there. Setting my shoulders and lifting my head, I confidently walked across the hall and climbed the stone stairs, with my back itching from the threat of a called challenge.

The ruse worked and I reached the top without confrontation. The staircase opened into a wide passageway that extended around the reception hall and led to several smaller corridors where private rooms and meeting chambers were located. I was uncertain of which way was west, and the west wing, so I randomly turned to the left. Trusting that energy vibrations would alert me to the correct suite, I strode along the first hallway and past several doorways before the passage ended in a solid wall. The process was repeated for the second and third corridors, each remaining empty as guests and staff were occupied with the festivities on the lower level. The fourth corridor shared the format of the previous three but with the addition of a narrow staircase at the far end leading to a higher level. I hesitated, debating whether to investigate or explore the opposite wing. Cursing the wasted time if I was wrong, I retraced my steps and continued to the next hallway, resisting the urge to look down onto the reception area to see if I had attracted anyone's suspicion.

I felt the faint tingle of energy when I approached the first passageway. It would have been easily ignored had I not been specifically searching for it, but grew reassuringly stronger when I entered the second corridor. My heart quickened in response to the call of the power. The first door opened easily into a functional sleeping chamber with a comfortable bed, a pair of upholstered chairs and a chest of drawers. The room was unremarkable and unlikely to have been selected for a king so I moved to the room opposite, which was similarly furnished. The energy signature remained persistently diffuse, giving me confidence I was in the right area while providing no clear direction for me to go. I continued to the central pair of doors that revealed suites containing a reception room separate to the sleeping area but, again, neither seemed suitable for Lindvane's king and I rejected these as well.

The final door on the right bore a sturdy handle above a thick lock to suggest a more appropriate chamber for a high-ranking guest. My suspicion was confirmed when I hesitated, my hand hovering above the handle, and found the buzz of magickal protections. The power maintained a gently pulsing rhythm, unlike that associated with defensive sigils but still provoking a mildly unpleasant sensation. I grasped the handle and, although I encountered no stinging backlash, the door was frustratingly locked. I was certain the crystal Delaina desired was within this room so I twisted the handle with more force and pushed against the thick door. I had little hope that the door would yield but sought to test its resistance while I considered ways of picking the lock without my tools.

'One moment,' came the muffled reply from inside the room.

The empty corridors had deceived me into ignoring the possibility that someone would be waiting in Hayton's suite and I rapidly recalculated my options. I had no way of knowing who I would be facing but after my fight with Nyx, I was reasonably confident in my reflexes and aimed to exploit their initial moment of confusion.

The door opened to a man of average height and build. He was covered in faded blue tattoos that marked his bald head and almost half of his face. He was dressed in the livery of a steward but I had no doubt that he had been, or still was, a warrior and his role here involved more than ensuring the rooms stayed warm. I immediately struck, punching him in the throat and forcing him back into the room. His eyes grew wide when I removed all the air from his lungs and denied him the opportunity to respond. I kicked the door closed behind me and the guard fell to his knees, instinctively clutching at his neck while he struggled to breathe. An unlit oil lamp had been placed on a narrow table beside the door and I snatched this, smashing its heavy base against the back of his head as hard as I could. He dropped to the floor with a muffled thud.

I stood over him for some time to convince myself that he was unconscious and not dead. The lamp rattled in my trembling hand and I felt unreasonably shaken by the brief assault. The man had succumbed more to the blow to his skull than the magick I had forced on him, but I still felt profoundly uncomfortable with my reactive tactic. Echoes of Drey's disapproving voice whispered that I had used my power against the founding principles and it would not go unpunished. I was being foolish. I had spent months abusing magick and the Gods had not seen fit to punish me for my transgressions, but the doubt remained that at some point there would come a suitably harsh reprimand.

I replaced the lamp with exaggerated care and began to search for the artefact. I concentrated on the persistent hum of energy but its sense of *wrongness* was dispersed throughout the suite and confused my attempts to locate it. I scanned the room, visually looking for the appropriate places to hide such a valuable object. There was nothing obvious within the reception room so I chose to start at the furthest chamber and work my way back.

The pressure in my head intensified when I entered the garishly lavish sleeping area. I approached the chest of drawers and fought the increasingly uncomfortable sensation, knowing I had found what Delaina was after when its vague familiarity shifted into sharp focus. I had felt the characteristics of this energy's warning before. The insistent suggestion that I leave this place and that this power was not for me. Telling me to run while I had the chance, with an undercurrent of hatred. It was the sensation I felt every time I went near a temple.

I carefully opened the second drawer from the top, finding no lock or sigil to deny my access. It seemed Hayton was less cautious with his artefacts than Baila's priests, simply hiding this one within the folds of a tunic. The wooden box was a little larger than the size of my hand, carefully crafted with dovetailed joints and delicate hinges but with no other ornamentation to declare its significance. I placed it gently upon the chest, keen to see the crystal despite its persistent warning and my growing apprehension. I slowly eased open the lid and shivered with the sudden chill that swept through my body. I instantly recognised what the box contained and what I had been sent to retrieve for the Queen of Hilman.

'Oh, this is not good,' I breathed, while dire implications raced around my head. 'This is really not good.'

It was more crudely cut than the one I had seen before and of a size that would easily fit into the palm of my hand. I stared sadly at the addition of the faint black lines that threaded through the crystal and looked so much like the vines of corruption that choked my mental barriers. I curled my hands into fists beside the wooden frame, no longer wanting to touch the container, much less the stone which nestled on golden silk inside it. Trembling, I gathered my fleeting courage and closed the lid on the pale-yellow crystal that provided an auditory link to Villermir.

CHAPTER TWENTY-TWO

The box fit snugly inside one of the hidden pockets at the front of my gown. I disliked remaining so close to the vile object but was not prepared to leave it with Hayton. I was undecided whether Delaina knew the power of the artefact she had requested or the ramifications of her possessing it, but I could not see how I could prevent her from obtaining it. Owl had shown that there would be no way of hiding the item in my cell, and that was assuming I could avoid any suspicion regarding the contents of a subtly bulging pocket. I was reluctant to leave it hidden elsewhere within Peverill Hall, but I was becoming increasingly aware that I was running out of time before the guard would awaken or someone else discovered me and raised the alarm. I pushed against the chest of drawers in frustration and exited the bed chamber, hoping a suitable solution would present itself before I was required to hand the crystal to the queen.

I warily stepped around the guard, who was still sufficiently unresponsive and left Hayton's suite. I walked down the corridors scanning for any viable niche or crevice, unsurprised when I was forced to reject all of them. A servant passed me when I approached the staircase but I trusted my shield of noble arrogance and he reacted with no more than a mildly confused frown. I paused at the top of the stairs, my hands clasped loosely at my waist in an attempt to obscure the interrupted outline of my gown, and looked down onto the reception hall which had grown busier in my absence. Nallin waited for me at the base, with her arms folded in annoyance and her scowl deepening as I descended.

'You were supposed to stay close to me,' she hissed when I joined her at the foot of the stairs.

'No. I believe you were not supposed to let me out of your sight. And, I daresay that two people sneaking around Averill's house would be more noteworthy than just the one.'

She flicked a glance towards those closest to us and lowered her voice further. 'You found it.'

'It wasn't there,' I lied.

She dropped her gaze towards my pocket. 'It was a statement not a question and your response insults us both.'

I shrugged. 'It was worth a try.'

'Hardly.' She straightened her shoulders and turned to towards the ladies' chamber. 'The queen is waiting for you.'

I followed her to the receiving room where Laryn was still quietly singing to entertain the assembled women. Hilman's queen effortlessly dominated the room, standing close to the centre and surrounded by an attentive clutch of admirers. Her white gown with the vibrant inserts visually declared her as separate from those wearing more subtle, softer shades. She chatted benignly with a few and smiled benevolently at others, selecting those she favoured and rejecting those she felt were insufficiently worthy of her attention. Her subtle political positioning was interrupted once she became aware of my arrival.

'Leave us,' she commanded, provoking a ripple of respectful curtsies before the women fluttered away. Laryn rose to follow them but Delaina raised a hand to stall him. 'You may stay, Laryn. I have no doubt that you will hear of our conversation anyway.'

The older man returned her smile, suggesting a close relationship between the two, and gave a small bow of obeisance. 'Of course, my queen.'

Nallin followed the last of the guests to the door, closing it behind them and taking a guarding position that faced me. The queen regarded me coldly and I concentrated on not fidgeting while I stood under her judgement. She made me wait for several heartbeats and I used the time to frantically search for ways I could deny her the crystal. Ones that sounded more sophisticated than *you can't have it*. Eventually she lifted her head slightly, causing me to meet her stare.

'You have something of mine.'

I had run out of time for a more elegant response so decided on the truth. 'I don't think you should have it.'

She narrowed her eyes. 'And what makes you think that your opinion is required? You have completed the task I gave you and now you will give it to me. There is no discussion to be had here.'

'Do you know what it is?' I protectively cupped the box in the palm of my hand, still hidden within my pocket. 'Do you know what it does?'

The queen flicked a glance towards Nallin but did not seem troubled that Laryn was also listening to our conversation. 'I am aware. Not that it is any concern of yours.'

'Then you should know how dangerous it is. You cannot use it.'

Her voice deepened and she leaned towards me to clearly convey the threat. 'Do not presume to tell me what I can and cannot do.'

I glanced desperately at Laryn, hoping for some form of assistance, and found that his head was tilted as if to consider my words. Delaina may be aware of the artefact's powers but how many others knew what it was capable of and what its use by the queen would mean for Hilman? The minstrel had some magickal ability and may be able to feel the tainted energy of the crystal. Perhaps his queen would listen to his counsel despite having rejected mine.

'I've seen one of those before,' I began carefully, testing how far I could challenge her. 'This one is smaller but it has been corrupted. I fear that makes it more dangerous.' She drew a breath to dismiss me and my warning but I persisted, glancing towards Laryn to ensure he was listening. 'Villermir is very particular about who he gives those to. If he wanted you to have one, he would have given you one.'

The queen did not react to the naming of Villermir, confirming that she was fully aware of where the crystal had come from and what that entailed. She held out her hand.

'Give me the crystal before I deem you no longer valuable and I instruct Nallin to kill you for your insolence.'

I half-turned towards my guardian to see she was already holding a dagger in each hand and an expression that suggested she would gladly comply with the command. I could see no way of refusing the queen any longer and despondently retrieved the box. I hesitated for as long as I dared before placing one end into her outstretched hand, continuing to hold the other end while I raised my gaze to meet her angry eyes.

'I'm pleading with you. Please listen to me. You cannot use this. You cannot touch it and let Villermir know you have it.'

She snatched the box from my hand, leaning in with such a look of malice that I took a reflexive step backwards. 'You seem to have forgotten your position here so let me remind you. You are my captive. You live purely at my pleasure and that is running perilously thin. Understand, should you no longer serve my purposes, I will sell you to whomever offers me the biggest profit.'

She stormed across the room and I made one last attempt. 'Nothing good will come of this.'

The queen, however, no longer acknowledged my presence. Nallin smoothly opened the door and Delaina swept into the reception hall, greeting the women outside with a regal smile as if nothing of significance had occurred in their absence. My guard's blades were concealed once more but her hostile glare remained. I turned to Laryn, hoping he at least would understand my fear about what the crystal could unleash. My hopes of an ally faltered at his flat expression.

'She is my queen,' he stated, closing any further discussion.

I felt completely deflated. Nallin came to collect me, slipping her arm around mine in restraint tight enough to leave bruises. The women had started to return to the room and the tense atmosphere melted with their light gossip filling the space.

'We should return to the ballroom,' she suggested, smiling politely when we bypassed a group looking to intercept us. 'You will have been missed.'

'I find I am no longer in the mood for such festivities,' I protested weakly. 'Can we not leave?'

'That would raise too much suspicion and you have already provided enough of that.'

I obediently allowed her to guide me back to the busy hall. The cheerful noise jarred sharply against my guilt at giving Delaina the crystal, despite being unable to think of any way in which I could have prevented it. I found the colourful masks threatening and judgemental, and the need to escape crawled over my skin like a swarm of insects. I distracted myself by looking at the stage. Averill was talking to an increasingly annoyed Hayton while Hulce circulated amongst the noble guests, laughing loudly at his own jests and being inappropriately tactile with the women. Delaina had returned to her seat beside the high priests and I noticed that the one I had spoken to earlier was conspicuously absent. My anxiety increased with the crystal being so close to Villermir's priests but neither showed any undue interest in the queen, engaging her only in polite conversation.

'I appreciate that you do not have the skills to blend with such refined company,' growled Nallin. 'But could you at least remove the scowl. People are starting to notice.'

I no longer cared to maintain the charade and wanted nothing more than to escape this writhing snake pit, but I understood that encouraging further suspicion would not help and I had no desire to become more memorable for when my theft became apparent. I relaxed my expression into a more neutral appearance, although I could not resist the opportunity to jab at my chaperone.

'Perhaps it would help if you stopped crushing my arm.'

She glowered at me, suspecting some trick, but could find no reason to doubt my intentions and reluctantly released her hold. She remained close while we made our way to the central area and aimed for a mixed group of six, but I used the crowd to gradually increase the distance, frequently allowing people to pass between us. Learning from her earlier oversight, she repeatedly checked to ensure I was still nearby but made no comment and seemed content that I was being sufficiently obedient.

I did not have to wait long before I saw my opening. Hayton had finally grown tired of his son's antics and abruptly interrupted his conversation with Averill to leave the platform. He did not attempt to hide his anger and strode through the guests to where Hulce was gesticulating animatedly to his group of attendants. He threw his arm back and narrowly missed the king's face, unaware his father was beside him. All eyes within the ballroom turned towards the confrontation where Hayton reminded his King-in-Waiting that he represented Lindvane and to act accordingly. A small gathering of retainers followed the king when he stormed out of the hall, passing close enough that I could use the distraction to meld into the crowd while Nallin's attention was elsewhere.

I was unwilling to remain in the main house should Hayton check for the crystal on returning to his chambers. I felt certain some alarm would be raised on finding his abused servant and knew my time was running out, increasing the urgency. I slipped into the reception hall and avoided the entrance where the capable staff would remember my early exit. I bypassed the ladies' receiving room, having lost any trust I had that Laryn would assist me, and headed for the quieter area at the rear of the house. The few servers who passed kept their gaze dutifully lowered and I took the servants' corridor behind the staircase without incident.

My fine gown and elaborate mask drew more attention than I was comfortable with. Guests had little cause to visit this section of the building and my presence was uncommon and, therefore, noteworthy. I rejected the option to hide and wait until after the festivities when the house would be much quieter, with the fear of imminent discovery once Hayton raised the alarm being too big a risk for me to take. Once again, I trusted the expected noble arrogance to cover my deception and snatched an empty tray from a startled server, muttering about unacceptable standards and glaring angrily at anyone who dared to look at me. The technique proved remarkably effective and I reached the kitchen again without incident.

As at Liegeport, Peverill's kitchen bustled with the frantic activity of serving a grand occasion, being rigidly kept just below total chaos by the sharp commands of the head cook which sent junior staff running in all directions. I found it easy to remain overlooked and slipped into a back storeroom that opened into the rear courtyard. I snatched a plain, unremarkable cloak to cover my expensive gown and gratefully ripped off the ornate mask. I was strangely reluctant to carelessly discard the decoration and clumsily held it in one hand while I grabbed a kitchen knife with the other, escaping into the cool night air.

A simple door on the far side of the courtyard led away from the illuminated house and into the shadow of the stables. The horses nickered quietly in warning when I skirted around the timber building, but no one came to investigate and I remained unseen. I left the estate and followed the road back to Peverill, staying off the gravel path to remain hidden within the shadows, although anyone who had need to travel that way was already at the royal house. My soft slippers were not designed for navigating rough ground and I cursed them every time a sharp pebble pushed through their thin soles. I had two tasks to complete before I could leave the town and disappear into the surrounding countryside; obtain more practical clothing and retrieve my weapons. I would not leave without *Saorsa* although I had no idea where she would be stored and, wherever that was, I doubted it would be easily accessible. Clothing would be my first priority, the decision being confirmed each time a stone stabbed into my foot.

The town was blissfully quiet after the sensory chaos of the ball and I relaxed into the familiar embrace of night-time alleyways. It was late but the day had not yet turned and there were still a few people walking purposefully along the streets. They rarely looked up from the direction in which they were heading, however, and I found it easy to avoid their attention. The problem I faced was knowing where to go. Peverill was similar enough to other towns that I could predict the merchant sectors from the labourers', where the barracks would be and where I would find the taverns, but I did not know the place well enough to identify appropriate targets within these areas. Where there would be dogs to alert my presence. Where people would still be awake or sleeping lightly and would hear the quiet sounds of my entry. Where I would find what I needed and where would waste my limited time.

I aimed for the labourers' section, deciding that, midwinter or not, many would have already retired ahead of a dawn start to tomorrow's working day. It would also be the best place to obtain the hard-wearing, practical clothing I would need to resume my life as an outcast. I entered a modest market square, bordered on three sides by merchant houses. It boasted a guildhall that was large enough to occupy much of the final boundary, decorated with skilled stonework to declare the authority of its guild.

A pair of Averill's soldiers emerged from a side street and started to cross the open space, chatting causally. They did not appear to be actively patrolling or looking for escaping captives, but I was unwilling to tempt the Fates and slipped into the nearest alley before they could notice me. A number of small stores lined both sides of the avenue and I crouched within one of the doorways, disturbing the rats at the far end of the passage. I tracked their voices while the two men approached, watching when they passed by the opening of the alley, then walked out of sight. I waited several heartbeats after their voices faded to be sure they had gone, then silently rose and moved back towards the square.

I had taken no more than a single step before movement to my side caused me to turn sharply. My reflexes had lifted my arm before my brain understood what was happening, reacting to the dull glint of a blade which aimed for my throat. I grasped my attacker's forearm but was pushed back into the wall. The dagger pressed far enough into my skin to draw a bead of blood.

'I said you would never make it to the town gates,' hissed Nyx, her mouth close to my ear. 'You barely made it a third of the way.'

'I hadn't realised it was a test. I would have tried harder.' She responded by adjusting the angle of the blade, opening the cut so that more blood seeped from the wound. 'Careful. I'd hate for my blood to stain Owl's pretty gown.'

Her eyes flicked down to the soiled hem and torn shoes that protruded from it. 'I think you have already succeeded in ruining it.'

The taller woman released the dagger's pressure slightly and I snatched at the opportunity. I wrapped a foot around her leading leg and shoved her backwards. Unbalanced, she stumbled and I followed through with a palm to her chest while I twisted the knife away from my throat. She felt herself fall backwards and grabbed my cloak to ensure I fell with her. We slammed to the ground and I smashed her wrist into the dirt, hoping to dislodge her grip while I fumbled to retrieve the kitchen knife. Nyx maintained hold of her blade, bashing her elbow into my cheek and forcing me to topple off her.

We regained our feet and warily circled each other. The fighter smoothly blocked my exit when I moved to escape the alley.

'Let me go, Nyx.'

'You know I can't do that.'

'I can't stay here.'

'That's not your decision to make.'

I had backed towards the far end of the passageway, aiming to lure her into thinking I was planning to leave via that exit. She took the bait and circled to block me, exposing the route back to the square. I lunged for the opening she had just presented and darted past. She reacted quickly, diving for my legs and tackling me to the ground so that we landed in a tangle of limbs. I turned to punch her in the face, loosening her grip on my legs and allowing me to kick her away. Without thinking, I created a wall of air and slammed her against the wall in frustration.

'Don't make me kill you!'

Nyx remained silently defiant while I held her pinned with an invisible force, but I could see the fear in her eyes. I shamefully withdrew my magick and released her from its restraint, watching the fear become swiftly replaced by disgust. I had confirmed all her reasons to resent me. I had used magick to subdue her, aligning myself with the despised priests who used magick to control those they deemed a threat. I represented everything in an enemy she had no way of challenging. The unfairness that gifted some with the advantage while others suffered. I had stoked the fire of impotent rage that continually burned within her.

'I vow that it will be me that kills you.'

The part of my mind that ached for oblivion stirred and I released a short, cynical laugh. Once again, I had delivered a powerful weapon into the hands of an enemy and once again, I was unable to stop the repercussions of that.

'You think I don't want that? You think I don't know that everything I touch turns to crap?' I opened my arms wide in invitation. 'Well, here I am. Go ahead and finish this.'

She hesitated, as I knew she would. Killing behind the veil of righteous anger was different to making the calm decision to end someone's life when you had time to consider the consequences, and Nyx was not one to take that path. I lowered my arms with a deflated sigh. I watched her face while she battled her desire to kill me with her duty to her queen. Her duty was predictably triumphant.

'You have to let me go.' She opened her mouth to protest but I continued, raising my voice. 'Listen to me. You have no idea what your queen is playing with. This goes beyond royal politics and selling me to the highest bidder. Villermir will destroy this town to get at me. You fear *my* power? Villermir is so much more powerful. And he's never going to make a deal with Hilman. He takes want he wants and crushes anyone who would get in his way.'

'You lie.'

'You've seen what he has done. He has ripped your kingdom apart. Torn up the ground like it's a sheet of smudged parchment. He's even corrupted the weather. You can't deny that it is uncommonly warm. There's drought in winter!' My thoughts spiralled around the corruption that seeped through the kingdom and I spoke more to myself when I continued softly. 'The land is dying. How can Delaina think that she can negotiate with that?'

'Lies!'

Nyx roared her denial, launching herself at me to drive the blade into my chest. I twisted to avoid the threat but the weapon caught in my cloak and she was pulled towards me when I turned. We stumbled back to the wall and, abandoning her tangled blade, she smashed her forehead into my nose. I felt a moment of sharp clarity when the tissue gave and blood flowed into my mouth. She immediately followed with a dizzying blow, slamming the heel of her palm into my forehead and sending my head crashing into the wall. I became disorientated, with my senses seeming to dislocate and my body no longer feeling attached to my mind.

Fighting the effects of a broken nose and a bashed skull, I aimed to slice across her ribs but it was a feeble attempt and did little damage. She squeezed my wrist hard enough that my fingers grew cold and the blade fell from my hand. Not content with merely disarming me, she slammed my head into the wall a second time. My legs turned to water and buckled. I collapsed, hitting the ground heavily, and my vision blurred as the alley swam in and out of focus.

'Are you done?' Nyx asked, standing over me. 'Or do I need to crack that thick skull one more time and carry you back to your cell?'

I felt blood drip from my chin and a dampness at the back of my head. A wound on my calf throbbed and my cheek had swollen following the contact with Nyx's elbow. My vision refused to settle and my head felt ready to burst. I pushed away the knife that had fallen from my numb fingers.

'You will regret this,' I warned quietly. 'But I can't stop you without the fear of killing you. And it seems neither of us is prepared to do that tonight.'

Having been half-dragged, half-carried back to the cell, I released my frustrations by attacking anything moveable in the room. I swiped at the pitcher of water and basin that rested on the small table, sending them crashing to the floor. The table followed and I smashed it against the wall. Still raging I turned towards the bed, ineffectually tossing the soft pillows before ripping the sheets and overturning the mattress. I roared at the bed, grasping the sides of the frame, but my anger was already subsiding and I suddenly lacked the will to destroy it. A numbness seeped through me and I accepted that my failing to protect people was nothing new. I slumped to the floor to curl among the torn linen and broken furniture.

Sleep eluded me, with my mind offering countless suggestions of how I should have handled the situation differently, and so I felt the first tremors when the land started to move. The shards of ceramic rattled and the deep rumbling intensified to send vibrations up my spine. I watched the debris from my tantrum quiver upon the shifting floor and I instinctively braced myself against the wall, but I found no comfort there with the stone shifting behind my back.

The surges increased in power, causing the bed to pound against the ground when solid earth rippled like a gentle tide. The walls visibly shook in rhythm to the rolling floor and everything in the room danced to an erratic beat. The force of the tremors caused me to rock uncomfortably between the floor and the wall. The waves grew stronger. I scrambled over sharp pottery and splintered timber, ignoring the sting when they stabbed into my hands and knees, and aimed for the relative shelter of a corner while the bed jumped on the undulating floor.

The walls cracked and I protectively covered my head while dust filled the air. A thick black line traced raggedly across the stones behind me, splitting the carved fresco at the far end before dropping to finish two hand-widths above where I was cowering. The wave was immediately followed by a more powerful surge that sent the bed skidding across the room towards me. I was unable to find the purchase I needed to move out of its way and it crashed into my shoulder and the curve of my ribs. Although I had turned to take the force of the blow on my side, it still connected with enough force to knock the air out of my lungs. I remained pinned while another violent tremor shuddered the wall behind me, cracking lower to cut across the narrow window. The shattered glass sprayed lethal shards into the room and I cringed with my arms protectively shielding my head.

It took several moments for me to accept that the quake was over. I carefully pushed the bed away, with my shoulder and ribs protesting at the movement. The cell was a mess. The remnants of my initial destruction had been joined by chips of stone from the two large cracks and shards of glass from the broken window. All had been thrown around to litter the room and a fine mist of dust covered everything. The bed stood defiantly undamaged amongst the chaos.

The carnage had the unexpected effect of suppressing my earlier apathy and motivated me to take back an element of control. I gathered strips of torn linen, cleaning the cuts made by flying glass and broken ceramics. I bound the deeper wound on my arm and, belatedly, attended to the gash on my calf muscle that Nyx had inflicted at some point during our fight. I retrieved my clothing, removing the dust before changing out of Owl's ripped and stained gown. I replaced the mattress and laid the garment on it, arranging the pendant so that it lay nestled within the fabric; I had lost the mask at some point during the night. Using my feet, now protected by thick boots, I pushed the sharp rubble into a corner and added the remains of the table. I bundled the linen beside the pile of waste and retrieved the pillows that had escaped with minimal damage. I placed them alongside the gown, releasing a few feathers from a small tear when I brushed away the dirt. I surveyed the room and took a measure of satisfaction from the order I had restored.

Having finished distracting myself with tidying the room, I sat on the bed and tried to consider my limited options. I scratched at the cuts on my hands that had started to itch and repeatedly turned my thoughts away from the convenient timing of the tremors. I considered Owl to be my best hope for orchestrating another escape attempt. *The queen has used the crystal.* If I could convince the child to help me, I would need to overpower the soldiers guarding my cell and those defending the gates. I was uncomfortable with the thought of having to use magick against them but could see no alternative. *Villermir knows you are here.* It would have to be soon but they would expect me to make another attempt. I worried they would expect Owl to be a potential ally and prevent her from attending me. *Villermir will come for you.*

I startled as the door opened, standing up while I frantically tried to convince my panicking mind that Villermir could not have come here so quickly. I was surprised to see Nyx in the doorway, but understood the fear which lay just under the surface of her rigid posture. She frowned slightly at the neat piles of debris but soon returned her attention to me and the reason she had come.

'You need to go.'

'Go where?' I asked tiredly, sitting back on the bed. 'I warned her not to use the crystal. How much damage has it caused?'

The older woman entered the room. She was unable to control her agitation yet remained undaunted by my association between the tremors and the gem I had stolen for her queen. I was sure she had already made that connection.

'You have to leave Peverill. You have to get as far away from here as you can.'

I gave her a challenging stare. 'You're just going to let me go?'

The proud fighter tossed her head like a frustrated horse. 'You can't stay here. It's too dangerous for you to be here.'

'For whom?' I asked churlishly.

I could not fully believe that she would release me so easily, but she did seem genuinely distressed by the violent shaking which had rocked her town. I chose to accept her suggestion before she had time to reconsider.

'I will need my weapons.'

'There isn't time. The queen has hidden them well. I don't know where they are being kept. It would take too long to search for them.'

318

She hesitated for a moment before removing her dagger and passing it to me, hilt-first. I doubted she would be foolish enough to hand me a blade if this was a ruse but I still took the weapon warily, immediately reversing the handle into a defensive grip. Her posture relaxed slightly at my implied acceptance of her request and turned to look back into the hallway. Owl scurried into the room carrying a bulging sack and a thick cloak, and wearing a warm cloak of her own above travelling leathers.

'No.'

The fighter glared at me. 'You will need her to get out of Roebaneswood. She can ensure you avoid the patrols.'

'Look at her! She's already terrified. I'm not going to take her further into danger.'

'And what happens to her, any of us, if you get caught and taken by Villermir's priests? How well do you think that will go for Peverill?'

I clenched my fists in frustration, knowing that she was right. I vowed to ditch the girl at the first opportunity but would not waste time arguing and I nodded in defeat.

Owl darted her wide eyes between the two of us. 'Can we go now?'

I shot one last poisonous glare at Nyx before reaching for the cloak. 'Yes, Owl. We can go now. Why don't you lead the way?'

The girl retained rigid hold of the bundle and I followed her down the corridor and towards the stairs. There were several cracks running along the walls and a large section of stone had fallen into the reception hall. The furniture and few items of decoration lay scattered across the floor. Women stood dazed, huddled in small groups as they sought answers for the destruction, or perhaps they just needed the comfort of being with others. Many regarded me with suspicion when Owl guided me past them and out into the courtyard.

The devastation of Villermir's attack was more apparent outside the building's protective walls. Most of the raised gardens had shattered, with soil and plants tossed around to cover the pathways or scatter over the grassed areas. Deep trenches had been gouged into the turf where the ground had twisted and buckled. I glanced over to the shrine to find that while many of the rocks had been fractured or displaced, the water still serenely flowed. The heavy gates to the compound were, remarkably, still intact although one had a long crack running down the centre. A subdued guard drew back the retaining bolt and allowed us to pass into the town without comment.

It was still dark but the streets were crowded with people. While a few were attending the wounded or clearing away debris, many seemed to gather in the meeting places as simply areas of relative safety. They no longer felt safe within their homes after the walls had shaken and the roofs had collapsed. People wandered aimlessly or stared at the wreckage of their shattered lives. We passed a woman being comforted while she sobbed in grief in front of a collapsed building. I wondered how many had been trapped inside the timber structure when it had crumbled and crushed those still within it. I followed Owl and we quietly made our way out of the ruined town.

Owl selected a narrow trail that wound around the base of the hill and across the rolling pastures that extended behind it. The sun rose in front of us, muted behind the low cloud. The open fields offered no concealment for the passage of two travellers, one of which was a child, from the curious shepherds who had risen with the dawn to check on their flocks. I would have preferred to have travelled west into a more rugged landscape, and away from the encroaching pirates and their shamans, but accepted that danger awaited me wherever I went and Owl's path aimed between two rocky hills and towards a welcoming forest which would provide good shelter.

My eagerness at entering the trees slowly faded when we journeyed further into the mottled light of the woods. The track started at the trees' edge as a defined path capable of accommodating Owl and I walking alongside each other, but when it snaked between the brambles and bracken, it grew narrower and seemed to be one rarely used. I needed to push through the more overgrown areas to break a path for Owl, while the twists and turns confused the direction until only the slow journey of the sun confirmed we still aimed eastward. I took some comfort that, with the trail being infrequently used, we were unlikely to encounter any of Baila's soldiers searching for two runaways, and I was content to trust Owl's greater knowledge of the terrain and Hilman's military routines.

The path finally opened to become a gravel track and I was able to get some sense of how far we had travelled. We had climbed to roughly a third of way up the hill, with a thick forest carpeting the lower slopes while those above became increasingly craggy. There were defined areas of woodland separated by large slabs of rock, where the steepness of the stone restricted access to the small birds which clung to their cracks and crevices. I could see the sheep fields and small farms dotted below, with Peverill being hidden behind the far hill. We continued around the curve and soon returned to the smothering cover of forest, where the trail narrowed again to cut through thickets of bramble and gorse.

A nagging concern itched at the back of my neck while we climbed higher. I could see an open section of track poking out above the treetops and we appeared to be aiming for that. The pale gravel showed sharply against the bright evergreens below and the dark stone of the hill, creating a funnel with sheer rock on one side and a steep drop on the other. Owl had been quiet for most of the day and startled when my question broke the silence.

'Have you taken this trail before?'

The girl shook her head. 'No.'

'But you are sure this is the right way? We seem to be spending more time going up than moving away from Peverill?'

'This is the way,' she confirmed, although not as confidently as I would have liked. 'Just past that open section there, the track starts going down again.'

I remained anxious despite having no evidence that there was danger ahead, but we had committed to this path and I had seen no other that had branched off in a more convenient direction. We continued to climb the gentle incline, snagging against thorns and squelching through stagnant puddles, and I dismissed my pessimism as a result of the unfavourable terrain.

We emerged from the trees and stepped onto the gravel track I had seen earlier. It extended for several paces before disappearing around the curve of the hill and was wide enough for three people to walk abreast, although the section was not as exposed as I had assumed and my feelings of unease returned with some force. The tree trunks originated from further down the hill so that their branches were almost level with the road but the slope was significantly shallower than I had expected. The rock-face was also more jagged than it had appeared, with deep cracks which were large enough to hide a man in their shadows.

I slowed my pace, moving closer to Owl and grasping her arm to keep her near me. My skin prickled and I rapidly scanned for threats; this was a perfect place for an ambush.

'How do you know about this trail?'

The girl picked up on my cautious tone and looked at me with anxious, wide eyes. 'I was told to bring you this way. I was to follow the track through the sheep fields. Follow it through Ryvan's Pass and then go on to Hare's Run where someone would be waiting to take you out of Roebaneswood.'

'Who gave you those instructions?' She hesitated, stammering quietly when I stared at her. 'Owl! Who told you about this trail?'

'The queen,' she blurted, reluctant to betray a confidence. 'Queen Delaina told me herself. She was very specific. I was to take this path and no other.'

I closed my eyes briefly with my fears being confirmed. 'Oh, Owl. Why would the queen tell you that?'

The girl was clever. I watched her face while she considered my question and reached the same conclusion. Her face paled and I retrieved the knife that Nyx had given me, pulling Owl so that she stood directly behind me.

'Stay close,' I instructed.

I turned back to the way we had come but it was already too late. Two men, dressed in the dark uniforms of Baila, emerged from the trees we had just passed and blocked our retreat. Three more scrambled out of the scrubby bushes and up the slope. I turned so my back was to the rock-face, placing Owl protectively behind me while I faced the threat of another three soldiers appearing from around the bend to trap us. I compared my one small blade to their combined weaponry, concluding that it was woefully inadequate and I would need to use alternative methods to defend us. I cursed Delaina and her foolish use of the crystal, having no doubt that she would have betrayed me but could not forgive her casual sacrifice of Owl.

'Let the girl go,' I called to the men who cautiously crept closer, encircling me to pin me in front of the stone barrier. 'I presume you know who I am and what I am capable of. Let the girl go and we can discuss how this will end.'

A soldier from the group who had come from further up the trail stepped forward to distinguish himself from the others. A little older than the rest, he had closely shorn hair and a thin scar which emerged from his stubble to extend across his cheek. He slowly withdrew his sword and a cruel sneer pulled at his upper lip.

'You've been a very bad girl,' he purred. 'I'm going to enjoy watching you get what's coming to you.'

'The child has nothing to do with this,' I persisted, trying not to declare my desperation. 'She's nobody. Let her go.'

'I'm not sure you understand the situation here. You are in no position to demand anything.'

He flicked his eyes to the group opposite him, signalling the start of the fight. The two soldiers advanced towards me, metal sighing when they drew their swords. Their action was swiftly copied by the other two groups and they closed around me. Any apprehension I had about using my magick was reduced to a slight tension within my guts and this was easily ignored. I focused on protecting Owl while the girl clung to me, scared by the violence pressing in on us.

I created a fireball and I briefly noted the hesitation in the nearest soldier before throwing the rotating flames towards him. The chaos was short-lived and I turned to face the rest, using another fireball to push them back. I used compressed air to dislodge a rock the size of my head and brought it crashing down, narrowly missing the snarling leader. I aimed another, smaller, stone at him and struck him on the side of his head hard enough to draw blood. My small advantage soon vanished and the soldiers closed, preventing me from controlling them for fear of harming Owl. I was restricted to the use of my blade and I defended with slashes and slices, parries and punches. My reflexes saved me more often than the ineffective dagger, and I twisted and dived to avoid the lethal blades coming at me from all directions.

'Enough!'

Everyone stopped and I took a breath to swiftly assess the situation. I was ringed by a wall of steel, but the threat barely registered when I realised that Owl was no longer beside me. The soldiers nearest to me parted to create a channel through which I could see the shaven haired thug, and I stared in despair. He had seized Owl, with one arm twisted behind her back and a thick hunting knife cutting into her neck. Silent tears streamed down her face while she tried to squirm free without pressing further against the knife. Blood seeped from the long, narrow wound to soak into the collar of her cloak.

'As entertaining as this is,' he gloated, 'the Supreme High Priest is an impatient man and we have a long way to travel. Regretfully, we do not have the time to enjoy playing with you.'

His eyes flicked to a soldier standing behind my left shoulder before returning to hold my gaze. His smile stretched spitefully and I cried out. I had taken no more than a pace before he dragged the blade across Owl's throat. Bright red blood bloomed along the gash, gushing as the blade bit deeper into the soft tissues of the child's neck.

I fell to my knees. An ice-cold blade stabbed into the base of my neck but the momentary flare of pain was instantly smothered by a numb detachment, and everything shifted.

CHAPTER TWENTY-THREE

It felt like a dream, an awful dream, but I knew I was awake and watching a scene that continued to play before me. I could see Owl, discarded like a pile of unwanted rags. I could see the soldiers still standing around me and those I had killed lying on the ground. And yet, it was all different. The colours were wrong. Everything appeared as if viewed through a window that had been covered in brown dust so the details were blurred under a sepia mist. I felt separate and removed.

I felt the cold touch of the knife at the curve of my neck where it met my shoulder, stabbing through the tissues to rest against the bone of my shoulder blade. It provided a disturbingly bright focus in a muted world. The information received from the outside of my body was restricted to the smudged images I could see, with no awareness of anything beyond that immediately in front of me. There was no sound of voices. No smell of burnt flesh. No acrid taste from charred clothing. The only sensations I could feel were the freezing touch of the blade in my shoulder and a consistent, crushing pressure in my chest.

My perspective shifted and I felt a moment's dizzying disorientation as the images rocked. I looked down at feet that no longer seemed to be attached to me. I had no concept of my limbs and had not thought to stand before assuming the position. I could not feel the tension within the muscles maintaining my balance. I could not feel the firmness of the ground beneath my boots. It felt like someone else had control of my body and I was merely an observer.

The pressure in my chest was building. A sucking void that pulled my awareness into its black pit with promises of a sweet release should I submit

325

to its will. I resisted, concentrating on what I could see and what I believed to be real. I focused on Owl in search of the anger that had always given me strength, but I failed to find anything other than a slight curiosity. I experienced nothing more than a mild confusion, removed from events which seemed to be happening to someone else. The scarred man walked towards me. His red hand still carried the blade and I watched a drop of Owl's blood slide from its point. He stopped with his face close to mine and his dark eyes sharp with disgust. I concentrated on his lips and they moved in the patterns of speech, but I could not hear his words and I was unable to understand what he said. He stepped back, turning to look at a dead soldier, before swiftly turning back to me. He raised his arm as he rotated, with the back of his hand moving towards my head.

The image spun and I was now looking at a ground that was much closer than it had been. I seemed to have fallen but I could not feel the ground beneath me. My thoughts were slow to make the connection that he had hit me. I felt no pain from his strike. I did not feel the gravel that must have been pressing into my knees. I only felt the cold numbness in my shoulder and that was fading to a distant concern, overshadowed by the intense pressure within my chest.

The ground receded, more slowly this time and without the vertigo, and I appeared to be standing once more. The images lurched when I followed those in front of me towards the curve in the trail, my feet taking each step without any conscious instruction. Curious, I willed myself to stop but the limb no longer existed in my mind and my feet continued walking without hesitation. I explored my options to see what control I had retained and found that, while I could not move my head, I did have some influence over the focus within my fixed field of vision. While my head stubbornly faced forward, I could drift my sight in a direction of my choosing. The process was slow, and the image frequently jumped back to the centre, but I could gradually shift my sight to obtain more detail from the edges of my vision.

The effort needed to obtain that small measure of success was exhausting and with my energy fading, the chasm within me increased its influence. The seducing darkness consumed the centre of my body and I was teetering on a ledge while my awareness drained into its emptiness like a waterfall. My soul was slowly being eroded like a raging river tearing at its sandy banks. I fought against its pull but the more I focused on the gaping abyss, the faster I flowed into it. My essence felt stretched and thinned while my *self* shrank.

My thoughts frayed and I could no longer separate what was real and what was conjured from fear. I desperately grasped for a direction, struggling to remember the tainted images of the hillside. I fought to isolate what I could see from what I was feeling. I battled against every rational thought that screamed for me to stay focused on the void that was trying to absorb me. I gathered each strand of my scattered will and turned my sight away from the drowning darkness.

It was merely a suggestion. There was no physical action to shift awareness from the ethereal realm of my mind and soul, to the hostile world of soldiers and a dead Owl, but it was enough and it gave me a heartbeat of clarity to see the stained forms of the trail in front of me. Gaining confidence from having resisted its drag, I repeated the action. Again and again, I snatched my attention from absorbing emptiness and clutched at disjointed images and confused information. The pressure of the void was relentless. It pulled with an overwhelming desire to fold in on myself, to implode and dissolve into nothing. My will to resist faltered. I questioned why I was denying its call.

I was sucked into the suffocating black hole and became smothered by the sensation of sinking into thick, viscous mud. After a moment's panic, the feeling changed and became unexpectedly calming. All my fears drifted away and my mind settled in the acceptance of the inevitable. I was held in a space that had no beginning. No ending. Just was.

Time had no meaning in this place. It could have been an eternity or a heartbeat, but gradually some definition formed within the black expanse. My weightless floating hardened into a supportive containment. The colour became sharper, shimmering slightly from an unseen light. Crisp edges formed to create an endless landscape of impossibly high walls, set at irregular angles where they pressed against each other. I was enclosed within spiky shards of jet. I was trapped within an obsidian crystal.

My crystal prison was alluring. It promised no past and no future. No pain and no guilt. It offered the oblivion I craved, but even this complete isolation could not prevent the memories rising like bubbles to the surface. First to visit was Owl, full of plans for her future. After a while she was joined by Z'hara, fiercely beautiful and ready to fight any injustice. Those memories, inevitably, turned to Vallori. Calm, patient and steadfast. My *pháirtí*. My safe harbour. Then there was Drey, with his organised, meticulous, inquisitive guidance. These memories brought comfort. A warm acceptance, where the details were softened over the distance of time and I could fondly remember their influences on me.

While those recollections were a muted landscape of a misty dawn, Kade shone like the sun breaking through the cloud. His memories were vibrant, persistent and urgent. Full of his passion and humour. The visions came as a reminder of what I was rejecting. He called to me, drawing on distant fragments of duty and loyalty, and scratching at my mind to see my seclusion for the prison that it was.

My thoughts remained directionless and I had no control over what memory would appear or how long it would last, yet I gradually regained some sense of *self* and with it came glimpses of reality. The flashes of awareness came infrequently and generally followed a memory of Kade. The shutters of a window would momentarily open and reveal visions of the world, before they closed and I became imprisoned within the crystal cage once more. The infrequent, fleeting images showed dry, flat landscapes, where spring flowers struggled to emerge from the dusty soil and deep gouges tore across fields to expose the dark, peaty earth.

Z'hara, Drey and Vallori gave silent reassurance, encouraging me to accept the truth in what I was seeing. The land screamed with an injustice that could not be ignored. Kade's presence was more insistent, forcing me to remember that I was needed, that the Three Kingdoms required a protector, and I needed to reject my incarceration. I desperately wanted to please him but it was so difficult. My thoughts kept slipping away. The harder I tried to force my awareness, the tighter the crystal held.

I used the memories of my friends to anchor me and started small. I imagined a crack in the towers of darkness that surrounded me. It was just a scratch, no thicker than the whisker of a hound, and yet I had caused it and that meant I could take control. It was an imperfection I could push at, making it larger and making it wider. Despite my awareness frequently drifting back into soporific oblivion, the periods of clarity gradually became more frequent. Sounds started to accompany the images when the number of cracks increased. The noise was faint and confusing, like being submerged under water, but it added some context to the disjointed visions. Many muted voices surrounded me and I heard the dull, rhythmic thud of horses' hooves. Smell and taste returned when I widened the seams, although these did little to enhance my understanding of where I was or where I was being taken.

My frustration started to build and I found that the returning emotions could be used to channel my efforts. I rammed my irritation into the small crevices and shards splintered from the black walls. I repeated the process over and over, each pillar falling to reveal further corridors of dark crystal.

Touch was the final sense to master and the cavern was a network of cracks and scars before it returned. It was less helpful than either the clouded sight or the muted sound, focusing primarily on aching shoulders and an uncomfortable pressure on my wrists. The sun's heat was unquestionably warmer than at Peverill and the knowledge fuelled the nagging discomfort that the energies were being increasingly corrupted. Echoes of Kade rattled around the cavern, repeating that I should not ignore this insult.

I escalated my attempts at smashing the walls of my containment, shattering the barriers in front of me which were endlessly replaced with more shimmering darkness. The images failed to provide any meaningful information so I ignored their distraction and obsessively destroyed the constricting stone. Unable to draw on any magick or access any energies, I relied on my imagination. Create a crack. Push it wider. Shatter the crystal. Break the wall. Again. And again. And again. Create the crack. Push it wider. Shatter the crystal. Break the wall.

My repetitive actions were violently interrupted by a sharp stab of fear. I was alerted to the threat without having been aware of the information coming from my limited senses. Anxiety choked my concentration and I struggled to access any vision or hearing. I frantically fought the increased pull of the void, with the offered oblivion becoming perilously attractive once more. I reacted to a danger without knowing what form it took, just the deep, primitive warning that I was in trouble. I dragged my thoughts away from the overwhelming lure of the abyss and my sight returned. I saw flashes of a tiled corridor. A wooden staircase. A richly furnished study. There was nothing that would explain the screaming peril that persistently clawed at my memories, forcing me to remember. I knew this place and I feared it. I strained to find the source of my unease but it remained just beyond my grasp.

A face loomed in front of me and the connection snapped into place. Villermir's face was pulled into sharp angles and thin hair framed his features when he leaned closer. His eyes probed into mine while his lips moved, and I strained to understand the words from the dull, monotonous sounds my ears provided.

'—truly remarkable.'

He stepped back, revealing bony shoulders which were covered by a dark robe. He lifted his hand and the blade embedded in my neck blazed with an intense pain. My senses erupted when the black knife flew into his upturned palm and I fell to my knees, overcome by the assault of sensations. I tensed against the ropes restraining my wrists, needing to cover my ears with my hands and block out the hurtfully loud sound of tapping. The noise of the wind blowing outside the window sounded like a raging gale and the breathing of the soldier beside me rasped like sand in my ears. I closed my eyes but the light still stabbed through their lids in a piercing display of red and white flashes. My joints ached, my muscles protested at the abuse that had been ignored for too long, and my head pounded painfully.

Gradually, the onslaught faded and my mind regained the ability to filter out the unimportant sensations, allowing me to focus on those that warned of danger. Villermir was still speaking.

'Stop being such a barbarian, Daigan. Remove her restraints. If she wanted to kill you, she could do it easily enough without the use of her hands.'

The scarred soldier, the one who had murdered Owl, leaned over me where I knelt on the ground. His expression clearly showed his distaste as he withdrew his thick hunting knife, the one that had killed Owl, and moved in to cut the ties. I raised a knee, placing my foot firmly on the polished wooden floor, and chose the moment when the rope fell free to push up and back. My limbs felt clumsy and it was a feeble strike, but I felt a satisfying crack when the back of my head connected with his face. He cursed thickly around a nose already bruising. I turned towards him, repeatedly clenching my fists to pump feeling into my fingers and the blood returned with the agony of countless needle-stabs. He did not wait until I had recovered and advanced with his weapon raised.

'Enough.'

One word, quietly spoken, was sufficient to hold our aggression to stares of mutual hatred. Villermir flapped his hand at the soldier in dismissal.

'Daigan. Go and do something useful.' He emphasised his point with a cold glare when the man hesitated. 'You are dismissed, Captain.'

Daigan rammed his blade back into its sheath in frustration and stormed out of the room. I waited until he slammed the door closed behind him before returning my attention to the Supreme High Priest. Without the sepia filter, the sharpness of his face revealed an emaciated appearance. His pallid skin stretched over the clearly defined bones of his cheeks and jaw, and his eyes were set deep within their sockets. Villermir had always been lean but his robe was open to reveal a noticeably skeletal frame, with claw-like hands protruding from his sleeves. He rested against the heavy desk and, despite the mocking smile curling his lips, he did not look well.

'Oh, Tallen,' he purred. 'You are so delightfully feral. Look at you. You are as bruised and battered as an over-ripe apple that has been kicked down the street.'

I felt awful and was in no mood for his games. 'Why am I here? Why have you not killed me already?'

'Kill you?' He looked genuinely surprised. 'My dear, where did you get that idea? By the One God's grace, why would I want to kill you?'

My head throbbed and I distractedly rubbed my forehead to relieve the pressure. I swayed when I briefly closed my eyes and took a quick step back to rebalance myself. Villermir noticed my weakness and indicated a chair in front of the desk, close to where he was standing.

'Where are my manners,' he continued in the unsettlingly charming manner. 'Please sit before you fall.'

He moved a beaker closer to the edge of the table, inviting me to both the seat and the refreshment. His smile faded when I hesitated. I remembered the previous occasion where he had offered a drink to demonstrate his power over me.

'It's just water, Tallen. Amongst other things, you are dehydrated. Sit. Drink.'

He was right. Much of my disorientation would be due to the lack of basic sustenance so, regardless of his motivation, I accepted both the chair and the water. Villermir waited patiently while I drained the cup. His smug smile returned when I placed it back on the desk.

'You are such an intriguing puzzle. Given your freedom and what do you do? You chose self-destruction by attacking my priests, my soldiers, my temples. Impressive at times, I admit, but foolish. You provoked an army to hunt you down as if you were a rabid boar. And even that wasn't destructive enough for you. You abused the flow of energy until it burnt away your physical form.'

'Seems I'm not the only one to do that?'

His smile hardened for a heartbeat before he inclined his head in acceptance of the truth. 'The feeling is exhilarating, is it not? Such damage you voluntarily inflicted on yourself and yet, when your freedom is taken away. Well, then you fight like a daemon.'

He glanced down to the desk and I followed his gaze to the dark blade he had removed from my shoulder. The thin, polished dagger finished abruptly in a short stub where there should have been a hilt. The blade's surface was so completely black that it shimmered like a pot of ink. Absorbing all the light and drawing me into its endless darkness.

I jerked back, having unconsciously tilted forward towards the artefact. I needed to blink several times to break the lure of the crystal, turning to look at Villermir who also seemed to be captivated by the weapon. A wistful expression had softened his face, remaining for a moment before he smoothly removed his attention from the dagger and returned to regard me.

'Do you know what this is?' he asked.

'Infinity Stone.'

He smiled, pleased that I understood the manner of his trap. 'Such an alluring crystal. Obsidian with the power to capture a person's soul. Confine their minds and subdue their thoughts. Even while sitting on this desk it can seduce, can it not? The more ability the person has, the stronger the spell. The more you resist, the greater the pull. A fly caught in a spider's web. You should not have been able to resist its effects. The lure is compelling when gazed upon. Embedded within you, its control should have been complete.' He inclined his head, studying me as if I was a particularly vexing riddle. 'And yet, you were aware. Before I removed the blade, I saw your eyes. You were aware.'

I failed to see his fascination. 'It served its purpose. I'm here. Was that why Owl had to die? So you could see if your toy worked?'

He frowned. 'An owl died?'

'She was just a girl,' I snapped. 'She was nothing to you. You could have easily taken me from Delaina's cell. Why play at giving me a taste of freedom only to trap me on a random trail on a random hill? Were you hoping to break my will because, honestly, that's been shattered for some time.'

The priest pushed himself away from the desk and paced the room in irritation. 'That game was not of my making. Hilman's queen planned that particular distraction.'

I huffed a bitter laugh. 'She defied you?'

He stopped pacing to glare at me. 'Delaina is ambitious, not foolish. She was to retain you until Daigan and his men could collect you, but she did not want them being seen entering Peverill. She was more concerned with preventing an insurrection than demonstrating the appropriate obedience to the One God. She still believes she can balance the wishes of her people with the authority of Baila. She will need to be dissuaded of that opinion.'

'Destroying half her town will probably help with that.'

He returned to rest against the desk, leaning back and folding his arms while he assessed me. I tried to defiantly return his stare but, shamefully, dropped my gaze after a few heartbeats.

'I feel you misunderstand my intentions. The damage caused was… regrettable. The connection to the Empathy Crystal amplifies my frustrations. I withdrew as soon as I felt it release the power, but I understand the repercussions were quite extensive.'

I scoffed at his careful use of language to distance himself from the effects of his destruction. 'What's one more town after you have damaged so many others?'

His face darkened. 'You think to judge me? Would you not do all in your power to serve the needs of your Gods? To protect those you hold close to your heart? Have you not caused pain and suffering for less?'

He paused while I considered his words. Words that echoed those of our previous conversation, before being halted by Megin. Words spoken in my mind to confuse what was real and what was imagined. Words that evoked layers of guilt and obscured what was fact and what was fear. I glanced back at Villermir and he gave me a small smile of encouragement.

'We walk a different road to that taken by most people. I daresay, we are the only two who truly know what it is to be favoured by a God. It is a difficult path, is it not?'

'My Gods do not require me to corrupt the energies and destroy the land.'

'Do they not? You are a Dragonslayer. Is it not your purpose to remove those who oppose your deities?'

'My purpose is to destroy daemons.'

'It may have started that way but that was not how it ended. Have you not heard the stories told of the Rebellion? How, once that threat was removed, Dragonslayers turned to other targets? You turned on your own creators.'

'It seems you have had time to study.'

He inclined his head, accepting the compliment despite it not being my intention. 'The fall of your Gods is a fascinating read.'

'The Gods have not fallen,' I denied loyally. 'They choose not to interfere.'

He smiled indulgently and I grudgingly accepted the naivety of my protest. 'All Gods crave power, Tallen. It is the only way in which they can exist. The more that people worship, or fear them, the more powerful they get.'

'That sounds dangerously close to heresy.'

He shrugged. 'I do not fear your Gods as some in the priesthood do. I know the immensity of Baila. I have felt his authority. Your Gods are as nothing compared to that.'

'I wouldn't be so sure.'

'Can you not see how Baila's Will brought you to me? First to Liegeport, where your talent was encouraged. Now here, where we can use that ability to build a new world.'

'What are you talking about? Drey took me to Liegeport. You brought me here.'

'Indeed. Guiding you to where you need to be. I should have seen it earlier. I should have been more involved with your training when you were younger.' He started pacing again. 'But I had to focus on building his religion. Spreading his word and gathering his devoted throughout the Three Kingdoms. We should have been working together, I see that now.' He turned sharply to face me, surprising me with a genuine smile. 'But you are here now. And with the start I've made, we shall complete this new beginning and all will see the glory of Baila's vision. Everyone will join us and rejoice.'

Baila's Supreme High Priest took a breath and I watched the pious fervour slowly drain from him. His eyes dulled and his shoulders dropped, becoming more of a tired old man than a powerful sorcerer. He seemed to realise how his sudden outburst bordered on madness and frowned, glaring a challenge for me to contradict him. For a moment I had felt the truth within his words, a connection between us based on faith and magick, but the sense of danger had returned to swirl around me. I became acutely aware that I walked a narrow ledge. I would remain relatively safe only while Villermir believed I could be of use to him. It was depressingly similar to the situation I had just left at Peverill, although the consequences of failure here meant more than just my death.

If Villermir's choice of torture for my previous visit to Burford had been fear, it seemed he had selected a very different tactic this time; that of luxury.

I was escorted from the meeting by a quiet acolyte who refrained from looking at me. He led me through the reception hall and up the bare stone staircase, away from the cell where I had been previously held. I quickly suppressed memories of the torments I had suffered and the reason I had voluntarily entered Villermir's base of power, focusing instead on the bland ordinariness of the country house. Burford Hythe was the ancestral estate of Hayton's family, having been the home of his uncle before being occupied by Villermir, and the building held onto echoes of its regal history with impressive architecture and skilled stonework. The atmosphere, however, had been replaced with one of a religious retreat with sombre acolytes silently walking the halls, many carrying scrolls or leather-bound books to remind me of the scholars studying on the Holy Isle.

I was taken to a room that was comfortably furnished, reflecting the indulgence of Villermir's study rather than the functional austerity in evidence elsewhere. The door was locked behind me. It was a simple mechanism and I could have easily opened it, although no thoughts of escape were considered while I stood for some time barely daring to believe what had been given to me. The room was spacious and fed into a smaller one. Two large, decorative tapestries hung from the walls and added to the thick rug covering much of the floor to create an invitingly warm space. A window, free of restraining bars, cast soft light onto the dark wood table placed in front of it. A high-backed chair was located to each side. The chamber was dominated by an unnecessarily big bed where a heavy fur cover had been folded back to expose thick linen sheets, carefully tucked around the well-padded mattress. An array of pillows and cushions clustered at the head of the bed and settled against a beautifully carved rest, the same wood as that of the desk.

I resisted the powerful urge to launch myself onto the promised comfort of the bed and went to investigate the side room, releasing a small whimper on discovering the steaming bath waiting there. Soft towels had been arranged neatly on a small chest, beside a pile of clean clothes. Candles had been placed around the windowless room to create a relaxing glow and scent the air with a subtle perfume. I did not care that these luxuries were meant to bribe my cooperation, I eagerly scrubbed myself clean in the bath before sinking into a dreamless sleep nestled within the bed's downy embrace.

Sunlight streamed through the window when I was woken by the click of a turning key and the release of a lock. A thin acolyte entered, followed by a boy of around nine summers who carried a plate of oat biscuits and a mug of steaming tea. The man regarded me silently while the boy placed the meal on the table and then moved to the bathing room, quickly returning with his arms full of towels and my discarded clothing.

'His Supreme Highness has requested your attendance,' he stated quietly. 'I shall wait outside to escort you.'

He offered a hint of a bow, seemingly more habitual than respectful, and ushered the boy from the room. The door closed behind him, remaining unlocked, and I scrambled from the bed to devour the biscuits. I looked out of the window while I sipped the hot drink, frowning at the lush green gardens which extended as far as the bordering woodland. Pockets of bright colour studded the emerald carpet as bluebells, daffodils, snowdrops and primroses bloomed in the morning sun. It was a disturbing contrast to the last time I was at Burford when the ground had been locked in the sleep of winter.

I dressed in the clothes that had been provided and pulled on my own boots before opening the door. The acolyte was waiting patiently for me, his hands clasped loosely in front of him.

'Please follow me.'

His soft tone barely disturbed the smothering hush of the hallway and he quietly turned and walked towards the staircase, expecting me to follow him. There had been no soldiers guarding my room and I saw none while I retraced the path to Villermir's study. The Supreme High Priest was seated behind the table, writing in a leather-bound ledger, and I was left to examine his workspace after the acolyte mutely withdrew. A large, annotated map hung on the wall behind him showing details of the Three Kingdoms. Comments had been placed beside the larger towns and sketched lines extended far into Faulknar. A tall window flooded the room with light and highlighted another, unaltered, map that hung on the wall opposite. Bookcases flanked the door behind me, but my attention was drawn to the double-doored cabinet nestled within a recess beside the iron-grated fireplace. The low hum of warding energies suggested it contained interesting artefacts. Villermir's personal treasure trove. My thoughts of what delights he had hidden within were interrupted by a polite cough. I turned to see him watching me with a small, satisfied smile on his face.

'Good morning, Tallen. I hope you slept well.'

'The room is certainly more comfortable than the last one you offered me.'

The smile faded and he sighed at my challenging tone. He hesitated for a heartbeat then swiftly rose, causing me to take a reflexive step back. He lifted his hands, palms facing me in a gesture of peace, and he walked around the desk to stand in front of me.

'I mean you no harm.'

'We both know that's a half-truth at best,' I replied, conceding that he, personally, had yet to show any aggression towards me. 'Why am I here?'

'Walk with me.' He indicated the door behind me. 'I have something I would like to show you.'

Villermir guided me out of the house and into the gardens I had seen from the window. The carefully manicured grass. The islands of colour where spring flowers displayed for the passing insects. The thick hedges that danced with the flittering of small birds. The bright sun that warmed my back while we strolled along a gravel path woven between the bright foliage. It all felt uncomfortable after the violent corruption of the land I had seen in Hilman and the reports of devastating drought throughout Lindvane.

'It's almost as if we are in late spring,' I wondered aloud.

'We are barely past midwinter,' he confirmed, his eyes flashing with pride.

'This cannot be.'

'You, of all people, should know that nothing is impossible,' he corrected, misinterpreting my concern over its creation as a lack of belief in his construction. 'You drew power into yourself. I redirected it into a garden of perfection.'

'You raped the land for this? Everything is dying so you can have an extended summer?'

'Come now,' he scolded. 'Drey taught you better than that. Energy cannot be destroyed. I have merely repurposed it. Life may be reduced in one area but it flourishes in another.'

'When was the last time you stepped outside of Burford? Your perfect gardens are surrounded by drought. Rivers have dried up. Landslides have collapsed the sides of mountains. That's a bit more than a reduction, don't you think? How can you believe that your selfish greed is merely a redirection?' I viewed the bounty of life before me with a heavy sadness. 'Why are you showing me this?'

He hesitated, a slight frown creasing the skin between his eyebrows. 'I would like for you to understand. I believe you have had some experience of sacrifice and may be the only person who could appreciate what I am achieving here.'

'You are creating an illusion here,' I persisted, struggling to find the motivation behind the madness. 'Why would you cause such devastation just so you can control this small space?'

'This is just the beginning.' The tall, lean man clasped his hands in a gesture of frustration. 'This is evidence of what can be done. Of what the Three Kingdoms can become.'

'But you've ravaged the land outside this bubble. You've drained all the land's resources to create a haven that would take barely a morning to walk across it. There's nothing left to take.'

'Think, Tallen! I expected more from you than this.'

His sharp tone recalled the crushing disappointment that he had fostered in me as a child. He took a breath before continuing in a milder manner.

'You know how magick works. The balance is always maintained. What is taken from one must be given to another. The drought in Lindvane is the partner of the rains falling on Faulknar. The disrupted land in Hilman is the release of the pressure generated here. I am merely weaving the threads of energy into a new tapestry. In time, what I have created here will extend throughout Lindvane. And beyond.'

'How do you hope to achieve that? Look at you. You've consumed your physical form channelling that much power. You'll die before you transform a quarter of the kingdom, much less—' I stopped, the connection finally being made. 'That's why you need me.'

He smiled, satisfied that I had accepted the scope of his plan. 'Sustaining the flow of power is exhausting, is it not? Both the physical toll,' he swept his hand down his emaciated body,' and the drain on your will. Tell me, do you find the pull of oblivion as intoxicating as I?' The desire to dissolve into that vast expanse of power. To be so completely absorbed. Sacrificing your brief, meaningless existence to the eternity of such a powerful entity.'

His eyes glazed over in a religious rapture but I felt disturbed by the truth within his words. I had accounted my spiralling descend into self-annihilation, fuelled by the taint of self-loathing, as being a product of my own guilt following the death of Z'hara, my failure to protect the people from the persecuting priests, and my inability to stop the slaughter caused by the Gallowglass daemons. Megin had suggested my suffering had been fed by that of the land and now Villermir claimed there was more than my own shame. That my abuse of power had been at the core of my despair. It was the truth I had been avoiding, and I could feel Drey's condemnation like a sharp-edged rock lodged within my chest.

'Why?' I asked quietly.

The passion had left Villermir's eyes and he regarded me with a contemplative expression. 'The Empathy Crystal is presenting some resistance. I'm having to fight against its influence as well as that of the land. It is consuming my reserves faster than I can replace them. I'm hoping that the crystal will respond more favourably to you.'

Ignoring the dull fatigue at his blatant abuse of the Empathy Crystal, I clarified my question. 'Why spend so much energy on recreating the land? What is the point? Surely you could use the power more effectively elsewhere.'

'You would have preferred that I had crushed Faulknar?' He smiled at my angry scowl. 'We are alike, you and I. I believe we both feel that we have something to prove. To ourselves, perhaps. To others, certainly. But also, to our Gods.'

'Baila wants you to grow pretty flowers?'

The Supreme High Priest's face hardened at my overt disrespect. 'My biggest mistake was to leave you in the hands of that druid. Filling your head with the contemptuous disinterest of obsolete Gods. Your Gods abandoned a world that they left flawed. Hunger. Disease. Imperfections that cause suffering and grief. It is time to finish what they rejected.'

'As I see it, the suffering is caused by you. Your religion. Your priests. Your intolerance.'

'There is much work to be done. Much resistance to overcome. I admit, I have not been able to monitor the action of my more… passionate priests as closely as I would have liked. They share my ambition, though perhaps a little too enthusiastically at times. With your assistance, I'm sure things can move faster and more will join us in the paradise we build.'

'Why would I help you destroy everything the Gods created? Why would I help you oppress the people of the Three Kingdoms into your elitist system of control?'

Villermir tilted his head in a parody of paternal concern. 'Oh, Tallen. Let me show you the glory that is to come. See how wonderful it will be when we are all living within Baila's Grace.'

He stepped towards me, raising his hand as if to cradle my face. I quickly withdrew and assumed a defensive stance, knowing he did not need to touch to gain access into my mind but hoping my clear rejection would discourage him. He closed his fingers into a loose fist and dropped his arm. He gave me a nod of acknowledgement and backed it with a small smile of depreciation.

'My apologies. It appears my enthusiasm can also cause me to act hastily. We have sufficient time for you to understand his aim and appreciate that this is the rightful path. You will come to see how this will benefit everyone.' His smile widened to become more conspiratorial. 'Have you not wondered at the tales told of the utopia ruled over by your Gods before the Rebellion? Are you not tempted to regain those idyllic days? Without the petty squabbling of your deities, of course.'

It was a tempting image but I would not believe that his intentions, and those of his God, were so benignly benevolent. I struggled to accept that Villermir's motivations were so altruistic.

'Why are you doing this?'

His smile slipped. 'I told you. We will correct the mistakes of your Gods and create a bounty that can be enjoyed by all.'

'No. Why are *you* doing this? What has your God promised you?'

Villermir stood very still. His mantle of authority subtly fading to reveal the elderly scholar that he could have been, had he not chosen the teachings of Baila. He regarded me with his slate eyes clear of hidden intentions while he considered whether to answer my question.

'We are a product of our raising, are we not?' he began carefully. 'You stand here today with your thoughts, ambitions, desires forged by Drey and Laken.' A smile of sympathy flickered over his lips at my involuntary reaction to his naming of Laken. 'We are so very alike. What would you do to have a moment with him? To show him what you have become. What you have achieved. To take back those years that were denied you.'

I remembered the ceremony where Sheehan had called the dead and given me that moment with Laken. My eyes stung with the tears I refused to shed in front of Villermir.

'What has he promised you?' I asked again quietly.

'My father.'

CHAPTER TWENTY-FOUR

Villermir left, abruptly finishing the conversation, and I was given the freedom to walk the extensive gardens of the estate. A few acolytes and young boys tended the decorative plants and the ornamental hedges, with no soldiers patrolling the grounds. It would have been easy for me to slip into the woodland and make my escape, but my contempt for Villermir's arrogance was immediately followed by the realisation that I did not want to escape. Ignoring the fact that I had been readily betrayed in Hilman and I had no doubt that an army of informants, not mention suitably coerced townspeople, would quickly reveal my location to the nearest temple, I was tired of running. I had dreaded being dragged back to Burford and Villermir for so long that, now I was here, I felt a little deflated. The lazy flight of the insects dancing from flower to flower was hypnotic and I could almost forget about the desecration that lay beyond the estate boundaries. My obedience had been cheaply bought by a hot bath.

A middle-ranking acolyte was waiting for me when I returned to the house, interrupting his instructions to a more junior assistant to address me.

'Your presence is requested in the library,' he stated coldly. 'Follow me.'

He turned sharply, accepting that I would follow, and led me further into the building. The library was a long room and was bathed in light from several tall windows. Dark wood bookcases stood proudly against the walls to house countless leather-bound volumes and rough-edged, loosely coiled scrolls. Narrow tables divided the space and these were currently occupied by a senior priest and two acolytes, each making notes on scraps of parchment concerning the appropriate points of interest within the texts scattered around them. Villermir sat in a corner, highlighted by the sunlight coming through the window behind him. A low table separated his thickly padded chair from a matching one placed opposite him. He passively watched me cross the room, with a hint of a smile resting on his lips. The intensity of our previous encounter had faded completely and he politely rose to greet me.

'Tallen. Thank you for joining me.' He indicated the empty chair. 'Please. Sit.'

I was unsettled by the return of his genteel hospitality and his elderly grandfather demeanour, but I indulged his charade and graciously accepted the seat.

'Can I get you some refreshment?' he asked pleasantly, with the acolyte hovering the appropriate two paces away. 'A cool drink, perhaps. Some fruit?'

I declined both and Villermir flapped his hand at the acolyte in dismissal. The younger man respectfully bowed before leaving, a gesture repeated by the other acolytes at the Supreme High Priest's harsher command for them to leave. The senior priest scowled at the interruption to his studies and gathered his things more slowly than the younger scholars, but he complied with his superior's wishes without a discourteous delay. Villermir waited until the doors had closed before turning to me with a disconcertingly charming smile.

'My apologies for earlier,' he began. 'It has been a long time since I spoke about my father to anyone other than my God. I was rude with my abruptness. Please forgive me.'

'It was nothing,' I replied cautiously, trying to determine the intention behind his suddenly amiable manner.

He dipped his head in superficial humility. 'My relationship with my father is very personal, as I am sure you can appreciate. However, having contemplated on the matter, I feel you may benefit from its discussion. It may help you to understand what I am aiming to achieve here.'

His voice lowered into the relaxing tones of a sermon and I found myself settling into the comfortable chair, intrigued to learn of the man within the monster I had created.

'My father was a formidable man. Juddenaire. There's a name to be respected.'

I had not heard of the name before so I doubted that the man had achieved any success of note, however, I accepted that respect could be gained from a number of small deeds and I allowed Villermir his filial pride.

'He was a stern man with a clear sense of what was right and what was wrong. He was a committed devotee of Baila when the God was considered little more than an unremarkable prophet. From an early age, he knew the truth. He knew the teachings came not from a mortal man but were the scriptures of the divine.'

'And you followed his example.'

The priest's face tightened with the recollection of a memory. 'He held himself to very high standards and expected them in others. As with many, I rebelled against my father's strict practices and I needed to be shown the Truth within his customs. The need for sacrifice to purify the soul and accept the God's Grace. Sometimes we need to be bathed in fire before we can feel its warmth.'

'I think your priests have taken that concept a little too literally.'

He met my gentle challenge with a level gaze. 'Sometimes literal is what is required.'

'I do not agree.'

He took a breath and leaned back in his chair. 'Your Gods have infested people's minds for generations. Their rules of balance and fairness. Of the freedom of choosing your own path. Tell me, Tallen. Where has this freedom of choice taken you? A system of the rich privileged suppressing those that go without. A world of hunger and disease, of pain and suffering.'

I shifted in my seat, uncomfortable with his biased interpretation. 'A system that you and your priesthood exploit. You have caused more pain and suffering—'

'Don't be disingenuous. The system is prevalent within the earliest records and I do not doubt its influence before then. Long before the legends of Baila claim that he walked the earth and the first emergence of your pantheon. Those with power, money and strength will always dominate those without any of those traits. It is within our nature to take what we need and protect those we cherish. We are designed to fight with everything we have, from kings to slaves. The motivation stays the same. Only the scale differs.'

'You're saying that we are doomed to repeat the same mistakes. So why go to all this trouble? How is Baila so different that you would replace what already is?'

He leaned forward again as if to include me into a confidence. 'The problem with your Gods is that there are too many of them. They squabble like siblings fighting over a broken toy. They are jealous. Petty. You cannot rule by ceding to every member of a council. The king makes his decisions alone.'

'Or queen,' I countered petulantly.

He paused, considering me. 'Everybody wants to be dominated, Tallen. They want the tallest, the strongest, the smartest to lead them. They want to feel safe and secure, knowing that they will be protected from the dangers of the world. Trusting that their problems will be effectively dealt with. That someone understands the chaos of living and can guide them to a better future.'

'And that someone is male?'

A smile danced over his lips. 'You are possibly the most powerful being that has existed for generations and yet, you have spent your life searching for protection and guidance. First Laken, and then Drey.' He held up his hand to halt my protest. 'We all crave that paternal support. That unquestionable belief that a father can protect us from the nightmares of our imagination. My father's methods may have seemed extreme. Even within his sect of believers, he was considered fanatical. But that was because they were bound by the indoctrination of their ancestors. Unable to throw off the shackles of free choice and self-determination. My father had the clarity of vision to know that there can only ever be one God. That the One God is the path to true peace.'

'And that's what you think you are achieving?' I asked quietly, failing to see how his belief in benevolent paternal guidance fit with the oppression and corruption I had witnessed in his priests.

'There is much work to be done. Resistance is to be expected. I also resisted the teachings of my father but I have come to see that this is a better way and, in time, others will too. There is a comfort to be found in structure and conformity. Accepting your place within a system that benefits all, negates the need for the petty emotions of envy or jealously which can cause so much suffering. There is a simple pleasure in appreciating how everything fits together and accepting your role within that.' He released a sad sigh. 'It is regretful that some require... harsher methods to see the wisdom of Baila's truth. Once gathered into his Grace, they will see that it will be worth the transitory discomfort.'

A pressure in my head was building. I tried to determine whether Villermir truly believed in this idyllic future or whether he was convincing himself that his violent methods of coercion were justified. Everywhere I looked involved pain and suffering, and I doubted his God could eliminate that any more than mine had.

'Why destroy the land?' I asked, focusing on one small element within the vastness of his madness. 'How can that be part of Baila's plan?'

His face flushed with pious pride. 'Baila offers a land untouched by heat and drought, by frost or flood. Do you not agree that this estate is close to perfection? A temperate climate. An abundance of natural resources. No one need starve. No one will go cold. A place of beauty and plenty, and all that is required is an acceptance of Baila's will.'

'While the rest of the world suffers in a land from Mobis's Hells as you leach all its energy.'

He frowned in frustration. 'My inability to harness the Empathy Crystal's full potential has slowed my work. With you by my side, we should be able to extend the boundaries further into Lindvane. Food can be grown in the surrounding farmland to support the community. There will be room for all within Baila's protection.'

'This was your father's vision?'

'My father believed in a paradise within the shelter of Baila's mercy. I have been blessed to be the one who has created the beginnings of that dream. Together we can make it a reality for all.'

'And when complete, Baila will return your father to you? Your father will be raised from the dead so he can congratulate you on how impressive you are. So he can tell you, how very proud he is of you.'

Anger flared in his grey eyes in response to my mocking tone but he swiftly controlled his emotions, the whiteness of his knuckles within his tightly clasped hands being the only sign of his annoyance.

'I admit, I do yearn for my father's approval and I eagerly anticipate his return so that he can see the manifestation of his vision. But that is not my primary concern and it is disrespectful of you to suggest otherwise. Once you have accepted his Truth, you will understand the importance of the work I do here. What we will accomplish.'

I tilted my head, trying to decipher the twists and turns of his motivations. 'And you believe Baila can do this for you? I doubt that it is an easy gift to accomplish.'

'No more than returning the young Faulknar from Mobis's realms.'

I sat very still, fearing the hidden threat in the lightly spoken words. I was not surprised he had remembered the event but I could not see how my retrieval of Kade, done purely on instinct, was the same as what he was hoping for.

'I can't do… I don't know how…' I stammered, unwilling to repeat the horror of travelling to Mobis's domain, particularly as I now knew the Fate had been aware of my trespass. 'This is not the same. His soul was still here. Almost. I just needed to reach… How long has your father been dead?'

I was not sure I wanted to know what I was being sent to retrieve. Kade had been in Mobis's Hells for a matter of moments and had not returned unchanged. I doubted that Villermir's father would be the man the priest remembered. My unease grew, with his eager smile scaring me more than his anger had, and I felt he had taken my question as my implied acceptance.

'My father was taken from me just after I had joined the priesthood but that is of no consequence. Baila will reconstitute his body. You will collect his soul.'

A chill shuddered my body at the tone of our conversation shifting from one of a spring paradise for a congregation of blissful believers, to that of the gruesome resurrection of someone who had been dead for many years. I searched for the insanity that must reside within the man, finding nothing but unquestionable belief. He had total conviction that his God would shelter and protect all who joined him, and that Baila would return his father in reward for his fantastical creation.

'I cannot return your father to you.'

'You will,' he replied with absolute confidence. 'Baila will channel my father's soul through you into the body that he will have remade. You will accept the Grace that he has bestowed upon you and you will accede to his Will.'

'Have you considered my request?' Villermir asked pleasantly.

He had given me two days to reflect on what he had demanded of me. I had rejected the option of reviving his father as being improbable, if not impossible. My retrieval of Kade had been reactive and I had no idea how to repeat the feat. I debated the role of Baila extensively, however. The addition of another God into the established pantheon was not a difficult concept to understand but it sat uncomfortably, seeming a little too convenient for the promotion of a narrow view of how lives should be lived. Villermir's view of how lives should be lived.

'Why do you believe that Baila is separate from the Gods?'

The Supreme High Priest tilted his head, surprised by the question. 'Because he is.'

'That's your interpretation. He could equally be an aspect of Drunst, using you to cause chaos throughout the Three Kingdoms. Or perhaps Camlun, feeding the flames of war.'

His expression softened to one of looking at a child who had failed to understand a simple message. 'I *know* because I have seen his Truth. Have you been honoured to gaze upon your Gods?' He smiled. 'I see that you have. Is it so hard to believe that I, also, have been blessed with divine communion?'

He was frustratingly logical about his beliefs and my arguments sounded weak. Could I claim my faith was true and his was not? Could anyone claim to know the ways of deities? I could argue that Baila was a reflection of my Gods as readily as I could maintain that he was created by Villermir's desire for control. Was I so certain that all Gods were not just our limited imaginations trying to understand the unknowable power of that we call magick? I moved to easier concepts.

'Why should I help you? You terrorised my childhood.'

Villermir appeared genuinely shocked by my comment. 'Why do you say that?'

'Because you did. You took every opportunity to bully me when I was growing up in Liegeport.'

His face creased with concern. 'Is that how you remember it? I'm sorry you feel that, it was not my intention.' He held a hand up to stall my protest. 'I may have been a little stern. Strict, perhaps.'

'As your father was strict? Using fear to focus the attention?'

'You needed clear boundaries. Drey let you run wild. Your power could have caused untold damage, had I not instilled in you some restraint. You required discipline and control.' He sighed, and I wondered how much of his reasoning was his father's. 'My methods may have been firm but I could not afford to fail you.'

I blinked. 'Fail me?'

'Please, Tallen. Sit.' He indicated the chair opposite to where he sat at his desk, lying his hands flat on its surface when I refused. 'Let me try to explain. You had the potential to be something far more powerful than we had seen in generations. I admit, I thought Drey a fool to be talking of dragons but, nevertheless, I feared that without guidance you could release immeasurable harm. You were a child. You could have been influenced by dark forces and I knew I had to instil in you a clear sense of what was right and what was wrong.'

'Drey taught me what was right. You just showed me how I was wrong.'

I was becoming less sure of myself, feeling I was standing on shifting sand while Villermir's words sowed seeds of doubt into my memories. I felt the need to defend myself, to make him understand how he had victimised me. I started to question whether it was I who had victimised him. I had used him as a convenient focus for my confusion and frustration, twisting his actions into something I could hate. I had made him the monster so I could avoid confronting the monsters within me.

'I'm sorry if that was how you felt,' he continued. 'It was never my intention for you to fear me. I would have liked for us to have worked together, but perhaps my frustration at Drey being so lenient with you, and my anxiety at what damage you could cause yourself, meant I was firmer than was necessary. Maybe, if we had spent more time together, I could have explained my concern for you.' He smiled indulgently. 'But you made quite a show of avoiding me.'

I felt an unwelcome twinge of guilt. I had not hidden my dislike of the priest and had been rude and disrespectful on many occasions, sullen and petulant on others.

'But the last time I was here,' I persisted, albeit hesitantly. 'You tortured me.'

He shook his head. 'I merely opened the door to the torments you contain within you. What you saw were the beasts of your own making. The latent evil that lies deep within the core of you. You needed to see the danger that you present and that how, without boundaries and guidance, these temptations could have overwhelmed you.' He paused to ensure I was listening. 'As I believe they did, during your campaign against Baila's devoted. You have a darkness inside you that can result in the downfall of kingdoms. Without control, you can inflict immense suffering. You cannot afford to ignore that part of you.'

A small part of my mind wanted to scream that he lied, but the larger part remained in silent judgement.

'But you killed Kade,' I offered quietly, desperately.

Villermir sat back in his chair and clasped his hands loosely in his lap, patiently waiting while I re-evaluated my memories and the assumptions I had based on them. Deflated, I slumped into the seat that had been offered earlier. I kept my eyes lowered, not wanting to see the look of triumph in his eyes, but fearing I was still transferring my prejudices onto his actions, I lifted my gaze to find an open expression of concern.

'I remember that feeling,' he said softly. 'The rearrangement of what you believe to be true. My father showed me the Truth and I have embraced the comfort of following Baila's Will. I had hoped to be the one to show you that Truth, but perhaps you needed to touch the darkness before you could truly see the evil you possess. Whatever the path, you are here now and we can start to rebuild the world as Baila commands.'

I shook my head slowly back and forth, unable to find the words to deny him now I no longer trusted my own decisions. At that moment, Villermir appeared to simply be a tired, old man who had pushed himself too far in pursuing a legacy of which his father would be proud. My suspicions, while reduced, were not completely rejected and my caution was reawakened when he continued.

'We have talked much of my father. Perhaps it would be appropriate to talk of yours.'

My heart stuttered, then raced faster to make up for the delay. 'What about my father?'

A smile flickered at the edge of his mouth at the focus that had returned to my eyes, and the challenging tone that once again hardened my voice.

'You asked how I could be so sure that the One God was not an aspect of your pantheon. Knowing what I know now, it would appear your father played a larger role in that than I had understood. The power of Dragonslayer blood. His abilities were largely dormant, of course.' He broke away from his private musings to look at me. 'Did you know that your power is reflected in your eyes? The renewed link to your dragon has allowed your true colour to shine through. The connection had remained hidden for generations, diluting your father's eyes from your vivid amber to his pale hazel.'

My mind spiralled while I tried to determine the association between Villermir and my father, and why this had not been revealed until now. Unable to find stability, I grasped at his last comment.

'How do you know the colour of my father's eyes?'

He smiled benevolently. 'Hael and I were once close friends.'

'You lie!' I snapped, unwilling to corrupt thoughts of my father with those of Villermir.

'Not at all. He was a student of mine and, while he rejected the teachings of Baila, we remained friends. We spent much of our time discussing faith and the nature of the divine.'

I knew very little of my father but found it difficult to accept that he could have known Villermir, much less had a relationship with him. The priest's views ran counter to everything I believed about my family and I struggled to find any common ground on which the two men could base a friendship. Villermir had created enough doubt in my assumptions however, that I readily conceded I could also be wrong in this.

'In the course of our studies we discovered a number of texts relating to ancient rituals and arcane summoning rites. Darker magicks that spoke of powers beyond our comprehension. That offered insight into the answers we sought. We each possessed some magickal aptitude and were both keen to discover if we had the skill to summon a God.'

'Gods should not be summoned,' I murmured, fearing where this was leading.

'Indeed. But I don't think we truly believed we would succeed. I mean, if the rituals worked then the priests and druids would still have been routinely performing them to prove each other wrong. Instead, the instructions had been left to gather dust in an obscure library vault.' He shrugged. 'Perhaps we were naive, and the event certainly frightened your father, but to witness the glory of the divine...'

The Supreme High Priest let his thoughts drift, caught in the memory of whatever he had summoned. Having been visited by The Lady on more than one occasion, I could appreciate the overwhelming majesty of a divine presence and the heart-stopping awe that it evoked.

'What did you do?'

My question interrupted his memories and I saw the focus seep back into his eyes. A weak smile rippled over his lips although he could not completely dislodge his expression of loss.

'We summoned a God. The ritual was laughably simple. An incantation. A few herbs. The sprinkling of powered minerals. And, of course, the blood. We added our blood to the mixture, a lot of blood, and used it to paint the required sigils that created the protective space. Imagine our surprise when a form started to take shape. Expanding in size and detail until Baila, in all his celestial glory, was standing before us.'

I did not need to imagine. I had seen that ritual performed, only it had not been Baila who had been summoned. I did not want to dwell on that memory but I was still morbidly fascinated by Villermir's tale.

'Having been gifted my faith from my father's teachings, I felt no fear in Baila's presence and readily accepted what he asked from me. But Hael screamed as if Mobis had stood in front of him. He was unprepared for the One God's judgement and failed to receive his blessing. I have come to believe that your father saw a reflection of his own daemons, as yours were revealed to you. Something broke in Hael that night and he was never the same. More timid. More haunted. He refused all my requests to repeat the ritual, eventually running to Faulknar and severing our friendship.' All illusion of the fragile, old man disappeared as he pinned me with a determined stare. 'I was never able to complete the ritual without your father. It was not until discovering your heritage that I came to realise his Dragonslayer blood was the key ingredient.'

I felt my heart race in response to his clear intent to use my blood to perform the summoning rites once again and grant him direct access to his God.

'It was many years later that I learnt of his family at Methhold. Perhaps his rejection by Baila drove him into the arms of your mother and her overt faith in the old Gods. I tried to reclaim him, to return him to the comfort of Baila's scripture. I reached out to him.' He paused, watching me carefully. 'But he resisted. And I'm sure you know of how the soldiers reacted to his refusal.'

I felt sick. The destruction of my village, of my family, had been the result of Villermir's ambition. It brought back vivid memories of that day. I could hear the screams. I could smell the smoke. I could taste the ash.

'He knew it was wrong,' I stated, more to convince myself than to disprove Villermir. 'He would never have helped you.'

'Indeed. He chose his death and that of his village rather than accept the inevitable. Tell me? What did his sacrifice bring? What did the waste of all those lives mean? You survived to sit here before me. Together we will build what your father was too afraid to comprehend.'

'No,' I whispered.

'It is inevitable,' he repeated. 'Baila has brought you here so we can build his paradise. So that all can live within his Grace.'

'No,' I stated firmly.

His expression grew harder and it was echoed in his tone. 'Do not make the mistakes of your father. Avoid the torments he suffered and embrace Baila's Will. This is your destiny, Tallen.'

I was tired of being told what my destiny was. It seemed everyone had their own interpretation; Villermir, Drey, the healers on the Isle of Serpents, Sálaforn and her Gallowglass shamans, Luella and her Moon Warriors, even Megin and the Goddess. Different shades of ambition but all wanting the power I possessed. I was ready to reject them all.

I gained strength from the determination to resist Villermir's plans for me, and this allowed me to see past the comfort and security of the illusion he had created at Burford Hythe. The pleasure I had previously enjoyed in the carefully maintained gardens basking in the unnatural spring soured, revealing the distortion of energies and the arrogance in Villermir's design. I explored further from the house to discover the boundaries of his influence and found the reason for my apparent freedom, confirming that I remained a prisoner despite the absence of soldiers, locked doors and barred windows. I could approach no closer than fifteen paces from where Villermir's influence ended and barren scrubland pressed against the lush, green grass of the estate. No physical border prevented my escape but powerful wardings stabbed into my mind, crippling me with pain when the nerves throughout my body erupted in burning agony. I could not build my defences strong enough to provide even the smallest protection from the assault and I would be left exhausted for some time after any attempt.

It seemed that Villermir had been aware of my investigations and his manner had changed at our next encounter. His charming, cajoling demeanour had been replaced by one of barely contained rage. He angrily paced the study, glaring murderously at the interruption when I was brought before him and causing my escorting acolyte to swiftly scuttle away. I clenched my fists behind my back, hoping to prevent him from seeing the fear his manner provoked, but my evident defiance was sufficient to further twist his face in disgust.

'Why do you insist on such foolish resistance?' he demanded, his voice rigidly contained to avoid shouting. 'Why must you remain determined to stay blind to the opportunity given to you? You should be on your knees in gratitude, instead...'

He could not finish his sentence, apparently unable to find the words to sufficiently express his displeasure at my disrespect. I remained silent, unsure of what to say and certain that I would provoke his wrath no matter what was spoken.

'All I ask,' he continued after he had calmed himself, 'is for you to assist in the creation of Baila's vision. A return to the glorious time of the Ancients, under the benevolent care of the One God. A time of cooperation and peace. A vision that would end all pain and suffering. His guidance would bestow purpose and all would know the comfort that brings.' He stopped pacing to face me. 'We would be the Favoured ones. You would complete your purpose. By my side, you would protect and care for those who embraced his Will.' He slammed his palm onto the desk, making the items placed upon it rattle and causing me to take a step back. 'And yet, you insist on defying me in this!'

'Because it is wrong,' I replied quietly. 'Because we don't deserve that much power. No one does. People should be free to make their own choices.'

'Spoken like a Favoured,' he sneered. 'They toppled their Gods so the people could have free will. How well has that freedom served them?'

I could not find the appropriate words to defend my ancestors' decisions despite knowing that Villermir would take my silence as a measure of victory. He paused for several heartbeats before appearing to have come to a decision.

'Follow me.'

He marched passed me, making to leave the study, but waited until I had turned in implied obedience before opening the door and exiting into the reception hall. He ignored the main staircase and led me to a smaller set of steps that led to the corridors hidden below the house. I did not remember using this access but knew it would take me to the rooms where Villermir had played with me, and the cold, dark cell where I had been kept. My heart beat painfully fast at all the horrors that could await me and the sudden claustrophobia raced through me like a tide of hot air, causing sweat to bead at the base of my neck and between my shoulder blades. I dug my nails into my palms and concentrated on not bolting back the way I had come. I focused on Villermir's back, following the movement of the fabric while he walked, and the way he casually flicked his hand to light guiding candles. The shifting shadows produced another layer of menace within the narrow corridor, seeming to call the creatures of my night-terrors.

I stepped into a bare hallway and glanced nervously at the stone staircase situated in the far corner, which would lead to the hateful cells. Villermir did not hesitate, turning away from the steps to open one of the rough doors and striding confidently into the darkened room. He swiftly illuminated the room with a warm glow, but I needed several deep breaths before I found the courage to follow him. The ghosts of my sessions in that room crowded around me. Monsters of my making, he had said. Perhaps, but I still feared what may be waiting regardless of whether they were of my imagination or created by the sorcerer. Visions of the fires that scorched and the insectile creatures that skittered returned to haunt me, while the daemons that slashed sneered at my cowardice.

'Foolish girl,' grumbled Villermir, quieting thoughts of those past terrors enough to allow me to refocus on my current situation. 'I offer you paradise and you snap at my hand. Just like your obstinate kingdom, you would fight every attempt to gather you into the glory of the One God. Why do you insist on making me do this to you? Hayton and Averill have accepted his Truth and yet I am still forced to crush those who would rebel within their realms. Why is it so hard for people to embrace the peace offered to them?'

I was finding it hard to concentrate on Villermir's ramblings. The anxiety I had felt before entering the room had built into a pounding pressure in my head. Dissonant energies writhed within the confined space and scratched at my skin while a painfully high tone pierced into my mind. The previous horrors of that space refused to leave and pressed closer with their threats of torment, yet their persistent presence seemed to mask that there was something more menacing trapped here. I forced myself to respond to the priest's complaints.

'Peace? Your priesthood is founded in fear. You rule as a tyrant.'

'Tyranny?' He gave a short, bitter laugh. 'You should look to your king before making such accusations. Baila's teachings have spread throughout Lindvane and Hilman without the blood that has been shed as a result of your king's stubbornness. People across those two kingdoms have heard the message of the One God, and have seen the evil hidden within the traditional ways and the old Gods. So much more effective at gathering them into the embrace of Baila's Will than the brutal costs of war. Averill sees this. Hayton understands this. Yet, Faulknar and his self-righteous dukes insist on sending their men to a slaughter. Does that sound like a just ruler who cares for his people? Obstinate fool has condemned them all to starvation rather than accept a Baila priest onto his council. He is forcing me to destroy his kingdom, just to avoid admitting he is wrong.' The Supreme

High Priest had been pacing the room in his agitation but stopped abruptly to stare at me, religious fervour sparkling in his eyes. 'You. You are the key to everything, don't you see? You can stop all of this. Bring Faulknar into his Glory and you will cease the killing of all these men.'

I was tempted to highlight that women were dying as well, but it was too petulant a remark when considering the scale of Villermir's madness. The priest continued, striding over to stand uncomfortably close to me.

'With the final kingdom welcomed into the Truth, we can focus all our energies on creating his paradise. A land of perpetual summer. A land of peace and prosperity.'

'And with you ruling over it like a God,' I mocked.

I was still distracted by the distorted energy permeating the room and failed to react when his face spasmed in rage; a brief warning before he struck with the back of his hand.

'Step carefully,' he snarled. 'You may be of use but I will not listen your blasphemy.'

The blow had been forceful enough to knock me back a pace and I felt my anger ignite beneath all the fear this room had provoked. I rubbed at my stinging cheek and all the confusion he had coaxed over the preceding days peeled away.

'You almost had me believing you,' I stated calmly. 'You had me thinking I had misread your intentions towards me as a child. That it was not as bad as I remembered. That I had stained your actions with my own fears of inadequacy and worthlessness. You had me doubting myself so much, I almost believed you were creating this paradise to provide a better future. A return to the fabled time of the Ancients.' His face twitched and he clenched his fists as if to restrain himself from hitting me again. 'But that's not it, is it? You're a bully, Villermir. Always have been. A mean-minded old man whose ambitions would see you rival the God you claim to worship.'

He raised his arm to strike again but I was ready for him this time. I raised my own arm, placing my palm to face him in a parody of the arresting gesture. I used the action to focus a small protective shield of air that effortlessly absorbed the blow when he smashed his fist into the invisible barrier. He repeated the impotent act in thwarted frustration.

'You thought to coerce me into being your partner because you were afraid you would no longer be able to dominate me. You were right to be afraid. I'm not a child anymore, Villermir. I'm not so easily intimidated.'

He leaned closer to menace me. 'Are you sure about that? Perhaps a demonstration of Baila's power will convince you to submit to the winning side.'

Villermir turned sharply and went to the long, low, dark-wood cabinet that ran the length of the small room. It was the only furniture within the space. He crouched in front of the central section, hiding its contents from my view when he opened the door and selected an item. I gasped at the sudden distress emitted from the writhing energies trapped within the room, their agony assailing me with the savage pounding of hail in a winter's storm. The priest rose slowly, carefully placing the object on the surface of the cupboard and pausing, reverentially, before moving to one side and allowing me to see his treasure.

'What have you done?' I breathed, horrified at what I saw.

Cradled in a shallow wooden base lined with folds of buttercup-yellow silk, lay the corrupted form of the Empathy Crystal. It was smaller than I remembered. Irregular, sharp edges spread across its surface where slabs had been chipped away. This had created the auditory crystals Villermir used to gather information and give instruction to his contacts throughout the Three Kingdoms. The sight of such defamation caused a physical pain to rip through my chest, but the violations which turned my blood to ice were the black tendrils wrapped around the stone to cage it. Dark veins, such as those which smothered the protective barriers of my mind. The lines of pollution I had seen infiltrating the diseased land. The foul vines that had caressed Kade's neck in my drug-induced vision.

I shifted my focus from the physical marks on the crystal to the power signatures that were radiating from the defiled stone. Malevolent darkness seeped from the artefact like questing fingers and reached towards the aura surrounding Villermir's hand, resting a cradling finger-width from the crystal. Small specks of black flared between the two points, like tiny flakes of ash. Surprisingly, the pulsing emanated from Villermir rather than the Empathy Crystal. I drew back my focus to include the rest of the priest's aura, appalled to find it shifting and twisting as though it contained countless ebony eels, all weaving around his body or snaking down his arm towards the stone. Black shadows coiled around his throat and thin spikes speared into the base of his skull. Dark threads infrequently passed under the skin of his face while his blissful expression reflected the faint, creamy glow of the crystal.

'She offers so much,' he said wistfully, 'but demands such a high price. Shall we see if she is more accommodating for you?'

He turned to face me with one hand remaining to hover over the abused stone. He extended the other, reaching to grasp my throat despite being on the far side of the room, and cords of vile darkness flowed from his fingertips. They crossed the distance between us and wrapped around my neck. I instinctively clawed at their constriction but the coils were insubstantial and my scrabbling fingers could find no purchase. I felt the foul essence probe into the base of my skull, flooding my mind with despair. My awareness flowed along the tethering lines, curling around Villermir's abhorrent consciousness before submerging into the lemon hue of the stone. I desperately tried to separate the pure crystal light from the dark corruption, but I was falling too fast and I could not hold onto the golden, empathic strands surrounding me. My mind felt stretched and thinned, dragged by a rapid current over vast distances while images of rivers and mountains, forests and lakes, flashed around me. Landscapes covered in a buttery haze were slashed by tendrils of black blight and I saw how the energies of the land fed into these vines, drawing the power contained within the soil and the plants into the Empathy Crystal.

I was swept back into the current with dizzying speed, my awareness buzzing with the forces passing through me. Within the crystal matrix, the energies seeped away like the exhaling of a breath. Grass was made to grow and flowers forced to bloom. Water was called into dry streams and shrinking underground reservoirs. Rains clouds were diverted to ensure unbroken sunlight bathed my creation. I pulsed between a broken and dying land and that of the oasis I was building. Stealing the health from one to nourish the unsustainable bounty of the other. Pushing the boundaries of unnatural fertility further from Burford Hythe and into the surrounding countryside. The power channelling through me was intoxicating. My mind sang with the energies swirling around me and the forces that danced to my command. I felt like a God!

The thought shattered the ecstasy and I became painfully aware of the unconscionable desecration I was causing. I resisted the pull of energies, slowing the pulsing transfer of power until the current became still. I fought against the binding veins that threatened to tear me apart and pulled them into myself, gathering them as a fisherman would gather his nets. The flow of energy started to reverse and I pushed the yellow light away from the encroaching darkness. Clouds gathered and flowers wilted while I repaired broken land and reopened waterways. I heard the faint echoes of a scream but I ignored it as irrelevant. My confidence grew and I diverted rain-laden storm clouds from a drowning Faulknar to the drought-parched wastes of Lindvane, careful to release the water steadily to avoid flooding.

My effort faltered, stuttering, and I felt my mind being crushed by Villermir's presence. His will fed into the vile snakes that wrapped around the crystal's matrix, squeezing my awareness within the yellow glaze into the foul veins which sucked at my independence. I felt trapped within their grasp and they drained my defiance, turning the energies back and destroying all that I had achieved. I clung to the empathic matrix, pushing its glow against the constricting embrace of the vines. Power flowed back and forth while light battled dark, neither maintaining the advantage for long. My will against Villermir's. The strength of the crystal against that of the hated tendrils. The current stalled as the two sides fought to control the land's energy.

It snapped.

The presence in my mind vanished and I had the nauseating feeling of being dragged, at some speed, back into my body. The lemon glow faded from my vision, with the crystalline structures and images of distant landscapes replaced by the room at Burford. Villermir staggered away from the Empathy Crystal and the black cords whipped through him, severing his connection from the artefact and from me. A high-pitched note reverberated around the stone walls within the confined space, and I covered my ears with my hands in a vain attempt to block the noise. The crystal rocked in its cradle, resonating with the sound and vibrating faster when the note's pitch intensified. Villermir screamed, echoing the one I had heard before, and reached towards the stone to prevent it toppling off its cushioning base.

The crystal shattered and a rain of lethal shards flew across the room, embedding into Villermir's shielding palm and piercing my arms. But the sting of my wounds ceased to matter when I saw the extent of the damage caused to the sacred stone. The Empathy Crystal was scattered around the room in an uncountable number of small, sharp, golden pebbles.

CHAPTER TWENTY-FIVE

Villermir was furious. His face was flushed and his hands contorted into claws. He roared in anger and I was sent flying across the room by a blast of compressed air.

'You've ruined everything!' he screeched, raising his hands for another attack.

I was ready for him and welcomed the chance to vent my own raging emotions. His gale hammered against my shield but I maintained my position and returned with a volley of fireballs. He deflected the flames, scorching an outline in the stone wall beside him, and I took his moment of distraction to send another clutch of fireballs at him. He extinguished each one with a puff of smoke before returning with a blast of air that bounced off my shield and crashed against the wall behind me, cracking the stone and showering me with dust and grit. I adjusted my tactic, attacking with a stream of fire to deny him the opportunity to douse the flames as he had done with the spheres. The blaze separated to flow around him, encasing him in a fiery orb, and my face tightened with the heat of the blaze while the priest remained unharmed.

The ground rumbled. A heartbeat later the floor opened with a giant crack that raced from Villermir towards me. I jumped to the side to avoid the hole he had created when the crevice widened to unbalance me. The priest immediately followed with another blast of air, aiming for the area previously damaged so that numerous sharp stones burst from the wall to pelt my head and shoulders. I twisted to avoid the pebbled hail and I pulled the air from Villermir's lungs in an attempt to suffocate him as I had done to his priests, but his power was much greater and he easily blocked access to his chest. He flipped the flow of power to siphon my energies towards him, gaining strength from my assault as he neutralised the threat. I mimicked his tactic, and the push and pull of our contest lasted several heartbeats before I was able to snatch control. The impact of my wall of air made him stagger back a few paces and I pounced on this slight weakness to direct another stream of fire towards his head. Once again, he readily deflected my attack but the inferno greedily engulfed the long cabinet and the timber burst to send lethal splinters flying across the room.

Villermir roared with fury while his artefacts melted and cracked. The energies released swirled in turbulent whirlwinds and both Villermir and I snatched at the power they offered. I released my gained strength in a single blast, slamming into the floor at the priest's feet to create a crater filled with unstable gravel. Villermir slipped and fell to his knees but did not lose concentration. He returned my brief advantage with a sustained assault of fire and a river of flame containing all the colours of a phoenix raced towards me. Its heat turned the room into a furnace. I smiled; fire was my element. I breathed in the energy of his gift as if inhaling a pleasant aroma, then returned it as a white-hot inferno. The room shimmered in the haze of the hellish firestorm we had created and flickering glare turned our faces into daemonic masks.

While we continued to battle with air, earth and fire, the priest started the next phase of his attack and pierced into my head like a rapier. The destruction of the Empathy Crystal and the severing of my connection to it had cleared the polluting vines from protective barriers, and they stood strong and unblemished. Denied easy direct access, Villermir came at me like a dust-storm and a wall of darkness rolled towards my defences. Black ropes twisted together to form battering rams that punched into the walls surrounding my vulnerable *self*. I was forced to divide my attention, protecting my body from his physical attacks while rapidly repairing the cracks to my mental barricades. His foul tendrils snaked in to exploit any weakness and I spread layer over layer of sigils, embedding them within a tapestry of energy while Villermir's mind continued to press and gouge and prod and scrape.

The room rocked when our two barriers of air hammered into each other. The concussive waves slammed into the walls and pelted us with stinging debris. We were both bleeding from multiple small cuts where flying stonework evaded our shielding defences, and there were numerous areas of charred or smouldering cloth where flames had penetrated our protections. These minor distractions we ignored and we continued to swipe at each other. Fireballs flew while the floor rippled. Walls crumbled and the air was choked by clouds of dust.

A storm wave of malevolent darkness smashed into my mental barriers and demolished several layers of defence. I cried out as the black vines clawed and raked and slashed into my mind. I frantically gathered the scattered energy threads and rewove sigil upon sigil upon sigil, twisting the cords of power into solid walls.

A single vein stabbed into my core and all became still. I floated in a landscape uninterrupted by any form or structure. No sound disturbed the unnatural silence and I felt utterly alone within the featureless expanse. There was a subtle *wrongness* permeating throughout the space and a sense of unease lingered just beyond my reach. I followed the irritation to its source. Villermir.

'You're going to have to try harder than that,' I taunted, ejecting him from my mind and slamming the walls closed.

A sinister smile twisted his lips and his eyes flicked to the doorway. The shock wave caused by the destruction of the Empathy Crystal and the impact from our magick had summoned his priests and acolytes, and the first to arrive hesitated on the threshold. Their faces showed their horror upon seeing the carnage we had caused. Thick stone walls had crumbled and the room was strewn with the splintered remains of the wooden cabinet and broken or twisted artefacts.

I dismissed their distraction and Villermir renewed his attack. His wall of fire collided with my blast of air to create a roaring vortex, while he relentlessly battered against the barriers defending my mind. With my concentration already divided in two, I had failed to recognise the threat in the third assault. The meekly pious priests and acolytes found a latent courage and charged into the violence to protect their Supreme High Priest. They were hopelessly outmatched and yet they fought with whatever meagre magick they had. Their efforts were as noticeable as the bite of fleas against the tempest that Villermir and I had created, and they were quickly left bloodied and broken. Their defiance was extinguished soon after it had begun.

The needless slaughter added another layer of spite to the battle and we intensified our attacks. It was time to finish the fight and I drew on the power buzzing around me to fuel my blasts of air, my rivers of fire, and my shredding of the ground. The shaking produced within the confines of the room reverberated throughout Burford Hythe and the energy pulsed in waves of destruction. The walls cracked and popped where fissures radiated throughout the stonework. The ceiling split into a network of craters and crevices. The ground buckled and roiled like an angry sea. Devouring flames were whipped into frenzied whirlwinds, lashing against the protective domes we formed around ourselves. The bodies of Baila's faithful were incinerated when the fire raced out of the room and through the corridors to consume the building. Flammable furnishings and combustible texts fed the ravenous beast while we remained cocooned within the hellscape of our own making, compelled by our obsession to annihilate the other.

I drew on more power, clawing wild energies from the chaos and weaving them into a complex tapestry which combined my essence with that I had taken. I contained a seething mass of power that built in pressure until I felt I would erupt with the glory of a fire-mountain. I shimmered as vibrations tore through me and I strained to control the untamed forces.

I felt a moment of detachment and floated slightly above my body. Movement slowed to an expectant pause. All became quiet and still. I released my hold.

Time and sound slammed back into place and the power exploded. A thunderous wave of total devastation raced across the room and its concussive tide smashed everything it connected with. Ripples of destruction radiated from me with incomprehensible speed. The walls burst outwards. The ground shattered. The ceiling collapsed. Burford Hythe crashed down on top of me and buried me under a mountain of rubble.

I was cradled in a sphere of darkness but this was not a void of black oblivion or an obsidian prison of crystal. I was safely protected in a cave of broken masonry and cushioned on a blanket of dirt. Small stones pressed into my side and dust tickled my nose while I lie curled within my bubble, deep under the ruins of Burford.

The destruction of the Empathy Crystal had eased the despair into a dull ache of grief. I no longer felt the torments of the defiled land and my mind was my own, left to consider my actions with clear thoughts. I could not be certain of how much of what I had done while I crossed Hilman had been influenced by my connection to the land's suffering, and how much had been my own selfish desire. Relishing the enticement of power and justifying my actions as retribution. The accusations and validations danced through my thoughts until I was forced to accept that I had twisted protection into something much darker.

Thoughts of protection melted into those of *Saorsa*; the virtue of my dragon-blade. The bright thread of her loss weaved through all the other griefs, with her call remaining subtle but persistent. I knew I would have to search for her. The priceless blade had been kept safe by my family for generations and my shame at having lost her pressed into my chest. I did not welcome the thought of returning to Peverill, or crossing Lindvane in order to get there, but the decision to return for my sword was uncontested. I would do whatever it took to retrieve her.

I was less certain about the appropriate action to take regarding Megin. I was a Dragonslayer, created to hunt daemons with my dragon, and to join with her was such a tempting option. And yet, there was too much for me to comfortably hide in the simplicity of destroying monsters. People were hurting and the land was damaged. There were injustices that needed to be amended.

I intermittently heard the rumble of masonry moving and settling within the collapsed building, although it seemed very far away and of no concern of mine. I felt safe, nestled within my den and disconnected from the world beyond that. I knew that at some point I would have to emerge from its comforting embrace but the motivation was stubbornly absent and I remained curled, letting my thoughts drift where they willed, while I listened to the creaks and sighs of shifting stone. Shingle rattled when it slipped into spaces and settled into crevices. A boulder toppled with a deep thud and another struck a neighbouring stone with a sharp crack. The sounds moved steadily closer to where I was sheltered, maintaining my protective bubble with barely more effort than a thought. I knew it could withstand further collapse, although the knowledge that an unstable building was pressing down on me was still a little disconcerting. I began to listen more closely to the music of the cracks and pops, the rumbles and moans. I felt for the vibrations that travelled through the ground, resisting the urge to search for weaknesses within the energy networks woven throughout the structure. Time, that had seemed endless, now weighed heavily while I waited for the next creak.

The grating noise of dragging rock sounded perilously close, reverberating around my cave. I extended my awareness beyond my sphere, snaking through the debris in search of inconsistencies and irregularities, but stopped abruptly at the detection of a clear energy signature. A person. My stomach clenched in response even though I accepted the foolishness of my fear. I had just reduced a building to rubble, I should have no fear of someone searching the ruins, and yet the dread lingered. I scouted for others who may be waiting but find no one else. The person was diligent and persistent, scrabbling at an area for a while before moving to a new section. The action was repeated over and over. Slowly moving closer.

Dirt became dislodged and covered me with a fine layer of dust. I curled myself tighter, bringing my knees up to my chest and wrapping my arms around them. The stones shifted and settled against my barrier of air while I gathered my energies into a taut coil of power. A rock was pulled away to reveal a patch of light, blindingly bright after having been entombed in darkness for so long. Long fingers curled through the gap to prise away the stones until the space was wide enough to accommodate both hands, digging at the barrier like a terrier at a mouse's hole. I waited, poised to attack, and then blinked at the face that peered in.

'Vallori?'

His face sagged. 'Tallen.'

'What are you doing here?'

He gave a small smile. 'That is a long story and perhaps we should get you out of there before I begin. Are you hurt?'

I shook my head. 'I'm fine. I'm unharmed.'

His face disappeared and he resumed his burrowing at the hole. The rough rocks added more cuts and scrapes to his already bloodied hands, enlarging the cavity until it was big enough for me to crawl through. He reached in to assist my exit but I just stared at his outstretched hand, suddenly needing to distance myself from its questing grasp. Confused at my delay, Vallori reached further forward until his head blocked the light and became haloed by an irregular circle.

'What's wrong?' he asked quietly, finally able to see me when his eyes adjusted to the dim light.

My mind was overwhelmed with the emotions that had surfaced upon seeing him. I had never once considered that he would come for me and I was unprepared for the conflict that rapidly fluctuated between joy and shame. I desperately craved the calm reassurance his memories had provided when I was trapped within the Infinity Stone blade, but too much had happened for me to believe that it would be offered or that I should accept it. I was not ready. I could not return to a life beyond my self-imposed isolation, much less the complexities of facing Vallori.

'I can't,' I whispered. 'I just can't.'

His sigh stabbed into my heart to widen the cracks already laced within it. He withdrew, removing more concealing rubble until he was able to awkwardly crawl through. He glanced nervously at the masonry hovering above him, before shuffling and contorting himself and finally shifting so he could wedge himself next to me. He hesitated for a moment, studying my face while I avoided looking at him.

'Oh Tallen,' he said softly.

The quiet acceptance of his words broke all my defences. The tears flowed unchecked and I struggled to breath around the crushing pressure within my chest. He wrapped his arm around my shoulders and I collapsed into him, soaking his stained shirt. I sobbed for all my guilt and shame, and for all the hurt and suffering I had caused.

'I'm sorry,' I mumbled, my voice muffled by folds of cloth where I lay cradled within his lap. 'I'm so sorry.'

'There'll be time for that,' he replied gently. 'I believe your question came first and I owe you an explanation of how I came to be here.'

Emotions flared weakly but I relaxed into the soothing tones of his deep voice and the hypnotic rhythm of him stroking my hair.

'I followed you through Hilman. You left a big enough trail that it became easy to predict where you would be, albeit always arriving after you had left.'

I tensed at the reminder of my savage destruction, causing Vallori to tighten his hold and prevent me from bolting. He quickly realised that the reflex was unnecessary in the close confines of my fox's hole and relaxed his embrace, resuming his tale. He used a familiar strategy that allowed me to be silent while he talked. He lulled me into stillness with the cadence of his words and calmed the turmoil within my head. As he always had.

'I was heading south-west towards Elmeth when everything went quiet. I arrived just before midwinter but there had been no reports of you for some time before then. I asked. I demanded. I bribed. I threatened. No one was talking beyond the general gossip concerning raiders and priests. The only burning was done by Baila's faithful, not to them. Their control is more subtle, the closer you get to Lindvane, but it is there nonetheless. Many are too frightened for idle chatter, much less that concerning Baila's devoted. These are challenging times for travellers, particularly for those asking unpopular questions.'

I shifted, concerned that some of the wounds on Vallori's hands were older than those caused by digging at the rubble.

'Peace,' he chided. 'I easily avoided the soldiers sent to detain me. It added some excitement into a chase that had become frustratingly dull, but I was unwilling to waste time debating ideology with those fools. I declined to linger and left Elmeth in the general direction in which you had been travelling. I had almost convinced myself I had taken the wrong path when I found a village nestled at the base of a hill. Before his mother could chase him away, a young lad gleefully described, in more detail than he could possibly know, how two of Baila's finest soldiers had been callously attacked one night in a farmhouse beside the large landslide. Could have been bandits. Could have been a small band of resistance. But such an isolated attack suggested a single fighter caught unaware. I had gathered no clearer options so I took a chance and followed the least-travelled trail to see where it led.' He chuckled softly. 'Nowhere. It led nowhere. No one had seen anything. Travelling merchants were scarce, much less those having no obvious reason to roam. The tight control of the priesthood means there is rarely a lifted purse of coin, and targeted attacks or any form of insurrection have been completely suppressed. I spent a very tedious few days jumping from tavern to market to washhouse to another tavern. And achieved nothing.'

Vallori paused, allowing me to appreciate his heroism in facing such a burden. I smiled at his indulgence, the smile widening in appreciation of his deft manipulation of my mood. He had effortlessly banished my troubles for a time with talk of his adventures.

'It must have been awful for you,' I mocked, sitting up so I could see his satisfied grin.

'It was terrible. But on the third, fourth, fifth tavern? I forget which one—'

'Too much drinking in taverns will do that.'

'Indeed. At some point, I met a very interesting man. One who still travelled the roads carrying news and telling stories.' He paused, ensuring that I knew to whom he was referring. 'Laryn apologises for his inaction. He had not fully understood the costs involved. He told me of the tremors that had destroyed Peverill.' He hesitated again. 'Is that what happened here?'

I took a breath. The small space that separated us suddenly seemed too wide and all that I had been ignoring crashed back into place. The spell that Vallori had woven unravelled with the reminder that we were confined within a cave under a small mountain of stone.

'No,' I replied quietly. 'I did this. We fought and I brought his house down on top of him.'

'Villermir.' He grumbled the name and I nodded in confirmation. 'I haven't found him. It doesn't mean he's not here. I found several bodies… but none were him.'

I was unsure of how I felt about that, at having caused his death or for letting him escape. Neither excited a spark large enough to bother me when so many other hurts pressed in to seek precedence. Vallori shifted and I readily snatched at the diversion.

'I'm sorry,' I repeated, although lighter in meaning than my earlier apology. 'This cannot be comfortable for you.'

My den was snugly created to fit me and Vallori was taller, with a bigger build. He had folded up into the confined area and sustained the cramped position for some time without complaint. He shrugged off my concern.

'The numbness in my legs is less of a worry than the knowledge that the only thing keeping the remains of this building from falling on my head is your concentration.'

'We're safer in here than we are out there,' I countered, imagining the bordering woods crawling with Baila's soldiers. 'But you do just have my word for that. Go. Get out of here and stretch your legs. I will follow. I promise.'

He could not completely hide his look of relief but still hesitated before moving. 'Laryn understood that his apology would bring little comfort, in light of his queen's actions. So, he charged me with delivering a gift to you.'

I frowned, unable to determine what manner of gift he could possibly give to compensate for Delaina's betrayal. 'Well, go on then. Let us go and get this gift.'

He awkwardly twisted his stiffened body out of the hole and I scrambled after him, squinting against the brightness while I stretched my back. I stared at the devastation I had caused. Large blocks of masonry had been thrown across a vast area and rubble was piled in tall mounds. A regular pattern of trenches had been scraped into the debris where Vallori had methodically searched for me, having had no clue if or where I would be hidden beneath the ruins. I turned in a slow half-circle to view the full impact. Burford Hythe had been reduced to a massive mole's hill of broken stone and splintered timber. The top half of one the heraldic bears, previously having crowned the entrance, was discarded amongst the rubble and it felt strangely like an insult.

Vallori waited for me at the edge of the channel he had excavated to reach me. The extent of the damage to his hands and arms was clearly evident in the sunlight. His stained shirt was no longer white and his trousers were covered in small cuts only partially obscured by layers of pale dirt. My attention, however, lingered on his hair. He had hacked it bald after Z'hara and the crown of his head had grown back in irregular patches. He had maintained the shaved area above his ears and at the base of his head to display the new blue tattoos.

'Why?'

He frowned down at me. 'Why what?'

'Why did you come for me?'

'You are my *pháirtí*. Did you think the vows we shared were empty words?'

I looked up into Villermir's unnaturally perfect blue sky and tears threatened again; I had not expected such loyalty and I very much doubted that I deserved it.

I lowered my gaze to see a long, narrow bundle held horizontally before him, carefully wrapped in a blanket of sheep's skin, and my heart raced in anticipation. I scrambled up the small slope of shingle with my feet slipping in my haste to reach him. He smiled and held out the offering, holding it in both hands to support its weight while I quickly unfastened the ties and flipped back the skin's edge. The light flared on *Saorsa's* hilt where she laid with my other weapons atop the soft, dark-brown leather of my Moon Warrior jerkin. I snatched at my sword, craving the feel of the embossed dragon pressing into my palm, and the flash of her ruby eyes filled me with a contented warmth. She was back where she belonged, with me.

Vallori had kept the horses safely tethered within the woods bordering the estate. I followed him along a dusty track where the snowdrops and bluebells added splashes of colour in the muted sunlight, while the birds trilled indignantly at being disturbed. Vallori's black mare whickered at his approach, head-butting him forcefully in the chest when he moved in to scratch at the base of her ear. I stopped a few paces from Trefin and she flickered her ears back and forth in mild agitation. Animals had never responded well to me but, apparently, I could form deep attachments to them and I felt unexpectedly pleased that the little roan was here and looking well. The brave mare snorted softly when I carefully invaded her space, slowly reaching up to scratch the warm area under her mane. She nibbled at the ties of my tunic and I lowered my forehead to rest on hers, closing my eyes and relaxing into the comfort I gained from the contact.

Vallori was already mounted by the time I reluctantly withdrew from Trefin and sat with his wrists loosely crossed over the pommel of the saddle. He had been watching me closely, a slight crease in his forehead, but quickly softened his gaze when he saw me notice and sat a little straighter in the saddle.

'Where should we go?' he asked.

The question took me by surprise. I had assumed he had arrived with a plan and I felt a flutter of insecurity at the thought of once again being surrounded by enemies, despite now having Vallori with me.

'I don't know. Hilman, I suppose. I assume the raiders have not gone home and taken their shamans with them.'

Vallori raised an eyebrow. 'You want to travel across half of Lindvane to go back to Hilman?'

His tone was playfully mocking and I suspected that he had come with a plan after all. 'You have a better suggestion?'

'There's a particularly troublesome band of raiders much closer than Hilman. If it is pirates that you seek, we could be of use there.'

I looked at him and he maintained my gaze, watching while I considered his proposal. 'You want me to go back to Faulknar?'

'There is much need for a Moon Warrior in that kingdom. They stand alone against the combined forces of Baila and the Gallowglass shamans, not to mention Lindvane's forces. They need your help. And you will have to return at some point.'

There were too many ghosts that I was unwilling to face for me to contemplate returning to Faulknar. I shook my head, as much to dispel the uncomfortable memories as to convey my refusal.

'I will not be welcome there.'

Vallori tilted his head with an expression that seemed to question whether I would be welcome anywhere within the Three Kingdoms, but the flippant gesture was swiftly replaced by a more serious one which addressed the reasons for my reluctance. I had said little about my time at Faulknar and of those who would be waiting there, and we both knew there was much I had not shared. The silent accusation of raggedly cut short hair and the damage to hands he would not let me heal meant I would agree to whatever he decided. It was the very least that I owed him.

'I would gladly take you far from here,' he offered softly. 'Leave the Three Kingdoms and never look back. Do not think I am unaware of how much you have already given. But I fear we have run out of time and events are occurring beyond our control to stop them. Our futures are balanced on a blade's edge and without help Faulknar will be consumed. They cannot withstand all that is pressing in on them for much longer. Are you prepared to let your kingdom fall?'

My kingdom. Despite all the years I had spent away and the irrevocable damage I had caused, she was still my kingdom. I could not bear the thought of her being oppressed in the manner of Hilman and Lindvane. The fact that I had abandoned her twisted sharply in my chest and added another layer of guilt to my, already considerable, burden. Vallori was right. I could no longer delay and it was time for me to atone for the harm I had caused.

'Of course,' he continued. 'Getting into Faulknar should prove challenging enough. The kingdom is under siege, with any areas of the border not swarming with The Army of Truth, being sufficiently controlled by Hayton's soldiers. And the coast is blockaded by Gallowgla ships. Nothing is getting in or out.'

'The marshes will still be open. They won't be able to control movement through there.'

'There is a reason for that. That place has been long abandoned by the Gods. We would spend days turned around by the network of peat bogs until we were irretrievably lost. That's assuming we weren't drowned in the swamp or sucked into the endless mud, leaving no trace that we were ever there. There are no safe paths through that hellscape.'

I wickedly grinned at him. 'Don't believe everything the fen-folk tell outsiders. There are ways if you know where to look. I can get you through.'

We left Burford when the sun was starting to descend and its warmth softened the tense muscles of my back. We rode along a deserted road through a landscape of flat farmland that extended to the horizon in every direction. I had removed a light cloak from the pack fastened to Trefin's saddle and used it to obscure my distinctive features, although the disguise was mostly unnecessary. The farms of Lindvane were attached to large fields and those we saw were infrequent and sited some distance from the road. Many appeared unoccupied. Vallori explained that Burford had developed a reputation for being *unnatural* and this had probably encouraged those closest to the estate to move to more acceptable locations. It was sad to see fertile land abandoned when so many were starving.

Vallori tried to sustain light conversation through much of that afternoon but eventually gave up when I offered little more than single word answers. My *phàirtí* was easy company and he accepted my brooding without comment, yet I found it difficult to banish the nagging shame his presence provoked. I had done too much and caused too much pain for me to sit comfortably beside him and gain pleasure from his aimless commentary. I knew I was being ungracious and rude but I could find nothing to say that would not sound arrogant or sullen or foolish or judgemental. I deliberated for so long over each response that the moment passed, and my silence added another insult to my deepening shame. I avoided looking at him, not wanting to see more hurt or undeserved understanding, and stared out over the vast expanse of beige. Clouds of dust swirled over the dry land, uninterrupted by the stunted growth of spindly crops struggling to reach the rich peat layers hidden beneath thick blankets of bleached soil. The lush gardens and vibrant colours of Burford Hythe already seemed a distant memory.

The strength of the wind grew when the afternoon slipped into dusk. The low clouds of dirt that danced over the fields became whipped into small tornadoes, collecting pebbles and sticks to become lethal vortices. The horses grew restless and frequently tossed their heads, with dust caking around their nostrils and grit entering their ears or irritating their eyes. The sky darkened with thick grey clouds but no rain fell to dampen the dust-storms. We were unwilling to encroach on a farm despite their apparent disuse, so camped in the shelter of a tattered hedge as dry-lightning illuminated the darkening sky. The streaks of white seemed a pale imitation compared to the rivers of daemon green.

'These storms are occurring more frequently,' Vallori remarked quietly while I watched the fluorescent light dance amongst the clouds. 'There's been one each night for the last few days. No rain, just wind and cloud and lightning.'

'The energies are readjusting without the influence of the Empathy Crystal. Villermir was using it to redirect power into Burford.'

He nodded in the deepening gloom. 'Creating the unnatural spring. I suppose the stone is buried somewhere under all that rubble. Will Villermir go back for it?'

I picked at an area of dry skin beside my thumbnail. I thought of the black tendrils extending from the priest, wrapping around the precious stone and threading his corruption throughout its matrix. I had given him the initial connection to the crystal and from that he had been free to violate it. The silence grew uncomfortable with Vallori waiting for me to answer his question.

'Villermir will not go back for the Empathy Crystal. It's broken.' I spoke quickly, wanting the words gone from my mouth. 'I destroyed it.'

I had pulled a small flap of skin from my thumb and caused it to ooze a bead of blood. I wiped the fluid away, welcoming the gentle sting as a distraction from Vallori's stare. I squeezed my thumb to produce another blood-bead just so I could swipe at it again. I raised my hand to chew at my thumb and cause more damage.

'Tallen,' Vallori scolded, sharp enough to interrupt my nervous habit.

I folded the seeping thumb into my fist to avoid the temptation of continuing to play with the traumatised skin.

'Everyone makes mistakes.' He raised a hand when I took a breath to protest. 'But you keep letting yours consume you. You let them taint all your decisions.'

My thumb itched and I surreptitiously rubbed it along my palm hoping Vallori would fail to notice.

'You insist on picking impossible fights,' he continued, 'just so that, when you inevitably lose, you can use it to confirm your belief that you were going to lose anyway. That you always lose. By the Gods, Tallen. Stop being so selfish?'

I blinked. 'Selfish?'

'You are so self-absorbed that you take all the blame for yourself. For everything. It's always your fault. You never leave room for anyone else.'

It was so unusual for my *pháirtí* to get angry that I had taken his stillness to be his normal calm acceptance, but his rigid control had masked a tension threatening to erupt. He was furious. I should have known. I should have remembered. While Kade and I raged dramatically, Vallori had always become sharply focused. The threat was more deadly because it was held hidden within his silence.

Nevertheless, I had some suppressed anger of my own and wondered which, of my many inadequacies, had caused such an extreme reaction. My reply was edged with spiteful provocation.

'Oh, I do apologise for having been so possessive over my failures. I shall try to be more generous and share my crap from now on.'

'You think you don't share your crap?' His voice remained low but was also barbed with the intent to wound. 'You leave an avalanche of crap in your wake while you go chasing after the next disaster to dive straight into. You are so obsessed with righting every wrong that you never consider those around you. We're just left to watch while you burn everything to the ground, not knowing whether this will be the time you finally succeed in getting yourself killed.'

'What do you want from me?' I snapped back. 'Would you prefer that I dragged everyone down with me? Would getting everyone burned along with me be so much better?'

'We would follow you anywhere. Your friends—'

I threw my hands up in exasperation. 'That's the whole point! I can't have you following me like some stupid, imprinted gosling. I'm the one who has been given these powers. I'm the only one who has even the slightest chance against Villermir and the shamans and their daemons, not to mention Sálaforn and her cursed wraiths. And yet, you blindly follow into the danger when you don't have a hope of beating it. I can't have that. Don't you see? I can't have that.'

'That is not your choice to make.'

'It's the only choice I've got. I can't watch anyone else die because I'm not good enough.'

Our expressions were hidden in the darkness while our accusations radiated like heat between us, but my last comment seemed to suck the air out of the night. The silence that followed hung heavy with accusation. Vallori replied in a voice so quiet that I could almost convince myself that I had not heard him.

'So, you would leave again.'

The short statement was so full of pain that it left me raw and exposed, and my guilt, so carefully buried under the anger, tore open again. I despaired at ever getting him to understand the responsibility I felt and the reasons why I could not continue to hurt him.

'You said it yourself, I'm too destructive. I cannot be around other people. It's safer for everyone for me to be on my own.'

'I travelled across two kingdoms to find you and, within less than a day, you talk of leaving.'

'I never asked you to do that.'

I heard him shift. 'You never ask, Tallen. You just assume. You just make the decisions and everyone else has to live with them.'

'What do you want me to say? What could I possibly ask of you that has not already been given?'

'Why did you leave?'

I sighed in tired resignation. 'I've already told you. I—'

'You've offered the excuses that you tell yourself. For once, tell the truth. Why did you leave me?'

I closed my eyes even though he was already effectively hidden in the dark. *Please don't do this.*

'I couldn't save her.'

'Of course you couldn't,' he snapped back, her ghost lingering so heavily between us that he did not require explanation. 'No one expected you to.'

'I'd brought back others. I saved them but I didn't save her.'

'Z'hara's injuries were too extensive. It was not the same.'

'No. It wasn't.'

I prayed that I had said enough to satisfy him. That he would accept my sorrow and shame and guilt, and he would let the conversation fade. But he would not relent.

'Then why did you run?'

Please don't make me say it.

'It was not the same because I did not have a reason to deny them. With Z'hara... Maybe I wanted... I gave up too soon. I hesitated when I should have fought harder.'

'That's not it.'

'I felt so guilty.' I dug a nail into the traumatised wound of my thumb, hoping the pain would distract from the words. 'You were not mine to take. You belonged to her. I should never have come between you.'

'You never did. She understood completely and she loved you too.'

It had become so hard to breath. I curled my knees into my chest and hugged them tightly, rocking back and forth while I tried to limit the damage his persistence was inflicting on both of us.

'I was jealous of what she had with you.'

'That's not it,' he repeated.

'Vallori, please.' I resorted to pleading in an attempt to get him to stop. 'How can this help anything? I'm sorry. I'm so, so sorry. I would give anything to change it if I could. I would give everything to give her back to you.'

'I needed you.'

'You never needed me,' I denied. 'You are so much more than I could ever hope to be. What could I possibly offer you?'

'Z'hara was my joy. My future. But you are my *pháirtí*. You are half of my soul and you ripped that away from me when I had already lost too much.'

Tears rolled silently down my cheeks. How many times can a heart shatter and still keep beating? I knew I had caused him unforgivable pain but I had not understood how deeply I had embedded the knife.

'I couldn't...'

'Couldn't what?' he demanded icily. 'Couldn't face your groundless guilt? Couldn't deal with your relentless doubts? Were you so afraid to show that you were not perfect? That you didn't, after all, have the powers of a God?'

'Please stop.'

'What was it, Tallen? What was so terrible that you had to leave when I needed you the most?'

I bit down on my lip so hard that the skin split. My mind screamed for me to be silent and that confessing would help no one, but I had already lost him. There was nothing more for me to lose and he had asked for the truth.

'You're right, I was a coward. I couldn't bear it. It just hurt too much. I couldn't look at you and see that much suffering. You were so full of pain, your body shook with it. You've shorn your hair, Vallori. I know what that means and it's a constant reminder of what you've lost. Of how I couldn't save her for you. All my abilities and I could do nothing to stop you from hurting. Your whole body cried out and I couldn't make it right. So I left. Because I couldn't watch you collapse into such grief and be helpless to make it all go away. It was too much. It was just too much.'

We sat for a long time, frozen in our own sorrow. The pain of losing Z'hara was intricately woven through all the hurts we had caused each other to create a tapestry of longing and regret, of missed opportunities and shared guilt. It created a gulf that was too wide to endure. Eventually, Vallori rolled over onto his side and pretended to sleep while I wished for all the ways in which this should have been better.

CHAPTER TWENTY-SIX

The distance between Vallori and I reduced during the days we spent travelling to the marshes, with interactions becoming less forced. Conversations started to last more than a sentence or two and the intervening silences were less awkward and uncomfortable. The tension in my back faded and I felt we had achieved some form of understanding despite nothing having been explicitly said.

While our relationship changed, the landscape stubbornly remained a dry, dusty covering over an endless expanse of sparse, stunted crops. The flat land exaggerated the sense of desolation, with the uninterrupted sky seeming to press down on us while we rode along the long, straight road. The hedgerows that separated the large fields were poorly covered in brittle leaves and these were readily shed by the gusty breeze, leaving multiple gaps where small birds declined to nest in favour of more sheltered locations. Occasionally, the monotony was broken by a hare loping across the ground, with its colouring blending in with the brown field so that only the movement alerted to its presence. Less often, a scraggy copse would be sufficient to nurture life and small birds chased after low-flying insects before a predatory hawk had them darting to the shelter of the trees.

We saw no other travellers on the road and it remained empty, stretching towards the horizon in both directions. The vast sections of arable land required a large workforce to manage it and the farms bordering the trail grew into sprawling settlements yet, with the crops failing to thrive in such arid conditions, most had left to seek better fortunes elsewhere. The few people we saw, labouring in their yards or nurturing their failing crops, were reluctant to draw attention to themselves and we all pretended to ignore each other while warily watching for any sign of threat.

The fields became smaller once more when we approached the marshes, with almost all of them abandoned and looking to have been that way for some time.

'It seems we have come to the end of civilisation,' I remarked when we passed yet another deserted farmhouse.

'The legends of the fen are enough to discourage most people,' Vallori replied quietly. 'And now they're facing the threat of crop failure, not to mention the hostile army on the other side of the swamp.'

I twisted in the saddle to look at him. 'Are you afraid of the marsh wraiths?'

He flicked an irritated look at my mocking grin. 'I know enough to appreciate that if the land does not want us there, it can make our crossing very unpleasant. And we are highly likely to get lost and wander forever in that maze of peaty bogs.'

I laughed at his uncharacteristic pessimism. 'Don't worry. I'll keep you safe.'

He declined to respond and I thought back to my first crossing of the fens. The marshes separating Lindvane and Faulknar sat at the northern edge of the fenlands, creating a triangle of swampy wetland before transforming into the mud flats which bordered the coast. They were considered distinct from the more flooded areas that surrounded the Isle of Serpents, but they were part of the same vast water reservoir which stretched across half of Faulknar's western border and extended for several days' ride into the interior. The defences I had encountered crossing to the Isle of Serpents would be less invasive in the marshes but would still be able to confuse and haunt those who entered unprepared. The network of sucking bogs and poorly defined walkways would be sufficient to trap and drown many, without the torments of the mind where you would imagine those you had lost, pleading for you to join them and tempting you into the swampy depths. I may have been flippant with Vallori and dismissive of his fears, but I appreciated his caution and did not enter the wetland lightly.

The ground became steadily damper. Moisture that had been trapped within the peat under a thick layer of dust, now rose to the surface. Even the prolonged drought could no longer suppress its influence, initially as a softness that maintained an impression of the horses' hooves, and then as patches of water which refused to seep into the saturated ground. A thin mist leaked out of the ground to float around the horses' fetlocks, gently swirling around their limbs while they walked. The fringes of the wetland were a marshy grassland but further in, areas of dark water reflected the sky and a thicker mist curled around their edges. The place seemed to be sullen and brooding and I appreciated how effective this was as a deterrent. We had seen no soldiers despite being so close to Faulknar's border, and this was before the additional defences I knew were waiting for us.

Vallori and I had become warily silent within the oppressive atmosphere. I turned to look back and found the open landscape of Lindvane had become completely obscured by the deepening mist. There was no trail to guide our way so I lowered my defences and felt the energies protecting this hostile wilderness. My sensitised sight flared with the signatures of small wading birds feeding on the worms and eels that slithered through the swamp, now completely hidden from normal sight by the fog. Ripples of shimmering light radiated from the liquid displaced by our horses' hooves and exposed a network of connected waterways that spread throughout the marshes. Vallori cursed softly when his mare stumbled into a deeper puddle and the horse snorted at the sudden loss of firm ground, splashing as stinking, muddy water grasped her leg.

I took a breath to ignore the distraction and relaxed back into the world of power signatures and energy lights. Gentle murmurs of sound lapped at the edge of my awareness while I searched for a safe path through the bog. The eruptions of colour that flared from disturbed water created a confusing landscape of shifting boundaries and tangled mesh. I could find no clear direction in which to travel.

'We should dismount.'

The fog swiftly swallowed my words to maintain the smothering stillness and I turned to face Vallori to confirm that he had heard. He gave a quick nod before dismounting. His lips were pulled tight and the muscles of his jaw were held rigid. His eyes darted around, searching for something or perhaps seeing things that were not truly there.

'How bad is it?' I asked gently.

It took some effort to remove his gaze from the shapes he saw in the fog and look at me, offering a hint of a smile.

'Bad enough that I would be racing back to Lindvane if there was another way into Faulknar.'

'I don't think that's an option anymore,' I offered apologetically. 'Do you want me to lead Mikkla?'

He paused, tilting his head for a moment to listen to the sounds of the swamp, before focusing back on me. 'No. Not yet.'

I led the way from one tufty tussock to the next, tentatively placing weight on my foot before trusting it to hold me. I followed a meandering path that relied more on instinct than any visual clues that it was the safest option. I frequently glanced at Vallori to ensure we had not been separated, while he stared intensely at Trefin's rump.

After an indeterminable amount of time, I finally accepted I was no longer able to distinguish between solid land, albeit one which sank alarmingly whenever I stepped on it, and that of sucking marsh. Mud covered as far as my knees from repeatedly sinking into bogs, where it had required the tugging on Trefin's reins to be able to extricate myself. On more than one occasion, I failed to find suitable passage and we were forced to retrace our steps, with both Vallori and the horses being unnerved by the retreat.

Unsure of my welcome, I tentatively reached out to the guardians of the wetland. Although I was not an Aqualine, my elemental control of water was sufficient to allow me a connection which could grant us safe passage. I clearly understood that this connection was a privilege and not a right, and that our crossing was in no way guaranteed. I respectfully offered my request and waited, feeling the density of the air around me shift while it was considered. I glanced at Vallori, wondering if I had led him into a miserable, watery grave but, fortunately, I was not kept waiting long. I smiled, with equal parts of relief and amusement, when a troop of water sprites burst from the dark water to leap and tumble in unrestrained delight. I bowed to them with respect and gratitude, to which they replied with mocking imitations before scampering over an unremarkable stretch of marsh. The water rose up to the waists of their shimmering, rainbow bodies as they skipped and danced away from me. The last two creatures turned back when I hesitated, beckoning me to follow, but knowing of their trickster nature, I nervously stepped forward and braced for the plunge that would topple me into a stinking, peaty pit. The water extended no further than a hand-width above my ankle and I took the second step with more confidence. I turned back to Vallori to confirm he was following and found him stationary, staring at the dark water with obvious dread and unable to trust that the path would hold his weight.

'Vallori?'

'I think you need to take Mikkla now.'

His voice was strained and he gripped his mare's reins tight enough for his knuckles to show white. Slight tremors rippled through his rigid muscles as he fought the ghosts that had been sent to haunt him. I carefully stepped around Trefin, collecting a lead-rope from my pack before attaching one end to Mikkla's bridle and the other to the back of Trefin's saddle; when I led Trefin, Trefin would led Mikkla. Vallori continued to grasp his horse's reins like they were the only thing saving him from falling into the abyss, which I had to concede that they probably were. He still lacked the will to step on the unknown path and Mikkla would repeatedly pull him forward until he had to move to prevent himself from falling.

'How do you know this is the right path?'

I suspected he asked the question so the sound of our voices would mute those only he could hear, rather than truly seeking an answer.

'Can you not see them? The sprites are leading the way?'

I grinned at their reckless antics but trusted the trail they showed me. Vallori closed his eyes, quickly realising that it made the temptations worse and resumed staring at the roan's tail.

'I see nothing but fog and water and...'

'I forget you have a shocking lack of ability,' I mocked, intentionally provocative to distract him from the visions that tormented him.

'I have some.'

'Really?'

'I can empower a spell.'

'Useful.'

'I can heal minor wounds.'

'Very helpful.'

'I can feel the energy lines and see auras.'

'You are truly blessed.'

I saw a flicker of a smile and was grateful that the tactic was working. I talked to him about the elements, specifically water. I explained how I had asked and been granted permission to navigate the protected waterways. It was information he already knew and I occasionally challenged him with questions to ensure he concentrated on me rather than those who would lead him astray. His replies remained terse but he answered correctly and I believed I was offering him some solace.

We continued to follow the sprite procession while the sky darkened and the dry-lightning illuminated the fog. The ghostly landscape transformed into an unsettling image. Shadows lunged at us, highlighted by erratic flashes of diffuse, vivid light, before fading back into the featureless gloom. Even the carefree sprites slowed their dance, several holding hands like young children frightened by the storm. The murmuring crowded in to taunt me with promises of safety and shelter, peace and acceptance. I raised further layers of defences to keep the wraiths as indistinct beings rather than the distressing voices of Laken and Kerk, Z'hara and Owl. I found myself imitating Vallori's studied attention, focusing on the fluctuating forms of the water sprites while he focused on Trefin. My distracting narrative repeatedly faltered and there would be long periods of silence when we battled against the lure of the swamp.

Eventually the light shifted and became the sustained muted brightness of dawn. We were surrounded by dull, grey water that reflected the low, grey cloud which smothered everything further than a few paces away from us. I had no idea where we were or in what direction we travelled. I wondered if we were being taken in a large, never-ending circle but quickly dismissed the disturbing thought, unwilling to consider the consequences of that.

Gradually, mercifully, the scenery changed again so that darker shapes developed some distance in front of us and I strained to separate form from fog. I convinced myself we were heading towards this feature, and took comfort from the fact that we finally seemed to be moving towards something more substantial than the ever-present ghosts who lurked in the mist.

'Do you see that?'

Vallori's voice startled me despite being little more than a croaked whisper. I saw nothing except an ocean of different tones of grey.

'You need to be more specific,' I replied tiredly.

'Ahead of us. To the right. The horizon seems to be moving.'

I resisted the urge to respond with an irritable observation that everything was shifting and swirling, blinking several times instead to sharpen my eyes against the relentless gloom. The darker shadows guiding our direction had deepened into more solid forms and now resembled distinct shapes that were clearly separated from the background grey, yet I failed to see how this could be the anomaly Vallori was referring to. I stared in the direction he had indicated for some time, trying to determine what shifting movement could be real and what was simply an illusion of the swirling fog.

It was too consistent for me to dismiss. The looming shadow had divided into smaller, elongated shapes that bobbed up and down in a blurry imitation of our rhythmic strides. The slightly rounded shapes merged and overlapped before pulling away to become separate once again. I was so intrigued by the strange sight that it was some time before I realised that I had failed to answer Vallori's query.

'Yes,' I said belatedly. 'I see them. You are not imagining them. Or, perhaps, we've both lost our wits.'

I turned to face him. He wore the slight crease of a frown and did not respond to my poor humour, but I was relieved to note that his gaze was clearer and the tension had faded from his face.

'If we were not stuck in this Godsforsaken swamp I would say those shadows were people.'

I returned my attention to the shifting shapes, unsure of whether to be pleased we had found others or fearful of who was waiting for us. I drew *Saorsa* and heard the echoing sigh when Vallori drew his blade. We had no way of knowing whether we were to face a friend or an enemy but the relief at discovering somebody, anybody, was too great to consider avoidance. Whatever we encountered, it promised to be real and this was infinitely more appealing than the wraiths who called to us.

The sprites vanished when the path became clearly defined and we were able to confidently make our way. Sounds drifted into voices and then formed into words. General comments were made cursing the bog and the fog. Names were called and answered. Disagreeable remarks were made concerning the unrelenting dreariness of the marshes. Accents that were Faulknar.

A man stepped out of the gloom less than five paces from me. I instinctively stepped in front of Trefin, raising *Saorsa* as he lifted his sword, both of us wide-eyed with surprise at seeing the other. I heard Vallori curse behind me when another stepped out of the mist.

'By the Gods,' grumbled the second. 'This place has you all jumping like fresh recruits. Hold fast, man!'

The older man stopped abruptly, staring at me while I stared at him. The grey hair, cropped savagely short to his scalp, was more white than silver and a matching beard covered more than half of his face, yet the familiar blue eyes still shone with perpetual bewilderment.

'For the unholy love of Mobis,' he breathed. 'Tallen? Is that really you?'

'At your service, Lord General.'

Two more soldiers emerged from the fog while I unsuccessfully tried to control my ridiculous grin.

'Pah,' he bustled. 'When have I ever tolerated that Lord General nonsense? Especially with you.' He flapped at his amused guard. 'Have you not got anything better to be getting on with? Standing around with your mouths open wide enough to catch flies.'

'No,' they smirked. 'Not really.'

Their general growled at them and they reluctantly disappeared back into the mist. He continued to stare at me with a mouth open as wide as those he had just criticised.

'Fearsome Father. What in the God's name are you doing here?'

'I've come to offer my services, such as they are and if you would have them.'

'It's cursed well about time! I was being to think you would never show your face.'

I bowed formally and respectfully. 'My apologies.'

Keenan stared at me for a moment longer, still unable to believe I was standing before him, before his face split into a wide smile.

'Welcome home, Tallen.'

The Lord General guided us out of the marshes and we returned to more solid ground, albeit one which was still waterlogged. The mists receded until the view opened into a landscape of short grass and thick hedges, a sharp contrast to the dust fields we had left on the other side of the swampy barrier. The chill wind blowing from the north made me pull my cloak tighter around my body, emphasising the unnatural change in climate between two kingdoms less than two days' ride apart.

'So how would you prefer that I address you?' asked Vallori when Keenan took a breath from grumbling about the marshes, the weather, and his incompetent soldiers. 'Would the use of your rank by a stranger offend as much as when used by a friend?'

The older man regarded Vallori, noting his shorn hair, his scraped knuckles, his fighter's poise and his array of weapons. Having completed his assessment, he turned to me and judged my faded bruises before making his decision.

'Keenan will suffice for you too,' he replied with a small nod. 'Rank helps to get things done without the need for endless discussion. But respect should be earned, not given because you managed to survive long enough to warrant promotion.'

'Or because you are the king's brother,' I teased.

He stopped walking and looked at me with a curious expression that deepened the lines around his eyes and mouth. He held himself very still and the sudden change from his customary, blustering complaint to the rigid stillness was discomforting.

'What is it? What did I say?'

He continued to stare, breathing hard, for several more heartbeats before his expression softened. 'You've been gone too long. How could you not know?'

'Know what?'

He sighed, then lifted his head and resumed walking. 'Kyllian's dead. Died a little under three years ago.'

It was my turn to stop. I was stunned, not only by the content of the news but also because I had not heard of it before. The Sanctuary of The Moon Goddess was not that isolated, Luella must have been aware and had chosen not to tell me. My annoyance was swiftly countered by the fact that I had not talked about Kade, I could hardly blame them if they followed my lead and not told me of Kyllian. All these thoughts were swiftly dismissed, with my mind focusing a different issue. I hurried to catch up with Keenan.

'Kade's king?'

I struggled to match the obviousness of the statement with the memories of how much he had hated the thought of being crowned. How caged he must feel at having been given the responsibilities he never wanted.

'A lot has changed while you've been gone. As if this cursed war is not enough, the boy seems intent on destroying himself and ripping the kingdom apart in the process.' Keenan flicked a scowl at me. 'Perhaps you can talk some sense into him.'

'Me? I'm the last person he's going to listen to. Why aren't you at Liegeport? Shouldn't you be counselling him, not hiding in the fen wastelands?'

Keenan sharply turned on me, stabbing a finger towards me in clear ill-tempered frustration. Vallori took a step to place himself between us but I stopped him with a small nod. Keenan had a right to be angry at me and I had no right to accuse him, when I was the one who had abandoned my kingdom and my king. My criticism had held more than a touch of self-condemnation.

'You think I haven't tried? What do you think got me banished to this miserable, stinking swamp? Sure, there is fighting enough to warrant my presence but it is no coincidence that he sent me to Kingsport. The boy's message was clear enough for all to see it.'

'Are things that bad?'

He took a deep breath, releasing the anger to leave resignation and exhaustion. He attempted to give me a weakly reassuring smile.

'They are not good. But you're here now.' He glanced over at Vallori to include him in the sentiment. 'Maybe you can offer a fresh insight.'

We had arrived at the temporary camp and further discussion was interrupted by Keenan's guard attending to our needs. Our horses were taken with the promise of oats and water, along with a thorough groom to remove the mud and ensure any injuries were appropriately cared for. Vallori and I were offered a hot tea that was just as gratefully received. We sat on our folded cloaks to provide some protection from the damp ground, appreciating the opportunity to rest legs which still ached from having to fight through the sucking marsh. Vallori did most of the talking, describing the politics within Hilman and Lindvane when Keenan questioned him on the situation beyond Faulknar. My *pháirtí* graciously glided over my part in agitating Baila's army and increasing recruitment, with men eagerly enlisting to fight the evil I represented.

'Well, something has certainly stirred up a hornets' nest,' Keenan concluded. 'Reports from all over have started talking about large numbers of soldiers aiming for our borders.' He caught the look shared between Vallori and me, narrowing his eyes in suspicion. 'You?'

I shrugged. 'Maybe.'

He threw his head back and laughed, his humour returning for the first time since I had mentioned Kyllian. 'Why am I surprised? You have always made a habit of seeking out trouble. Sadly though, I suspect it was inevitable. You may have hastened its arrival but this slowly festering war had to burst at some point.'

He slapped his hand onto the ground in a prelude to rising, claiming we did not have time to be gossiping like fishwives when there was a war to be won. He barked orders at the five attending soldiers who had already anticipated his commands. They grinned indulgently, as if he was a cantankerous uncle, while he complained about their traitorous lack of respect. Vallori watched it all with a slightly bemused expression.

The camp was quickly disassembled and we soon picked up the track that would lead us to Kingsport. The road widened from a muddy trail into a clearly defined route, telling of a prolonged history between the prosperous port and the fenlands which had supplied it with reeds for thatching and eels for trade. The ground was soft with trapped moisture and the horses' hooves made little sound as we headed towards the coast, travelling under an expansive sky of low cloud which prompted Keenan to comment on the rarity of that cloud not dumping its load of rain. He told of large areas of fen succumbing to flooding due to the persistent rainfall, confirming Villermir's claim of relocating Lindvane's moisture to fall relentlessly on Faulknar. Farmland had been lost under unworkable levels of water while any crops they did manage to salvage, quickly spoiled with moulds ravaging the perpetually damp stores. Disease spread rapidly through both people and livestock, with malnutrition and overcrowding exacerbating the effects of the thriving infection.

Vallori carefully suggested that conditions should start to improve soon, and efficiently avoided the reasons behind his confidence of a spring which should have been some way off still. Keenan remained pessimistic so Vallori guided the conversation towards Faulknar's capacity to resist Lindvane's advances. Hayton's troops, boosted by a significant number of Baila's soldiers, had pushed far into the kingdom. A narrow corridor remained along the north, from Kingsport to Haign, but below this almost a quarter of the land had been bitten into. There were a few isolated pockets where Faulknar still maintained a presence, although most of the western border had fallen so that Lindvane was now advancing on Havering, depressingly close to the centre of the kingdom. The south was less heavily threatened, with the main thrust aiming towards Liegeport and the king, but even there, persistent raids claimed lives and destroyed morale. The eastern towns were overwhelmed with refugees, fleeing their villages and the surrounding countryside for the relative safety of larger settlements. What land had not been drowned by the constant rain had been abandoned by people too frightened to farm there.

We were forced to leave the road when it disappeared under flooding so severe that it extended as far as I could see, creating a vast lake which covered a significant portion of arable land. We headed east for a time before being able to change direction back to the north, and the terrain sloped steadily upwards when we made for the cliffs bordering the northern sea. I smelt the change in the air, feeling cleaner and fresher despite the smothering low cloud and the musty sodden turf. I tasted the first hint of salt and, reflexively, took a deeper breath to grasp at its familiar scent. Despite my apprehension at the welcome I would receive, I found myself eager to look upon the fierce beauty of the north Faulknar coastline and the crashing waves which battered against the towering cliffs.

My pleasure dimmed when the coastline become clearer and we turned to run parallel to its edge. I had initially dismissed it as a reflection of my own concerns, but it became increasingly noticeable that the relaxed atmosphere within the group had been replaced by one of brooding concentration.

'Of course,' Keenan stated grumpily, confirming what I did not want to acknowledge. 'Lindvane is not our only problem.'

I had known there would be pirates. There had always been intermittent raids and Vallori had told me that this had increased in Faulknar, along with the entire eastern shore of the Three Kingdoms, but I had denied their existence in a desperate attempt to believe it was not true. Not so close to Kingsport. Not so many. They waited just beyond the sandbanks that protected this portion of coastline, an endless barricade of low ships with distinctively shaped sails. Vallori's back was held rigidly straight.

'They're off the coast from here to the Nalton Ness estuary,' Keenan continued. 'Smugglers have managed to maintain some of their routes, obtaining much needed supplies from over the water here into Lindvane, and further down the coast into the Traveller's lands. Much of the coast has been deserted, though. Left for the pirates to take whatever they want.'

He was silent for some time and I knew he was referring to the people taken as slaves as well as the taking of food and bounty. The raiders had caused sufficient harm when people still had the will to oppose them, their destruction would be significantly higher with free access to the kingdom and a people weakened by war and hunger.

'We retain three main centres of defence. Stanmouth is relatively calm, being too far south for the raiders to make the extra effort. The worst of the fighting has been here and, unsurprisingly, at Liegeport. Both being on a direct path from Gallowgla as well as being politically important.'

'Both containing a valuable prize,' offered Vallori. 'Perhaps the king's intention was to divide the royal line and split the fighting.'

'That's kind of you to say, lad, but that's not the reason. My fool of a nephew sent me here as a warning to me and those who would sympathise with me. Besides, Kingsport is prize enough without a discarded Faulknar in residence. It has always been the kingdom's gateway to the north and remains so despite being severely diminished. If we ever get help from outside, it will come through Kingsport.'

We continued along the cliff-top road and I soon saw the first signs of the tall stone buildings that dominated the docks. The ever-present threat of the pirate ships became a less urgent concern against my growing anxiety at the thought of seeing Tawpin again. Despite having no evidence to support my theory, I was irrationally convinced that he would know of the horrors I had inflicted on Hilman. That I had them etched on my face and branded onto my soul for him to clearly see. I had no doubts that he would consider me a traitor following my refusal of Kade's request in the Northlands. He was ever loyal to Kade.

My nervousness agitated Trefin, who shied at everything from a startled ground-bird to an errant gust of wind. Keenan grumbled about my poorly trained horse while Vallori frequently stared at me, inviting me to open the discussion of why I was so restless. I ignored both of them and concentrated on calming my flighty mare, succeeding only in making her more reactive with my increasing frustration. Keenan finally lost patience when Trefin kicked out at his horse after I had pulled harshly at her mouth upon seeing the western town gates.

'Mobis's Torments, Tallen. What has got into you and that banshee of a horse?'

'It will be fine,' Vallori reassured me. 'Whatever is waiting for us, we'll face it together. And you've faced much worse.'

Keenan's eyes grew wide. 'That's what you're worried about? You think Tawpin won't welcome you? Tawpin?'

I smiled apologetically, knowing he was right yet still unable to shake my fears. 'He has every right to turn me away. I have not always treated him as he deserves. And there are things that I have done...'

He huffed dismissively. 'Aside from the fact that the Earl refuses to see the bad in anyone, he can do with all the friends he can get right now. You will be welcomed. Do not doubt that.'

'The Earl may be generous,' called one of Keenan's guard, 'but his lady may not.'

I turned to see the stocky soldier grinning and he winked at me. Keenan's groan confirmed he was the focus of the soldier's comment.

'Leyn's going to throttle me,' he whined, rolling his eyes but relenting to explain. 'I'm supposed to be resting. Resting! Confounded woman. Does she not know there's a war on?'

'I'm sure she's well aware of that,' I chided, remembering the formidable and very capable woman. 'Why does she think you should be resting?'

Keenan huffed again, sounding more like a petulant child than a lord general and an uncle to the king, and causing everyone to smirk at his discomfort.

'Got struck on the head and was laid low for two days,' supplied the soldier helpfully. 'The lady instructed him to rest so that he could recover his strength.'

'Recover my strength!' the Lord General blustered. 'Does she think I'm one of her mewling brats, that she can order me so?'

The soldier ignored his ill-temper and gleefully continued. 'She ordered everyone to prevent him from engaging with the Gallowglass. Forcibly confining him to his rooms if necessary.'

'Pah! As if anyone would listen to her.'

'You listened to her,' continued the guard mercilessly, and earning a murderous glare from Keenan while the other soldiers sniggered. 'You felt a sudden need to review the marsh defences rather than openly comply with her wishes.'

'I'm a guest in her home,' he defended weakly. 'It would not do to be seen to undermine her authority. Despite how ridiculous her demands.'

Keenan remained sulking until we arrived at the western edge of the port where, despite the pitiful expanse of temporary accommodations which housed the increasing population of refugees, the tension in his shoulders melted. He and his soldiers were acknowledged by a few, but we were mostly ignored by people trying to salvage what they could of their lives and their pride. The west gate sat within the wooden fortifications, facing the wet fenlands extending from the port to the muddy estuary, before degrading into the inhospitable marshes. The two sentries looked bored until we approached, and their cheerful welcome lifted the quiet mood within our group. A coin flared in the afternoon sunlight when it was tossed by one of the guards to her smiling companion.

'I would say it's good to see you returned,' she called out, 'but I waged you had run south to avoid the lady's wrath.'

The victor pocketed his winnings, gleefully adding, 'I knew the Lord General was brave enough to handle a scolding and being sent to his chambers with no supper.'

'Yes, yes,' Keenan grumbled, albeit lacking the normal sharpness of his tone. 'Very amusing. Remind me to place the pair of you on latrine duties for the foreseeable future.'

The guards laughed freely, ignoring his ill-tempered scowl, and the gentle teasing continued while we made our way towards the bridge leading into the main town. Such comments were not restricted to those who may have fought alongside their victim and had, perhaps, developed a mutual respect. Everyone, from merchants to guild administrators to labourers, felt comfortable goading the royal. He was even heckled by a couple of young boys, bold enough to comment on the various punishments Leyn would dispense. Keenan faced them with a frosty glare and a cutting remark but there was an amused pull at the corner of his mouth. I felt some pride in the atmosphere cultivated in Tawpin's home and that he still nurtured the humour in his people, even with the harshness of war closing in on him.

The town was busy, not only with the activity of so many people crowded into the streets and squares, but with the normal routines of the port. The merchants sold what they had and the people bought what they could. The stalls were less bountiful than those I had seen in Hilman but trade was constant. Conversations were loud and I frequently heard laughter. The odour of fish mixed with the briny tang to the air, declaring the port's reliance on the sea. Saltwater fish, shellfish and seaweed were the main commodity although there were also freshwater fish and eels brought in from the villages further upriver. Supplies of grain and vegetables were noticeably scarce with the port's isolation far from the more fertile fields of central and southern Faulknar, and Keenan had told of the submerged land to the east of Kingsport where arable farming had previously been able to supply the town. Villermir's prolonged rains had limited the availability of food as much as the surrounding armies of Lindvane, Baila and Gallowgla. Despite all this, Tawpin's people continued to work and trade, making the most of what they had. *Toughest people in the kingdom*, he had once claimed, and they were proving their earl to be correct.

Leyn was standing at the top of the stone steps that led into the port's main meeting hall. She was dressed in functional leathers, with the only acknowledgement to her rank seen in the quality of the richly embroidered tunic which buttoned to her waist before flaring to brush against her knees. The colour was an unusual shade of forest green that shifted into subtle shades of blue as she breathed. It was a beautiful garment, but its splendour was overshadowed by Leyn's rigid posture and crossed-arm irritation. She fixed a challenging stare upon Keenan while our horses were collected and we assembled before her at the base of the steps. The sea breeze ruffled her short, curly hair while she made us wait, prolonging the Lord General's discomfort.

'You were told to rest,' she stated eventually, the acoustics of the square projecting her voice. 'Did you mistake my instructions to be optional?'

I saw a couple of Keenan's guards purposefully looking at anything other than each other, or Leyn, or the victim of her scathing accusation. To his credit, Keenan faced her with his head high and wearing an unrepentant expression where I would have been reduced to the demeanour of a disobedient child were I in his place. He took a breath but Leyn continued before he had the chance to defend himself.

'And don't think to use the welcome return of Tallen as an excuse.' She acknowledged me with a slight dip of her head but did not delay further chastisement. 'You had no way of knowing she would be there when you disobeyed me.'

'My lady—' Kennan began.

'My lady?' she mocked. 'The man who refuses his title seeks to use mine in appeasement.'

Her comment caused a ripple of mirth to spread through the soldiers and I suspected their general would reward this with a variety of distasteful duties being suddenly allocated to them.

'My lady,' he repeated. 'My apologies for sneaking off like a thief but you knew perfectly well that I was never going to comply with your command. There is too much at stake for me to sit around while good people are dying. So, if you are finished with having your fun, perhaps we can move on?'

An amused smile crept over Leyn's lips and she tossed her head in defeat. 'I suppose I should be grateful that you ran away from the fighting instead of charging towards it. But Keenan, you are too valuable to risk yourself so needlessly. Go to the healers. Get your wound taken care of, I am sure you will have opened it up. And get someone to check if you've done any permanent damage to your thick skull. You can deliver your report when we dine this evening.'

Keenan's face showed obvious affection and he bowed with full respect before taking his leave, his soldiers trailing along behind him. Leyn's face showed similar fondness when she watched him go, turning to me with a warm smile and beckoning me to join her. She grabbed me in a firm embrace as soon as I was in grasping distance, much to Vallori's amusement, and restrained me long enough for me to slowly relax and return the gesture.

'Oh, Tallen,' she breathed, holding me at arm's length with a hand placed lightly on each shoulder. 'It is so very good to see you. Tawpin is so pleased that you are here.'

'He is well?'

'Works too hard. Doesn't eat enough.' She smiled indulgently. 'But yes, he is well.'

She hooked her arm around mine and guided me into the building where several people quietly hurried, occasionally acknowledging Leyn with a respectful nod.

'We have much to catch up on,' she continued while she led me up the wooden staircase to the open gallery that encircled the lower floor. 'I hardly know where to start but perhaps we should begin with introductions.' She turned to Vallori. 'Please call me Leyn. I'm the Countess of Kingsport—'

'Taw's married?' I blurted, causing her to laugh.

'Yes, he is. Although, I have to admit he did not have much choice in the matter.'

I grinned, knowing that Leyn would have organised the whole process. It was the best news I had heard in a very long time. I liked Leyn, and her calm practicality was the perfect match for Tawpin's chaotic nature.

'Congratulations. I'm pleased for you both.'

'Really?' Leyn stopped to look at me with concern causing a small crease in her forehead. 'It means so much to me, both of us, to have your approval.'

'Of course. Someone has to keep Tawpin in check.'

The tall woman beamed before turning back to Vallori, who introduced himself without explaining anything about his relationship to me. Leyn narrowed her eyes at the oversight and I knew she would challenge me about it at the first opportunity, but she was polite enough to let the matter slide and proceeded to inform him, in great detail, about how much trouble Tawpin and I had caused as children. I was in no doubt that she was enjoying my embarrassment.

Tawpin had his back to us when we entered his study. He was hunched over a large table placed in the centre of the room, where a map had been unfurled and held open with random books and discarded tankards. There were a small number of men standing around the table and I smiled when I recognised Mace. I was pleased to see one of Kade's former guards, but the big man wore such a strange expression when he looked up and saw me that I felt my smile fade. Tawpin noticed his focus of attention and turned.

'Magpie!'

He greeted me with the full force of his toothy grin, to which I replied with a ridiculous expression of my own. I could hardly believe that my oldest friend was standing in front of me, with his uncontrollable hair and his mischievous sea-green eyes. I would recognise his face anywhere. But the moment lasted a little too long and we both noted the differences that had developed during the time we had been apart. Leyn was right, he was tired and he was a little too thin. His quick humour had dimmed with the stresses of managing his earldom and the griefs he shared with his people.

'You've changed,' he said quietly.

'I grew my hair.'

He threw his head back and laughed with the sound I remembered so well. I no longer cared that he was unaware of the things I had done and the person I had become. I rejoiced at being with my friend and hearing his distinctive laugh.

'Oh, Magpie,' he grinned. 'I've missed you.'

He crossed the room in three long strides and gathered me into a fierce embrace that lifted me off my feet.

CHAPTER TWENTY-SEVEN

We spent time discussing the situation in Kingsport, postponing our stories until a more appropriate time. Tawpin and Leyn explained the threats that faced them; both civically, with the constant need for food and shelter to meet the requirements of a growing population, and militarily, with the frequent raids by the Gallowgla and the menace of Lindvane slowly advancing from the south. I watched Vallori join the conversation. He was primarily a warrior and he instinctively understood the challenges presented. His council was heeded and I noticed the beginnings of a relationship built on mutual respect developing between him and Mace. The two would be formidable on the battlefield.

Dusk was darkening towards night when Leyn called for a conclusion to the war council. There was much left to discuss but she argued that the specifics could wait until the next day. We had enough of a plan for now and it was time to address other matters. The tall lady smiled at me and I knew she could no longer resist the call of sharing gossip. Mace was invited to join us and, unexpectedly, we retreated to Tawpin's family home on the edge of the old town. Taw and Leyn hounded Vallori and me with questions about how we met and what we had been doing, wanting a precise account of my story since leaving Kingsport almost seven years earlier. There was so much I did not want to confess that my answers were often unnecessarily blunt. Vallori graciously carried most of the conversation, sketching a rough outline that answered their questions without revealing any detail. He carefully guided the discussion back to the politics of Hilman and the pockets of resistance there, adding insight into his journey across Lindvane and the tight control of Baila throughout that kingdom. He engaged Mace in military tactics and strategic options so that Tawpin or Leyn would have to interrupt if they wanted to focus on more personal matters. Tawpin finally gave up when we approached the Kingsport estate, declaring he would find out my seedy little secrets before long even if I maintained my refusal to indulge him. It was light banter and, for the first time in what seemed a long while, I felt accepted and content.

Lord Jardine, Tawpin's steward, greeted us on our arrival and guided us to a comfortable dining hall, dominated by a long table which was capable of accommodating many more than just the six of us. Keenan was waiting, already seated with a glass of wine, and we were ushered in and arranged around one end of the table. Leyn had excused herself, returning moments later carrying two babies swaddled in soft blankets and an infant waddling beside her who gripped her mother's tunic to maintain her unstable balance. The young girl, who had masses of Leyn's curly hair, beamed at seeing Tawpin and trotted over to embrace his leg.

'All girls,' he bemoaned, fondly cuddling his elder daughter.

'My bloodline runs true,' shrugged Leyn, handing one of the babies to Keenan. 'My father desperately wanted a boy. There were six of us before he finally admitted defeat.'

She passed the other baby to Tawpin, collecting her older daughter while the men dutifully cooed over their girls and Vallori and Mace grinned at each other. The household staff brought more drinks and small savoury pastries that could be easily nibbled while one arm was wrapped around a small child. The conversation revolved around the antics of the girls, with Tawpin boasting of the trouble the older one was causing already. The regret was clear in both his and Leyn's eyes when the children were collected for their beds.

We continued with light conversation and Tawpin's efficient staff brought the main meal, consisting primarily of fish yet being more flavoursome than anything I had tasted for several days. Leyn teased Keenan mercilessly, causing him to bluster ill-temperedly while we all knew he welcomed the attention. The atmosphere was comfortable and inviting and it felt good to consider myself among friends.

The mood was interrupted before we had finished the main course when Jardine apologetically ushered in a young woman who was still covered in mud and horsehair.

'My apologies,' the steward repeated. 'But I felt you would want to hear this news without delay.'

'Of course.' Tawpin turned to the messenger. 'What have you to report?'

The woman saluted formally, bowing first to Keenan and then Tawpin, before delivering her report to the Lord General.

'Your Grace, Earl Kingsport. I regret to inform you that Witcham's Ford has been taken.'

'Mobis's Hells!' Keenan banged the table hard enough to rattle the plates and causing the messenger to startle.

'Those that could, have retreated to Two Holes,' she continued. 'All of Lord Stanton's lands are now under Lindvane control.'

'That brings them within three days' march of here,' Mace stated quietly. 'We don't have the numbers to fight on two fronts if they decide to look here instead of at Liegeport.'

We all fell silent, thinking of the implications of Kingsport defending against both Lindvane and Gallowgla. Leyn thanked the woman for her report and instructed Jardine to provide her with refreshments.

'Curse the boy!'

'Keenan,' Leyn cautioned softly.

'Fearsome Father, I mean it. He concentrates too much on Liegeport and leaves the dukes fighting on the border with whatever they can muster. We should be pushing back as a combined force, not sitting around waiting until each estate is picked apart. Fool will see his kingdom burn before he gets his fight at Liegeport.'

'And this is why you were exiled here,' reminded Mace.

Tawpin turned to me with a weak grin. 'I have been officially labelled as an enemy of the court. I may have told the king exactly what I thought of him.'

Keenan continued to grumble, albeit with less force. 'Cursed witch is to blame for this. You'll see I'm right.'

'Breya?' I asked, unable to believe she would be spiteful enough to destroy Faulknar.

Keenan shook his head. 'Always thought she would be the one to rule the boy. Never thought I'd say it, but I wish that were the case. At least our queen understands her duty to her kingdom.'

'Greenwood was one of the first to be lost in this more aggressive, sustained assault from Hayton.' Leyn absently stabbed at the neglected remains of her food. 'She felt the loss keenly, and with everything else...'

'The years have not been kind to Breya,' Tawpin agreed. 'She is no longer the petty, ambitious girl we knew.'

'She's still ambitious,' corrected Keenan.

'True,' replied Leyn with a small smile. 'I doubt she is capable of being anything other than that. But much of her spirit is gone.' She shared a look with Tawpin before turning back to me with an expression of intense sympathy. 'After she lost her second son... She does not birth easily and Keevan caused significant harm. It was feared that she would never maintain another pregnancy. But this one has held so far.' She made the old gesture to avert evil. 'Merciful Mother that it remain so.'

'Who would have predicted that Breya would be selfless enough to be such a caring, nurturing mother,' commented Tawpin quietly.

'It has been very hard for her,' agreed Leyn. 'And it has taken a heavy toll.'

'And those cursed rumours haven't helped,' grumbled Keenan.

'What rumours?'

'A whole stinking pile of nonsense. As if people haven't got better things to gossip about. Not a shred of truth to base their lies upon.'

'Peace.' Leyn spoke softly when Keenan's face flushed with restrained temper. 'No one believes the stories. Not really. And certainly not those who know Breya and Kade.'

'Kyllian's death was suspicious,' Tawpin clarified. 'He had been in perfect health but within days he sickened and died. There was no obvious reason for it. No injury that had turned sour. No contagion in the court, or even within Liegeport, that he could have succumbed to. The speed of his decline seemed... unnatural.'

'Poison?' I was already certain of the answer.

'That's the popular conclusion,' Tawpin confirmed, ignoring Keenan's rumble. 'Breya has always been so conspicuously ambitious that it was inevitable suspicion would centre on her. But there is a growing faction that blames Kade for his father's death.'

'That's ridiculous,' I blurted. 'Kade would never.'

My conviction in Kade's innocence faltered in the silence that challenged my denial. Even Keenan stared at his plate and avoided looking at me.

'You can't be serious,' I persisted. 'Their relationship wasn't perfect but you can't believe he would do that?'

Tawpin reluctantly raised his gaze, looking at me with a pained expression. 'Once, I would have been as confident as you. But now? He has been so isolated. So twisted around himself. Now, I'm no longer sure what he's capable of.' He sighed sadly. 'He is very far from what he used to be.'

'And not one of you stayed to defend him?'

Vallori shifted in his seat at the harshness of my accusation but did not comment. Tawpin shamefully lowered his gaze while Mace played with his table-knife.

'Why do you think we have been ostracised to this stinking marshland,' growled Keenan. 'No offence meant.'

Tawpin waved a hand in dismissal. 'None was taken. I would be with him as well if he would allow it.'

Keenan rumbled deep in his chest but it was Mace who answered the original question.

'Erula.'

'Erula?' I spluttered.

'Who is Erula?' asked Vallori.

'A nobody,' growled Keenan.

'A Traveller I met in Liegeport,' I explained. 'Erula had gathered a band of female fighters and had come to join Faulknar against Lindvane. I don't see how she would be advising Kade?'

'When Kade returned from your *adventure*,' continued Tawpin, obvious in his frustration at not being told the details, 'Hagan returned to Liegeport to be with him.'

'We all went back to be with his Grace,' Mace resumed. 'Erula and her fighters came with us.'

'Muris stayed,' corrected Leyn. 'And Iffan.'

Mace inclined his head in acknowledgement. 'But most of us followed Hagan. They were difficult times but, looking back, at least we had Kyllian to keep the kingdom together. Kade was angry. So angry. At everyone. Us. His father. Breya. Somehow Erula managed to position herself to always be at his side. Supporting his view no matter how unreasonable he was being. Sympathising with him when we challenged his spite and his tantrums.' The big man flicked a look at Keenan, knowing this was close to treason, but Kade's uncle simply continued to glower. 'It happened so gradually. No one took it seriously until she had forced out everyone who was loyal to him. We never noticed until it was too late. By that time we were effectively, and completely, removed from his council. Hagan refused to be chased away but he is rarely heard. And when the king died...'

'Kade is your king now, boy,' Keenan chastised gently.

'Then it's cursed time he started to act like one,' Mace snapped, stabbing the knife he had been playing with into the table in frustration.

Leyn smiled at his apologetic expression, waving away his apology. 'It is not the first wound this table has sustained. I doubt it will be the last.'

'Who knows how much of his attitude is due to her influence and how much is his own spiralling descent,' commented Tawpin. 'No one can get close enough to tell. But in public, she feeds his fears and fans the flames of his prejudices.'

'To what end?' I asked, struggling to understand how it could have gone so wrong in the time I had been away. And how Erula was at the heart of it.

'Chaos, as far as I can see,' offered Keenan.

'Power,' suggested Leyn. 'There are many who would seek the king's ear.'

Mace merely shrugged. 'Whatever her reason, she has him so isolated that he listens to only her counsel. I see no other reason for him to abandon his kingdom in order to fortify Liegeport, other than at her request.'

'He denies her with regard to Baila, at least,' defended Tawpin loyally. 'She may not advise surrender to Hayton but she would have us all pray to the One God.'

I could not believe what I was hearing. I did not remember Erula being overly pious to either doctrine, and the war with Lindvane was so enmeshed with Villermir and his faith that I failed to see how you could advocate for one without conceding to the other.

'True,' accepted Keenan. 'The boy still shows some stubbornness there.'

Leyn smiled at the older man. 'I wonder where he gets that from.'

He flicked an appreciative smile at her attempt to lighten the mood but continued with tired resignation. 'Although he still refuses to expel those flea-infested priests that fester like a seeping wound, seeding intolerance and hate throughout the kingdom. He may remain true to the Gods but he gives no favour to those that join him there. He accepts that Namori witch's faith and refuses to provoke a holy war between the two religions, but he remains blind to the civil unrest when communities turn on each other. Each claiming their way is the true way and squabbling amongst themselves when they should be looking to the enemy marching across our land. I don't doubt many of Baila's followers are aiding the Army of Truth, providing the information that lets them walk in and claim vast sections of the south.'

'We don't have the resources to ferret out the informers,' Mace continued. 'Not without sinking to the levels of persecution reported in Lindvane and Hilman. And if we do that, what is it we're fighting for?'

'And while you're being distracted fighting each other, not to mention

Hayton and Baila's armies,' added Vallori quietly, 'the real enemy sneaks in to exploit the advantage.'

'Approaching armies I understand,' grumbled Keenan. 'Civil unrest I understand. But what it is those pirates bring, that's beyond my comprehension.'

The presence of the Gallowglass off the coast had been discussed earlier, along with the wraith army which could kill without suffering any harm from Faulknar weapons. The pirates had kept their shamans hidden and protected within the ships, so Vallori had explained how the ghosts were summoned and how they could be managed with fire. We did not feel the need to burden them with the knowledge of where the spectres came from and what happened to those who fell to the unnatural host. It was a small mercy that the daemons rampaging across Hilman were absent from Faulknar, but I would not trust that this would hold and despaired at the woeful inadequacy of one Dragonslayer when they arrived. We all descended into a heavy silence, trying to think of ways in which we could resist such a combined assault. We had insufficient numbers to effectively control Lindvane and the Army of Truth. We had insufficient power to resist the Gallowglass' monsters. We had insufficient will to turn against our neighbours and stop the rot that festered within. We needed allies where there were few to be found.

'Tallen?' I looked up to see Tawpin watching me closely. 'What are you thinking?'

I gave him a depreciating smile; he always knew me too well. All eyes turned towards me and I shook my head in denial.

'I'm sure you have already considered it. You would have done it by now if it was a viable option.'

'Considered what?' he prompted.

'I think it may be time to call in some favours.'

I slept late the next morning and weak sunlight flooded the chamber when I awoke. The bed had been comfortable and I had missed a night's sleep whilst trudging through the marshes, so I had yielded to my exhaustion and slept soundly. I could hear the gentle sounds of Tawpin's staff performing their duties and enjoyed the opportunity to lie and do nothing, but my conscience did not let me linger for long and I reluctantly threw off the soft blankets, washed and dressed, and then left in search of Vallori and the others.

The household staff worked quietly and diligently, hurrying through the building on their errands. Most acknowledged me with a respectful dip of the head but still refused to meet my gaze. I saw no sign of Leyn or Tawpin, or even Keenan or Mace. I was starting to get concerned that Vallori was absent when Tawpin's steward approached me.

'Lady Tallen,' he greeted pleasantly, smiling at the expression on my face. 'I know. Lord Keenan is similarly annoyed. But it's an old habit and it feels impolite to omit people's titles.'

'I'm not sure I have a title. And I'm fairly sure yours would exceed mine in any case. *Lord* Jardine.' He inclined his head in humility. 'Have you seen Vallori? Or Tawpin? I can't seem to find them.'

'Earl Kingsport and your companion have returned to the meeting hall to continue their council. You have been invited to join them.' I thanked the steward and turned to leave but he continued. 'May I provide you with some refreshment before you go? Or perhaps one of the lads to accompany you?'

I gently declined both food and escort, appreciating the simple pleasure of walking into the port without the fear of recognition. The morning was cool, with a chill sea-breeze that gusted strong enough to knock me off balance on occasion. People strode purposefully to their destinations and I was grateful for my cloak, which provided enough anonymity for me to be dismissed as just another fighter in a town full of soldiers. I felt no threat from those I encountered but I was unsure if my treasonous act was common knowledge, and I was unwilling to give Tawpin any more trouble than he already had.

I soon arrived at the central square and entered the hall without challenge. A quick enquiry to a passing scribe confirmed that the council was being conducted in the same room as the previous day, and I quietly entered Taw's study where reports from overnight were being discussed. Tawpin, Vallori and Keenan stood around the table with their backs to me, while Mace and two other senior soldiers had their heads bent over the map. I smiled to see another of Kade's guard standing between the two soldiers, with Kutan's fair hair being as unkempt as it had been when we had escorted Kingsport's earl home. He looked up to see me and grinned while he continued his report. Keenan caught Kutan's change of attention, turning to see who had arrived and triggering a ripple of raised heads as they turned in my direction. Tawpin greeted me warmly and introduced me to the Lords Pellin and Just, who barely acknowledged me.

Kutan concluded his report regarding the positioning of the Gallowgla fleet further east along the coast and was released. He leaned in when he passed me, his mischievous grin returning.

'I see you have returned. Was that brave or foolish?'

His comment left me wondering whether he welcomed my return or not but I had missed the chance to ask, being drawn into the discussion involving my suggestion during the previous evening. Two sets of messengers had been sent south with the hope that at least one from each group would be able to avoid Lindvane's army and deliver the message. The group travelling further south would be least likely to succeed, needing to cross an entrenched border of Army of Truth fanatics in addition to Hayton's forces. Lord Pellin questioned the wisdom of sacrificing riders with no guarantee of the requests being accepted. Keenan silenced him by demanding to know if he had any better ideas.

The debate rocked between the need for offensive assaults or defensive consolidation. Vallori said little but his eyes rarely strayed from the map and I knew he was considering different strategies and determining potential options. Keenan and Mace argued for attack. Pellin and Just petitioned for caution. Both risked increased losses while neither promised decisive gains, either through the improvement in the supply of resources or the expulsion of hostile forces. The stalemate surrounding Kingsport threatened to continue regardless of what was decided.

The conversation stalled and then stopped when the men ran out of ideas. Tawpin rubbed his eyes and stretched his back, suggesting that we should take a break. He was turning to one of the pages who sat against the wall when we heard raised voices from the reception hall, echoing around the gallery that encircled it. We all turned towards the door when heavy footsteps raced up the wooden staircase, with the thin rug doing little to muffle the sound. We waited expectantly while the scout hurried through the open doorway, his face flushed from the cold wind, and bowed to Keenan and Tawpin.

'Lord General. Earl Kingsport. My lords—'

Keenan flapped a hand with impatience. 'Yes. Enough of all that. What news?'

'Pirates, my lords. They've breached Sterret Sands.'

Mace was three paces towards the door before Tawpin called him to a halt.

'Patience, Mace,' Tawpin cautioned calmly before turning back to the scout. 'What numbers? How long ago?'

The details of the raid were swiftly provided and pages were sent running to the stables to ready the horses and then to the training ground to collect Mace's guard. Keenan grumbled about heading back to the miserable swamp before being told that he would not be going, with everyone too wary of Leyn's scathing reprisals. Pellin and Just remained quiet, reluctant to commit their soldiers when their lands lay to the east, and with Tawpin conceding that he could not stop Mace from going even if he tried, he instructed him to lead the assault. The big man had family in a coastal fishing village and he had gained a reputation for defending the resilient communities that were the focus for many of the pirates' raids. Valloori and I did not need to discuss whether we would go. It was why we were there.

By the time we left the hall, our horses were waiting in the main square. Kutan had returned with his brother and around twenty others, including Muris and Iffan. The scout had reported three landing craft so we should be evenly matched. I nodded to Dru and the women, receiving a small smile from Muris, but there was no time for reunions. The sound of horses' hooves striking stone echoed around the square and we set the horses to canter out of Kingsport.

Most settlements bordering the port were located to the east where more fertile land could be farmed and the tall sandstone cliffs provided protection from onshore gales and stormy seas. Sterret Sands was one of four communities who worked the mud flats of the western coast and it was the only one still populated after the others had abandoned their homes for the promised safety of the port. The raiders had largely ignored this insignificant village, protected by treacherous sandbanks which could strand a ship or rip the hull out of a boat, and Sterret Sands had continued to harvest the mud's seaweed and razorshell clams to provide much needed supplies for the overcrowded town.

The horses' hooves thundered upon the sandy-turfed road that bordered the beach and ran all the way from Kingsport to Sterret Sands. The dunes on our right sloped gently down onto dark sands, where sucking mud waited to claim any who were unaware of the dangerously shifting tides around this section of coast. Strong gusts of wind buffeted the ground-birds that had startled when we raced past them and whipped up grains of sand to sting our faces and irritate our eyes, but these distractions were ignored as we charged towards the defenceless fishing village.

We saw the smoke first. The north wind blew the dark clouds away from our approach and the settlement was still hidden behind the curve of the coast, but there was no mistaking that we had arrived at the raid. I instinctively leaned forward in the saddle, trying to coax extra speed from Trefin even though she was already galloping at full pace. The beached boats of the pirates were visible a moment before we heard the yells and cries of the attack. The dull sound of steel striking wood confirmed that the fishing community lacked even basic farming tools with which to defend themselves.

I drew *Saorsa* and aimed for the nearest raiders as they chased and slashed, stabbed and burnt. Some villagers tried to escape to the beach but most ran for the marshes that lay further inland, and the invaders split into two groups to eagerly pursue them in preference to the meagre loot offered within the dwellings. We adopted their strategy, dividing when we charged into the chaos, and I steered Trefin towards the larger group at the south of the village. I briefly noted that Vallori, Dru and Kutan were with me before I engaged with the first raider. The pirate roared in challenge when I leaned over him from the saddle. He managed to absorb my initial strike with a two-handed hold on his broadsword and my nimble mare rotated on her hind limbs to allow me to follow with a slash across his back. The raider twisted to meet my attack but he was unbalanced. I dragged *Saorsa* down his blade to bite into his wrist and blood gushed from the deep wound. I reversed the angle of my blade and sliced into his neck.

I turned towards my next target. A terrified young woman was being dragged by her hair and stumbled when she was hauled backwards. The raider struck the woman across the face in an incentive to get her moving, and I fixed onto my prey. The pirate dropped her captive when she saw me aiming for her. She calmly removed the axe that was strapped to her back and with sword in one hand and axe in the other, she planted her feet and bravely waited for me. Metal screamed when the axe caught on *Saorsa*'s blade and I turned Trefin's rump sharply to avoid the slice that had aimed to hamstring her. Three times the pirate blocked my attack with either sword or axe before I could exploit a moment of weakness. I removed my foot from the stirrup and kicked her in the face, sending her staggering back several paces. Trefin skipped sideways to keep me within striking range and, while she was still dazed from my kick, I goaded her into over-reaching with her axe. I caught the swing of my blade and rotated my wrist to stab into her chest.

The raiders had been unprepared for a mounted response and, with fighting on foot never going to defeat those on horseback, they had quickly decided to retreat to their boats. I followed the withdrawing pirates, guiding Trefin through the smouldering village before waiting at the edge of the beach to assess the second assault. One boat had already launched and was battling the incoming tide while Mace's soldiers cut down those aiming to follow them. It had been a short and decisive attack. Dead raiders littered the beach while we seemed only to have suffered minor injuries. The fishing community's casualties were mainly targeted at the very young or the very old, with few who could mount a defence despite their lack of effective weapons. Based on what I had seen with the young woman, I suspected the raiders had come for slaves rather than slaughter.

Vallori walked his mare over to join me, and we watched the small boat crest the last breaker and aim toward the Gallowgla ship waiting beyond the sandbank. Mace's guard efficiently dealt with those left on the shoreline, taking weapons and small items from the dead raiders, attending to the wounded villagers, and organising the others into meaningful distractions. Vallori and I left them to their work, content to remain on the edge of the dunes until called to assist.

Mikkla shifted her weight and I turned towards Vallori, finding a questioning frown creasing his face. Following his gaze, I saw the rowboat was almost halfway to its target and was slowly approaching the sandbanks marked by a lighter shade of blue-grey sea.

'They're almost to the ship,' I commented.

Vallori agreed distractedly before raising his arm to point at a mark slightly to the left of the retreating boat. 'But what's going on there?'

Beyond the Gallowgla ship, and a little further to the west, were a pair of sail boats. They were smaller than the sea-faring ship but significantly larger than the rowboat. A flaming arrow was released from the Gallowgla ship and arced towards the nearest of the two boats. The target was too far away and the arrow fell harmlessly into the sea, but the intention was clear and the new arrivals were not allies of the raiders.

Gradually, more on the shoreline noticed the strange craft and stopped to watch. The onshore wind filled their sails and they raced towards the smaller boat, maintaining a safe distance from the threat of arrows when they passed the ship and moved to intersect the vulnerable boat. The pirates were steadily advancing towards safety but were forced wide into the safe channel between the sandbanks. The delay was sufficient for the new arrivals to position themselves between the landing vessel and their ship. More arrows were released with a few, aided by the gusty wind, travelling far enough to land in the boats and ignite the oiled sailcloth. The fires were quickly doused but the threat remained, and they waited until they had moved further away from the ship before lowering their sails and reducing their speed. They separated to flank their prey, while their target could do little except shout insults and brandish their weapons. The pirates had not thought to take arrows for a raid on a vulnerable fishing village while their attackers were well prepared and now launched a volley of their own. Trapping the boat between their two larger vessels, they were now close enough to pick off individuals. The pirates never stood a chance and the battle was soon over, with those who had jumped into the sea to avoid the rain of arrows being leisurely taken when they surfaced until none remained.

One of the boats continued approaching the defeated vessel, with a sailor jumping into the craft once close enough to secure it with a towing length of rope. The other boat had turned towards the shore and the rhythmic stroke of oars drove it swiftly towards us. A tall, dark man stood at the prow, raising his arms in triumph and roared so loudly that he could be faintly heard despite being so far away.

'That is a big man,' Vallori commented absently while we remained fascinated by the strange event, watching until the boat was close enough to allow the identification of individuals. 'Is that Bear?'

I laughed. 'I don't know how but I believe it is.'

I dismounted and walked Trefin towards Mace who waited, still mounted, by the shoreline. Vallori followed and we stood by the big soldier while the boat crested the first of the breakers. Bear grinned manically at the prow with Nash seated behind. Mace was still tense in readiness to confront this new threat and the small movement of raising his sword to his horse's shoulder was enough to call his soldiers to him.

'Hold,' I requested. 'These are allies.'

Mace turned to look down on me with clear suspicion. 'And how do you know that?'

Vallori answered with a small grin. 'Because those reckless fools are our friends.'

Mace stared at us for several heartbeats, but eventually dismissed his guard with a nod and they returned to aiding the villagers. The vessel was now within hailing distance and Bear boomed a greeting.

'You found her then?' he yelled at Vallori, having to suddenly grasp the side of the rocking boat when it slammed into a breaker wave and unbalanced him.

'I did,' Vallori yelled back.

'Never doubted it.'

'Liar.'

Mace remained focused on Bear throughout the exchange and had not yet sheathed his blade. I repeated my assurances, guaranteeing that they were not a threat until, reluctantly, he grunted his acceptance. He called for a pair of soldiers to attend to our horses and dismounted, and the three of us waited for the boat to crest the last wave. Mace and Vallori waded in to assist when two sailors jumped into the surf, all four tugging the craft onto the beach. Bear levered off the side to leap from the boat while Bonash disembarked more carefully. They had splashed noisily to the beach before I noticed an oarsman with long, dark hair curled by the damp air. I shook my head in disbelief when he turned, amused blue eyes and a small grin greeting me.

'Elyos? By the Gods, what are you doing here?'

He bowed expansively. 'I wasn't going to let that overgrown ox have all the fun.'

Organising the relocation of the villagers back to Kingsport took longer than I was expecting. A few refused to abandon their homes, but Mace soon convinced them that they were too vulnerable to further attack and he would leave none behind. Many more were unwilling to leave behind valued possessions and no one wanted to leave their dead. Driftwood was collected to add to the smouldering shacks. It was damp and smoked horribly but, eventually, we succeeded in getting three large fires blazing hot enough for the funeral pyres. We left the raiders for the scavengers.

Our journey was slow, only being able to move as fast as the slowest walker. The elderly and the injured were given horses with room made in front of the saddles for the youngest. Mace and Dru retained their mounts, with the courtesy offered to Bear, Bonash and Elyos. Each declined, knowing there were those who needed the horses more, and Vallori and I walked with them. I joined Bear and Nash, finally getting the opportunity to hear their news.

'What are you doing here in Faulknar?' I asked, still not quite believing it. 'Are things so quiet that you thought to cross the length of Hilman and Lindvane, just to annoy the Gallowglass pirates here?'

Bear smiled, new scars and fresh wounds showing on his face. 'Vallori was the one to suggest it and it seemed discourteous to let him go alone.' His smile faded and he watched my *pháirtí*'s back, silently walking beside Elyos a few paces in front of us. 'He would not be dissuaded from going to find you and he felt I would draw too much attention if I accompanied him through Lindvane.'

I grinned at the man towering over me. 'Now why would he think that?'

'I have no idea. But as he was determined to go on his own, we agreed to a compromise. If the Gods allowed, we would meet in Faulknar. All accounts suggested that this kingdom could do with the services of a Moon Warrior or two. I did not expect you to be waiting for us when we made land.'

'A day earlier and we would not have been. We've only just got here ourselves.' I shook my head. 'And you thought the sea route was the best option? Fighting them on land was not enough, you thought you'd irritate them in their preferred arena instead?'

He rumbled a laugh. 'I admit, I normally find travel by boat tediously dull but not this time.'

Bonash looked up from entertaining a small boy to share a look with Bear before resuming the game.

'What?' I asked suspiciously.

'We had some help,' he dismissed quickly, refusing to give further explanation. 'Travelling down the coast was the quickest way. And at least those cursed daemons can't walk on water.'

I nodded in agreement before realising the intonation of his words. 'Wait. That sounds depressingly like you're saying that the wraiths *can* walk on water.'

We walked in silence for a while and my thoughts returned to the daemons. I had abandoned the Hilman people to those monsters.

'How is the fighting in Hilman?' I asked quietly. 'Faulknar certainly could do with the aid of another Moon Warrior, but can Hilman afford to lose you? And Elyos?'

Bonash was chasing the young lad and making him giggle. Bear smiled indulgently at the pair's antics before returning to address me, watching me carefully to gauge my change of mood.

'Hilman continues to face many different threats,' he started carefully. 'Not just those from Gallowgla. Did you find what you were looking for?'

'I found Villermir.' It was not what he was asking but it was close enough. 'The weather should fall back into its normal rhythm soon. The land is no longer under attack.'

'I felt the shift and we saw the lightning storms as we travelled south. That is good.'

'It came at a price,' I cautioned. 'The Empathy Crystal is destroyed. I destroyed it.'

He considered for a moment before continuing. 'Better that than the corruption it was forced to endure. What now of Villermir?'

'We could hope that he was buried under Burford but I don't believe he was. His influence will be reduced without the crystal and it is unlikely he will still be able to directly communicate with his informants throughout the Three Kingdoms, but he still has an army of fanatical soldiers and a priesthood of vindictive zealots. He has more than enough power to complete the destruction of Faulknar.'

'Do you feel the need to search for him?'

I had spent time reviewing my options concerning Villermir but had come to no firm conclusion. With the land able to heal itself, I felt no pressing need to address the Supreme High Priest and whatever trouble he was planning. I had abandoned Faulknar for too long. The daemons may be missing but the shamans were here with their wraiths, and I considered it only a matter of time before they brought their beasts to join them. I could not shake the feeling that the sorcerers off Faulknar's coast were holding back for some reason, although I intended to exploit that caution.

'No.' I said at last, looking towards the ships anchored beyond the sandbanks. 'There will be time for him later. I suggest we deal with those pirates and their shamans. It's time Faulknar was rid of these unnatural armies so it can focus on the natural ones.'

Bear nodded in agreement and we lapsed into a more comfortable silence, considering how we could possibly achieve such an ambitious aim. The big man continued to watch me with a strange expression on his face until I confronted him about it. He flicked a look at Vallori before turning back to smile at me.

'It's good that you have returned to your pack, Tallen.'

The dark Moon Warrior dropped back to walk with Nash and I was left to watch Vallori's back. I saw him repeatedly glance towards the ships. They had a distinctive line that sat low in the water and their square sails were unusual enough to remind him of a home he had left a long time ago. Several flew a dragon banner in differing forms or colours, perhaps declaring allegiances or familial attachments, or perhaps to appease their Gods. I did not see the black dragon of Freisholm. I considered asking him if there were any he recognised, but I had enough secrets of my own to go poking a stick at his.

CHAPTER TWENTY-EIGHT

It was dark by the time we arrived back in Kingsport. Dru stayed to organise the villagers into the refugee camps located to the west of the port, directing his brother and most of Mace's guard in the many tasks required to settle the new arrivals. The remaining soldiers, along with Muris and Iffan, left after crossing the bridge into the main town and took Elyos's fighters to the barracks. Only Mace and Elyos, Bear and Bonash, Vallori and I remained to climb the stone steps into the hall. Staff hurried in quiet efficiency and Mace led us, without hesitation, to the commotion coming from the rear of the building. A wall of noise battered us when we entered a room full of shouting, cursing, laughing, and drinking soldiers along with a few clerks and officials. The soft smell of warm bread smoothed over the sharp brine of the fish broth to remind me that I had not eaten since the previous evening.

We pushed through the crowded space to join Tawpin and Keenan. The two men were sitting with a small group, leaning in over the long table in order to be heard despite being a short distance from the neighbouring table to provide some degree of privacy. Mace and Bear barrelled their way through the chaos and we made easy progress in their wake. Elyos moved to walk alongside me and leaned in with a mischievous grin.

'Mace and Bear look similar, wouldn't you say?'

'I suppose,' I answered suspiciously.

'I'd wager they are related.'

I rolled my eyes, having forgotten his joy at provocative gossip. 'Don't be ridiculous. Bear is from Hilman. Mace is from a fishing village a short distance east of here.'

'Perhaps their father was a sailor. Perhaps he was one to seek comfort wherever he docked.'

He looked at me with such an eager expression that I could not help but laugh. 'I suppose that would explain Bear's fondness for sailing.'

'Exactly,' he crowed, hitting me on my arm and gleefully ignoring my sarcastic tone.

Elyos was clearly enjoying being surrounded by so many people. I gratefully snatched a mug of ale from a passing server while Tawpin's advisors tactfully withdrew to allow us room at his table.

'This is where you chose to receive counsel?' boomed Bear after brief nods of introduction.

'A man has to eat,' Keenan commented before turning to address Mace. 'You seem to have found three more strays. This is turning into a competition.'

'Then I appear to be winning.'

The big man grinned at the Lord General before formally introducing them to Tawpin. He waited until we had all been seated and supplied with drink before delivering his report on the raid and the resettlement of those from Sterret Sands. Tawpin and Keenan nodded their agreement that no one was to be left behind, and Tawpin thanked the men from Hilman for their assistance in preventing the pirates from returning to their ship.

'I would like to know how a group of fighters landed on my shores,' encouraged Tawpin when Mace concluded his account. 'And for any news from Hilman that could aid our cause.'

I was also keen to hear about those I had left there, and to continue the conversation Bear had carefully avoided earlier about how they had managed to evade the many pirates who patrolled the coast of both Hilman and Lindvane. I fought the drowsiness brought on by the warmth of the hall and the effects of the ale, with a mellowness seeping into my muscles and crowding at the edges of my thoughts, and I concentrated on Bear while he recounted his story. He frequently looked at me or Vallori when he talked of matters that would be news to us.

'Hilman is still beset by the shamans' daemons as well as their wraiths,' he began, giving a brief description of the battles with the monsters which I remembered well. 'But we managed to acquire a significant number of ancient weapons that can deliver a meaningful blow to the creatures. As well as creating a few of our own.'

He flicked a brief look at me when Keenan seized on the idea of enchanted weapons. 'Are these blades effective against the wraiths? Do you think we would have some in Faulknar?'

'The blades only seem to work against the daemons. Sluagh's ghosts appear to be immune to all except fire and, even then, the flames only irritate unless you can get them hot enough. But there is no reason to believe that there would not be charmed weapons in Faulknar. And they certainly work well against Gallowgla pirates.'

'The resistance have managed to create a barrier that extends along most of the coast,' continued Elyos. 'We've been able to prevent the daemons from advancing too far inland. And those that do are discouraged from going further.'

'We?' asked Vallori. 'The resistance were disconnected, isolated groups. There were not enough to allow an effective covering of that much territory.'

Elyos grinned. 'Carys can be very persuasive when she wants to be. The runners who were sent to locate swords also went to recruit, despite Sheehan's protests. My devious sister has developed a network that has united most of the resistance. By both fair and foul means, she has managed to get everyone working together. She is quite the accomplished liar.'

'She is related to you,' I smiled back, enjoying his obvious pride.

I also held a significant amount of respect for the spirited young woman but to have coerced unity into such a disparate group of strong-willed individuals was outstanding. To achieve it in so short a space of time told of uncommon skill and determination. I was glad Carys was on our side.

'That's impressive,' confirmed Vallori.

Bonash smiled modestly at Bear. 'This may have helped.'

He flicked a coin at me, which I caught instinctively before realising what it was. I dropped the disc onto the table as if it was red-hot, resulting in a row of confused expressions from Tawpin, Keenan and Mace.

'It's all right,' Nash encouraged. 'You can pick it up.'

I cautiously grasped the coin by its edges, still reluctant to touch it more than was needed to examine it. I looked at the face of Averill, stamped into the metal disc along with the stag of Hilman. I turned the coin to look at the reverse side and the hated symbol of Baila, but the image was not quite as I remembered it. I looked closer and saw subtle differences to the distinctive oval with its radiating rays. The central symbol was plumper so that it had become more of a circle. The harsh lines extending from Baila's mouth had

414

been softened, each with a slight curve and a subtly rounded tip. I rubbed the surface with my thumb, confirming that a central mark was a cipher embossed into the metal and not a scratch due to frequent handling. I looked up to see Bonash watching me. His small, humble smile was ruined by the pride showing is his eyes.

'You clever little man,' I smiled back.

Bear playfully shoved Nash's head. 'Carys is not the only one who can be devious.'

'The thought of all those coins, slowly siphoning the will from any who touched them.' He caught the token when I flipped it back to him and critically examined his work. 'It bothered me. I wanted to find a way to stop it.'

'We started stamping our own coins,' continued Elyos. 'When the runners went to search for ancient weapons, they would exchange the currency. Bringing the Baila coins back for repurposing before being returned into circulation.'

'Averill's likeness is remarkable,' commented Vallori, examining the coin he had been given. 'It is so similar to the original. Your crafter is talented.'

'It took a while,' Nash admitted. 'People rarely look closely at their coins and Baila's image is so stylised that we knew we could alter that without too much concern. But Averill and the stag were key. His official image is so familiar that any deviation would be noticed. Causing people to look more closely and we couldn't have that. Once we had completed the template, we made multiple casts so that forges all over Hilman are now stamping their own coins.'

'But how does having your own coins help with organising opposition to daemons?' queried Tawpin, taking back the conversation.

'The rune,' I said quietly, smiling at Bonash. 'Truth.'

Bear grinned at me, appreciating my understanding of Nash's cleverness, before answering Tawpin. 'It doesn't. Not directly. Baila's coins are used throughout Hilman to steal the threads of people's souls. They sap their will, making them compliant and obedient to the whims of the priests. With control over the narrative, they convince everyone that talk of daemons is just exaggeration and that Baila will protect any who are appropriately devout. Unless you have seen one of those monsters, it is easy to dismiss the danger and carry on with your life.'

Bonash nodded in agreement before adding, 'The changes to the imagery would be enough to interrupt the flow of energy to the priests, reducing their power of persuasion. But I wanted more than that. I wanted people to see the truth, so I added the sigil into the design and Bear empowered the casts to that some of its influence would be stamped into each coin.'

'Anyone handling our coins,' Bear concluded, 'will see past the priests' rhetoric and finally realise what is happening to our kingdom.'

'Our camps along the coast are growing in number to be a credible threat to the pirates,' continued Elyos. 'And they realise that we need to work together if we are to stand any chance of containing the daemons. A few people further west are acting to limit the prejudices and hate stirred up by Baila's faithful, and we're building networks of sanctuaries for those who are persecuted.'

'That's good work,' interrupted Keenan. 'And you have managed to make it down the coast right under the noses of those pirates. Can we expect more of you? We might not have daemons but we have horrors enough that we would not turn away extra hands.'

Elyos shook his head. 'We have achieved much but we are still relatively few. Averill remains dedicated to Baila and Lindvane's war. We have our own battles to fight. The best we can offer is to try and keep Hilman's armies occupied within their own kingdom and discourage Averill from joining Hayton against Faulknar.'

'But sailing down the coast is an option?' persisted Keenan. 'If we called, would your people answer?'

'It would not be easy.' Bear shook his head, echoing my protests from earlier. 'We may not face the daemons on the water but there are still the wraiths. Not to mention that Gallowgla has been pirating the waters of the Northern Sea for countless generations. Their ships are strong and manoeuvrable. If they attack as a combined force, I'm not sure anything could get through.'

'We were small and tried to sneak past,' Elyos agreed. 'And we would have not made it without its help. Yours, I assume?'

He looked expectantly at me, ignoring the warning glare from Bear. All eyes turned to me; Tawpin and Keenan looking confused, Bear and Bonash showing sympathy, Vallori merely waiting. Mace, however, was the one that captured my attention as he wore the same expression he had when I first saw him in Tawpin's study.

'What help?' he asked softly, in contrast to the tension contained within his body. 'What is he talking about?'

'It was magnificent,' Elyos resumed, unconcerned with Mace's suddenly dangerous mood. 'All red and purple and shiny. Like it was covered in countless gems and jewels and precious stones. Oh, its wings. Two of those pirates' ships placed end-to-end could comfortably fit beneath one of its wings. The downdraft alone was enough to raise a wave taller than their masts. It was the size of a mountain but as graceful as a hawk. And its fire.'

'Elyos!'

Bear's sharp tone was enough to halt Elyos's awestruck ramblings but the wonder at encountering a dragon remained in his eyes. An awkward silence permeated through the group and I kept my gaze lowered to the table.

'But it was magnificent,' he persisted.

'She,' I commented quietly. 'The dragon is a she.'

'He was right,' Mace growled.

'You have a dragon?' Keenan blustered. 'I thought the boy exaggerated. But you really have a dragon?'

I looked up at Tawpin, finding him watching me with a sad expression tightening his face. Keenan continued before I had a chance to explain.

'For the love of Mobis, girl. Why didn't you say? This changes everything. Hayton's army cannot stand against that.'

'No,' I refused gently.

'Precisely,' agreed Keenan, misunderstanding my comment. 'Not a chance. This cursed war will be over before we know it. Hah!' He slammed his fist onto the table in his excitement.

'No,' I repeated more firmly. 'Megin is not for you to use as a weapon.'

The Lord General looked at me as if I had slapped him. 'That's ridiculous. You're a Dragonslayer. Is that not what you do? Use your dragon to slay the enemy? Of course, it's a weapon. And a powerful one at that. We should have had this long before now.'

'She's a creature of the Gods. She fights for the Gods, not for us.'

I turned to Tawpin with the silent plea that he, at least, would understand. Which, of course, he did.

'This is it,' he said softly, as if only talking to me. 'This is why you didn't come back. Kade asked you for her, didn't he?'

'Kyllian asked for her,' I correctly weakly. 'Demanded, actually.'

'And you refused?' Keenan accused, suddenly realising the implications. 'You refused a command from your king. That was treason.'

'I am aware of that, Lord General.'

'She'll kill us all,' muttered Mace, and I was not entirely certain whether he referred to me or Megin. 'His Grace was right to build defences. She'll kill us all.'

I turned to Tawpin. 'What defences?'

'Kade came back talking about dragons and how one was going to destroy Liegeport.'

I closed my eyes against the memory of Kade's vision where he had seen Megin incinerate countless people within the royal port. He had been ashamed of his visions then, believing them to be a product of his brief time in Mobis's Hells. It seemed he now regarded them as prophesy and was convincing others of his fears.

'He's fortified Liegeport with tall towers and immense ballistae, capable of shooting arrows large enough to injure a dragon.'

Mace shook his head in slow arcs. 'I thought he had lost his mind. Thought he'd been enchanted by that Traveller sorceress. But he was right. He's been right all along.'

I addressed Tawpin again, believing him to be the only one who might understand. 'Do you see why I can't call her? She's not...' I struggled to explain myself. 'She's not of our time. She wasn't created to fight for or against the armies of man. She was created to fight daemons and that's where she needs to stay.'

'A cursed waste,' Keenan grumbled. 'Good people are dying and you refuse to use your dragon to stop all this madness.'

'I can't control her.'

'Can't or won't?'

I took a shaking breath. 'She's too powerful. Too wilful. I can't control what would happen.' I looked at Elyos, hoping he would understand the dangers hidden within the gifts of the Gods. 'She's too wild for any of us to predict the outcome of using her. I can't guarantee that she would see the difference between friend and enemy. Kade could be right. In asking her to defend Liegeport, she could end up destroying it.'

I would not place Megin in the path of Kade's arrows but did not feel anyone would listen to my concerns for her safety. She was a dragon. All they could see was how she could be the answer to all their problems. I looked at each of their faces when we fell into an uncomfortable silence. Bonash played with the coin that had offered so much hope before talk had turned to my dragon and overshadowed his masterful achievement. Bear watched the men of Faulknar and assessed those in the room as if already planning a hasty retreat. Mace stared at his tankard, recalculating all he had believed and wondering where his loyalties should now lie. Keenan glowered in frustration at the loss of such a decisive weapon and being unable to force me to reconsider. Vallori watched me to determine how I would react, when I had no idea how to proceed from here.

Finally, I turned to Tawpin who was also watching me closely, albeit without the caution of Vallori. A small smile sat comfortably on his lips and he gave me a wink when he caught my gaze. Despite his carefree nature, he had always understood the complexities of divided loyalties and the burdens of important decisions. He understood the competing passions that raged behind obligation and duty. And he understood people.

'I have had way too much to drink to talk about dragons,' he declared, although he showed no signs of intoxication. 'I will be shamed by childhood nightmares if we don't lift this discussion and I suggest that this is a subject to be reviewed at another time. I have been embarrassingly neglectful in welcoming our new friends and decree that we shall, henceforth, give them a traditional Kingsport reception.'

Tawpin raised his tankard in salute to Bear and Bonash, Elyos and Vallori, while Keenan complained about the foolishness of Kingsport's earl. The Lord General, however, joined in the toast and took a deep swallow of his ale, cautioning Mace not to let Faulknar's honour be disgraced until, finally, the big man also drained his drink. More drinks were called for and Tawpin wove an elaborate tale about the Blue Boar and how he single-handedly overthrew a pack of dockers who had commandeered the tavern. It was not how I remembered the event, but the story worked to dispel the sombre mood. Soon Tawpin and Elyos were trading ever more unlikely accounts of bravery and heroism within the confines of a tavern, prompting Vallori to question whether having the two of them in the same room was a wise idea.

The wine and ale flowed freely and was sufficiently effective in suppressing unwelcome thoughts of Megin and Kade. I embraced the fun instigated by Tawpin and mercilessly encouraged by Elyos. Even Mace finally succumbed to the inevitable when Bear challenged him to a competition of strength, resulting in frantic wagers being exchanged throughout the hall and ending with several items of broken furniture.

I smiled at Bonash talking at Keenan while the older man looked greatly confused. Nash had started gesticulating in an attempt to explain more clearly but the old soldier just blinked, seemingly having lost all thread of the conversation some time previously. A loud cheer rattled around the room and Tawpin stood on a table, raising the arm of Mace and declaring him the champion while Bear shouted that there had been cheating and unfair advantages. Elyos called for another bout, proclaiming that Bear would certainly win the next contest. More wagers were exchanged.

Vallori came to sit beside me where I perched on a table. He grinned at me, shaking his head at the noisy banter between Elyos and Tawpin while they goaded Mace and Bear.

'So, this is a normal welcome from the earls of Faulknar?' he asked, having to lean closer to be heard.

I smiled affectionately at my first and most treasured friend. 'Normal for Tawpin.'

The attack came the next morning. Perhaps it was in retaliation for the events of Sterret Sands. Maybe it would have happened anyway. Whatever the reason, the assault was big and it aimed to crush the defiance out of Kingsport.

I awoke to the sounds of shouting and running feet while the soft grey light of dawn was still lingering. My head pounded painfully from the excesses of the night before and I groaned at the unwelcome intrusion. I reluctantly rolled out of bed to determine what was causing all the commotion, barely making it halfway across the room before Vallori burst through the door.

'Get dressed,' he commanded. 'Gallowgla has attacked.'

He left as quickly as he had arrived and I lost little time in dressing for battle, checking twice that I had all my weapons before following him down the stairs and towards the main entrance. The reception hall was an ants' nest of activity, with orders being shouted while those leaving jostled with those arriving. I scanned the crowd for Vallori but found Tawpin instead and elbowed my way through to him. I waited while he gave instructions to guard the storehouses that contained the food so desperately needed to supply the town, and to ensure water-chains were organised to prevent the spread of fire. Having sent them running, he turned to me.

'The raiders have surrounded the town. Ships have come in the night and they have attacked on three fronts. The docks are burning and they are pushing into the town. They've also sent bands to the east and west, pushing through the camps. They've sent their ghosts.' He turned to address a scout who reported of a breach in the south wall, commanding that Pellin needed to send more soldiers to support that section before resuming his report to me. 'I've sent Keenan and Mace to the west. Vallori and your friends have gone east.'

I nodded and made to join them, taking only two paces before I stopped and turned back. 'Stay safe, street rat.'

'You too, Magpie.'

I gave a quick nod of agreement before rushing out to find Vallori. The town was a confusion of people running in all directions and several knocked into me in their haste to find safety. I pushed my way across the square where the soldiers trying to move towards the fighting were hindered by families trying to get away from it. I heard the sound of connecting steel and found my first fight within three streets of the main square. I emerged from the alley to find Vallori facing two raiders while one of Tawpin's soldiers faced another. My *pháirtí* had despatched one before I had gained half the distance, finishing the other as I joined him. We both turned to assist the Kingsport fighter but his opponent was already dead. He dipped his head in acknowledgement before running off to find more enemies.

'You could have waited for me,' I complained mildly.

'I was going to wait by the east gate but these had already broken through. I felt obliged to correct their rudeness.'

'Shall we go and find more to educate?'

Vallori dipped his head in a formal bow, extending his arm towards the street exit with an invite to search for more pirates. I accepted his invitation and we aimed for the town's walls, soon encountering the frustrations of fighting in an enclosed space. Our advance was hampered by the mass of people who were funnelled into the streets and alleyways, clogging any access to the gates. They surged against us as we pushed our way through, with those fleeing from the camps adding to those already there. Small clashes erupted periodically, with people taking their fear and frustration out on those closest to them, and the chaos allowed the raiders to merge with the crowd and enter the town.

We were still some distance from the eastern exit when a sudden tide of people swept towards us. The crush was dangerously fuelled with fear turning into terror, and any who stumbled were mindlessly trampled by those who followed.

'The gate will have fallen,' shouted Vallori, our progress slowing to virtually nothing. 'We will not be able to get out this way.'

'We should head for the docks,' I called back. 'We might be able to get out along the sea wall.'

We pushed across the flow of people, finding it only marginally easier than when trying to fight against it. The streets that led to the docks were less crowded than those that ran directly to the gates but they were still chaotic, with Vallori and I repeatedly separated. The clash of steel became a focal point and we increased our efforts to reach the pirates who had invaded the docks. Gradually, the proportion of townspeople within the mass shifted so that I saw more soldiers. Those not having escaped to the centre of the port now chose to hide in the hope that the invaders would not find them. My advance to the sea wall became tortuously slow and I engaged with pirate after pirate, a new one quickly replacing each one I cut down. I consistently moved towards Vallori to ensure we always remained in sight of each other while numerous small battles continued to separate us. The Gallowglass tried to push us back but we managed to slice and punch our way forward, becoming completely submerged in the fighting. Step by hard-won step, we crept closer to the seafront and the chance to escape the port to aid those fighting within the refugee camps.

We fought through to the half-moon walkway that opened onto the docks and the extent of the invasion became clear. I cursed loudly. Vallori finished his opponent with a thrust to the pirate's guts before turning to see what had provoked my comment, repeating my curse along with a few of his own.

'Seems we have found the ghosts.'

The space was designed to be a pleasant route taken for a stroll on a summer's evening while watching the seabirds dive in search of fish. Now, the proud statues on the merchant houses looked down in horror as Kingsport's soldiers tried to defend against the pirates swarming over the jetties. The ring of colliding swords echoed around the stone buildings, adding to the cries of those maimed and dying. The blackened skeletons of the port's ships, destroyed long before the current attack, stood in silent sorrow while Sluagh's green army marched amongst them and claimed their deathly sacrifice. Kingsport defences were overwhelmed by the combined assault of devastating numbers of Gallowglass raiders and the unstoppable wraiths.

Clenching my jaw, I waded into the battle with Vallori by my side. The restricted space and the mass of bodies forced me to concentrate on the direction in which I sent my fireballs, so I could accurately enflame the ghosts without harming Tawpin's fighters. My defence against the raiders who targeted me was compromised as a result and I reacted instinctively rather than strategically. Vallori covered any gaping deficits and, within our small section, we managed to stop the flood of pirates into the town. Our minor victory provoked the raiders to attack us with renewed force, increasing the numbers who opposed us while preventing any allies from reaching us.

Intense pain stabbed into my heart. My chest refused to move, clenched in spasm as an echoing agony sliced across my belly, my ankle and the back of my skull. My body felt crushed by the multiple assaults and I fought to remain standing while my mind frantically searched for the source of the injuries.

Vallori killed the pirate who sought to take advantage of my sudden incapacitation, then grabbed my collar and dragged me into the building behind us. He braced the door closed while I collapsed against a wall, coaxing my lungs to accept small volumes of smoke-filled air. Vallori crouched down in front of me.

'Where are you hurt?' he demanded, concern hardening his tone. 'Show me.'

We both searched for wounds that could debilitate me, dismissing the numerous superficial ones. The echoing discomforts were fading but the excruciating pain in my chest remained. I feared to look at my fist, protectively clenched over my heart, certain I would find a fatal amount of blood seeping through my fingers. I peeled my hand from my chest to find no sign of injury. I saw my confusion reflected in Vallori's expression.

A timber beam crashed through the ceiling and released a cloud of sparks when it landed less than five paces from where I was sitting. Hungry flames licked at the hole, seeking to devour the lower floor while the space filled with dark smoke. The acrid air brought fresh tears to my eyes and provoked painful coughing from my abused lungs.

'We can't stay here,' Vallori warned. 'Can you stand?'

I nodded and took his offered hand to help me rise. I had to resist the urge to curl around the pain despite knowing there was no physical wound, and I forced myself to follow Vallori. We emerged into a narrow alley that ran behind the smouldering building and joined a small battle that filled the constricted space. The Kingsport soldiers were outnumbered and badly needed our assistance, but I could offer little more than a distraction as each concussive blow I received threatened to darken my vision and rip open my chest.

Slowly the discomfort eased and I was able to attack more effectively. I carved and sliced and stabbed, occasionally releasing a fireball into any wraiths that entered the alleyway. Those we killed were endlessly replaced by more and we became trapped within a ring of hostile steel. Tawpin's fighters were systematically picked off until only three remained to stand by Vallori and me. We protected each other's backs, forming a circle that faced the enemy, but we were unable to effectively swing our long blades while the pirates were lethally efficient with their short-handled axes. I used my dagger to block a thrust from my opponent, committing to the follow-through and vulnerably exposing my side to a slice with his axe.

'Hold!'

The pirate obediently stepped back at the bellow and, seizing the unexpected advantage, I rotated my wrist to swing *Saorsa* around to slash at his neck. Vallori grabbed my arm as the command was roared again. I glared at him, momentarily redirecting the fury of my thwarted attack at him, but he just shook his head and refused to release his hold. He turned back to the head of the alley that opened onto the docks and, while I appreciated the chance to catch my breath, I did not trust the strange truce. And I disliked the rigidly contained calm suddenly adopted by my *pháirtí*.

A ripple of sideways movement flowed towards us and the owner of the deep, nasally accented voice became incrementally revealed. He was a tall man and brown hair could be seen above his fighters as he made his way through. Vallori's grip was painfully tight on my arm. I turned to see that his face had drained of all colour and his head trembled slightly with restrained rage. By the time the raiders parted in front of me and I could see the blue tattoos and the forked beard, I had recognised the pirate who stopped just beyond a sword's length from me.

'What have we found here?' he asked, grinning with evident pleasure. 'The Gods have truly delivered me a gift.'

I took a breath to answer the Gallowglass captain who had captured me and taken me to Freisholm, but Vallori addressed the man first.

'Bellator,' he spat the name like a curse.

The pirate laughed. 'Come now. No one has called me that for a very long time.'

'Bane is her name for you.'

He smiled indulgently. 'Ah Vallori. My valiant brother. You must learn to let go of these long-held grudges. They will cause you to lose your hair.'

He narrowed his strange, ice-pale eyes at Vallori's shaven head and the tattoos of mourning, and the brothers maintained a look that lasted several heartbeats. The intensity of their gaze made me feel uncomfortable, an intrusion on something intimately personal, and I gently released my arm from Vallori's grip. The small movement swung Bane's attention towards me and the mocking smile returned to split his beard.

'Little sparrow. You've learnt a few tricks since we met last, hey? I am not surprised the Gods have paired you two together.'

'Why are you here, Bane?' demanded Vallori, dragging his brother's attention away from me and back to him. 'I thought Liegeport would be more to your taste?'

Bane shrugged. 'I go where I am sent.'

'Always her plaything,' he scoffed, ignoring Bane's darkening expression. 'Is she here?'

'Of course.' He returned to stare at me. 'She was very excited a few days back. Just before the dry-lightning and the sea shuddered like a wet hound. The grandmother cackled so hard I thought she would crack in half.'

'And the wraiths are hers?' Vallori persisted.

Bane flicked him a glance but immediately returned to address me. 'My brother delights in declaring the obvious, little sparrow. You remember her monsters?'

'I remember raising the Fates,' I corrected.

'The monsters were a gift.'

'The Gods do not give gifts.'

A small smile danced over his lips. 'They do if you know how to please them.'

'Sluagh will not stay appeased for long,' Vallori interrupted, drawing an irritated look from his brother. 'Her price is not one you would wish to pay.'

'And what would you know, little brother? Your cowardice prevented you from embracing Sálaforn's tutelage and your embarrassment at such a public weakness caused you to run from your land and your people.'

Vallori had taken a step towards his provoking brother before realising what he had done. Bane smiled in triumph.

'She's bleeding you,' I stated softly, breaking their bitter exchange.

Bane was wearing a thick leather jerkin, oiled so heavily that it shone even in the weak light. He wore no shirt or tunic and his bare arms were exposed to reveal countless scars amongst the blue tattoos. Several were old reminders of past battles but many were more recent, and some showed the scabs and inflammation of fresh wounds.

He rolled a cold stare towards me. 'As she did with you.'

'I did not give willingly.'

The corner of his mouth twitched in a ghost of a smile. 'And that is why Sluagh's army does not dance for you.'

'This is wrong, Bane,' protested Vallori. 'Can't you see this is madness?'

The pirate captain tilted his head back to look at him. 'Says the man who would dance with a Dragonslayer. Do not be so quick to judge, brother. Your she-wolf plays with those forces you do not wish to understand. Can you claim that your path is better than mine?' Having subtly chastised his brother, he returned to me. 'You gave so little of your blood, the crone had to be creative. Turns out that a drop of your blood when added to a beaker of mine is sufficient to raise a horde of Taranis's daemons and an army of Sluagh's wraiths. You opened the door for her. I keep it open.'

I assessed his aura; the crone had been clever. His colouring remained healthy yet there were traces of her influence threaded throughout. She had controlled the amount she drained, ensuring he would not sicken and she could continue to milk him. Her calculated abuse sickened me. He may be my enemy but he had always been honest with me. And he was Vallori's brother.

'I don't want to kill you,' Vallori pleaded, provoking a mocking laugh.

'As if you could? You could never beat me when we were boys. And I am so much more now.'

Before Vallori had a chance to reply, a warning shout sounded from behind us and I turned to face the exit that led further into Kingsport. The

426

screeching cry of stressed metal was immediately followed by the frantic pushing within the group of raiders who had blocked our retreat. Unsure of which threat to address, I returned my attention to Bane who was, once again, sharing an intense look with his brother. I flicked back and forth between commotion behind me and the pirates in front, momentarily frozen with indecision. Bane's men were equally conflicted, nervously shifting while they considered whether to confront the new threat or continue to obey his command. Finally, Bane broke the uncertainty by bowing formally to Vallori.

'Until next time, little brother.' He called for the retreat, glowering when the raiders' responses were delayed by their confusion. 'You would think to question me? Me!'

Shamed into action the pirates withdrew, ignoring us in their haste to comply. Vallori and I turned to engage the remaining raiders who were trapped between us and the rampaging disorder scything through the alley. Relief and panic collided when I eventually realised the cause.

'Move!' I yelled at the three remaining Faulknar fighters. 'Get out of the way.'

I shoved the nearest one towards the far wall, cursing at the other two to follow while I pulled Vallori with me towards the opposing wall. The fire had taken hold of the storehouse and flames plucked at the smoke billowing from the destroyed roof. Vallori stared at me as if I had suddenly lost my wits, then his eyes widened in understanding. Elyos was barrelling through the raiders, causing devastation like one of the daemons we had fought together. He was lost in the uncompromising fury of his *miann cath* curse, ringed in a half-moon by his fighters who effectively guided him towards a target. One of his guard pulled a Kingsport fighter out of Elyos's way, simultaneously shielding the other two, while the others efficiently dealt with any raiders who managed to escape Elyos's wrath. The unstoppable force carved towards the docks and Vallori and I stared, stunned, at the trail of carnage they had left behind.

Vallori recovered before I did, shoving me forward to where Elyos had created a temporary respite at the head of the alley. We emerged to join the fighting that had continued without us. My senses were overwhelmed by the noise and stench of the slaughter, contained within the curved walkway which separated the storehouses and guildhalls from the jetties of the docks. Wraiths glided silently through the madness and I sent fireballs hissing into any I could see, carefully balancing my desire to incinerate the abominations whilst avoiding Tawpin's fighters. My flames added to the fires started by the raiders throughout the waterfront, and the billowing smoke heightened the chaos with the onshore wind blowing the acrid clouds further into the port. I had no attention to spare for managing that problem, so both raider and fighter were left to take whatever advantage they could within the confusion while I concentrated on those in front of me.

I swung *Saorsa* in wild circuits with enemies pressing in on all sides, hacking and ripping and gouging and severing. I tightened my grip on her hilt with hands covered in blood and tissue. I used a shield of air to divert a burning section of timber that fell towards a group of retreating soldiers, pushing it into the pursuing Gallowglass while I slashed across the neck of the pirate before me. I blinked blood from my lashes and blocked the strike from my right, pulling back to smash *Saorsa*'s hilt into the face on my left, then kicking out at the knee of the one aiming to stab Vallori in the back, while he battled two more. Again and again, I pierced and punched and carved and clubbed. I attacked each featureless obstacle caught within range of my blade, no longer considering them as individuals who had homes and families and ambitions. I cut into each one with no more concern than I would give to the log chopped into firewood. I thought of nothing except staying alive and protecting Vallori.

Step by viciously bought step, we advanced towards the docks. Sálaforn's spectral army had unexpectedly withdrawn to leave a more evenly matched contest between raider and defender. Both sides were exhausted and the port was littered with hazards that repeatedly caused fighters to slip and stumble. The frenzy of the earlier conflict slowed to a relentless toil as muscles cried out for energy and lungs screamed for air. In a battle of attrition, those defending their homes will often find the motivation to outlast those coming for bounty. The tide turned and we started pushing the pirates back towards their boats. The momentum grew until there was a clear line between the advancing soldiers and the retreating invaders. We smelt the victory, gaining confidence from the knowledge that it is difficult to fight an effective withdrawal. The pirates' disadvantage gave strength to our tired limbs and we pressed harder to seal the rout.

A shrill whistle cut through the air and rebounded against the damaged buildings. The pitch was raised until it became painful and effectively halted the fighting when everyone flinched. I scanned the waterfront in search of the whistler's location. The seawall curved around the harbour and several sets of stone steps led down to the jetties. Those closest to the wall were hidden from my view but where they extended further out, I could see the pirates' boats moored amongst the blackened hulls of Kingsport's destroyed fleet. A few had already departed and fled, full of raiders, to their awaiting ships and my gaze swept across the processions of pirates that still sought to escape. Piles of crates had been scattered along the causeways, protected by being sufficiently far upwind of the flames to avoid burning with the rest of the docks. One of these piles had been hastily arranged to form a platform, upon which stood a tall Gallowglass whose dark hair whipped around his face in the erratic breeze. He was too far away for me to clearly see his features but the sight of him tugged at a memory. I dismissed the distraction, more concerned with why he had halted the fighting and exposed himself to a hostile army. His voice carried when he addressed his confused audience.

'People of Kingsport,' he began.

The memory flared and I recalled Kade's arm being vindictively smashed by this pirate in Freisholm. I felt my lips pull back into a snarl and I pushed several soldiers out of my way to get closer to this hated bully. A fireball formed in my hand, causing more to jump out of my way.

'You have fought well this day,' Harke Calderson continued in a heavily mocking tone. 'I regret I must leave you now. But I leave you with a gift so you will remember me.'

His smile was stained with such malice that I thought my chest would burst from the desire to incinerate him. He looked down to the group of pirates who surrounded him and his smug smile rippled into one that oozed contempt. A broken fighter was manhandled within the crowd before being dragged onto the platform. The captive's back was towards me but the quality of his tunic suggested he was someone important, and that he was being paraded as a statement of power. I refused to consider who the victim was and would not acknowledge the colour of his bloodied hair. A shocked denial rippled through the Kingsport fighters when the man was turned to face us. The fireball evaporated, forgotten, and my soul turned to ice.

No. No. No. He's safely protected within the meeting hall.

Tawpin was held up by two raiders, no longer able to support himself. His broken hands grasped weakly at his belly, pitifully trying to protect the wound that, even as far away as I was, I could see was severe enough to expose guts. The dark material of his tunic hid any wounds to his chest and arm, but his face exposed the brutality of his capture. It seemed that every bone had been broken under skin stretched tight with bruising. One eye was hidden beneath swollen lids and the suggestion of a smashed cheekbone, the other drooped while blood flowed freely from a gash which split the eyebrow. Red stained his blond hair from the crown of his head to the wisps that stuck to his torn lips and misshapen jaw, both covered in the blood which seeped from a broken nose.

I inhaled a breath and felt the air, filled with innumerable shards of glass, stab into my chest. My mind closed down, unable to process what I was seeing. My body became disconnected and separate. All except the shearing lacerations gouged with every breath. I stood, unable to move, while the bastard grabbed Tawpin's hair and pulled his head up. Taw's mouth fell open in a silent gasp of agony, no longer having the strength to resist.

'Your leader,' he spat, 'could not even die with his sword like a true warrior. This is who you chose to lead you?'

He released Tawpin's head, which slumped back against his chest, and looked out across the ruins of the docks. He nodded his head slowly, approving of what he saw.

'Know this, people of Kingsport. I shall return. And when I do, I will finish you.' He drew his sword, twisting his wrist so the blade flashed. 'But first, I promised a gift. I shall rid you of your weak leader.'

The guards supporting Tawpin released him and took a step back. In the heartbeat it took for the Earl of Kingsport to fall, Harke slashed his blade to cut from the base of the ear to the opposite collar bone. Tawpin dropped to his knees and his head toppled forward to bounce against the platform. It rolled macabrely, finally resting an arm-length from its body.

There was a moment of stunned silence before an eruption of furious denial. If the pirate had thought to cower Tawpin's people, then he had gambled in error. Incensed by the horrific execution of their earl, his soldiers roared with rage and surged towards the retreating raiders. Alongside sword and dagger, anything that could be lifted was thrown and everything within reach was used as a club. The fighters descended into an impassioned mob and their retribution was stoked to new levels of viciousness. Any not already within the fleeing boats were trapped within the storm of violence that tore into the remaining pirates.

The massacre flowed around me. All I could see was Tawpin's defiled body, left discarded like a rancid fish. Somewhere rage and grief hammered against impenetrable walls but I felt nothing. Nothing existed except his wretchedly battered body. The image of the docks faded from my vision to leave me isolated in a silent world of muted colours.

I walked slowly towards what remained of Tawpin, stopping to kneel a short distance from him. I wrapped my arms around myself to resist the ridiculous urge to stick his head back onto his body, as if he was a broken toy which could be mended with a small twist of twine. I wanted to hold him but it felt grotesquely invasive when he had been so badly hurt. I wanted time to reverse and for Tawpin to be whole and healthy again. I refused to move, feeling it would confirm what had happened and signify some form of acceptance. I would not accept this.

I felt her appear behind my shoulder but it was some time before I could acknowledge her. The Goddess's calm presence grated against the desecration of Tawpin and I found it hard not to blame her for her lack of action.

'He did not deserve this,' I stated coldly.

'Do any?'

'He was never a part of this.'

'Perhaps.'

Her bland acknowledgment sparked an anger that was buried deep below the numbing haze. 'Fix him.'

'That is not for me to grant.'

The ember flickered, yearning to ignite. 'Then make him whole. I'll retrieve his soul myself if I must.'

I heard the soft rustle of her silk cloak when she shifted in response to my tone. 'Would you choose Villermir's path?'

'In a heartbeat if it would bring him back.'

She remained quiet, allowing me to consider the implications of my brash statement but I would not retract it.

'Bring him back,' I demanded. 'You owe me this.'

'Do not presume to value your obligations.' I turned at the rebuke and looked at a face as uncompromising as granite. 'That is not how this works.'

'Then make it so.'

She regarded me with glacial eyes. The ember spluttered and spat yet failed to kindle the anger I desperately wanted. I was too weary to fight for the passion I needed to confront her.

'I can't do this anymore,' I pleaded. 'The price is too high.'

Her expression softened and I was reminded of the many faces of the moon; the powerful warrior and the gentle nurturer, the relentless surge of the tides and the subtle fragrance of night-blooming flowers. The ember gave one last, small, flare and was extinguished. The Goddess clasped her long, pale fingers in front of her waist and tilted her head slightly.

'And yet it is yours to pay.'

I slumped back onto my heels and returned to mourn Tawpin, unwilling to accept her sympathy. I shook my head slowly.

'It's too much. You've taken too much.'

'And what, exactly, have I taken?'

Her warning tone had returned with its icy accusation but I no longer had the will to care. In the emptiness of all I had lost, I stabbed at an old hurt.

'You denied me my father.'

She huffed and I turned to see an un-Godlike toss of her head, rippling the white hair draped over her shoulders.

'That,' she dismissed casually. 'Would you have preferred to have known about his relationship with Villermir? Would you have been more open to Villermir's counsel? Would you have repeated the mistakes of your father?'

'You took away my choice,' I persisted weakly. 'You didn't need to take away my memories.'

'You are a Dragonslayer. You have a job to do. It is not your place to question how you are used to achieve that task.'

'So, you get to take everything from me? What's next? Liegeport? Drey? Kade?'

'And you bear no responsibility for these things? You would deny your culpability for the easy answer of blaming the Gods. You have the powers of the Favoured. You have gazed upon the faces of Goddesses. Do not think these things are given freely.'

'Then take them back.'

She became as still as a glacier, considering my petulant comment with frosty irritation and, despite her lack of overt expression, I felt her displeasure. Her clear eyes pierced into my soul and pinned my core with her dissecting scrutiny. The touch was subtle but all-encompassing and I knew I had gone too far. In my smothering grief, I had ignored the peril of challenging a God. I had rejected her will and refused the destiny she had claimed for me. I belatedly realised that she would not release me without consequence and if I considered obeisance to be too high a price, how much more would be required for my disobedience. What else did I have to lose. What was left that had not already been taken or tainted by her ambitions.

Vallori.

'No,' the Goddess stated, seeming to answer my panicked thought. 'I will not remove your powers. You are still my Warrior and you still have a task to complete. You do not get to refuse that.' She withdrew her probing review of my character. 'However, as you insist on denying her, I revoke your status as a Dragonslayer.'

The Lady withdrew and the chaos of the docks returned to batter my sensitised nerves and overwhelm my senses. I knelt beside Tawpin's abused body while the sea-breeze chilled my skin to pimple-flesh. *Saorsa* lay on the ground, having fallen from numbed fingers. Her ruby eyes were dulled with silent condemnation. None of it touched my awareness. I felt entombed within ice. An unimaginably deep void had swallowed my soul. The total, absolute *nothing* extended without end, sending violent tremors throughout my body. Megin was gone.

Chapter Twenty-Nine

The wind blew cold fingers beneath the warm cloak and I shivered, perched on the edge of the roof with my legs dangling over into clear air high above the town. The ruins of the docks were hidden by distance and the night, although the smell of ash still lingered in case anyone thought to forget. Soft noises drifted up from the meeting hall below me, punctuated by sudden laughter or drunken singing which would make me flinch. My eyes stared at nothing while I revisited the events of the day, again and again.

I had retreated to the rooftop when I could no longer tolerate being around others. I had provoked numerous fights with those I deemed insufficiently respectful at the loss of their earl, jesting and celebrating life while Tawpin's body was being prepared for his funeral rites. I had also caused several more arguments with those I deemed too conspicuously mournful. He was their earl but he was my friend. They had no right to their grief when mine remained chained and dormant. I could not bear the dignified sorrow of Leyn's pain and avoided her completely.

Bonash was another I avoided. After the intensity of the attack had faded, the cause of my strange debilitation had become wretchedly apparent. I had been told of the marks given to Moon Warriors so that we would always have a connection no matter how far we were separated, and I had been warned of the effects that the *gifts* would inflict upon the death of a Warrior. Bear had been defending the refugee camp to the east of the port. The fighting there had been savage, involving a large number of pirates and their wraiths. Most of those who had fled to Kingsport for protection had been slaughtered and countless souls had been recruited to Sálaforn's ghostly army. Half of the force that rode out to save them had also been taken. Bonash had been surrounded and was bleeding heavily from a wound carved into his shoulder. Bear would never have left him, and he had bullied his way to Nash's side in a desperate attempt to protect him against impossible odds. Nash had explained, white faced, how the big-hearted warrior was stabbed from behind, with the sword piercing his back to exit through the centre of his chest. Bear had bled out almost immediately. The raiders had laughed at the small man's grief, rejecting him as no longer being worth the effort it would take to kill him.

Keenan and Mace had ridden to the west and a similar scene had greeted them there, although the losses of both refugees and soldiers had been fewer. In each encounter, the raiders had unexpectedly withdrawn from the camps despite maintaining a clear advantage. The reports were consistent; Kingsport's fighters had been on the verge of collapse when the wraiths suddenly vanished, seeming to be a signal for the raiders to return to their boats. I could not shake the nagging suspicion that we were being played with, as a cat plays with a mouse, but failed to find a reason why they would choose not to destroy us when they had the opportunity.

And then there was the return of the pirate captain. Bane. Vallori's brother. I was unsure of what I felt about that. I rocked between his presence being a strange coincidence and random twist of fate, and the meddling of the Gods towards some unknown aim. Sálaforn's use of his blood to supplement mine did not bode well for my weak hope that the shamans would exhaust their supply and be denied the means to summon their daemons. I did not dare believe Bane's comment that I had opened the door so a simple blood sacrifice would now be enough to keep it open, maybe indefinitely. I found it unlikely that the sorceress would bleed such an important warrior when other, more mundane, supplies would suffice. I worried that it meant Bane's blood was somehow important or special. I feared for Vallori, should his blood hold the same potential.

The thought of my *pháirtí* seemed to summon him, and I turned towards the sound of his soft footsteps on the narrow walkway behind my perch. He hesitated for a few heartbeats before sitting beside me, careful to avoid hanging his legs over the roof's edge.

'You didn't need to come,' I offered as a small apology. 'I would have come down soon anyway.'

'I doubt that. You've been up here most of the night. And you are shivering. You should have come down long before now.'

I did not have to explain why I had escaped to the highest point in Kingsport or why I remained there long after most had retreated to their beds. Too many thoughts crowded my mind and I had always sought the peace that could be found above the noise of others. I shied away from the other reason why I was drawn to heights.

'At least you didn't run this time?'

It was said lightly and there was no accusation in his words, yet they still had the power to cut. 'No. No more running. Where would I go?'

He considered for a heartbeat. 'Well, the worst place you could go would be to Sálaforn and my arrogant brother, so probably there.'

A small smile tugged at the corners of my mouth. 'I'm not sure she would want me anymore.'

Vallori turned his head to look at me, my choice of words causing him to frown. 'What do you mean?'

I continued to stare into the anonymous night. I was not ready to share that particular wound so chose to stab at his instead. He had introduced the topic.

'Did you know your brother was here?'

'If Freisholm had come, it was possible he would be with them. But Bane has no allegiance to any except her and I had not thought she would come to Kingsport.'

'You were not surprised that I knew him. That he was the captain who took me to Freisholm.' I tried to keep the bitterness out of my voice and failed. 'Have you always known?'

'If Sálaforn wanted you, she would have sent him to fetch you.'

'So, you knew.'

Too many sorrows, all so much bigger than that one. I did not want to take my pain out on him. Not him. Not now. I continued in a softer tone.

'Why Bane? Why did she choose him? Was it simple convenience or was there something more?'

Vallori remained silent, looking out into the darkness while he considered his words. 'I have often wondered that. Our parents are simple farmers. We were not important. Both Bane and I could fight well enough, but so could everyone in Freisholm. As far as I could tell, there was nothing that marked us as different. From the beginning, I could tell I was only of interest to her because of my connection to Bane. We had been inseparable once. If she had me, she would have had him.' He flashed a brief smile. 'He was too wild to waste time on an old lady's stories but I was intrigued. Within the hard, mundane world of Freisholm, she shone like a beacon. Surrounded by ancient mysteries and arcane magick. She drew me in and Bane followed. But he was always her first choice, and she was relentless. Giving him gifts and flattery. What boy doesn't want to be told that he is better than the rest? What boy can resist the lure of power and destiny?'

'You.'

He shook his head. 'I was not her target. I'm not sure I could have resisted if she had turned her attention to me. As more than bait to snare him.'

'And Bane will give her whatever she wants. Including his blood to raise her monsters.' I tightened my grip on the ledge with fear tightening my chest. 'Will it be enough for her? Will she come for you?'

'I don't know how she is using my brother's blood, and I would not be so quick to believe what he says. It is a big claim to say that she is using his blood to summon the daemons. Sálaforn was using blood sacrifice long before she could summon daemons or wraiths or the Fates. Whatever she is using Bane for, I doubt it's good but it doesn't have to be connected with daemons.' He turned to challenge at me with a questioning look. 'As to whether she will come for me. I think I'm overshadowed by her desire for you. So, stop evading my question. Sálaforn would not *need* your blood if she was using Bane's as a substitute but you said she would not *want* you. Why wouldn't she want you? You are a Dragonslayer. She would not turn away that much power.'

I tried to distract him with weak humour. 'You know, you would be easier company if you weren't so cursed clever.'

He was not fooled. 'What happened at the docks? One moment you were by my side and the next you were at the far side of the jetty. Beside Tawpin. What did the Goddess want with you?'

He was far too clever. How could I explain that I had been so stupid and had thrown away our best chance of defeating Villermir and Sálaforn. He had named me true when he called me selfish.

'You're right. Sálaforn would never reject the power of a Dragonslayer. But I don't have that power anymore. It's like I've lost half of my body. I can't access it. I've tried but it's just not there. Not like it was. A Dragonslayer without a dragon is just another... what? Sorceress? Witch?'

'Moon Warrior?' he suggested loyally.

I thought of Bear. 'I'm not sure that will be enough. What am I if I'm not a Dragonslayer?'

'I don't understand. How can you stop being a Dragonslayer?'

'I demanded a boon from the Goddess.' I released a brief, self-mocking laugh. 'How did I think anything good would come of that? I demanded that she returned Tawpin to me. And for my arrogance, she took Megin.'

I could not look at him. I could not face the accusation, the disappointment, the betrayal. I gave enough of that to myself, I could not take it from him. Not now. I'd lost Tawpin and I felt so alone without Megin, I could not bear the thought of him abandoning me too. But I had no right to ask him to stay. I had left first. And I now understood the cost of that.

'I can't believe that the Goddess would be that—'

'What? Petty? You've not been paying attention to the legends. Megin's gone. There's nothing. A big, gaping hole of nothing. Even when I sent her away and refused contact, she was still there. Curled safely deep inside me. Even before I knew I was a Dragonslayer and she existed, there was always this feeling.' I pressed the heel of my hand into my chest as if, if I only pushed hard enough, I could feel her again. 'But now there's nothing. Just nothing.'

Vallori remained quiet. I listened to his breathing, trying to determine his emotions. Trying to predict his reaction.

'I don't understand how that is even possible,' he stated quietly. 'And I would never confess to knowing the ways of the Gods. But I find it hard to accept that they would leave Dragonslayers dormant for countless generations, only to deny you when the need is greatest. Maybe this is only a temporary reprimand.'

I wanted to believe him. With every fibre of my body I wanted to believe him, but the void that had opened on the Goddess's judgement was too real. To absolute. It was as if Megin no longer existed. As if the Goddess had refrained from killing me and had taken Megin instead.

The despair I had felt on being separated from her was nothing compared to the thought that Megin was dead. My mind shut down and a crushing weight constricted my chest. I could not breathe. My vision tilted and dark shadows crowded in at the corners. My ears rang with the thundering pulse of my heart, hammering against my ribs, trying to escape my chest. I tipped forward.

Vallori grabbed my cloak and dragged me away from the edge. I grasped his wrists painfully tight, fearing the connection was the only thing preventing me from toppling into the grasping pit of madness. I focused on the contact, trying to relax my throat and allow air into my rigid lungs. One small breath. Then another. Gradually the noise subsided and I heard my *pháirtí* repeat the familiar phrases; I was safe, he was with me. My panic slowly gave way to numbing shame.

'Are you back with me?' he asked.

I nodded, relaxing the pressure within my grip but still unable to release the hold on his wrists. I took a careful, deep breath, briefly closing my eyes with relief when the air moved freely.

'Sorry,' I began. 'I'm so sorry.'

'I think we are far beyond apologies by now.' He gave a flicker of a smile. 'But can we, please, get off this cursed ledge?'

The message came from the last person I had expected to contact me. Breya's network of informers was efficient, to have taken the news of my arrival at Kingsport and return with a summons within a few days. Her request to meet was not presented as urgent and Vallori tried to insist that I stayed for Tawpin's funeral rites, but I saw no reason to delay and gladly took the excuse to leave the grieving port.

The horses were keen to leave a town that still smelled of ash and death, and we let them have their heads to race around the edge of the ruined eastern refugee camp. We continued for some time until slowing to a walk along the once fertile land that was no longer farmed. Many of the fields had reclaimed the water now the rains had stopped, leaving a sucking, clay-rich mud which clung to the horses' legs and threatened to pull a shoe or strain a tendon. We turned inland, along roads that were still submerged in several sections. The level ground either side of the track shimmered like an immense mirror with the water reflecting the vast, pale blue sky. As with Hilman, Villermir's corruption could be seen in the long channels that disrupted the earth and the dark lines scored into the peaty turf. We rode past several deep craters that had been gouged into the ground, some of which had flooded to create muddy lakes. The energies within the land hummed with repair but much of what was done through the misuse of the Empathy Crystal would remain.

We travelled late into the evenings with the unspoken desire to cover the distance as quickly as we could. There were few people on the road to delay us, although those who were made for a sorrowful procession. We saw no signs of the raiders once we had moved off the coastal road and Hayton's army was still some way to the south, but the coming threat of war hung in the air and corroded the confidence of even those who had not had direct experience of the fighting. Talk of rumour and imminent doom was spreading like a plague and people had responded by moving their families to safer locations. All headed towards Liegeport, with the news of Kingsport's most recent attack already deterring people from claiming sanctuary there. Most carried few possessions and food was scarce. Vallori managed to find some mushrooms that continued to thrive in the damp conditions, and we shared what we had with those who were most in need. We intervened when those who were also hungry tried to take more than their due from those less able to defend their meagre stores. We travelled alone whenever we could and bypassed villages that refused entry to all outsiders, many of which had not escaped Villermir's attention. Mounds and crevasses scarred the farmland, extending to disrupt the primitive defences which had been erected to protect those inside the walls. The gaps had been hastily repaired to discourage those who came to petition for shelter, but they would not withstand the organised force of a hostile army.

After four days' travel, we finally turned off the main road leading to the royal port and onto the trail which led to the woods surrounding the woodcutter's cottage. And it seemed I still feared Breya's barbed tongue. Trefin responded to my tighter control on her reins by repeatedly tossing her head, noisily rattling the bit within her mouth. I tried to concentrate on my breathing, telling myself that I was being foolish, but my nervousness refused to settle and Trefin continued to react to every movement within the bracken and brambles.

'Why here?' asked Vallori. 'It seems an isolated place to hold council.'

'Breya has a distinctive sense of humour,' I replied caustically, dismissing Vallori's raised eyebrows with a quick shake of my head. 'This place has some significance. I spent time here.' I gave him a small smile. 'The first time I ran. No, the second time. First time was not a pleasurable experience but the second set the habit. I was content here.'

'Maybe she has chosen it to be neutral territory?' he offered, ducking to avoid a low branch which hung over the trail.

'I doubt that.'

We emerged from the tree cover and crested the small rise that overlooked the clearing in which the cottage nestled. The single-storey structure was showing signs of neglect and I wondered sadly if any had come here after I had left. The forest was encroaching towards the rear of the property, while long grass and the stems of tall wildflowers reached questing fingers up the walls. The cottage was well-built and, despite the evidence of disuse, had remained intact. Thin trails of smoke rose from the single chimney when we walked the horses down the small hill.

'I'll settle the horses and set up camp at the far end of the meadow,' Vallori said after we had dismounted.

'I'll not be long.'

'Perhaps. But we will not be leaving tonight. You will have as much time as you need.' I turned at the tone of his voice and found him grinning. 'You should wear this.'

He took my Moon Warrior cloak from the pack attached to Trefin's saddle and held it out to me. The rich, black material flowed open effortlessly to reveal the dark purple lining.

'I don't think—' I started to protest.

Vallori thrust it towards me in a gesture I could not deny. 'She may be a queen, but you are a Moon Warrior. She should show you the appropriate respect.'

I smiled at his generous suggestion, suspecting that Breya would be reluctant to show me respect regardless of what I wore, but appreciated that it could provide a different kind of armour, able to deflect a preconception as effectively as my leather jerkin would deflect a knife. With a heaviness caused by my complicated relationship with my Goddess, I graciously settled the cloak over my shoulders. I had not expected to find the level of peace it gave me and wondered again at the complex nature of The Lady's gifts.

I walked towards the cottage, confident that I was no longer the street rat Breya would be expecting and that I would no longer be intimidated by her. The door creaked open and I entered the single room. My boots sounded loud on the wooden floor, shattering the hushed quiet and destroying my short-lived resolve not to be intimidated. The hem of the cloak had swept a trail in the light dust covering the floor, but the room had been tidied. Fresh rushes had been placed around the single bed, the narrow table, and the two roughly cut chairs that I remembered from my stay all those years ago. The clean mattress and fresh linen that covered the timber frame, and a small, finely carved chest were new additions. The floor covering released a subtly pleasant aroma and I could detect no damp or mustiness. Dimmed light came in through the two small windows and from the flickering glow of a fire, above which water simmered gently.

I had taken less than two paces from the doorway before I was fiercely embraced by the reason for the cottage's cleanliness. Tarra had always been kind to me and evidently her feelings had not changed. The small, round woman hugged me tightly, smelling faintly of lavender, and maintained the hold longer than I was comfortable with. I gently removed her arms and she took a step back to appraise me.

'Tarra,' I greeted with genuine warmth. 'It's good to see you.'

The older woman gently patted my chest, with tears threatening to spill down her plump cheeks. 'It's been too long, Tallen. Too long.'

She sniffed noisily, dabbing at her eyes, and tapping me once more on the chest when she passed me on her way out of the cottage. I watched her go with an amused smile, waiting until she had closed the door before turning to address the remaining occupant of the room. Breya stood beside the hearth, partially hidden in the shadows. As always, I was more aware of her regal presence than her physical appearance, although her beauty had not diminished during the time since I had last seen her. I felt a flicker of annoyance that she still held such power over me, but gained some comfort from the knowledge that she did that to most people. She was easily the most beautiful person I had ever met. Her long, blonde hair fell gracefully over her shoulders. Her violet eyes were concealed within darkened sockets, but their shape effortlessly enhanced her pale complexion and the flawless perfection of her face. Her slender fingers rested against the stone of the mantle above the fire, its embers casting a flickering light over a golden gown which fit snugly over her narrow waist. Forcing myself to look beyond her carefully cultivated majesty, I saw that she was noticeably thinner than I remembered. To the point of being gaunt.

'The robes of The Lady suit you.' Her imperious tone forced my attention to her face and away from any frailties.

'Why have you summoned me, Breya?'

I heard the petulance in my voice and cringed at such an obvious display of intimidation. She chose to ignore my churlish tone and merely regarded me familiar contempt. The silk of her dress rustled softly when she shifted position slightly.

'I summoned you as your queen. It is time that you stopped playing at whatever it is you have been doing. It is time you honoured your obligations.'

'And what, exactly, would they be?'

'Not this.' She flicked her fingers dismissively at my cloak. 'A priestess? Drey will be so proud.'

'I don't believe you have brought me here just so you can play your games. So, what is it that you want from me?'

She declined to answer but continued to study me, considering me in the same way she would assess the merits of a recently purchased horse. The contempt in her eyes had gone, however, and the water was noisily boiling over the fire, so I obediently removed two, dust-free mugs and a small container of tea from the shelf. I poured the hot liquid and stirred the leaves until the fluid darkened. The calm routine of familiar actions made it easy to ignore Breya's scrutiny, and I breathed in the released aroma of feverfew while I agitated the leaves. I left the hot water on the stone hearth and carried the steaming mugs to the table, taking the chair facing Breya. I finally acknowledged her, sending her a challenging stare to accept the spare seat and the offered drink. She hesitated a moment longer, before sighing in defeat and joining me at the table. She glared a challenge of her own when she saw me frown at her hands, daring me to comment on their tremble when she grasped the mug.

'Things are different in Liegeport. It is not the place you remember.'

The mockery and arrogance had left her voice to leave one that contained more than a hint of tiredness. She wrapped her thin fingers around the cup but did not drink, her eyes losing focus to picture the town where we had grown into adults.

'People have lost their pride,' she continued. 'The streets are no longer safe during the day. No one walks at night unless heavily armed. People fight over what little there is, turning against friends and neighbours. Even family, on occasion. Strangers are treated with distain, readily stabbed for a crust of bread.'

'I heard,' I said gently. 'I saw some of it on the journey here.'

She looked up from the untouched tea. 'He is not the man he was. He has turned from his allies. His friends. He listens to bad counsel while refusing all others.' Her voice turned harder. 'He needs to remember his heritage and start acting like the ruler his people need him to be.'

'I understand but I don't see how that relates to me. You are his wife. You made sure of that,' I added bitterly. 'If he will not listen to you, what chance do you think I have?'

'Do you think I would be here if I had any other option,' she snapped back. 'I do not make a habit of begging. Especially from you.'

Deep resentments rose effortlessly to the surface in response to her provocative barb. 'You've found yourself in quite the mess, haven't you? Needing to ask for my help in giving counsel to Kade when it was you who first turned him against me. How bitter is that drink tasting now?'

'You would have turned him into the court jester. Encouraging him to be bard. A wastrel.'

'He would have been happy.'

She gave a sharp laugh. 'Happy? You think *you* would have made him happy? Since he came back from your last little quest, he trusts no one. Is suspicious of everyone. He sees plots and schemes in every conversation.' She narrowed her eyes in blatant accusation. 'What did you do to make him condemn you as a traitor?'

I took a deep breath, forcing my fingers to spread out over the table and prevent them from balling into fists. These were old wounds that would not be healed cleanly. There was no benefit to scratching at these scars.

'And that's the point,' I continued in a quieter tone. 'He will not listen to me.'

The fight had drained from Breya as well, leaving her subdued and unexpectedly vulnerable. It was an uncomfortable image in a woman I had never thought to see such a weakness.

'You must make him listen. I can think of no one else who could get through to him.'

'I hear he listens to Erula.' I prodded carefully.

Faulknar's queen was too proud to hiss but I saw the cost of her restraint. 'That poisoned witch. She feeds him lies and condemns any who would oppose her. She's isolated him from any who would talk sense, leaving him with no counter to her narrative. She shows him treachery in every comment. Every gesture.'

'But why would he believe her over you? Or Keenan? Any of his advisors?'

She raised a finely arched eyebrow. 'I believe spell-craft would be more suited to your talents.'

'You think she has enchanted him?'

I did not remember Erula as having any particular abilities and had not sensed any power within her, but I had not been looking. I had believed her to be the friend she had claimed to be. Perhaps she had ensnared Kade as easily as she had fooled me.

'I know that since she has been at his side, his mood has grown increasingly erratic. His temper is quicker to provoke. His rages are more spiteful. He spends prolonged periods behind closed doors, morose and sullen, where even I cannot gain access.' She hesitated. 'He frequently talks to people who are not there.'

A memory flared of a drugged vision where I had seen him pacing his chamber, talking to evil spirits. 'Who?' I asked quietly. 'Who does he speak to?'

'What does it matter?' Breya snapped back. 'The man no longer has control of his wits. If they did not fear his temper so much, they would mock him as a fool. What importance is there in the names of the ghosts he confesses to?'

'You are probably right,' I conceded, but I could not dismiss the suspicion that Erula's hold went further than bad counsel and that she was somehow the cause of his torments.

'He talks to you.'

'I'm sure he does,' I replied flippantly, still distracted by thoughts of Erula and missing Breya's change of tone. 'I'm sure he curses me to every one of Mobis's Hells.'

'No,' she denied softly, causing me to look at her when I finally caught the shift. She gave me a flicker of a smile. 'Well, yes. But that's not what I mean. When he's not raging, he talks to you. It is why it has to be you. Much as I truly hate to admit it, it has always been you. I'm staking my kingdom on my belief that he will listen to you.'

Tarra came soon after, claiming that the queen needed her rest and shooing me out of the cottage. Breya gave the expected display of annoyance at her attendant's fussing, but I could tell it was superficial and I was reminded of how tired and weak she appeared. I was hustled out of the room before I had the chance to assess her aura, vowing to check at the next opportunity, and left the women to their mild bickering. I retreated to Vallori's camp where he was boiling water, declining the offer of a drink while I continued to fret over Breya's condition.

'What did she want?' he prompted after a prolonged silence.

I shrugged. 'Same as Keenan. She thinks I can talk some sense into him.'

'And you still don't believe that you can?'

I thought of the happy Kade, *my* Kade, singing in a tavern and playing with his audience as delicately as he played his lute. I remembered how he had taught me to trust. And to love. How we had shared everything and readily confided our secrets. The memories moved seamlessly into how it had all soured, ending in betrayal and hurtful accusations. If he was as angry as they were claiming, I knew that temper would be aimed at me without censor.

'He will not welcome me back.'

Vallori shrugged. 'Since when have you taken the easy path?'

I dipped my head in acknowledgement, content to leave that decision for another time. 'Perhaps. But for now, I'm more concerned about Breya.'

'I thought you didn't like her,' he teased.

'Confounded woman won't even let me hate her in peace. She's trying to hide it but I know something eats away at her.'

'Do you think it's unnatural? Tarra mentioned that she has recently born a child and the birthing was not easy.'

'And Leyn mentioned that this was not the first complication. You are probably right and she is just exhausted. I'll do a full assessment when Tarra lets me back in.'

We spent the rest of the afternoon hunting although we were unsuccessful. The needs of hungry people had reduced the available game and what remained was extremely cautious. We settled for an evening meal of dry biscuits and foraged nuts, frequently looking towards the cottage.

I awoke the next morning to the dawn call of the forest's birds and the unexpected smell of cooking eggs. I sat up to find Vallori agitating the congealing meal, with several cracked quails' eggshells scattered around him.

'By the Gods, where did you find those?' I asked, my stomach rumbling in anticipation.

He grinned smugly and refused to share his secrets, passing me a bowl of warm, fluffy eggs instead. I ate quickly, appreciating the fact that I had a spirit-badger for a companion and would never lack food. I followed the meal with a steaming mug of tea, sweetened with honey from our supplies, while I waited for signs that those in the cottage were awake. I had almost finished when Tarra emerged, placing a bundle of linen to the side of the door and crossing the meadow to join us. The usually cheerful woman appeared weary and gave only a sad flicker of a smile as a greeting. Vallori handed her a bowl of eggs, which she immediately passed to me.

'Take this to her,' she requested. 'Make sure she eats.'

'Are you all right?' I accepted the bowl and helped Tarra settle by the fire.

'I'm fine,' she dismissed with a flap of her hand, while convincing no one. 'Just don't overly tire her, please. I know how it is between you two. And she will pretend she is stronger than she is.'

'What is wrong with her?' I prompted, ignoring the warning look from Vallori. 'Why is she so frail?'

She looked at me sadly. 'That's not my place to say. Just call if I'm needed.'

I shared a look with Vallori before I left, hoping he would be able to obtain more information while I was with Breya. The air felt cool when I entered the cottage. The windows had been opened to catch the morning breeze, but its freshness could not quite displace the faint odour of sickness. Breya sat at the table in an elegant rose gown, with her hands resting on the table's top to expose the bones of her wrists where they extended beyond the sleeves. The light from the windows harshly defined her protruding cheek bones and the sharp angle of her jaw. I assessed her aura to find the reds and oranges of her health and vitality had dulled to a muddy amber. My concern at seeing the disturbing shades of her aura must have shown on my face and she straightened, using her tongue as a familiar weapon to deflect my pity.

'Shed your robes already,' she declared. 'Old habits of being a street rat are hard to shake, I see.'

'The clothes do not always reflect the manner of a person,' I replied defensively. 'The most expensive gowns can cover a frozen heart.'

Her lilac eyes flashed dangerously and, heeding Tarra's warning, I chose to defuse the tension by placing the eggs in front of her.

'Tarra says you should eat these.'

I pushed the bowl a little closer to her and took the seat opposite. Breya tugged at the cuffs of her sleeves, which refused to cover her pale wrists, and stared at the food while making no move to eat.

'Breya,' I prompted. 'Are you going to tell me what is happening here? Why is Tarra so worried?'

Faulknar's queen pushed the bowl away in annoyance. 'Tarra is always worried. That's her job.'

'No,' I persisted. 'Tarra fusses and frets. This is different. And your aura—'

Breya stopped me with a frosty stare. 'Complications following childbirth are not uncommon. That meddling woman would have me confined to my bed. I do not have the patience for that.'

'Let me heal you.'

'You will do no such thing,' she snapped, before softening when I maintained her gaze. 'This is not the first time. After Kennet, the births were increasingly difficult. Each one causing a little more damage. Kallie was so small and delicate but I was warned not to have any more. What is a queen, if not to provide heirs?' She looked down at her hands, seeming to forget I was listening when she became lost in her sorrow. 'I lost two before Keevan. Oh, he tore into the world. He would have made a fine prince. But he lasted only a few days before he was found, dead in his crib. I did not believe I would carry another, but here we are. Koburn is sickly. I do not expect him to live much longer. My body is unable to provide milk for him and he refuses to suckle on his nurse.'

She drifted into silence, folding her hands to mask their tremor. I felt I was intruding into her grief and diverted my eyes to look around the cottage. The bed sheets had been freshly changed and there appeared to be fewer rushes covering the floor. I suspected that Breya had gained little rest overnight and I worried again about her physical health, which would not have benefitted from her journey from Liegeport.

'At least he will have Kennet and Kallie,' she said suddenly, causing me to startle.

'Kade?'

The ice returned to her stare. 'I know what you think. What everyone thinks. But I was never unfaithful to him.' Her expression softened again. 'I never hated him that much. He would not have understood. He understands loyalty and duty.' She raised an elegant eyebrow at me. 'And love. He never understood ambition.'

We slipped into an uncomfortable silence, each remembering Kade as a younger man where his passion for the future burned brightly. That was until his brother had died and his future had shrunk to that of a King-in-Waiting. A privilege he never wanted. I took a deep breath, knowing that such thoughts would achieve nothing.

'Why did you come here, Breya?' My question prompted the return of her distain. 'Surely you would have been better staying with your children.'

She tossed her head in irritation, causing ripples to cascade down her golden hair. 'That would be nice. Kade's paranoia runs deep. He claims I am poisoning his children against him. Me? The poor creatures are terrified of him and his anger. I rarely get to see them and when I do, it is always in the presence of her.'

She spat venom into the last word and I despaired anew at the madness that had made Kade unrecognisable from the man I knew.

'But in your condition—'

She cut me off again with a glare that challenged me to discuss her *condition* further. 'This is family business. There was no one else.'

'And Drey does nothing?'

'Drey is powerless to intercede. Kade mistrusts me but he is openly hostile to the old druid. He is convinced Drey is plotting to kill him and has banished him from court.'

'Erula?'

'Undoubtedly. Kade refrains from accusing Drey directly but the witch spreads lies and gossip to discredit him at every opportunity. She would have him burnt like the heretics in Lindvane if she could. Kade continues to refuse her, but I suspect it is more in fear of the druid's power than due to any loyalty he may have once had.'

'How did it all get so bad?'

She gave no respite. 'I believe that was you. He has had night-terrors since you came back without the Empathy Crystal. He's been preparing for a war against a dragon since he came back from the Northlands. A dragon! Each time he has left with you, he has come back worse. What is it you do that drives him into such madness?'

I could not deny her judgements but spat back nevertheless. 'And yet you call on me. To do what? Save him?'

'Believe me, I would not be here if I had any other choice. You caused this. Fix it!'

She went to stand but swayed violently and collapsed back into the chair. Her skin had faded to a deathly shade of grey and her breathing was more rapid than it should have been. I rushed to her side but she flapped me away, unable to draw the breath needed to dismiss me.

'Let me heal you,' I pleaded, preparing to connect to her aura.

'Don't...' she rasped. 'Don't... touch... me.'

'Breya, please.'

'Leave.'

'I am not leaving you like this.'

She continued to glare at me and I knew my presence was causing her more distress. Growling in frustration, I hurried over to the door and shouted for Tarra. The older woman came running with Vallori and cried in distress when she saw the condition of her charge, scolding me for not having called for her sooner.

'She won't let me heal her,' I tried to explain.

'You should leave,' Tarra demanded.

'I can help. Let me help.'

'Make her... leave,' Breya gasped, causing Tarra to fuss over her with impotent concern while she repeated her command for me to go.

Vallori grasped my arm, shaking his head at my silent plea. 'It is not what she wants. We should go.'

Reluctantly, I let Vallori lead me from the cottage and Tarra gently guided Breya to the bed.

CHAPTER THIRTY

I never tired of looking at the beauty of the hourglass lake that rested in the shadow of Cloud Mountain. The ancient trees hugging the shores rose above an early mist that still lingered to cover the bracken and grasses, making the lake appear to be cushioned by the cloud which permanently wrapped around the base of the mountain. The moon was still visible, complimenting the weak sun at my back where I sat on the narrow gravel track. I let the timeless tranquillity seep into me and clear all other thoughts from my mind. The craggy mountain was said to have been there since the time of the Ancients and I did not doubt that the lake had partnered it during all that time. I felt small and transient in the presence of all that history.

I was chilled by the cool dawn air and huddled further into my priestess's black cloak when Vallori's footsteps recalled me back to the present. He stood at my shoulder for a while, waiting for me to acknowledge him, before sinking to sit beside me.

'We should leave,' he prompted softly.

'I know,' I replied, despite showing no sign that I was ready to depart.

We sat for a while longer and each silently considered the events that had driven me to my solitude. Breya had died when the dusk had deepened into night. She had not stopped bleeding since the birth of her son four days before and the short journey to the cottage had taken the last of her strength. I had raged at Tarra, demanding to know why I had not been called. In my frustration, I had spitefully accused her of denying me the opportunity to heal the queen. She had tried to explain that it was not want Breya had wanted but I could not hear her as I mourned another death I was unable to prevent. It took Vallori's flare of temper to shame me into realising that I

451

was being hurtfully unfair, and I had retreated to the lake to avoid upsetting Tarra further. If I was being honest, I left because I could not bear to witness her grief so soon after Tawpin.

'It is known as Cloud Mountain,' I said eventually. 'But the old name for it is *Arach Beinn*.'

Vallori turned his head to look at me. 'Dragon Peak? That cannot be a coincidence.'

'Legend claims that a dragon is buried deep within it.'

'Perhaps that is why you are drawn to this place?'

'Perhaps.'

There were other reasons but many of those reminded me of Kade and I was unwilling to address those just yet, wanting to retain the calm I had gained from my vigil. My small measure of peace evaporated, however, when Vallori returned to the reason why he had joined me at the water's edge.

'You don't have to come,' he offered. 'We could return to Kingsport.'

I had no more desire to return to the pain waiting at Kingsport than I did for that waiting at Liegeport, but I had made my decision during the night.

'No. I'll go with you to Liegeport.' I talked to the water while he remained quietly watching me. 'Despite seeming to disappoint you with every step I take, I still don't fully trust myself when I'm not around you. I feel like I'm spinning and just a breath away from losing control. The only fixed point I have to focus on is you and without you, I fear it will all unravel.' I turned to give him an apologetic smile. 'I need you to be my guide. My conscience, I suppose.'

He nodded seriously with a slight frown of concentration. 'You mean, you need me to be your *pháirtí*?'

I scowled at his smug grin. 'You can be such a horse's arse at times. And for that, you do not get to escape your responsibilities as my *pháirtí* just yet. I'm in no hurry to return to Faulknar's capital but the Gods seem to be pushing me in that direction. You will never let Tarra bear Breya on her own and I need to be by your side, so we go to Liegeport.'

Vallori gave a brief nod of acceptance, offering a small smile of approval.

'Of course, all scenarios suggest that when I do finally meet Kade, he will either kill me in an eruption of rage or publicly execute me as a traitor.'

'I will not let that happen.'

I shrugged. 'With your hair, you'll be too busy stopping him from killing you as a pirate.'

The journey back to Liegeport took most of the day. Tarra had performed the initial death rites, having expected Breya's decline and brought the required herbs and oils with her. Once tenderly bound in her funeral shroud, she was lifted to sit cradled before Vallori on his mare; neither he nor Tarra would see Faulknar's queen returned home bundled over her horse like a sack of oats. I closed and secured the cottage before taking a position some distance behind them. Tarra frequently checked on Vallori's hold, still unable to relinquish the care she had given since Breya was a child.

The land surrounding the royal port was depressingly familiar, with Villermir's disrupted landscape acting as a background to the human toll of displaced families. The road became crowded with refugees long before the town was visible. News of the approaching Lindvane and Baila armies circulated freely with people exchanging their reasons for seeking the safety of the king's port. Most came from the central areas of the kingdom and had accepted the unknown perils of pirates over the known horrors of an invading force. People had fled long before any hostile soldiers had arrived, carrying their possessions in wagons or handcarts or packs on their backs, and their leaving allowed the march of the enemy to continue unimpeded. There was seldom talk of the defending fighters, suggesting little faith in Faulknar's outnumbered and overmatched army. Vallori and I shared frequent glances on hearing the demotivating gossip that confirmed our concerns. The final stand would be at Liegeport and, if we failed there, there would be no recovery.

The sun had sunk low by the time we crested the small rise west of the town and I looked upon Liegeport again after so many years. I pulled sharply on Trefin's reins, causing her to toss her head when I forced her to stop. The port had changed so much that I needed a moment to process it all. The tall spire of Baila's temple could still be seen, defiantly claiming its importance and maintaining its imposing presence, but its ability to dominate was greatly reduced by the extra layers added to the town's walls which now concealed most of the buildings from outside view. The barrier was tall and thick, and I could see soldiers patrolling the walkways which ran behind the sharp points of the timber posts. The distance had reduced the guards to the size of toys but I did not doubt they would be heavily armed and ready to answer any threat. Numerous dark shadows throughout the walls suggested holes where archers could deter any who came too close.

The training camps that had housed Kyllian's conscripts during the initial escalation of the war, and had been so shocking to me on my previous return to Liegeport, were lost under an ocean of temporary structures used to accommodate the endless tide of refugees. Timber shacks were scattered amongst canvas shelters, suggesting the camps had been occupied for some time. I suspected there would be equally chaotic scenes within the town where people sought the safety provided by the walls. The healer inside me despaired at the knowledge that such densely packed spaces would allow disease to flourish and spread freely throughout the camps. Many of those aiming to avoid death by escaping the invading armies would succumb to gut-rot and red fever long before the enemy arrived.

All of these changes failed to provoke the dread that clenched my belly and crept up to choke the back of my throat. Enormous towers soared above the high defensive walls, placed at each corner to ensure every aspect was covered. The platforms contained no roof so they could provide a lethal defence against an airborne attack. The solid weapons looked dreadfully large even at so far a distance, their size would be horrifying when standing next to them. The thick cords had been pulled tight and the iron points on the hateful, thick arrows glinted in the light of the setting sun. The weapons were notched and ready for my dragon, and I was certain they would remain permanently waiting.

We made slow progress toward the town gates. Any advantage we gained from being mounted was swallowed by the press of people trying to get into the overcrowded port, frustrating our efforts so that the sun had set before we reached the wall. Angry complaints flowed around us, often aimed in our direction, and the intensity of those increased when we approached the guards. Despite the persistent crush to force us into a single line of travel, we maintained the position of riding alongside each other so that the increasingly agitated Tarra was protected between us. The presence of a shrouded body did nothing to ease our passage with people too concerned with their own needs to spare any sympathy for those already dead.

'Halt,' called one of the many soldiers guarding the entrance to the town. 'No one is getting in tonight. Go seek what shelter you can find. Gates will be closed until dawn tomorrow.'

He resumed pushing the refugees back from the gates so he could make his retreat while another flicked his gaze up at our horses' approach. He opened his mouth to repeat the instructions of the first guard, but stopped when he saw me. His eyes went wide in recognition and his hand moved to free his sword. Alerted by his actions, all turned towards us and we were quickly surrounded by a barrier of pointed steel. Those seeking entry wisely decided to abandon their attempts.

Tarra cautiously nudged her horse a half-length in front of Vallori and me, hoping recognition of her would defuse the hostility. 'Please. Let us pass. The king needs to know of his queen.'

A ripple of uncertainty travelled through the guard. They would have been informed of Breya's departure with Tarra two days previously and would have realised who was cocooned within the shroud held protectively by Vallori.

'The king will want to know of our arrival,' he prompted quietly.

The guard who had initially called the closing of the gates stood straighter having made his decision. He informed us that we would be allowed inside the town's defences but Vallori and I would go no further until the king's captain had been called. Despite the occasional muttering that called me a traitor, the guards were professional and efficient. We were quickly hustled through the gates, instructed to dismount and our horses were taken. Tarra gave us an apologetic look when she left us restrained behind many blades, but her primary concern was never in doubt and she followed her queen. I felt Vallori relax beside me, free to face the threat of a hostile welcome without the burden of protecting Breya's body.

I waited impatiently, trying not to provoke those who openly condemned me with their stares. Our weapons had not been requested and I suspected this was to prevent triggering a violent refusal from two obviously well-trained fighters. Sheer numbers would ensure we would be swiftly subdued but the cost would be high and one I doubted they would be willing to pay. I gained some degree of calm by having *Saorsa's* weight at my hip, despite having been denied her song since the Goddess's rejection and the loss of Megin. I feared that my blade would also reject me but I continued to handle her safely and without the bite she normally gave to those who touched without consent. I folded my arms to resist the temptation to rest a hand on her hilt, understanding the action was unlikely to be viewed favourably by those who watched with nervous eyes.

Eventually, a tall soldier wearing Kade's lightning strike crest strode angrily towards us. I was relieved to see it was Hagan, and trusted Keenan and Mace's assessment that he would not kill us where we stood. He glared at me in obvious irritation while I aimed to look suitably apologetic. It seemed adequate and he swiftly dismissed me to address Vallori.

'Pirate?' he demanded.

I had the foolish urge to remind Vallori that I had predicted he would prove the greater risk at being perceived as a raider, but his rigidly calm expression quickly deflated my dark humour.

'I am no threat to you,' he replied carefully.

'That remains to be seen.' Hagan assessed him a moment longer before sighing in tired resignation. 'Come on, then. Let's get this over with.'

Kade's captain guided us through a disorganised town that was as crowded and pitiful as the camp surrounding it. The clean streets and colourful markets had disappeared under the squalor of too many people crammed into too small a space. An inadequate number of sour-smelling torches fitfully illuminated the streets, leaving the alleys to skulk in menacing darkness. Having welcomed the anonymity of night for most of my life, I now found it unsettling and my hands stayed close to the hilts of my weapons.

Overlying the changes in the town where those of the people within it. I had expected to see the constant presence of soldiers but many did not bear the crest of Kade or Faulknar. Mercenaries walked the streets of the royal port with disturbing authority, needing only a glare to send people scurrying out of their way. I understood why our weapons had not been confiscated, with everyone carrying a blade and freely using them to threaten. Tempers were short and multiple confrontations erupted around us while Hagan strode without pause. The arrogance of the mercenaries and, more depressingly, Faulknar's soldiers clashed with the fear and frustration of the townspeople so that pushing and shoving frequently turned into slapping and punching. Unable to challenge the trained fighters, people turned on those around them to provide a vent for their anger. Small acts of violence fluttered throughout the town, targeting anyone marked as different because of their clothing or their accent. As always in times of stress, the weakest got bullied by those with more power. It was a situation I had seen too often, but the realisation that the atmosphere in the heart of my kingdom reflected that seen in Hilman still stabbed sharply. It was a long way from the relaxed, easy welcome I had experienced at Kingsport.

We turned the corner and the royal house stood before me. Light blazed from every window to garishly proclaim the status of the king to those unable to afford even the cheapest tallow candles. It was shockingly insensitive and did not bode well for my encounter with Kade. The pair of white stone lions stood in proud defiance of the decline they witnessed, alongside the two sets of soldiers guarding the entrance. The sentries closest to the door stiffened at our approach but did not comment when Hagan marched us past without acknowledging them.

The house was surprisingly quiet, with only a few household staff drifting through the reception hall. Their attention remained firmly fixed on the floor and Hagan did not address them. He led us directly to the large meeting room at the rear of the house where two more soldiers flanked the heavy oak door, each wearing Kade's personal crest and holding a ceremonial spear. They showed no surprise when Hagan stepped aside so I could approach alone, but sliced down their weapons with frightening speed when Vallori made to follow me. We both froze with the lethally sharp blades crossed less than a finger-length in front of his chest.

'Not you. Just her.'

Vallori glared his annoyance at the guards, receiving paired expressions of casual disregard in return. Hagan rolled his eyes before carelessly clapping Vallori on his shoulder, causing my *pháirtí* to flinch.

'Come with me,' Kade's captain instructed tiredly. 'We have much to discuss.'

Vallori made no move to leave, but Hagan had the muscle of an experienced fighter and had no trouble in pushing him back along the corridor. I gave a small smile to see Vallori herded like a recalcitrant child, then turned back to the imposing door. I hesitated while the guards withdrew their spears and resumed their positions, taking a steadying breath before throwing it open.

The room was blindingly bright with an excessive use of candles, lamps, torches and braziers adding to the light of the well-fuelled fire. It was uncomfortably hot and the air was heavy with cloying scent and smoke. Thick tapestries and a large rug trapped both the heat and the smell so that, while the room was meant to give an impression of wealth, it became one of grotesque over-indulgence.

I evaluated the people within the room. Another two soldiers stood behind me where I had entered the chamber, wearing the king's personal crest and carrying ceremonial spears to match those outside. Two more flanked the exit at the far end of the room. None of them acknowledged me, maintaining an alert posture which focused on nothing but was aware of everything. Grateful for my weapons should I have need of them, I dismissed the guards as I had the ostentatious display of power.

The danger was in front of me and they remained silent while I concluded my assessment. Despite the oppressive heat, Kade was dressed in a thick, black tunic over brushed leather, black trousers. The bones of his cheeks and wrists were prominent and angular. Stubble covered the lower half of a face that looked tired and pale. His hair was longer than I remembered and was contained behind the beautifully engraved, silver circlet that proclaimed him as king. His brown eyes had lost their warmth and stared blankly at me while he sat with one leg thrown carelessly over the arm of his throne.

Erula stood beside him and had one hand resting possessively on his shoulder. She was dressed in a long, black gown threaded with strands of silver. Her dark hair was arranged in plaits that curled around her head and down her back. She also wore a silver band around her forehead, although hers was purely decorative and lacked the royal status claimed by Kade's. She regarded me with undisguised contempt.

'You should not have returned.'

I chose to address Kade, ignoring her and her comment, which provoked an irritated pinch to her mouth. 'I came to return your queen. She passed to the Halls last night, in case you were interested.'

He gave no flicker of emotion. No acknowledgement. No surprise. No grief. He just sat, silently watching me. I felt my anger glow at his dispassionate apathy.

'Is that the only reason you are here?' continued Erula. 'Are you not here to swear fealty to Faulknar? Or do you remain a traitor to your king?'

I turned to face her, seeing a smile curled with malice. Any trace of the woman who had claimed to be my friend was chillingly absent.

'Cleverer people than you have tried to snare me in that net,' I cautioned. 'But what of your loyalties, Erula? Who do you swear allegiance to? Because you have done little to benefit Faulknar.'

Her mouth twitched in amusement. 'Perhaps I should command my guards to remove your traitorous head. For the benefit of Faulknar.'

I flicked a look at the soldiers, who had not reacted to her possession of them. 'Your guards? They bear the mark of the king.' I returned my attention to Kade. 'Does she speak for you now?'

Kade remained silent and still, his expression of apparent boredom at odds with the intense gaze he never removed from me. My mind screamed for him to do something but he continued to passively allow Erula to control the situation.

'The king does not question my loyalty,' she purred, squeezing his shoulder in an obscene display of familiarity. 'I have the authority to kill you, here and now.'

'And I could incinerate you with a thought.'

Her mouth twitched again with the pleasure of seeing me play to her game. 'And confirm all the rumours? All the prejudices he has of you?'

'The rumours you spread. The lies that come so easily to you. Were you ever my friend or was it a performance from the start? Was any of it true?'

She threw her head back and laughed. 'Of course it wasn't true. You were just so pathetically desperate for a friend, how could I resist?'

Kade failed to react, either to defend me or deny my accusations. I feared he was aware of her manipulations and had accepted them, but it seemed more likely that he simply did not care. He appeared incapable of feeling anything.

'Why?' I asked, starting to accept he was under some form of spell. 'What do you gain from this?'

She smiled indulgently, walking behind Kade's throne to stand on his opposite side. She retained one hand on a shoulder throughout the movement and my suspicions flared. I relaxed my gaze to visualise the energy patterns, forcing myself not to react to the corruption evident in Kade's aura. His natural energies were almost completely smothered by thick cords of constricting darkness. The black mass heaved and squirmed, crushing his resistance and providing devastating evidence of why he lacked emotion.

I moved on to assess Erula, feeling an urgent need to break her malignant hold on him. Her energies were surprisingly intact, with black tendrils woven delicately through her aura but showing none of the suffocating pollution seen in Kade or Villermir. I wondered if she was fully aware of her destructive schemes, finding no evidence for the transfer of corrupting energies seen with Villermir's control over the Empathy Crystal. Erula's dark vines remained quiet despite the raging malice seething within Kade. That she held some malicious influence over him was not in doubt but it appeared different to that wielded by Villermir.

'You have so little understanding of the powers involved here,' she continued, having taken only a moment's pause to cross behind Kade. 'The rewards are beyond your imagination.'

'I can imagine a great deal,' I countered. 'What have you been promised? A kingdom? Powers? Who's playing you, Erula? Villermir?'

She huffed in contempt. 'That fool? He can't even kill you!'

'Does Baila speak to you as he does the fool you claim Villermir to be? That false God has promised the Supreme High Priest the resurrection of a loved one. Is that your reward as well?'

Her dark eyes narrowed in warning against my mocking tone. 'There are things much older than Baila.'

I flicked a look at Kade, who was still watching me intently. 'Did you get him to kill his father?'

She smiled viciously. 'Never send a boy to do a woman's job.'

Her comment was dangerously close to an admission but I was distracted by a sudden flare of anger in Kade's eyes, so transient I almost convinced myself I had imagined it. He swung his leg off the arm of the high-backed chair to place it firmly on the ground, straightening his posture and shrugging Erula's hand off his shoulder as he did so.

'Leave us,' he commanded.

Erula tensed with annoyance and her smile became too fixed to be genuine. I resisted the temptation to gloat. She flicked her hand irritably at the guards.

'You heard your liege,' she instructed. 'Leave us.'

Kade continued to fix me with a stare. 'All of you.'

Erula's cheeks flushed and she tensed her jaw in anger. I permitted myself a small, smug smile to add to her displeasure, childishly satisfied when she glared at me with impotent frustration. I waited until she had followed the soldiers out of the far exit before I tore into Kade, completely ignoring my earlier certainty that he had been ensorcelled by Erula.

'For the love of Mobis, Kade! What is wrong with you? You just sit there while your kingdom descends into a stinking pile of horse crap. Your people are starving. Your soldiers are beating up the desperate. You have mercenaries ruling it over everybody. Curse you, you spend money on candles that should be spent on your people. How can you not care about this?'

He remained infuriatingly passive throughout my rant. 'Where is your dragon?'

'Fearsome Father. Wraiths are crawling across your shores and you are still back at Wyrm Island. My dragon is not a threat to you.'

'We both know that she is.' A hint of emotion tightened his eyes. 'After what you did to me, you cannot deny this truth.'

I had started pacing, twisted by old wounds despite having accused him of living in the past.

'After what I did? You mean, saving your miserable hide from Mobis's Torments? So, you came back changed. That is not my fault. Do you not think that simply going to Mobis's Seven Hells would be sufficient? Perhaps I should have left you there.' I growled in frustration. 'That is not the biggest concern here, Kade. You should be less consumed with what did or did not happen in Mobis's hell and worry more about the Gallowglass and the two armies marching towards you. What are you planning on doing about those?'

His head twitched and his hand seemed to flick involuntarily. His mouth twisted into a poisonous sneer. 'What would you suggest I do?'

'I don't know. Maybe you could have your soldiers care less about your royal arse and send those mercenaries to fight the enemy instead of your own people. That might be a good place to start.'

I knew I was being unfair, countless fighters were dying in the attempt to slow Hayton's advance, but I threw my barbs carelessly as I sought to provoke a reaction from him.

'My resources are not limitless. Wishing it will not make it so.'

'Then go looking for more. There are plenty who hate Gallowgla and Baila as much we do.'

His face darkened and his hand jerked again, although he paid it no attention.

'Allies are difficult to trust. Even those considered friends can betray you.'

'Oh, don't be such a child. You're a king, start acting like one.'

He did not respond and his gaze drifted to the floor. His head tilted, listening to someone who was not there. I repeated my question, my tone making it more of a concern than the accusation thrown previously.

'What is wrong with you?'

Kade's attention snapped back to me with enough venom within his glare to compensate for his earlier unemotional state.

'I am not the problem here. You are. You have always been the problem. You are the betrayer.'

He leaned forward to emphasise his point, failing to control the repeated twitching of his head. The fear I would not be able to break Erula's spell started pressing with an urgency within my chest. I could accept his rejection of me but I could not leave him as her twisted puppet, where his only options were apathy or paranoia.

'Please Kade. You have to fight this.'

'And why should I listen to anything you have to say?'

'I know you are still in there, trapped inside yourself.' I searched his eyes for any sign that would support my claim. 'Remember what is real.'

'Who are you to talk of what is real, witch. You have no loyalty to any but yourself. You manipulate for your own ends. You curse us all.'

'That's not true.'

'I stand alone, surrounded by carrion who would sell my throne and feed me to their dogs.'

'That is not true.'

His erratic movements became more evident with his increasing agitation despite the rigid set of his muscles where he tried to contain his anger.

'Everyone has betrayed me. Everyone!'

The fresh fear of losing Kade collided with the raw pain of Tawpin. 'Tawpin died defending you! Can you not even care about that?'

Kade pushed against the heavy throne and crossed the chamber in long strides. The speed at which he approached caused me to take a reflexive step back but he stopped within a pace of me. He trembled violently while he fought to keep still. His face was held in a mask of fixed control, with his dark eyes ringed by the shadow of exhaustion. I could see the marks that had been hidden by the high collar of his tunic. The tattoo had been completed obscured by the vile, dark fingers that wrapped around his neck and reached into the back of his skull, providing visible evidence of the corruption which writhed within him.

Knowing the slightest wrong move would result in a dagger in my guts, I cautiously raised my hand to touch the foul vines. Kade quivered like a startled deer but made no move to stop me. I gently touched his collar bone with my fingertip and gasped when an agonising sting pierced my finger. I quickly withdrew my hand but the pain was already receding, leaving behind only the faint image of a black stain.

'Go,' he growled, deathly pale from the effort of maintaining control. 'Get out of my sight.'

'Kade–'

'Go!'

I scuttled backwards and fumbled at the door in my haste to escape. I closed the door behind me and rested my back against its sturdy oak, closing my eyes in despair for Kade's torments and in relief at escaping his temper without injury. I opened my eyes to see Vallori sitting on the floor, his back against the wall opposite me.

'What happened to the plan?' he mocked mildly. 'The one specifically stating you should not antagonise him?'

I smiled. 'I thought you were with Hagan?'

'He was called away.' Vallori stood and stretched his back. 'He suggested that we visit Drey. Said he had found lodgings in North End.'

'North End?' I did not like the idea of Drey staying in the most brutal section of the port. 'What's he doing in North End?'

We left the royal house with soldiers carefully monitoring our exit. Hagan would have issued a command to ensure we were not detained but it did not stop them expressing their suspicion and distaste, and I was grateful to leave the building. We were tracked by countless pairs of wary eyes while we walked through the town, and the quiet caution descended into open hostility once we reached the market bordering the slums of North End. Many of the stalls had been smashed and there was refuse littered throughout the square. Too many people were huddled in corners and sheltered doorways, having nowhere else to go. We entered the first alleyways within the undefined boundaries of the sector and the chaotic arrangement of shacks and poorly erected dwellings pressed in to create a shadowy, claustrophobic world. My anger simmered at the thought of Drey being forced to live here. A man of his stature. After all he had done for Kade.

I hesitated after only a few streets. The haphazard manner of the buildings and the maze of alleyways were designed to confuse those who were not familiar with the area. We had seen very few people and those we had refused to talk to me. I had no idea where we would find Drey and knew we would get hopelessly lost before too long. Vallori raised a querying eyebrow at the delay but refrained from commenting. I was cursing Hagan for not giving clearer instructions when a small child emerged from the shadows, of perhaps seven or eight summers and hidden under roughly shorn hair and mismatched, overly large clothing. Suspicious eyes looked out of a grubby face to flick nervously between me and Vallori.

'Drey had me watch for you. Said I should bring you to him.'

I had no better option so, although the child may have been a scout taking us into a trap, I requested that they lead the way. We were guided through twisting passageways where people lurked in the shadows and regarded us with a blatant contempt over a thinly covered threat of violence. I assessed every face, every noise, every corner for potential danger while my muscles ached to draw steel. It may have been our weapons or more likely the presence of Drey's runner, but no one approached to deny our passage or steal our possessions.

Eventually, the child stopped outside a two-storey building made of stained, roughly cut timber. The lower floor windows were shuttered and barred, and no light shone from the upper windows.

'He said you'd pay.' Our guide held out a begrimed hand.

'He did not,' I replied, tossing a coin anyway.

The mischievous grin confirmed that Drey had already settled the fee before the child promptly disappeared back into the concealing shadows. Vallori had already tried the door and left it open for me to enter first as Drey's guest. I kept a cautious hand on the hilt of my dagger and stepped into the darkened hallway. In glaring contrast to the royal house, no spare candles were used for a welcome. A small oil lamp released a sour odour from a narrow shelf beside the battered wooden stairs to allow some degree of safe footing. The dim glow of another filtered down from the upper level.

The top of the stairs opened into a narrow corridor with a long, faded rug. I walked past two closed doors, with another at the far end of the hallway. I considered whether Drey was the only inhabitant of the building or if others skulked behind the closed doors, and whether they would be a threat. The final doorway beckoned with a gentle light.

Drey sat in a threadbare chair by a meagre fireplace, where a small cauldron gently steamed over its flames, and another was placed opposite his. A narrow bed was topped with a thin mattress and crumpled sheets. There was no table, but a crate had been used to house a precarious pile of books while more covered the floor surrounding it. The room was shamefully basic.

'Don't just stand there,' Drey instructed. 'Come in. Make yourselves a drink.'

He gave me an apologetic smile when I hesitated in the doorway, unable to accept what he had been reduced to. His voice was softer than I remembered and thin hands cradled his mug, but his posture showed the greatest change. The confident, blustering man had been replaced by one who slumped within his chair, unable to hold my gaze. He looked crushed. He looked defeated.

'Tallen,' he scolded mildly. 'You are embarrassing me. Come in and introduce me to your friend.'

Shamed into action, I entered and allowed Vallori to follow. He introduced himself to Drey and chatted lightly while he collected two mugs from the rough mantle and retrieved the container of dried leaves. The men spoke of trivial things while I could not stop myself from staring, despite Drey's frequent pleading looks.

'What have they done to you?' I demanded.

Drey sighed and twisted in his chair to fully look at me, still only one pace from the door. His bushy eyebrows drew together while he assessed me, critically evaluating more than my appearance. The familiar behaviour quietened my concern, confirming that while his body may look diminished, his mind was still sharp and his eyes still held the power to make me squirm. His gaze lingered on my hands and wrists, showing below the leather vambraces, and I had to resist the urge to fold my arms and hide the faded scars.

'You've changed,' he said at the conclusion of his review.

'So, everyone keeps telling me,' I retorted churlishly. 'Stop trying to avoid the question. How could you let this happen? You deserve better.'

'There is no deserve. You, of all people, should know that. There is what you have and what you make of it.'

'Merciful Mother. How could things have gone so badly wrong? Faulknar is turning on itself. Liegeport had become so hateful that it's hard to know where the town finishes and North End begins. There are mercenaries on the streets. Mercenaries! Keeping order with the point of a blade. In Liegeport!'

'I am aware, Tallen,' Drey confessed quietly but I was not ready to listen.

'Then why are you not doing anything? Why are you hiding in this rat's hole while Kade... You have all the knowledge from your books. Why are you not using it to stop the wraiths? You are a healer. Why are you not helping people?'

'Tallen,' Vallori warned sharply but I barely heard him.

'You were here. You must have seen the changes. Must have known where it was headed. There must have been ways in which you could have stopped this. Instead, you just sit there. Like a tired old man who no longer cares what happens to his people. What gives you the right to give up?'

'Tallen!' repeated Vallori.

'What?' I snapped back. 'This is not a good day and I do not see it getting better any time soon.'

Drey held up his hand to stall Vallori's retort. 'I have found it is quicker to just weather the storm.'

His amused smile and gentle mocking were more effective than Vallori's disapproval in making me see how unfair I was being. I stopped my agitated pacing and sat heavily on the bed. Drey's face softened into an expression of concern.

'May I suggest that you accept the tea Vallori has kindly prepared for you, and ask me of your true concern.'

'I'm sorry,' I apologised to both, remorsefully taking the tea. 'I have no right to lay blame when I have plenty of my own.'

I distractedly rubbed at the finger that still faintly tingled after the contact with Kade. I tried to organise all the problems we faced, to find the most urgent and discover ways of dealing them. There seemed so many.

'I don't know how she's doing it,' Drey stated quietly, gazing into the fire.

I smiled, unsurprised that he had ignored all the noise and found the hurt which pained the most. 'Is she the only one doing it? Do you think someone is assisting her?'

He shook his head, lifting his gaze to address Vallori as well as me. 'I'm not even sure of that. You were right to question why I did nothing to stop it. I have asked that many times but remain unable to find anything to stop. I don't know how she is controlling him.'

It was clearly understood that Erula exerted some form of control over Kade's behaviour and Drey would have also looked for the energy transfer I had failed to find.

'I had my suspicions when you told me of your first meeting. Do you remember? She went to retrieve your sword but refrained from touching it. I felt it odd and suspected she was more than she seemed, but I saw no latent ability within her. And with all that came next.' He shook his head sadly. 'I have reviewed that memory from every angle and can see nothing to predict she could achieve something like this.'

'I would have suggested the Empathy Crystal but with that destroyed.' I shrugged. 'There should have been some improvement.'

Drey's eyebrows raised. 'I felt the change in energies. The crystal is destroyed?'

'I was trying to prevent Villermir from using it. We fought over it.' I offered an apologetic expression. 'It broke.'

Drey gave me a flicker of a smile. 'Still breaking things, I see. Perhaps you have not changed that much.'

I dipped my head in acknowledgement before returning to the problem. 'I saw no siphoning of power from the ground and if she's not accessing energy from the crystal, then how is she doing it? The corruption wrapped around Kade's aura matches what Villermir has spread through the land and what he threaded through the Empathy Crystal, but I felt its influence fade when the crystal shattered. Kade still has thick cords woven throughout and they run deep.'

Drey leaned forward, revitalised by our conversation. 'Maybe there is some residual effect that still lingers within him. Maybe his time with Mobis has made him more susceptible to its influence.'

'Perhaps. It would explain the visible traces on his skin.'

'He has visible marks?' asked Drey eagerly.

'You don't see them?'

'It has been some time since I have been allowed close enough to our king to assess his aura, much less the state of his skin.' He waved away my concern. 'If these marks reflect Villermir's control over the Empathy Crystal, can we assume he is orchestrating Kade's madness?'

'It has his style written all over it, but I'm not sure. I don't see why he would go through all that effort. What does he have to gain?'

'I agree,' continued Drey. 'I do not see Villermir's hand in this, other than as a general puppet-master. I still feel Erula is the key but that leaves the question of where she is getting her power. Kade is not without training. She should not be able to control him. Could she be getting that from Villermir?'

'Perhaps. But how? Villermir needed the auditory stones to relay his instructions over distance. Could he use them to focus power? It would explain the targeted attacks on the Isle of Serpents and Peverill.'

The arguments went round and around. We traded theories and suggestions about how Erula could be gaining her power; what methods

Villermir could use to transfer energy over the distance that separated them, what artefacts could be used to store power for her to subsequently release, what abilities would she need to access and shape the energies bound within the land, and what knowledge would she need to twist those energies into manipulating Kade. We offered endless possibilities but had no evidence that any of them would work, much less were being used. We eventually ran out of ideas and lapsed into a deflated silence.

'Putting aside how she is getting her power,' asked Vallori, having remained silent throughout our long discussion. 'How is she using it to control Kade? And stop scratching your hand.'

I looked down at my palm, finding it covered in red welts where I had been mindlessly clawing at it. The tingle in my finger had spread further into my hand and I had been fussing at the itch while I had talked with Drey. I relaxed my vision to determine if there were any abnormal energies but all remained healthy and vibrant. I re-evaluated whether Erula's physical touch played a role in her malign influence over Kade, something had irritated my hand after I had touched him, but I tiredly dismissed this as my own frustrations creating connections where none existed. I raised my gaze to find Drey sharing a smile with Vallori.

'You should keep him close,' the old druid instructed me. 'But Vallori raises a good point. We have been focusing on where she is getting her power when, perhaps, we should look to how she is using it.'

'We know how she is using it. To control Kade. To break his mind.'

'But how is she doing that?' Vallori persisted. 'From what I've heard, Kade is not without defences. He is not without power of his own. How did she get in? Why does he not resist her? How is she maintaining that control?'

'Those are interesting questions, lad,' commented Drey sadly. 'Ones that suggest I did not train him sufficiently.'

'Well, if we've reached the point where we walk the trail of self-blame, I'm sure his visit to Mobis's Hells gave her the means of entry.' I flicked a look at Vallori. 'Seems I'm quite good at opening doors that should have remained closed.'

'That was Villermir,' corrected Drey. 'Not you.'

'But it was me who brought him back. And I brought him back changed.'

Drey and I slipped into personal thoughts of self-recrimination, each considering our share of the blame for Kade's madness. Vallori refused to let us wallow.

'May I suggest that we avoid the traps of what has been and look to see what is. How do we break her hold?'

I looked to Drey and grinned. 'There is a reason I keep him close.'

CHAPTER THIRTY-ONE

We were given rooms adjacent to Drey's. Despite the suspicion and hostility seeping out of the North End, it seemed its people appreciated the services Drey was giving to the sick and the needful, and they had treated him with respect. He explained that the rooms' usual occupants had lodged elsewhere so that he could greet his guests with some privacy. His eyes twinkled with a hint of his old mischief, admitting he may have encouraged their fears of his magick.

'You're up early,' he commented when I joined him by his fire.

'As are you,' I replied, gratefully accepting the offered tea.

'Couldn't sleep,' he dismissed lightly. 'You?'

'Bad dreams.'

He frowned. 'True dreams?'

'Past dreams. Old events twisted to haunt.'

We had talked late into the night trying to find a way of breaking Erula's hold on Kade, yet found no inspiration on how to do that. I had retreated to my bed but shadows moved at the corners of my vision and had prevented an easy slide into sleep. The dreams started with remembered scenes from the Blue Boar where Kade had entertained his adoring audience with songs and music. The warm companionship of Kerk and Tawpin, as well as my prince, quickly descended into a familiar litany of accusation and shame. The old sorrow of Kerk's death collided with the raw pain of Tawpin's. Kade's happy, vibrant character twisted into the hateful contempt he now favoured. I awoke feeling bone-achingly weary.

'We will get him back,' Drey prompted quietly after I had lapsed into a brooding silence.

I gave him a small appreciative smile. 'Am I that obvious?'

'He is constantly on my mind as well. I failed the boy,' he confessed sadly. 'In his time of need, I failed him.'

'There's plenty of blame to go around.'

'Indeed. Enough to drown in. So let us not linger there.' He gave me a sly grin. 'Tell me about this warrior you have brought us. Gallowglass, I would guess. Does he have abilities?'

We talked comfortably about lighter topics, grateful for the excuse to avoid current concerns with news of what had happened during the time we had been apart. Drey was excited to hear about the Sanctuary of The Moon Goddess while being slightly offended that he had been unaware of such a place of knowledge and learning. He told me of how the visions of Megin's attack had fuelled Kade's obsession with building defences against her. He described how the plans to deter Lindvane's invasion had been thwarted by the unexpected numbers Hayton had brought against Faulknar. We discussed the wraiths and I talked of the daemons that rampaged across Hilman. Vallori had joined us and he spoke of Sálaforn and our suspicions regarding her involvement. I told them of Villermir and of his connection to my father, looking for evidence that Drey had known and being relieved to see his genuine surprise. Drey confirmed the damage the Supreme High Priest had done to the land's energies and what had been done to try to mitigate against the worst of the corruption. We had reached the fall of Kingsport when Drey interrupted the flow of our conversation.

'Keys,' he said sharply. 'Do I have to remind you that I require you to listen to the conversations of others, not to listen to mine?'

'Keys?' asked Vallori as the street rat who had guided us the day before curled around the doorframe.

'He can open any lock,' explained Drey, trying to look sternly at the boy but failing. 'It makes his services very useful but he finds it difficult to stick to agreed instructions.'

Thoughts of Owl stabbed painfully at seeing yet another child being pressed into schemes bigger than those they should be made to handle.

'Got a message,' the lad stated, poking in his ear with a grubby finger.

'From whom?' Drey prompted.

'The lady in the big house. The Traveller.'

'Erula?' I demanded harshly. 'Why are you talking to Erula?'

Keys looked at me like I was the stupidest person he had ever met.

'Didn't. Spoke to Pockets, who spoke to one of the stable boys, who spoke to a page, who spoke—'

'Yes, yes,' interrupted Drey irritably. 'What is the message?'

'She wants to meet you.' He pointed at me to ensure we understood the invitation was meant just for me.

'I don't suppose you know why?' I asked while Drey blustered that it was not a good idea for me to go.

The lad shrugged. 'But for an extra coin I'll guide you out of the End.'

Vallori smiled at the child's opportunistic offer but agreed to his terms.

'No. Not you,' repeated the boy. 'Just her.'

The two men started arguing with each other, Vallori claiming that there was no way I would be going alone while Drey insisted that I should not be going at all. Keys stood patiently, chewing a filthy nail while he waited for his coin.

'I'm going,' I stated after I had let them dance for a while. 'It's our best chance of finding out what she is doing and how she's doing it.'

'It's a trap,' persisted Drey.

'Probably. But it could also be the only opportunity we get.'

'You're not going alone,' confirmed Vallori.

'She's not going to tell me anything with you there. If we want her secrets, she needs to feel in control. She needs to think that I am unaware of her trap and that she has me exactly where she wants me.' I turned to Drey, hoping to find an ally. 'If she is using an artefact, this will be the best chance I get to find it.'

Drey had been placing me in danger to obtain magickal items since I was a child. It was easy for me to prod this part of his character, and I took sad satisfaction to see his eyes lose focus as he considered the ways I could exploit this opportunity. His head started to nod in agreement when he recognised the possibilities. I ignored Vallori's frown of disapproval.

'Vallori does draw attention,' Drey muttered to himself, and I knew the decision was made.

'This is madness,' Vallori growled at me. 'We have no idea how she is controlling Kade. She could just as easily start manipulating you.'

'Peace,' I offered gently. 'I have much better defences than Kade and I know the threat she poses. I'll be fine.' He opened his mouth to protest. 'I'll be careful.'

I knew Vallori did not agree with my decision but did not think he would stop me. We maintained each other's gaze while he searched for arguments I would not quickly dismiss.

'I would like to talk with you further,' Drey continued, oblivious to our silent contest of wills. 'I would hear more of Bane if you would allow.'

'Of course you would,' I retorted, my tone made harsher by the shame I felt in manipulating Vallori. 'You're itching to know how to exploit any power locked inside Sálaforn's apprentice.'

I did not need to hear Vallori's sharp hiss to know I had been callously unfair. Drey sunk into his chair, returning to the defeated old man I had seen the day before. My final, unintentional but effective, twist of manipulation would ensure Vallori stayed. He would never leave Drey alone to nurse the hurt I had just inflicted.

'I'm sorry,' I apologised weakly. 'I did not mean that.'

'Just go,' Vallori dismissed and I hastily left with Keys.

The boy guided me back through the maze of dirty streets and alleyways, and the oppressive atmosphere made me startle at moving shadows and the rustle of rats. Keys left me at the accepted border of North End and I continued along the less ominous paths through the town, although my uneasiness refused to settle. Every stare felt hostile. Every conversation carried threat. Every sudden move seemed to be reaching for a blade. I cursed myself for being foolish, dismissing my anxieties as a product of a haunted night's sleep, but could not shake the feeling I was being followed by indistinct shapes and I ached with tension by the time I reached the royal house.

I was denied entry by crossed spears, as Vallori had been excluded from my meeting with Kade.

'I've been summoned by Erula. Let me through.'

The guards remained unconvinced. 'I doubt the King's Confidante would waste her time with one such as you.'

I blinked. 'King's Confidante? That's what she's calling herself?' I received the edge of a spear being moved closer to my chest in reply. 'Perhaps you should send someone to check. Just to be certain.'

After a moment's hesitation a runner was sent to confirm my claim, returning with breathless speed with the instructions for me to go straight to the old druid's suite. I scowled at the disrespectful tone given to Drey's rank, but settled for assuring the guards that I knew the way and dismissing their suggestion of an escort. As with the day before, the household staff gave me little more than a brief, fearful glance while the soldiers who patrolled the building were more obvious with their disdain. Their hands gripped the hilts of their weapons, but none challenged my passage and I quickly made my way to the upper corridor and to Drey's chambers.

I was becoming increasingly frustrated at my persistent paranoia. Even within the house I was reacting to flickers of movement at the borders of my vision, only to turn and find nothing there. I heard voices that whispered from locations where no one was standing. I turned sharply at the call of my name, finding only a surprised maid, and started to consider whether it was more than my heightened imagination. I was feeling echoes of the torments that were stalking Kade and briefly wondered if Erula's influence would be felt by all who had magick, quickly rejecting that possibility. I had not been so reactive the day before despite standing close to him. I finally accepted that the witch was building her trap and her sorcery was aimed specifically at me. I remembered my casual dismissal of Vallori's warning that I could be so easily manipulated.

I opened the door to Drey's outer room and all thoughts of Erula vanished. The space had been systematically destroyed and there was broken furniture lying across the floor. Smashed ceramics and shattered glass lay amongst torn ledgers and ripped scrolls, scattered throughout the damaged timber. I found the mess more distressing than the destruction, being such a sharp contrast to the order and cleanliness that Drey had carefully maintained. Erula's shadows seized on my distraction. Ghosts leaned in to taunt me, oozing malice and contempt despite being no more than the blurred outlines. The shades circled like predators controlling their prey, silently menacing but making no attempt to attack.

Forcefully ignoring my instincts that screamed to attack the wraiths, I calmed my breathing to see beyond their forms. I looked for an energy tether that would lead back to the enchantress, but the ghosts constantly melted and reformed so it felt like grasping at water. Each strand dissolved as soon as I touched it, reforming in another section of the shade. I changed tactics and spread a net of energy, containing the elusive threads within a defined area where I could track their movements more easily. The whispers grew louder as I followed a strand beyond Drey's public chamber, into the room which had once been mine, and out over the central portion of the house.

The door slammed shut behind me and my concentration splintered, causing the thread to slip away. I cursed, returning my attention to the room and the unwanted interruption. I had expected to see Erula or more likely a runner to confirm she was busy elsewhere, and stared for several heartbeats before accepting who was blocking my exit.

Rolyan rested against the closed door. He had lost none of his intimidating presence and his fighter's bulk promised to deliver the cruelty tainting his expression. The muscle at the corner of his left eye twitched while he leered at me. I continued to be distracted by the circling ghosts despite knowing the real peril came from the vicious bully in front of me.

'What do you want, Rolyan?'

His lecherous smile widened. 'So many things, little rat. So many things.'

'Did Erula send you?' He dipped his head in smug acknowledgement. 'Do you belong to her now? What has she promised you?'

He dismissively waved his hand in the air. 'Oh, the usual. Money. Power.'

I twitched when a shadow floated in towards me, so close that the rounded shape of its head brushed the side of my neck. I felt neither cold nor the sting of energy, just a gossamer touch of *something* that made my skin flinch.

'Breya could no longer give you the influence you crave,' I stated, forcing myself to concentrate on the bigger threat, 'so you readily changed your allegiance to Erula.'

He casually pushed away from the door and took a step towards me, smiling when I took a reflexive pace back in response.

'An effective business arrangement.' He took another slow, deliberate step and I willed myself to remain still. 'One that has presented me with such a delicious reward.'

My mind whirled in chaos. There was too much danger coming from too many angles. More ghosts reached in to touch and caress, causing my body to cringe away although no harm was being inflicted. I could not ignore the shifting motion of the shadows even though I knew I should concentrate on the man who stood in front of me, waiting for the perfect time to strike. Despite not wanting to know the answer, I asked the question anyway, forcing my mind to focus on Rolyan.

'And what reward has she given you?'

His face twisted into an expression of such depravity that I took another fearful step back and my heart hammered against my ribs. He smiled in poisonous triumph, moving to within an arm-length of me.

'You, of course.'

His hand shot forward and grasped my throat. My mind shattered. His fingers dug into my flesh and squeezed. The wraiths crowded in. Surrounding me. My lungs protested, demanding more air. I heard Erula's voice chanting ancient words. Rolyan's face was pressed close to mine. I could smell stale ale on his breath. Faces formed within the shadows.

'She instructed me to kill you. But I think I will have some fun first.'

He whispered close enough to my ear that I could feel his lips. The ghost-faces gained definition. Recognisable features. My head pounded from the lack of air. Dark specks floated throughout my vision. I smelled cedar and rosemary. His lips touched the point of my jaw.

'I have waited so very long for this. I will take everything from you. I will make you beg, you whore.'

The chanting echoed around my head – *bamfer, bine, brik*. The faces were so disappointed in me – Laken, Tawpin, Kade. I felt a hand and the tearing of my shirt. I saw flames reaching up out of a brass bowl. Such sad eyes – Laken, Tawpin, Kade. Sad, disappointed eyes. Their faces swirled in and out of focus. They would not stay still. They moved too fast. There was pressure on my hips.

My anger ignited, blasting away the smothering ghosts and dissolving the faces of Laken and Tawpin and Kade. My vision cleared and returned me to Drey's ruined chamber. Rolyan was on top of me. His lips. His hands. His body. I could not be distracted by the ghosts. I had to silence the voices. He had to be stopped.

I cracked my head into his nose and used the pain as a focus. My arm was released when he rose to punch me and I clumsily blocked the strike. I called on my power to burn the bastard and flickers of flame sparked within my palm in answer to my call.

I was slammed back into the vortex of shadow. The wraiths returned to twist around me with renewed malice. Plucking and poking with skeletal fingers. Laken, Tawpin, Kade. Cursing me. Shaming me. Hurtful accusations. I spiralled deeper and deeper.

Bamfer. Bine. Brik.

I targeted Erula's voice and followed the trail back to the brass bowl. I reached towards the odour of ritual incense. I found her. Her palms held upwards, eyes closed. Repeating the chant – torment, bind, break. She softly rocked while she weaved her spells. She was mine.

I flared an arrow of pure energy at her heart. Her eyes snapped open as she recoiled from my attack. She hissed in anger and her chant became harsher and more desperate. Power surged into her words, crushing my mind to a single point of resistance. I sharpened that restricted focus into a point and stabbed energy into her with white-hot precision. She screamed. The bowl exploded, showering her with burning debris. She fell backwards and my mind snapped back to Drey's chambers.

Rolyan was knelt over me, with his head thrown back and his eyes almost closed. Looming over him was Kade. Real Kade, not the ghost Erula had sent to haunt me. My eyes widened when I saw him raise his sword. I watched in horror while he swung the blade down in an arc, slicing deep into Rolyan's neck.

Rolyan's body collapsed on top of me. His head was twisted in a sickening angle and his blood flowed over the bare skin of my belly and thighs. Kade stood with his sword still raised, visibly trembling.

'I warned him,' he snarled. 'I warned him.'

'Yes,' I replied carefully, unsure whether his righteous anger would turn on me next. 'Yes, you did.'

Kade continued to stare at Rolyan's body while his tremors slowed into infrequent twitching. The madness drained from him and he lowered his blade, turning to reveal Hagan. Kade's loyal captain stood watching his king with his hand gripping the hilt of his dagger so tightly that the veins protruded from his skin as thick, blue cords.

'Deal with this,' instructed Kade, before marching out of the room.

Hagan waited until I had covered myself, holding together my torn clothing, before quietly asking. 'Can you help him? Can you return him to what he was?'

'I don't know,' I replied, equally subdued. 'Perhaps. I will try.'

I hugged my knees tightly pressed into my chest and surveyed the damage done to Drey's chamber. I could not stop shaking.

'Can you tidy the room? Not just... But the furniture. The books. Drey would not... '

The tall man walked over, offering me his hand and giving me a tired smile when I accepted it. 'I don't know. Perhaps. I will try.'

Breya's funeral rites were completed at sunset. The occasion was rushed and lacked the elaborate statement she would have expected. Few were in attendance, with most having more important concerns than observing the internment rituals of a distant queen; the easy relationship between the townspeople and the royal family, which had been so integral to Faulknar rule, had ceased some time ago. Those who did attend stood in small, isolated groups and there was little interaction between the different factions. An additional level of hostility was aimed at Drey. Poorly concealed mutterings about his unwelcome presence had followed in his wake when we made our way along the gravel path to the cliff top. Drey and I stood alone at the edge of the meadow, while Vallori remained several paces away with his arms folded and stubbornly refusing to acknowledge me.

'Don't be too hard on him,' Drey said gently.

'It's not me who is sulking.'

I had returned to Drey's lodgings and retreated directly to the room I had been given. I had washed and scrubbed and scrubbed again, and I had avoided the two men until it had been time to leave for Breya's ceremony. The scratches and bruises were easily hidden under clean clothing but my swollen cheek remained visible, prompting Vallori's anger when I told the barest detail of what had happened.

'He blames himself for letting you go alone.'

'I know. But it was not his choice and he is not to blame. How many times do I have to tell him that? Besides, it turned out that I was not alone.' We both turned to look at Faulknar's king. 'Seems he's still capable of watching my back.'

Drey huffed, grumbling without conviction. 'Kade is not a reliable ally and should not be relied on to save you.'

'He's buried deep, but he is still in there. With Kyllian and Tawpin, and then… Maybe his anger is his own. If I can just get him angry enough.'

'Or maybe you could avoid tempting the edge of his blade?' Drey looked at me with his bushy eyebrows raised high on his forehead. 'Perhaps we should try removing Erula's influence first?'

'A simple spell.' I shook my head in disbelief. 'How did we miss such a simple spell?'

'We were so busy looking for more elaborate schemes that we overlooked the basic techniques. Any hedge witch can act as a conduit with the right combination of words and potions. We may not know where she is getting her power but now we know how to stop her from using it.'

I studied the Traveller who stood demurely a pace behind Kade, and tried to determine whether she would be capable of exerting any influence without the ritual I had seen during her attack on me. I was certain her possessive touching was a way in which she could manipulate him and frowned at the thought of her coaxing his emotions while they stood listening to the eulogy. I distractedly rubbed at my hand that was no longer tainted.

'The lady does not look well.' Drey interrupted my thoughts having seen the direction of my gaze. 'You delivered quite the sting.'

'That's the least she will be getting from me.'

Drey tensed at my tone but I would not apologise. I chose to ignore his frown of concern and continued to watch the source of my smouldering hatred.

'I do not claim to understand all that you have gone through,' he started carefully. 'But the road you are contemplating rarely ends well. Do not lose yourself to hate.'

'Your warning comes too late,' I informed him. 'I have been travelling down that road for some time. Erula's fate will barely touch the surface.'

Drey had no reply and we stood in an uncomfortable silence while I watched Coen conduct the service Baila required. The celebration of a person's life and the comfort of knowing their soul travelled to the Halls of Lower Gods were absent. Rigid stoicism was expected from all attendees while the High Priest cautioned that the ways of wickedness would deny entry to the One God's paradise. Coen's elaborate posturing and gestures exposed his appreciation of the control he held over the occasion.

The lowly clerk had swiftly risen to the position of High Priest of Liegeport, a role previously held by Villermir. I remembered him as an insipid, grovelling little man with no more ambition than that needed to extort taxes from all he could. He had risen uncommonly fast, and I wondered whether this had been due to his obedience to Villermir or his cultivated relationships with the Faulknar heirs, with both Kerk and Kade having sought his counsel.

'Breya would have hated this,' I said.

'I fear our queen stopped caring about such things some time ago,' he replied sadly. 'Her ambitions were eroded by the Fates long before Erula shattered her reputation.'

I glared again at the witch standing next to Faulknar's king. 'Breya told me of the children. That Kade had denied her access. Erula's work, I would wager.'

'Indeed. Rumour and gossip were used to discredit the queen. But it was the children who broke Breya. I believe that she would have seen her death as a welcome release.'

I turned sharply to look at him, rapidly re-evaluating Breya's refusal of my healing along with Tarra and Vallori's calm acceptance of it. I found it hard to believe that such a proud woman would accept defeat so easily, but I had skimmed around that void too many times to deny its appeal.

'Do you think they travel to the Halls without the proper rites?'

The druid smiled briefly. 'I do not believe the Gods would turn away those who would wish to enter. The rituals are often more about our own experience. Offering the comfort of companionship and of familiar routines. I doubt the Gods need to be placated or bribed with our ceremonies in order to grant us their peace.'

I considered the different expressions of faith, with the inclusive embrace of my Gods clashing with the privileged rejection of Baila. Did either path run true or were they just a mere reflection of our own fears and desires. I watched Coen preside over the austere occasion and wondered whether his performance was any more effective than ours. I bitterly concluded that the Gods would do what they wanted to do, regardless of us.

'How did that snivelling weasel get to be High Priest?'

Drey chuckled. 'Perhaps his potential was always there, waiting for the opportunity to ignite. Maybe he was as blind as we were, his talents lying hidden beneath his insidiously, subservient demeanour. I suspect he received a nudge when Villermir fled Liegeport. I have often wondered whether Coen was selected to be Villermir's successor because he was not perceived as a rival or whether the Supreme High Priest was aware of his talents all along.'

'You think Villermir had a hand in this?'

'I was able to confirm that Coen was in the possession of an auditory crystal.'

'They were all part of the Empathy Crystal,' I commented regretfully. 'You should have seen it, Drey. Villermir had chipped away at it as if it was no more than a piece of flint.'

'I fear there is no end to that man's meddling?' Drey shook his head sadly. 'A shared resonance would explain the connection and with Coen receiving instructions directly from Villermir, none of the other priests would be able to deny him. He used his opportunity well, systematically discrediting his competition.'

'Including you?'

'His campaign was quite effective. I had shown my intentions too clearly upon discovering his link to Villermir and I suddenly became the target for the people's fears and frustrations. The reason for the king's paranoia. Coen is a gifted orator and his sermons were greedily consumed. Within weeks, the port had changed from a tolerant mix of faiths to one that was zealously proclaiming Baila as the One True God.'

'Do you have Baila coins?' I asked, suspicious at the speed of change. 'In Hilman, we found coins that were stamped with Baila's image. The priests were using them to siphon the energy and sap the will of any who touched them.'

'Clever,' breathed Drey, immediately understanding the implications.

'Fortunately, I have a friend who is also clever.' I smiled smugly. 'He put the rune of truth in the centre.'

'Oh. That was well thought.' Drey's eyes widened with appreciation and his enthusiasm softened the stab of grief at remembering Bear's role in the scheme. 'The coins of Faulknar are still Kade's. Despite his problems, of which there are many, he would not allow the priests such a public endorsement. Erula cannot push him that far. No. I fear that the attitude of the people involves the simple need for guidance in the face of horrors they are ill-equipped to comprehend. Faulknar has known peace for generations. Now, we have war and wraiths. While their king stays silent, they look to another and Coen is taking full advantage of that.'

The first good news came three days later. Drey and I were sitting in his room, joined in a trance to track Erula. We had spent many hours over the preceding days monitoring her movements while she sought to influence Kade and concluded that when she was physically with him, she was reliant on human manipulations to coax his desires and taunt his fears. Drey remained unable to access the king's mind, having done this easily before Erula spun her web of control. He cursed passionately when we were forced to watch the energies that swirled around the Kade, trying to determine when he was being controlled and being constantly frustrated by being unable to see how those energies affected his behaviour.

A direct line between Erula and Kade was more apparent when she was alone. As with the attack on me, her spell-work created cords of energy that wrapped around her victim and I was certain this was the cause of the night-terrors and ghosts which haunted him. We had decided to extinguish this torment. Drey would attempt to access Kade's mind while I sought the source of her power. I was immersed in a tangled tapestry of light. Black threads pulsed with flashes of vibrant green, twisting and snaking within the larger matrix of colours. Behind the mesh of illuminated strands was a background of faded red that throbbed in time to the witch's slow heartbeat. I dismissed all except the dark vines, seamlessly moving to another when I lost a thread in the mass of shifting energies. I worked slowly and methodically, remaining hidden while the power of the chant absorbed her awareness.

My attention drifted towards Vallori. He had become agitated but not from boredom. I lost my connection to the black thread at the sound of his curse.

'Concentrate,' demanded Drey.

Trusting Vallori to deal with whatever had upset him, I returned to start my exploration again. Erula's pulse remained steady and she remained unaware of my presence. I carefully separated the coloured strands and exposed the first black vein, letting it guide me from the sorceress to the source of her power. The thread wove around the mesh of distracting lights, twisting back on itself several times on its meandering path. Erula's core energy signature grew steadily brighter and I tracked the vine towards her centre. Green pulses, at a different rate to her heartbeat, flared along the black network to swell the cords with dissonant energy. I pushed against the rhythmic forces that swirled around me like a strong tide. I tentatively extended my connection.

The flare of Vallori's anger shattered my control. The vivid landscape of energies was swiftly replaced by the muted light within the room, causing a moment of nauseating disorientation.

'The last summons you brought resulted in a great deal of harm.' Vallori's voice was menacingly quiet. 'Would you betray us a second time?'

Quickly touching the ground, where I sat cross-legged opposite Drey, I dispersed the excess energy and regained control of my awareness. Drey had also ended his connection and was scowling in obvious frustration at the interruption. We both turned to Keys, who bravely remained at the door despite Vallori's hostility.

'By the Gods,' grumbled the druid irritably. 'What is it, lad?'

The boy flicked a glance at the glowering Vallori before addressing his message to me. 'Soldiers have arrived from the west. Was told to fetch you.'

'What soldiers?' demanded Vallori. 'Who sent you?'

Keys darted another cautious look at him before returning to me. 'I was just told to fetch you. I'll wait in the alley.'

The child ran down the hallway before he could be questioned further but I doubted he would have the information Vallori wanted. I rubbed my forehead where an ache was developing and went to fetch a beaker of water for myself and Drey.

'Erula's work?' Vallori asked.

I passed Drey the grounding drink. 'I doubt it. She's too busy creating ghosts to dance around Kade.'

'Which we should be preventing,' Drey reminded me querulously.

'Later,' I pleaded. The water had not eased my headache but had, at least, settled my turbulent energies. 'She's blocking me far more easily than she should be. She should not have access to that much power.'

'And you should have enough power to extinguish her like snuffing out a candle. But here we are.'

Vallori remained wisely silent while Drey and I glared at each other and I waited for Drey to admit that we were both exhausted and frustrated, neither being an appropriate state with which to perform magick. After several stubborn heartbeats, he closed his eyes with a sigh and acknowledged our need for rest. I turned to Vallori.

'I can't hide away while Faulknar is at war,' I commented quietly. 'We should see what new soldiers have arrived.'

'And why they requested you.' He maintained his stare to emphasise his point. 'I'm going with you.'

I grinned wickedly. 'Of course. Drey and I seem to be doing all the work. It's time you made a contribution.'

Keys had waited for us outside Drey's building. He sullenly led all three of us to the edge of North End, repeatedly looking at Vallori, before transferring us into the escort of Pockets. The older boy had gained his name from the numerous compartments sewn into his clothing, from which he withdrew various items in exchange for the information fed to him by his ragged group of street children. Coins, gems, food, even a small toy. Each item was appropriately selected to buy loyalty, although I noticed a fair amount of affection was freely traded as well.

We were guided towards the section of Liegeport that housed the labourers and the taverns along the town's shoreline. The jumble of buildings were better maintained than those of North End, although not by much. The overcrowding had extended throughout, with people curled under blankets in any form of shelter they could find, and the alleys were dirtier than when I ran them as a child. We walked in silence while we were watched by defeated eyes.

Pockets left us at a building that matched all the others in the alleyway, informing us that the strangers waited for us in a room at the rear before disappearing into the shadows. The interior contrasted considerably with its stern outer appearance. It buzzed with activity, with men and women carrying bundles of linen or crates of supplies, or rearranging furniture. Several smiled pleasantly in greeting, carefully stepping around us.

'Looks like they are planning on staying for a while,' commented Vallori.

We obediently made our way to the small room at the back, finding the door open in a clear invitation but still hesitating on the threshold. A lively counsel was being held where multiple people talked at once. A small woman had her back to us but the tightly curled, red hair that escaped every attempt to contain it was unmistakable. I saw a smile creep over Drey's face and I answered him with my own, broad grin.

'Not content with the chaos in your own domain,' Drey accused mildly, 'you've come to cause mayhem in mine.'

The Mother Priestess from the Isle of Serpents turned and greeted us with a joyous cry. 'Ah! It is good to see you. Please come in. Be welcome.'

Sutha had crossed the space before we had taken more than a pace into the room, enclosing Drey in a tight embrace which he hesitantly returned. I grinned foolishly at the exchange, finding myself relieved that the old druid finally had an equal upon whom he could share his responsibilities. I had not appreciated how he had faced his concerns alone until I saw the change in his posture in response to her presence. Sutha turned to me next, greeting me with a similarly fierce hug before turning to Vallori. He remained passive while she regarded him in an assessment that judged more than his physical appearance. He held her gaze without candour and she rewarded him with a small smile.

'Blessed be, Warrior.'

He dipped his head in respect. 'Blessed be, Priestess.'

With the formalities completed, the small woman beamed up at him and grabbed him in a firm embrace. He hesitated for a moment, but then generously returned the gesture.

I smiled wickedly at him when the two separated, shrugging with false apology. 'She does that. I probably should have warned you.'

She led us to a narrow bench beside a wall where we could talk without being disturbed by those hurrying to and from the room or be distracted by the rapid conversations of the new arrivals settling into their new accommodation. Drey and Vallori flanked Sutha while I sat, cross-legged, at Drey's feet.

'It is very good to see you,' began Drey. 'But what, in the Goddess's name, are you doing here?'

The small woman looked down at me. 'I came at the Dragonslayer's call.'

'I didn't... I wouldn't... It wasn't for me,' I spluttered, embarrassed that the Isle of Serpents' Mother Priestess had come as if I had whistled for a hound. 'I called for Kade. Faulknar could do with your assistance.'

Her face softened, releasing me from her gentle mocking. 'I swore that I would come when you called. And here I am.'

I had sent two messages from Kingsport asking for aid. The Isle of Serpents had been one, although I had forgotten the promise Sutha had made when she first informed me of my triple heritage as an Empath, Moon Warrior and Dragonslayer. I had not intended to test her oath, merely hoping that her knowledge and magick could counter those of the shamans and help control their wraiths. The second message was more of a gamble and, as Lindvane tightened its grip, I did not expect that one to be answered. Sutha was here, however, and that was unexpectedly good news.

'You are most welcome,' confirmed Drey. 'There is much work to be done.'

'Indeed.' Sutha returned her attention to the druid. 'Our king has sunk deep into his dark waters.'

'Erula,' I snarled. 'The witch has him haunted by ghosts that crush his will. She's twisted him to the edge of madness.'

'From what I hear, he has extended beyond that.' She maintained her gaze on Drey. 'But the enchantress is not his only torment.'

'I had not forgotten,' Drey replied quietly.

'The remnant from Mobis's realm is woven tightly around our king,' she continued. 'Does our binding still contain it?'

'The tattoo has changed,' I answered. 'The design has been lost under a featureless mass of black. He has corruption visible throughout his energies.'

The priestess frowned. 'The protection was only temporary, although I had hoped for longer than this. Pollution of his aura was to be expected.'

'It's more than his aura. There are visible cords running under his skin. They enclose his neck and reach up into his skull.'

I recalled the obscene caress of its tendrils and my head ached trying to determine whether the malignant influence was Villermir, or Erula, or whatever I had brought back from Mobis's Hells. The silence stretched while we all considered how much corruption had spread throughout Kade and the effect it must be having on him. It had been lethally entwined when we had travelled to the Isle of Serpents, how greater the peril now that its presence was visible even to those without magick.

'I've failed him,' whispered Drey. 'I was meant to protect him and I have failed in every aspect.'

Sutha reached over and took his hand, capturing it within the support of both of hers. She looked at him with such tender compassion that it ached to witness it. She maintained the contact until Drey was forced to accept it.

'We do not face one foe,' she advised quietly. 'One man cannot be expected to counter that. No matter how talented he is.'

Drey placed his free hand on top of Sutha's. 'Thank you, my friend.'

'We are here now. You have our assistance.'

The druid and the priestess shared a look that was intimate and I turned to watch those in the room to avoid intruding. The atmosphere was animated and the conversations were loud, but still the commotion occurring in the corridor outside could be heard. The noise travelled closer, becoming recognisable as an argument regarding the unsanitary nature of large towns. I shook my head in amused disbelief and turned to Vallori, finding him grinning back at me.

'All I am saying,' persisted Elyos, crashing into the room, 'is that there should be a limit to the number of people allowed to remain in any one area.'

'People are trying to find safety,' countered Bonash patiently, while looking apologetically at those who had turned to glare.

'I know that,' Elyos dismissed with a flap of his hand. 'It's more a general point. Too many people cause too much stink. It's just nature. Too many wolves and the pack splits.'

He turned and found us sitting by the wall, staring at him with bemused expressions. He slapped Bonash on the chest hard enough to force the smaller man back a pace.

'Look who we've found discarded in a corner,' he declared loudly. 'Tallen. Tell Nash I'm right. Too many people is not good for general good health.'

'Regardless of your viewpoint,' I replied, 'I will always defend the opposing view on principle.'

Elyos clutched his chest and staggered back a pace. 'Ouch.'

The two men joined us and I made the introductions to Drey. Elyos explained how Sutha had arrived at Kingsport with healers and scouts in response to my summons. Bonash added that the additional seers helped to mitigate much of the shamans' presence, and confirmed that Leyn had not been left unprotected when Keenan and Mace had withdrawn their fighters to escort the priestess to Liegeport.

'Keenan's here?' I spluttered.

'He went straight to your king,' confirmed Elyos with a malicious glint in his blue eyes.

I grinned back. 'Oh, I would pay a lot of coin to witness that exchange.'

'The Lord General has gone to request that we set up an infirmary here by the water,' continued Sutha, ignoring Elyos's and my childish glee. 'We have most of Nathair's healers. The king cannot refuse our services.'

'There are many reasons why Kade would refuse,' I denied. 'Not least because Keenan is the one asking.'

Drey glared at me as if I was a misbehaving infant. 'Regardless, I feel that we should provide those services. They are sorely needed.'

Our conversation drifted towards reports from Sutha's scouts that told of increased numbers of Lindvane soldiers moving into the south-western regions of Faulknar, joining with Baila's Army of Truth in a coordinated campaign to push further north towards Liegeport. Elyos confirmed that the infrequent attacks from Gallowgla kept the coast on nervous alert, despite many ships having also moved towards the royal port.

'What are they waiting for?' asked Elyos when the conversation slowed to private contemplation. 'With their cursed shamans, the pirates could finish us with a couple of organised assaults. But still, they strike as individual groups.'

'It's the same here,' I confirmed. 'More ships keep coming but they only attack with one band, occasionally two, but never more than that.'

'They're waiting for reinforcements,' Vallori said quietly.

Sutha nodded. 'I suspect the Warrior is correct. Gallowgla has always been seen as an opportunist. We see their presence here as simply exploiting the advantage our war has given them. I fear that this is not the case. I fear Gallowgla marches to Lindvane's drumbeat.'

Before a reply could be offered, Bonash tilted his head, reminding me of a bird searching for worms. Not even Drey doubted that he listened to the power that threaded throughout the land, waiting patiently with the rest of us for what the quiet man had discovered.

'The shamans are gathering their energies,' he advised. 'There will be an attack. Around the curve of the coast. Perhaps, half a day's ride from here.'

Elyos looked at me and grinned. 'Shall we?'

'If you leave now, you may get there in time,' Nash offered.

'We should let Keenan know,' cautioned Vallori. 'We will need his support.' He glared at us in frustration. 'At the least, we should collect Mace and his guard.'

Elyos and I were already halfway to the door. Elyos turned back to Vallori in an exaggerated gesture. 'Are you afraid I will steal all your glory?'

His barb hit true and I knew Vallori would follow without further complaint.

'A Warrior, a Dragonslayer, and a *miann cath*,' observed Sutha. 'I believe the Gods will be enjoying this.'

Drey huffed. 'The Gods should be protecting us from the young and their incessant foolishness.'

CHAPTER THIRTY-TWO

I was kept busy during the following days as the different needs each vied for my attention. Sutha created her infirmary in a warehouse not far from her lodgings and the centre of her network. Unsurprisingly, Kade had not agreed to Keenan's request and the shouting was heard beyond the royal house, but neither had he prohibited it and so the infirmary went ahead. Sutha and her team were left to conduct their affairs with no interference from Kade's soldiers or the mercenaries. There was a great need for her skills. All made their way to a building stripped of the empty crates that had once held luxuries, and was now filled with neat rows of mattresses for those needing care and healing. Fighters wounded by raiders lay next to those injured from the increasingly vicious beatings spreading throughout the town. Those suffering from the diseases of overcrowding were sent to the canvas shelters erected along the walkway between the storehouse and the seafront, where the sea breezes gave some relief from the stench of decay and contagion. Sutha's healers were kept busy and Bonash, Drey and I helped whenever we could.

Bonash had gained an effective gathering of his own. Using the knowledge learnt from the resistance in Hilman, he had taught the Isle's seers how to predict the engagement of the shamans. Some had stayed at Kingsport but enough had followed Sutha to Liegeport, and their talents proved extremely helpful. Much of the damage inflicted by the pirates was due to their tactic of choosing targets with no predictable pattern, attacking and retreating before we could mount a response. Nash's scrying meant we could react before the raiders could escape to their boats, allowing us to be much more effective at protecting the vulnerable fishing communities who were vital in maintaining Liegeport's supplies. In addition to the advanced warning, Sutha's priests and priestesses were able to disrupt the energies the shamans used to control the wraiths, creating disorder within the ghostly army and reducing the number of reaped souls. The advantages given by both groups were hard to ignore and suspicions were suppressed enough to reluctantly allow their presence during the councils of war.

The fragile suspension of hostilities did not extend to Drey, Vallori or me. Erula's rumours had been thorough and, as we spent more time away from North End to work at the infirmary, we were frequently subjected to verbal attacks. Vallori and I, with our clearly displayed weapons, discouraged the more physical expressions of people's distrust but we received no welcome from those we healed or those we fought beside. Their attitude was uncomfortable and frustrating, but I had too much occupying my time to dwell on their unfair judgements. Vallori and I frequently rode with Elyos and his fighters to relieve our irritations through the bashing of pirate skulls. With the support of those from the Isle of Serpents, I was no longer alone in battling the unnatural forces unleashed by the shamans and that allowed me the simple pleasure of physical aggression. *Saorsa* still refused to sing to me but she cut just as deeply.

I joined Sutha and Drey to work on Kade whenever I was not healing or fighting. Now that we knew Erula's connection to Faulknar's king, we could interrupt her spell and provide some relief from his demoralising ghosts. Breaking the spell was not difficult but we remained unable to block her access to the vast power that channelled through her. She was as frustrating as the pirates, with each success at severing her connection to Kade being quickly negated by another enchantment. My role became reduced to repeatedly thwarting her attempts and was as tiresome as blowing out a candle that refused to be extinguished. While I forced Erula to concentrate on me, Sutha and Drey were able to address Kade's malignant shadow. They carefully rebuilt the protective wards within his tattoo, reinforcing them again and again when they became overwhelmed by the corruption woven through his energies. I was able to quieten his torments for a while, but the black tendrils persisted to stab at his anger despite all attempts to contain it. The king's rages continued to be volatile and he found little peace no matter what we tried.

Hayton maintained his advance through the rest of the kingdom. The armies of Baila and Lindvane had fought as separate forces, with Lindvane primarily pushing from the west while the Army of Truth marched up from the south. They had divided our resources with the need to defend both fronts. Faulknar's soldiers had been driven back so that they now faced a continuous line reaching from the marshes and fens of the west to the estuaries of Stanmouth in the east. The noose was tightening around Liegeport with almost two-thirds of the kingdom now beyond our reach. The invading armies had no interest in talking hostages or slaves, and those who had not been able to reach safety had been systematically slaughtered. Everyone felt the constricting pressure of the relentless advance as the coiling of a spring, twisting tighter and tighter within our chests. It was inevitable that at some point our line would break.

The call came that Lindvane had pushed through at Marten's Ford, two days' ride south of Liegeport. Keenan's company were sent to assist the soldiers who had been flanked, with the instruction to halt the enemy's flood through the gap. The Lord General was not going to leave his nephew's side again, despite all the commands to the contrary, and sent his captain in his stead. Bodax welcomed us as cheerfully as he had in the marshes, extending his invitation to Elyos and the fighters from Hilman. Mace and his guard, including the brothers, swelled our numbers and we left the town in a thunder of hooves. We pushed the horses harshly and rested little so that we were able to shave a half-day off the journey's time and arrived a little after dusk on the following day.

We made for the camp that had been erected to the west of the breach, finding orderly rows of tents and the busy activity of fighters overlaid with the harsh ring of a smith's hammer. Soldiers and mercenaries. Men and women. Young and old. Experienced fighter and new recruit. All melded together with expressions of determination covering those of exhaustion. Our mounts were efficiently collected by the young stablehands, while our company was taken for food and rest. Bodax and Mace were required to report to the camp's general, and Keenan's stocky captain suggested that I should also attend. As I was going nowhere without Vallori, the four of us were escorted to a shelter situated in the centre of the army's base.

The door flap was held open for me and I entered to find the main area filled with soldiers huddled over a collapsable table. Their attention was focused on a frayed map, with fingers jabbing at various points while the relative strengths and weaknesses of the two sides were discussed. Mace strode over to clasp Slicer on the shoulder, who still wore the ever-present broadsword that had earned him his name. The two friends greeted each other warmly.

The general had his back to me with his head bent over the map. He finished his instructions to one of his captains before turning to acknowledge Mace and address the rest of us. My heart raced when I recognised a face that had been marked by too many scars. A face showing more creases around his eyes from the years of hard fighting. Sharp blue eyes that contained an amused glint. He relaxed his formal posture, dropping his shoulders and shaking his head slowly in disbelief.

'Well met, Tallen nic Duane.' His wide smile added more creases around his eyes. 'It has been a very long time since I've seen those strange orange eyes.'

I stood frozen in place. So many emotions clambered for attention that I was unable to focus on any one of them. Tears threatened to spill down my cheeks while I drank in every detail of someone I had not expected to find.

'Fearsome Father, girl,' Gheth said impatiently. 'Get over here. I have need to confirm what my eyes are telling me by holding your tiny bones. And Laken will return to haunt me if I just leave you standing there.'

My legs finally responded and I quickly crossed to Gheth's open arms. I fell into his firm embrace, bunching his shirt in my fists when unexpected memories of Laken threatened to buckle my knees.

'Come now,' he said after too short a time. 'We have a war to fight.'

I reluctantly released my hold and took a step back, studying the changes in his face. 'You should learn to move out of the way of swinging blades.'

'I'll try to remember that,' he replied with an indulgent grin before turning to Bodax. 'What news from Liegeport?'

We exchanged information, finally arranging for a combined assault to begin at dawn and we were sent to seek whatever rest we could find. Gheth caught my arm when I made to leave.

'It will be good to have your talents, Tallen. We have much need of them.'

A low cloud pressed down on us the next morning and its fine mist of rain added to an already oppressive mood. Both armies had gathered before the night had faded to grey in anticipation of the inevitable battle; Lindvane knew their advance would not remain unchallenged while Faulknar knew they could not leave the enemy at their rear. I expected it to be a bitter struggle from which Gheth's soldiers would not retreat. Vallori rode by my side and Elyos held position nearby on an agitated bay. The Hilman was uncomfortable with the thought of riding the gelding into battle and his frustration was felt by his mount. All three of our horses had been battle-trained and had faced violence before, but it still stung his principles to take a horse into such danger.

'It looks as if Lindvane and Baila have become friends,' commented Vallori while we waited for the signal to engage.

A long line of soldiers faced us with the image of Baila interspersed within the ranks carrying Hayton's boar. The two imposing armies presented a united force that aimed to intimidate and demoralise those fighting for a kingdom that stood alone. The Army of Truth that opposed us here was not that of the inexperienced fanatics we had encountered on the border of the Northlands, and there would be no adherence to the rules of the game played there. These showed the organisation and discipline of fighters who had gathered years of experience, seamlessly integrated into the ranks of Lindvane's soldiers. I assessed our own lines and found no lack of discipline or determination there.

Elyos's gelding shied sideways and I felt the whispering touch of gathered energies. In alarm, I scanned the rear of the endless ranks of hostile soldiers but saw no evidence of shaman involvement. I turned a questioning look to Elyos whose expression confirmed that he had felt it too. Vallori cursed and I followed his gaze to the west.

'It would appear we now know why the Gallowglass were waiting,' he commented grimly. 'Their reinforcements were coming up from the south.'

The hatefully familiar mist coalesced behind the invading armies. We had not thought to consider that Gallowgla would align with Lindvane and give their aid to an inland assault, despite Sutha's warning. They had no need to risk pirate lives when their daemons could rampage amongst those of Lindvane and Baila. I echoed Vallori's curse, drawing *Saorsa* as the monsters solidified and the call to engage sounded across the battlefield.

The orderly advance of the enemy disintegrated in response to our mounted charge. We crashed through their front ranks, cleaving left and right as we trampled others under our horses' hooves. Pockets of fighting spread throughout the first lines of contact and the horses pushed through while the enemy closed in behind us. Our mounts were forced to stand, shying sideways or turning to expose their hind legs when threatened, hampered by the close press of fighters. My blade slashed again and again at all within her reach. Elyos's bay flailed wildly, unnerved by the danger surrounding him with a rider who struggled to control the erupting battle-lust. The *miann cath* quickly abandoned the attempt, dismounting and turning the horse loose to fend for itself before merging into the heaving mass of battle.

The ground shook when the land-daemons crashed through the Lindvane lines and thundered towards us. I sent fireballs arcing into the sky at the bird-daemons that swooped down to spear our soldiers with their pointed beaks. Trefin swung round to kick a Baila fighter in the face, twisting back for me to silence his cries with a back-handed slash across his throat. I kicked out at another who dared to grab at my mare's reins, clubbing him with *Saorsa*'s hilt before slicing into his shoulder. A horse-daemon cantered past, breaking bones when it tossed its head. I could not manoeuvre Trefin to intercede so tore a crater into the soft ground, causing it to stumble and fall in a tangle of limbs. Unable to reach the monster, I liquefied the earth under the beast, causing it to sink as if engulfed by a swamp. It was completely covered before I solidified the ground once more. A blade swung towards my chest, forcing my attention back to the dangers surrounding me, and I had no time to see whether the daemon would remain entombed.

I was never a strong rider and I found myself having to concentrate on controlling a frightened Trefin within the surrounding enemy, rather than being able to deal with the daemons. Despite my mare working courageously to defend my rear and keep me in the saddle, I was unable to split my attention to cover so many factors. Saying a quick prayer to the Gods to keep her safe, I followed Elyos's example and turned her loose. I ran towards the nearest daemon, defending against those who opposed me by reflex while manipulating the elements. I moulded the earth, stiffened the air and created barriers of fire. I confused and delayed the monsters until I could finish them with *Saorsa*'s hungry blade. I slipped and darted and twisted my way through the mass of fighting, chasing down one creature after another. Green mist surrounded me, diluted by the fine spray of rain into glistening emerald droplets.

It took until late in the afternoon before we had pushed the enemy back far enough to allow an adequate defence of the line. The fighting had slowed to an exhausted exchange of blows but neither side had the motivation to press the advantage once it was clear the breach had been repaired. The daemons faded with the shamans having depleted their resources and gradually the armies withdrew to a joyless truce. Trefin had been trained well and I found her not far from where I had abandoned her. She was surrounded by soldiers with smashed heads, many of which showed the half-moon imprint from her shoes. She shied when I approached and stamped her front hoof in agitation. I huffed a short, incredulous laugh.

'You stand firm against enemy soldiers who want to hamstring you and daemons that want to disembowel you, and yet you shy from me?' I reached out to scratch at the base of her ear. 'I'm trying not to be offended by that.'

She snorted in a release of tension, blasting me with a puff of warm air as she reached her head forward to nibble at the ties of my jerkin. I was still resting my head against her forehead when Vallori joined me, leading Mikkla who had a deep gash over her shoulder. I narrowed my eyes when I saw that her rider was equally battered. A dark bruise surrounded a narrow cut at his hairline and the ragged slash that had opened his upper arm was still bleeding.

'Let me heal you,' I persisted when he twisted away from my reaching hand.

'There are those who need your skills more.'

I sadly accepted that truth and let him guide me to where a temporary shelter had been arranged to treat those most seriously injured. I was pleased to see that Gheth had several healers in his company and together we worked on those who struggled to maintain their grip on life, while others were left to cauterise and dress the many open wounds. Most of the night had gone by the time I had finished and was escorted to the general's shelter for much needed food and rest.

'Daemons?' I asked, gratefully slumping into a chair. 'How long have you been facing those monsters?'

'Not long.' He dismissed his attendant and poured me a drink. 'There was a change after the dry-lightning storms. We were used to facing either Lindvane or Baila, but then they started combining their forces. It was almost as if they were holding back until then. The unwelcome addition of those horrors is a new development.' He grinned at me. 'Your arrival is timely.'

I remained quiet, avoiding his gaze while I nibbled at the bread and cheese he had provided. He tilted his head at me and his smile slowly faded.

'I know you can't stay, Tallen.'

I looked up at him with an apology. 'I'm needed here. I hate having to abandon you.'

He huffed quietly. 'I have been fighting this war for a very long time. I have no plans of leaving before the end. You do not have to worry about me.'

'Sorry, General.' I smiled sadly. 'I am unable to obey that order. I will continue to worry about you until this cursed war is over.'

'With what they've started throwing at us, I fear that may be sooner than we planned.' He sighed. 'You should be with him. He has perilously few friends left to watch his back.'

Gheth was one of the last links I had to Laken. 'I would stay. If it was any other than him, I would stand with you.'

Gheth smiled softly. 'I know. But your destinies have ever been entwined. Go and protect our king.'

Valloni and I left just before noon the next day, along with Bodax and Mace and each of their companies. Elyos and his fighters remained to counter the threat from the daemons as best they could. His battle-fury was more suited to the open battlefield than the restricted spaces within the port, where there was the risk of the townspeople getting caught in his path. He did not hide his relief when Gheth enthusiastically accepted his assistance and was already organising runners to source ancient weapons when we rode out of the camp.

We did not tire the horses and returned to Liegeport in no great haste. I felt the tension tighten my shoulders the closer we got to the port and I sharply missed the easy company of Gheth and his soldiers, uncorrupted by the gossip and lies which infested the town. I ignored the look of distain from those guarding the gate, grateful they had restricted their distaste to ill-tempered scowls and had not prevented us from entering.

'I refuse to do anything until I have soaked in a bath,' I declared.

'You need to care of your horse first,' Valloni corrected.

I rolled my eyes at having ruined my moment. 'After I have cared for Trefin, I refuse to do anything until I have soaked in a bath.'

A mischievous smile flickered at the corner of his mouth. 'You should resupply your herbs and ointments.'

I groaned in frustration. 'You are no fun. Stop being so sensible.'

'Apparently, one of us needs to be and it seems destined that I'm the sensible *pháirtí* while you are the *pháirtí* who goes looking for trouble.'

'That's not fair!' I cried in protest. 'I have not gone looking for trouble in ages. Well, for a while. I haven't gone looking for trouble today. And, you have to admit, trouble finds me more often than I go looking for it. And Elyos is worse than me.'

We continued to bicker while the horses were settled into their stalls and we made our way to the waterfront, my bath having been postponed until after we had reported to the infirmary. The building was unusually subdued and our return was greeted with sad smiles or embarrassed avoidance. I feared the sombre atmosphere was the result of a large attack, involving many casualties. I straightened my spine and prepared myself for a prolonged healing session.

Vallori entered the room first and I had to stop quickly to avoid knocking into him. My fear sharped with his sudden, coiled stillness and I followed his gaze to see Drey sitting on a bench beside Bonash. Drey's right hand was bandaged and his posture was stiff and protective. A large bruise spread along his jawline and the skin was pulled tight around one eye with swelling. His robes covered the signs of other injuries from my critical assessment but I did not doubt that there would be a significant number. I pushed angrily past Vallori and stormed over to the two men.

'What happened?' I growled.

'Now, don't fuss.' Drey carefully turned his head to look at me. 'I'm fine. Just a few bruises that will soon fade.'

I turned to Nash and repeated my demand. 'What happened?'

The smaller man flicked Drey an apologetic look before answering. 'He was attacked.'

'I can see that,' I snapped.

Bonash continued patiently. 'The day after you left.'

'Cowards. Who?'

'There really is no need to concern yourself,' Drey persisted.

'Erula?' I accused, ignoring the injured man's weak protests.

Nash shrugged. 'Perhaps. Her frustration at our interference has added a new level of spite to her rumours. But they bore the image of Baila.'

'Coen.'

Drey went to wave his bandaged hand in dismissal but quickly corrected himself with a brief grimace. 'Coen feels threatened by the work we are doing here. Despite the best efforts of those two snakes, people are remembering the kindness of the old ways and that is desperately needed at the moment.

It is making them question the rigid doctrine of the One God. Coen simply sent a pair of his thugs to remind me of his power.'

'It was more than a pair,' Bonash corrected quietly.

'I hope you helped them question their mistake?' I demanded of Drey.

He gave me a mildly embarrassed smile. 'They may think twice about attacking an old man.'

'And a few that will not be thinking anything at all for some time,' confirmed Nash with an expression that bordered on affectionate pride.

'Curse that festering priest to the Seven Hells of Mobis.' I slumped onto the bench beside Drey. 'This has got to stop. How are we supposed to defend against external enemies when we have those within Liegeport seeking to frustrate our every move?'

Drey raised an eyebrow at my exaggeration, wincing when the gesture pulled at the skin of his damaged eye.

'I fear there is not much we can do to discourage Coen and his flock of bullies. But perhaps we can irritate Erula a little further.'

Bonash shook his head. 'We've discussed this. It's too dangerous. And that's assuming we can even get close enough to find out if what you suspect is true.'

'What are you taking about? What's too dangerous?'

Vallori huffed. 'You managed to last a full morning before you went looking for trouble.'

'Hush,' I replied. 'You are not going to let this pass any more than I am.'

'There may be a way of snapping the witch's power supply,' began Drey, intentionally ignoring our comments. 'The energy source is old. Ancient. More powerful than that of the land.'

I frowned. 'A God? Baila?'

'That is my assumption. I have a text somewhere that mentions the possibility of harnessing the power of a God. I never paid it much attention because why would anyone want to channel that much raw energy.' His eyes flashed with excitement. 'But maybe Erula would be foolish enough to try.'

'Drey,' I cautioned softly, not wanting to remember the last time I had seen his books. 'Your chambers have been destroyed. If your information was there, it has been burned or torn beyond repair.'

'I am not a complete fool, Tallen. I did see what was coming and placed all but the most banal documents in the tower. They are warded against all except Kade. I have not lost that much faith in him.'

'Your tower is beyond our reach,' protested Nash. 'We cannot obtain the text even if we assume it has not been destroyed.'

'I can get us in.' I grinned at Drey.

'You?' Vallori blurted. 'The person the guards would most happily spear as a traitor? Along with a druid who has been marked by two sorcerers, one of whom may be channelling a God.'

'Keenan will get us in,' I persisted, continuing to look at Drey and ignoring Vallori.

'Of course.' Drey enthusiastically slapped his thigh then cursed when he struck a sore area. 'No one is brave enough to disobey the Lord General. Especially in his current temper.'

Vallori sighed in defeat. 'I don't suppose we would be fortunate enough to be interrupted by Gallowgla and their unnatural creations. I fear those threats would be less likely to kill us.'

'Good point, young man,' replied Drey, standing up to slap the warrior on his chest. 'We should leave at once.'

Despite my confident claim that Keenan could grant us access to the royal house, I had not truly believed he would be able to achieve it. Keenan's temper, however, had become perilously shortened with the frequent, violent arguments with his king and there was not a soldier in Liegeport willing to cross him. He cursed and berated and threatened while the guards swiftly moved to obey his commands. We received poisonous glares and fists were tightened around weapons in impotent frustration, but we were granted entry into the building.

'Hagan wants a word with you, boy,' Keenan instructed fully expecting Vallori to follow him, and his face hardened with barely suppressed anger when Vallori hesitated. 'Don't make me tell you twice.'

I urged him to go and he reluctantly accepted the inevitable, understanding that Keenan could have us restrained in chains as easily as he had gained us entry. Drey and I swiftly made for the stairs after the two men left, not wanting to linger without the protective presence of the Lord General. We arrived at his chambers without incident but Drey paused with his hand resting on the door.

'I can do this alone,' he said quietly.

I was in no rush to enter the room. Although I had mocked Vallori's *sensible concerns*, I was fully aware of the dangers we faced. Rolyan may have been gone but there were many others who would eagerly take his place to gain favour with someone as influential as Erula. Drey understood my reluctance and graciously gave me an excuse.

'It would be beneficial if you could distract our enchantress while I engage in magicks.' He smiled. 'I believe you would enjoy the opportunity to take counsel with Erula.'

'There are one or two topics we could discuss.' My smile faded. 'Be safe, old man.'

He flapped his hand in dismissal and opened the door, calling back to me while he entered. 'Try not to cause too much trouble.'

I left Drey to mourn his ruined chambers in privacy and I scanned for Erula's distinctive signal within the turbulent energies flowing around the royal house. I crossed to the opposite hallway, following her current towards the suite that had once been claimed by Kyllian. It would have reflected the witch's inflated sense of importance for her to claim chambers meant for a king, but I admitted it was more likely she would be there to tighten her web around Kade. His presence would complicate matters, and I was in no hurry to encounter his temper, but not to the point where I would abandon the opportunity to call her to account for her meddling.

I passed the chambers that had been Kade's, finding the door slightly open and quiet muttering coming from within. The king was not with Erula as I had assumed and I eased the door further open to find him pacing the outer chamber. His hands were pinched white in tight fists while he marched across the room. His head jerked in an achingly familiar gesture, mumbling words too quiet for me to understand. He was completely alone. No guards protected him and he was without even a dagger to defend himself if needed. He turned and saw me, twitching when he raised his head. His face creased in distaste.

'It would seem that my guards should be disciplined for their slovenly behaviour,' he declared coldly. 'Do you feel an execution would be sufficiently motivating, considering the filth they have let seep into my house?'

Ignoring the hurt caused by his comments, I carefully took two paces into the room. He took a defensive step back, before glaring a challenge for me to comment on his unintentional display of vulnerability.

'Perhaps. They've tolerated your decline.' I flicked a hand to my forehead. 'Tell me, when did Faulknar's king need a crown to demand the respect of his people?'

He growled in response. 'Why are you here?'

'I thought that would be obvious. Look at you. Somebody needs to save your miserable hide.'

'Save me? Incinerate me would be closer to the truth.' He narrowed his eyes at me and his lip curled in a scathing hate. 'Where is your dragon?'

'For the love of Mobis, Kade! Forget about my dragon. You have real enemies at your gates. You're a soldier. Why are you not out there, fighting alongside those who are willing to die for you?'

'Forget your dragon?' His voice dipped dangerously low. 'Is it so easy to forget what you did to me? I know what the real enemy is. I have seen it.'

Kade's visions had begun after I tore him from Mobis's Hells. Visions of a dragon, *my dragon*, breathing fire over Liegeport. I could not believe that Megin would destroy innocent people so wantonly but the doubt remained. Kade's defences were not the only reason I wanted to keep my dragon far from the royal port.

A violent tremor shuddered through his body and he closed his eyes, fighting against the forces which had been sent to break him.

'Go,' he whispered through tightly clenched teeth. 'Leave me.'

'Who do you see?' I asked gently. 'What do they say to you?'

He wiped a hand across the back of his neck where sweat had darkened his collar. He stared at me with tightly controlled anger.

"My father tells me that which I already know. That you have betrayed me and will destroy the kingdom that fostered you. That the druid will bring foul magick to ensnare the souls of my people, condemning them to burn in eternal torment. He instructs me to execute you both.' His smile held a cruel malice. 'He provides detailed account on how I should do it.'

I heard the echo of Erula in his words but was not given the opportunity to tell him so. A blinding flash of blue light blazed throughout the building and the structure shook violently, showering dust from chipped stone. My vision danced with after-images. I looked to Kade but he was already running, pushing past me and out into the corridor. I swiftly followed him to the shattered remains of the door to Drey's chambers.

I froze on the threshold, unable to process what I was seeing. Hagan had replaced the ruined furniture as I had requested, but this was now littered throughout the room in twisted timber and torn fabric. The door to his private chamber, and which led to the tower, was hanging by a single hinge having been scorched with the image of a large flame. Lying in its shadow was the contorted body of Coen. His robes were still smouldering and his long, lank hair was singed, framing a face fixed in a mask of agony.

Kade knelt in the outer chamber. His hand was holding one drained of colour, his other hand cradled the head. My mind frantically repeated that it was all right, everything was going to be all right. The fact that I could not look at Drey suggested otherwise. There was a lot of blood. Too much blood.

It took an extreme amount of effort to force myself to look and bear witness to the unthinkable act that Coen had committed. Tears streamed down Kade's face as he accepted what I could not. A large gash carved into Drey's skull and showed white bone within a pool of crimson blood. An irregular circle of bruising covered the deformity of his neck where the small bones of his throat had been crushed, causing the dreadful rasp which accompanied each shallow, infrequent breath. His robes were soaked with blood and a dark, ruby puddle was slowly spreading across the wooden floor beside him. The wound would be large and deep. It was pure strength of will that had kept Drey from joining his Gods.

He was still alive. I should help him. My body refused to move.

I assessed his wounds again and my thoughts slowly accepted what I was seeing. A wound below the ribs at the point where the energies converged – *the draining of life's blood*. The crushing of the throat to obstruct the passage of air – *the stilling of life's breath*. The blow to the skull to expose the brain – *the releasing of life's soul*. Three distinct ways of ending life. Each sufficient to make the kill. The triple death. Coen had given Drey the threefold death.

My heart clenched painfully. Drey opened watery eyes and struggled to focus on Kade. The two men exchanged a heart-shatteringly intimate look. Whatever my relationship with Drey had been, it was a faint shadow compared to the bond between Kade and his mentor. His protector. His friend. The moment made more terribly unbearable by Kade's treatment of the old man over the past few years.

'You know what you are,' Drey breathed, making barely enough sound to be heard. 'The fool gave me the... the threefold death. The greatest gift.'

Drey closed his eyes, and I waited in agony before he took a rattling breath. Kade dropped his head onto the knuckles of his hand, his tears falling to run across his skin and onto Drey's. He lifted his head again when Drey clawed in a second breath.

'You were born a bard,' he continued weakly, having to pause before he

502

took the next breath. 'Trauma made you a seer.' He fixed Kade with a look of such harrowing tenderness. 'With love, I make you a druid.'

With a cry that tore at my soul, Drey rolled onto his side. He brought up his free hand and slammed it into Kade's chest. Kade threw his head back in a silent scream. A flare of sapphire illuminated Drey's hand and seared its image into Kade's chest. The transfer of immense energy radiated from the contact to bathe Faulknar's king in a corona of golden light. The power granted by the triple death, which Coen had wanted to take for himself, combined with Drey's dying soul to pierce into Kade's being and infuse every one of his cells. A terrifying screech split the air when Drey's gift collided with the corruption enmeshed within the king. Kade's spine arched and his arms were forced back. A dark shadow was ejected out of his back, writhing with twisting tendrils to form the outline of the man. It hung in the air for several heartbeats while it shifted and shimmered, then burst into a spray of bright blue droplets which rapidly faded.

Kade slumped forward, curling protectively over Drey who refused to breathe no matter how hard I willed it to be. The new druid's aura blazed with a golden hue that contained the remnants of Drey. All that he had been now resided safely within Kade. The weight of the legacy, generously given, bowed the young man's shoulders and he sobbed in distraught agony.

I could not stop shaking. My mind could only offer fragments of thoughts. I continued to stare at the piteously vulnerable, broken body of Drey and the devastatingly defeated posture of Kade. The corruption that had polluted his energies since I had retrieved him from Mobis's Hells had been completely expelled, but the cost had been unconscionably high. I could not accept that this had been a good outcome.

My anger answered my distressed soul with a comforting familiarity. I blamed the Gods and the Fates for allowing this to happen. I blamed Villermir and Coen and all the despised priesthood. And I blamed Erula for tormenting my king when he was already damaged.

I left the chamber and was halfway along the hallway before I was aware of where my feet were taking me. The twisted energies of Erula's spell had dissipated but her core pulsed urgently. I smiled a predatory grimace; she knew I would be coming for her. I kicked the door, shattering the latch and adding to the debris created by the earlier destruction. The brass bowl and ritual herbs had been discarded in front of the fire, unremarkable amongst all the other scattered artefacts. I disregarded them as unimportant and strode to the private room on the left. Erula yelped when she saw me, dropping the clothes she was hastily packing. I used a barrier of air to slam her against the wall and pin her suspended above the ground. I took my time to cross the room while she visibly fought to suppress her terror. I stopped a pace in front of her and wondered why I had taken so long to squash this insignificant, little bug.

'Your king is broken,' she spat with a shaking voice. 'Shattered beyond repair.'

I calmly created a fireball and set it slowly spinning above my palm. I watched while she squirmed against the pressure I pushed into her chest, taking no satisfaction from her struggles. I tracked the tears that leaked from the corners of her eyes when it became increasingly harder for her to breathe.

'You tried to break him,' I stated quietly. 'You failed, but it cannot go unpunished.' I ignored her whimper. 'I should flay the skin from your body. I should crush your bones, one by one, while you scream your throat bloody. I should rip out your spiteful heart and hold it pulsing in my hand while I tear it into excruciatingly painful strips. I should make you regret that you ever came to Liegeport.'

And yet I did none of those things. I held her suspended, completely at my will, while my rage offered countless ways in which to make her suffer. But the flames of my anger did not reach the surface. I was unable to connect with such righteous passion. A quiet part of my mind reminded me of Drey's sacrifice and I found myself unwilling to disappoint him.

I held Erula pressed against the wall for a long time while the turmoil seethed and demanded to be released. Eventually, I extinguished the flames of the fireball and quenched the witch's life with an equal lack of effort.

Dawn rose over the sea in a dazzling display. The light cast a soft glow around the shadows of the Gallowgla ships, stretching beyond sight in both directions, lines upon lines to encircle Faulknar. The seabirds glided on the wind, screaming their indifference as they searched for fish. The gentle murmur of the awakening port wrapped around me while I sat on the seawall, my legs high above the water.

I had left the royal house without returning to Kade and aimlessly walked the streets for most of the night. I was unwilling to return to North End and the memories of Drey that waited there. I had no desire to encounter Vallori and his endless sympathy, and I was not good company for anyone else. I had withdrawn to the dispossessed people of the town who understood loss and anger and defeat. I became lost within those who understood the struggle of having to continue.

I turned to see Bonash waiting cautiously before he approached at my invitation. He sat beside me, looking out over the waves and tracking the flights of the birds.

'A lot of people are looking for you,' he scolded mildly. 'Vallori is ready to stab anyone within reach.'

We sat in a comfortable silence for a while before he tried again.

'More ships have arrived overnight. Hayton rides up from the south. It will not be long before we see his banners.' He sighed. 'Bear would have hated missing the end.'

My mouth twitched in a sad smile. 'He would have hated the thought of Mace stealing his glory.'

The small man released a quietly amused laugh before the sombre mood drifted back. 'I'm sorry about Drey. It was an impressive thing that he did.'

I briefly closed my eyes but the loss had dulled to a persistent ache at some point during the night. 'I think he was looking for a little glory of his own.'

'I find it hard to see the glory,' Nash confessed tiredly. 'Just the hurt. The best I can hope for is to maintain some shred of honour. I hate to think that Bear would be embarrassed by me. I'm not a warrior like him.' He took a shaking breath. 'It should have been me.'

I turned to face him. 'Don't say that. Don't ever think that. And Bear would never be embarrassed by you. He was so proud of you and what you accomplished. Nash, you are the cleverest person I know.' I thought of Drey. 'And I have known some very clever people. And you are a good fighter, despite what you think.' He shook his head in denial. 'You know I'm not just saying that to make you feel better. I would gladly have you by my side when we finish this, but that is not where you are strongest. You know your place is with Sutha and her team. We need you to control the shamans. We would have already lost without your aid there.'

'People are dying and I remain sheltered behind walls. I feel so useless.'

I sighed, trying to find a way to make him understand. 'The fighters get all the praise. They get stories told and ballads sung about them. But that does not negate what you can do. Hilman would have become enslaved to the priests if it were not for your coins. Sluagh's army would be marching across Faulknar, claiming every last soul, if it were not for your team of seers. Do not think less of your abilities just because they are silent.'

He remained quiet for a while before turning to give me a small smile. 'Thank you.'

I grinned. 'And besides, someone has to tell our story. I expect you to tell anyone with ears about my cursed, glorious destiny. Win or lose, people should remember. And I will accept nothing less than a twelve-verse ballad with a rowdy chorus.'

Bonash shook his head with an exasperated grimace. 'I'm a worse singer than I am a fighter. I propose a grand tale that will be told for generations.'

The mocking smile faded from my lips and I thought of the real possibility that I would not live to see the end of this war, and how I calmly accepted that fate.

'Tell me your story,' Nash continued, still caught up in the illusion of the Three Kingdoms being safe from conflict and where people could listen to a long tale by a warm fire. 'Tell me all the fabulous details so I can craft your saga of unbelievable feats.'

And so, I told him. I told him everything. I talked of Drey and of Laken. Of Kade and of Breya. Of Kerk and of Tawpin. Of Villermir and the Isle of Serpents. Of Freisholm and Sálaforn and Bane. Of the Goddess. And of Megin. I told him of all the things I had done that I could never have told Vallori. I made peace with my past and moved forward to meet my fate.

CHAPTER THIRTY-THREE

The attack came before dawn, with the darkness adding another layer to the hellish scene with the fires glowing vividly against the indigo sky and green wraiths emerging from the black shadows. After weeks of individual, randomised strikes, an organised assault involving countless pirate ships had increased the confusion and fear within those who had been targeted first. Multiple raids were sent to both the docks of Liegeport and along the surrounding coast. Every fighter was roused as we were forced to divide our numbers into three. One third rode north-west to cover the coast between Liegeport and Kingsport. One third rode south-east to defend the stretch between Liegeport and Stanmouth. The final third remained to protect the port and the town. We were stretched perilously thin.

Vallori and I raced to the docks, shoving and elbowing people out of our way while they pressed into the overcrowded town and the safety they hoped to find there. The chaos was worse outside the gates. The docks had been distinctly separate when I was a child, their industry sited away from the royal town with a grassy common land separating the two. Precariously unstable timber dwellings now covered the area closest to the town walls, with these replaced by tented shelters when we got nearer to the docks. The most vulnerable had only thin blankets to protect themselves from the cold. All those desperate people now pushed towards the gate in a frantic attempt to gain shelter within the walls. We fought against the tide of terrified people and treated them harsher than they deserved, but it was impossible to gain any progress without cursing and shouting and pushing them out of our way.

The disorder changed at the docks. Any who did not need to be there had already fled, leaving only the soldiers and pirates to clash in a purer form of madness. I was engulfed in the fighting soon after entering the wide streets that led directly to the jetties. The design of Liegeport's docks had developed as its own centre of commerce rather than as an extension of the town and, as a result, the fighting was different to that in Kingsport. The streets were large enough to accommodate wagons and this allowed us to fight within small companies rather than being restricted to individual skirmishes. Vallori and I joined a group of around twenty who had formed a barrier to confine the raiders by the waterfront. We were outnumbered but able to maintain an unbroken line between the buildings on either side. It was a dangerously weak defence, and we were only able to hold because the pirates were prevented from attacking us with more than a few at a time. We fought savagely with the knowledge that if they broke through, they would quickly overwhelm us.

Wraiths stalked throughout and were not restricted by the confines of the streets. They would appear behind us to present a potentially lethal distraction, in addition to the deadly threat of weapons which could not be turned by steel. Children, too young to fight but too old to remain with their mothers, were used as runners to relay messages between different groups and take reports to those coordinating the defence from the royal house. They also proved immensely useful at brandishing pitch-soaked torches at the skeletal ghosts. The flames were not hot enough to incinerate the creatures but they were effective at causing enough delay for us to dodge out of their spectral grasp while still concentrating on the attacking pirates. Curiously, the wraiths often appeared sufficiently frustrated that they would seek easier prey elsewhere. On one occasion, I saw them being herded into a burning building where the fires had reached the required intensity to ignite them. The children darted everywhere and were surprisingly efficient at containing the threat of these unnatural enemies.

I sent a fireball into a group of wraiths that had evaded the fire-brandishing runner to close in on a soldier on my left, causing those on that flank to flinch away from the sudden flare of heat. The raiders sought to exploit the opportunity and I used a blast of air to stun them, giving the soldiers time to recover. In the heartbeat taken to deal with those on my left, those to my right pressed in to take the advantage. Vallori deflected the blade that aimed for my vulnerable side and used the same swing to deal with the pirate who meant to impale him. I brought *Saorsa* round with a slashing swipe that cut across the face of my attacker and caused him to stumble into the path of Vallori's sword. The two pirates were instantly replaced with fresh fighters and we were forced back a few paces. I tightened my grip on *Saorsa*'s hilt as concussive forces travelled up my arms and I absorbed the violent impact again and again. All I saw was the enemy in front of me and Vallori fighting beside me. Slice and parry. Slice and parry.

A tug pulled at my jerkin. I turned and swept my sword in an arc to confront the threat. Only the small size of the runner saved her from decapitation.

'By the Gods!' I roared. 'I almost took your head off.'

'The king requests your presence,' she declared impertinently.

'Don't touch people when they're fighting,' I growled, still full of the need to kill raiders.

'He says it's urgent.'

I grabbed the child's shirt and pushed her backwards more roughly than was necessary. The defending line closed seamlessly behind me while I challenged the girl.

'Tell me. Quick.'

She had seen too much conflict and was not intimidated by my anger. She gave her message clearly and concisely before running off to deliver her report to others fighting within the docks. I cursed in frustration but could not deny Kade's summons. Vallori stole a quick glance when his opponent fell, also retreating out of the line at my apologetic expression.

'Daemons,' I explained briefly. 'Stay if you're needed here.'

He gave a short grunt in reply, immediately following when I turned back towards Liegeport.

Trying to get back into the town was more frustrating than it had been leaving it. During the time we had been fighting, the flood of refugees had compressed to a heaving mass which blocked access to the gate. Our pleas to make room quickly descended into shouted threats. People were reluctant to let us through, angry that two more would be between them and the shelter they sought. Soldiers who should have been fighting the enemy were, instead, having to forcefully maintain order while preventing all except the runners from getting in.

With the use of increasingly violent verbal and physical means, we finally passed through the gate and ran to the royal house. The war council was being held in the formal hall, having been stripped of its ostentatious rug, tapestries and candles. A wall of noise greeted us while runners darted about like agitated insects. Several tables had been provided, each with a map detailing a sector of the fighting. Reports and instructions were filtered to the appropriate table and the senior soldiers who surrounded it. Kade roamed around the room, stopping briefly to talk with those in a group before moving on to another. I was unexpectedly pleased to see that his crown had been removed, and that Hagan had resumed his rightful place a step behind his king. We were within a few paces of the two men when Kade noticed our arrival. He launched straight into his instructions without greeting.

'Lindvane has pushed through the line and is marching towards Liegeport. Two companies remain between them and us but the rest are having to fight a retreat.'

He marched over to another table expecting us to follow him, which we obediently did. He reviewed the map and the placement of counters laid upon it with a deepening scowl while he continued to address us.

'Gheth is holding ground at Warren's Heath. We will join him to slow the advance, giving the other companies time to rally.' He looked up at me. 'It's time I saw these cursed daemons and what a Dragonslayer can do about them.'

'Through the Gods you will,' stated Hagan, taking a heartbeat before looking up from the map to stare at his king. 'You are needed here.'

I held my breath. Kade had not been openly challenged without responding with an explosion of temper in a very long time. Everyone within hearing distance had stilled, waiting to see if he would retaliate. Many expected that to be at the sharp end of a blade. The moment held for several heartbeats while the two stared, Hagan with casual determination and Kade with irritated frustration. Eventually, Kade tilted his head with a sigh of defeat. He turned to me, holding my gaze for a moment before giving me the commands to relay to Gheth.

'Tallen,' he called when I made to leave. 'Make sure you come back and report to me.'

'Yes, my liege.' I made a formal bow before turning back to see Vallori's amused grin. 'What? He is my king.'

Horses were waiting for us at the bottom of the stone steps. The one allocated to me shied when I approached but there was no time to fetch Trefin. I channelled its apprehension into speed and we raced south out of

Liegeport to join Elyos. We bullied our way through familiar scenes that extended around the perimeter of the town. Crowds of people clogged the roads and the desertion of the camps carried a frantic undertone with pirates now pushing in from the coast. We saw no signs of fighting, but the sounds of conflict drifted on the wind and were sufficient to cause panic.

Having pushed through the camps, we then had to negotiate the barriers placed between them and the encroaching armies. Liegeport had not been designed for war and held only one defensive wall, albeit one that had been extended to become a double ring: one of stone, one of timber. To protect against this weakness, traps and deterrents had been laid to discourage a large-scale assault. There were long rows of stakes, rammed at an angle into the ground so that their sharp points would impale any charging horses. Numerous small trenches had been filled with sharpened sticks to pierce any who fell in. Several shallow mounds of earth had been placed to interrupt a disciplined march of organised troops and expose the enemy to our archers when they crested the shallow rises.

We carefully guided our horses through the deadly obstacles and then thundered towards a battle depressingly close to the royal port. We had scarcely made it through the barricades when the terrain gave us glimpses of the flapping banners. Once we saw the blurred outlines of the armies, we urged our mounts to deliver extra speed, knowing we would not need their stamina for much longer. We both fought daemons better on foot.

We lost no time looking for those in command, with our target clearly visible. Bird-daemons circled, screeching their challenge to those they flew over. Horse-daemons stampeded, creating chaos in the wake of the carnage they caused. Man-daemons rampaged, tossing soldiers as if they were cloth dolls. It took a heartbeat to determine a cloud of green mist hung over the right flank, where Elyos and his fighters would be engaged with the monsters. Infrequent plumes of green rose from various points within the left flank, where a thin covering of enchanted weapons dealt with the threat in that area. The central section seemed the most vulnerable and I aimed for there, with Vallori a step behind having made the same assessment.

I slashed and hacked at any who came too close but most I left to Vallori and the Faulknar soldiers who had moved to assist us. These were experienced campaigners who had been fighting for effective captains for many years. They needed no guidance to adapt to my magicks and they allowed me to work against an enemy they could not defeat. I was protected within a bubble of relative calm while I pushed through the battle, stalking daemons and letting a silent *Saorsa* drink their blood. I created a tapestry of fire, air and earth to herd the beasts towards me. I corralled several to charge at me at once, dancing in a rhythm which was so familiar that I did not need to hear my blade's song in order to follow her music. I rotated and lunged in a sweepingly graceful blend of movements that had been perfected to dispatch the beasts with the minimal number of strikes. I destroyed them again and again and again.

The horns called for the retreat and the trio of short pips repeated across our lines. The sun had passed its apex and was descending towards the west, and we had left little impression on the enemy with the area still swarming with an unopposable number of invading soldiers. The daemons continued their riot of destruction and I despaired at the sight. The battles within Hilman had relied on the limitations of each shaman's power, but teams of shamans would be able to summon their monsters beyond the endurance of the individual. The combined strength available from so many pirate ships would mean they could continue long beyond our ability to resist them. We did not have the troops needed to fight through and threaten the sorcerers. We did not have enough runed blades to deal with their daemons. We were being slaughtered by the combined armies of Gallowgla, Lindvane and Baila. We withdrew back to Liegeport, crushed by the heavy knowledge that we faced an insurmountable struggle.

The battle ebbed and flowed and our days fell into the routine of fight, rest, then fight again. The war became one of grinding repetition while we tried to maintain the little we had left. Unable to remain within our walls and force the enemy into a protracted siege, we pushed out, day after day, to defend those still desperately vulnerable outside the town. We fought rabidly, driven by the knowledge that if we retreated to the walls, they would soon fail and we would never recover. So, we rode out, day after day, to engage on a battlefield trampled to mud and sodden with the blood and waste of dying fighters and horses.

We faced attack from all sides. The Gallowglass barricaded our shoreline, sending raiders and wraiths from the north and east where the coast curved around the port. The main force of Baila's army pushed up from the south, infiltrated with soldiers from Lindvane and supported by the shamans' creatures. The daemon threat continued along the south-western front, where Hayton had based the bulk of his army, and up the western edge, where Hilman had arrived with its troops. Kingsport was now isolated and surrounded by the enemy, kept under siege. If I was in any doubt that the final gambit was in motion, reports confirmed that all the main players had arrived to witness our fall. Hulce fought alongside his father and Averill closed in from the west, while Harke and Bane caused carnage within the docks. There had been no sign of Sálaforn or Villermir, but I did not doubt they were there and gloating at our misery.

I took a long swallow of watered ale and inspected my bruised knuckles and the discoloured welts on my hands. The hall was busy with runners delivering their messages and then leaving with more instructions, while captains delivered reports on the status within their section of the fighting. The atmosphere remained subdued but surprisingly calm as clear routines and procedures ensured an efficient order in sharp contrast to the chaos of battle. I was mercifully overlooked where I was slumped on a bench and I scratched at a scab that had started to itch, waiting for the weak drink to soften the persistent ache in my muscles.

I watched Vallori quietly talk with Hagan and the two men shared a gentle tease. I forced myself to concentrate on the positives that were hidden beneath the heavy gloom of the war. Vallori was battered but had managed to avoid serious injury, as had I. Parin and Etard had been killed by Lindvane soldiers some time ago, but Iffan and Muris were safe with Leyn, still under siege in Kingsport. All of Kade's original guard still fought under Mace or Gheth.

And then there was Kade. I softened my focus to confirm, yet again, that the black shadows that had surrounded him were gone. His tattoo had darkened back to the design given to him at the Isle of Serpents and its protective sigils emitted a faint glow. The twitching had stopped following the death of Erula and the removal of her ghosts. His gaze remained clear and focused, although he was still angry, and petulant, and grumpy, and cantankerous. I smiled; he was a passable reflection of his uncle.

My assessment of Kade was distracted by a commotion outside the hall. One last company had come from the west, managing to avoid being trapped when Hilman advanced. The soldiers had been provided with rest and refreshment on arrival, and it would appear their captain had now come to report to the king. I turned to the doorway to see if it would be someone I knew, blinking in disbelief when I saw two people I recognised well.

Luella and Carys walked into the room, both travel-stained and weary but, impossibly, standing in Faulknar's war council. Carys smiled at me before touching Luella on the arm and leaving to report to Kade. The Northlands' sanctuary's High Priestess walked over to me.

'Close your mouth,' she scolded with some amusement. 'You have a reputation to maintain.'

I obediently did as she commanded, before opening it a heartbeat later. 'Merciful Mother, what are you doing here?'

Her smile faded. 'I felt Bear's flare. As did Kien. We would not leave you to face this alone.'

'But you should be in your sanctuary.'

'Should I?' An indulgent smile rippled over her lips. 'I have faith that it will survive without me. Kien is more than capable of managing its needs. He was ready to come to your aid but he has seen his share of fighting. This is my time.'

Luella was a gifted leader and a knowledgeable teacher, and she was seen as a mentor to many at her sanctuary. It was easy to overlook that she was also a Moon Warrior who had been trained to fight for her Goddess. I flicked a look at Carys who was delivering her news to Kade and the priestess followed my gaze. Her forehead creased in a slight frown when she appraised Kade.

'I will get my time with your king. For now, Carys can tell him what he needs to know.' She returned her attention to me. 'And we have much to catch up on.'

Luella explained how the pain I had felt when Bear had been killed was also felt her and Kien, both knowing what that meant and prompting her decision to leave the sanctuary with a company of its warriors. The Army of Truth had abandoned the border with the Northlands and had travelled south, eventually joining with the force invading Faulknar. Carys's reputation had spread far across Hilman and Luella had gone to meet her, finding that the exodus of Baila's army had been reflected in Averill's. Hilman had been stripped bare of troops to advance on Faulknar and had left behind only the minimal number needed to maintain order. And it seemed, the armies were not the only ones to have fled. On meeting Carys, Luella had learned of the resistance's role in managing the threat of the Gallowglass shamans' daemons and wraiths. The Moon Warrior had been impressed, but unsurprised, by the measures instigated by Bonash and Bear with regards to the enchanted weapons and the runed coins. Her fighters had quickly mastered the techniques used to identify and disrupt the shamans' energies, although there had been few left in Hilman to challenge.

Luella paused before turning to look at me with a piercingly uncomfortably gaze. 'The entire east coast of Hilman has been destroyed by dragon's fire.'

My mind quickly rejected that statement. 'That's impossible.'

'And yet I have seen it. Everything within two days' ride of the shoreline has been incinerated. The whole area is an ashen wasteland.'

'Megin would never...'

Luella's voice turned harder and more accusatory. 'Why would you let your dragon unleash such devastation?'

My mind spun with the thought of such damage being caused by Megin. Echoes of Kade's fear and his visions of Liegeport's destruction floated through my thoughts and chilled the blood in my veins.

'I don't control her,' I protested weakly.

'That is a poor excuse and you know it. You are bonded with the creature. She could not have done such an act without your knowledge.'

I closed my eyes, fearing I knew the answer. 'When?'

'Carys confirmed that your dragon had been sighted for most of this past year. Rumours of her before then. She had been seen as a sign of hope, being able to kill both daemon and wraith. But she has moved to doing it with horrifying efficiency. Her ruin made no exception. Not for daemon nor human. Gallowgla or Hilman. She razed everything. Nothing was left.'

I opened my eyes to look at the older woman and her mask of controlled anger. Her disappointment settled with a comfortable familiarity over my shame.

'When?' I repeated.

Luella narrowed her eyes in sudden understanding. 'A few weeks ago. What happened?'

I watched her face carefully while I told her about my rejection by the Goddess. I had been given the most wondrous gift and I had thrown it in my Goddess's face. I deserved all the judgement Luella gave me and more beyond that. The High Priestess remained silently watching me for some time before her face softened.

'Your dragon has not been sighted for a while. Whatever she is doing, she seems to be doing it away from the Three Kingdoms, for which we can take some comfort. I suspect she is hunting far out at sea as our voyage to Kingsport was remarkably uneventful.'

'You were at Kingsport? Are they well?'

She smiled at the eagerness of my questions. 'They were in surprisingly good spirits when we left them, considering their situation. The Lady Kingsport is a remarkable woman, and she does not surround herself with fools. They have been preparing for a siege for some time and, assuming the invaders do not press their advantage, they will be able to hold for as long as necessary.'

I gladly pursued the safe topic of impressive women and informed her of the work Sutha was doing here in Liegeport. I had suspected that the two women shared many similar traits, and this was confirmed as Luella questioned me about the healing performed at the Isle of Serpents and the magicks performed in defence of the royal port. The High Priestess indulged me for a while before fixing me with a stare that held the power to make me squirm.

'And how are you, Tallen?' she asked with a touch of steel embedded within her tone.

'I'm fine.' I cringed at my petulant tone.

'Is that so? Have you continued with your meditation exercises? Of course not.' She released a frustrated sigh. 'With the backlash from prolonged use of your powers. Not to mention being surrounded by all this suffering.'

I rolled my eyes at the familiar liturgy. 'I'm fine.'

'I can see your aura, Tallen. You are a long way from fine. You cannot plough your way through every obstacle and expect there to be no consequences. Have you learnt nothing?'

I picked at a scab on the back of my hand. 'Vallori says I'm being difficult.' She raised a questioning eyebrow. 'He may have called me less flattering names. I'm just so angry. All the time. I know everybody is tired and stressed, but I just can't seem to stop myself taking that anger out on everyone around me. I regret it as soon as the words leave my mouth but it's always a heartbeat too late.'

'And Vallori?'

We both looked over to where he was discussing strategy. 'He gets it more than most.'

'You are who you are, Tallen. You are surrounded by pain. Faulknar's pain. Accept that there is a reason for what you are feeling.' She waited until

I turned from Valori to look at her. 'He was chosen as your *pháirtí* for a reason. Do not shut him out.'

Carys had finished her report to Kade and walked over to join us, allowing me to avoid acknowledging Luella's advice.

'It's good to see you again, Tallen.'

She greeted me with a warm smile, which I returned having found myself unexpectedly pleased at her arrival. 'And to see you. You and your fighters are very welcome.'

She shrugged in dismissal. 'They were getting lazy with all the fighting having moved south. And speaking of fighting. I'm to join my idiot brother.'

'Don't let him fool you,' I replied, grinning at the thought of a spirited reunion. 'He will be very glad to see you.'

She moved to leave but hesitated for a heartbeat. She turned back to face me with a curious expression on her face.

'Elyos has found a purpose. He is no longer feared or resented. And he has gained quite a following of those who believe in him. I will be forever in your debt for that.'

She gave a brief nod and left before I had the chance to reply. I stared at the doorway after she had gone, reviewing her words and whether I had played any role in changing the resistance fighters' attitudes to her Gods-touched brother. I was certain that he had done most of the work by himself. With a sigh for the tangled web of the Gods I turned back to address Luella with my conclusions, finding her assessing me with a critical eye. A ghost of a smile settled on her lips.

'Maybe you are not always what Valori calls you.'

The banners could be seen from the town's walls. The golden, rearing crowned stag of Hilman and the tusked boar of Lindvane. Even the eagle of Gallowgla, carrying its salmon, was scattered throughout, making Baila's image conspicuous by its absence. The lions of Faulknar faced impossible numbers but they were standing anyway. Archers, cavalry, pikemen and foot soldiers. All had gathered to oppose each other in grim determination. The clash of metal and the screams of the dying could be heard by those still exposed within the refugee camps and by those who cowered within the town's walls. A tenuous barrier of spikes and pits separated the people of Liegeport from the vast wasteland where the armies met, crashing together again and again until darkness and exhaustion forced a temporary reprieve.

I had wanted to go south to join Elyos and Carys. I was informed that there were daemons throughout the battlefield and I would be sent wherever the need was greatest. Vallori wanted to defend the docks where the Gallowglass had secured a base and were able to effectively push out along the coast. He was told that he could not be spared to pursue his feud with his brother. In the end, Kade ordered us into a compromise that satisfied neither of us. We were sent to the south-western section, the centre of the battle, where Keenan was targeting the Lindvane king.

The battle was brutal and chaotic. Any attempt at order and structure became impossible in the immediate and overwhelming need to confront those directly around you. Tactics and strategies became quickly discarded with instinct and reaction controlling the fight. Awareness became restricted to a ring of sweaty, bloody bodies, with those who were more than two or three paces away being dismissed as not currently relevant. The mass heaved and surged as one giant beast; inhaling when we gained the advantage, exhaling when we were forced to retreat. We fought over the same patch of land that threatened to trap our feet in its noxious, gelatinous mud.

I threw a fireball at a bird-daemon, knocking it towards me and bringing it close enough for *Saorsa* to slash at its neck when it aimed to spear me in retaliation. The crash of its body when it fell to the ground caused several to stumble before the creature dispersed into a fine, green mist. Frantic scrabbling ensued with those who had fallen forced to defend against those who would take opportunity presented. Most did not live long enough to rise. The man-daemons caused wanton carnage where they rampaged through the tightly pressed crowd. They smashed and crushed without concern as to which banner their victims fought under. Vallori and I had been forced apart soon after submerging into the turmoil but I intermittently caught sight of his shaven head when the monsters dissolved into emerald rain. I turned my attention to the creature on my right, using a tunnel of air to push fighters out of my way while I raced towards it. I dropped to my knees to avoid its swinging arm, using my momentum and the wet ground to slide between its legs, slicing across its hamstrings when I passed through. The creature twisted to face me, dropping its head to roar in anger and blasting me with its foul breath. I pushed up from the ground, extending my sword in a two-handed thrust through its jaw and into its skull. I was lifted into the air for a few heartbeats when it recoiled, dropping lightly to the ground when it melted.

In the thunderous noise of battle, I became inexplicably receptive to sounds that should not be audible within the clamour of steel and the roar of hostile cries. Elyos had mentioned that despite the chaos of his battle-lust, he would often recall the smallest detail such as a facial tattoo or the engraving on a sword's hilt. It seemed I had the same strange ability, involving sound. Above the screams of the horses and the bellows of the daemons, Keenan's shouted challenge pierced through to urgently capture my attention. I turned and saw the Lord General astride a blood-stained, grey battle-horse, rearing in agitation within the ring of Keenan's honour guard. Hayton was less than five horse-lengths from him, riding a battle-horse of his own which sprayed white foam through bared teeth. Keenan roared again, too far away for me to hear his words but the intention was clear and Hayton responded. Lindvane's king kicked his mount into a high rear and then charged.

Cursing against the sting of a raw throat, I swung my blade in lethal arcs to create the passage I needed to get to Kade's uncle. A horse-daemon aimed to delay me but was soon nothing more than mist. I roared in frustration when I saw another turn towards Keenan and his men. The beast was in no hurry, casually using its horn to disembowel with its weaving head, but I was still some distance from being able to protect them. I released a stream of fire, causing those around me to flinch away from its heat and open a path to allow me to race towards the daemon. I created a crater in front of the monster, hoping to turn its attention to me, but it clumsily leapt over the obstacle and continued towards the Lord General. Keenan and Hayton clashed and the two circled each other, clubbing with giant broadswords. The defeated man I had seen in Peverill was a long way from the warrior-king that attacked again and again, wrapped in a mantle of rage.

I reached the horse-daemon as it crashed into the outer circle of Keenan's defence. I slashed at a soldier who had thought to engage me, almost severing his head from his neck in my fury, then quickly resumed my focus on the daemon. I forced a river of fire into it, scorching its flank and finally drawing its attention to me. It bellowed while I stood my ground, waiting for its inevitable charge. I braced my feet and raised *Saorsa*, preparing for the curving slice that would carve open its neck. My primal grin widened when it lowered its head and came at me. It ran straight, no longer pausing to take victims from those it passed. It thundered directly at me. I easily stepped to the side when it raised its head to gore me, and *Saorsa* whipped down to bite deep into its neck.

Between the heartbeat of being dealt my killing strike and the creature's evaporation into a harmless mist, the beast twisted its head away from me. It lifted its nose in a sweeping curve, raising its point to gouge into the soldier who was unlucky enough to be within its range. The hateful horn pierced through the soft tissues of Bodax's back, stabbing up into his chest as the daemon dissolved into green droplets. I screamed in frustration. Keenan's captain folded over his horse and fell to the ground.

His collapse revealed the Lord General performing the same manoeuvre in reverse. His blade slid into Hayton's guts and pushed into his chest. The two men locked eyes as Keenan rammed the blade further into the king until the hilt pressed against his belly. The tip of the sword could be seen extending beyond Hayton's shoulder blade when he slumped forward to rest his head against Keenan's chest.

I had retreated to the space created between the battle and the spiked traps, where Faulknar's soldiers could catch their breath away from the fighting. I had greedily drained a beaker of water and was almost finished with the second when I heard the news; our king had left the protection of the town and had come out to fight. I cursed foully and I threw the cup away. I stomped over the young fighter who had shared the information, grabbing the front of his battered jerkin.

'Where?' I demanded, shaking the lad when he nervously stuttered. 'Where is the king headed?'

'South. To the Army of Truth.'

Cursing again, I roughly pushed the boy away. Hagan had sworn to keep his king within the royal house, tying him to a chair if required. There would be only one reason for Kade to defy him, and then not even his stubborn captain could prevent him from engaging. Villermir had come to join the fight.

Without thought for Keenan, who I had been sent to protect, or Vallori, who I had promised to stay near, I grabbed the nearest horse and galloped towards the main force of Baila's army. It was uncertain whether I raced to protect Kade or because I wanted Villermir for myself, either way, I was going to find the Supreme High Priest and finish this.

The horse's fear of me was channelled into its speed and it bolted behind the fighting. I allowed it to run with only minor corrections to its direction while I concentrated on the energies being emitted from the chaotic battle and looked for the distinctive flare which would identify Villermir. The air vibrated with a kaleidoscope of colour, with the multiple auras from the dying blending with the dispersing matter of the daemons. Golden threads wove throughout, sent by the spell-weavers of Sutha and Bonash to ensnare the darker strands of the shamans, snatching their control away from their monstrous puppets. Countless shades drifted with the souls of the fallen rising into the realms of the Gods. Black and green cords twisted and tangled and trapped these energies, staining their vibrant power. So many colours shifted and shimmered as energy bled from the massacre.

A flare of tarnished copper speared into the sky. Villermir had released his power. I pulled harshly on the horse's reins and turned it towards the despised beacon. We crashed through the rear ranks, scattering Faulknar soldiers who leapt out of the way. The horse snapped at the faces of those around it and we barrelled deeper into the fighting. *Saorsa* slashed from side to side, cleaving into any who tried to delay me. I paid little attention to these distractions and aimed directly for the hated priest. I kicked and roared and smashed with *Saorsa*'s hilt while Baila's faithful pressed in to impede the battle-horse's advance. Too impatient to allow the beast to muscle through, I slid from the saddle and used my small size to dance around the obstacles placed in front of me. Faulknar's soldiers quickly realised what was occurring and hastily created a rolling shield around me. Soldiers to each side engaged the enemy when I passed, closing back in behind me once I was through. Soon enough, I saw him. Standing within a ring of his black uniformed fanatics.

I threw a fireball at the poisonous head. Villermir batted it aside by reflex before turning to see who had dared to attack him. A reptilian smile creased his face when he realised it was me. He sent a wall of air in greeting and I raised one of my own to shield against its impact. The force divided to pass around me and smash in those nearby. I immediately countered with a stream of fire, which Villermir's barrier doused into a rain of sparks that ignited the clothing of the soldiers who surrounded him. Our initial attack effectively cleared an area around us that was over five paces wide, making it feel like we were alone.

Contempt oozed from the priest while hatred radiated from me. We evaluated each other, debating whether to strike first or allow the other to reveal their strategy. Villermir pulsed with a power I had not seen in him before. He tilted his head in amused arrogance, confirming he was aware of my assessment. Impatient to crush him, I created a whirlwind and sucked up all the pebbles that were near him, exploding the stones into lethal shards to pelt him with a stinging hail. He dismissed my attack with a wave of his hand, but some of the pellets had struck true and blood seeped from a number of small cuts on his face and neck.

His contemptuous smile was replaced by a frustrated snarl. He withdrew the water within the muddy ground to trap my feet in solid rock. I felt the disorientating sensation of liquid being pulled out of my tissues while my lungs filled with the fluid that would drown me. I sent multiple white-hot fireballs towards his defences while I compressed the air around him into a whip, slicing across his face with a savage flick. Air rushed back into my lungs when Villermir's concentration wavered, and I immediately followed through with a stream of fire which made the air scream when it clawed around the priest's barriers. A twist of his wrist sucked the air from my flames, extinguishing them as if snuffing out a candle to leave curling wisps of dark smoke.

His responding blast of air slammed into my protections with enough force to send me flying backwards. I swiftly scrambled to my feet but Villermir did not press his advantage. He waited patiently for me to rise.

'You are not as strong as you were,' he noted. 'You cannot hope to win, Tallen. Just surrender to me and all this can stop.'

'I'm not afraid of you anymore,' I snapped back.

'That's hardly the point. Your greatest fear has always been yourself. Always so afraid of your powers. Always so scared that they, that you, are evil.' My sullen silence provoked another gloating sneer. 'The mind of the child is so malleable. So easy to fill with monsters and danger. While the mind of the adult is so rigidly fixed. Trapped within layers of habit and belief. Unable to break free from the fears created in the child.'

I screamed an incoherent denial and sent a massive ball of flame into the ground beneath his feet. I crushed the earth into a powder that ignited in the heat of my inferno. The burning sand sucked at his legs, instantly cooling into spikes of glass which stabbed towards his limbs. I roared again in frustration when he remained protected by his defences and the glass knives shattered harmlessly before reaching his skin. He replied to my assault with a mountain of air that pressed down on me, crushing against my barriers and forcing me to my knees. I desperately grasped at his energy, crying out as the pain of his corrupted power burned like molten metal throughout my core. I twisted his attack and slammed it back at him. His defences were ill-equipped to block his own energy and did little more than soften the blow when the forces smashed into him.

We both rose painfully to resume our combative stances, with feet apart and hands raised.

'I will flay your king while his enslaved people watch.'

I screeched like a banshee, compressing fire into a white-hot spear. I twisted a vortex of air around it so that it spun in hungry, seething destruction. Villermir replied with a rod of pure energy, crashing into my spear with the deafening crack of shattered power. The air shimmered around our connection, crackling with white-blue lightning and screaming with the forces contained within the writhing energies. My body howled in protest at the effort needed to push against Villermir's attack. My face pulled back into a mask of agony as I struggled to contain his power.

'No!'

Kade's anguished cry broke my concentration. My energy stream wavered and Villermir's power slammed into me, instantly igniting all my tissues so it felt as if every cell within my body burst from the pressure. Scalding forces splintered my aura into a rainbow of sparks. I fell backwards, my head cracking on a rock, and my awareness shattered into nothing.

CHAPTER THIRTY-FOUR

Megin screamed in anger and the shards of my awareness snapped back to show the vibrant colours seen through a dragon's eye. The battle passed below me at frightening speed. I saw Kade slide off Mael and run towards my abandoned body. He collapsed to his knees beside me, rocking as he cradled my unresponsive shell. Villermir sent a blast of air at the Faulknar king and I cried a warning, but my protest was impotently silent, buried deep within my dragon's core. Megin released a river of fire and incinerated a wide, terrible path towards the two men. The intense heat within the wall of flames caused the air to shimmer. I frantically pleaded, to Megin, to the Gods, to anyone, but I was unable to stop it.

Kade's power ignited with the gift given to him by Drey. Curled protectively over my body, he raised a hand to centre a domed barrier, completely covering the both of us. Megin's fire engulfed his defences and the shield glowed with a blinding light, with flashes of lightning sparking throughout. My dragon continued to soar over the battlefield and I could not tell whether Kade remained unharmed. I begged her to return to him but Megin seemed not to hear me. I tried to fight but there was no structure to my containment. No boundaries for me to push against. There were only my thoughts to offer the hope that I was not dead and lying next to Kade.

Megin banked to the left, releasing another stream of flame and turning two companies into smouldering embers. She made no distinction between Faulknar's soldiers and those they were fighting, all died within her inferno. Vast sections turned to ash and she created a dark trail towards Liegeport. I watched in helpless despair when she aimed her fire at the town and those who cowered inside. Bells rang the alarm but the overcrowding meant there was nowhere for the people to hide. I screamed for Megin to stop but she would not heed me. The refugee camp melted under her blazing assault.

The ballistae within the towers had remained attended despite the threat of multiple armies, and they were already pointed at the sky. The ratchets had been cranked in readiness and a giant arrow tracked her progress. It was released as soon as Megin flew over the wall, but the iron-tipped harpoon skimmed harmlessly over the scales of her belly and crashed into the town below. She responded to the small distraction by casually flicking her tail into the timber structure, smashing it effortlessly into lethal splinters while the four men fell to their deaths. Three more arrows speared towards her. One slipped over her scales while the other two missed their target completely. All three crushed bones when they descended onto the crowd.

We continued past the leaping flames of the burning town, fanned into whirlwinds of igniting sparks by the downdraft of her massive wings. She turned towards the docks and screamed a challenge that caused the air around us to shudder. I saw Faulknar's soldiers battle Gallowglass raiders while trying to avoid the dreadful touch of the wraiths. Most were too busy to acknowledge the terrifying vision that hurtled towards them. Megin released her fury and storehouses exploded, incinerating ghost and human with equal lack of concern. There was nothing I could do to stop her. She glided beyond the jetties to the pirate ships barricading Liegeport's coast. They jumped into the sea to escape the fires, but their vessels threw flaming debris in a lethal rain and both raider and shaman died under Megin's onslaught.

Megin banked right and flew back towards the land. The presence of daemons provided a target for her wrath and she scorched large tracks, carving blackened roads between the sections of fighting. The stench of burnt flesh sickened the air already polluted with the foul odour of blood and waste. Sour smoke rose in dirty plumes to create a night-terror scene of total devastation. Megin hunted. The screeching cries of the bird-daemons added to the chaos and the panicked stampede of land-daemons increased the carnage.

My vision dipped, and the shifting colours twisted and rotated before finally settling. I stood on the small rise west of the port and looked over the smoking battlefield. The colours were bright and garish and lacked the range of subtle shades seen with Megin's eyes. I viewed the battle with a mildly curious detachment, as if looking at a moving tapestry or an expertly crafted wall-painting. The noise of the fighting was subdued, with only a faint hint of the ash and blood and burning bodies to tell of the massacre.

I felt the Goddess beside me but could not turn to face her. Tears slowly tracked down the face this reality had given me while I witnessed the unconscionable loss of human lives. So many of which were being taken by Megin.

'I can't control her,' I accused quietly. 'You took her from me and I can't stop what she's doing.'

'Her destruction is not because of that,' she denied. 'She cradled your awareness. She was aware of your pain. Her actions are driven by her anger.'

'At whom? There are so many innocent people. Some are my friends.'

'She is angry at the Gods.'

She declined to acknowledge my questioning expression, much less explain herself. Her ice-blue eyes continued to track Megin. My dragon passed over the town once more and then moved on to the golden banners of Hilman. I watched the Goddess closely.

'You can't control her either?' I guessed. 'You're afraid of what she can do?'

The Goddess responded with the slightest tightening of her hands. 'The dragons stubbornly remained beyond the influence of the Gods. An oversight that was corrected with the creation of the Dragonslayers.'

'Megin was created to kill daemons. Can she kill Gods too?'

'No,' she replied sharply. 'Not directly.'

'What do you mean?'

The Lady paused, considering me for a moment before extending her hand in a graceful gesture. 'Look.'

I looked back at the slaughter surrounding Liegeport, seeing the desperate fighting and the devastating toll. Overlaying this terrible image were strands of silver and gold, rising from the countless bodies and drifting into the sky.

'The Gods exist because of the soul gathered upon the death of a believer. Small amounts are obtained from prayer and ritual, of course, but our power mainly comes from the release of energy when the body dies.' Her voice hardened. 'If your dragon kills everyone, there will be no souls left to sustain us.'

I clenched my fists. 'That is what all this is about? All this pain and suffering? We fight your religious wars so you can claim your tithe of souls?'

'Do you think we watch passively while you destroy yourselves? Look again.'

Another layer of power was revealed. Four more Gods joined the Moon Goddess on the small hill and watched the violence of the battle, each wearing robes in the colour associated with them. Arduinna raised an eyebrow in acknowledgement when I stared, open-mouthed, at being so close to that many deities. I recovered to an awkward embarrassment after a few heartbeats and followed their example by returning my attention to the fighting. Sparkling threads appeared in response to the presence of the Gods: gold, silver, sapphire, emerald and ruby. The shimmering cords wove into a beautiful tapestry around those fighting for Faulknar and the Hilman resistance. Those fighting for Averill and Lindvane were trapped within a net of pulsing black vines, with flashes of green rippling along the malignant strands. The Army of Truth seethed as a roiling mass of darkness.

'Do not think we have left you unprotected.'

At the Goddess's words, the image narrowed to show individual battles. Kade continued to oppose Villermir, exchanging spears of air and walls of fire. Villermir's aura was choked with the foul corruption of Baila's dark tethers.

'No,' corrected the Goddess. 'Not Baila. The one he claims as a God was merely a seer and a prophet. That one's meddling summoned a Fate and he has kept Taranis well fed on the souls of his followers.'

I recalled the monsters that Sálaforn had conjured in Freisholm and saw the towering Fate with dark-skinned blemishes standing behind Villermir's right shoulder. Taranis casually rotated the wheel in his hands and human-like creatures twisted and writhed along its rim.

'There is more here than the fate of your kingdom,' she continued while I stared, enthralled by the terrifying vision of Taranis. 'Villermir has called Taranis. Sálaforn has summoned Sluagh. Mobis looks to collect all and create a wasteland to match his Hells. We are here because of this.'

It required a considerable amount of effort but I managed to drag my attention away from the Fate and looked to Kade. Faulknar's king was wrapped in a shell of golden sunlight: the protection of the Sun God. Standing beside the king, beyond the range of the magicks thrown by the two men, was Luella. The High Priestess of the Goddess's sanctuary and her Warrior. She was swathed in the silvery glow of a full moon: the protection of the Moon Goddess.

The image drifted swiftly across the battle to where the Hilman resistance fought the Army of Truth, resting on Elyos and Carys where they stood close to each other and challenged the stampeding daemons. Carys was surrounded by a halo of soft emerald light: the protection of Arduinna. Elyos was enclosed within a bubble of ruby-red: the protection of Camlun. The huntress and the warlord.

The scene moved again, taking me to the waterfront at the edge of the town where Bonash and his spell-weavers battled the shamans. They were positioned in a circle, surrounded by burning debris, within which Sutha sat in a deep trance. The healer was bathed in the soft, sapphire embrace of her Goddess: the protection of Nathair.

My vision pulled back to encompass the complete battle and the suffocation of Liegeport.

'How does this end?' I asked. 'How can I make it stop?'

'You have completed your task. This will end as it is supposed to.'

'How can you say that? We're losing. Faulknar will be overrun. The Fates will take everything. I need to go back and fight. They need me.'

'The role of a Dragonslayer is not just to control their dragon,' she replied sharply. 'They are also kingmakers. Your task was to choose the rightful king. You have gathered to you those who were needed to bear witness and they will support your decision. Kade will unite those faithful to us regardless of whether he survives this day. Your presence is no longer required there.'

I turned to glare at my Goddess. 'You cannot expect me to abandon him.'

The Lady faced my stare with glacially pale eyes. 'You are my Warrior. You serve at my command. The future of the Gods is assured and you are no longer required to intervene. You will sever your heart's connection to these people. You now exist beyond that. You will call your dragon and your soul will meld with hers, to act as I require it.'

Megin would be returned to me but I had to renounce Kade.

I was reminded of a dream where the Goddess had told me to choose between my heart and my soul, with the decision having already been made for me. My soul was owned by my Goddess and she expected my obedience. I thought of Breya and of the time she had tried to force my loyalty by having me swear fealty to her. It seemed I was destined to repeatedly make this choice. I smiled.

'You should not have sent me to your sanctuary.' She remained rigidly still. 'You ask me to choose between my heart and my soul. To go back or stay with you. Kade does hold my heart, but you do not have my soul. That belongs to another. The vows of the *phàirtí* are old and they hold power. They are not easily broken, not even by you. You cannot compel me to stay here and I choose be with them. Kade and Vallori. Heart and soul. You have to send me back.'

A sharp pain stabbed into the back of my skull and I dragged air into my sluggish lungs. I opened my eyes to my own vision, albeit with two images of the smoke-filled sky overlapping when they swayed slightly from side to side. The deafening noise of battle slammed into my pounding head to confirm that I was once again lying on the ground outside Liegeport.

Safe? queried Megin urgently.

Every cell in my body erupted with the relief of hearing her again. *Safe, my beloved. So please stop killing everybody now.*

Her answering call ripped across the battlefield. I carefully rolled onto my side, feeling as if I had been kicked in the chest by a battle-horse, and swallowed against the nausea caused by the disjointed swimming of two images. The air slammed above my head with a piercing whine and reminded me that Kade still fought Villermir.

'It seems that I concentrated on the wrong whelp,' goaded the priest, pushing a flare of energy towards the king. 'Your Dragonslayer turned out to be less of a threat than the legends foretold.'

Kade answered with a barrier of air that glowed when the energies smacked into it. 'You may have poisoned her mind to fear you, but I suffer no such constraint.'

He tore a trench between Villermir's legs, causing the older man to stumble and break the flow of his energies. Kade's barrier raced towards the priest and Villermir was forced to react, twisting as he pushed the threat to the side. The two men traded blows, with all four elements used to distract and defend while energy flares sought to stab into the other's core. I staggered to my feet, aiming to assist Kade, but maintaining an unstable stance required such intense concentration that I was unable to do anything else. I noticed Villermir toss his head when he saw me rise from my supposed death.

'Perhaps she is stronger than she seemed,' he said quietly, before resuming his baiting. 'Your Dragonslayer's ghost sits at your shoulder.'

Faulknar's king had not seen me stand but he had dealt with enough

529

ghosts and he was not going to be distracted by more. Villermir's comment awakened all the frustrations and fears that Erula had stoked, igniting them into a single point of rage. In a terrifying reflection of his crest, Kade called a spear of blindingly white lightning. The crack of power, caused by the containment of such an impossible amount of energy, tore out over the battlefield and sounded far into the distance. The blaze of raw power stabbed through Villermir to snap into the ground beneath his feet, twisting the priest like burning tinder. Kade roared in fury and the lightning vanished, leaving an after-image burned onto my vision and the acrid smell of spent forces.

I blinked repeatedly to clear my sight, looking up to see two monstrous, leathery-skinned Fates standing beside Villermir's charred body. Mobis tilted his bald head slightly towards Taranis, dipping his horns in a subtle challenge. The Fate of Torment gave a half-bow in appeasement and withdrew. Mobis slowly rolled his head to look at the fallen priest, continuing the action to fix me with his terrifying stare.

'You owe me a soul, Dragonslayer.'

His deep voice reverberated painfully within my chest. He slowly lifted his hand and the blackened, twisted soul of Villermir rose with the gesture. Mobis closed his fingers around the middle of the shade, causing the creature to writhe. Perhaps trying to escape. Perhaps in agony. I felt a numbing lack of concern for either option. The Fate regarded its struggles with mild curiosity.

'Consider the debt paid.'

Mobis vanished, taking Villermir's soul to his Hells. Kade bent to collect his discarded sword, his mind already turning from the dead priest to the threat of his fanatical soldiers. He staggered when he straightened, overcome by the exhaustion which followed the use of so much power, particularly in one not trained to channel that much energy. I went to assist him but stepped back when he thrust his blade toward me. I ached to see the pained expression that haunted his face as he perceived me as a ghost.

'Peace,' I said gently, raising my hands to show that I held no weapon despite knowing his mind had gone beyond that. 'It is me. I have a double-image and skull-splitting pain to attest that I am real. I am not a shade, Kade. It is really me.'

His expression melted my heart and he dropped his sword again. He quickly covered the distance between us and pulled me into an urgent embrace, cradling the back of my damaged head. I crushed my hands against his leather armour, pressing against him as hard as I could. I was overwhelmed by the need to touch him. To hold him. To feel the solid shape of him. My whole existence compressed down to the physical connection of his body and I breathed in the sweet smell of him.

'My liege,' interrupted Hagan, who had come to stand by my side. 'May I suggest that you stop throwing away your sword. You are going to need it.'

I grinned into the warm darkness at the curve of Kade's neck and reluctantly moved away from him. He captured my face with both hands and stared into my eyes for several heartbeats, before releasing me with a small smile and accepting the sword offered by his captain. Luella joined us, placing her hand carefully at the base of my spine. The flow of healing was unasked for but gratefully received. The two images drifted into one and my balance returned so I no longer had to concentrate to maintain it. The pounding pressure in my head dulled to a level where I could ignore it. I gently removed her hand, declining any more healing.

'There will be time for that later,' I promised.

She withdrew, briefly placing a simple touch on my shoulder, and I turned to retrieve *Saorsa*. I looked at the devastation that had been caused by Megin and the combined magicks of Villermir, Kade and myself. A large circle of scorched earth extended several paces around us. Blackened bodies were scattered within the charred ring, some still smouldering or reduced to glowing embers. The fighting continued beyond this but soldiers on both sides refused to cross a boundary that blatantly declared unnatural forces.

We naturally assumed a barrier around Kade and rejoined the battle, Luella and I on each side with Hagan defending the rear. The sanctuary's High Priestess was majestic to watch, fully displaying her skills as a Moon Warrior. Her calm, organised character was readily transferred into an effective, killing attack. Each strike was considered and precise so that no effort was wasted. She fought with the silent grace of a hunting owl, captivating in the beauty of her perfect manoeuvres. Soldier after soldier fell to her blade while she maintained a fluid pose and an unhurried rhythm. Her style reflected Vallori's thoughtful precision, but Luella had elevated this to a much higher level. Kade and Hagan were also skilled in the use of weapons and the four of us wrecked ruin as we carved into the invaders. And *Saorsa* sang for me once more.

An explosion punched into the air, loud enough to cause everyone to flinch. I turned towards the sound and saw a mountain of dark smoke rise above the docks, its base glowing with the orange of reflected flames.

'Vallori,' I breathed, instinctively knowing he was in danger.

I turned back to Kade, torn between the need to protect him and the urgent necessity to find Vallori. Faulknar's king wiped the sweat from his forehead and flicked his gaze from the towering smoke to me.

'Go,' he instructed. 'They will have need of you there.'

I tossed my head in frustration. The docks were on the other side of the town and I would not reach Vallori in time if his life was truly in danger, but I could not ignore the tugging insistence which demanded I go to him. Luella moved to stand beside Kade and she was soon joined by Hagan, both understanding my conflict.

'Go to your *pháirtí*,' she advised gently. 'I will protect your king.'

I turned to Hagan, trusting his decision regarding Kade's safety. He would not let me go if he thought his king would be at greater risk. He gave a brief nod of agreement. It was all the confirmation I needed.

I had hoped to obtain another horse, as I had done when racing to engage with Villermir, but there were no mounts available. I impatiently snatched a drink and surveyed the battle. We had drifted further north so, while the easiest route to the docks was to circle south around Liegeport, this would now take significantly longer than punching through the crowded town. I considered both options, frozen by the indecision of whether to wait for an incoming messenger's horse or to start running with the hope of gaining a ride at some point along the way.

I could no longer delay. Cursing in frustration, I chose to run through the town as this presented the shortest route. I had taken less than ten strides when Sucellos gifted me with a blessing. A messenger came thundering in with reports and orders, sliding her horse to a halt not far from me. Before the mount could be given to the next runner, I had grabbed the reins and vaulted into the saddle. I ignored the shouts of protest and the jostling alarm of the horse, and jabbed my heels into its belly to force its flight towards Liegeport.

The ruins of the refugee camps, destroyed by Megin's fire, failed to hold my attention and I rode straight for the smoke still rising up from the docks. People jumped out of my way while the pulsing ache in my chest urged me to demand more speed from the tired horse. I barged through the town's gate, yelling for everyone to move but not hesitating to see if they did. My frustration seethed whenever I was delayed, dodging around obstacles within the chaotic space and twisting back on myself when I was unable to take the direct path to the rear gate.

My attention was caught by movement at one of the timber towers, where its arrow still aimed at the sky in preparation for Megin's reappearance. My dragon had smashed one of the towers into splinters and another had been destroyed by flames. Megin was currently hunting pirate ships and their sheltered shamans, so I targeted the tower overlooking the sea first. I sent a warning fireball into the tower, close enough to send the archers scrambling to safety. I followed it up with a stream of fire fuelled by my increasing agitation. The hated weapon melted in the heat of my inferno and I repeated the process with the final tower.

Safe, I informed Megin.

Always safe, she replied arrogantly. *They have forgotten how to fight dragons.*

I finally passed through the second gate and was able to give the horse its head, gaining speed as we galloped towards the burning docks. The air was thick with smoke and ash, with over half of the buildings having been destroyed by Megin's sweeping assault. The plume of black smoke hung heavily over the far end of the port, leaving a strange island of calm between the two blazing sectors. The streets swarmed with Faulknar soldiers, Gallowgla raiders and the silently menacing wraiths. I sent arrows of flame into the ghosts and hacked at the raiders while frantically searching for any sign that would help me locate Vallori. I resorted to shouting, calling out his name, and demanding of anyone I encountered whether they had seen him.

'Tallen!'

I turned the horse sharply enough that its hooves skidded on the slick surface of the road. I grabbed a fistful of its mane to balance myself while it scrabbled to settle beneath me. By the time it had recovered, Kutan was pushing towards me, wiping his face free of the gore which covered him.

'Tallen,' he repeated. 'Vallori is two streets over. There's debris everywhere, you'll never get through on a horse.'

'Where?' I demanded, sliding out of the saddle.

My knees buckled when I hit the ground so that, for a moment, my hand on the horse's mane was the only thing keeping me standing. Kutan snatched at a runner when the child tried to dodge past.

'You know where the Warrior is?' he asked, receiving a quick nod in confirmation. 'Take her.' He turned back to me with a warning. 'He was badly hurt.'

The urgent ache flared again, turning into a clenching need that would not be denied. I followed the child and we twisted, clambered and evaded our way to an alleyway guarded by a number of fighters, including Dru. He led me through the relative calm of the sheltered area, where a ragged group of soldiers curled over to recover their breath or crouched to attend the wounds of those slumped against the walls.

Vallori was collapsed against a discarded crate, his eyes tightly closed while a pair of fighters fussed over his injuries. They had applied bandages to the open wounds on his thigh and forearm but I could see, even at this distance, that these were the least of his concerns. His breathing was painfully slow. His stomach was sucked in with each heaving gasp while his chest barely moved. His face had gone beyond pale to the blue-grey colour that often preceded death. I skidded to a halt beside him, falling onto my knees.

'What happened to you, big man?' I asked, unable to hide the worry in voice. 'I hope you weren't thinking of leaving me.'

One corner of his mouth flickered in a weak smile, but his eyes remained closed as he concentrated on snatching what little air he could into his failing lungs. I cradled his head with one hand and rested the other lightly at the base of his ribs. I fought the urge to blast him with healing and carefully wove my energies around his aura, searching for the fatal wound. Several broken ribs had been pushed in and their sharp edges had torn the tissues of his lungs, which were unable to inflate and filling with blood. I blessed the stubbornness that had kept fighting for so long. I flooded his body with energy to reduce the need on his compromised lungs, then worked to repair his ribs and drain the pooled fluid. Once content that his breathing had stabilised, I moved to address his other injuries, finding many that were significant but not immediately concerning. I brought together the smashed shards of his forearm, moulding them so they would hold under pressure. I moved to the deep thigh wound and wove the sliced muscle back together. I had turned to a more superficial gash over his hip when he pushed me away and broke my concentration.

'Enough,' he cautioned hoarsely. 'You have done enough.'

He took a deep breath to justify his claim and I rocked back to sit heavily on the ground. My head spun while I settled my energies, supporting Vallori's clam that I had spent more than I could afford. I looked at the other soldiers in the alley; we were all pushing beyond safe limits. I gave my *pháirtí* a grin that masked my fear at how close he had come to dying.

'What are you doing here?' I chided gently. 'I left you with Keenan and Mace.'

He shrugged a shoulder. 'You went to claim your sorcerer. I came to claim mine. Sálaforn was stirring up trouble in a storehouse on the south side before your dragon destroyed the building. Somehow the witch slithered away.'

'Is that so? Well, with Kade stealing Villermir from me, perhaps I can have Sálaforn instead.'

'Kade?' Vallori did little to hide his surprise. 'Seems the boy is good for something after all.'

I gave him a withering look then I helped him rise, maintaining my grip on his hand for an extended moment once he was standing.

'Tell me true, can you fight?' I continued when he opened his mouth to protest. 'We both know you are going to anyway. If you have any doubts, let me heal them before we stick our heads into the viper's nest.'

I held the hand of his damaged arm and Vallori squeezed my grip hard in reply. 'Shall we go?'

We left the alley and aimed for the devastation of the southern sector. Sálaforn had moved to the pirate base within the port rather than remain safely offshore and raiders had formed a dense barrier around a row of merchant houses, with the space seething with wraiths. We battled for a frustratingly long time without getting any closer to finding our target. In desperation, I created a wall of air and compressed it into a force that stunned all within hearing range. We exploited the moment of hesitation and pushed towards the buildings.

I had barely made it past the first house when Sálaforn stepped out of one further along the street. She was guarded by Bane and I heard Vallori growl in challenge before Sálaforn released her energies in a crackling spear, aimed solely at me. I defended with a shield of air but the contact forced me back a few paces. I pulled my face into a feral snarl and replied with a blazing fireball, sending it hurtling towards the crone.

Sálaforn, unexpectedly, jumped out of its path and the blast seared into the wall behind her, leaving a blackened stain. My grin widened at the realisation that she had no access to elemental magicks, and it turned predatory when I released another fireball which sent her scuttling away like a wrinkled spider.

In answer to my arrogance, she sent a rod of pure energy spearing towards me. My defence split the air with a crack that left my ears ringing and the acrid scent of abused energies floated on the breeze as bitter incense. Her stream of energy persisted and I fought to contain her power. My strength wavered and I briefly wondered at how her ability far exceeded what I had expected.

I cursed myself as a fool. I had seen Mobis and Taranis, Sluagh would surely be watching as well. I relaxed my focus and saw Sálaforn's aura, caught within a web which pulsed with the colour of her skeletal army. The effect was more subtle than Taranis's controlling black cords, but it was clear that Sálaforn danced to Sluagh's drumbeat. I followed the writhing strands where they left the sorcerer's body and flowed towards a space some distance behind her. The hideous, emaciated, sagging form of the female Fate mocked me with a fearsome grin.

I divided my power, roaring with the effort required to hold against the crone's assault while sending a stream of white-hot fire towards her puppet-master. The creature laughed.

'Your fire will not harm me, Dragonslayer.'

My flames caressed the dark, wrinkled skin of her body as if wrapping her in fine silk. My abilities would never be enough to stop a God. Their power was inconceivably greater than mine. It was an endless stream, constantly maintained through the souls of their worshippers.

My concentration faltered and I swiftly twisted away when Sálaforn's strike broke through my barriers. My arm burned as the energy brushed past me, bursting into deadly sparks when it hit the ground. The soldiers who had followed to assist Vallori and me screamed with the freed energies tearing through their bodies. I had no time to mourn their loss. I now knew how I could defeat the Fate and would not delay in acting upon it. My dip in concentration had been caused by the understanding that Sluagh's power came from her connection to Sálaforn and the devotion she received from the shaman. All I had to do was reverse the flow.

I created a mesh of elemental energy. The core was a rotating fireball, my primary power. I wrapped a matrix of air around the flames to create a basic barrier and then covered both in a layer of water. From the slowly turning sphere, I extended a rod of water to channel the excess energy into the ground. And then I pulled. Sensing my distraction, Sálaforn sent another spear of blazing energy towards me and I adjusted the position of the fireball to intercept her attack. My creation crackled and spat. Her power was sucked into my sphere and the sorceress's energy was siphoned into its matrix within a few heartbeats. My hungry globe demanded more while the power drained into the earth and diffused harmlessly throughout the soil. Sluagh hissed as her powers were dragged from her through her connection to Sálaforn, but she was designed to absorb power and could not prevent its escape. My fireball burned brightly and more energy was sucked into its whirling vortex, contained within the layers of air and water before flowing into the ground.

Sálaforn screamed when her Fate severed the connection. The backlash forced the crone to her knees while her body blazed in a whirlwind of green sparks. My fireball collapsed into a shower of white sparks with the loss of its sustaining fuel and I staggered forward with the release of pressure. I took a deep breath to refocus my energies while a pounding headache threatened to crush my skull. It took several heartbeats before I could stand without my vision tilting.

Soldiers and raiders continued to fight around me but I no longer saw any wraiths. *Saorsa* demanded to taste the shaman's blood and I found no reason to refuse her. I abandoned the easy kill of incineration for the pleasure of driving my blade through the witch's shrivelled heart. Without removing my focus from her retreating back, I carved through her protective guard and stalked towards my prey. My exhaustion had been replaced by exhilaration with my quarry being so close, still staggering from the sudden withdrawal of Sluagh's power and leaning on the arm of a pirate. I swiftly gained on her. I pulled back for a slice that would open her rotting belly, but *Saorsa* struck a blocking blade and released a scream of tortured steel. I roared in frustration, turning to see who had dared to defy me.

'She is not for you, she-wolf.'

Bane stood perilously close, easily holding my blade. I twisted to release, angling my sword to cut up at his wrists, but he parried with infuriating arrogance. I clubbed at him in impotent rage. Sálaforn was escaping while he mockingly taunted me into a blind fury. *Saorsa* whistled through the air and we clashed again and again.

He was momentarily distracted, with his eyes flicking to a point over my shoulder. I seized the opportunity and drove all my remaining strength into the swing that would open his neck. I sliced my weapon down into the killing blow, but *Saorsa* crashed into a barrier with another wailing screech of protest. Two blades halted her attempt at carving into Bane's throat.

'I do not need you to fight my battles, little brother.'

Vallori maintained his blocking grip. 'That is not why I do this.'

The two men stared at each other for several heartbeats before Bane withdrew his sword. I trembled with unspent aggression but had calmed enough to reluctantly accept this was Vallori's battle, not mine. I also withdrew my blade and allowed Vallori to lower his.

'The two of you are tightly twisted around the Fates,' he continued quietly. 'I would not tempt them further.'

Bane took a deep breath and released it in a long sigh. 'More than you know, little brother. Do you understand yet? The prophecy is unfolding. Sálaforn is The One. She has been foretold.' He flicked a look at me. 'She is not for you to take, little sparrow.' He returned to Vallori. 'Come with me, brother. You have a place in this. You belong with us.'

'You know I cannot.' My *pháirtí*'s hand shook with a barely noticeable tremor while the two shared another long, silent exchange. 'You should go. Take your witch and leave. Do not rely on my restraint should we meet again.'

Bane's face clouded and the muscles of his jaw tensed, looking at me for a heartbeat before addressing Vallori once more. 'Until we meet again then, little brother.'

Bane strode away, whistling a command when he reached the end of the street that had his fighters obediently following him. I turned to face Vallori, but my attention snagged on the sight of Harke's body lying several paces behind him. Vallori twisted so he could see what had delayed me.

'I have avenged your friend,' he stated coldly.

I stared at the mess that had once been Harke. His head had been cleaved almost into two equal halves. I did not want to think of the anger that had fuelled such an attack. For Vallori to have caused so much damage. He stood silently beside me, allowing me the time to accept that Tawpin's killer was dead.

'The raiders are withdrawing,' he said when I looked up. 'We are done here. We should join Elyos and contain the daemons.'

'That's a good idea,' I replied carefully, not knowing whether his rigid control remained from the encounter with his brother or the violence shown towards Harke. 'Lead the way.'

We followed the flow of soldiers who had made the same decision and moved south. I felt no satisfaction at the retreat of the pirates but numbly welcomed the unrestricted path back to the battle still encircling Liegeport. The massacre continued with no concern for the dispersing ships. The shamans who summoned the daemons showed no sign of joining their departing kin and the monsters rampaged despite the absence of the wraiths. The sun was sinking towards the west and I saw my exhaustion reflected in those around me. I despaired over how much longer this madness would last now that Villermir and Sálaforn had been lost from the battle. The invading armies continued to fight as viciously as before, and we would not surrender. We would fight until this was finished. We would either win or we would all die trying.

A wave of unrest rippled through enemy to cause a moment of uncharacteristic confusion. The event revitalised our efforts but the experienced soldiers soon recovered and our advantage stalled once more. It took some time before the news filtered through and I became aware of the reason for the interruption.

'Reinforcements have come from the south,' explained a breathless runner when Vallori and I took a quick rest.

'Faulknar's broken through?' Vallori queried.

The girl shook her head. 'No. The line around Liegeport still holds despite the pirates leaving and half of Hilman's army deserting after their king was killed.'

'Averill's dead?' I asked, welcoming the news that both kings were now gone from the battle. 'What about Hulce? Has he submitted?'

She shrugged. 'I've heard no news of him. Still being protected from having to do any actual fighting by his ring of guards, I suspect.'

'So, who is fighting at the rear?' Vallori asked.

The runner smiled. 'Horses. They're flying the horse.'

'Namori?' Vallori shook his head in disbelief. 'That banner has not been flown in a very long time.'

I gave a soft laugh. My second request had been answered despite all the challenges to deny it. Not the least being the many years since Eldiss had challenged Kade to determine his right to rule, and whether the Travellers would support Faulknar's fight. I looked over the battlefield, unable to see our new allies but taking comfort in knowing they were there.

I scanned the slaughter that stretched to fill my entire view. The enemy forces were showing no signs of retreat despite the removal of Villermir and Sálaforn, Hayton and Averill. We had a dragon and spell-weavers to counter their shamans and daemons. They had no answer to Kade's druidic powers or that of two Moon Warriors.

'Why do they continue to fight?' I asked tiredly.

The girl had run off to share her news and gather more information, and Vallori refrained from answering having no more knowledge than I. The fanatics of Baila clung tightly to those of Lindvane and Hilman. The belief in their God would prevent them from surrendering. Their God who was simply a prophet. Their devotion fed the needs of Taranis and it was Taranis's daemons that stayed despite the withdrawal of Sluagh's wraiths.

'Enough of this!' I shouted, making Vallori startle. 'They continue to fight because they are as much puppets as Kade was to Erula. Sluagh is not the only Fate stirring this pot.'

'So, how do you summon a Fate and make it stop?'

I had an idea, although I doubted it was a good one. I did not have the powders or know the chants used by Sálaforn, but my blood had achieved it once and it was as good a place to start as any other. I sheathed *Saorsa* and withdrew my dagger, slicing into the fleshy edge of my palm. I squeezed the wound until blood dripped to the ground and soaked into the sodden turf.

'Taranis!' I demanded. 'Enough!'

'I am not one to be summoned like a disobedient hound, Dragonslayer.'

I blinked in surprise, but Vallori remained unaware of Taranis's presence standing behind him. The Fate spun his wheel of torment in one leathery hand and clicked the thick, blemished fingers of the other, snapping the connection to my blood. My hand stung with the backlash. I looked for the tether I could use to siphon his power but I was overwhelmed by the countless cords spreading throughout the battle. Each remaining shaman and every soldier fighting for Hilman, Lindvane or Baila had one or more restraining threads that pulsed energy towards Taranis. He exerted his will over them all and they fed him with their devotion. Taranis rumbled a gloating laugh.

'You cannot drain me as you did my sister,' he challenged. 'You may have severed my connections to Villermir and Erula but I have so many more. You will never be able to kill them all.'

540

He received power from more than two kingdoms. He would never relinquish his control and I could not break the ties that bound all who had invaded Faulknar, much less every man, woman and child who worshipped Baila and, unknowingly, Taranis. I could only think of one way to weaken him enough that he would withdraw and end the war, but the cost would be so dreadfully high.

I looked past the Fate to see my Goddess and her God. The Lady wore an expression of mild irritation but the Sun Lord smiled indulgently, gently taking her hand before giving a single nod in agreement. I called my dragon and she joined me. We released an impossible storm of fire, and the air burned. Our combined power smothered everything in devastating flames. I spread my arms wide while Megin soared over the battlefield. We spread a wall of all-encompassing, all-consuming heat from the coast on my left, over my ruined kingdom, and on to the coast on my right.

Mobis's Seventh Hell raged over Faulknar and Taranis's boom of angry thunder rattled the sky.

CHAPTER THIRTY-FIVE

It was not to be a celebration. How could it be when so many had died. The land was scorched for half a day's hard ride from Liegeport. The port and most of the town were little more than ruins, and those who were left had lost so much. Food was scarce, with the wine and ale well-watered. And yet. Despite overwhelming odds, Faulknar was still standing. Free from the meddling of Gods and Fates. Free to gather what remained and build again. And so, it was a celebration. A subdued and sombre one, but a celebration nonetheless.

I did not want to go. During the two days through which I had slept, news had spread until all knew what I had done. Most avoided my gaze, keeping their eyes lowered or taking furtive, fearful glances when they thought I would not see. Some openly stared, making me feel exposed and uncomfortable. Even those that knew me well were cautious, watching me carefully to see if I would erupt in a fit of temper and incinerate everything in sight. They were scared and they had every right to be. They had lived with their king's rages for years and I was unthinkably more dangerous.

But Vallori had asked and I could not refuse him, so I discarded my leathers and dressed in a simple gown. The cost of using so much magick still hammered within my head and sent tremors infrequently through my body, and my fumbling fingers took longer to fasten the laces and attach the amber earrings than they should have. I had questioned the wisdom of wearing orange, not wanting to highlight my unusual Dragonslayer eyes, but accepted that everyone knew what I was and changing the colour of my gown would not make them less afraid. I nervously soothed the front of the dress for the third time, decided I could delay no longer, and went to join my *pháirtí*.

The main hall had been cleared once more and a row of tables now extended the length of the room in a long line down the centre. Highbacked chairs stood neatly along each side, waiting for those who had been invited to attend the formal dinner. The seats remained empty, awaiting the arrival of our king, while the guests gathered in small groups at the edges of the hall, filling the space with quiet conversation. Candles had been generously used to illuminate the room with a warm, gentle glow, creating an atmosphere that was relaxed and welcoming.

I tucked myself into a corner by the entrance, appreciating the opportunity to observe before being noticed. Vallori had his back to me, engaged in conversation with Bonash, Luella and Sutha. He had draped his arm over the smaller man's shoulders, recounting some tale which had Nash flushed and smiling in mild embarrassment. I looked to the opposite side of the hall where Elyos stood close to his sister. Carys had been badly injured and her rigid posture told of the effort required for her to attend the event. Elyos was uncharacteristically subdued and overly attentive while she gently teased him. I doubted they would move far from each for a while yet.

At the far end of the hall was another couple who were unwilling to separate. Tarra tightly held Keenan's hand and pressed close to his side. They stood at the centre of the largest group and the meek woman seemed overwhelmed by the attention she was getting. Keenan was quietly supportive with frequently exchanged glances and a constant rubbing of her hand with his thumb. Since Kade's official acceptance of their relationship, claiming that Tarra was the only one with a hope of keeping him in order, the Lord General had showed a side of his character that very few had seen. Desperate to forget the horrors they had seen, people greedily snatched at their story, declaring it to be fit for a storyteller's tale.

Not all were there. A messenger had come to report that Kingsport was safe but the countess would be unable to attend the king for a few days yet. While the siege had held, Leyn had refused to engage with the army but there had still been losses from the continued pirate raids. She was needed to support her people while they recovered from the trauma of war, and this was repeated throughout Faulknar. Liegeport was not the only place to suffer and there would be a time later for the noble families to gather, when Kade would formally acknowledge the cost paid by their towns and ports.

I would have liked seen Gheth, Mace and Slicer but the intention had been to keep the event small and discreet, and few had been invited. The men, along with countless others, were being kept busy managing the royal port and I was content that they had survived with only minor injures which would heal well. Hagan had lost an arm and had been confined to the infirmary despite his loud protests. Dru was also there. He had stood by his brother when Kutan had been gored by a horse-daemon, and he had received injuries that were so severe it was unlikely he would have survived had he not received the prompt attention of gifted healers. His wounds would repair but the brothers had been inseparable. Many feared he would not recover, lacking the will needed to continue.

The unlikely sight of the Namori riding to our aid during that last, terrible battle had been recognised, however, and Eldiss had been invited to attend with two of his men. He noticed me watching him and separated from his group to join me. He greeted me with a mocking smile.

'You've grown some teeth since we last met.' He gave a small bow that held no hint of respect. 'If I'd known you were a Dragonslayer I would have given you more attention.'

'No, you wouldn't. You were very sure of your own importance.'

'True,' he admitted, turning to lean his back against the wall beside me. 'Still, you and your king have achieved something remarkable here.'

'We had help. Your arrival was much appreciated. The horse banner has not been seen in generations. You have achieved something remarkable yourself.'

He shrugged. 'Took so long to gain everyone's agreement that we almost missed it.'

'But you didn't. And for that we are grateful.'

We lapsed into silence, thinking about the final stages of the battle. The Travellers may have been the last to arrive, but they had fought courageously and had taken significant losses as a result. Those who survived, along with everyone else who had witnessed my horrifying firestorm, suffered from the night-terrors of being engulfed in flames. The inferno had greedily devoured every soldier polluted by Taranis, instantly incinerating the armies of Baila, Lindvane and Hilman. Within the blink of an eye, the shamans and their daemons ceased to exist. But amongst the hellscape of scorched land and vast swathes of bodies turned to ash, the God and my Goddess had protected each fighter, runner, groom and water-carrier who was loyal to Faulknar. Each had been contained within a shield of pearlescent energy that kept them safe from the intense heat of the fires. Faulknar's horses had not suffered a single singed hair as they stood, unnaturally calm, within the raging fire.

'I was sorry to hear about Drey,' Eldiss said quietly. 'He was greatly respected by the Namori. It has been agreed that we will train more *zorotas* as a tribute to his memory.'

'He would have liked that.' Thoughts of Drey were painfully linked to those of Erula. 'Did you know? Erula claimed to be your cousin. Did you know she came to Faulknar to influence Kade?'

'I have many cousins, it is hard to keep track of all of them.' He raised a hand when I made to protest. 'Erula was a distant relative and no, I did not know of her plans. I have heard she was difficult as a child. Ruthlessly ambitious. I do not think she was mourned when she left.'

'You did not send her.'

'I did not.'

I released the tension in my shoulders, turning to him with an apologetic smile. 'I need to know how she came to cause so much harm. The other pieces of the puzzle box are in place. I understand Averill and Lindvane. Even Villermir. Why would she do it?'

'I will ask. We owe you that. But we may never know and I suggest you let this lie. Let the Namori deal with the Namori.'

I promised to try as Vallori came to join us. The two men greeted each other, clasping forearms.

'A Dragonslayer and a Warrior,' commented Eldiss. 'The Gods have truly touched Faulknar.'

'Don't forget the *miann cath*,' Vallori countered, dipping his head towards Elyos.

Eldiss shook his head in disbelief. 'A fine tale to tell by the fire.'

'Indeed.' Vallori turned to address me. 'Your king is becoming noticeably absent. Perhaps you should remind him that he is awaited.'

I held his gaze. 'I might not come back.'

'I trust you.' He rolled his eyes at my expression. 'Go before I change my mind.'

The logical place to find the missing king would be his chambers. He had remained in those he had used as a boy, refusing to take his father's suite, and I made my way hoping to find him there. I paused at the top of the stairs. My earlier thoughts of Drey were still close and I felt I should address that particular ghost. I had not returned to his chambers since that day, with the room holding too many dreadful memories, but I could not avoid it forever and now was as good a time as any.

The door had been repaired and stood open, with a soft light coming from the outer chamber. I was not sure why anyone had cause to be in there so I entered cautiously. Much of the furniture had been removed and new rugs covered the floor. The flickering light from a small lamp made the room seem sad and empty. I resisted the urge to look for signs of the damage that had been caused, both during Rolyan's attack and that of Coen. Another, fainter light came from Drey's private rooms.

Taking the lamp, I continued into the smaller chamber which would be permanently associated with dried herbs and potions, expecting to smell their familiar scent. They had been removed a long time ago and the room was as forlornly bare as the outer one. The light came from the tower and the soft noise of someone moving confirmed Kade's presence; no one else would be there. I left the light on the empty bench and climbed the pale stone steps. I had been quiet and he remained unaware of my presence, giving me the time to watch him slowly turn the pages of a book.

The tower was filled with all the books, scrolls, crystals, artefacts and eclectic trinkets Drey had collected, with every table, shelf, chair and ledge covered. The floor was equally cluttered, leaving only narrow passageways between sections to allow easy access to the treasures. His entire work had been safely hidden, protected from all except Kade. I breathed a sigh that was almost a sob when I saw a scorched painting of an emerald dragon. He had held a lifetime of precious memories in this room.

Kade turned at the sound and smiled when he saw me. He was dressed in formal black, with the white collar of his shirt showing at the neck of his tunic. The contrasting purple slash hung from one shoulder across his chest to rest on the opposite hip and was the only overt sign of his status, the crown having been returned to the treasury once more.

'My liege.' I gave him a passably graceful curtsey.

'My lady,' he returned, giving me a more graceful bow. His eyes sparkled in the lamp's light. 'Everything is here. He kept everything for me.'

'Do you remember that?' I asked, indicating the picture. 'When I burnt it?'

He laughed. 'The time you exploded the tower.'

'The day you found out the name of my sword.'

His smile slowly faded. 'By the Gods, we were reckless. How did he ever survive us?'

We were silent for a time, remembering, before I broke the mood with the reason I had sought him.

'Your guests await you, my liege.' I grinned. 'Keenan is holding court and he still hasn't forgiven you for giving him Lindvane?'

'"*Never asked for a cursed kingdom, boy*",' Kade blustered in an accurate impression of his uncle. 'Someone had to take it. He killed Hayton so they will accept his claim through right of war. I don't think anyone will mourn the loss of his wastrel son. Fool couldn't even die regally.'

Hulce had been poorly suited to war and his guard had performed an admirable feat of protecting him during the battle, mainly by blocking the incompetent prince from any attempt at fighting. It seemed that not even his horse could tolerate the man, and had crushed his skull when Hulce fell trying to avoid a swooping bird-daemon.

'Hayton's line has ended,' Kade continued. 'But there is a niece. Handera's daughter was an infant when her father was killed. She will be raised as Keenan's ward and inherit the crown after him. The kingdom will revert back to Lindvane but it should no longer be a threat by then.'

'I can't imagine Keenan having the patience to rule,' I grinned, playing with a small crystal. 'And there's Tarra. Surely there is only so much bluster a kingdom can take.'

Kade laughed. 'I would have happily paid a ransom to see the look on her face when he told her. She's good for him and they've waited long enough.'

'And Hilman? Have you reached a decision about that?'

His forehead creased while he considered his options. 'Are you sure about Delaina?'

As with Lindvane, Hilman had lost its king but it had retained its queen, preventing the clean solution of replacing Averill with a Faulknar duke. The tensions that simmered within Hilman ran close to civil war and these passions would easily ignite with the wrong choice of ruler.

'Delaina is favoured by her people,' I replied carefully. 'She is ambitious and capable of manipulating any situation to her advantage. But she has no love for Baila and will protect her kingdom with everything she has. We just need to convince her that aligning with Faulknar is in her, and her kingdom's, best interests. Carys can manage her ambition and Bonash can temper her intellect. I still believe it is the best option.'

Kade nodded, considering again my proposal, and I felt certain he would soon accept Delaina as a client queen. I pushed him further.

'And the priests? What will you do about them?'

'After your display of the Gods' power, I doubt anyone will have the courage to deny them. The priests will lose their authority and over time, Baila will probably fade back into being a prophet.'

I suspected that the Gods would be satisfied. The pantheon will, once again, share the power that was too great for a single deity, and I had to accept that. Kade looked tired and sad as he surveyed the legacy Drey had left him. Despite all the obstacles that had been thrown at him, I knew Drey would have been proud of the king Kade had become.

'We should go. Your people are awaiting the High King of Five Kingdoms.' He grinned at my mocking tone. 'Which is ridiculous as two are not even kingdoms. The Namori have never sworn fealty to a king and the Northlands are a bunch of squabbling seabirds. I have no idea how Luella has managed to bind the clans and gain their consent to pledge their fealty to you.'

'Enough,' he laughed. 'I'm coming.'

I continued to tease him as he followed me back to hall. 'And if you behave tonight, tomorrow you can come with Vallori and me to hunt dragon bones on Cloud Mountain.'

Surprisingly, Kade agreed to my suggestion. The following day saw the three of us taking a much needed break from the war's devastation to ride through the unharmed beauty of the forest below Cloud Mountain. Megin waited for us on a rocky projection at the summit and I relayed her memories of the mountain's creation while we rode amongst the mist shrouded trees. Squirrels scurried to the safety of the pine branches when we passed, and the harsh call of jays protested at our unwelcome intrusion from oak and sycamore. Fawn-coloured deer wandered onto the path ahead of us, twitching their ears and noses before deciding we were to be avoided and bounding into the shelter of the tall bracken. I found it easy to forget the present and drift within Megin's tales of the past.

My glorious black and gold nestling was killed by those hateful arrows, Megin grumbled, displacing several rocks when she flexed her claws. *As if I would fail to learn from his death and fall to their iron bite.*

I refrained from using Megin's emotive language regarding Kade's defences, choosing to focus on the story rather than her accusations.

'The last time dragons flew over Faulknar, the contest was between humans and the Gods. The Dragonslayers and their dragons were sent to subdue the rebellion.' I looked at Kade, knowing that he would have read the accounts in order to build his towers. 'The people had fought dragons before and knew how to kill them. A glorious black and gold dragon flew too close to the town and was fatally struck by a harpoon.'

You are not telling it correctly, Megan criticised, shaking like a wet hound in irritation when I ignored her.

'He fought against the pain of his massive wound and struggled to stay conscious as his blood rained down on those below.' Megin snorted at my embellishments. 'He finally succumbed to his injuries, crashing down with enough force to send a crater's worth of soil and rock into the air. The dying dragon lay within the hollow while the displaced earth floated down to cover him. The funeral mound was so high that it created a mountain.'

Vallori grinned at my wondrous tale, content to be caught within its spell. 'And so they called it *Arach Beinn*. Dragon's Peak.'

Kade remained cynically unconvinced. We teased him gently, creating ever more incredulous accounts of how the mountain was created and the number of dragons buried within. We had placed a dragon's hoard of treasure beneath its rocks by the time we dismounted to rest the horses, having risen above the perpetual mist to where the forest thinned. Sharp stone walls bordered the trail before opening into a large plateau of rugged turf and wiry heather. We decided to linger a while before making the descent.

We tethered the horses and left the treeline. Vallori kicked at a root that had poked through the soil. 'Look,' he said enthusiastically. 'Dragon bones.'

'You are such children,' Kade responded testily having tired of our teasing. 'It's just a tree root.'

Stupid ape, retorted Megin. *Look again. Those are the bones of his wings.*

I bent down for a closer inspection, brushing away some of the dirt that concealed it. The pale structure was covered with numerous narrow lines of a darker shade, as if the edge of a quill had scratched along its surface. I wiped away a little more soil at one end to reveal rounded extensions, which did look a lot like the knobbed projections of a very large finger joint.

With a little encouragement, which mainly involved stroking her vanity, I encouraged Megin to join us. I grinned at the expressions of awe on my companion's faces when she settled at the far side of the wide ledge, but still found myself sharing their sense of wonder when I looked at my dragon. I had not seen her for so long and marvelled anew at her beauty. Her colours were pale in reflection of her placid mood, with a soft rose underbelly and a duck-egg blue covering her back and wings. Her dark amber eyes watched us with mild interest and she lowered herself into a position similar to that of a contented cat. She flicked her serrated tail so that it curled around her body and the arrow tip rested lightly over her foreleg. I felt Kade tense beside me when Vallori stepped forward and cautiously crossed the clearing, but Megin's defensive frill remained close to her neck and her colours stayed pale. She did not caution me to stop him and lowered her proud head at his approach. Kade released a long-held breath when Vallori slowly reached up to touch her cheek.

I slapped Kade on his shoulder, making him startle. 'She's not going to eat him.'

He huffed in denial. 'That remains to be seen.'

We settled on the springy turf to watch my *pháirtí* scratch at the base of one of Megin's horns as if she was an overgrown horse. Her lips crinkled in a way that I could almost convince myself was a smile, while Kade continued to scowl beside me.

'What?' I asked eventually.

'Why does he get to touch her?'

'Now who's acting like a child?' I scolded gently. 'Perhaps she's willing to let him touch her because he didn't try to kill her.'

'She tried to kill me first.'

'True.' I remembered Kade's first encounter with my dragon. 'Drey and Sutha could not separate you from Mobis's corruption. All she saw was daemon.'

His expression softened slightly but not by much. I followed his gaze and tracked it to Vallori rather than Megin.

'Are you jealous of him?'

He hesitated for a few heartbeats before answering. 'He's made quite a reputation for himself as the Warrior.'

'Sutha has a way of naming people,' I commented before quietly addressing his misplaced resentment. 'The Gods named me a kingmaker, Kade. As well as fighting their enemies, Dragonslayers were to have a role in ensuring the continued worship of the Gods by choosing the *rightful* king. Do not compare yourself to him, you were chosen by the Gods.'

'Chosen by you,' he corrected.

'The Goddess may have guided my steps and allowed me to gather assistance along the way, but don't discount your part in this. You stayed true to your Gods and, in doing so, shone like a beacon for Luella and Carys and Elyos. Sutha and Eldiss had both tested you, remember? They may have come at my call, but they would not have stayed if they had not found you worthy. Do not consider yourself lacking. You are a Druid King! One of those has not been seen in a very long time.'

Kade paused again before asking the question I suspected he had been brooding on from the start. 'But you will leave. With him.'

'You know I can't stay. Your people need to heal and my presence will only act to remind them of what I have done. Vallori does not have the responsibility of Faulknar. He is free to follow me, although why he continues to do so is still a mystery to me. He has some healing of his own to do and I am his *pháirtí*. It is long past time I started being one.'

I hesitated, considering how to describe something I barely understood myself. How I had denied my Goddess for the two men on this mountain.

'Sutha named my triple heritage at the Isle of Serpents. Everyone has seen my dragon and knows me as a Dragonslayer. Those that have fought beside me will know of my abilities as a Moon Warrior. The third aspect, however, is more silent and easily overlooked. Even the Goddess forgot that I am an Empath.'

'But he doesn't?'

'No. I don't think he does.' I took a breath. I was not explaining this well enough. 'When Villermir did what he did—'

'When he killed you.' Kade's clarification held ice within its tone.

'I wasn't dead. Not really.'

'I was there. You were dead.'

'Either way, it was meant to stay like that. I was expected to reject my connection to… this existence. I was to join with Megin and fight where the Goddess commanded it. But I refused her. For a second time, I rejected her. When it came to it, I could not deny my Empath calling. I would not be separated from my heart or my soul. Not even for my Goddess. You are my heart, Kade, but he is my soul. Do not ask me to choose between you.'

Kade remained silent, watching Vallori, and I thought about all those who had shaped my decision. The strong women of Luella, Carys and Sutha, even the fierce determination of Delaina and Nyx. I thought about those that had been favoured by the Gods. Of Elyos and Bear, and of Drey and

Kade. I thought of those who had been manipulated by the Fates. Of Erula and Villermir and Sálaforn.

Kade gave a twitch of a smile and I turned to see Megin lifting her nose to send Vallori crashing to the ground. Considering all that had happened, and all that I had done, I felt blessed to feel the warm sun on my face and know that those of my heart, my soul, and the very fibre of my *self* were safe on this mountain with me.

EPILOGUE

The cold wind blew around her and the clouds raced across the sky. The feeling had persisted for days and she was finding it harder to ignore. The insistent pull felt deep and ancient. A primitive call that promised the fulfilment of a need when she already felt complete.

She pushed off the cliff and spread her wings to catch the warm current of air that would lift her high above the clouds. She travelled east, over the familiar waters where she had hunted the pirate ships and those who summoned the hated daemons and green ghosts. She flew further than she had gone before. Her muscular body appreciating the prolonged exercise.

She continued. Passing over a land that was grey with the stones of mountains and rocky valleys. The beauty of the bleak landscape was highlighted by the dark indigo waters of long, narrow lakes. The jagged peaks of the mountains slowly smoothed into forest-covered hills and then into open valleys dotted with cattle and sheep.

Still she continued. Her giant wings beat a slow, regular rhythm while the rolling hills and gentle valleys rose once more into towering peaks and cavernous canyons. The pointed summits of the ice-mountains poked through the clouds with each one pressing against the next in an endless range. It seemed that she flew over a raging white sea. The air was so crisp that it felt like inhaling frozen water and it sent a pleasant tingle through her deep chest.

The ice-mountains eventually softened into verdant, round-topped peaks and lush valleys, bejewelled with sparkling waterfalls and shimmering lakes. The clouds had dispersed so the cobalt sky reflected in the waters below. Eagles glided on the warm currents far below her, reduced to small streaks of colour by distance and to insignificance when compared to her majestic size. She screeched a reply to their squawking calls, causing them to scatter from her shadow.

The fertile valleys faded and her body made its first gentle protests. Wing muscles ached from the extended exertion but the compulsion to continue would not be ignored. She soared over a landscape that had faded from vibrant shades to a bland carpet of pale-yellow. Tall grasses baked under the blazing sun, swaying gently in the unhindered breezes which swept across the plains. Large herds of horses bolted from her silhouette and she amused herself by dipping low to heighten their panicked flight.

She did not stop to eat. Her belly clenched intermittently but the need to continue tolerated no delay. She flew on, over the vast ocean of grassland that was undisturbed by hill or lake. Time became meaningless beyond the rhythm of her wingbeats and the slow passage of the sun. The call to join became a living serpent within her chest and it wrapped snugly around her heart.

The plains finally ended at a bright azure sea. The calm waters looked like coloured glass and she lowered her flight, aiming towards the chain of islands embedded like gems within it. The serpent squeezed in time with her rapidly beating heart when she glided over the first island. A single, pointed peak arose from the centre, with its black rock crowned with a cap of white snow. An array of vibrant colours surrounded the mountain as plants thrived in its dark, fertile soil.

A screaming cry split the air when she flew to the larger second island. Her blood enflamed in answer to that recognised sound. A sound she had not thought to hear again. A sound she had thought lost for so many years. A sound that sent a surge of energy through her tired muscles. She increased her speed.

She paid no attention to the second island other than to note that the black mountain there had no pale covering. It had no covering at all. Just a deep, black crater. A fire-mountain.

She sped towards the next island. The largest within the chain. She descended further to skim over the small, sparsely forested mountain near the coast and aimed for the cluster of three tall peaks further inland. The central one having the sharp cut sliced across the top, declaring it a fire-mountain.

She was still some distance away when five shapes erupted from the dark shadows between the mountains. Vibrant colours flashed in the glow of the setting sun and five dragons flew towards her, arranged behind the largest like the head of an arrow. She bellowed a warning and the lead dragon challenged back, raising his head and breathing a river of fire into the sky above him.

They were closer now and she could identify their markings. Three females and a male followed, all smaller than the lead male. Their scales shone: cobalt blue, ice white, raven black and sun gold. Iridescent colours that shimmered over bulging muscles as they flew towards her. None were able to compete with the glory of the lead dragon who displayed the colours of the phoenix.

She reared when they approached, exposing all her talons in preparation for the fight. She cried again and was answered by the screams of all five dragons. She tensed for the collision. The lead dragon sped towards her, but he turned at the last moment to twist around her. His nestlings followed his example and she became enclosed within a revolving ring of bejewelled muscle. Neck-frills were extended and throat-sacks were engorged. They circled her, hostile and wary, but there was no attack.

She slowly lowered her neck-frill and her action was matched by the lead dragon a heartbeat later. The four dragons pirouetted at the display that signalled the intent not to fight. They flowed around each other in complicated patterns, leaving the phoenix-dragon to hover in front of her.

Welcome, little one. He rumbled. *It is time.*